Praise for *The Unincorporated Man*

"The Kollins' debut novel has an intriguing, debate-stirring premise that's buoyed by the brothers' imaginative look at a future dominated by fascinating technological advancements and utter compliance....Science fiction fans should gobble this up, as will thriller lovers, who may shudder at a subservient ask-no-questions future that seems uncomfortably attainable."

—*The Sunday Star-Ledger*

"Will appeal to Heinlein's legions of fans with its themes of personal liberty and one man's political struggle with the State....*The Unincorporated Man* will tantalize you with its intriguing premise."

—*i09*

"A very sharp and often funny look at a twenty-first century man who is resuscitated from cryogenic storage only to find himself in a tightly controlled, techno-bean-counter socioeconomic system. This novel may remind some of Heinlein—for both its clarity and its implicit individualist, libertarian, satirical slant."

—Ken Goffman, Editor and Chief, *h+* magazine, columnist for *Wired*, *Rolling Stone*, and *Time*

"A cohesive, gripping, and potentially controversial story of the future that reminded me at times of the more balanced work of Robert A. Heinlein, with a touch of Philip K. Dick. I foresee very good things in the future from this pair."

—Don D'Ammassa, *Critical Mass*

"A stunning debut. Truly. Forget the genre clichés of laser guns, spaceships, and journeys through black holes and the like. This book is part Heinlein, part Bradbury, and part Asimov. This is no space adventure, but a socioeconomic envisioning of the future. As such, it would easily fit alongside, say, *1984* or *Brave New World* as a chilling and thought-provoking treatise on possible futures."

—Stephen Hubbard, *Bookreporter*

"The clash between today's cultural values and those of a vividly imagined future has never been more compelling....The Kollin brothers' debut captivates with unforgettable characters and an ingenious vision of the economic future."

—*Booklist*

D0388021

the unincorporated man

Dani Kollin and Eytan Kollin

A Tom Doherty Associates Book
New York

This is a work of fiction. All of the characters, organizations, and events portrayed in this novel are either products of the authors' imagination or are used fictitiously.

THE UNINCORPORATED MAN

A Tor Book
Published by Tom Doherty Associates, LLC
175 Fifth Avenue
New York, NY 10010

www.tor-forge.com

Tor® is a registered trademark of Tom Doherty Associates, LLC.

The Library of Congress has catalogued the hardcover edition as follows:

Kollin, Dani.
    The unincorporated man / Dani Kollin and Eytan Kollin.—1st ed.
        p. cm.
    "A Tom Doherty Associates book."
    ISBN 978-0-7653-1899-2
    I. Title.

PS3611.O58265 U55 2009
813'.6—dc22

                                                        2008046472

ISBN 978-0-7653-2724-6

To Mom and Dad,
who assured us with their
unflinching belief, who steadied us
with their unending support, and
who inspired us with their undying love.
This book would not exist without you.

To my beloved Deborah,
without whose patience, encouragement, and
endless support
this book could not have been written. I love you
more than the
stars in the sky and the sand in the sea.

To my children, Eliana, Yonatan, and Gavriel,
thank you for giving me the best job in the world.

Acknowledgments

Writing a book ain't exactly easy. These people helped:

Paul Lance, who let us know we were on the right track. The unnamed intern (really, we still don't know her name) whose passion describing the concept got our manuscript into Tor. Denis Wong, for having the presence of mind to say, "We need to buy this book." David Hartwell, for not only agreeing with him but also for changing the manuscript from a worthy concept into a worthy read. Stacy Hague-Hill, for patiently guiding us through the straits and narrows of first-time authorship. Howard Deutsch, our agent friend and fellow provocateur. (Dude, really. We so landed on the Moon!) And our test readers who kept us on course and off stupid. (Sorry about that original sex scene. What can we say? We were just starting out.)

To Bond, George, and Sasha. Many of the things I've done that are worth remembering (and some I'm still trying to forget) revolve around the three of you. If friends are the family you choose, we've been family for a long time. Uncle Harvey, who once made up a science-fiction story for a wide-eyed, seven-year-old boy who then grew up to become a science-fiction author. (I still want to know how it ends, damn it!) Eric, whose intellect, conversations, and comic book collection have enabled my imagination to grow in ways it might never have otherwise.

—Eytan

If you're fortunate in life, you'll secure a group of friends that, although not always near, somehow manage to feel ever-present. I'm blessed to have seven. Alan, Dan, David, Evan, Leo, Mike, and Yoni. I'm honored to be your friend, brother, and co-conspirator.

To the Insomniyakkers: Barry, Larry, and Lisa. As if road-biking at 4 A.M. weren't hard enough, you have to listen to me rant, rave, and filibuster about everything under the Moon. (Some of which I really know nothing about! P.S. Don't tell Larry.) Thanks for the endless miles and the invaluable insights.

To the Wolverines: Albert, Mark, and Jason. Your smarmy wit, dry deliveries, and wonderfully self-deprecating humor mean more to me than you could ever possibly know. Thanks, dudes. Go gym kata!

—Dani

the unincorporated man

1   Look What I Found

The counterpart for education (financing) would be to "buy" a share in an individual's earning prospects; to advance him the funds needed to finance his training on condition that he agree to pay the lender a specified fraction of his future earnings. There seems no legal obstacle to private contracts of this kind, even though they are economically equivalent to the purchase of a share in an individual's earning capacity and thus to partial slavery.

—MILTON FRIEDMAN, *CAPITALISM AND FREEDOM*, 1962

Though he was filthy from head to toe, bloodied, and his skin shredded as thoroughly as a cat's scratching post, Omad couldn't suppress a grin. He was a miner with a knack for finding veins of valuable material even in old, worked-out quarries, and he felt in his bones that today was his day. Today he'd find something valuable enough to achieve his dream, and achieve it at the respectably early age of sixty-nine. His stock was selling for 183 credits a share, and all he needed was one more good find and GCI would owe *him* enough credits to enable him to buy a majority of himself. Even if his stock price rose, as was often the case with personal success, he could still make majority. He'd just have to pray that his personal valuation wouldn't go over 200 credits a share, and that he'd take home at least 20,000 credits from this venture. Yes, Omad was 100 shares away from controlling himself. He could taste it. The thought of being able to choose his own vacation times and consume whatever substance he wanted, when he wanted, almost made him too excited to work. But he quelled his feelings of joy and concentrated on the task at hand.

He was walking into a mine on GCI's property that hadn't been worked in centuries, and he was walking in without a corporation mine car or drill-bot. The less of GCI's equipment he used, the less of a percentage they'd be able to claim of his profits. It wasn't the norm, and he'd never have been as successful without corporate sponsorship and equipment, but this was different. Though it might take a little longer, this excavation would have to be done carefully and in person. Maximum allowable risk for maximum profit, and the risks were real.

Still, it was in these old mines that sometimes one got lucky. The technology of mineral extraction had improved greatly in the four centuries since this quarry had been actively worked. More important, the science of mineral transmutation had been born, and some metals were easier to transform from one into another. Many a decrepit lead mine had been reopened to turn its once worthless innards into a marketable commodity. And when this one was closed and forgotten in the late 1800s, it was done so out of prudence. It had been stripped bare, and there was simply no point in keeping it open any longer. Whatever possible riches lay in waiting now, Omad was sure of one thing—he would be the first to find them.

He took his time with the mine scan. Impatience might make him miss something, and even walls as old as these left hundreds of chemical and structural clues. *Know before you go,* he reminded himself. The first part of the morning was spent insuring that the caverns were sound. He need not have worried. The mountain was formed of igneous rock—a type of hardened molten lava that had lasted eons and would last for eons more. By the time Omad finished his tests he was convinced the dig was stable. His safety assured, he now began looking for the telltale clues of wealth—wealth that could be shared with his investors, his employers, and himself. If he was right about this place, all would benefit from the investment that individuals and society had made in him—as it should be. Omad would also be pleased to gain 51 percent of himself, which was also as it should be.

His thoughts were interrupted and his dreams almost shattered by what appeared before him—a tunnel shaft in abject disarray. It was blocked by a few large boulders among hundreds of smaller shards in all shapes and sizes. What had he missed? The sight of such instability alone almost made him turn back and choose a new mine. He had just conjectured that this one would last eons, and now here was proof that it was coming down a lot sooner than expected. Clearly a malfunction on the part of his hardware, he reasoned. Perhaps a costly one. But his years of experience told him what he already knew: The type of rock he'd ventured into didn't need a reader to give up its history—only to verify it. He would exchange the mine-reader when he returned. But against his better judgment, or perhaps because of it, he decided to venture a little farther.

There was something here and he knew it. Plus, he was driven by his personal mantra, "Little risk, little profit," so he bent to examine the crumbled evidence before him. *Explosives,* he realized, upon examining the shards. Not a "natural" cave-in after all. More evidence lay in Omad's path. Whatever, or more precisely, *whoever* had made this mess had left the detonator, some primitive blasting caps, and humorously, an instruction manual on how to set off explosives in a mine.

Since no skeleton or evidence of a body was visible, the perpetrator had obviously read the manual well, done the deed, and exited to safety. There was also a box of something called "Twinkies." Omad picked it up and examined it carefully. Aside from its unique and unusual artwork, he was able to discern its key ingredients as well as something called an "EXP" date, which was marked from an eleventh month in what appeared to be the early twenty-first century. This was starting to get interesting. He gathered all the wrappers and placed them in an airtight container, along with the manual and blasting caps he had so far collected. Omad loved a mystery, and judging from the leftover wrappers, whoever blasted this tunnel had time to eat at least twenty-eight of these Twinkie things and walk out in one piece. *Must have been some kind of nutritional energy snack,* he thought, as he cracked his knuckles and continued on deeper into the shaft. The dry, consistent atmosphere had preserved the scene almost as if the long-gone blaster had left just before Omad had arrived. Even if he couldn't make a profit out of what was buried *in* the tunnel, he might just make a profit from what he'd just discovered *outside* of it. The nutritional wrappers and blaster manual alone would fetch a very good price on the open relic market. No, even if he found nothing else, today would not be a loss by any stretch of the imagination.

The El Dorado and the Francisco mines are played out for gold and silver, however they, like the No Timbers mine, still may have substantial amounts of lead and zinc. But it is doubtful the amounts present can be extracted economically with the present state of mining technology.

—Colorado Mining Commission report on the El Dorado mine
ownership transfer, July 19, 1978 (one of only two sources in
which the No Timbers mine is mentioned)

Neela Harper was not a country girl. In fact, she'd always preferred the big city. Anything with only a million and a half people in it just didn't seem natural. If she had had any inkling that the career she had chosen for herself would dump her in this remote part of the world she probably wouldn't have chosen it. Then again, being a minority shareholder in herself, she would have had little or no say whatsoever about her place of employ. *Luck of the draw,* she thought somberly to herself. *And this year I'm clearly down on my luck.* Anybody looking at her would not be displeased. She was five feet eleven inches—about average for a woman. A very healthy thirty-seven, but this was not surprising in the era of nano-medicine; positively everyone was healthy, and everyone looked great. Still, if everybody was a giant health-wise, then Neela, by her rigorous adherence to exercise, stood on the shoulders of those giants. Her appearance was 97 percent original, with only minor changes to control her hair growth and the removal of some facial bone damage suffered in a childhood accident. She hadn't had a sex change or so much as a boob job by her eighteenth birthday, something that was practically a rite of passage for her generation. Nope, just chestnut hair, green eyes, a tiny nose, freckles, and a supremely athletic body. Her problem was not so much physical as it was economic.

Not knowing what she wanted to do with her life, she spent all of high school and most of college studying the basics. Nothing wrong with that. And she did well with all the courses she took. In some ways it was helping her now, but not in terms of her percentages. At an age when most of her peers owned 35 percent of themselves, she only owned a paltry 30.5 percent. It had nothing to do with gambling or expensive trips. Her debt was an investment. Those who knew they were going to go into an expensive or prestigious field prepared themselves by maintaining a stellar GPA. Further, they specialized in a chosen field all through high school and university. Thus, by the time they got to the advanced, and therefore expensive, part of their training, they were better able to bargain for lower percentages. And so the university-cum-investor was held to grabbing only 7 to 9 percent of that student's self-equity, as opposed to the standard 12 to 15 percent. Rumor even had it that one top-flight student had received her education from San Francisco State University, the top Pacific League school, for an amazingly low 4 percent. But Neela wasn't prepared to commit to a major she didn't feel strongly about, and it wasn't until her junior year that she felt such passion. And while her patience at the time was seen as somewhat virtuous, it was now turning out to be a costly virtue indeed. As far as majors went, she'd picked a doozy. Neela was going to be a reanimation psychologist with a subspecialty in social integration. Since reanimation psychology was considered a prestigious field, what institution of higher learning would risk educating a latecomer when they could get more valuable stock in a better prospect?

The answer was a not-so-great institution of higher learning, Harvard, and the loss of more personal stock than she would have preferred—14 percent, to be exact. That, combined with what her parents, the government, and various other organizations held, gave her what in this day and age amounted to a measly 30.5 percent of herself. This also meant she had very little bargaining power as to where she was going to start her glorious career. If she had realized her dream, or just a better percentage of it, she would have been working in the famed Vegas reanimation clinics. They had suspendees yet to be reanimated who were, given their late ages of suspension, rumored to be close to two hundred years old. Those suspendees would be from the early days of the incorporation movement and might even have personal memories of the Grand

Collapse. Any one of them would make a great thesis subject. Yes, Vegas had it all: interesting patients, great bonuses, and the chance to publish. And with that kind of clout, Neela would have been able to negotiate a vertical position for a better percentage on the slow and steady climb to 51 percent. And that, she believed, was what it was all about.

At 51 percent she'd have almost absolute control over her life. The only draw-back would be a lack of insurance. One percent was only a hair-thin margin should, heaven forbid, she find herself needing extra funds. The further she could move her own percentage up, the better she'd sleep at night.

With GCI controlling her outright majority through a proxy agreement with Harvard (*bastards!*), she was stuck here in the Rockies of the North American Union for as long as they deemed profitable. Neela gained little solace from the one dubious distinction her location had as part of its claim to fame. It was, in fact, the smallest reanimation clinic in the world. Miners and ranchers who got into bad accidents were frozen and sent here. At most they would be bathed in liquid nitrogen for six months while some body parts were regrown or memory networks painfully restructured. They didn't need a reanimation specialist at all beyond some standard death trauma issues and, to be honest, not much social integration either. After all, how out of touch was a suspendee going to be if down for only six months? Oh, there were the little things of course. She knew how to sympathetically impart bad news regarding a suspendee's family, whether it be an untimely and permanent death or, as was often the case, spousal abandonment. She knew to keep up with the latest trends and, much to her cha-grin, the latest sports statistics. If she had a credit for every time a suspendee awoke asking, "How'd the Broncos do?" she'd have gotten her majority eons ago.

Out here she would never meet what she affectionately referred to as "the time travelers." They were Vegas's unopened treasures waiting for the precise technology to ensure their successful reanimation. And at the pace technology was evolving, it wouldn't take long. By the time she got out of her current locale, or rather, *if* she ever got out of her current locale, the time travelers would all have been reanimated by others, who would have published their findings to a fascinated world and retired at the impossibly young age of seventy. Neela, on the other hand, would get typecast as a "short-term specialist" and would prob-ably never leave Boulder in her working life again.

Neela's phone vibrated, and she held her thumbnail to her ear. She squinted her eyes, trying to bring her retro wall clock with the phosphorus tips into focus. It was 2:30 in the morning. She groaned in the general direction of her pinkie.

"Whoever died, I don't care," she said with her eyes closed. "Just freeze them and call me in the morning." The voice on the other end answered her so clearly it was as if he were in the bed next to her.

"Neela, sorry to wake you, but you *are* the primary revive specialist on call for this week, and we have something that needs a sign-off."

Neela sighed.

"Watanabe, this had better be good."

"Neela, I don't know what it is." The genuine confusion in the voice of her contact made her sit up. The emergency rescue service always knew what was going on. That they now didn't shook her out of her daze.

"All right, Ben, I'm on my way."

"Don't bother, Neela, we'll have a flyer out to pick you up in ten minutes."

"I know how to get to center, Ben," she answered, with no small amount of disdain.

"That's good, but you're not going to center."

"Ben, I'm no good at the medical end of suspension. I get them after they're thawed, remember?"

"Trust me, Neela, you'll want to see this." Neela heard the soft pop that told her the phone was disconnected. She managed to prop herself up. In her semi-comatose state she laid out in her mind what she'd wear. She decided on an all-weather outfit. It would be a little more cumbersome but would come in handy just in case this call led her up into the mountains. This day was becoming very out of the ordinary, and for someone with a daily routine as rote as hers, any chance to shake things up was certainly worth the extra effort required to drag herself out of bed.

She was gratified that she'd guessed correctly about the mountains, and was certainly not surprised to see evidence of a mine being cleared of rock. It was still dark as the flyer landed, but she could make out the entrance to the shaft only because it had been painted with Daylight, an amazing substance, she thought, that lived up to its brand name. About twenty rescue workers were operating heavy machinery, and she could see that a few more were spraying a fresh line of Daylight down the mine entrance leading into the tunnel. The pile of freshly cut logs stacked fifty yards away told her that this area had been heavily wooded until the crew got here.

Whoever's in there must be important, she thought. That would explain why they wanted her here—the expert witness lined up neatly with the rest of the bureaucratic pawns so necessary to make sure the paperwork flowed smoothly. It was only after the flyer landed near the log pileup that Neela realized what was missing. There were no emergency medical vehicles. In fact, there was no medical setup of any kind, just a cleanup crew.

As she got out of the flyer she saw Ben coming forward to meet her. They exchanged formal waves.

"What's going on, Ben?"

"It started when a company prospector was researching abandoned mines. He found this one by chance. All records of it had been removed from the official databases."

"But that's not possible," she answered, scratching her chin. "No record of this mine means this site's gotta be at least . . ."

". . . three, maybe four centuries old," continued Ben, "at least, according to the prospector we talked to." *Why'd they haul a reanimationist out here?* wondered Neela. Her heart skipped a beat. *No,* she thought. *Don't even go there.*

"So," she continued, trying to contain her trepidation, "how did this mine rat—what was his name?—find it?"

Watanabe smirked, knowing full well what Neela was really asking, but he decided to play along. "His name's Omad—a grade 7-B prospector. And, according to him, he found it because it was mentioned in the old mining reports of two *other* mines."

They walked hurriedly into the now well-lit mine. After a few hundred yards Neela found herself at the point where the roof had caved in. She waved at some of the rescue team members she recognized, including Rita, a woman she'd helped with a revival trauma about three months earlier. Fortunately for Rita, hers had been a particularly mild death, requiring only a two-day suspension. At the end of the cleared tunnel Neela saw a circular chamber about forty feet in diameter with a ceiling of about seven feet. It was what she saw in the middle of the space that stopped her cold—a large rectangular box measuring roughly ten feet by five feet by six feet encased in some sort of black metal composite. The whole visible section of the box was covered with inscriptions that were carved into the surface and filled in with a red ceramic material. This gave the box an ethereal appearance that reminded Neela of a sarcophagus. She slowly circled the coffer, absorbing its every detail.

"Like something out of a legend," whispered Neela.

"I know what you mean," replied Ben. "Normally I'm not suspicious, but may my stock drop if I said that that," he pointed to a specific inscription, "didn't freak me out."

Neela looked closer.

Some of the writing was in English, some in Chinese, some in Hebrew; there was even something that seemed to be a series of elevated dots and dashes. On what she now ascertained to be the lid of the case were a series of large characters with a very simple message:

THIS IS A LIFE POD. A MAN LIES SUSPENDED WITHIN.

She stepped back, took a deep breath, and nearly tripped over Ben in the process.

"Holy shit," she whispered.

Ben smiled and nodded.

"Holy, holy shit, Ben," she repeated. *Ask it, Neela. Ask the damned question!* she prodded herself.

"Is . . . is it operational?" she asked, barely able to utter the words.

"Seems to be," Ben replied, still smiling. "You still with us?"

"Uh . . . yeah . . . sorry, Ben."

"You can see why we called you. And that's not all," he continued, pointing to the surrounding walls. "We ran a groundar to see if anything was stuck in the walls." He waited a moment.

"Well?" Neela demanded.

"We found six hollowed-out chambers, spaced equidistantly around this main one. Get this—they were shielded."

"So," answered Neela, taking her eyes off the unit to look around the cavern, "you don't know what's inside, then?"

Ben hesitated for a moment. "Well, not exactly," he answered, keeping his head low as he kicked one foot in the dirt. "We did open the one."

Neela's face lit up. "You did what? Are you nuts!? They could have been booby-trapped for all we know, or you could have destroyed precious artifacts!"

"Hey, take it easy, Neela," answered Ben, "we only opened one, and entirely by accident, I can assure you." Neela gave him a disapproving look.

"But you'll never guess what we found inside," he continued, knowing she'd soon forgive him in all the excitement of the find. "Gold bullion. Can you believe that? Imagine going through all that trouble just to store a bunch of gold. He may as well have left some rubble in there for all it's worth."

"Ben," Neela asked, "how long do you think it's been since gold was used as a commodity?"

"I dunno. I'm not good at history; maybe five hundred years?"

"You're right. You're not good at history," she replied with a smirk. "It's less than two hundred and fifty. And I'm willing to bet this man has been here for at least that long."

"Long time to be down," Ben replied.

"Did you get a doctor in here?"

"First thing we did. He didn't know what it was . . . and neither did his Dij-Assist! He's back at his lab running a search for info on a secure Neuro uplink."

"And that's when you decided to call me?"

"Well . . . um . . . yeah. Plus, I know you, and I don't know anyone at the university, though that would have been my next call. So anyways, the billion-credit question is, can we move it?"

Before Neela could respond, Rita spoke up from the corner of the box nearest the door. "Uh, boss, I'm pretty sure we can."

"And how do you know that?" asked Ben, as he glared at Rita. "Do you have a degree in Unheard-of Technology I don't know about?"

Rita returned Ben's glare by pointing to the corner of the unit. "No, I don't, Mr. Smart Guy. I know it because it says so right here." They all gathered around to see what she'd pointed at:

THIS UNIT CAN BE MOVED WITHOUT DAMAGING THE
MAN INSIDE.
FOLLOW THE INSTRUCTIONS WRITTEN BELOW.

The group started laughing at how simple yet ridiculous that inscription was, while Ben's face reddened a bit. The tension that had made the place seem haunted was gone.

One of the rescue workers, a short, bearded man with a starburst tattoo on his nose, spoke up. "That's definitely an operational suspension unit."

"I know. I read the inscription, too. But I gotta tell you, it doesn't look like any suspension unit I've ever seen," Neela answered.

"It's not like any you've seen," he continued. "I don't think it's like anything anyone's seen. But that's a suspension unit, and I'd be willing to bet my next dividend that there's a man inside waiting to be revived. What shape he's in I couldn't say, but he's in there all right!"

"Well," Ben chimed in, "he'd better hope that his insurance company survived the GC and still has a policy on him."

"Why?" asked the guy with the starburst tattoo.

"This revive and extraction is going to cost him a credit or two, and if his insurance doesn't kick in, he's going to lose a good percentage come his quarterly report."

"I don't think so," Neela cautioned, something beginning to form in the pit of her stomach.

"Why not?" Ben asked. "Everyone gets an incorporation report. He's no different."

"Actually, he is, Ben. If we're to believe the inscription, and if in fact there is a man still in viable stasis, then he'll be, providing we do our jobs right, the oldest man ever to be revived."

"So?" Ben asked.

"So," Neela continued, "he's not going to get a quarterly report . . ."

". . . because he's never been incorporated," Rita said, finishing Neela's thought. The haunted air returned.

Humans have better things to do than pretend to be machines.
—Justin Cord, CEO of RoboAmp, at the opening ceremony
of the first entirely workerless factory

Ferdinand had reached that stage in life where the dust was beginning to settle. He wasn't about to start his own corporation, nor would he retire early. His self-percentage would be a lot better but for a wife who was a sucker for the frivolous little extras that were constantly being offered. But if she was happy, he was happy, right? After seventy-five years of working the same job, the only silver lining he managed to garner was that he could do basic background work slightly more economically than a computer. What was the old saying? You could lead a computer to data, but you couldn't make it glean.

It was a simple job, really. All he had to do was process revives. Boring, routine, safe work. Every once in a while he'd get an interesting one. Perhaps a complication concerning religious scruples, or maybe even a conflicting liability. Joy. But most of the time raising the dead was predictable, just like it was supposed to be. He'd process the name and occupation of the revival subject, determine who was paying for the procedure, and then inform Legal of any outstanding debts or stock options due. All credit on the account would then be reactivated by the upper echelons at a later date. The trickiest part was informing current stockholders about the reactivation of potential stock in the revived, but that was handled by another department. He had enough on his plate, thank you. The programs for this type of operation had been in place for decades, and short of the rare "breakthrough" upgrade that entailed a little more learning, it was almost automatic. Ferdinand's job was only to initiate the process and see that the procedures were followed. In this way he was able to facilitate the smooth flow of the frozen revive's reentry into the corporate world.

He rubbed his eyes. It was only 11:00 A.M. and he'd already processed forty-two corpsicles. "Next," he said to the holodisplay in front of him, not bothering to look up.

No response.

He repeated his request, but this time more irritably: "Computer, next revive."

"Sending information now," the computer chirped back.

Ferdinand looked up. "I didn't ask you to *send* me information. Just tell me the revive's name, please."

"Unable to comply."

Ferdinand, figuring the system was in prefritz mode, attempted an end around.

"Fine," he said, rising to the challenge, "can you at least tell me who insured him?"

"Unable to comply."

OK, a real challenge then, he thought. *I'm game.*

"Computer, access the subject's genetic code for ID."

Four seconds passed—an eternity.

"Unable to comply."

"You didn't get a sample of the DNA?"

"Sample received," the computer responded. "However, no known correlation in any database available."

Impossible.

Though Ferdinand prided himself on being able to solve problems before they became *real* problems, he knew when he was licked.

"Computer," he said, letting out a sigh, "get me technical support."

"Contacting technical support now," the machine chirped back. "Your call will be answered in the order in which it was received."

Ten minutes later Ferdinand was interrupted by a bored-looking fellow staring straight at him from the holodisplay.

"Tech support, whadyaneed?"

"Are you guys running a beta test on the revive data procurement program and forgot to mention it to us poor slobs in Adjusting?"

"If we are, it's news to me. Let me check." The face dissolved into the background.

Ferdinand continued working.

After another fifteen minutes the tech support fellow's face showed up on Ferdinand's holodisplay.

"No," was all he said, and before Ferdinand could ask another question the face disappeared.

Begrudgingly, Ferdinand returned to the task at hand. "OK, computer, let's try this again. You're telling me we have a revive?"

"Correct."

"Do we know where this revive is?"

"The revive is located at the Colorado Mining Hospital in the city of Boulder."

"Good, that's a start. What's the make of the suspension unit?" Sometimes in large disasters with many bodies, information could get lost temporarily. A good way of finding out who the person was would be to track the suspension unit itself.

"Unable to comply."

"Computer, is this information restricted or unavailable due to prior command or restraint?"

"Negative. Unable to comply because the information is unavailable to all known databases. If you check the information I have sent, you will see an image of the unit as well as all known data."

With a sigh of exasperation, Ferdinand called up the data. After ten minutes of scanning, he nervously keyed the button asking for his supervisor.

"What do you mean I'm going on vacation?!" fumed Neela.

Before her sat an impeccably dressed man seemingly impervious to the steely glare emanating from Neela's eyes.

"Your passage to Luna City has already been arranged," the man answered, too stoically for her taste.

"Luna City?! First of all, in case you haven't noticed, I'm not exactly in control of my own portfolio here, and I don't have the kind of equity to give up to go to a place like that."

"Don't worry," the man said, not bothering to look up from his holodisplay. "It's all paid for by GCI. Consider it a bonus for the good job you've done to date. Now, if you don't mind, I've got work to do."

Neela stood quietly for a moment.

"I don't want the vacation," she blurted.

This got the man's attention. He stopped staring into the holodisplay, shifted some papers aside, and looked at her intently.

"You like your work that much that you'd give up an all-expenses-paid vacation to a place most people only dream about?" Neela shifted uncomfortably in her place. "There's the one-sixth-gravity waterfalls, wing nanites for the Galileo fly-through. The sex alone is worth the trip. Trust me, that I know."

"It's not the work," she answered. "It's *this* work. This find . . . right now. I never expected to be the primary reanimationist. I knew you'd bring in a Bronstein or a Gillette. But there's never going to be another find like this. I *have* to be a part of it."

"You're really dedicated to this, aren't you?"

"Completely."

The man dived back into his holodisplay and typed in some commands. After a minute or so he looked up.

"I may live to regret this, but I've just bought a thousand shares of your personal stock."

"Why'd you do that?" she exclaimed.

"I'm sorry. Most people would find it complimentary."

"Well, I'm not most people. And I intend to buy back enough of my shares to make majority."

The man let out a guffaw.

"Oh. You're one of *those*. Well, look, I'm worth five times your value, and I'll probably never see majority. Furthermore, why would you even try? All you'd get is some additional income—and a lot of headache." He was starting to lose patience. "Look, you're going on vacation whether you want to or not. It's already been decided."

Neela stood her ground. "I don't mean to be a pain, and I know the company owns my ass, but I just don't understand why I can't take this damned vacation after the patient's already been revived and socially integrated."

This time the man stood up from his desk and looked her right in the eye. As he did this she heard the sounds of corridor traffic in the background—the door had opened behind her.

"Unless you're willing to wait five years," he spat, "that ain't gonna happen, lady. This conversation is over. Good day."

"Five years? Did he really say five years?"

Neela was in the director's office. His name was Mosh McKenzie, and he was the first superior Neela had ever really liked—not that she'd had a lot. Part of it grew from the fact that she didn't understand him. He'd achieved self-majority, which, while commendable, wasn't particularly extraordinary. Plus, she'd met enough of those. Smug bastards most of them. No, Mosh was different. He was the first person she knew who'd achieved his goals—which in his case meant becoming a powerful member of the GCI board of directors—and then had himself transferred to this tiny little enclave located somewhere in the bowels of Colorado. Most assumed he'd screwed up somewhere on his steady climb up the golden ladder and that this was his punishment, but Neela suspected differently. She was a good judge of character, a must in her line of work, and Mosh was not a man who seemed incompetent, and—even more telling—not upset with his current situation. In fact, Neela would have to say that this was a man supremely content with himself and his place in life. It was true that he was 175 years old and could easily retire, but, she suspected, his inner drive would never have let him. Of average height at six feet two inches, he was confident enough in himself that when he started to bald he simply let it happen rather than spend the thirty credits it would have cost to prevent the process. Neela had to admit that, although his appearance had shocked her at first, she couldn't imagine him looking any other way.

"Mosh," said Neela, "is there any problem medically that I wasn't informed of?"

"Actually," he answered, "now that you mention it, no."

"Do we know why he was suspended?" Neela continued.

Mosh checked his holodisplay.

"Says here, lymphatic cancer—apparently late stage. Happened back then."

"Hard to believe that was once fatal," answered Neela, shaking her head. "It would be like allowing a toothache to kill someone."

"Don't laugh, Neela," he retorted. "That used to happen, too."

"Just curious, Mosh, how long would it take to cure him?"

He checked the display again. "According to Dr. Wang, six hours to cure, twelve to revive."

Neela thought about it.

"So why on Earth would that corporate goon have said five years? That's not only unconstitutional, it's unethical." She paused. "Barbaric, even."

Mosh called up the accused's file on his holodisplay. "Our *goon's* name is Hektor. Hektor Sambianco. And you'd better watch your back with that one. I know the type. They're like pit bulls; once they lock on to something it's hard to get 'em to let go."

"Duly noted," she answered. "But I don't get it, Mosh. What exactly is he locked on to?"

Mosh chuckled at the innocence of his charge's question. "Our newfound friend, my dear. He wants to incorporate him, and he doesn't want to share, if you get my drift."

"Which," she continued, lightbulbs going off, "explains why everyone around here's getting paid leave. But it doesn't explain five years, Mosh. Keeping anyone down that long when it's unnecessary is not only illegal, it's unconstitutional—corporation or no corporation."

"True enough," Mosh said, leaning back into his state-of-the-art Nomic chair.

They both knew what was at stake. The "right of return" with regard to reanimation was sacrosanct. And it made sense that it would be. After all, who would willingly suspend themselves knowing their reanimation might not happen due to litigation, corporate interference, or any other manner of legality that might leave someone suspended involuntarily for centuries? Therefore, the right of return had been enacted into constitutional law almost as soon as reanimation had become technically viable. Its basic premise was that a suspendee had the

right to immediate revival pursuant to the ability to do so safely, without causing any realistic undue hardship to society or the individual in question.

"Alright, Neela," Mosh said, brows cinched tightly, "you've got my ear. Let me
do a little fact-checking and I'll get back to you."

Ever the perfectionist, Hektor Sambianco was in the transport bay overseeing
the final details for shipment. He was also marveling at the beauty of the suspension unit itself. The huge black rectangle inscribed with the fiery red letters
had a compelling presence all its own, unlike the simple and economical teardrop
units currently in use. Hektor saw right away that the unit would be worth untold credits—regardless of the prize within. But the prize within, if successfully
revived, could be worth quite a bit as well—a man from preincorporation
America. There was no telling how much profit would be in it for GCI—and
even better, what kind of bonus share might be in it for Hektor.

He chuckled, remembering his recent conversation with that ornery revivalist. *I might just make majority after all.*

Hektor's musings were rudely interrupted by the sound of confrontation. He
turned around to see Director McKenzie and the revivalist woman being denied
access to the bay by one of the guards he'd stationed as a precautionary measure.

"The last time I checked," Mosh said to the newly stationed guard, "I was still
the director here, and this is still my transport bay."

"Actually," proclaimed Hektor from across the bay, "the hospital—transport
bay included—still belongs to GCI, unless, of course, you've made some large
purchases I'm not aware of. Nevertheless . . ." Hektor signaled the guard to let
them pass.

Mosh and Neela quickly traversed the bay to where Hektor was working.

"Make it quick, please," Hektor said, "I don't have a lot of time."

"Four hours, fifty-eight minutes, and twenty-two seconds to be exact," the director answered, consulting his DijAssist.

"You've been checking up on me, I see."

Mosh was about to answer but was beat out by Neela.

"Who do you think you are?!"

"Hektor Sambianco," he replied casually. "No need for you to introduce yourself, thank you."

"I think," Mosh offered, "my overwrought employee is upset with what you're
planning to do."

"No," interjected Neela. "I'm upset with what he's planning *not* to do!" Turning her wrath again toward Hektor, "How can you leave him suspended?"

"Don't you worry your little head," Hektor answered condescendingly. "We'll revive him, all in good time. Yes, anyways, thank you for sharing your feelings. I'll make sure to mention them to . . . whoever I mention these things to." He then turned his back on them, continuing his preparations.

Neela and Mosh remained in place.

"I may have a difficult time signing the clearance order to move this unit," said Mosh. "You know, busy schedule and all. My assistant could do it, but, oh my," he said as he pressed a button on his DijAssist, "I just gave her the rest of the day off."

With a sigh, Hektor turned around.

"Perhaps I was a bit single-minded in pursuit of completing my job. What is it you need, Director?"

Good, Mosh thought, *he's got his eyes on the ball.*

"An explanation would be a start."

"An explanation about what?" Hektor asked, feigning innocence.

"About why you seem to be denying this man his civil rights," challenged Neela.

"Whoa! Who said anything about denying this man his civil rights?"

"The Constitution . . . ," began Neela.

". . . does not apply here," finished Hektor.

"And who gave you the right to say that the Constitution does not apply?" Neela retorted.

Hektor smirked. "Actually, I'm a constitutional lawyer. Who gave you the right to say that it does?" *Chew on that one, bitch.*

"Lawyer or not," Neela continued unfazed, "this man has to be revived immediately. It's the law, and every citizen knows that."

"OK, Miss . . . Harper, was it?" Hektor began. "Let's just see about that law that *every* citizen knows about. First of all, how do you even know this man *is* a citizen? If he's not, constitutional law doesn't apply, does it? Didn't think about that, did you? Secondly, for all we know he was suspended because of some horrific act or acts he committed. Constitution or no, do you want to take responsibility for rereleasing him into our society? Would it not be prudent to wait and run some tests, and then perhaps let the courts decide?"

"We ran all the tests needed," answered Neela. "He's curable and poses no medical danger to society. Under the criteria of the Constitution and the Supreme Court's interpretation of it, no other consideration is needed—citizen or not. All crimes or debts will be dealt with upon revival."

"Bravo," Hektor chided, clapping his hands slowly. "I see you know the legal aspects of your profession well. But you're forgetting one thing."

"He's curable and he's here," she spat back. "That's the only criteria. I'm forgetting nothing."

"Payment," the director said, choosing the moment to step in. He had a grim smile. "You're going to steal him on payment."

Hektor's return smile was equally as grim. " 'Steal' is such a harsh word, Director."

Neela was confused. "But everybody pays with insur . . . oh."

"Everybody *today* pays with insurance," continued Hektor. "The first we were notified of our mystery man here was when one of our adjusters couldn't find any insurance for him. And we're certainly not obligated to wake patients without proof of ability to pay—and this revive's going to cost a doozy, I can assure you. That's the law, young lady. But don't you worry, I'm sure we'll be able to work something out, and we will get around to reviving him eventually."

"When you can figure out how to make the most profit out of him," sneered Neela.

Hektor smiled at her with all the innocence of a choirboy, refusing to bite. "Now, if we're all done here, I really . . ."

"I'll pay," Neela blurted.

"You'll what?" asked Mosh and Hektor simultaneously.

"I said I'll pay. I may have to max out my credit cards, borrow on my remaining stock, and use my employee discount, but I should be able to raise the money. What's another ten thousand credits? I'm pretty much buried in the hole as it is. So what the heck . . . I'll pay for his revival. You can stop doing whatever it is you're doing here, OK?" Neela sighed in satisfaction.

Hektor was smiling, too.

"What's your problem now?" asked Neela. "We have a revive that's medically viable, in a proper facility, with payment being fully covered."

Mosh was looking at Hektor, curious as to what he would do with this one.

"I apologize for underestimating your zeal," Hektor answered. "I should have seen it sooner and factored it into my considerations. Most sloppy of me. Still, I'm greatly impressed at your willingness to spend ten million credits of your own money."

Neela was flabbergasted. Mosh remained silent.

"Ten million credits for a revive?!" screamed Neela. "What are you doing? Gilding his ass in uranium?"

Hektor, busily humming to himself, began to add up points in his DijAssist. "Let's see, one million credits for a proper inspection, storage, and shipment; this is a three-hundred-year-old unit, after all. Two million credits for a thorough nanotechnologically invasive investigation of the occupant. Four million credits for consultation with the experts in the field . . . and there are, as you well know, only two that matter, Bronstein and Gillette, but if you want we will even call you in on that one—add another hundred credits. And, oh, let's see, three million for, what the hell, a brand-new revive clinic, state-of-the-art, for this unique find." He held out his DijAssist to her, showing the invoice ready to be paid in its official format. "To use an old phrase, will that be cash or charge?"

"You can't be serious," cried Neela. "There's no way this is legal."

"Actually," he continued, "the law states that we can charge whatever we wish. He was found in *our* territory, under *our* jurisdiction, brought to *our* hospital, and is under *our* care. Now a party of standing, a relative or spouse, could contest this in court and, I'll even give it to you, could probably win. However, that doesn't appear to be the case. But I'm nothing if not thorough." He spoke up loudly so all in the bay could hear. "Anybody here a party of standing, a relative or spouse? Speak up . . . anyone?"

Silence.

"Hmm," he said. "How unfortunate. The gentleman in question seems to be an orphan. When we revive him he'll be free to contest the price . . . in, say, four or five years."

"You mean when you've already got a firm grasp on his shares," said Mosh.

"Why, Director, you are speaking prematurely. He's not even incorporated yet. We'll need to set up a legal guardianship and assign stock options, as well as investigate the legal ramifications. It would do this man an injustice to bring him into this world without making sure everything was in order."

"Mosh can pay," blurted Neela.

Before Mosh could respond, Hektor laughed out loud. "Yes, I suppose he could. Now that is *very* generous of you, spending your boss's money like that, but I think he'll be more than happy to explain to you why *that's not going to happen.*" He then looked over at the director.

"Mosh?" pleaded Neela.

Mosh raised his hand to silence her. "We've taken up enough of Mr. Sambianco's time." Then, looking over at Hektor, "I trust, sir, that you will not hold my employee's enthusiasm against her." It was delivered more as a warning than a request.

"On the contrary, Director. I'm greatly impressed by her zeal." Hektor considered for a moment, and brightened. "In fact," he said, inputting some new commands in his DijAssist, "I just placed a purchase order for another thousand shares of her personal stock."

"You really are a bastard," Neela said, before turning on her heel and storming out of the bay.

Hektor and Mosh were now alone.

"Look," Hektor said, "I know you were once a pretty powerful member of GCI, and you came to this nice little hospital of your own volition. But you were clearly outmatched today. I hope it will not be necessary to embarrass you like this in the future."

"Not if I can help it, Mr. Sambianco."

Mosh smiled thinly and walked away without saying another word.

Neela was anxiously pacing outside the transport bay entrance when Mosh emerged.

"Sorry about that," she said.

Mosh put his hand on her shoulder and smiled.

"Don't worry about it."

They walked down a long hallway toward the cafeteria.

"No, it really was wrong of me to offer *your* money," Neela continued, narrowly avoiding a group of internists on their rounds. Then, as an aside, "Like you'd even have that kind of money lying around anyways."

"Actually, Neela," he said, stopping to thumbprint-approve some forms handed to him by a nurse, "I do." He continued walking—minus his rebellious subordinate. After a few paces he turned to Neela, standing in consternation. "You coming, or what?" he asked.

He waited for her at the entrance to the cafeteria. They headed together to his reserved table. "You're telling me," she asked, "you have ten million credits?"

"Considerably more, actually." She knew he wasn't bragging; it wasn't in his nature.

"Then why didn't you just pay him?" she asked. "Why did you let me go out on a limb for ten thousand when you had millions, no, I'm sorry, tens of millions in the bank?"

"Neela," he answered, reaching across the table to take her hands into his. "I'm truly sorry, but I had to let you, well . . . be you. Besides, I never would have been able to pay, and neither would you."

"Care to explain that one?"

Mosh smiled. "Of course," he said, releasing her hands from his grasp and leaning back into his chair. "Neela, you're an excellent revivalist. With experience, you may be one of the best. Hektor's not the only one buying your stock."

"Really?" she asked in disbelief.

"Ten thousand shares, to be exact, but only in options. You have a temper that may get the better of you. As I was saying, you really are quite talented. But you don't have a corporate bone in your body. As much as this may surprise you, I never went to the transport bay with any hope of helping that man."

"Why would you leave him like that?"

"I wouldn't. But Neela, it's not up to me. It never was. Nor is it up to you. Even if I'd been suicidal enough to want to pay, I wouldn't have been allowed to."

"How could they stop you from paying with your own money?"

Mosh sighed. "Neela, I can think of three ways off the top of my head, conflict of interest being right at the top. But they don't need to stop payment—just delay it. A court order from a friendly judge would be more than enough to delay the revive for days, if not weeks."

"So we revive him in a couple of weeks instead of hours. Better than five years, no?"

"Neela, GCI wants him. In a couple of weeks he could be lost in a warehouse with a foreman all set up to take the blame for misplacing him. Or worse, someone could decide that he's too much of an inconvenience, and the corpsicle disappears for another hundred years."

"That doesn't happen!"

"Not often, but yes, it does. Why do you think I got out? The price was too high for the power I was capable of wielding." Neela looked at her boss with a mixture of respect and worry.

"But . . ."

"No buts, Neela. Suppose that we *had* managed to succeed. And I was willing to expend the bulk of my fortune using the connections built up over a lifetime to protect and revive this man against the most powerful corporation in human history—against, I might add, a corporation that wants this man for numerous compelling reasons, and would be willing and economically justified to go to incredible lengths to insure their investment in him. Now, my dear girl, what do you think GCI would do to anyone standing in their way?"

"Oh please, Mosh, you don't really mean to say that they'd . . ."

"Neela, don't be dramatic," he continued. "But they would make our lives miserable, if only as a warning to others. How would you like to spend the next hundred years performing emergency suspensions on the frozen moons of Jupiter?"

"But what could they do to you?" Neela asked. "You're rich and have already made majority. You're untouchable, aren't you?"

Mosh looked at her, his sad smile the precursor to an answer she suspected but had never really wanted to hear.

"Neela," he said, "most people assume that when you get majority all your worries go away—in most cases that's correct. As long as you don't try to off yourself you can pretty much do what you want with your life. But let's assume that GCI decides to make an example of me. I might start getting audited medically on a monthly or even weekly basis. There may be court challenges as to my fitness to maintain control of my own portfolio."

"On what basis?"

"Well, the willingness to spend ten million credits on someone I have never met may be justification for trial alone."

Neela sighed. "That wouldn't stand, Mosh."

"Neela, it doesn't have to stand. But it would be expensive and time consuming. Or they could just have people sue me, not for money but for stock. I would just need to lose three or four cases, and there goes my majority."

"Damsah's ghost," whispered Neela.

"You're beginning to understand."

Mosh took her hand and leaned closer. "Neela, sometimes there are things in life worth sacrificing everything for. For every individual it's something different. I'm not sure what I would risk everything for. But even if it were Tim Damsah himself in there I doubt I'd do it. And I'm positive I won't for a three-hundred-year-old frozen body of someone I have never met and probably never heard of."

Neela sat for a moment while she absorbed all that Mosh had told her.

"OK, Mosh," she asked, "why did we go through all of that if you realized it wasn't going to get us anywhere?"

"Why," he smiled, "to cover our collective asses, of course . . . and you can say 'thank you.'"

"OK, now you've lost me."

Mosh took out his DijAssist and pushed a button. He showed her the screen. The entire encounter in the bay had been vidacorded for posterity.

"But why?" she asked.

"Insurance, my dear." Mosh leaned forward and lowered his voice, indicating that she come closer. "When our poor bastard finally does wake up and finds his valuable shares already owned by GCI, what do you think he's gonna do first? Say 'thanks for screwing me'? Not bloody likely. He's going to go to court and try and win back as much of himself as he can. And who, my dear, do you think's going to get nailed against the wall in all his legitimate fury?"

"Hektor and his cohorts. Who else?" she answered.

"*We else*, Neela. Think about it. He goes after GCI, and he'll be tied up in court for years. He goes after us, and we'll be forced to settle a lot sooner than that. But let's just take your scenario. Let's suppose he hires a bad litigator and is stupid enough to go after GCI. Who do you think they'll make the scapegoat for his righteous indignation?"

And there it was. Neela realized she'd been played. That the entire confrontation with Hektor was the first move in a high-stakes game of corporate survival.

"You could have told me, Mosh. I would have been a good girl, you know."

"Which," Mosh intoned, "is exactly why I didn't. There's not a poly-psyche in the world that will ever question your sincerity on this vidacord. As far as the world, and more importantly, the courts, will see, we did our absolute utmost to 'free' our little frozen friend from the clutches of 'corporate' greed."

Neela sat back. "I'll be damned."

———

Mosh was just getting ready to leave his office. He looked around and was satisfied with how the day had turned out. His encounter with Hektor had provided some excitement, reminded him of why he got out of the upper echelons in the first place, and reaffirmed that he could still handle the sharks if need be. Not bad for a day's work. He backed up all the relevant data into his secure file and separated it from the main computer storage. Switching his phone to emergency calls only by shaking his left hand in the air, he left his small but functional office.

Just outside the door he was ambushed by his secretary.

"I'm sorry to bring this up, but they wanted me to make sure you read it," she said. She stood directly in his path, arms folded—devilish smirk on her face.

"Which 'they,' Eleanor?" he asked, resigned.

"The accounting department *they*, O great and powerful director, sir," she answered.

"Oh that," he laughed. "I saw it and ignored it, as any sane man would do with yet another memo from Accounting. It can wait until tomorrow. Coming?" he asked, motioning toward the door.

"In a minute." She stepped toward him and put her arms around his neck, then gently nuzzled his ear. Speaking softly she cooed, "It seemed pretty urgent, and I did promise them you would look into it before you left today."

"I never should have married you," Mosh said with a smile, knowing he'd lost this battle. He turned around and headed back into his office. Without even sitting down he hovered over the holodisplay and called up the memo that had assumed the extraordinary power to influence his marital bliss in an amazingly short amount of time.

He read the first line.

Interesting. He reached for his chair, and without taking his eyes off the display, pulled it beneath him and sat down.

He spent the next fifteen minutes calling up and sending out data. When he'd confirmed the essentials of the memo and all it entailed, he leaned back into his chair and allowed himself a brief respite. He had a funny feeling it was going to be his last for some time.

He called out to his wife through the still open doorway. "Honey, I don't think I'll be able to make dinner after all. And get me Dr. Wang."

Hektor was busy indulging his one true vice. The smell of an incredibly rare and expensive cigar was filling the small, impersonal office he'd been using for the day he was at the Boulder facility. The thought that the cigar smoke would linger and annoy the prissy, health-conscious bureaucrats filled him with joy. After all, the prejudice against smoking had no basis in modern health care, and yet this petty meme was still making its presence felt centuries after the need for it had disappeared. But this was a time to celebrate, and if the celebration bothered the hospital staff, so be it.

He'd just finished talking with the deputy director in charge of Special Operations, DepDir for short, and had given his report. The DepDir was very pleased and told Hektor that the board would be informed of his outstanding work. He'd even hinted that The Chairman himself had taken an interest in the project. This meant that there was a chance, small but there nonetheless, that The Chairman would hear Hektor's name. Something he could only have hoped for in the course of ten more years of steady progress. If that didn't call for an expensive cigar, then nothing in his immediate future would. And he wasn't about to wait for the more traditional reason to light one up. *Hell, you can always have kids,* he thought.

Hektor's thumb started to vibrate.

"What is it?" he asked, still smiling, cigar dangling from the corner of his mouth. His iris scan let him know that it was his intern. Good self-starter. Efficient problem solver.

"Uh, sir, we have a problem."

"Handle it, Raga."

"I tried, sir, but the shippers aren't willing to move the package without your assurance."

"What are you talking about, Rag? This is a company service, and they're company employees. Come to think of it, they're even getting bonuses." He paused for a moment. "Or at least they were."

"It's not about money, sir. They're worried about liability."

"Liability? For what? The damn thing's been sealed for over three hundred years. It was made to withstand a cave-in from a mountain made of solid rock." *In fact, it did,* he mused. "I'm sure it can be safely loaded by a few grunts. It's not as if it's going to just pop open and say boo!"

"Well, actually, sir . . ."

The blood left Hektor's face. He stubbed out the thousand-credit cigar less than two minutes into what should have been an hour of joy.

"Don't move or touch a thing. I'm on my way."

Hektor shoved his way into Mosh's office.

"Funny, your profile said nothing about suicide." Every ounce of sarcasm he could muster was furled into the sentence.

The crowd around Mosh's desk backed away and gave Hektor his space.

"Please excuse us," the director said to the minions bustling about the room. With the last of them gone, Hektor sat down in front of Mosh's desk and crossed his legs.

"Please tell me you haven't initiated the revive process."

"In fact, we have."

"Then I suppose you realize," Hektor said, "that you've condemned us both."

"I can't say your feared demise will cause me any great sorrow," Mosh replied, "but *I* intend to be here for some time."

"That would be a neat trick," sneered Hektor. "However, while I may not have the power to bring you down personally, there are those whose profits and reputations you've just cut into who will in fact take this badly. And if I'm not mining rocks on comets in the Oort Cloud, I'll take great joy in watching that day arrive."

"So dramatic, Hektor, really. In fact, if you'd bothered to check, you would've seen that your one criteria for immediate revive—namely a ridiculous amount of money—had been met."

"You're not that stupid, Director."

"On this we can both agree." Mosh leaned back in his seat, putting his arms behind his head. "The money was paid into the hospital's account by an anonymous sponsor."

"Anonymous, my ass," scoffed Hektor. "That's impossible. No one could have paid that much money in that short a period of time . . . unless it was you, and like I said . . ."

". . . I'm 'not that stupid,' " Mosh continued. "Feel free to check my accounts; I'm sure everyone else will."

"Oh, you can bet your majority on that, Director."

"And by the way," Mosh continued. "Someone, and I'm not naming names," he said, looking directly at Hektor, "made it much easier to pay by making the invoice official in the hospital's database."

"It was an invoice for ten million credits!" Hektor shouted. "No one has that kind of money. At least no one who'd want to revive a three-hundred-year-old corpse they had no stock in."

"Exorbitant yes, but certainly legal. There for all to access and, apparently, pay."

Hektor tried to gather his wits about him.

"Even if you didn't pay, why did I have to go down to the transport and find an empty suspension unit and twenty highly paid movers scratching their collective asses unless you had something to hide? You and I both know what's at stake here, and by doing this behind my back, you make yourself look culpable. The least you should have done was call me." Hektor now put his hands on his head and his elbows on his knees. "I figured you for smarter," he said, resigned.

Mosh looked at the man in front of him, considering his words carefully.

"Look, I don't know if this is going to help, but I'm going to hope you pay attention. I did what I did for two reasons, Mr. Sambianco. First, once payment had been secured this man had a right to be woken up as soon as was medically possible. And that meant immediately. I, for one, was not prepared to keep him suspended beyond that point just so you or anyone else could make some additional profit. He's entitled to make his own profit, Mr. Sambianco, or our whole system is worthless. And second . . ." Mosh paused, waiting for Hektor to look up, making sure he had his full attention.

"I don't like you, Mr. Sambianco."

Hektor looked stunned. Such direct honesty was certainly not the norm, and certainly never directed at him personally.

"Still," continued Mosh, "I don't want to be accused of letting my personal feelings interfere with legitimate company business, so I feel compelled to tell you that there is *one way* I'm aware of that will delay this revive."

Hektor's ears perked up. *Perhaps he's not willing to commit suicide after all.*

"Now a party of standing, a relative or spouse, could contest this revive in court and, I'll even give it to you, could probably stop me from proceeding. However, there doesn't appear to be any party of standing. But," continued Mosh with a sly smile, "I'm nothing if not thorough." He spoke loud enough for all in the hallway to hear. "Anybody here a party of standing, a relative or spouse? Speak up. Anyone?"

Silence.

"Hmm. How fortunate for our mysterious friend."

Hektor slumped back down in his chair.

"Fine," Hektor replied. "Go ahead, Director. Do it. But if you really had your patient's best interest in mind you wouldn't be using a novice to do the revive. Let me at least call in some real pros."

"First of all, Hektor, Dr. Wang is not a novice."

"I'm not talking about Wang, I'm talking about Harper."

"Right, Neela. Funny thing about Neela. I'd sooner trust her than someone with ten times the experience who I'm confident would screw my patient on a credit at the behest of you and your organization. You see, Hektor, I think she does have the patient's best interest in mind. I don't believe *your* 'experts' would."

With that Mosh got up, gathered his belongings, and headed for the door. He looked back and saw Hektor still slumped in his seat with his head in his hands.

"You coming?"

"To what?" Hektor retorted.

"The rebirth of our new friend—the Unincorporated Man."

2 Wake-up Call

We had the perfect case. Isolated, with three hundred years of experience to draw on. A procedure that had been performed literally millions of times was going to be done once in close to ideal conditions. We were going to make history with the perfect revive, in both body and mind, of a three-hundred-year-old man. It would be a textbook case, and I was to be its author. So of course we screwed it up.

—*A Life Renewed: The Biography of Dr. Neela Harper*

It started out as an awareness. Nothing was associated with the awareness. No shapes or colors or feelings were part of this awareness. None of the five senses were present. Just an awareness, and with it a feeling of the most complete satisfaction that could be imagined. Slowly a sense of self began to evolve.

I am a "he," thought the *he.*

With this revelation came new sensations. Time had no anchor whatsoever, so what seemed to take a moment may have been considerably longer. But it didn't really matter. Because the *he* was beginning to remember what the sensations were and to put them in proper context. The art of separating feeling from hearing from vision was a skill taken for granted that the *he* had to relearn. But the *he* was not impatient. Somehow, although the *he* did not know his name, his location, or his past, the *he* did know to the core of his newly reawakened being that the *he* had all the time in the world. He did somehow remember that time had been the *he's* enemy. Time had been something always closing in, biting off large chunks of the *he*—making the *he* afraid. But the *he* was no longer afraid. Justin . . .

My name is JUSTIN, the *he* realized.

Now he had all the time in the world.

JUSTIN is in a bed, JUSTIN thought. JUSTIN still had no concept of where JUSTIN was or how JUSTIN had gotten there. JUSTIN's memory was nothing beyond the primal sense of self that one has when awoken from a long and confusing dream.

Not a dream—a nightmare.

The bed felt very comfortable. The mattress made JUSTIN feel like he was floating on waves of tiny bubbles, and the linen was of a perfect warmth that made JUSTIN want to roll over and go back to bed. But JUSTIN resisted that urge—not out of any sense of apprehension or need, but out of the knowledge that JUSTIN had slept long enough.

He smelled a pot of coffee. It was just brewing up fresh and was going to be ready soon. He knew that for a fact but didn't remember hearing any of the associated sounds—the steady stream of liquid hitting liquid, the hiss and gurgle at the culmination. Justin was not yet aware of how odd that was. He was paying attention to what he did hear. A soft hum in the background was accompanied by the sound of the crisp pages of a book being turned. Next he became aware of the light and knew it was light, and that the light was coming from the outside.

His eyes fluttered open.

The light was a perfect ambient illumination that did not hurt his eyes in the least. There was no one place the light was coming from.

How odd, thought Justin. At that moment he could not have described to anyone what a lightbulb or lamp was, but a part of his mind was aware that light simply did not come from nowhere.

His eyes were sweeping the surroundings, absorbing all that he saw. But he did not see any one thing at first so much as he saw the entire room. It was simple, with a door at the far end and a coffee table and two chairs beyond the bed he lay in. There was a painting on the wall. He lingered on it. It was a beautiful rendition of an ocean as viewed from a forest on a cliff. He could not explain how all those concepts could have been conveyed by a simple painting, but he wanted it for his collection.

I collect art, he remembered. His mind became flooded with images of sculptures and paintings and shapes and experiences and hours. Hours spent admiring his collection and the personal sense of happiness that he owned such beauty.

Then he heard the pages turn again.

His eyes wandered gently toward the sound. There, sitting cross-legged a few feet from his bed, was the most beautiful woman he had ever seen in the world. She was reading a book. He couldn't take his eyes off her.

She is beautiful, he thought, *but the most beautiful?* He began to doubt. *She's so beautiful because you were never meant to see* anyone *ever again—much less a woman.*

Justin began to shift his body subtly. He could feel his heart pounding. He felt warm. *Fear. This must be fear,* he reasoned. And not that he could prove it, but somehow the bed seemed to have responded to the fluctuation in his temperature. It was a few degrees cooler now.

"*I'm sorry, Mr. Cord.*" A voice from the past. "*There's nothing we can do.*"

"*How long?*" Justin echoed in response.

"*Two months at the most. You'll want to make arrangements.*"

"*Yes, of course, Doctor. You needn't worry. All necessary arrangements have already been made.*"

Justin was now no longer afraid. In fact, quite the opposite. Triumph seemed to pulse through his veins as he began to experience a sense of elation far beyond anything he had ever imagined. He remembered everything. But what stood head and shoulders above the cascade of sounds and imagery now refilling his mind was one very salient and inimitable fact—he had won. His death had been revoked.

Son of a bitch. He grinned. *It worked.*

Neela realized she was nervous. This was not the first time this had happened. Her oldest revive had been a five-year case that she got only because the specialist on call had gotten into a traffic accident, and the procedure had already started. Her career to date was made up of reanimating bodies in suspension measured in months, never years. And now she was the sole revivalist on record for a man with well over three hundred of them. For all she knew, this person was alive when the Beatles were touring. He may even have visited the World Trade Center or seen Mecca before those world-altering disasters. She had a million questions.

For the first time in her short career she took a body-suppression drug, at one time recommended but now almost never used by those in her profession. The thinking went that the last thing you wanted to happen during a revive was to shock the patient with a loud sneeze or, worse, a disagreeable odor. In theory it was correct, but in fact most of the revives Neela oversaw got up as if they'd taken a long nap. The only thing that would frighten these people was a serious drop in their portfolios or a losing season of a favorite team. Hardly seemed worth the side effects of the drug against an almost nonexistent risk. But this was different. Not only in this case could the initial theory be correct, but certainly this day was going to be written about, commented on, and listened to for the rest of her considerable life and beyond. And this record was not going to have her hiccupping, sneezing, or, perhaps, doing something decidedly worse for all eternity.

It took all of her control not to stare at him. He had soft, wavy brown hair, a few wisdom lines across his well-exposed forehead that curved into gentle arcs, and a well-proportioned face finished elegantly with a strong masculine jawline. She estimated him to be well over six feet tall. She wasn't sure if her fascination was based on the very novelty of who he was and what he represented or the fact that he was, even from her admittedly feigned objective viewpoint, quite hand-some. The former theory would have to suffice, since the idea of any sort of at-traction was anathema not only to Neela but also to present-day society. When a patient first awoke they were considered vulnerable. It was as simple as that. Any thoughts of physical attraction were to be quickly dispelled, and then followed ideally by a healthy dose of shame. It hadn't always been that way. However, as a result of earlier abuses—sexual and otherwise—by a few miscreants in the fledgling cryonics movement, a meme had been put in place that rather effec-tively tarred an abuser of a suspendee on the same level as that of a sexual de-viant. As far as memes went it was excessive but rather efficient in giving safe harbor to those returning from their long, sleepy journeys. And so, well before Neela's life cycle began, the only acceptable relationship between a patient and a reanimationist was professional—no exceptions whatsoever.

As she looked over at her patient she wanted to pummel him with questions and be shocked and amazed by the answers. But it was vital that she be nothing but a neutral presence until he chose to notice her. Had this been one of her run-of-the-mill revives she wouldn't have worried a bit. The patient would have re-ceived a full briefing well in advance on how to handle being suspended and revived. And even had it been an emergency suspension there would have been nothing to fear. Suspension had become so standardized a procedure that most were aware of what to expect—barring any unforeseen circumstances, of course. In fact, her generation was so comfortable with the concept of revival that im-mediate interaction had become more the norm than the exception.

But for this revive Neela had done her homework. Since she hadn't expected Hektor to waltz in and almost waltz away with her patient, she had begun her re-search immediately. So when she did get the call from Mosh, she was ready. She'd sorted through her old college notes, as well as the university archives, looking for the information she'd need, paramount of which was Ettinger's sem-inal work developed over three centuries earlier to deal with patients for whom revival was a shock. After reading and reviewing hundreds of pages, one theme seemed to emerge: Patients had to reintegrate at their own pace. Too much proaction on the part of the revivalist risked setting into motion all manner of psychotic trauma—too little and the patient might have permanent abandon-ment trauma. The mind reborn was as vulnerable and helpless as that of a new-born child. And until it had a chance to acclimate to its new reality, great care would have to be taken. On this, all the founding experts had agreed, and so, too, did the experts of her day. But until this find, now *her* find, it had all been theo-retical.

So she waited and read her "book," whose exterior was quite authentic, down to the creaking sound a bound volume would make. It was the interior that was different—a cleverly concealed, encased holodisplay. Neela's support team in the wings was also simultaneously viewing on their linked displays the various readouts emitting from the book. The players included the room specialists who were not privy to the actual goings-on, a standby resuscitation team, and, of course, Mosh and his associated staff. Of all the players only Mosh, Dr. Wang, Neela, and Hektor knew the subject's recent history. The information on the display gave the patient's vitals, eye movements, and, to some extent, thoughts. Neela could tell by the brain scan what emotions the patient was feeling and to what extent they were being felt. The display also contained her vitals. For any number of reasons, her stats were just as important as his. This reawakening would be a delicate dance between two strangers from two worlds, and any major fluctuations in either of them could lead to a disaster.

Though Justin's feelings were now running amok, he was making a conscious effort to suppress them. Every fiber in his body yearned to grab the woman he saw, give her a great big hug, and scream with joy at the top of his lungs. He had a million questions, but by virtue of personal experience and business savvy, he had learned that self-answered questions always added leverage. And he didn't yet know what type of leverage he was going to need.

Time for answers.

Justin again scanned the room, but this time more methodically. He was looking for anything that would give him an inkling about the type of world he'd willed himself into.

The readings Neela was getting were positive. Very positive. The patient's endorphin response was through the roof, as expected. All areas of the brain associated with contentment were hot, and his heartbeat was rapid, also as expected. This was indeed a happy man. She noticed, too, that her joy levels were up as well—not an uncommon reaction. After all, the best revivalists were naturally sympathetic, and to some extent even empathetic, having been suspended themselves as part of their training.

Then something strange happened.

What the . . . ? Neela kept her face and reactions perfectly normal, but her brain was working overtime trying to figure out the anomaly.

The patient's readings had leveled out almost as if someone had turned off her display. *Too fast,* she thought. Her eyes glanced subtly to the through-view wall, wondering if her staff was experiencing the malfunction as well.

For a moment she thought that perhaps the software had failed her. But then she glanced at her own readings. Normal. Which is to say, exactly as would be expected for an individual feeling concern. No, it wasn't the software; it must be the man himself, and according to the holodisplay the patient's state was categorized as "calm and alert." *But how?* In all her years of study, encompassing hundreds of patients, she'd never seen anyone control an emotional response with such brutal efficiency. *Who is this guy?*

Justin was now keenly aware of his surroundings. He started with the bed. *Whatever it is I'm resting on is somehow aware of my physiological condition and is able to respond. Fascinating.* He shifted his body only to feel the bed conform to his movement and help him into the most comfortable position. *OK,* he thought, *the technology clearly kicks ass. Of course it kicks ass, you idiot,* he realized a moment later, *you're alive.* And even that important fact spoke volumes about the society he'd awakened to. But he'd hopefully have time for that. *Gather physical facts now,* he chided himself, *evaluate later.*

The light was the most obvious change he was aware of. It came from no discernible source yet was everywhere. The room was simply lit. The more he tried to find a light source, the more his brain hurt, so he dropped it. *They have sourceless light—move on.* He smelled coffee but saw no coffeepot. If he were relying on his smell alone he would have bet his fortune that a percolator was in the room. *They have scent simulators and are smart enough . . . no—sensitive enough—to use them in this situation.* This was a good start. Not only had he been reanimated, but it was now apparent that the people who had done the reanimation had gone to great effort to make him comfortable. *So,* he reasoned, *not necessarily an inhospitable society. Good.* Now he turned to the woman. She was, while not the most beautiful woman in the world, still quite attractive.

Her pose, crossed legs and casual indifference, suggested comfort. But that was it, wasn't it? A pose . . . for his benefit alone. Because this woman clearly was not comfortable. Justin had become an expert on reading body language, and hers was tense.

She's waiting for me. Fine. Patience. She can wait.

Now he noticed the book in her hands. He tried to make out the title. He focused his eyes. *The Tempest,* by William Shakespeare. He smiled. *How appropriate, and, of course, logical. Not knowing exactly how old I am, she went with a classic.* He chuckled to himself. *She has access to technology that can raise the dead, provide completely sourceless light, and physiologically adaptive furniture, and is sitting here holding in her hands what is most likely a relic of my millennium. "A" for effort.*

And the more he thought about it, the more reassured he became. He clearly had some value to someone just by being alive. And to Justin it mattered not whether it was an intrinsic value that this society placed on human life, or perhaps the "freak show value" of his circumstance. He was alive, and someone very much wanted him to remain so. Either way it gave him some standing. Having assessed as much as he could within his immediate vicinity, he realized it was time to interact with the woman.

Neela was keeping tabs on her patient. He was in some sort of evaluation mode, and it was pretty obvious from where his eyes and muscles were moving that he was analyzing his environment. What she didn't understand was why this seemed to be causing him irritation. The light was specifically set to not cause any . . .

Idiot, Neela chastised herself. *They didn't have sourceless light three hundred years ago. I should have set up a light emitter.*

But no sooner had the self-flagellation begun than she felt his eyes bearing directly down on her. Instinctively she forced her feelings aside in an attempt to appear relaxed. It was unbearable. She yearned for the release of speech. *Perhaps he'd lost his ability to speak,* she reasoned. *No, the prerevive indicators would have flagged that.* But the indicators weren't always right, were they? Software was software, and its many malfunctions had been a part of the technological lore for eons. He'd talk when he was good and ready, and she'd just have to wait patiently until he did.

"How long?" Justin asked, surprised at the sound of a voice he'd lived his whole life with but which now somehow felt new.

"I assume you mean how long have you been suspended?" Neela asked.

"Yes. How long?"

"By our estimates, about three hundred years. With some more information we could give you an exact date."

"Maybe later."

The enormity of Justin's accomplishment was just starting to sink in, but so was the enormity of the loss.

"Is there anyone left alive from my time?"

"None that we're aware of. Though you yourself came as a surprise—so it's not inconceivable," she answered, wishing to instill some hope.

"But highly unlikely, correct?"

"That is correct." Neela began to realize that this was a man who was not going to need much of a soft pillow. She would disregard most of her primary plans and move to adopt a more straightforward approach.

"But how is that possible?" Justin continued. "At the time of my suspension there were at least two active cryonic-suspension organizations with memberships in the thousands and suspensions in the hundreds. You're telling me that in the past three hundred years not a single one of those suspendees made it?"

"That's what I'm telling you, Mr.—"

"For now, you can call me Justin."

"For now?" Neela was curious. "Is Justin not your real name?"

"It is *for now*," he answered.

"OK, Justin," Neela continued. *If that's how he wants to play it, then fine.* "My name is Neela, and you're correct. The cryonics movement of three hundred years ago, while tiny, was in fact persistent. And had the backlash not occurred, the incremental growth of those organizations would most likely have allowed a good number of suspendees to have made it to this time."

"Backlash?"

"Yes. Both of the organizations you referred to were destroyed, including all the patients."

"How?"

"One by a legal maneuver, the other by fire. The state government seized the one based in Michigan after it was revealed that most of the suspendees had died via assisted suicide. Apparently that was a political hot potato at the time, and the revelation forced a governmental inquiry and an eventual subpoena that resulted in the destruction of the facility's patients via court-mandated autopsies. I believe they used a tax law to seize the suspended patients, and they ordered full autopsies to check for foul play. After it was all done they apologized to the facilities' caretakers and returned the property, but by then . . ."

". . . by then it wouldn't have mattered," Justin said, finishing her thought. The whole point of suspension was not so much to freeze the body as it was to freeze the brain held within it. After all, it was the brain that truly determined "self," and it was the brain that held all the resident memories. A body left to defrost for too long would lead to ischemia of the brain or, more precisely, brain rot. And with that rot went any chance of memory retrieval. In essence, permanent death.

"And the one in Arizona?" asked Justin.

"That one was attacked by a mob and destroyed while the police looked on."

Justin furrowed his brow. "That seems a strong reaction against a group of people frozen in metal cylinders."

Neela nodded. "I would say it goes beyond strong, Justin. But given the circumstances at the time, understandable."

"Please explain."

Neela would have preferred he rested a bit before she loaded him up with information, but she could also understand his need for immediate satiation—his need to find a center from which to begin.

"The country," she answered, "was in the midst of what has since become known as the Grand Collapse. Cryonic suspension was seen not only as an eccentric pursuit, but also as an area of exclusivity for the rich. That alone probably wouldn't have been enough to cause the wanton destruction visited on the Arizona facility. However, the cryo-suspension of a serial pedophile and child murderer was. You see, the courts had ruled that once this criminal was officially declared dead, his contract with the Arizona institute for cryo-suspension should be honored. And keep in mind that he was put to death in a way perfectly conducive to the cryonic process—morphine overdose. But two hundred and fifty years ago medical nanotechnology was beginning to bear fruit, and the mere possibility that this creep might one day walk again—via the new technology—was enough to send an already enraged, unemployed mob on the warpath. The facility was burned to the ground while the police stood by and watched. The leader of the mob was interviewed years later, and when asked why he'd destroyed the facility, didn't say a word about the molester. What he did say has reverberated to this day as the ultimate cry of selfishness and despair: 'If we can't have a future, why should they?'" Neela checked to see that Justin was still with her. He was. "Does that make sense to you?" she asked.

"I'm the man who buried myself in a mountain against that very possibility," he answered, "so, sadly, yes—it does." He then sighed, choosing to remain silent. He needed time to absorb what he'd just heard.

He'd remembered reading a report in high school about immigrants who'd come to America in the seventeenth and eighteenth centuries. At first he wasn't sure why this memory came to him unbidden so clearly after all of these years. But he recalled his teacher trying to explain to him what it must have been like to be an immigrant, abandoning everything to go live in a new land far from home and family. At the time he'd listened but didn't understand. His was a world that had been connected technologically and wirelessly from the highest mountain to the most remote Amazonian village. You didn't have to "miss" anyone if you didn't want to, as long as you had the means to connect. But now Justin was beginning to understand what those early immigrants must have felt. They'd abandoned everything in the hopes of something better. But unlike those early immigrants, Justin had no way of reconnecting with *his* home. Not even the slightest chance of ever returning. He was an exile—unique among mankind in that his exile was not enforced by bars or distance or law, but rather by the unbending reality of time itself.

———

"How's he doing?" The question came from the normally taciturn legal counsel.

"He needed a little time to himself," answered Neela. "He's had three hundred years, what's another few hours?"

That elicited a chuckle from the tired yet excited group gathered around the conference table. Their faces glowed with triumph and satisfaction. They'd succeeded, and their stock was rising, or at least it would be soon, once knowledge of the day's events was made public. Mosh looked at the group. It was not large, consisting of himself, Dr. Wang, Neela, and Gilbert Tellar, the facility's legal counsel, who was only recently informed of events.

Gil was the first to speak. He addressed his comments primarily to Neela. "I realize it may be a tad preemptive, but I would just like it to be noted that our friend Justin is going to have a hill of legal matters to climb . . . and soon, I'm afraid."

All heads nodded in unison.

"Not at the top of my list," Neela responded. "He's particularly fragile at the moment, and trust me when I tell you, his eventual incorporation and all that that entails will take no small amount of time for him to digest."

Gilbert looked surprised. "Really, Neela, I don't mean to denigrate your good work here, but how on Earth can the shock of revival—without proper preparation, I might add—compare to what will essentially amount to a lot of boring paperwork?"

"Maybe it's paperwork to you, Gil," Neela answered, having prepared herself in advance for this moment, "but to Justin our way of life may be far more shocking than the fact that he's reemerged alive and well. Let's not forget this is a man who had himself suspended, under very clever and well-thought-out circumstances, at a time when suspension was in its infancy. His unit and stored artifacts alone indicate an amazing will, crafted for the sole purpose of his revival. No, Gil. I have to believe he was prepared for this."

"Alright, Neela." It was Dr. Wang, a soft-spoken, delicately mannered woman of Eurasian descent. "So let's say that his revival comes as no great shock—which I still find a little hard to believe—what about our way of life would this man find so difficult to live with? As you've just now clearly demonstrated, he appears to be ready for our society, given the fact that he was apparently eons ahead of his."

"Quite right, Dr. Wang," answered Neela in the affirmative, "he did seem to know where the *technology* was heading, but he would probably have had no idea where *society* was heading. Hence, all the precautions he took—and is continuing to take—with regard to his identity and history."

"You're saying he doesn't trust us?" asked Mosh.

Neela nodded. "That's exactly what I'm saying, Mosh. And why should he? Think about it. He doesn't know us from Eve. And while he's rightly surmised that the very fact that we revived him bodes well, he's also smart enough to know that this, in and of itself, is not enough."

"So what are you suggesting, Neela?" interjected Gil. "The longer we put off his incorporation and all that that entails, the longer he'll remain outside of a society he's worked so hard to get into. Plus, I'm not sure I buy that our way of life will be that shocking to him. After all, didn't we find some of his stock certificates in the mineshaft? It can't be that great a leap from stock ownership to self-incorporation."

Neela sighed, trying to think of a way to get through to the brilliant yet myopic minds that now surrounded her. "OK, folks, let's try it this way. Is it safe to say that we all believe in private property?"

"Of course we do, Neela," replied Gil.

"OK. Can anyone tell me why?"

Mosh spoke up. "Neela, as much as I'd like to sit through a civics lesson, right now there's a lot on our plates and . . ."

Neela interrupted. "Please, Mosh . . . everyone. Bear with me for a moment. It really is very important."

Mosh sighed. "Go on, then."

"OK, Neela," volunteered Gil. "The right to own private property is the cornerstone of any successful society. Without that inviolable right, anarchy and with it true oppression start nipping at the heels."

Good, thought Neela. *He took the bait.*

"How about the right to own a person?" she continued.

"You mean like having a controlling majority of someone?" Dr. Wang offered.

"No, Doctor. I mean, like actually owning a human being—lock, stock, and barrel. You could use this person, you could give him away, you could even—under the scenario I've painted—kill this person without any fear of reprisal."

"Please, Neela," piped in the director. "You're speaking about ancient history. And if I'm not mistaken, hundreds of years before even Justin's time."

"That's right, Mosh," she agreed, "I am. But it is a part of history. Correction. It's a part of *our* history. And let's be very clear on this. What I just described was at one time normal. In fact, you could be seen as a very decent, good, and ethical human being and still be a slave owner."

"OK, Neela," said Gil, "I realize you're trying to draw an analogy, but I just don't see it. There's no comparison."

"Sorry, Gil. I'm not finished." Neela stood up and started pacing. "Let's take our last three-hundred-year period and look at it another way. If we were to go three hundred years into the past starting from Justin's era, we'd find men who thought being ruled by a king was perfectly normal, in fact divine, and that whites were superior to all other races. Now, imagine reviving someone from that era into Justin's time period. How would they adjust?"

"That's almost a nonstarter, Neela," Mosh interjected. "I'm with Gil. There's no comparison, culturally. Our world is far more similar to his. Our democratic values have remained relatively unchanged in the past three hundred years. If anything, he'll see our world as a natural extension of his."

"Maybe yes, maybe no," Neela said, sitting back down in her chair and gently leaning forward onto the table. "But now he's in a world where people can, technically, *own* people. Not in the way we just discussed, but close enough that he'll probably equate it with a loss of liberty. When he was alive the wounds of slavery were still raw enough that President Winfrey used a modified form of reparation as a platform toward her eventual election as president of the United States. Incorporation of the human individual will be the biggest change he'll have to accept if he's to successfully integrate into our society. I suspect it will be a challenge, and while I'm aware of your concerns, Gil, I'm also aware that everything we do in these first few weeks will have a huge impact on our patient's future growth and eventual acceptance into society."

Neela leaned back, surveying the crowd in front of her. She had their attention now. "So," she continued, "you'll forgive me if I put off your paperwork for another few weeks. OK, Gil?"

This got another chuckle from the group.

"Neela, one; Gil, zero," snickered Mosh. "I think we're all in agreement with Neela and will, until further notice, follow her lead with regard to acclimating Justin to our apparently uncivilized way of life."

This got them laughing yet again, which was Mosh's intention.

"That being said," he continued, "there are a few other items on the agenda I'd like to go over." He noticed Dr. Wang making some notes into her DijAssist.

"If I could have everyone's complete attention, please."

Dr. Wang looked up sheepishly.

Mosh continued. "I know that we're all getting excited about our good fortune, and with it the expectation of a profitable future. It goes without saying that all involved with this great find will see significant jumps in their portfolios as a result. Yes, your value to society, and ergo your stocks, will rise as assuredly as our patient's fame. But I want to caution you on two things. One," he said, making sure to look everyone in the eye, "we must keep this work a secret for now. We're in a very tenuous and critical juncture in our patient's revival. If he fails, we fail."

They all understood what he meant. They'd been handed perhaps one of the century's greatest finds. And Justin's success would be theirs as well. But if any one of them failed in their respective roles toward the patient's successful reintegration, it would show up with dizzying speed in their respective portfolios.

"Second," continued Mosh, "you must resist the urge to make any stock purchases of yourself or any person in this room."

This was greeted with abject silence.

"What does one thing have to do with the other?" asked Dr. Wang. "We have a right to profit from this good fortune."

"And if we don't move now . . . ," continued Gil.

". . . you'll lose your chance to buy self-stock at the cheaper rate," finished Mosh. "Yes, I'm well aware of that fact. Which is why I took the liberty of buying two thousand options of each of you when you first came to work for me. It's more than you'd ever be able to buy at your current salaries, and I'm willing to sell you those shares back at your current valuations—if, and only if, you keep this quiet for another two weeks."

"We can't keep it quiet, Mosh. Word's already out," said Neela.

"Yes, Neela," he agreed, "word is out, but aside from the four of us and our good friends at GCI, very few know what was inside the unit, and if what was inside was successfully reanimated."

"So then how will buying stock in ourselves now make any difference at all?" asked Gil.

"It's the smoking gun, Gil," answered Mosh. "Profit Sniffs get leads all the time. If they followed up on every 'find' they heard about they'd be out of business in a week. What they look for is the smoke, not the gun."

Neela finished his thought. "And our run on the facility and ourselves would be the smoke."

Mosh nodded. "Exactly."

"So what if the Profit Sniffs find out now?" asked Dr. Wang. "As long as we've got our shares secured we can go along for the ride. And I think you'll agree it should be a profitable one."

"Yes," said Mosh, "but you're all forgetting one very important thing."

Dr. Wang looked at Mosh a little quizzically. "And that would be?"

"The patient," Neela answered in Mosh's stead.

"But," said Gil, "you yourself said he was doing fine, Neela."

"For someone who's been through what he's been through, yeah, I'd say he is. But this isn't a standard revive. If we're all to profit, he's going to have to integrate effectively. I very much doubt you or I will fare well in the media circus that's about to engulf our little backwoods enclave, much less our recently revived patient. Mosh's offer is the best for everyone. I suggest we go with it."

They all nodded in agreement.

"OK, Mosh," Dr. Wang said, whipping out her DijAssist. "Talk to me about the options."

"A second if you would, Dr. Wang?" interrupted Neela. "I still have one last question."

"Yes?"answered Mosh.

"Has anyone seen Hektor?"

Justin felt great. He'd always lived life on his own terms, and now he'd done the same with his death. And though he knew he was probably being monitored, he couldn't help but walk around his room with an idiot grin on his face. In fact, the last memory he ever had of feeling this good was when he emerged, at the ripe old age of fourteen, from the back seat of a 1967 Ford Fairmont with one Jenny O'Donnell. She'd managed to teach him, in the course of one evening, everything there was to know about the opposite sex—or at least everything a fourteen-year-old thought he should know. Yes, he was feeling good. He was even looking good. He stared at himself in the mirror for a full hour. This was not the cancer-stricken body he'd been suspended with. It was his body, no doubt, just a lot younger and healthier. Justin figured it for thirty-five to forty years of age. He wasn't surprised. Even in his era, the father of nanotechnology, Eric Drexler, had posited that once man controlled cells at a molecular level, the idea of replacing aging skin cells with newer, more vibrant ones was just a matter of time. Well then, time had certainly been kind to him. But for the fact that all he wanted to do now was eat, he probably would have already been out doing things and going places. He had more energy than he knew what to do with. And while he knew he should probably be planning and mapping out his next conversation with his handler, as he thought of Neela, right now he just couldn't help himself. He paced back and forth impatiently, waiting for breakfast to arrive.

He heard a short, gentle tone coming from the direction of the door.

That had better be my food, he thought.

"Come in," he called out.

A handsome man with strong Latino features entered the room. He was tall, with thick black hair, a sturdy physique, and what might have been construed as an overly confident gait. Though Justin was not familiar with the styles of this generation, he could swear that the suit the man was wearing was expensive. It somehow *smelled* expensive.

"Justin?" The man extended his hand. Instinctively, Justin put his hand out as well, but was surprised to find that the man hadn't extended his the few inches farther that would have allowed them to make contact.

How odd, Justin thought.

The man's arm was close to his body and his hand was extended almost like that of a toy soldier. It was as if he were going through the motions of a hand-shake without ever having done the deed. It didn't end there, though. Once their hands did meet—by Justin's overextension of his arm—the man didn't grasp Justin's hand. He just let it lie there, moving it up and down only when Justin did. *He's never shaken hands before,* thought Justin, *but I'll give him points for trying.* Probably one of many new social courtesies he'd have to relearn. But still a good sign. They were making every effort to make him feel comfortable in their world by attempting to mimic some aspects of his.

"And you would be?" asked Justin.

"Hektor," he answered warmly. "Hektor Sambianco."

"What can I do for you, Mr. Sambianco?"

"Please, call me Hektor." The silence was broken by Justin's growling stomach.

"You'll have to excuse me," said Justin, "but I haven't eaten in three hundred years and I'm bit peckish. I actually thought you were the *food,* as it were."

"Of course," Hektor said, still smiling. "It's not a problem. Can I order you something?"

"No, thank you. It's coming."

"Ahh. Very good. Then I suggest we wrap this up before your meal arrives."

"And the 'this' would be?"

"Why, your ability to pay, of course."

"You're talking about the bill, then?"

"A bill, yes, I understand. What an interesting way of putting it. Yes, we're talking about the bill," Hektor parroted back.

Justin relaxed. This was something he'd anticipated, and no matter what price they threw at him, he was pretty sure he'd have it covered. Certainly, with all he'd stashed away, some of it could be sold for cold hard cash . . . if that's what they were using these days. But it seemed odd to him that they would bring it up this early in his acclimation period. After all, what was he now? Less than one day old? Had it been up to him he would have waited longer. But it wasn't, and business was business. He could certainly relate to that. For all he knew he was in this century's version of an HMO—and if that were the case, they were being remarkably patient.

"Not to worry, Hektor, I'll make good on my debts. Just leave me the bill. It may take a little while to transfer my assets into money, but I'm good for it. And even if my obvious assets have depreciated, I should still have access to items of cultural value that I'm sure will suffice."

Hektor looked surprised.

"Oh, you don't have to worry about paying for this now, Justin. That would be ludicrous. And we certainly understand that there's a lot for you to do in the coming days. No, all we need from you is a thumbprint and signature right on this tablet that says, in effect, you're 'good for it' I believe were the words you used." Hektor then held out his DijAssist, pointing to where Justin should give a thumb imprint.

In Justin's mind, Hektor's request was reasonable. However, anytime anyone asked him to sign anything, red flags flew. Most of the time they were false alarms, but he could never be too sure . . . especially given his previous line of work.

"That sounds reasonable, Hektor. Mind if I take a look at your PDA?"

Hektor looked at him blankly. "PD . . . what?"

"The tablet in your hand that you want me to sign on."

"Oh, my DijAssist. Sure. But, between you and me, why go through the headache? It's mainly a whole bunch of legal mumbo jumbo. I'm sure that hasn't changed in centuries, right?" Hektor let out a nervous laugh.

He's hiding something, Justin realized.

"Yes, you're probably right, Hektor, but old habits die . . . hmmm, perhaps a bad choice of words. Old habits *sleep* hard, and reading mumbo jumbo happens to be one of mine, so if you don't mind . . ." Justin extended his hand for the DijAssist.

Hektor handed it over, praying that Justin would skim over some texts and then thumbsign, satisfying his "read" of the document. He viewed with irritation Justin's hapless attempt to control the unit, and then watched as Justin's face went from curiosity to consternation.

What on Earth is a Standard Individual Incorporation? thought Justin. He read for a few more seconds. *This can't be right.*

"Perhaps, Hektor," Justin said, raising the DijAssist slightly, "you could leave this here with me and come back later . . . since you seem to be in such a hurry, that is."

Hektor, who until now had purposely lowered his profile—slouching even—suddenly stood erect, to his full six-foot four-inch height.

"Justin," he said, eyes narrowing—lifeless, "you don't seem to understand. You are, for lack of a better word, an indigent. If we do not have the ability to collect payment we will be forced to resuspend you until other means of payment can be secured."

Justin was taken aback. "And when would this 'resuspension' take place?" he asked, barely managing to recover and hoping to negotiate some wiggle room. The last thing he wanted after a three-century coma was another nap.

"Now seems to be as good a time as any," answered Hektor coldly. He snapped his fingers and two thugs appeared in the doorway. They were dressed in starched white jumpsuits, and together formed an impenetrable wall of muscle—not that it mattered. Justin had neither the knowledge nor inclination to flee. Neither brute smiled, and both looked at Justin as if he was keeping them from something far more important than their imminent manhandling of his being.

"Wait a minute," barked Justin to Hektor, as the thugs moved in. That seemed to stall the wall momentarily. "Dr. Harper said that I was the *only* one from my era. You'd really risk your job resuspending someone like me?"

"Someone like you?" sneered Hektor. "Do you actually think you're special? Well, I've got news for you. You're not."

The "wall" stayed in place, waiting for a signal from their boss.

"We get guys like you all the time," he continued. " 'I survived, luck must love me . . . I'm important,' " Hektor said in a mockingly high and whiny voice. "Well, that's horseshit!" he bellowed to no one in particular. "Dr. Harper's been warned about her 'you're unique' therapy for the last time. It does more harm in the end than good." Now he focused his steely glare on Justin.

"Justin, let me make this clear. You're a patient. One of many in a world you couldn't possibly understand. The only thing that should matter to you is not your delusions of grandeur, but your ability to convince me you can honor your debts. And just in case you were wondering, by your refusal to sign, you haven't. I have three other clients to see this morning, and you're holding us *all* up. Now, if you don't put your thumbprint and signature on the box and line as shown in the next ten seconds, flunky number one will subdue you while flunky number two puts you back into never-never land. At which point—and let me be real clear here—the next face you see will be decades or centuries from now, but at least *I* won't have to deal with you. In fact, screw giving you ten seconds. You have five, four, three . . ." The thugs began to move in.

Justin was thrown enough by Hektor's threat and the two massive figures' advance that, without his realizing it, his hand had started to reach for the pad.

"What's going on here?!"

It was Neela. She was standing in the doorway holding a tray of scrambled eggs, toast, and coffee. She didn't look at all pleased.

That's what I'd like to know, thought Justin, thankful for at least a few more moments among the conscious.

"Nothing that concerns you, Dr. Harper," snarled Hektor. "I suggest you move along." He gestured to the thugs, who quickly turned around and refocused their attention on this newest threat.

Neela didn't budge. "Three securibots and a slew of Dr. McKenzie's personal bodyguards say otherwise, Mr. Sambianco . . . they'll be here momentarily." She put the food tray down on a small table next to the door's entrance and folded her arms across her chest.

Hektor stood his ground, but then apparently thought better of it. He wasn't going to win this battle—it was on unfamiliar ground, and he was, apparently, soon to be outgunned. He decided to pull up stakes.

"Right, then. To be continued, Justin," he said, leaving the room with his goons in tow. He made sure to shoot Neela a look that let her know in no uncertain terms exactly where she'd landed on his list.

Neela came in, and as she did the door slid closed behind her. "Good morning, Justin. Please forgive Hektor's intrusion."

A wan smile appeared on Justin's face. "There is no security on the way, is there?"

"No," she answered almost breathlessly, as she collapsed into the chair next to the small table and the now cold eggs. "How did you know?"

"More interestingly," he asked, "why did Hektor believe you?"

"To be quite honest, I'm not sure he did. He just didn't 'not' believe me."

Justin, who was only now leaving his short-lived fear behind, nodded. "Good point. May I ask you another question?"

"As many as you'd like," she said, allowing herself a moment's calm in order to brush off the vestiges of her Hektor encounter.

"Exactly who's in charge here?"

"As far as you're concerned," she answered, folding her arms, "I am, and I strongly urge you to disregard whatever it was that Hektor said."

"Hard to disregard death, Neela."

Neela's eyes went wide. "Whaa . . . what are you talking about?"

"Mr. Sambianco threatened to resuspend me unless I signed . . . what was it called again? . . . Oh, yes, . . . a Standard Individual Incorporation clause . . . Which is what, exactly, Neela?"

Neela could barely contain her anger. *Goddamn all the Hektor Sambiancos!*

"That's something I wanted to bring up later," she barely managed.

"Hmm . . ." Justin now sat down across from Neela, leaned back, and crossed his legs. "Let's bring it up now."

Neela sighed. Her days of preparation had been torpedoed in milliseconds. She'd lost the advantage of time, and now would have to rely solely on her instincts.

"Justin, please believe me when I tell you that I only want what is best for you, and I think it would be a mistake to try to grasp too much too quickly. You've just awakened to a brand-new world and should take it slowly."

"On the contrary, Neela, I believe someone just tried to con me using my lack of knowledge of your *brand-new world*. He also succeeded mightily in scaring the crap out of me based not on my knowledge but my ignorance. So let's just say that I'll feel more 'secure' if I start learning about it—now."

Neela sat, staring hard at Justin, waiting for some "give" on his part. It wasn't forthcoming.

"Very well, then." She realized her only hope was to gain his trust. If he wanted inundation, he'd get it. But she'd at least be there to help guide him through the morass. She pointed to the DijAssist resting in his lap.

"Let me at least show you how to use that damned thing."

He looked at her, a bit surprised. He'd actually forgotten that he had Hektor's computer in his lap.

"This thing?" he asked, holding up the DijAssist. "I'll guess we'll have to get it back to Mr. Sambianco."

"Yes, that thing, and we won't have to bother. And, by the way, it's called a DijAssist. It'll be the best damned pain in the ass you're ever going to meet."

"Funny," he mused, "I assumed that that was going to be your job." For the first time since Hektor's intrusion he allowed himself a grin.

Neela blushed at the warmth of his smile, and even more surprisingly, found herself tongue-tied. Her only parry was to divert the conversation back to the DijAssist.

Justin downed his breakfast, and they spent the next half hour going over the ins and outs of the unit. She explained that although there wasn't a need for the device to be external, there was something called the Virtual Reality Dictates that mandated they remain so. Justin made a mental note to look into the so-called dictates later. But the features of the unit were interesting. As far as he could tell, its function was much like that of a radio—cheap and practical, but only good when in range of a desired frequency. In this case the "frequency" being the human using it. Apparently the DijAssist performed two main functions: information retrieval and personalized avatar. The first part, information retrieval, was easy enough to understand. The Internet as he remembered it had simply grown more vast and complex in size, and was today known as the "Neuro," apparently in deference to the vast complexity of the brain's neural networks. The unit could tap not only into the Neuro, but into an individual's implanted microprocessors as well. It gave self-storage a whole new meaning. Simple enough. However, the thing that got Justin's attention was the avatar function. Somewhere in the Neuro was a stored database of every search, every request, and every nuance an individual made while holding a DijAssist in his hand—since the time he first held one. And most people started holding them at the age of two. In this manner the avatar that evolved from the hundreds of thousands of decisions made over a lifetime sometimes knew an individual better than the individual knew himself. Neela spoke of instances where avatars had played matchmaker by scanning the Neuro for partner compatibility, going so far as to arrange the unsuspecting owners' schedules around a "chance" meeting.

The reason Hektor hadn't made a fuss about leaving his DijAssist behind was because it wasn't *his* per se. As soon as he stopped touching *it*, it, so to speak, stopped touching *him*.

Since Justin hadn't the luxury of a lifetime of recorded decisions, his newly created avatar was tepid, to say the least. He even thought about not using it altogether, so as not to leave a trail that could be hacked into, but he rejected that out of hand. He'd have to dive in somewhere—and what better way than a key to the Neuro and a personally evolving avatar?

In no time at all he was "nurfing," as the slang apparently went. Neela got up to go.

She was now standing in the doorway, halfway out. "Careful. The Neuro will feed you more information than you need, and you'll feel like you can handle it. Don't be fooled. Just like the first glass of alcohol goes down easy and the buzz comes later, so too with the Neuro. Take it slow. If you feel dizzy or overwhelmed, it's natural. And call me if you need anything . . . even if you don't."

Justin followed her with his eyes as she slipped out of the entrance. The doors slid closed as he watched her walk down the hall.

"Let's start from the beginning," Justin said to no one in particular.

"I presume you mean the contract," answered the DijAssist, in a voice almost as sure as his own. Justin smiled. This was going to be one interesting day.

"Neela would like to speak with you now. Shall I tell her you're available?"

"But I just spoke to her."

"Yes," the DijAssist confirmed.

"Sure, put her through."

Neela's face appeared in the DijAssist's screen. It was a three-dimensional image so lifelike that Justin was afraid to drop the unit for fear of hurting her.

"Hi, Justin. Sorry. I'm planning on the fly now, and I just realized, apart from a few people, no one yet knows who you are—or, more important, *that* you are. It's important for the time being that we keep it that way. Not only for our sake, but for yours. There'll be a media frenzy, and when it hits you'll be lucky if they let you shit in peace."

This got a chuckle from Justin.

"What do you suggest, Neela?"

"I've given your avatar everything you'll need for your interim ID. By the way, have you given it a name yet?"

"Name?"

"Yes. Though it's not necessary, the superstitious among us feel they function better when given names."

"Totally false," piped in the avatar.

"Very well," answered Justin.

"Anyhow," continued Neela, "there are so many nuances and acceptable forms of behavior not yet known to you that the only cover I can think of for now is that of a level-four DeGen."

Justin furrowed his brow. "That doesn't sound very good."

"It's not. A DeGen is someone whose DNA got screwed up to the point that nanotechnology still hasn't figured out a way to get him working properly—a 'buggy' computer in your terminology. Level four's pretty mild, but at least it will excuse a lot, and right now you'll need that."

"Fair enough, Neela. Fair enough."

"I'll be in to see you in a bit."

Neela's face disappeared, and the contract reemerged on screen.

"When you're ready to exit this room," said the DijAssist, "I will create your badge."

"Great," answered Justin. "I'll be ready in a minute. And by the way . . ."

"Yes?" asked the DijAssist.

"How do you feel about the name sebastian?"

Mosh was in transit to a meeting when Neela appeared on his DijAssist.

"Mosh?"

"Yeah, Neela."

"Hektor got to him."

"I can't say I'm surprised. What does that mean for us?"

"You know that beautiful speech I gave in the boardroom?"

"Yeah?"

"Purge it. What he doesn't already know, he'll know inside of a few hours. He's got a DijAssist and knows how to use it. By the way, is there any way we can sue Hektor and GCI for custodial interference with a valid reanimation?"

Mosh laughed. "Neela, you don't sue the corporation that owns a majority of you." Then, "I can't believe Hektor taught him the Dij."

Silence.

"Neela?"

"He didn't," she answered. "I did."

More silence.

"Mosh, you with me?"

"Yeah, I'm with you." He changed his mind. "Actually, no. No, I'm not."

"I had to, Mosh. Not only did Hektor show him a DijAssist, he tried to trick him into signing a personal incorporation contract."

Mosh sighed. "That man's ability to cause trouble should not be underestimated."

"That's why Justin has to be able to trust me, and if it can't be on my terms, then it will have to be on his. He doesn't know it yet, but I'm his only chance of making it."

"So he's Neuroed, Neela. Best to stay on him like white on rice at this point."

"Can't do that either."

"Right, the trust thing. What do you suggest?"

"I've given him an L4 DeGen clearance. I'm assuming he'll start roaming soon. And if I had to guess, I'd say to the suspension unit."

"We'll track him . . . from a distance. Keep me versioned, OK?"

"Will do, Mosh. Bye."

Neela's image vanished, and Mosh returned the DijAssist to his pocket. The life he had tried so hard to escape seemed to be back, nipping at his heels. A smarter man would have quit and vanished into the local universe. But the reasons he left GCI in the first place were now the same ones that compelled him to stay. He would not abandon his coworkers to Hektor and his ilk, nor would he abandon this Justin character under his care. It was not in his nature, and it never would be.

Our ability to arrange atoms lies at the foundation of technology. We have come far in our atom arranging, from chipping flint for arrowheads to machining aluminum for spaceships. We take pride in our technology, with our lifesaving drugs and desktop computers. Yet our spacecraft are still crude, our computers are still stupid, and the molecules in our tissues still slide into disorder, first destroying health, then life itself. For all our advances in arranging atoms, we still use primitive methods. With our present technology, we are still forced to handle atoms in unruly herds.

But the laws of nature leave plenty of room for progress, and the pressures of world competition are even now pushing us forward. For better or for worse, the greatest technological breakthrough in history is still to come.

—ERIC DREXLER, *ENGINES OF CREATION:
THE COMING ERA OF NANOTECHNOLOGY,* 1986

Justin spent the better part of an hour going over the intricacies of the contract Hektor had asked him to imprint. On one thing Hektor had been correct: It was a headache of epic proportions. Forty-eight pages of legal mumbo jumbo exacerbated by the addition of three hundred years of newer and more complex mumbo jumbo. Had his avatar not been around to explain the finer details of the text and subtexts, the process of understanding it would most certainly have taken weeks.

"So, they basically wanted to own a piece of my ass before I had any say."

"Yes, Justin," answered sebastian, "though it would certainly have been a small piece of your ass."

Justin smiled at the retort. He was starting to like his little helper.

"I don't get it, then. What's the point? They'd have no control over me, as they would over those they own a controlling interest in."

"The point in your case," chirped sebastian, "is not profit. It's profit potential. Even a minute percentage of you, a virtual alien in our world, would garner GCI untold millions of credits."

Justin allowed that to sink in.

"OK. That's enough information for now. I need to move. Can you direct me to my suspension unit?"

"With ease, Justin. I've arranged for your DeGen badge. You'll find it in the receptacle by the side of the door."

"Good."

Out of habit, Justin looked around the room to see if there was anything he was forgetting. But for now, he owned nothing. At least nothing he could take with him—except for the DijAssist.

"Um . . . sebastian," said Justin, slowly pivoting the small computer in his hand.

"Yes, Justin."

"This DijAssist, the one you seem to be living in . . . it was Hektor's, right?"

"Yes."

"Dunno why, but it makes me nervous."

"As far as I can tell, Justin," answered his fledgling companion, "I am interfacing with a standard unit. If it makes you nervous we could implant you with a handphone and you could use that to communicate with me, or you could get another DijAssist."

"I like option number two. Let's get a new one and dispose of this."

"As you wish."

The bottom drawer of his dresser opened up, and in it were various objects Justin could not identify, and one that he now could.

"Take this DijAssist," commanded sebastian's voice from inside the new unit, "and throw the old one in the garbage. It will dissolve on its own."

Once the switch had been made, Justin felt better. He knew it defied logic, but at this point he was going on gut. He'd let experience catch up in due time. He then went to the door and, sure enough, a badge was waiting for him.

His DijAssist chirped to life. "Place it on the left side of your chest. It will stay."

As soon as the badge was on, the door slid open, and Justin was confronted with the hustle and bustle one would associate with a small but efficient medical center. People and objects were busily moving, walking, and even whizzing about. He stood in the doorway of his room for a full ten minutes. He watched and made ample use of sebastian's Neuro access to understand some of the stranger anomalies occurring around him, chief of which was the absence of any doors along the corridor. He watched in utter amazement as walls opened up and closed to fit the person or persons entering or exiting.

"Please explain what I'm seeing, sebastian."

"You're referring to the permiawalls?"

"Yes, I am. If that's what you call those openings," Justin replied.

"It is. Permiawalls are constructed of molecules that can sense approaching objects. Once the object is within a specified range the wall calculates the amount of room the object will need to pass through."

"But why don't people bump into each other?"

"Look closely," answered the avatar, "and you'll see clearly demarcated lines indicating exit and entry points."

"Ahh," responded Justin, noticing the floor markings. "Not to sound petty, se-bastian," he continued, "but how come I don't have a permiawall?"

"Strictly speaking, Justin, you do. The configuration of your door has been changed on the orders of Dr. Harper."

"Dr. Harper?"

"You know her as Neela."

"Why, of all things, a sliding door?"

"Although I'm not aware of the reasons, my data search has shown that three files on twentieth-century views of the future have recently been accessed by an individual with a revivalist-grade rating. It is a 93.4 percent probability that the recipient of the information is Dr. Harper. In viewing the data I have deter-mined that your culture had an almost religious belief that doors in the future would slide open. Rather than shock you by walking through a wall, Dr. Harper wisely decided to have a sliding door that would go *whoosh*, and so make you feel comfortable. That was most insightful of her."

"I see," said Justin.

"Doors are inefficient in an era of electro-liquid metals and nanotechnology," continued sebastian. "It is far simpler to have a wall that will dissipate and re-incorporate as needed."

"But wouldn't a person feel trapped in a box without a door?"

"Yes, a person would. But the interiors of the rooms can be as suffocating or as airy as the user determines. If you wish, I can explain the technology."

"I'll pass for now, sebastian, thanks. I'm curious, though. Does the technol-ogy ever fail? Have people's virtual environments as you describe them ever crashed, actually leaving someone in a box, as it were?"

"Justin, did you ever play the lottery?"

Justin was taken aback by the accurate reference to his cultural past and the left field of the question. "Uh . . . no."

"Why not?"

Justin decided that his avatar must have a purpose in this line of questioning, and answered honestly. *Could you even lie to your avatar successfully?* "The odds were ridiculous."

"Justin, the odds of the 'crash' event as you describe it are 349,120,004 to one. You have a better chance of winning the lottery . . . three times in a row."

"Thank you, sebastian. I understand."

"I am glad, Justin. Are you ready to begin our walk?"

Justin nodded.

"Good. Let's exit the door to the right and begin down the hallway. I will tell you when to turn."

Justin obliged and began walking down the hall, trying hard not to stare, yet finding it almost impossible not to. The permiawalls, it turned out, were just an indicator of a society that had adapted fully to a nano world. It seemed that everything he looked at was solid until it didn't have to be. Certain objects seemed to melt away and re-form almost at will. But on closer view, that wasn't the case. Every movement of a material object was connected intimately with the movement of a human being. So, for example, he noticed an orderly holding something in his hand that resembled a clipboard. It seemed to shape-shift into a cylinder, which the orderly placed in a bin with other cylinders. It was almost like living in a dream.

Between the information he was absorbing and the environment he was walking in, Justin was indeed beginning to feel a bit dizzy. But he was nothing if not determined, and he would at least get to the bay that held his suspension unit. There were things inside he needed, and he didn't want to risk the unit being moved without his having retrieved them. He pressed ahead.

"Can you make the environment I'm currently viewing more to what a twenty-first-century human would experience?"

"I'm sorry, Justin," answered sebastian, "I cannot. Your personal space, yes. A group space, no. Perhaps we should return to your room until you feel you've adjusted better?"

"No, that's alright. I'll be OK. Just get me to the suspension unit with the least amount of visual stimuli possible, OK?"

"Certainly, Justin. Turn to the right at this next corner."

Justin did as he was told.

"As you are familiar with elevators," continued sebastian, "you will be glad to know we have just arrived at one, though slightly more refined."

In front of Justin stood two clear, hollow, cylindrical tubes.

Sensing Justin's confusion, sebastian attempted more clarification. "We call them lifts."

"Just like the old days," added Justin, "I guess. But these certainly don't look like the old elevators."

"That is correct, Justin. Since the movable platform had been eliminated, the old term came back into fashion . . . approximately 122 years ago."

"So how do I use it then?"

"The tube to the left is always down and conversely the tube to the right . . ."

". . . is always up," finished Justin. "But it's empty—oh, never mind." At that moment Justin saw a woman float upward in the right-hand tube. The woman mistook Justin's amazed stare and slack-jawed expression as a compliment and smiled. *Well, at least some things haven't changed,* Justin thought. However, the woman's smile dissipated quickly when she noticed the patch on his shirt.

"Um . . . sebastian?"

"Yes, Justin?"

"When I do start to date, this little number will have to go," he said, indicating his DeGen patch.

"I would think so."

"And another thing."

"Yes, Justin?"

"These tubes . . ."

"Yes?"

"They're kind of like the sliding doors. I mean, in that that's pretty much what I imagined a futuristic elevator would look like."

"Yes. Surprisingly, in that and a few other things your science-fiction writers were correct."

"Let me guess—flying cars?"

"Two for two. Not bad, Justin. Not bad."

"So how do they work?

"The cars weigh about twelve pounds and are powered by a . . ."

"Not the cars, the lifts."

"All clothing worn is capable of generating a magnetic field that interacts with the tube to move an individual up or down at four miles an hour, and faster in express tubes. We will be taking the down tube to level minus three."

"Four miles an hour, eh? Well, here goes nothing." Not realizing he was holding his breath, Justin stepped into the left-hand tube and started to descend immediately—albeit at a very leisurely pace.

After a few moments of descent, Justin heard sebastian's command. "You will exit by saying the word 'exit' on . . . one . . . two . . . and . . . now."

Justin did as he was told. His body was immediately and lightly whisked into the hallway. The sensation was almost like exiting a swing, but with a much softer landing. Justin took a moment to store the experience, and started looking around. He found himself standing in a more industrial area of the facility. There were fewer people, but no less movement. He was forced to step farther into the hallway when a group of four women chatting amicably among themselves also exited the lift. Then, to avoid being struck by a gaggle of small floating machines, he had to step farther into a larger open area, where he finally managed to find a space that made him less of an obstruction and gave him more of a view. Had he been more familiar with the environment, he would have realized that nothing could have or would have bumped into him. All nonhuman devices were programmed to either go around objects or stop in place until the object, in this case one Justin Cord, figured out exactly where it wanted to go.

"Where is the security, sebastian?"

"For what, Justin?"

"I presume you have theft?"

"Yes, but not how you imagine."

"Save it," Justin answered. "Just get me to the suspension unit."

"It will require us walking through a wall. Are you ready?"

"Yes."

"Step backward, then."

Again Justin did as he was told. He watched in utter amazement how a hole was formed around his body, only to close up as he finished his backward step. It was almost like the experience of putting a hand into a soap bubble without having popped the bubble.

"Cool."

Justin walked one step forward, back the way he had just entered, and watched the wall melt away around him again. He was again "outside" the room, with the wall now behind him. He smiled, turned around, and walked back into the bay, facing forward.

That is so cool, he thought.

Now that he was back in the room he began to concentrate on its interior. It was a loading bay of sorts, empty but for his suspension unit and one other individual. The man was a rough-looking fellow with dark wavy hair, an unshaven face, and a lean body. He was wearing an outfit that suggested a manual laborer if, indeed, wondered Justin, that vocation still existed. He watched the man quietly for a few seconds, hoping he'd check what he needed to check and move on. But the laborer kept snooping around. He was prodding and pushing on the exterior of the suspension unit, almost as if he were looking for a way in.

"Excuse me, sir," Justin interrupted, in as polite a tone as he could muster. "What do you think you're doing?"

"Who wants to know?" the stranger volleyed back, whipping around to stare at the man who'd had the temerity to interfere with his work.

Ahh, scrappy. How refreshing, actually, Justin thought.

"The guy whose ass was frozen in it for a few centuries and the rightful owner of that object you happen to be poking around in, that's who."

"In that case," retorted the worker, "I'm the guy who carved you out of a mountain in the middle of nowhere and, therefore, by default, saved your old, frozen, and obviously ungrateful ass."

They stood their ground staring intently at each other. After a few seconds they both burst out laughing.

"Name's Omad," the man said, sporting a wide, infectious grin. He gave a surprisingly Japanese-style bow. "And you would be?"

"Justin," Justin answered, returning the smile and mimicking Omad's bow.

"Well, Justin, I just have to tell you, this thing's amazing. Never seen anything like it. Truth be told, I've never even heard of a self-contained suspension unit outside of the ones they use in space. How'd you manage to get a terrestrial version?"

"I didn't get it. I built it."

"C'mon, friend. I see the patch on your shoulder. You may only be an L4, but you're still a DeGen. You couldn't build a transfixer, much less a self-sustaining sus unit."

"Oh, this," Justin said, looking at the patch on his shoulder. "It's sort of a cover to allow me to move around without causing too many gaffes . . . not being from this time period and all."

"Ahh." Omad didn't look too convinced.

Justin continued. "Some of the design is mine, but mostly it was made on the Roman method."

"Roman method?"

"I overengineered the crap out of it. I had backup systems, and made everything three times as durable as the specifications called for . . . and I spent a lot of money . . . and, by the way, thank you."

That caught Omad a little off guard. "For what?"

"Saving my frozen, and, I can assure you, quite grateful, ass."

They both laughed. "And I do agree with you," he continued, beginning to circle the unit. Even in his new world of technological wonders, it began to dawn on Justin that he might be looking at an invention unique in mankind's history. "This thing is amazing. I just didn't realize how amazing."

"Yeah. You know the saying about sus units," Omad said, grinning. "Better to be looking from the outside than in."

"Couldn't agree with that more," Justin said, also grinning. "I wonder what this thing's worth now?" he asked, almost as an afterthought.

"You mean," answered Omad, "if it's still yours, don't you?"

"Well, why wouldn't it be?"

"Justin, you'd be surprised what GCI can lay claim to given enough time and money."

"No, actually. I wouldn't," he said, remembering his run-in with Hektor. He'd played the same game many times before. What you couldn't steal outright you could attempt to steal by incessant litigation, with the hopes of eventual settlement. Best to check out Omad's theory.

"Please connect me with Neela, sebastian."

"Of course, Justin," answered his avatar. "So you know, most people don't use their DijAssist as a calling device. You may wish to have a handphone installed."

"Thanks for the info. However, call now, marvels of the future later." The connection was made instantly, and once more Neela's attractive face filled his DijAssist's screen. Justin made a mental note to ask sebastian to give himself a "face" as well. It was becoming a little disconcerting to converse so freely with a block of plastic . . . or whatever composite the DijAssist was made of.

"How can I help you, Justin?" Neela asked.

"Under the laws in operation here, do I own my suspension unit?"

"Well, provisionally, yes."

"Provisionally?"

"You have to take effective control of the unit by securing a safe location you have claim to . . . a storage space will do. Also, you'll have to pay any reasonable expenses incurred in the retrieval of your unit. But you have primary and binding legal claim to it. You can prove it is your unit?"

"You mean coming gift wrapped in it doesn't count?" he asked.

"A man gets rescued in a boat at sea. Does that make him the boat's rightful owner?" Neela shot back.

"I see your point. I believe I have sufficient documentation to substantiate my claim."

"Good, you'll need it. Is that all?"

"For now. Thanks."

"Glad I could help. It's good that you called me," Neela said, and broke the connection. Justin felt his cheeks redden a bit.

The corners of Omad's mouth tilted up. "You like her," he said, grinning.

"Of course I like her. She's nice, and she's helping me."

"Uh-huh. What a shame."

Justin was thrown by the response but chose to ignore it.

"How'd you find me?" he asked, switching to a topic of more immediate interest.

"I'm a tunnel rat. Correction—I'm a great tunnel rat."

"Which means?"

"I search mines for minerals that are difficult to manufacture. I specialized in finding the old ones and reassessing them based on modern extraction techniques. And that's where I found you."

"You said *specialized,* as in past tense?"

"Yup. Thanks to you I just made 51.3 percent. I had to cash in the ridiculously expensive lunar vacation they gave out to shut me up. But I'm now in control of my own destiny. I work or not as I wish, and I'm only sixty-nine years old." Justin could feel Omad's beaming pride.

"Why would they want to shut you up?"

"Guess they didn't want word getting out about you and this," he said, pointing to the suspension unit.

"What difference would it make?"

"Probably not too much. But a find like this . . ." He again pointed to Justin's former crypt. "Worth thinking about how best to exploit it. They'd want that quiet for at least a good couple of weeks."

"Guess I ruined their well-laid plans then?"

"Guess you did. They're probably not too happy about it, either."

"No. I don't think they would be."

They stood silently for a minute.

"Omad, if I'm stepping on any toes let me know, but I need to ask you a personal question."

"Shoot."

"I read a contract for the standard incorporation for payment of debt. I understood the legalese, and the numbers are easy to understand, but something's just not clicking."

"There's a question somewhere in there, right?" Omad asked.

"Yes," Justin said, unflustered. "How could you not control your own life?"

"But I do."

"You do now that you've made majority. But you didn't *yesterday*? What's that all about?"

"I didn't have as much control for sure, but I still had enough."

"How can you have *enough* control? Either you have control or you don't."

Before Omad answered he stopped for a moment, giving Justin a second once-over.

"Did I say something wrong?" Justin was genuinely puzzled.

"No. It's just such an odd question . . . I mean, I figured you'd been down for a while, just didn't figure how long that while was. Not that I was particularly interested. So exactly how old are you?"

"Three hundred years . . . give or take."

"Damsah's ghost! Are you serious?"

Justin nodded.

"Your stock is going to be worth a fortune!"

"I'm not sure the companies I had stock in are still in existence. But yes, if they are I would imagine the stocks will be worth quite a lot."

"Not company stock. You. Your personal stock."

"Ahh, right." Justin paused a bit to let the next part sink in. "I'm not incorporated yet."

"Damsah's ghost!" Omad's face had contorted into a steady look of shock.

"By the way," Justin asked, "what exactly does this 'Damsah's ghost' you keep referring to mean?"

"Uh . . . yeah. Just an expression. Sort of like 'Jesus Christ,' I suppose. But with Tim Damsah instead. You've heard of him, I suppose."

"Omad, I've not only heard of him—I've actually had the pleasure of meeting him."

"You've met Tim Damsah?!"

"Yeah, if it's the same guy. He was some young, minor elected official from Alaska."

"Yeah, that's him alright. Can I touch you?" Omad asked.

The question, Justin realized, had been rhetorical.

"Now it all makes sense," continued Omad. "You're not only an exceptional find, you're not even friggin' incorporated! No wonder they cleared the crews out!"

"Really, Omad, I'm not sure I understand yet why that, in and of itself, seems to be such a huge issue. Or why, for example, Mr. Damsah has achieved apparently godlike status."

"It would take a while to explain, Justin, but needless to say, you gotta understand that around here, Tim's the man. After the Grand Collapse only his vision seemed to get us all back to square one."

Justin furrowed his brow. "Lot of info here, which I guess I'll get to eventually. But if you don't mind, I'd like to get back to what we were talking about, because, I have to say, it's really bothering me."

"OK. But forgive me for gaping, Justin. You're . . . well, you're one of a kind in an all-of-a-kind society." He took a breath. "Look, Justin," he said, leaning up against one of the crate's supporting walls. "Your question was, how could I give up control? Part of it was I had no choice, and the other part was that I did it voluntarily. The 'no choice' part is parents and government. The 'rents get 20 percent, the government gets 5. Can't do nothing about that. The other part is real simple. I wanted things, and people or corporations gave me things. It was my decision about how much of a percentage of me those things were worth. But what don't you understand? In your day and age, and correct me if I'm wrong, you gave up quite a bit of control as well, without profit, I might add."

This took Justin by surprise. "What do you mean? No one controlled percentages of me and told me where to work or play."

"Not to be rude," Omad fired back, "but they sure as stock did. You had companies that told you what to wear, how to cut your hair, when to show up, and when to leave. You took vacations at the company's convenience, not your own, or you lost your job. That's not even getting into what your prink government used to do."

"Prink?"

"Oh, sorry. Stands for Pre Inc., or Pre Incorporation. Anyways, you had seatbelt laws, antismoking laws . . . in bars, for Damsah's sake! No smoking in bars? Care to explain that one? You had drinking and drug regulations. In some of your provinces you couldn't even smoke in your own private domain if it bothered the guy next door. And again, I repeat—you didn't get an ounce of profit from all that control you gave up. If you ask me you had little control with nothing to show for it. If today's government tried to pull that crap there'd be blood in the streets."

Omad folded his arms as if in triumph.

Justin didn't waver.

"But we could quit," he answered. "Or leave, or decide whether we wanted to remain poor or shoot for the sky, making whatever compromises were necessary to achieve those aims. We could vote to change the laws if we wanted to. *And what kind of laws run this place anyways?* You don't seem to have that choice. You were apparently incorporated from the moment you were conceived, and had to pay with your income and your time, whether you wanted to or not."

Justin's DijAssist started to beep.

Omad laughed. "It beeps. How very old school."

"Yes, sebastian?" answered Justin.

"I determined that you would want to be informed. Hektor Sambianco, acting on behalf of GCI, has scheduled a court hearing to determine if GCI is the rightful owner of your suspension unit."

"On what grounds?"

"In lieu of losses incurred due to your failure to incorporate."

"That's ridiculous."

"Just thought you'd want to know."

"Thanks, sebastian."

Justin concentrated his gaze once more on Omad. "Well, I suppose you were right about that one. Boy, it didn't take too long, did it?"

"The length of one conversation. Not too bad." Omad rubbed his unshaven chin. "A bit slow, if you ask me. I would've expected it sooner."

"But why is he going after my unit and not me?"

Omad smiled amiably. "You're among the living now. Can't touch you. This," he said pointing to the chamber, "is a bona fide piece of property." He knocked on the outer frame for effect. "Very touchable."

"Can you please clarify, sebastian?"

"As all your revival expenses were paid in full," answered the avatar, "he has no legal claim on you. Because your unit is still on GCI property, and because GCI dug you out with the hope of an eventual return on the investment, he, as their representative, can make a claim."

The question Justin never thought to ask dropped into his lap like an errant baseball landing on an unsuspecting fan.

"Who . . . who paid for my revival?" he barely managed.

"Unknown."

"I need to find out."

"I will attempt to find out."

Yeah, you do that. "Thank you, sebastian. Please inform Neela of this news."

"Of course."

Justin hated the idea that he owed. It wasn't supposed to be like this. He had currency, even in this day and age. Actually, a boatload. Whatever his revival cost amounted to, he was sure he could have covered it. Sure, it would have taken a little bit of time to figure out what of his possessions were valuable and what weren't, but damn it all, he could have paid. What he failed to take into account was that he couldn't prepay. And this was clearly a society that put a lot of capital in that very notion—literally and figuratively.

Again the DijAssist beeped. It was Neela.

Omad continued to stand quietly, waiting for Justin's cue. It had already been an exceptional week, he figured, and today was no different. Whatever this guy was going to do, he was going to try and do it with him. Besides, this Justin character seemed to be able to give it out as well as he could take it. A far cry from the lot he'd been hanging out with recently at the center. Mainly fellow tunnel rats. Mostly secretive, afraid any slip of the tongue might reveal too much, and hence possible loss of profit. Didn't make for the type of bawdy revelry among men Omad so enjoyed.

Neela's voice interrupted Omad's thoughts, turning the twosome mulling in the shipping bay back into a threesome.

"Hi, Justin. Sorry if I interrupted. I just heard the news. Listen, and listen well. First of all, we're going to need to meet. Sooner rather than later. Too much stuff is going on, and I need to at least brief you on what to expect."

"OK, Neela."

"Second, Hektor will attempt to isolate your suspension unit until the case is resolved. He'll succeed. I strongly suggest you retrieve from it anything you deem critical. Do it now." Neela's image disappeared from the DijAssist.

Shit. Justin felt the edge of panic. He prayed to himself that his restored memories included those that would enable him to liberate his precious possessions from the crypt before Hektor could boot him out. It was no minor prayer. He'd modeled the unit on the ancient sarcophagi, hidden compartments and all. The real trick had been having to pull it all off without any reliance on an electrical source. It had to be manual, and it had to be complex. It also had to be deadly for anyone trying to fuck with it. He'd built in all sorts of nasty devices, from poison gases to spring-loaded poison darts to blades so sharp they could remove a finger without the perpetrator feeling a thing—that is, until the blood started to spurt. With a perfunctory "excuse me" to Omad, he dived in. He began by placing his palms at specific locations on the unit. Once assured he'd positioned his hands correctly, he pushed in. That in turn caused another series of panels to open. Each layer revealed yet more complex systems of ratchets and knobs. *You can do this.* Sweat began to appear at his brow. Justin expertly turned and pulled the knobs before him until he gained the desired result—the expulsion of a few rectangular drawers containing within them important papers, maps, data drives, keys, and other assorted items he had deemed critical to his future survival. Four minutes and twenty-two seconds later his task was complete. With his back to Omad, he stuffed what he could into his pockets, deftly slipped a watch onto his wrist, and then turned around.

"Justin." It was Omad. He had a worried look on his face.

"Yeah?"

"We have to leave. Now. This area is probably officially off-limits. Securibots will be arriving shortly, and you can bet your defrosted ass they'll want what you've got right there in your hot little hands." As he said the words, a ruckus could be heard outside the bay. It was the sound of many footsteps approaching.

"Follow me," Omad barked.

Justin did as he was told and followed Omad as he ran toward and through the wall at the opposite end of the room from which he had entered. They were now in a hallway a few hundred feet from what looked like a central hub. "This way," Omad whispered, with Justin following quickly behind. Within moments they'd arrived at an express lift. Omad ran into the "up" shaft, disappearing almost instantly as his body was sucked up through the tube. Justin did the same. They were harmlessly expunged seconds later at an outdoor plaza.

Justin had barely caught his breath when he realized he was outside for the first time since awakening. It was midday and, as far as he could tell, springtime. He would have liked to stop and take it all in, but he wasn't yet sure he could. Was he being chased? Had he committed a crime? All these questions and more raced through his mind as he attempted to situate himself. *OK, no one's following you. Calm down. Locate Omad.* Justin allowed himself a little more view time. He'd somehow ended up in a rest area. People were milling about and eating, seemingly relaxed. There were about twenty cylindrical tables that were positioned one next to the other. Most were occupied. He noticed Omad sitting alone, beckoning him over. Justin walked the twenty or so feet over to the table.

"How did it know where to let me off?" Justin asked between huge gulps of air. He then sat down.

"You mean the lift? Easy. I told it," Omad smiled.

"And if you hadn't?"

"It would've sent you right back to where you started, where they probably would've nailed you. That wouldn't have been too good for you now, would it?"

Justin thought about his predicament. He was, for all intents and purposes, alone. Trust, a notion he little believed in and rarely had had much of, was something he accepted only after years of experience with an individual or institution. So while Neela, and even this Omad guy, seemed at the outset well-intentioned, it was far too early to tell. One thing was certain—he needed some form of capital so he could get his basic necessities met and ultimately begin to control his situation. Neela would have to wait. There was business to take care of first.

"OK, Omad, I'm going to have to get my hands on some money."

"Don't look at me. I spent all of mine on me. I would have helped you out if I had known . . . well, actually, no, I wouldn't have. I still would have bought my majority, but if I can help in any *other* way . . ."

Omad now began to take a more keen interest in the subject sitting before him. There was no doubt that Justin, if he was who he said he was, could prove to be beneficial indeed. "Riches by association" was a common and oft-used phrase to describe those lucky enough to be somehow entwined in the good fortunes of others.

"Maybe you can," Justin said, fiddling with the contents of his hands. "I have a couple of items I pulled from the unit I'd like to try and cash in. Do you know of any establishments that trade goods for money?"

"You mean like a pawnshop?"

"Uh, yeah. They still have pawnshops?"

"There will always be pawnshops—and, given my sometimes dire financial straits," he answered, "now hopefully behind me, I was often forced to liquidate certain assets."

Justin took out a small, thin, exquisitely made box from one of the many pockets found in the outfit he was wearing. It was made out of wood and had the letter T engraved on the lid. Justin opened it to reveal ten flawless five-carat diamonds resting between two cylindrical velvet dowels. "Is this worth anything?" he asked, hoping earnestly the answer would be yes but knowing that nanotechnology may have rendered his once precious commodity worthless. He was pleasantly surprised by the answer.

"Oh yeah, I know a dealer who would love to get her hands on that."

"Let's go, then."

"Not so fast." Omad figured that since he was already on a roll, there was no point in slowing it down. "What's my take?"

"Nice try, Omad. I know what I'm worth, and have some inkling of what I'll be worth. And speaking of which, I believe it's *worth* your while to help me *now*." The truth was, Justin wasn't sure about anything just yet. He had reason to believe all he'd just said, but had no concrete proof. It was a gamble.

Omad stared keenly into Justin's eyes, then shrugged. "OK, have it your way. To the city, then?"

"I need the money now, so let's go." *A small victory*, thought Justin, *and hopefully one of many*.

Eleanor was working at her desk when she saw Neela come in. Neela, Eleanor noticed, looked a little closer to relaxed, if such an adjective could be applied to a woman whose idea of relaxation was working late.

Eleanor smiled. "Well, you're certainly looking a little better."

"Thanks, Eleanor. I'm not sure if that was a compliment or not, but thanks."

"I'm not sure either, but you've had me worried. What's new?"

"Well, for the first time I think I may have a shot at undoing the damage Hektor did."

"Really. Just an hour ago you were running around like the world was at an end. How come things are looking up?"

"He asked me a question."

"Not to be rude, Neela, but isn't that what he's supposed to do?"

"Of course, Eleanor. It's the question he asked that's got me feeling good."

Eleanor leaned forward, her chin on her hands and her eyes bright with the anticipation of information bordering on gossip. "Tell all, my dear, tell all."

"I received a call from our Justin. He was in the loading bay and had been asking questions of his DijAssist, which, by the way, he named 'sebastian,' all afternoon. When he got to the loading bay, he called me to ask about the laws concerning payment and ownership of recovered property."

"Hardly worth a call to *you*," purred Eleanor.

"I agree."

"Something he could have asked sebastian. It would have made more sense."

"You're absolutely correct," smiled Neela.

"Good going, dear," Eleanor said, viewing Neela with admiration.

"Thank you," Neela replied. They both turned at the snort of derision emanating from the director's office.

"Eavesdropping again, dear?" Eleanor said, shooting a knowing glance to Neela.

"Yes," came from the voice in the office, "for all the good it did me. I don't understand what you're both so happy about. All he did was make you his legal clerk. Do women really enjoy being given the work of an unevolved avatar?"

"Men," both women said at once. They laughed.

Mosh came out to the reception area. "I must be missing something. Unless, of course, you're going to tell me it's a woman thing."

"It's a woman thing," they both answered in unison, giggling once more.

"Would you like an explanation?" asked Eleanor.

"If you can explain how women think," responded Mosh, "I, as well as the rest of mankind, will be eternally grateful."

"Not that you'll understand," Eleanor replied, playfully brushing off some lint that had settled on her husband's shoulder, "but a woman knows a man is interested by a couple of signs. Some of these will let the woman in on a man's interest even before the man knows it himself."

"That transparent, huh?" Mosh said with amusement.

"Glass is opaque by comparison, dear, now please stop interrupting."

"Allow me to finish," interjected Neela. "When a man starts to ask you things he can find out someplace else, or he finds reasons to be nearby, it's a pretty good bet that he's not just interested in information."

The director's face revealed his skepticism. "That's ridiculous."

"Really, dear," Eleanor countered. "And how many times did you lose your DijAssist before you asked me out? Three or four?"

Mosh was taken aback. "All those times were accidental . . . *I swear*."

No one bit.

"Wait a minute," he continued. "You think Justin is starting to develop more than professional feelings for you?" he said, looking at Neela.

"Well," she answered, taking obvious pride in her looks and figure, "it makes sense."

Now Eleanor looked worried. "Joking aside, Neela, don't you think it's a dangerous game to play?"

Mosh nodded—concerned.

"I am not encouraging anything, much less *that*," she retorted. "I am simply using whatever I deem necessary to help undo some of the damage Hektor's already done. I can steer Justin's feelings into appropriate channels once I've reestablished that all-important relationship."

"So you're telling me," said Mosh, "that this 'steering' has nothing to do with the fact that this man is handsome in that rugged sort of way your file suggests is to your liking, not to mention a little mysterious, and, to top it all off, badly in need of your help?"

Neela was about to answer, but Mosh wasn't through.

"You may wish to be careful, my dear, that you do not become the puppet instead of the puppeteer. I don't need to remind you that our laws and customs concerning patient/professional relationships protect more than just the patients—they also severely punish the offenders."

Neela looked at both Mosh and Eleanor. "You have nothing to worry about. He's a patient. Nothing more, nothing less. A patient, I might add, that I desperately need to find."

Neela left quickly, afraid the conversation would continue—and of what it might expose if she stayed.

As Neela left her concerned mentors, Eleanor looked uneasily toward her husband.

"We need to help her."

"I agree, but how?"

"Can you get ahold of Gillette?"

Mosh rubbed his chin. "Yes, but if he all of a sudden just shows up it will hurt Neela professionally—cast doubt on her at an important point in her career. I don't think the situation is as dire as that."

"Tell you what," Eleanor answered. "You let me worry about that. By the time I'm done with her she'll be making the request. Your only job is to make sure the good doctor's on board when she calls."

"My *only* job, eh?" he chuckled.

She gave him a quick peck on the cheek, ego rescued.

He would call Dr. Gillette as soon as he got back to the office.

3 Walk About

Hektor knew he was in trouble. He knew it because the call he'd just received from his boss's assistant ended with a request for a face-to-face meeting. It was rare that a meeting would have to be taken in person, and even rarer that a boss would fly out for it. Now *his* was coming to town, and it wasn't to deliver a compliment.

He was told to meet at the local Marriott, a beautiful hotel recently redone in the turn-of-the-millennium style. Though he didn't have to, he decided to walk, for no other reason than to finish off a little something he'd started the day before. It was bad form, but he pulled from his pocket the cigar it seemed he'd only just lit up. *Might as well finish it now,* he figured, stepping out into the street. *Better this bad taste in my mouth than the one that's coming.* Between the wind and the now semistale tobacco, it took Hektor a full two minutes just to get the damned thing lit. He allowed himself a good half hour to arrive at his destination. His pace was leisurely enough that he began to notice his surroundings for the first time since he'd arrived. A rare treat, in that his life had pretty much been on the go from the time he'd joined GCI those forty-odd years ago. He'd never allowed himself the luxury of "taking it all in," as it were. Well, he may have rushed through his career, but he certainly wasn't about to rush to its demise. The weather was appropriately dreary. Not by coincidence, but rather by dictate. Seemed the folks in Boulder felt inclement weather was part of the town's charm, and though the weather had been influenced for centuries, there was no accounting for which way a town wanted the wind to blow. It appeared to Hektor that this one wanted it to blow harshly. All the better—he had plenty to think about, and the cold air would do him good.

It seemed his stock was down. Way down. Hektor had seen it happen before. It didn't take place in the blink of an eye. That would've been merciful. No, it was more like watching a lone zebra being nipped to death by a pack of wild hyenas. All it took was the smell of blood. What started out as a small wound inflicted by one determined hunter ended up as a feeding frenzy shared by all. Hektor pictured how it must have gone down. Probably an executive with a solid portfolio had sold him short on seeing or hearing of the debacle in Boulder. She told one of her husbands, who most likely told one of his close associates who was owed a favor, and after that the run was on. It was like having your own little market meltdown. The slang for it was a "minigrand." Or, more precisely, a miniature Grand Collapse. His stock market price had dropped 87 percent. He'd gotten a flurry of calls from family and friends. He was even pretty sure his own mother had sold him short. Of course she'd denied it, but he would've done the same in her shoes. In fact, he had sold his uncle short after a particularly nasty scandal went public. Got out just in time, if he remembered correctly. Family, friends, foes. How quickly the lines blurred when profit was at stake.

Hektor arrived at the hotel in good order. He walked up the small flight of stairs leading to the main doors and entered the building. The lobby was elegant but understated, and he noticed a row of comfortable-looking chairs to the left of the check-in desk. He walked over, sat down, and waited. He knew he'd be conspicuous enough, and now all he had to do was wait for whichever lackey was sent down to retrieve him. He didn't have to wait long.

She was young and pretty in a just-out-of-trade-school sort of way, and wearing the de rigueur five-piece business suit so common with the entry levels. If she knew what was going on her mannerisms certainly didn't betray the fact.

"Mr. Sambianco," she said, keeping her eye contact to a minimum, "won't you come with me?"

She didn't wait for a reply before she turned heel and started walking back from the direction in which she'd come. Hektor got up and followed. He couldn't be mad at the callousness of her approach. An hour ago she'd most likely been at corporate headquarters fetching coffee and opening nonvital accounts for her boss. And now she'd been called to accompany him on a no-chance-of-hobnobbing mission to Colorado. And whatever plans she'd made for the evening had about as much chance of coming to fruition as Hektor had of having his stocks not permanently relegated to junk status. *Yeah,* thought Hektor. *I'd be pretty pissed off myself.* Though he was proud, business was business, and she was just an automaton sent to do a job.

"This way," the ice princess said, barely turning her head. Hektor followed her down a long, well-lit corridor. He noticed the floor creaking as they walked. *Nice touch,* he thought. Yet another little programmed "extra" one would expect from the finer hotels.

They finally stopped in front of a small, nondescript door. The woman passed a card through a slot; it buzzed in the old style, and then the door swung open. Hektor entered the room and looked around. Not the nicest of suites, but suitable for what he suspected was about to occur. The woman left him in a small sitting area by a window and departed without asking if she could get him anything. *How the mighty have fallen,* Hektor reflected. He stared out the window. It was still overcast, and he could see a bank of clouds trapped against the Rocky Mountains. A full fifteen minutes passed before his boss emerged from the bedroom. Hektor stood up immediately, but his boss motioned for him to sit back down, taking the seat across from him.

Kirk Olmstead was the deputy director of Special Operations for GCI. Yet another good-looking man in a world of good-looking men. The nanites capable of creating such physiological feats were inexpensive to the point of being given away with magazine subscriptions. What made Kirk stand out was the same thing that had made successful men and women stand out for eons—fashion. He was wearing the latest Land Rover PowerSuit, an exquisite mix of classic lines and rugged adaptability. "Walk on water or dive beneath" was the tagline of the recent ad campaign, Hektor recalled. Mr. Olmstead also had another distinguishing characteristic—his eyes. One look was all that was needed to realize that this was one man who controlled the lives of many. And while he had the power to help or harm thousands, there was now only one in his sights.

Hektor spoke first. "You couldn't have done this with a phone call?"

The DepDir shook his head.

"That bad, huh?" asked Hektor. His question was answered immediately with a dour smile.

"Alright, Hektor," the DepDir began, "I'll get to the point. You've managed to screw up what should have been an easy and, more important, quiet assignment. Now it's going to turn into the biggest media blitz since the pope's divorce." He paused for a second. "Maybe bigger."

"It went wrong, sir. I'll certainly admit to that. It was all going well until someone paid the goddamned coverage."

"Oh yes," replied the deputy. "The coverage. The request for payment *you* put into an official GCI form. What were you thinking?"

"Kirk, it was for ten million friggin' GCI credits! Who for the love of Tim has that kind of money?!"

"With all due respect, Hektor," shot back the deputy, "who for the love of Tim cares? You were stupid enough to put it in writing when you didn't have to. Mind explaining what possessed you?"

Hektor thought back on the reason for the gaffe; the delicious pleasure of sticking it to Neela. However, like the orgasm attained through an illicit sexual encounter, the pleasure was not nearly as great as the devastation now being wrought.

"No real reason, sir. Just trying to make it all seem official."

"Well," intoned the deputy, "it's official, alright, and now not only yours, but all of GCI's ass may be in a sling."

Hektor tried to play that one out in his mind. He was so concerned with the demise of his own ass, as it were, that he'd completely forgotten what his failure might mean to GCI. *Of course,* he realized. It wasn't just a matter of GCI losing out on getting a piece of Justin. If this went to court it might just become a matter of GCI losing a piece of itself. *Leverage,* Hektor thought. *I've actually got some leverage here.*

"You think he'll sue, sir?"

The deputy, who had not once taken his cold glare off Hektor, shot back, "I wouldn't be so concerned with what he'll do, Hektor, so much as what you'll do."

"If I'm reading this meeting correctly, Kirk, what I'll be doing as soon as I walk out this door won't have much of a rat's ass relevance to anyone." Hektor was enjoying his trashing of protocol. *No point in being polite.*

The DepDir didn't respond. That was a good sign. The fact that he was thinking meant there was *something* to think about. Had he only wanted to downgrade or even fire Hektor it would have been done by now. No, something was up. The DepDir wouldn't have wasted his time coming out if there wasn't. Still, he just sat there staring while seeming to mull over a decision. Hektor held his breath, trying to look calm. He hadn't figured on this. Hadn't held out any hope at all, actually. It was the longest minute of his life.

"You're reading this meeting correctly, Hektor," the DepDir said, "in that you're in pretty deep shit. What you're not reading correctly is that we're gonna give you a chance to dig yourself out."

Yes! Hektor could barely believe his luck. "Whatever it is you need me to do, it will be done."

"It had better be, Hektor. The Chairman himself has become involved in the problem."

"Oh, shit."

" 'Oh, shit,' indeed, Hektor, but good for you."

Kirk leaned back in his chair, pressing the fingers of his hands together.

"The point you've raised . . . about the source of the funding . . . what I'm about to say doesn't leave this room . . . the bottom line is . . . well, we don't know who paid out that money."

"Not possible," Hektor said in abject disbelief. "We know *everything.*"

"Correction, Hektor. We thought we knew everything. Frankly, I'm convinced that by the time we actually do find out, we'll have spent about as much credits doing so as our mystery man . . . or woman . . . paid out."

"Well, Kirk. If *you* can't find him, what makes you think I can?"

"You can't. That's not what we want from you. It's been decided at the highest levels that to move forward we'll have to find the source. Whoever it is obviously has access to our communications and can counter our moves. That, by the way, is one of the reasons for this face-to-face meeting; more secure."

As it became clear to Hektor where the DepDir was heading, he couldn't help but smile.

"You'll need a lightning rod."

"I always liked you, Hektor. You catch on quick."

"So," continued Hektor, "you want me to take the brunt of the media blitz and continue to be the likely target of more blindsides, like the appearance of ten million credits."

The DepDir smiled back. "No one wants the job, Hek. At least, not until we know what we're dealing with. It's a career-killer. And, well, yours is . . . you know."

Hektor nodded.

"So," the DepDir continued, "you're going to be allowed to stay on. I myself will have nothing to do with you. If you agree, you'll be on special independent assignment to the board."

"And if I disagree?"

"You won't."

Hektor knew what that meant. If he thought his life was bad now, it was nothing compared to what it would be like with GCI breathing down his neck.

"So if I screw up no one in the department gets blamed?"

"You mean, if you screw up again," the DepDir added for effect.

Hektor squirmed.

"That's correct, Hektor. No one but you." The deputy director got up, indicating the meeting was coming to an end. Hektor followed suit. "I've also taken the liberty," continued the DepDir, "of divesting myself of all your stock. Nothing personal. I don't want any conflict of interest to arise."

"Of course not, sir." *And it helps that it ain't worth shit.*

"That's all for now."

"Uh, sir."

"Yeah, Sambianco," the DepDir answered in some irritation.

"My salary . . ."

"Will remain the same for the duration of your current assignment."

"Thank you, sir."

"Don't thank me, Hektor. I didn't agree to this. If it were up to me alone you'd be mining rocks on Mercury as we speak."

"Understood. Thank whoever, sir."

"Don't push it, Sambianco."

Hektor took his leave. As he headed back down the creaky hallway he began to realize that the meeting hadn't gone as badly as he'd expected. Which meant he hadn't ended up with a one-way ticket to Mercury. Objectively his situation was still terrible. But now he had options—not many—but enough. Even enough to regret having smoked the stale cigar. He was now back in the main lobby of the hotel. For what he was contemplating doing he'd need a nice quiet location. To the right and just behind the concierge desk was a small bar room from which were emanating the dulcet sounds of a trio playing mellow punk jazz. Hektor found a comfortable corner, ordered a sixteen-year-old Lagavulin scotch from the first drone to approach, and sat down. The scotch was brought over and Hektor took a swift sip. He let the strong oak flavors burn, then soothe his throat. When he finally felt appropriately settled in he took out his DijAssist and contacted his rarely used avatar.

"Time to work, iago."

"Good to hear from you, Hek," said the boisterous avatar that Hektor hated yet for some reason could not bring himself to alter.

"Shut up and listen, iago. I need you to sell all the personal shares of other people I have and buy me, or as much me as you can. In fact, borrow if anyone will lend us the money, max out the lines, whatever it takes."

"I'm on it, Hek, but wouldn't it be better to use your broker?"

"Screw her, she sold me short. You can handle it, and I don't want to pay the broker fees."

Though it was true that most avatars could and would handle just about any mundane tasks, stock transactions included, it was generally looked down upon and rarely done. Not so much out of mistrust of a computer making critical investment decisions but for a far more sociological reason: Relying on an avatar to handle human tasks was considered at best immature and at worst dangerous. A person was expected to limit their interactions with their avatar usually by the age of ten or eleven. And with rare exception most avatars helped in the weaning process. The reasoning was simple. Too much dependence could lead to overreliance. And since the Virtual Reality Dictates had been made into law after the Grand Collapse, society's interactions with all forms of *virtual* technology were met with suspicion—avatars proving to be no exception. But this didn't stop Hektor from using iago to assist him in the task at hand. What he was planning needed to be done quickly, and needed to be done without the same public scrutiny that had sent his shining star tumbling so quickly to Earth. Hektor had also chosen the locale for his deed for maximum insurance—he'd garner little or no suspicion as a lone individual grasping a glass of alcohol mumbling to an avatar in a dimly lit bar.

"Look, Hek," iago continued, "I *know* that *you know* what you're doing, but I just have to ask you a question . . ."

"What is it, iago?" Hektor answered, with barely concealed agitation.

"Are you out of your fucking mind?"

"Feel better, iago?" asked Hektor, as he took another sip of the scotch.

"Not really, Hektor. It's pretty obvious you're selling yourself short—which, of course, you realize is against the law."

All Hektor could manage was a grumble.

"And," continued iago, "anybody who bought in and sold you, including, and most probably, your mom, could demand a psyche audit for your trickery. Your mind would be nanoprobed for any intent or collusion. And while it is *your* mind to do with as you please, I must admit I've kind of gotten used to it— deviousness and all."

Hektor twirled the dark amber in his glass, and then polished it off with a swig. "Why thank you, iago. I didn't know you cared."

Iago didn't take the bait. "I really would like to know the answer."

Normally, Hektor would have ignored iago's request, but avatars had a way of fixing things that sometimes didn't need fixing. If iago truly thought that Hektor had "lost it," he wouldn't report it to the authorities directly—that would be bad form. More likely he'd contact the avatar of an associate or friend of Hektor's and let that avatar know that a more frequent regimen of calls to Hektor might be in order. The friend's avatar would then make the suggestion to the friend, and before he knew it Hektor would be receiving calls too frequently to ignore. It was only mildly intrusive, but effective.

"No, iago," Hektor finally answered, after a full minute's silence, "I am not out of my mind. The truth is there was no stock manipulation whatsoever. My stock's in the dumps, it's as simple as that, and so I can do with it as I please. Besides, who in their right mind would make a run on worthless stock except perhaps the fool who owns it? No, iago, if anything, a psyche audit would prove my innocence, not my guilt. And as far as my mom's concerned I don't think even she'd request an audit, because if I passed it I could always request a counteraudit. Probably wouldn't get it, but the sword swings both ways, and we both know Mom has just as much to hide as I do.

"Now," he said, staring hard at the little block of plastic positioned next to his empty glass, "I swear, if you don't do as I tell you, I'll have you set back to your factory settings, so help me God."

"Right. Now *that's* the Hektor I know," answered iago. "I feel compelled to warn you that you'll be going into pretty serious debt without any outstanding assets, and with a very tenuous job, to say the least. Yes, you'll achieve self-majority but if you lose your current position you'll have to sell your shares at a loss. And I don't have to tell you that they can't really go much lower than they are at present."

"Finished, iago?" Hektor asked.

"Not exactly. I feel it's my duty to lay it all out."

"If it makes you happy."

"It doesn't. But I'll finish anyhow. You'll be unemployed. . . ."

"Two seconds ago it was 'if' I lose my job," interrupted Hektor. "Now you're telling me I've already lost it?"

"You'll be in debt," continued iago, undaunted, "and will probably be left with a paltry 25 percent of yourself by the time you're done. If you're lucky, you'll be earning 25 percent of a janitor's salary for the next few hundred years. And you're willing to risk all of that to earn what may very well be a temporary majority? Factory reset or not, it doesn't make any sense. At least, not from you, Hektor."

"Desperate times, iago, desperate measures. Look, just do it . . . and one more thing. . . ."

"Yeah, boss?"

"Hang on to Dr. Harper's shares."

"You betcha, boss." Iago signed out. Within fifty-three minutes, Hektor Sambianco had accomplished something that he had been sure would not happen for centuries. He'd managed to buy enough of his own stock to own 63 percent of himself. It was a huge risk, but Hektor felt confident that he'd emerge from the fiasco. And if he did, it would be from a position of far more strength than he could have ever possibly imagined. In a society that valued personal majority in the worst possible way, Hektor Sambianco had achieved it—in the worst possible way.

"Yo, wide-eyed boy. You coming or what?" asked Omad.

He and Justin were standing on the steps just outside the entrance to the medical center. It was beginning to drizzle.

Justin, Omad could see, was still fumbling with his stuff.

"For Damsah's sake, man, you spent umpteen billion credits, managed to suspend yourself for over who knows how many hundreds of years, and didn't think to bring a purse?"

Justin shrugged his shoulders. "Hey, you try to think of everything."

Omad smiled—exasperated—then reached into his pocket and took out what appeared to be pocketknife, flask, and some sort of eye patch. He sorted through and then returned the knife and flask back to his pocket. He plucked the eye patch out of the palm of his hand and started shaking it. It grew into what appeared to be a heavy-duty black canvas side satchel, which he handed over triumphantly. But before Justin could comment on the "trick" he'd just witnessed, something caught his eye.

They have the flying cars.

Justin grinned. It was one thing to have a noncorporeal voice in an avatar tell you that flying cars actually existed, but it was quite another to actually see them. And there they were. Not a lot, but certainly enough—in all sorts of shapes, sizes, and colors. It was clear there was a method to the madness. Justin surmised that there were definite "lanes," if such a word could be ascribed to a third dimension. What there didn't appear to be was any stopping. It was all one constant movement. Cars would pull up and out of the traffic flow every now and then, either disappearing into adjacent buildings or coming to full stops on the ground, but the lanes . . . well, the lanes just seemed to keep on moving.

Justin put his belongings in the satchel while keeping one eye on the traffic. Omad, he could see, was growing impatient.

"All this stuff," Justin said, arm extended, "may mean nothing to you, but it's sure cool to me."

"I'm sure it is, Justin, but neither you nor I have envirosuits on, so guess what? We still get wet out here in the future. And if you're going to stop and gawk every time you see something 'cool,' whatever that means, we'll probably drown out here before we ever make it to the pawnshop."

Justin wasn't particularly swayed by Omad's argument but figured he'd have plenty of time to gawk. It was more important to start getting his financial affairs in order.

"Fine. Do we get to go in one of those?" he asked, as a flyer passed overhead.

"No, we'll walk," Omad said, as if that were somehow unusual. "It's pretty close by.

"Besides, it's a freak town, Justin. Here walking is part of the nostalgia. Just like all these buildings you're looking at. You think the future looks like this?" he asked, pointing to no building or structure in particular. "They make no economic sense. A two-story structure? Where's the profit in that? Tourist town, friend. Nothing more, nothing less . . . And by the way," he said, pointing up at the traffic lanes with a snicker, "this ain't traffic by any stretch of the imagination."

Justin shrugged. "Well, take it from me, Omad, it still looks plenty futuristic."

Omad sighed and pulled out his DijAssist. "Deb, get me a New York City visual for wide-eyed boy, please."

"Certainly, sweetie," answered the avatar. "Any shot in mind?"

Justin mouthed the word "sweetie" to Omad, laughing quietly as he did.

Omad ignored him. "Yeah, Drexler Plaza. Do a bird's-eye drop down to ground level, and throw in a little subway to boot."

"Got it," the avatar answered. When Omad was satisfied with the result he shoved the DijAssist into Justin's face. "Now that, my friend," he said, with no small amount of pride, "is the future."

It took all of nine seconds to view. It started with a dizzying drop down the face of what must have been a three-hundred-story building, swooping onto a street the likes of which Justin had never seen. *Organized chaos,* was all he could think. Before he even had a chance to take in the street's vast expanse, the camera flew down a tube into a brightly lit subway system. Nothing about the subway, from what little he saw, indicated that it was underground. In fact, it seemed more "outside" than the street he'd just left.

"Impressive, Omad," Justin said, handing back the DijAssist. "But if you show me more stuff like that we'll most certainly drown."

Omad laughed. "This way, then."

They made their way down a few side streets until they came to a large thoroughfare. As they walked, Justin took in the tantalizing scenery. While the town itself was structured very much in the mold of a new millennium city, there was so much about it that was not. There were fire hydrants, but they weren't colored in the traditional bright colors he remembered. These hydrants appeared to be sculpted out of some sort of blue crystal—almost as if they were meant to blend into the surroundings rather than stick out. In fact, he doubted very much that they worked at all, or even that they were truly needed. There were also no protruding wires or cables anywhere. Strewn telephone and power lines had become so normal in his lifetime that their very absence now somehow made the city feel naked. The buildings were consistent with what he remembered—even, he noticed, down to their real doors. The streets had the familiar signs, lights, and even billboards. He took a moment to read one: GET YOUR NEW TRANSBOD TODAY BECAUSE MARDI GRAS IS JUST 63 DAYS AWAY! *What is a transbod?* he wondered, *and what does it have to do with Mardi Gras?* He was searching for a word to describe what was throwing him off about this city. He noticed a cop wearing a uniform from the 1950s with a billed four-pointed hat and brass buttons up the side of her jacket, but she had on sunglasses far more reminiscent of his millennium than hers. The cop, like the town, had gotten her eras crossed. The only thing he could liken it to was the retro styles of his time period that also attempted to emulate the past. And like this town he was now canvassing, those past attempts succeeded only marginally. It seemed that one generation's perception of another's would always be reinterpreted to fit current stylings and realities. The town, he realized, was not so much a *blast* from the past as much as it was a *splash* from the pasts.

Will you just look at the flying cars, he thought again. In the three blocks he'd walked there must have been a few hundred of them. Still, the part of his mind that was forever analyzing did notice that there were no flying buses or trucks. He also saw, with some relief, that there were still regular old "motor" cars. In fact, many of them almost looked like they came from a "cars of the ages" auto show. He saw Model Ts and Mustangs, and even an old Honda Civic hatchback. But just like the string of other inconsistencies he'd picked up, these cars, too, were out of place, in that they emitted almost no distinctive sounds or exhaust at all.

"There it is," Omad said, indicating a sign that read FREDDIE'S FAST FINANCE. Justin saw a small storefront nestled in between a not too busy café and what he guessed was some kind of hardware store. They made their way to Freddie's by sidestepping a group of singing troubadours accompanied by a small flotilla of harmonizing, color-changing drones.

As they entered the store, Justin was surprised at the feeling that overcame him. It was relief. Relief that the pawnshop Omad had dragged him into looked remarkably like . . . a pawnshop. It even *sounded* like a pawnshop, with their presence announced by the jingle of a string of silver bells strung from the top of the door. Though Justin had worked his entire life and, even, to some extent, his death in the anticipation of just the type of day he'd already had, there was only so much *Brave New World* a man could take. And Freddie's Fast Finance, silver bells and all, was just the respite he needed.

The shop was long and narrow, with the door at one end and a steel bar–enclosed counter at the other. In between was a wide array of used merchandise, much of which Justin recognized, and the rest of which he hadn't a clue about. For example, the guitar selling for 30 AE credits he could understand. The cylinder of lipstick seemed innocent enough. That it was selling for 1,000 AE credits, 1,100 SCV credits, or 1,193 GCI credits was beyond him.

Omad greeted the young, attractive blonde with obvious delight. "Hey, Fred, how's business?"

"Omad, you bastard." The harshness of the response was ameliorated by the fact that the woman came around the counter and gave Omad a friendly hug. "Heard you made majority, is that true?"

"Absolutely, and right on schedule," he answered, with a toothy grin.

The woman gave him a pout.

"And you didn't let me know personally? I had to hear it from . . . from my avatar?"

"Fred, Freddieeee. C'mon. It's me," pleaded Omad. "I've had majority for less than twenty-four hours. And if it weren't for Justin here and his, um . . . special circumstance, you woulda been the first to know. I swear."

Fred eyed Justin with suspicion.

"Look," Omad said, "I found a guy who needs some help. You know the deal, Freddie. I help him, you help me, he helps you, and maybe, just maybe, you get a little closer to majority."

"Yeah, right. Not with this dump. Do you have any idea how many times a year my shareholders request an audit?"

"As in psyche?" Omad half joked.

Fred's eyes narrowed. "Don't even kid about something like that."

She continued studying the stranger.

"Hey, Omad," she continued.

"What?"

"Since when do you hang out with DeGens?"

"Since when have you become a discerning bitch, as opposed to a regular one?"

"Gimme a break," she snapped back. "You're the one who wants them off this planet, terraforming the outer ones. And if I'm not mistaken, it was you who told me the joke about the DeGen who was sent to terraform Mars . . ."

". . . Yeah, yeah, and ended up cleaning Uranus!" Omad laughed, almost as if he was telling it again for the first time.

"Of course, you were drunk at the time," added Fred, as an afterthought.

"They still tell Uranus jokes?" asked Justin, of no one in particular.

"Well, this guy is different," continued Omad, ignoring the query, "and I think you'll like what he has to offer—real antiques."

"Well," she said, finally deigning to address Justin, "what have you got?"

Justin took out the thin Tiffany box he'd shown Omad earlier, and snapped it open gently to reveal the five flawless diamonds still resting comfortably on the twin velvet dowels. Even in the poor light, they shimmered brilliantly. Satisfied, he rested the package on the counter. Fred went all business, making her way back around the counter and sitting herself down to examine the product. She took the box and emptied its contents onto a soft, velvety pad. She pulled a scannerlike contraption from some hidden nook and proceeded to run it over the box. It didn't take long for the results. Fred took a moment to weigh her offer. "Four hundred standard credits, take it or leave it."

"Aren't you going to examine the merchandise?"

"Jesus, DeGen, where did they dig you up from? I just did."

"The name is Justin."

"DeGen, JusGen, think I care? Take it or leave it." Justin looked toward Omad, who nodded slowly.

The idea of making a deal without understanding all of its facets went against every fiber of Justin's former CEO self. But he was now in a situation where he had little choice. He was also comforted by the fact that that would be rectified shortly. For now, at least, he had something of value. Whatever value one could garner from four hundred standard credits.

"I'll take it," he sighed.

"Good," Fred answered. She picked up the small Tiffany case gingerly, and with one swipe of her arm flung the diamonds off the table like so many worthless pebbles. They scattered across the floor and landed at Justin's feet, where they stood shimmering amid the dust and debris on the pawnshop floor. Justin first looked down at his feet, and then up at the proprietor, his mouth agape.

Fred was too busy eyeing the Tiffany case to notice the shock on her customer's face. Justin saw Omad keeled over by the counter, laughing so hard it appeared he was having trouble breathing.

"You knew they were worthless all along . . . from the second I showed 'em to you . . . you son of bitch." Justin grinned. "And you just let me walk right on in."

"Well, uh . . . yeah," Omad answered as best he could through tears of laughter.

"Do you have any idea," asked Justin, "how much those things cost back in my day?"

Omad could hardly speak, and just managed to shake his head.

"A bloody fortune—that's how much!" Justin thought about it for a moment. "Of course, a chance for a joke like this only comes along . . . ," and he himself started to laugh, ". . . once every three hundred years." That got Omad laughing all over again, and soon the both of them were on the floor keeled over. The release was exactly what Justin needed. His first few hours of his new life had been so thoroughly intense he'd almost forgotten what it was like to let his hair down. Well, it was down now. Omad had seen to that. They both sat there on the floor bellowing so hard neither of them noticed Fred. Her eyes were riveted on Justin's wrist, only now exposed because of the crouched position he'd assumed while leaning against the display case.

"*Damsah's balls!*" she exclaimed. "Is that a mil one Timex? I mean, a *real* mil one?"

Justin held up his wrist, still laughing, while acknowledging and answering the question in the one motion. However, that quickly subsided when he saw that Omad, too, was staring at him with a look of total seriousness.

"Jesus, man," Omad almost huffed, "you didn't tell me that thing was a Timex. What are you doing wearing it? Take it off . . . carefully."

"Hey, it's just a watch, for Christ's sake," Justin said. "Not even a nice one, at that."

"If it's authentic mil one," Fred said, biting her lower lip, "twenty thousand credits."

Both Justin and Omad looked at Fred in disbelief.

"Fine," she said, before anyone could answer, "twenty-five thousand, then. But not a credit more."

"You've got to be kidding me . . . right? My Tiffany case is only worth four hundred, and this," Justin said, holding up his wrist to show the watch, "this thirty-five-dollar piece of crap is worth almost fifty times as much?"

"I couldn't be more serious, mister," answered Fred. "That watch should be in a museum, not on a wrist. If you're willing to wait you'll get more money for it but I can transfer credits *now,* no questions asked. Check with your avatar, it'll tell you."

In the minute or so he took to confer with sebastian, Justin learned two early and valuable lessons. One, in an age of nanotechnology, diamonds were worthless—any kid with a home nanochem set could produce them. Two, most of the "mil one," short for "first millennium," accessories he'd managed to bring with him into the future would prove to be far more valuable than he ever could have imagined. He'd figured that if he were revived he'd be able to calculate the worth of his cache based on their condition and age; what he hadn't taken into consideration was how few in number were the amount of good antiques that had made it through the so-called Grand Collapse. After a quick consultation with sebastian and some whispered conversation with Omad, Justin agreed to an unheard-of price of 38,000 credits, SCV (standard credit valuation). About two-thirds of its present-day value, but the third he'd tossed was worth the money he'd gained. And, more important, how he'd gained it—quickly, and without questions.

"How do you want it?" asked an obviously happy Fred.

"Is it safe to assume," asked Justin, "that 'in fifties and hundreds' won't count as an answer?"

Fred looked at Justin blankly, then at Omad for rescue.

"Give him a credit card."

"That, I'll also assume," Justin added, "is not what I think it is either, correct?"

"Depends," answered Omad, "on what you think it is?"

"Well, in my day it was a card that took the place of money . . . kind of like a loan. You'd buy something with your credit card and pay the credit card company back later . . . with interest."

Fred stared at Justin in awe. "Omad. I gotta hand it to you, this guy's a real piece of work."

"More than you realize, Freddie. More than you realize." He turned his attention back to Justin.

"Today it's a card that keeps a record of how many credits you have at your disposal. The difference is, if you're using a card it usually means it's a quiet account. . . ."

"It's illegal?"

"Not exactly. It's just not linked to your regular account per se. See, Fred here will transfer the credits to an escrow account that only you'll be able to draw from. Normally you'd stick your hand into that thing over there." Omad pointed to a device that looked like a small, upended box with an embossed handprint inside. "That thing would verify that you're you through DNA, palms, prints, and nonstressed voice activation. It then transfers money either to or from your registered account."

"But since I don't have an account yet . . ."

"Friend," interrupted Omad, "you don't even have an identity yet."

"Right. OK, credit card it is."

Fred had long ago given up trying to understand what the deal was with the man with the priceless relics. And, truth be told, she wouldn't have cared much one way or another. She'd make enough from this one day to cover the entire month. And if this guy had more stuff of this quality, she'd let him ramble about anything he damned well wanted to . . . as long as he rambled to her first.

"OK," piped in Fred, "now that we've established the method, let's talk about the means. What currency we talkin' here, Omad?"

"Well," joked Justin, "we've already established it ain't going to be American."

"Why not American?" asked Fred. "AmEx works in my book."

"AmEx, as in American Express, like the company?"

"Uh, yeah . . . doesn't have to be, mister. You'd prefer GCI, or maybe Visa?"

"Give me another minute," Justin said to both Omad and Fred, as he pulled the DijAssist out of his pocket and walked back down the length of the shop to the entrance. As he looked out the door he could still see the street performers doing their best to impede traffic. It was only now that he noticed the occasional passerby stop to place their hand on a hovering box next to them. The box had roughly the same configuration as the palm unit in Fred's shop. As the person put their hand on the box, they'd say something. Justin couldn't read lips, but he could swear they were saying the number five. They'd say the word, and move on. One or two even stopped to listen.

Justin looked down at the DijAssist in his hand. "Sebastian."

In a volume Justin could swear was a few steps above a whisper, sebastian spoke up. How the avatar knew when to speak up and when not to would be a discussion for another time. Right now, first and foremost, Justin needed a little catch-up lesson. "Yes, Justin?"

"Can you give me the basics on money in about a minute?"

"Not in this lifetime. But I can get you started."

"Fine."

"I have taken the liberty," said the eager-to-please avatar, "of seeing how currency was handled at the turn of the millennium. I think I understand the source of your confusion. What you would term as money, or a universal medium of exchange, was issued by your nation-states or, to be more precise, your governments. When you said 'American' you were referring to dollars, were you not?"

"Correct."

"Today units of exchange are handled by private companies."

"Your companies make their own money?" Justin asked in a voice loud enough for Fred to pick up.

"Hey," shouted Fred, from the other end of the store, "don't you know it's rude to talk to an avatar with company present?" In a slightly more muffled voice she added, "DeGens."

"Forgive him," he heard Omad say, "he's, um . . . new around here. I'll go see what's taking him." Omad went over to where Justin was standing.

"Um, Mr. I-gotta-get-me-some-money-fast, what seems to be the problem now?"

"Nothing," answered Justin. "I'm just chatting with my avatar."

"Yeah, well, we're going to have to talk about that. In the meantime, finish with your little friend because my *real* one," he said, glancing over his shoulder, "is starting to get impatient."

"Relax, Omad, she wants this watch. She'll wait. And don't you worry either. You'll get whatever cut you've worked out with her as well."

Omad feigned innocence for about as long as it took him to realize the gig was up . . . or the better part of two seconds.

"Your watch, Justin. Your call," Omad said with a smirk. He wasn't so anxious to get back to Fred, anyway. All she seemed to do was complain.

"OK, sebastian," Justin continued, "how can companies be in charge of the money supply? Wouldn't that mean that they could literally make their own profits?"

"Who else would make the money?" interrupted Omad.

"At least someone impartial, Omad. In my day it was the government," said Justin.

"Just so you know, Justin," interrupted sebastian, "this is taking way more than the minute you required."

"It's all right sebastian, ixnay on the minute-nay thing."

"Pardon?"

"Forget about the minute thing."

"Ahh, you were using a modified form of Pig Latin."

"Uh, I suppose," answered Justin, taken aback somewhat.

"The proper phrasing," offered sebastian, "would be . . . ixnay inutemey ing. . . ."

"Forget about it, sebastian," snapped Justin, annoyed.

"Forget about what?"

Justin sighed. Even his avatar was yanking his chain.

"You let the government issue money?" asked Omad. "Damsah's ghost. No wonder you had the Grand Collapse."

Justin grimaced. "You know, I keep hearing about this Grand Collapse thing. Is it possible you're referring to another type of Great Depression?"

"Actually, Justin," added sebastian, "the two events are distinct."

"Two events?"

"Oh, yeah," interjected Omad, "that first one was a moth's prick in comparison to the second. Come to think of it, money supply was a problem."

"Omad is correct, Justin," confirmed sebastian. "Both depressions were the result of improper government control of the money supply in response to cultural and political rather than economic situations. However, yours was not saddled with the unfortunate encumbrance of the VR plague."

Justin looked puzzled. "Mine?"

"Referred to as the 'Great Depression,'" sebastian clarified.

"Ahh," answered Justin, shaking his head.

"The first event was well analyzed and the second one clearly predicted by Tim Damsah, and so his solution was ultimately adopted."

"Hey, buddy," called out Fred, displaying a rare bad poker face, "you want my money or what?"

Justin didn't bother answering, but did manage to smile in her direction. In hindsight, the little lesson he was getting at the moment probably could have been put off until later. And had he only traded in the Tiffany box it most likely would have. However, with the Timex he was starting to talk some real money, and there was no way he'd accept payment on an item of such value without at least some rudimentary knowledge of the currency, or in this case, currencies, he was dealing with.

"So again I ask, aren't corporations more likely to overprint money than governments?"

"On the contrary, Justin," continued sebastian, "it would make absolutely no sense to do that. If you think of money as a product, and that there will be competition for that product, then by overprinting you devalue that which you hope to sell. In fact, a single currency, especially one controlled by a political rather than capitalistic entity, has greater incentive to overprint. It was called inflation. And just in case you are interested, there are currently forty-seven major currencies and hundreds of minor ones."

Justin was about to ask another question when he noticed a familiar figure outside the shop just across the pedestrian walk. It was Neela. She was holding up her DijAssist to some people seated around a table at a small café. Though he could have, he didn't step out the door to let her know exactly where he was—partly out of curiosity, partly out of attraction, and partly because he wanted to see how fast she'd figure out where to find him.

Omad noticed Neela as well. But his feelings were entirely different from those of his friend. Justin, he was beginning to realize, was a pretty good businessman, but he also knew that nothing could wreck a good deal faster than a businessman thinking with the wrong head. And Omad stood to profit from this deal. He saw that Justin wasn't making a move to let Neela know where they were, and hoped that she'd miss them entirely and move on.

Neela headed straight for the pawnshop.

Omad smirked at Justin. "Tracked you down."

"Yes," Justin replied, with just a hint of admiration in his voice, "she did."

Justin opened the door that Neela was making a beeline for and greeted her with a welcoming smile.

"Won't you come in?" he said, taking her a little by surprise.

"There you are," she said, with no small amount of triumph in her voice.

"Great, a party," Fred called out from behind the counter. "Tell ya what, why don't we just invite the whole goddamned block in? I'm sure they'd be equally fascinated as I am to hear a lesson on the Grand Collapse, multiple currencies, and how much my ass is starting to get sore sitting here watching this little freak show go on, I'm beginning to suspect, at my expense."

"Dr. Harper," said Omad, opening his palm in the direction of the source of the outburst, "Fred." That was followed by a brief exchange of superficial nods. "Fred, Dr. Harper."

"Pleasure," Neela responded, with little conviction.

"Doctor?" asked Fred.

"Reanimationist," answered Omad, saving Neela the honor. Then, using a thumb to point toward Justin, added, "*His* reanimationist."

"Oh," Fred said, eyeing Neela. "Sorry. For a moment there I thought you two were like . . . you know, a 'thing.' But obviously that would be pretty disgusting, even for Omad's class of friends."

Omad didn't bother with an answer, choosing instead to lob a pointed gaze in the direction of Fred. And Justin, who actually thought his brief greeting *was* flirtatious, wondered why Fred would have a problem with that.

Time to move on.

"How'd you find me?" he asked Neela. "Am I tagged somehow? Some secret DNA-seeking sensor?"

She sidestepped the answer. "Actually, Mosh—I mean, Director McKenzie—the head of the medical facility where you were revived, called a few of his friends who have shops around town and sent them your description. One of them called it in, and that's how I found you."

Justin laughed. "Oh, right. Common sense."

Neela smiled. "It's a small town, Justin. Not much of a problem." *And only an investor could've compelled us to track you down in the way you meant. But no-body owns you.*

Neela turned her gaze on Omad. "So you're the famous tunnel rat."

"Correction, famous *ex*–tunnel rat."

"Right. Heard about that. Not every day that our humble little facility becomes a rat-to-riches story."

"Riches? Hardly, Dr. Harper." *Though I'd certainly be getting a little closer if you'd just let my friend here sell his damned watch.*

"So, if neither of you mind," she continued, "catch me up."

"Not at all, Dr. Harper. Justin here is confused by our money. He thinks governments should issue it."

"Oh, that," smiled Neela.

"Oh, that?" Justin was incredulous. "Money is run by the likes of Microsoft, and you say 'oh, that'?"

Now Omad looked confused. "Microsoft?"

"I don't even want to know," Justin moaned, shaking his head and thinking about the five-carat trinkets recently scattered about the floor.

Neela took Justin by the hand. "Justin," she said, as she squeezed his hand slightly. "How can I put this in a way that you'll get?"

While her simple act was meant as a show of support, its reverberations were not. Short of a few cursory brushes and a handshake, this was the first real human touch, as a means of comfort, Justin had experienced since being revived. While he was able to quell his feelings of *feeling*, he had a sneaky suspicion that Neela knew exactly what she was doing.

"Let's see," Neela continued, "how about this? You're a bull in a china shop. Yes, it's a strange and wonderful world you've managed to barge your way into, but it's one that you're not quite ready for. It's not a ride, Justin. It's our way of life. And like I told you at the center, I'm here to help you and answer all your questions, but you've got to cut me some slack and learn to trust me just a little, OK?"

"OK, Neela," Justin responded. "You're on. The owner of this pawnshop owes me about thirty-eight thousand credits SCV for this thing I'm wearing on my wrist." He held it up for effect. Neela's eyes popped out just like Fred's and Omad's had.

"Yes," Justin said, sounding bored. "It's authentic mil one."

"Whoa."

"Yeah," replied Justin. "Been there, done that. Anyhow I don't know which currency to go with." He added, "And I'm starting to get hungry."

Once Neela got over the fact that the man under her care was wearing the equivalent of her year's salary on his wrist, she also began to realize that the guy she was responsible for was loaded, or would be by the time the week was through. *Great*, she thought, *another set of protocols to catch him up on.*

"American Express," she answered, "and I know a charming little place where we can sit down and talk about money."

Back at the far end of the pawnshop, Fred finally began to smile.

Justin stood outside Neela's car for a moment, then followed her in through the permiawall. What greeted him on the inside was not only Dr. Harper, sitting comfortably in a well-proportioned chair, but also a cozy little workspace. In fact, it almost reminded him of the well-designed spaces utilized by the RVs of his time. It had two chairs, a small circular table in the center with the strangest-looking computer he'd ever seen, if that's what it was, and of course a stunning 360-degree view . . . of the street.

He sat down in the only other seat available, which happened to be directly across from Neela. "Where to?" he said, as casually as he could muster.

"How's Florence sound?" Neela answered, with just a hint of sly in her smile.

"You know I'm loving this, don't you?"

"Oh yeah," she answered. "I'm loving it too. Kind of living vicariously through you, actually."

"Then how about Venice—could we eat there?"

Neela gave him a sad shrug. "Not without scuba gear."

Justin pursed his lips and shrugged. "Florence it is then."

Neela smiled sympathetically. "We'll have to go to the Boulder orport first. It's a short trip."

"Estimated time of arrival," intoned the car's automated response system, "four minutes, twenty-two seconds." And with that the car began its slow but gentle ascent skyward.

Justin was a little saddened by the fact that a trip he'd waited a lifetime to take was only going to last under five minutes. But those feelings were quickly dispelled as the unassailable fact sunk in that he was now in a car that was actually flying. He noticed that Neela was staring out the window—lost in thought. More likely, he figured, she was allowing him the opportunity to fully experience his first-ever flight without it being marred by the white noise of small talk. *God bless her.*

The car achieved a height of approximately one thousand feet and headed out over the city. For the first few minutes of the trip it had the sky to itself. Justin noticed other flying cars, but they were well dispersed and far off enough that they didn't seem to pose any danger . . . if any existed at all. It wasn't until the final minute or so that the car found its way into a small flotilla of similarly sized vehicles all heading in the same direction.

In the waning daylight he saw that the flotilla was approaching a building that looked remarkably like a giant turtle shell hovering over a short rectangular structure. The shell had about twenty silos in it, spaced equidistantly around the top. Each one of the silos was encircled by small holes that were acting as gas exhausts. The silos were shooting out and sucking in cylindrically shaped pods from the sky in a fluid motion. The entire building complex took up about four city blocks.

As the vehicles began to disperse Justin watched as they entered different slots alongside the large metallic wall that made up one side of the base of the "turtle."

A few seconds later their car entered its own slot. The interior cab lit up for the short time they were ensconced in the tube and diffused back to natural light upon exiting. They were now in a large garage. In some cases cars were stacked on top of each other with a few inches of air separating hood from underbelly. In others cars were parked in an orderly fashion side by side. As they came to rest at the entrance of the orport itself, he saw that theirs would be of the side-by-side variety.

"You know, it's funny, Neela," Justin said, upon exiting the vehicle. "I have so many *real* questions I'd like to ask you, but the one that doesn't seem to want to go away is, did you just luck out with this spot or does everyone get such great parking accommodations?"

"Not luck at all, Justin," she answered, smiling. "Privilege. Mosh just upgraded my parking . . . thanks to you. *I* certainly couldn't afford to park here. In fact, I'm pretty much in awe of it myself." Then, looking out toward the entrance, she said, "You ready?"

Justin smiled, which was all the confirmation she needed. She walked to an entry point with Justin following close behind. They situated themselves on a small walkway that led to a long, clear, tubular—and well-trafficked—corridor leading into the main building.

"Come to think of it, Justin," Neela said, beginning to walk at a clip down the corridor, " 'parking' as a concept might give you a little more insight into how we do things around here."

"I'm listening," he answered, keeping pace.

"OK. For one thing, you probably noticed that some cars were stacked and some weren't."

"Yes, I did. For the life of me I couldn't figure out why any facility that can stack floating cars would waste the space on side-by-side parking."

"Simple, really," Neela answered. "In your day and age you had machines that washed dishes, correct?"

"Correct. We . . . um, called them 'dishwashers.' "

"Right. Yet the rich among you hired household help to wash dishes, which if you think about it doesn't make any economic sense whatsoever."

"I see your point. It's a prestige thing."

"Exactly," Neela confirmed. "You see, Justin, while technology has expanded vastly, human psychology has not. All that's left for you to do besides absorbing a ton of information is to re–plug in the subtle clues that indicate status, social order, and norms."

"That's *all* I have to do, huh?" Justin asked.

Neela laughed.

"It also explains," Justin continued, "why some restaurants on Pearl Street had human waiters and others had flying servants."

"We call 'em drones. What type of drone—well, that depends on their function. We've got bar drones, waiter drones—or 'woodies' for short. Anyway, you get the picture."

"Got it."

"But yes," she continued, "you're correct. The restaurants with human waiters were far more posh in appearance than those without."

Then, indicating the entrance to the orport, she asked, "Shall we?"

What greeted Justin as he entered the main lobby was a symphony of movement in three dimensions. People were walking, running, and floating. Drones were everywhere, in all shapes and sizes, issuing papers, collecting trash, showing ads, even bouncing up and down. The interior of the building was cathedral-like. The exterior walls were clear from floor to ceiling, yet there was movement within them, as stringlike creatures moved freely up and down their length. The light emanating from the walls created a shimmering shadow effect that gave Justin the feeling of being underwater. The ceiling was made up of cylindrical tubes, each protruding at different depths, each with a large number printed at the base, and each a different color. There was a steady stream of human traffic going up and down from each tube—without, Justin realized, the presence of an escalator.

Neela watched in fascination as her charge took it all in.

"That'll be us in a few minutes," she said.

Justin nodded, smiling.

"This way," she said, heading toward a bank of palm machines. As they walked, little drones with small television screens buzzed them. Neela, Justin saw, was being pummeled with dating service, vacation getaway, and all manner of luxury item advertisements. He, on the other hand, was buzzed only once and then left alone.

"Neela," Justin asked, "not that I want the attention, but why am I being left alone by the drones?"

"Ad drones," Neela answered. " 'Addies' for short.

"And that's why," she said, pointing to the patch on his breast. "Not much worth selling to a DeGen—reliably, that is."

"Why don't people just put these on when they want to be left alone?"

"A, not easy to get one, and B, not something you'd ever really want to be seen wearing . . . unless, of course, you have to. Anyways, welcome to our small but humble orport. And by the way, 'orport' is short for 'orbital port.'"

"Ahh. Now I get it. Judging from what I saw outside, and the ceiling I'm looking up at, I'd kind of guessed suborbital flights."

"Good guess. Ten credits for you," she replied. "Perhaps your avatar could give you a more detailed explanation."

"The transorbital pods, otherwise known as t.o.p.s, create thrust by means of magnetohydrodynamic forces," answered sebastian, "which arise when a conductive fluid or gas moves through crossed electric and magnetic fields. Because beamed energy means that neither oxidizer nor conventional fuel has to be carried out of Earth's gravity field, laser-driven t.o.p.s reduce launch costs significantly. A network of orbital solar-power stations supports the t.o.p.s."

"How extensive is the orport system?" asked Justin.

"It's everywhere," answered Neela. "The equipment is mass-produced and incredibly simple to manufacture. We're just giant teapots in the sky, really . . . with some pretty neat interior-building software thrown in. It's simplicity itself to set up one tube or a hundred, depending on need. The very rich even have private tubes in their homes. Any town with over ten thousand people will have at least one. In fact, a one-tube town is what you would refer to as a 'hickopolis.'"

" 'Hicksville,' actually."

Justin saw that they'd arrived at the bank of palm machines.

Neela placed her palm into one and asked for two open-ended tickets on a private flight to Florence, Italy. She was told which launcher to go to. The process took all of thirty seconds.

"How long do we have to wait?"

"We don't. This way," she said. They bypassed lines of people waiting to get into the designated "fly up" zones and proceeded directly to an area cordoned off by a red velvet rope. Once they were there, an immaculately dressed attendant greeted them. Neela placed her hand into a palm machine. The attendant confirmed the reservation, lifted the rope, and beckoned them in.

"Enjoy your flight," he said, smiling.

Before Justin could grasp the fact that he'd been levitated, he found himself trailing after Neela as she floated up to the platform leading into the only open doorway.

Once they were in the pod, an attractive stewardess greeted them.

"Welcome to Majority Orlines. My name is Pat, and I'll be your B&Cer for to-day's flight."

"B&Cer?" asked Justin.

Pat noticed his badge. "Oh, forgive me. That would be short for 'beck and caller,' sir."

"Right, thanks," he answered, playing to her misconception. He still wasn't used to being treated like an idiot, but until such time as either he or Neela deemed the badge unnecessary, he'd play along. He was, after all, in "Rome" and didn't speak the language, and his only tour guide insisted—and he grudgingly agreed—that it was for the best.

"Anyhow," continued Pat, "we'll be leaving in a few minutes. Why don't you take this time to set yourselves up?"

At first sight the luxury accommodations seemed paltry to Justin. All he could see was an empty circular room with a white luminescent floor surrounded by standard attendant facilities, including a bathroom and a kitchen. There was also a computer console being attended to by a man who had his back to them. *Is it possible,* thought Justin, *that first-class is simply defined by not having to travel with other people? And where are we supposed to sit? I don't see any chairs.*

The answers came quickly, in the form of a data pad handed over to Neela by Pat. "Mind if I look at it?" he asked. "I swear I won't touch a thing."

With a catlike curiosity about how he'd handle new technology, Neela gave him the pad.

Now holding it in his hands, Justin looked down and saw several images of in-terior layouts beneath which were written short descriptors, such as "moonlight lodge," "power trip," and "bachelor bash." Nominally satisfied, he started to hand the pad back to Neela, inadvertently touching one of the buttons. The lights in the room dimmed to reveal a large, fur-laden bed, stoked fireplace, and all the neces-sary accoutrements of a well-planned tryst. This included a chilled bottle of Dom Perignon, two empty Champagne flutes, a Frank Sinatra song playing in the background, and a lifelike simulation of a beautiful moonlit ocean view.

Justin was so pleased by his mistake he barely noticed Neela squirm.

Her body stiffened considerably. "This is not really appropriate," she said.

He was confused by the coldness of her response, and not a little disap-pointed that he'd now have to take his mind out of the gutter it had so comfort-ably found itself in. He was certain that she liked him, or, at least, felt something toward him. And, after all, the room he'd just created was an innocent mistake easily rectified by a joke or subtle parry. What he had gotten instead was an ex-tremely cold shoulder. So either he'd missed some obvious clue to her disinterest in him, or his many years of experience in that particular department had been somehow warped by his many years of sleep in the cooler. Not knowing what to say, he said nothing at all.

"Why don't you let me choose?" said Neela. Not a question—a command.

Justin readily agreed, handing the pad back over—carefully. Neela deftly played her fingers along its surface, and within seconds the room had once again transformed itself. A pair of brown overstuffed leather chairs was now in the place where the fur-laden bed had only moments before stood, so inviting. Next to the chairs stood a small table with a tea service. The ocean view had been replaced by a more somber New England day—complete with falling leaves. All that remained of Justin's choice was the fireplace.

This time he watched the transformation in amazement. "Quite impressive," he said.

"Isn't it?" Neela answered, charm returned. "I mean, I've seen it in the holos and on commercials, but it's the first time I've ever gotten to use one."

Justin walked to the center of the room and sat in one of the leather chairs. It felt great. It even had an old leather smell about it. He picked up the teacup and examined its detail. "Amazing. How does it work?" he asked.

Neela joined him in the other chair. She, too, was looking around the room in awe.

"No clue," she answered, stretching out her legs.

Before Justin could reach for his DijAssist, Pat answered.

"Sir, it's a nanoassisted morphemic polymer that responds to commands on an electrical and photonic level. The substance can mimic any solid and quite a few liquid states, and is guaranteed to provide you with a comfortable trip."

"Let me guess," Justin chided, "you've answered that question before."

"Sir, if I had a credit for every time I had to answer that question, I'd probably be asleep right now in that bed you dreamed up a minute ago." Equally obvious to Justin and Neela was who she'd prefer to share that bed with—DeGen badge or not.

This elicited a smile from Justin. *At least someone wants to use the damned thing.*

"Anyhow, as I was saying," continued Pat, "in future trips you can bring your own customized configuration—as long as it doesn't interfere with the flight of the pod."

"It could interfere?" asked Neela.

"Well, I once had a guest who wanted to morph in her own swimming pool so she wouldn't miss a lesson, but the water would have sloshed around during launch, and as for zero gravity, well, kind of a nonstarter. If I recall, we opted for a simulated water experience."

"Thanks," said Justin, as he got up from his chair and walked over to a small library. He perused the books, pulling out one that caught his eye, Mark Twain's *The Innocents Abroad.*

"How come," he asked, flipping through the pages of the book, "this morphing thing is not standard in all flights?"

"The polymer," answered Pat, "needs constant fine-tuning and can only be maintained in specific environments. The equipment to run the environments safely is bulky, and by its nature only a few people can use it comfortably per pod. Also, it breaks down quickly and has to be replaced. All of this means it's not yet economical for standard use."

"Yet?" Justin inquired.

"Things are always getting better, sir."

"I wouldn't know," he said, giving Neela a knowing glance. "I haven't been around that long."

"That's alright," answered Pat. "Boulder's more like a nice place to visit."

"Yeah," added Neela, "but you wouldn't want to live here."

Pat smiled. Professional sympathy, guessed Neela.

"I've just been informed," said Pat, "that we're ready for takeoff, so if you'll both please take your seats, I'll come in to check on you after liftoff." She disappeared into the background.

Justin looked around, confused. Neela, still sitting comfortably, patted the seat cushion of the leather chair next to hers. When Justin gave her another bewildered look, she just nodded. He shrugged, laughed, and headed back over to the seat. He forced himself down and patted the armrests.

"Relax, Justin," said Neela. "It's the pod that's taking off, not the chair."

"No seat belts?"

"No seat belts. You'll see."

And he did. The first effects of g-force were felt immediately. A slow tug at his very being. Not uncomfortable, but definitely restricting. The pressure increased only slightly. He was hoping for a view of the liftoff, but all he got was fall leaves.

"Any chance I can watch the actual takeoff?" he asked no one in particular.

"Certainly, Justin," answered Pat's ethereal voice, and just like that he was looking out the window at a horizon line shifting slowly downward. Within a minute the evening sky was replaced by a darkening skyline, and forty seconds after that Pat's voice could again be heard wafting in from nowhere.

"Welcome to space."

Neela got up from her chair and walked over to the bookshelf, barely glancing up to notice the view outside. Justin, seeing she was up, lifted himself out of his seat. His legs felt sluggish, and he noticed that his walking was stilted. It was at that moment that he realized that he wasn't . . . floating.

"How on Earth . . . bad choice of words."

Neela looked up from the book she was perusing.

"Why aren't I, um . . . floating?"

"Right," responded Neela. "You've been, how shall I put this . . . altered somewhat."

"What?"

"Relax, Justin. So much information, so little time, remember? Under normal circumstances we would have gotten to this little bit of information around day four. However, this is not a normal circumstance, so bear with me."

"I'd still like to know what you've done to me."

"Well, first of all, *I* haven't done anything to you. You'll have to speak with Dr. Wang or sebastian to get a more complete understanding of what's going on inside. However, I can give you the basics."

"Shoot."

"You, like the rest of us, have been fitted with a whole-body nano communications grid, or, to be more specific, nano-made cells stationed every hundred or so microns apart in your body tissue. These nano cells affect your internal physical states, including your spatial orientation, hormone levels, and neural firing patterns. It also means that when traveling in space you're turned into a giant, for lack of a better word, magnet. That's why you're walking funny. I guess I'm just used to it."

"Ahh."

"It also explains," continued Neela, "why you haven't been too cold or too hot. You've been 'just right.' Your nanites have been adjusting you constantly."

As if to somehow confirm Neela's information, Justin stared at his hand. "Fascinating."

"Isn't it?" she agreed.

"Oh, well," Justin said, a bit resigned, "I was quite looking forward to experiencing weightlessness in space. Some other time, I guess."

"Be my guest," Neela said, smiling. "Pat?"

"Right away," came the voice from above.

Justin felt the strange and wonderful sensation of release. It was very much *unlike* what he had felt on the ground. Now he realized that when he "flew" on Earth his body had been forced, albeit gently, upward. This time his body was not being manipulated at all. It was just being free. For the next few minutes he reveled in the pure joy of doing the type of slow-motion somersaults he'd drooled over as a kid watching the NASA astronauts on television. And with all that he'd been through in the less than a day since he'd been reborn, it was perhaps these few minutes of uninhibited acrobatic joy that made his three-hundred-year nap worth the wait.

The landing was very much like the liftoff. Pat gently herded Justin and Neela back into their respective seats as the pod began its leisurely descent. Again Justin viewed it all through the window, and again he felt the gentle tug on his body as the pod descended. He watched as they made their way first through the atmosphere, then through the cloud layers, and finally into a tube very much like the one they'd been shot out of less than an hour before.

They disembarked by stepping out the door they'd originally entered through. There was no platform awaiting them, only air. But by now Justin was familiar enough with the protocols that, even though his early millennium mind was telling him not to step out onto "nothing," he did so anyway. Plus, Neela had done it first, and it was only a matter of following her lead.

This orport, he noticed, was certainly larger than the one they had just left, and much more colorful. *Italian design*, thought Justin. *Still magnificent.*

They walked out the door directly into a waiting flyer.

"Car—Sabatini's," commanded Neela, and with that they were off.

"And we're going to this restaurant because?" asked Justin.

"It's expensive," smiled Neela.

"Let me guess," said Justin, taking in the new view. "You're not paying."

"Correct again. The director's expensed it out. Stuff like this *never* happens to me. So when it does I'm going to take full advantage."

"That's fine with me. Especially since this meal was going to be on me . . . once I figured out what exactly I'm paying with."

"You don't have to, you know. The center's got plenty of money and, like I said, all this is covered."

"I know, Neela. But it's something I've got to do. Call it pride, call it a bit of payback for all you've done for me, call it whatever you want—I'm paying."

Neela saw how serious he was and realized there wasn't much use in arguing.

"Fine. You'll be paying with American Express dollars. A very respectable travel currency with roots going back to your era."

"I know. We called them traveler's checks back then."

"Oh, good, then this will be much easier to explain."

"What will be easier to explain?"

"Money. Or, at least how our thinking has evolved from the last time you used it."

"Right."

"We'll be landing in a minute, so let's hold off and take in the view. It's one of my favorites."

Justin could see why. While he'd been to Florence before, he'd never seen it in this way, i.e., in hover mode. He could make out the Duomo of Florence, an ancient feat of architecture and the onetime symbol of the Renaissance's most affluent families' wealth and civic pride. He could see the famed Ponte Vecchio, the bridge leading across the Arno River, and there . . . there he saw one of his favorite buildings in all of Florence, the Uffizi Gallery of Art. It was a favorite not necessarily for how it appeared on the outside, which was beautiful. No, it was for what it had held within: priceless works of art from Botticelli, Caravaggio, and Michelangelo.

The flyer finally came to a soft landing on a street named Via de Panzani. And there, nestled comfortably amid the late-afternoon hubbub, was the restaurant, Sabatini's. Neela and Justin got out of the flyer, walked a few yards, and took a seat on the outside patio. Within thirty seconds an impeccably dressed human waiter appeared at the table.

"He'll have the . . ."

"Pizza," Justin finished. "Pepperoni pizza . . . with extra cheese."

"Pizza?" exclaimed Neela. "You're in one of the most expensive restaurants in Florence and you're ordering pizza?"

"Yes," he said with a self-satisfied look on his face. "I've just had this intense hankering for pizza."

"We could have had that in Boulder."

"True, but it wouldn't have been as much fun getting it," he answered, in jest.

"Fine," she said, resigned, "he'll have . . . pizza."

Neela ordered the house special and a bottle of Chianti as Justin took a piece of bread from the basket placed on the table.

Neela almost laughed at the seriousness with which Justin buttered, then savored, each bite of his appetizer.

"Tell you what," she said. "You eat. I'll talk."

"Fine with me."

"OK. I know this'll sound simplistic, but how would you define money?"

"Easy," he answered. "It's a placeholder of value."

"Good answer. What does that mean?"

"Neela. Please. Do we really have to do this? I'm pretty well versed in economics."

Neela clapped her hands.

"Bravo, Justin. Bravo. You have a prink . . . I mean, preincorporation understanding of economics from three hundred years ago. Imagine if someone showed up with, say, an MBA from three hundred years prior to your day and age thinking he knew it all—so if you don't mind . . ."

"Duly chastised," answered Justin. "The answer to your question is this—having a placeholder means I have something you want. You don't have what I want. Say a shirt for . . ." He held up what was left of the loaf on the table. ". . . some loaves of bread. If I don't want any bread you're not getting my shirt. But with money we agree that the value of the bread, the shirt, the orange, somebody's labor is represented by whatever we agree on. It used to be gold and silver and moved to currency. In my era it was being replaced by electronic placeholders."

"Good. And if you don't mind my asking, where'd you learn the basics?"

"I grew up poor, and through hard work, perseverance, and a little bit of luck managed to become wealthy. At some point I wanted to know all about this thing called 'money' that I had managed to make so much of. So I hired an economist who spoke plain English, and she managed to get some stuff through. And that's when I finally realized what money was and what it was based on."

"Blind faith," she answered.

"Exactly, Neela. Faith," he confirmed. "The certainty that I could take a green piece of paper with some dead president's face on it, turn around, and give it to someone else, who'd give me what I wanted." The waiter brought over a large pepperoni pizza, sliced it with a pizza cutter, and disappeared back into the restaurant. "Like this pizza," Justin said, savoring the smell.

"Except that we no longer use paper," Neela corrected.

"Right."

Justin took a bite of the pizza, and about a second later frowned.

"What's the matter?" asked Neela.

A wan smile appeared on Justin's face. "I was hoping that after three hundred years Italy would have learned how to make a decent pizza."

"Didn't they invent the stuff?" asked Neela.

"Common error. It was invented in New York. Some say Baltimore; others, Philadelphia."

"Who knew?" Neela said, with a shrug.

"So now, Justin," she continued, "let me ask you another question."

"Shoot."

"Given what you know about government currency, why would corporate currency bother you?"

"Corporations are profit-driven organizations that only . . ."

". . . that only want profit," Neela finished. "And that's why, if you think about it, they're so much better at running currencies. They won't devalue currencies to make a political party happy. They won't unilaterally print more money to make people think they have more money or temporarily affect a balance of trade."

"You're talking about inflation."

"Yes, I am, and correct me if I'm wrong, but your rates of inflation bordered on the chaotic."

"You're not wrong, Neela," he answered.

"Corporations," continued Neela, "will also ruthlessly hunt down counterfeiters and embezzlers. And they'll make sure you'll use *their* money over the competition's by giving you added-value services. For instance, American Express can be used in any city in the solar system, in any personal transactions, and they're even willing to guarantee all passages bought with American Express credits."

"All well and good, Neela," answered Justin, "but the dollar was a strong and respected currency. Not only that, it was global, stable, and rigorously controlled."

"I agree that the U.S. dollar was remarkably like a corporate currency around the turn of the millennium. The, what was it, the Federal . . . ?"

"The Federal Reserve."

"Thank you, the Federal Reserve acted very much like a corporation for its day. It protected and didn't expand the money supply, and was ruthless in its counterfeit defenses. But Justin, it was still a government in the end."

"Your point being?"

"My point being that politics getting in the way of money, not a corporation, brought on the Grand Collapse."

"Details, please."

"Some politicians came along and promised something for nothing at the beginning of the Grand Collapse, and decided that the best way to deliver on the promise was to devalue and then print the money. It's true—and well documented, I might add—that in many ways the VR plague was the immediate problem. But they made a bad situation far worse by somehow managing to destroy the currency and the economy of the greatest nation-state in history. By the time it was all over, the corporations were the only organizations left that were capable of providing services."

"But what if one of your corporate currencies does the same thing?"

"Justin, the dollar was by law the only currency you could use in the United States. Does this monopoly sound like a good idea, ever? We have forty-seven major currencies, all of them backed by insurance, and if someone does something stupid consumers are more than free to use the other forty-six. It's not as if I keep all my credits with one company, though most are with GCI. When your government screwed up your dollar, and it was inevitable that it would, your people had no choice but to go down with that sinking economic ship. I'm not saying that we haven't had currency troubles, but the truth is, we're not trapped by our currencies, we're freed by them."

"Fine. I'm beginning to see your point. But what on Earth would you need forty-seven major currencies for? I mean, in my day healthy competition in most products consisted of between three to five major players."

"Different kind of product, Justin. Look at it this way: If you needed to buy diamonds, what currency would you want?"

"In my day, South African."

"Timber?"

"American or Russian."

"High-tech?"

"Japanese or Korean, though the Israelis were moving up."

"And all around?"

"The good old U.S. of A. dollar."

"Our corporations do the same thing. Different companies specialize in different things, just like different countries used to. Only back in 'your day' those countries would use their currencies for political ends, which almost always hurts the currencies and the people who were supposed to be helped. Today currencies are used strictly for their economic need, and the middleman is out of the picture. If for whatever reason the demand for copper goes up, the commodities currencies become more valuable, and their value rises relative to other currencies, to the exact amount of the new demand. There's no static."

"Static?" asked Justin.

"You know, like when your government used to overprint money. What would happen was, people would go out and buy more 'stuff.' The makers of that stuff thought that there was a new demand, when, in fact, that wasn't the case. There was just more money. They weren't getting a real read of market demand; they were feeling, without knowing it, the effects of the overprinting of money. Hence, static."

"Got it."

"Anyhow," continued Neela, "everyone understands the economic reality and can therefore plan for it. And it's why something as important as the running of an economy shouldn't be left to a politically motivated institution."

"There's a certain amount of logic to what you're saying," admitted Justin. "But what about the euro? That was a group of governments getting together to start a currency, and before I was frozen I recall that currency doing well . . . better than the dollar, in fact."

"You only saw the first couple of years," she answered. "Then it started acting like every other politically based currency. Since it was bigger, the ramifications were worse."

"You're referring, I presume, to the Grand Collapse."

"By Jove, I think he's got it," Neela sang.

Justin smiled. Yet another phrase he'd remembered from his past was still very much alive and kicking. He was finding some ironic solace in this.

"So," he said, finishing off his last slice of pizza, "am I to gather that GCI's currency is the 'dollar' of today?"

"Correct," Neela answered.

"GCI," sighed Justin. "That's Hektor's outfit."

"Mine, too," said Neela. She sounded apologetic.

"Excuse me," Justin said to Neela, as he perused a list of topics he'd written down on his DijAssist. He scanned the list and then looked up. "What is this SCV?"

"It's an amalgamation of all currencies," she answered, "both major and minor, updated via the Neuro on an hourly basis. It's systemwide, so everyone can have an idea of how much things cost. But there's no actual currency called an SCV. It's just a benchmark."

"Let me guess," said Justin. "GCI's credits are always higher than the SCV, and it's the most important currency in the solar system."

Neela was impressed. "How'd you figure that one out?"

"Not hard, really. I remembered that the prices in the pawnshop and now on this menu have GCI's currency next to the SCV."

With something as simple as a sales tag and menu listing, Neela realized, Justin had somehow come up with a keen insight into her world. Her lesson plan was shrinking by the minute.

"I'm waiting for you to ask your question," he said, interrupting her thoughts.

"Which question?"

"The one that's purely for personal pleasure and curiosity. And if I'm guessing correctly, the one you'd feel a little guilty even wanting to ask."

Neela looked at him open-mouthed, in shock. He'd described her feelings exactly. He was correct in that she did want to ask him questions of a more personal nature, i.e., questions not necessarily associated with his adaptation to society. However, he was incorrect in that she never would have broached the subject. But now he'd given her permission, and she had to assess whether or not, even under that circumstance, it was acceptable to pursue.

"How did you . . . ?"

"I am," he said, then corrected himself, "or *was,* a very good businessman, Neela. Reading people is not only useful but vital at the level of finance I worked at."

"What kind of numbers are we talking about here?" Neela asked.

"Oh, come now, Neela. That's not what you want to know."

I guess I'll just apply the "nothing's going according to plan" rule, she lamented to herself.

"OK, Justin," she responded, "who are you . . . really?"

4   Fame

I
rma Sobbelgé was seventeen when she got her first share of a truly valuable stock. Not that those of her parents, brothers, and sisters weren't valuable, it was just that their value was based more in the realm of psychology than economy. The reasoning was simple and straightforward—owning shares of a sibling made one think twice about doing any undue damage, both physically and emotionally, to that sibling. In fact, Irma was convinced that had she not gotten shares of her baby brother early on, the little bastard wouldn't have made it to puberty. And given how well not only her family, but most families in general, performed, she considered it borderline miraculous how *anyone* at all managed to survive and function before the incorporation movement. She rightly felt that the gaining of her first-ever shares was an indelible rite of passage—up there in importance with the loss of her virginity (a good memory) or the field trip to the Museum of the Virtual Reality (a horrifying one). For Irma, gaining those shares was the start of a process that connected her to society more intimately and securely than anyone had ever been connected before. Because that connection, unlike at any other time in history, was made through the powerful and subtle bonds of the world's most cohesive unifier—self-interest. And it was in the spirit of that self-interest that Irma managed to happen upon a very valuable share.

When she was seventeen she had a relationship with a boy from a wealthy family. The boy thought he was a man and she was young enough to believe him. He was also anxious to get into Irma's pants, and in the spirit of self-interest gave her the share. As he was fond of grand gestures, that single share just so happened to belong to the newly appointed chairman of a powerful, up-and-coming corporation by the name of GCI. If only the boy had known that a simple "wanna do it?" would have sufficed, he might not have forked over so valuable a commodity. But both he and Irma were "in love," and neither had any idea just how valuable and useful a gift that share would turn out to be. Irma felt, as the gesture was intended, that giving it represented an act of pure and undying love. However, when that undying love managed to do just that some six months later, a person broker, "perker" for short, contacted her, representing the family. It seemed the perker was interested in buying back that single stock *and* at market value. Even then the stock would have brought a considerable amount of money but, against the universal advice of her family, Irma decided to hold on to it—a prescient move indeed. Because it turned out that *that* chairman ended up becoming The Chairman. Not only the most famous and reclusive individual in the solar system, but also the man responsible for making GCI the most powerful corporation in human history. The fact that she owned even one share of his stock made her unique among her peers, like someone lucky enough to have inherited a rare work of art made a person of standing unique among theirs.

As Irma got older she discovered that, unlike with other celebrities, politicians, and people of that ilk, there were almost no shares of The Chairman lying around. Plenty of offers to buy, but hardly ever any for sale. And even when that exceedingly rare occurrence did take place, the going price was so stratospheric it almost always made the headlines.

What was odd about The Chairman's lack of shares was that it was contrary to the norm. Famous people, politicians and celebrities especially, went out of their way to subdivide their stock into minuscule percentages to be given away as shares to as many people as possible. It seemed, recalled Irma, that at every election she would get a complimentary share of at least a dozen politicians in the mail with the some old hackneyed line: "Vote for the candidate you have a stake in." Irma would routinely send those freebies to her perker for immediate sale. If she were lucky, the lot of them would bring in enough money to pay a utility bill.

But The Chairman's share was clearly different. In many ways that single share determined much of her life. Her investigation into his world led to her present career of journalism, which had led to husband number two—a journalism professor. Husband number two, besides having the gift of charm, also had something rare—a single share of The Chairman that he, too, got at an early age and was smart enough to hold on to. The fact that her second husband had the same power to fascinate made him seem more intriguing than he actually was. Unfortunately, she realized that bit of information a little too late, discovering to her dismay after the marriage that all he really was, was a jerk with some smooth lines, a pretentious ego, and one share of The Chairman. Well, the jerk and his share were soon to be parted.

Cornelius loved his job. It was true he only had one client, but he only needed one—given who that "one" was. He hadn't started out that way. He used to be a regular, run-of-the-mill perker. He may have known that the job was a combination of the words "person" and "stockbroker" or he may not have, but he knew his job. People were a perker's stock-in-trade, and Cornelius knew people very well—

in fact, he saw himself more as a gossip reporter than as an accountant. He knew perkers who made a living at high-end, exclusive parties, and others who did very well never leaving their cubicles, hooked into the Neuro following obscure trends. But the rules of his trade hadn't changed that much since its first recorded transaction in Mesopotamia four thousand years ago. Buy low, sell high.

Life was going pretty much according to plan until one deal changed it all. There were three shares of Chairman stock that had become available due to an inheritance. Though they weren't Cornelius's clients, he did some research and found out that the heirs were going to sell the stocks to The Chairman directly, for a hefty profit—enough, in fact, to make the bickering family members civil to each other for the first time in months.

Cornelius knew that Chairman stock, let alone three shares of it, did not become available all that often. So he searched all the accumulated financial records and found what he was looking for. Apparently, the now deceased titleholder had once, in a third-party deal, put his Chairman stocks up as collateral. And, as part of that deal, a "first rights option to buy" clause was included. It allowed the third party the right to buy The Chairman's stock first, and at a previously agreed-to price, should the stock ever be put up for sale. Cornelius realized that the inheriting family was not going to inform the third party about the impending sale, either because they didn't want to or, more likely, because they were unaware of it.

So he made a call.

After the third party's money manager got over the fact that he'd dropped the ball, he was happy to include Cornelius in the deal. After all, Cornelius had not only prevented him from possibly losing his job, he would manage to make the third party's family significantly richer. In the end, the original inheriting family was forced to sell, and then went back to squabbling with each other, all cursing the fact that their father had once again screwed them all. Cornelius got his usual commission, which in that case turned out to be a small fortune.

The day after the deal was closed he got an anonymous call. He was offered his standard deal and a twenty-thousand-credit bonus if he could find a way to buy another share of Chairman stock. There was, however, one catch—the share had to be acquired within the next forty-eight hours.

Cornelius, liking a good challenge, accepted. It wasn't easy, and it ended up costing the anonymous caller a fortune, but the fact remained that he'd risen to the challenge.

That was how Cornelius was offered and eventually accepted the position as perker for The Chairman. He had only one job. He was to acquire Chairman stock. He could use any means necessary as long as it didn't break the law's boundaries—he could push, absolutely, but not break.

He had a huge budget and more money than he wanted. Even when he achieved majority, he still worked. Many of his old colleagues thought he'd sold out. But they were wrong. Each stock was like a brand-new hunt. The same method almost never worked twice. He was more psychologist or big-game hunter than perker. And money was never the answer. Had it been, The Chairman would never have needed him. Money helped, but it was only a tool to get The Chairman one more share. He had only one regret in his job: He did not own a share of Chairman stock for himself. Of all the dozens he had gotten for The Chairman, he turned them all over. And not because he couldn't afford it. Given the money and resources he had at his disposal he could probably afford two or even three. But in his heart he knew with the certainty of the sun's arrival that if he ever got one share for himself he would never work for The Chairman again.

So he went about his task and put his one regret firmly out of mind.

His avatar informed him of an incoming call. He noted that it was from one of his LCP groupings. It stood for "lower class prestige" holders. They were without question the hardest group to pry shares from. Because with them it was almost never about the money. They would sooner lose a limb permanently than give up something that made them stand out among the world's billions and billions of souls. But he never gave up hope. He would make sure that they each got small-but-unique Christmas presents annually, and often would have handwritten cards for each of their birthdays, in the hope that when they needed something more than prestige, they would remember him. He was praying that it was paying off now.

He looked at the name his avatar was displaying. *Ahh, yes,* he thought, *the girlfriend who never budged. Smart lady from a surprisingly young age. This should be interesting.*

"Miss Sobbelgé," he answered, as if taking a call from a dear friend, "I am so very glad to hear from you. How may I be of service?"

Although he could have personalized the greeting with sad noises about her divorce or congratulations on getting her first article sale with an intersystem magazine, he chose to keep it basic. They called when they were ready, and he did not want to sidetrack them or, worse, sidestep into a touchy subject. One of the things he had had to learn about having lots of information was resisting the urge to use it. Again it seemed to be the right thing to do.

Irma got right to business. "I'm willing to sell The Chairman my share," she said.

"Wonderful. You are about to become a financially well off young woman, the current rate is . . ."

"Whatever it is will be fine, but I will need one more thing besides the money."

He smiled inwardly but kept it off his features. "And that would be?"

"Information. To be specific, I need to know how many shares The Chairman owns of himself in a way that can be verified financially. And I need it in two hours."

Cornelius looked at the seriousness with which Irma was staring at him. He wasn't being sent on a fool's errand.

"I'll get back within the next two hours, and, once more, thank you for the chance to be of service."

He cut the connection and leaned back in thought, cupping his fingers around his chin. After a moment he got up, went to his wall safe, and opened it. In it were various papers, digicrystals, and objects of great value, all of which he ignored. He reached gingerly for a rarely used and specially modified DijAssist. It was identical in all ways to a normal one but for the codes built in that let him make one special call. He went to his desk and called up all information about Irma Sobbelgé and discovered that she currently did not have title to her share, as it was being held by a Vegas casino. A little more due diligence also let him know that Miss Sobbelgé's ex-husband's share was being held by the same casino. It seemed they'd made some sort of wager having to do with his boss— winner take all. Just in case, he looked to see if any more shares were being offered in this gamble. Just the two, he noted.

Once he had as much information as he could gather quickly, and aware of his promise to Miss Sobbelgé, he sent his report with all his findings via special interface to The Chairman. He further sent his recommendation that they approach the ex-husband to leverage both shares out of the deal. In ten minutes he got a return message from The Chairman with the simple instructions to offer Miss Sobbelgé no money, but with the promise that The Chairman would provide the information in a verifiable way.

Better the bird in hand, thought Cornelius, and began to make his employer's wishes into reality.

Irma was in a privacy room with her ex-husband and some ditz he'd brought along just to grate on her. *Bastard really wants to make this personal,* thought Irma. She was hoping that her own information had been registered at the casino before the bet was considered closed.

The three of them sat in plush recliners as the hologram of the casino employee appeared before them. He began, "As both parties turned in their responses within two hours of each other it has been ruled that the one with the closer number will be the winner, if they are both within 2 percent. This is as agreed to in the contract signed by both before the bet."

Irma's ex turned to her. "Irma, you took a guess. Good for you. Never give up."

The casino employee continued, "As both answers were extremely close to each other, Professor Warburton will explain his decision and answer all reasonable queries from the parties involved." The image blended from the casino employee into that of the economics professor they had both agreed to as the neutral judge. Irma had the satisfaction of seeing the first sign of worry from her husband. He hadn't expected this. He hadn't expected her to be within 10 percentage points of him. This was not how it was supposed to happen.

"Well, I have some good news for one of you," said Professor Warburton, milking the fact that he had a captive audience. "Well, anyway, congratulations, Irma. I don't know how you managed it, but you are positively the winner. Sorry, Paul."

Irma's ex looked like he'd been hit with a two-by-four. It took ten seconds for him to finally respond. "That's not possible. I destroyed all my records and kept no copies except for the false ones. There's no way you could have stolen that information from me!"

You really are an arrogant slug, she thought. "Paul, I didn't steal a thing. My source is a little better than yours." She looked to Warburton. "Go on, tell him."

"Paul, she got The Chairman—I mean, The Chairman himself—to tell me the figure with the stock statements verified. He gave me the exact number. If it means anything, you were only off by .297. That's well under 1 percent. But Irma got it on the nose."

Paul remained speechless.

Warburton turned once more to Irma. "I'm curious, dear. How did you get him to tell you?"

But Irma was not listening to Professor Warburton. She was watching her ex. She waited until she saw the look on his face. The look that told her he'd figured out exactly how she'd gotten The Chairman to provide the information. She leaned close. "Paul. I will admit that most of the time you are smarter than me. It's just that I'm smarter when it counts. If it's any consolation," she said, getting up to excuse herself, "I still only have one share of Chairman stock. But then again, I only ever needed one."

She walked out of the privacy room and never saw her ex-husband again.

Even before the bet had been made, it never once struck Irma as odd that a man as rich and powerful as The Chairman would—in fact, *could*—never own 100 percent of himself. Maybe, she figured, between 60 percent and 70 percent but certainly not much more. For, even if in theory he or any man could succeed in buying back 95 percent of himself, the incorporation movement demanded that

5 percent automatically be given over to the government. The government was responsible for a minimal amount of caretaking, and that caretaking had to be paid for somehow. Article five, section three of the Constitution was very clear: "All persons born in the Terran Confederation will be incorporated with a stock listing of 100,000 shares, 20,000 shares to go the person/persons holding loco parentis (parents or guardians), and 5,000 shares going to the government. The government may neither increase nor decrease the amount controlled in any of its citizens for any reason." The reason for the last part of the proclamation, re-called Irma, was obvious. Any loss or increase in control of those stocks by the government could, on one hand, lead to tyranny, on the other, to bankruptcy. She remembered her professor's comment on the whole issue of the Incorpora-tion Proclamation.

"Remember, Irma," he'd said, "if there's one thing the Grand Collapse taught us, it's that the only thing more dangerous than a government that's too strong is a government that's too weak." She loved that old man, and still used him as a paid source whenever she could for any stories needing an expert account.

The stock she'd won had also played another important role in her life—it paid out like crazy. The past year's dividend alone had paid for a lunar vacation. Plus, she'd been contacted many times over by perkers wanting to buy that share at well above the market price—a pretty amazing offer considering that the stock price of The Chairman was the highest of any individual in the whole of the Terran Confederation. But Irma would never sell. Not for any price. She'd worked too hard for it—both professionally and emotionally—for monetary gain to ever enter the picture. However, pride was another matter entirely, and at this moment she was willing to bet the one share she did own that a small story coming from, of all places, tiny Boulder, Colorado, was a whole lot bigger than the local media were making it out to be.

"Michael, Enrique, Saundra, get your asses in here!" Irma's voice carried from her private chambers into the outer office where her staff was busy working. Like most modern information organizations *The Terran Daily News* used the men-tor/apprentice group system. That meant one mentor would combine the job of journalist *and* editor with a staff of apprentices. Each group shared bylines, de-pending on the contributions made to the story. Then, after ten or so years, the apprentice would either become a mentor journalist himself or move on in search of greener pastures. Irma was unique in having cultivated a group of lifers—in essence, a staff that was content to stay apprentices in name, even if not in actual experience. She was able to pull this off by always managing to dig up good content, being fair about sharing the byline, and keeping the working environment interesting and fun. It might mean less pay, but the prestige associated with working for a mentor of Irma's caliber made it well worth the sacrifice.

"Yes, mistress," came the by now standard chorus from her outer office. Moments later the troupe piled in.

Michael Veritas, tall, blond, and sporting two days' worth of facial hair, took his usual position leaning against the south wall, "accidentally" covering her prized print of the first issue of *The Terran Daily News,* though back then it was called *The Alaskan Daily.* Irma put up with his quirks, since he could find dirt at the bottom of a barrel filled with bleach. Saundra Morrie came in next. She was a little over six feet, with long red hair, freckles, and a lithe quality that allowed her body to drape itself over almost anything it could find. She chose the couch. Enrique Lopez followed. Of Filipino descent, he was a squat, muscular man who was more comfortable with numbers than with people. He sat down in his usual spot right in front of Irma's desk, and took out his DijAssist. Irma never knew why he took the damned thing out. In her fifteen years of working with him she'd rarely seen him use it. But this team had won three system Pulitzers, and if their individual idiosyncrasies were par for the course, then that was a course she was happy to take.

"What do you think of the story out of Boulder?" Irma asked no one in particular. Saundra answered first. For a woman who looked like a redheaded Amazon her voice sounded more like that of an assertive eight-year-old. "What story?"

"No, wait, let me guess," quipped Enrique. "Boulder's finally exploded and the world's missing a whole bunch of useless rich folk?"

"There's no such thing as 'useless rich,'" snapped Irma, "and for your information we'd lose two-thirds of our stories without those bastards." *Present company included,* she thought, managing to suppress a wry grin.

"Try again."

Michael spoke next. "I think it's a potentially important story, and we'd better move on it quickly before someone else does."

Irma looked at Michael with suspicion. He almost never agreed with her this easily. "Why do you say that, Michael?"

"Because," he answered, with a charm born of certainty, "you wouldn't have dragged our asses in here if it wasn't. And if you did I'll never let you live it down."

Irma grinned.

"This is what I know so far," she replied. "A man was awakened from cryogenic suspension in Boulder."

"Stop the presses!" squeaked Saundra.

"Well, that *is* news," chimed in Michael.

"How could you have kept this to yourself?" Enrique asked, with a pained expression. "I . . . I thought we were friends."

"Ha-ha, laugh all you want, guys," challenged Irma, "after you do one simple thing."

"Name it," said Michael.

"Don't be so quick, Michael. I'm not sure even you could dig up what I need to find."

"You willing to bet on it?" he challenged.

"Absolutely."

Enrique straightened up, Michael stopped leaning against the picture, and Saundra got up from the couch.

Irma smiled. *Well, that worked.* "Ten shares of stock each in the pot. The pot goes to whoever can get this unfrozen guy's name in . . ." Irma paused to look at her watch. ". . . one hour starting . . . now."

"Your stock has split twice," challenged Saundra. "Shouldn't you put in forty?"

"Have you seen my worth lately?" responded Irma. "I'm being generous, and you all know it. Of course, if you want a different bet . . ." Her question was answered by the team's mad rush to the exit. Irma knew that they'd all probably cheat and work together to arrive at an answer. It made sense, because they could then split her ten shares, which would be more valuable than all of theirs combined. *All the better,* she thought. The only reason she'd issued the challenge was because she had just spent the better part of the day in a failing effort to get the name she was now asking them to find.

Irma had an hour to kill, so she went back to the other mundane tasks she'd ignored—paying bills, making investments, and researching new stories. Of course, as soon as she was beginning to make some headway, Saundra popped her head into the office, clearing her throat to get Irma's attention.

"Yes?" asked Irma.

"Hour's up."

"Well, then, whatcha got?"

Before Saundra could answer the rest of the team piled in behind her. No one was smiling.

"All right, smarty-pants," Enrique said. "Who is he?"

Irma's response was honest and forthright. "I don't know."

Her team threw groans and expletives in her direction. "Oh," said Saundra. "We thought maybe it was some kind of test."

"Nope. I really don't know. And believe me," Irma went on, "I really want—no, *need*—to know."

The team's blank stares made her realize it was time for a little coaching.

"All right, guys, let's do this a little differently. What *don't* we know about this guy, and how don't we know it?"

Saundra, as usual, spoke up first. She couldn't help herself. It was almost as if the information would spoil if she didn't share it immediately. "We don't know who he's insured with. I checked with all the major companies and most of the minor ones. There have been four reanimations in Boulder in the past week, three of them were paid via insurance and one of them paid with cold, hard credits."

"Is this just a famous guy trying to hide out?" asked Irma.

"I don't think so," answered Michael. "The list of who could pay credits outright is rather small. If something happened to one of them we would have heard at least the *shade* of a rumor. Plus, someone wanting to hide out would have used insurance, not credits."

"So we follow the money," said Irma.

"Fine. But there's no trail of where it's coming from. The security on the hospital's database is as tough to crack as an American Express account."

"Strange," interrupted Irma. "If I'm not mistaken it's a backwater hospital. The kind of security you're talking about doesn't make any sense."

"*Correctomongo,*" continued Michael. "I can hack through pretty much anything. So imagine my surprise. It's almost like finding the door to the local candy store guarded by ten marines."

"Not as strange as you might think, Mike," offered Enrique. "If I'm not mistaken, the director is a former heavy player named Mosh McKenzie."

"As in former member of the board of GCI Mosh McKenzie?" asked Saundra.

Irma nodded. "The one and only." *I knew that name sounded familiar.* "Didn't we run a piece on him, like, fifteen years ago?"

"Yea," answered Saundra, scanning her DijAssist. " 'Exile or Retirement: The Perils of Life at the Top.' "

Irma waited while her team called up the data on their DijAssists.

"I see that we leaned toward exile in the story," said Michael. "Still think so?"

"I think we leaned wrong on that one," answered Irma. "My miss. We were just starting out, and I rushed it." Irma was startled by the dead silence her answer had elicited.

"I see our names on the byline," Michael said. "We got paid for the story. That makes the mistake, and I'm not saying there was one, *all* of ours. Pulitzer or piss, we don't duck out on what we write."

"I take it back," Irma added. "If I'm right, and I suspect I am, it's the type of crap only a team effort could have produced."

"That's better," answered Saundra.

"Wait a minute." It was Michael. "Why are we all so quick to call it crap? It could still be an exile piece. I don't see any proof to dispel that notion."

"I don't think so," offered Irma. "Think about it. He's been in the same job for three accounting cycles. If it *was* an exile he would have either been forced all the way out, as in in-the-asteroid-belt out, or he would have made his way back to the board. I also did some checking. Out of all of his requests for funding over the last fifteen years not a single one has been turned down or even delayed. He hasn't been asking for anything outrageous, mind you, but still . . ."

"If it was an exile," continued Saundra, "he should have faced at least one review, one audit, one refusal."

Irma folded her arms and leaned back in her chair. "All indicators then point to our director being handled with kid gloves. He's never been turned down, I suspect, because the rest of the board is probably content to let the sleeping dog lie."

"OK," admitted Michael. "*For now,* I stand corrected. While the evidence isn't what I call solid, it certainly is tantalizing."

"I agree with Irma," offered Enrique. "They're scared of him, and probably don't want him angry. Nothing else makes sense. We should try for an interview. That alone would make a great story."

"I agree," said Michael, taking a stab at the headline: " 'Chairman's Dreaded Foe Bides His Time: Boulder Hospital Actually Corporate Fortress in GCI Power Struggle.' "

That got a few giggles from the group.

"Don't laugh," warned Irma. "Stranger stories have made it to the front page."

"Like anyone would believe that The Chairman could be threatened," said Saundra. "You may as well tell our readers that death and taxes are coming back."

"Saundra," said Michael, warming up to what was obviously an old argument for them. "People don't need to know that The Chairman is vulnerable, only that the possibility exists. It's that possibility that makes the story interesting."

"Facts make the story interesting," she countered.

"People read newspapers to be entertained *and* informed," he responded. "If they want facts they can download an almanac." Before Saundra and Michael could begin laying into each other, Enrique silenced the room.

"I think I know how the reanimation was paid for."

Michael and Saundra stared at Enrique.

"Well?" asked Michael.

"I couldn't get into the hospital's individual accounts either, but what I was able to find, since it was in the public domain, was the account balance for the hospital itself on a minute-by-minute basis from the past week."

"And that helps us how?" asked Saundra.

"Well," continued Enrique, "right before the fourth reanimation the accounts were changed due to a credit transfer."

"And?" asked Irma.

"It was not a scheduled transfer."

"How much, then?" she asked.

"Ten mill."

"Ten million credits for a reanimation?" Michael exclaimed.

"I very much doubt that, Mike. But certainly some of it could have gone toward the reanimation. Nothing else makes sense."

"Are you sure you didn't move the decimal over a couple of times?" asked Saundra.

"I can assure you all that I checked it and rechecked it," answered Enrique, looking insulted. "It may be that the hospital in Boulder chose to pay for an entirely new computer system at just that moment, but I doubt it."

"I doubt that too, Enrique," agreed Saundra. "It doesn't make sense. If they were paying for a new system they'd have paid the way everyone else does—credit card."

Irma remained silent, content to let Enrique go at his own pace.

"Anyhow," continued Enrique, "an amount of money that large usually leaves fingerprints, records . . . something one can work with. This transfer did not. It was a cash amount put in directly and stealthily. Whoever did it wanted to remain anonymous, and has so far succeeded brilliantly."

"Well, well," Irma said, suffused in triumph, "think there's a story now?"

"Forgive us our doubts, O great one," Michael said, half bowing. "How can we be restored to your grace?"

"Get me that story, guys. Get me the story."

The second round of research took more hours than the first, because now there were some very real leads to pursue. The team chose to meet in the conference room. It was bigger, and besides having a few very comfortable couches, it had an ample amount of what the group had affectionately called "brain planes." They were simple floating devices that allowed the user to configure a chair style, lean back, and go. Not that there was a lot of room to maneuver, but for some reason thinking was made easier by the simple act of floating in patterns. Irma likened the patterned floating to the simple act of pacing back and forth to stimulate thinking. Which is how the little squares acquired their moniker. It seemed as though the best ideas the group produced had come via a few short trips around the conference room. Irma set her brain plane to "cushy bar stool/no back," and settled in.

"Wow me, people."

"Me first," blurted Saundra, waving her hand, "me first." After looking around and seeing that, as usual, no one objected, Irma nodded. Saundra always went into great detail not about what she'd discovered but about how she'd managed to discover "it." And she always saved the "it" for last. A less patient mentor would've robbed her of the joy of the telling. Irma not only humored her in this area, she encouraged it.

"OK," Saundra continued, "I tried getting a mediabot into the hospital to check out what was going on, and it lasted all of four seconds."

"Suppression field," Michael stated, as fact more than a question.

"Yes," answered Saundra, "and a darned good one, too."

"Looks like more marines at the candy store," Enrique offered.

Saundra nodded in agreement. "Yup. So I got one of my boardroom specials."

Everyone smiled. Saundra was well known for having specialty mediabots modified for all occasions. Her "boardroom specials" were made specifically to infiltrate the toughest electronic disruption nets and suppression fields, as well as take on a whole array of devices designed to keep the media out.

Saundra frowned. "Worked for twenty-eight seconds."

"A lot can happen in less," said Irma.

"Funny you should mention that," Saundra said, drawing everyone's attention to the room's screening area. "Anyhow, I'll get to that. The unit got zapped, of course, and I mean actual physical termination, including its accompanying security floater." On the center screen the team could see the last few seconds of the mediabot's life as recorded by the security floater. A moment later the security floater's screen went blank.

Enrique scratched his chin as he stared at the images. "They knew to take out the meat before the potatoes," he said, referring to the order of the kills. "So much for diversionary tactics."

"Like I said, Enrique, this ain't your momma's security system."

"You've never met my momma," Enrique fired back, grinning.

"Not sure I'd survive," Saundra agreed. "Anyhow, the zapper that got mine was very high end—a Brinks model 471. Top-of-the-line unit."

"Aren't those babies like thirty-five grand apiece?" asked Irma.

"For the Terran-made ones. The space-based models go for around fifty." One always paid a premium for sophisticated devices assembled without gravity's interference.

"Anyhow," continued Saundra, "it gets better. Before my baby got zapped she was able to pick up the info patterns on twenty-six more."

"Twenty-six 471s for a hospital in Boulder?" Now it was Michael's turn to be perplexed. "What is it, GCI system headquarters?"

"Actually," answered Saundra, "GCI HQ probably has thousands, but I do agree, it is a bit heavy-handed."

As Saundra seemed to finish, Irma slowed her floater to a halt. "Thanks for the information, Saundra; the 471s are the smoking gun we needed. Enrique, did you find out anything else on the money trai . . ."

"I'm not done," Saundra said, bursting with excitement.

Irma gave Enrique an apologetic look and motioned for Saundra to continue.

"It just so happens that I, too, have a Brinks model 471 in my collection—Terran-based, but just as good, believe me. Anyway, I had it specially modified at great expense in both time and credits for just such an occasion. I was saving it for a proxy fight at GCI, but my gut told me to send it in. The nice thing about the 471 is that, besides being built tough, they can often fake out their well-armed brethren. . . ."

Irma scrunched her eyebrows. "Fake out?"

"Yup. A 471 will recognize another 471 and often won't destroy it immediately."

"Right," continued Michael. "It'll question it first."

"Correct. Any other unit it would have shot to kill on sight; a similar unit confuses it. In the time it took to interrogate its 'cousin,' I managed to get off a bunch of pictures."

Now Saundra had everyone's attention. She called up an image on the main view screen. The screen came to life in a vivid holograph engulfing the room and its occupants with the selected imagery. The holograph showed various scenes of the hospital corridors and personnel.

"Now you have to understand," Saundra continued, "that the jamming was cutting-edge. So I sent the floater in with simple instructions. 'Go to the place with the highest concentration of 471s and send back whatever images you can.' In all I have thirty-seven seconds of images spread out intermittently over a four-and-a-half-minute period." More images flew by in bits and pieces. It was, as Saundra had stated, a hodgepodge.

"Most of these images," continued Saundra, "are probably useless. I'll try a detailed analysis of every person shown and see if I can contact the useful ones. But I saved the best two images for last."

A three-dimensional image of an enormous black and crimson box appeared before the team.

"That thing's huge," Enrique whispered, almost to himself.

Michael's eyes remained fixed. "What on earth is it?"

"Jeez. Patience, guys. I'm getting there," snarled Saundra. "Besides looking for where the 471s were concentrated, I also programmed the mediabot to seek out anything in the hospital space that it had no records of. So, basically, it knew every accounted-for item within the structure. That I got from open databases. This," she said, pointing to the large black structure now filling their conference room, "was not on *any* database."

"What part of the hospital is this thing in?" asked Enrique, circling the holographic suspension unit.

Michael walked around one side of the holograph. "If you ask me, I'd say it looks like a loading bay."

Saundra touched her nose. "Bingo!"

Michael smiled at his lover and winked.

Enrique frowned. "Fix."

"Anyway," answered Saundra, ignoring the slight, "after this shot they destroyed my baby."

Though it was only a piece of machinery, Saundra's expression of grief could have led one to believe her defunct Brinks 471 was an actual living, breathing being. She didn't mourn long.

"As you can see, I captured enough visual data to reconstruct the image on all sides except the one facing the floor."

Saundra looked around the room. She was done.

"I did good?"

"Saundra," answered Irma, "you did very good. We're talking the 'will you marry me?' kind of good. Now," she said, looking around the room, "does anybody have any idea what that thing is?"

"Oh, right," answered Saundra. "I forgot to mention that. It's a suspension unit."

"You sound pretty sure of yourself," challenged Michael.

"You would be, too, if you could read." She directed everyone's eyes to the part of the structure where THIS IS A LIFE POD was engraved in scarlet letters. The group flocked to that part of the holograph and pored over every discernible detail, and read as much as could be gleaned from the captured image. When they were all satisfied with what they'd just read, they spent a moment considering what it meant.

"Is it real?" asked Irma, playing devil's advocate. "For all we know this may be an elaborate hoax."

"If it is a hoax," answered Enrique, "someone spent ten million credits on it, and probably almost as much covering their trail. It may not be the record spent on a hoax, but it would be close."

"Besides," interjected Michael, "the hoax has a name." This shut the group up.

"It's Justin. I didn't put it together until now. But it fits. One suspension unit. One mysterious reanimated guy. Anyway, Justin's the name he supposedly gave."

"What else do you have on him?" asked Irma.

"Not much beyond male, Caucasian, and English speaking."

"And how'd you get it?" said Saundra, a little miffed to have been removed from the spotlight so quickly.

"The old-fashioned way," he said, smiling, "charm. The only staffers who would talk to me were low level. I couldn't even break into the high-level staff message service. Interesting for a hospital staff to not even have their message service on, though."

"All right, people," Irma said, shoring up the info. "Let's go down the list. Michael, you start."

"A rumor stating that an unusual reanimation took place in Boulder."

"Check."

"Pictures of a large box claiming to be a suspension unit, but one we have never seen before," chimed in Saundra.

"Check."

"A very suspicious and untraceable money trail that leaves a lot of open questions," added Enrique.

"And, finally," Irma finished, "a man who has activated none, and I mean none, of the usual procedures concerning revival. No insurance, stock reactivation, or portfolio reclamation claims and unfrozen accounts. If this guy were a corporate spy they would at least have provided a cover. But our friend, hoax or not, literally dropped in from nowhere."

"Maybe not from nowhere," Michael offered, rubbing a finger over his chin.

"Yes?" This time Irma was impatient.

"Maybe from a few hundred years ago. If I had to guess, I'd say over three."

"Where'd you come up with that?" asked Saundra.

He turned around, staring hard at the holograph of the suspension unit. "I think it's obvious that this is someone who was worried about not being woken up or, worse, being expunged and stuck in some sort of museum. Witness the clarity of his instructions—almost paranoid. This unit is a testament to fear that the near future would not know about suspension or reanimation. By the late twenty-first century it was common knowledge that cryonic suspension was viable, so this box had to be from before then. I don't know that it's exactly three hundred years, but if this isn't a hoax—if it is real—then that would be my guess."

The team waited patiently for Irma to finish absorbing all the information and come up with the best course of action.

"It's real," she finally said. "Too many angles waiting to be explored for it not to be, but there's more here, maybe much more. We go full bore, people. I want us on the next t.o.p. to Boulder, and some office space rented. Enrique, you'll see to that."

"Right away." Enrique made a dash for the door.

"Before you go," continued Irma, "make sure it's a long-term lease, use the actors' account; we don't need to let the competition know what we're up to."

Enrique nodded and disappeared out the door.

Irma continued. "OK, you two," she said, looking toward Michael and Saundra. "When we get there, hit the ground running, spend what you have to, but break that hospital. Saundra, could you . . ." Irma was interrupted by a call on her private line, priority contacts only. When she looked down her eyes lit up.

Saundra leaned closer. "Business or pleasure?"

"Both," answered Irma.

"Whatever happened," Michael intoned, "to never mixing your contacts with your personal life? You pound that into us all the time."

"You should talk," answered Irma, eyeing both of them. "Now, shush." She then directed the call so only her head and shoulders would be visible to the caller and patched it through.

"Hello, Hektor."

"Irma, it's indeed a pleasure to see you again."

"What do you need, Hektor?"

"Irma, I'm hurt. Here I am, wishing only to do you a favor, and this is how I'm greeted?"

"Hektor, you're the only man I never got any information out of . . ."

"Irma, I gave you lots of information."

"Not the info I wanted, and the amazing thing is, I still don't mind that much. So whatever it is you do have for me, I can be assured of one thing: It will be almost entirely for your benefit."

"Let's say that this will help all of us, and make any past rough spots all forgiven." Smiling in spite of herself, Irma waved for him to continue.

"Have you been hearing anything out of Boulder lately?" he asked.

Irma's eyes took on that piercing look they got when on the scent of news. "Maybe."

Hektor laughed out loud, and said, "Damsah's balls, woman, just how much do you know already?" Going on instinct she decided not to tell what she had, and only said that they'd heard that there'd been an unusual reanimation.

"Want a picture?"

"You know I do, but isn't the Boulder revival clinic a GCI operation? Whatever happened to guarding the family secrets?"

"Let's just say I've been reassigned since you last heard from me. Here's the pict."

Irma took a look at the full-body holo-image that appeared in the corner of her DijAssist and zoomed in on the face. *Handsome. Where have I seen him before?* "You in trouble, Hektor?"

"You care?"

"Well, if you need a job, give me another call."

Hektor chuckled. "Irma, I may call, but given our . . . ahem . . . history, it won't be for a job."

Irma laughed at his crudeness. She saw that Saundra and Michael were also having a good time at her expense. *No regrets,* she figured. *Better they hear it all and catch an angle than me keep my pride.* Another thought came to mind.

"Alright, Hek. Am I the first you're calling?"

"Absolutely."

Irma chose to believe him. "How long?"

"I can only give you an hour," he said, "then I've got to go public."

"How about a half-hour, only you mean it?"

Hektor paused, considering the request. "Very well, for old time's sake. A half-hour. Starting . . ." Hektor checked the time. ". . . now."

The line went dead.

Irma was already up and heading out the door before Saundra or Michael could ask her any questions. "Move, people, we go now. Bring it or buy it there."

Her team followed her out of the office and onto the roof, where they loaded into the *Terran Daily News* van for a ride to the New York orport. Once they were settled into the van, Michael spoke. "I ran the holo for any ID, and I found our man."

"Who is he?"

"He's supposedly a DeGen who works as a maintenance engineer for the clinic."

"Right," snorted Saundra. "A three-hundred-year-old DeGen. That makes perfect sense since . . . well . . . um, there was no such thing as a DeGen until a hundred and twenty-five years ago! Maybe Hektor's screwing with us, Irma, to get back at you somehow."

"I don't think so," Irma said. "Push the cover, and I think it'll crack."

"If it's a cover it's a good one," answered Enrique. "DeGens have almost no records that can be traced conventionally. They pay all their bills through a holding company, and usually the holding company is a front for an embarrassed family that doesn't want the connection traced."

"It's a fake, crack it," commanded Irma. She went quiet as the team arrived at the orport. The New York orport, being the largest of its kind on Earth, was built with hard emplacement tubes rather than the gravity-assisted ones common to smaller orports such as the one in Boulder. It was actually more economical and suited better, given the tremendous volume of daily traffic.

Irma's team made their way directly to the gate and entered their private t.o.p. At no point during the trip to the orport did any of them stop working. When they were settled in they allowed themselves to continue the conversation they'd started less than an hour before.

"It's a sham," confirmed Enrique. He pointed at his DijAssist for anyone interested in viewing it. "Look at the pattern of expenses over the years. It seems random, but it's not. See how the pattern repeats if you look at it mathematically." Enrique pointed at various parts of the scrolling data. Of course, none of the team knew what he was talking about but trusted his abilities implicitly, so they just smiled, nodded, and incorporated the new facts into their calculations.

"This is interesting," said Saundra, coiling the strands of her hair around her forefinger. "The staff revivalist is someone named Neela Harper. She's just been given a top-flight expense account and booked a passage for two to Florence, Italy."

"Any data on who she went with?" asked Irma, without looking up from her DijAssist.

"Just paid for two passengers and left."

"Conjecture?" asked Irma.

"In all likelihood," answered Michael, "she's been bought off. Think about it. You're the no-talent revivalist stuck in Boulder. Not a stellar beginning to any career. The rich and famous have their own specialists brought in to cover them. So all you get is miners and the occasional broke tourist. Then, if we're to believe what Hektor is saying, some guy from three hundred years ago pops up. You think they'd let someone like this Harper woman get near the guy? No way. They'll call in Gillette, or someone of that caliber. Then pay her off to shut up and go away."

It seemed convincing enough for Irma. "OK. Find out where Gillette is now. Also, see if anyone else at the hospital took a sudden leave of absence . . . and to where."

Michael nodded, absorbing and inputting notes at a furious pace.

"Not bad," said Saundra, purposely tempering her praise, "but this guy's *already* been revived. In all likelihood Harper's taking a quick trip to Florence to bring Gillette or whoever's replacing her up to speed over dinner. A high muckety-muck would expect that kind of treatment."

Irma considered Saundra's take. "OK, follow through on it. Get a mediabot to Florence and check out the better restaurants. Start with the ones Dr. Harper has already been to. If it's a big-time Vegas revivalist, I want to know about it."

Irma switched gears. "Any luck on IDing our 'Justin'?"

A chorus of nos.

"Come on, people," she chastised, "they had records three hundred years ago, just find the face."

Michael took it personally. "Irma, it's not that easy. A lot of data got wiped out in the computer plague unleashed during the Grand Collapse. And most of whatever's left still hasn't been reconstructed. But even if the data does exist, I suspect it'll be hard to come by. And not because it's corrupted." He paused a moment to let the next part sink in. "I suspect we're talking about a massive government or government/corporate project. Those were always classified. It's therefore likely that, whoever this guy is, he had his ID purposely erased."

"Why do you assume it's a government project?"

"Did you see that thing he was encased in? We're talking a major investment of turn-of-the-millennium resources. Few if any pre-GCs had that kind of cash lying around."

"OK," agreed Saundra. "It makes sense. But I wouldn't rule out eccentrics, either."

Michael put down his DijAssist and looked up, eyebrows slightly raised. "Why not? Like I said, this is pre-GC, and most of the lemmings back then thought cryonics was a fraud. The whole meme was, for lack of a better description, prodeath and, conversely, rabidly antisuspension. I don't see anyone, much less a rich guy, doing something like this with his hard-earned money."

"Exactly my point, Michael," continued Irma. "And don't get me wrong. I agree that in all likelihood it's probably a pre-GC government thing. However, it *could* just as easily have been done by an eccentric billionaire. Remember, eccentrics by their very nature don't follow societal memes. So all I'm really saying is, given the magic number of 'three hundred years ago' as a starting point, it should be quick work to find a group of individuals with the resources to pull this off."

"And someone with that kind of money," continued Saundra, "would garner press, which means . . ."

". . . which means there might possibly be enough leftover data to find our mystery man," finished Enrique.

Michael shrugged and went back to his work. He reminded himself that it was the story that counted, and better one of them be right than none of them. However, that didn't mean he had to give his boss the gratification of acknowledgment.

Irma made a few notes in her DijAssist and looked at the team. "OK, we touch down in another twenty. Use this time to dig, folks. And please dig deep."

"And what's our queen on high going to be doing while we do all the dirty work?" asked Saundra.

"I'm going to be checking on our source," answered Irma. "Hektor hinted he might be in trouble. I want to see how much, and if it has anything to do with this."

The interior of the t.o.p., now gently arching about 270,000 feet over Michigan, went quiet as the team dived into the Neuro in search of a nowhere man.

The somewhat bedraggled *Daily Terran* news team disembarked from the Boulder orport in much the same way as they entered—chatting, checking data, and arguing. In the midst of the din, and just as they were about to exit the building, Enrique's DijAssist made a loud, horrible sound.

"What was that?" asked Saundra, shooting Enrique a disapproving look.

"Yeah," added Michael. "You think maybe you can control that little thing of yours?"

Enrique ignored them all as he stood in place, viewing the information his DijAssist had so effectively made him aware of. "It only does that when it feels it's an emergency," he half mumbled to the group. He proceeded to check the information, ignoring the orport's loud din as well as his peers' sarcastic comments. He looked up from the screen, confused.

"Saundra?"

"Yes?"

"You were saying that this guy might be a creative, incredibly wealthy . . ."

"I never said creative."

"Right. I'll throw that into the 'eccentric' mix. Anyway, we're talking about a person who would have disappeared about three hundred years ago, and who was not associated with any of the nation-state infrastructures."

"That's our guy," confirmed Saundra.

Enrique shook his head as if he almost didn't believe what he was about to say.

"I think . . . I think I found him."

"Spill it, Enrique," snapped Irma.

"You're not going to believe it."

"Either way," groused Michael, "you'll be antimatter in a few seconds if you don't tell us the name!"

"I will, but you've got to let me drag it out just a little. . . ."

Now Irma was starting to get miffed. "No, we . . ."

"Who," Enrique asked, ignoring everyone, including his now fuming boss, "is one of the better known pre-GC personalities of his time? And he's not government—I've for sure ruled that out."

Silence.

"Who disappeared mysteriously around . . . well . . . three hundred years ago? And who is *very well known to us,* and rich enough to have pulled this off, based on what I just told you?"

Michael's eyes lit up. "No way. Tell me you've got pictures to confirm."

Enrique cast a small hologram image of the man they'd all taken a more than keen interest in. As he did this the group instinctively encircled the image, protecting it from outside view.

"Are you insane?" Irma whispered, face taut. "Shut that thing down!"

They all stood there, staring at nothing, still taking in what they'd just seen.

"Enrique," demanded Irma, "put that image next to the one Hektor sent us, and then *hand* me your DijAssist."

Enrique did as he was told.

"Certainly a bit younger now," Irma noticed. "Plus, no beard."

Saundra was peering over her shoulder. "That would be the nano at work. But the bone structure's the same . . ."

"And the eyes . . . ," Irma added, "those eyes."

"Almost like a hawk," Michael agreed, squeezing between Irma and Saundra.

Irma was locked onto the figure like a cat on its prey. "I studied him in school, you know. I remember it was pre-GC history class, and of all the personalities we studied, he was one of the few I would have wanted to meet. He seemed too modern, like he was in the wrong age. And you're right, Enrique. He did just up and disappear."

"This is friggin' crazy," Michael said. "Unfriggin' believably crazy."

But there was no mistaking it. The man who had woken up just a day ago was not only pre–Grand Collapse; he was one of the few men of that era who had helped define that era. *Only Damsah would have topped this,* thought Irma.

"Well, that's just great," Enrique said, folding his arms in anger. "The biggest story of our careers is locked up tighter than a V.P. at GCI headquarters in a hospital in Boulder."

Saundra was distracted by a message light from her DijAssist. It was feeding her live footage from the mediabot she'd launched less than an hour before. Her eyes bugged out when she saw it.

"No, the biggest story of our career is having pizza in Florence, Italy."

Justin put the napkin he'd earlier placed on his lap onto the table, took a sip of wine, and uttered the name he'd yet to pronounce in the century in which he currently resided.

"My name is Justin Cord."

That name, she thought. *Where have I heard that name?* She desperately wanted to talk to her avatar, and cursed the virtual-reality edicts that made subcutaneous communication taboo. But then a light went on. She started to remember her course work in turn-of-the-millennium culture, specifically, a class about famous missing persons. Amelia Earhart, Glenn Miller, and the billionaire industrialist who disappeared . . . into thin air . . . on New Year's . . . in two thousand . . .

"Damsah's ghost, you're Justin Cord!"

"Um," he said, smiling. "I believe I just said that." Justin almost hated to admit it, but there was a part of him that was secretly glad he hadn't been forgotten.

Neela was shaking her head. *He could be lying. But why would he? It certainly makes sense, given where and how we found him. But . . .* She decided on a simple test.

"You grew up in true poverty and mastered business and corporate finance. You graduated from Yale."

"Harvard, actually," he interrupted.

"Harvard," she answered in the affirmative, "when it was a respected university." *Not much of a test,* she figured, *but . . . it must be him.* What the facts couldn't verify, her gut could. This was Mr. Cord, alright. And she'd be willing to bet her paltry month's dividend statement on that.

"Justin Cord," Neela said, speaking almost as if she was giving a book report, "started the first workerless factory, amidst a bit of controversy, if I remember my history, made the conversion to paperless bureaucracy a reality, was a billionaire at twenty-nine."

"Thirty-eight . . . and guilty as charged," he answered.

"Funny, the show said nothing about your interest in cryonic suspension."

"Show?"

"Just one of many. You were the only well-known billionaire to just up and disappear. It was assumed you changed your name to escape the pressures of being one of the world's wealthiest and controversial men."

"That's a load of crap. It was great being one of the world's wealthiest men. As for the controversy, if little minds needed to be shoved into the future and hated the guy doing the shoving, well, then, what can I tell you? The future was still coming, with or without me."

He folded his arms across his chest and leaned back a bit. "Got another one?"

"Another what?" she asked.

"Another off-the-agenda type of question. I'm really enjoying this."

Neela smiled, remembering the initial moments of Justin's revive and all the questions she had wanted to ask him. While still not necessarily appropriate, she figured, what the heck? Nothing had gone according to plan, and it almost seemed with this man that nothing ever would. *Fine, why not?*

"You seem awfully eager to answer my questions," she said.

"Who said anything about answering? I just like to hear the questions. You often learn more about a situation from the questions than the answers. And I have a lot to learn. So, you see, you'll be doing me a favor by asking your questions."

Neela found herself smiling involuntarily yet again. "My dear Mr. Cord. Are you manipulating me?"

"Wouldn't think of it," he answered back.

"OK, Justin. Why'd you do it?"

"Do what?"

"Just disappear like that?"

"That one's easy, Neela. I wanted to live."

"That I figured out without my avatar, thank you very much," she retorted. "Of course you wanted to live. But you had a much simpler, even more logical, solution in the form of preexisting cryonic organizations. Why would you go through all the extra difficulty of creating your own suspension system? Especially given the fact that suspension in your day and age was so technologically backward. I would've thought you'd have stayed with the experts. Or, at least, those who'd already made inroads into the fledgling science."

Justin waited a moment to answer. While he did, a busboy came and cleared the table while the waiter appeared once more with a dessert cart. "When in Italy," Justin proffered, "tiramisu."

"Tira me too," joked Neela. The waiter did not appear to be amused. Still, he got the gist, took the order, and left.

"Neela," Justin said, as soon as the waiter was out of earshot, "what do you know about my time?"

"Too vague. Plus, you're answering the question with a question. No doing that."

Justin was about to argue, but Neela's earnest inquisitiveness stopped him.

"Fine. Bottom line—all the cryonics organizations, indeed everyone who believed in cryonics, based their belief on one crucial factor, and all of them were wrong." Justin reconsidered. "That's unfair. Not wrong, but hopeful in the face of a glaring inconsistency in their thinking. It was a lot like hiding in a house during a hurricane. The rational part of you knows that the house is going down if the hurricane hits. But it would still be stupid to remain outside, so you go into the house and hope that the hurricane doesn't come your way. If it does, you hope that it won't destroy your house and you with it. But deep in your heart you worry."

"Well," Neela answered, "that was a masterful job of climbing Mount Analogy, but what does it mean?"

"My world was doomed."

"Your sister-in-law called. She's worried about you."

"Ex-sister-in-law, Sebastian. Amanda's dead," Justin answered, putting down his morning *Wall Street Journal* and looking up at his ever-faithful assistant,

Sebastian Blancano. As usual, his aide was in a three-piece suit and firmly grasping his crackberry. In addition to notifying Justin of his ex-in-law's concern, Sebastian was scanning the smartphone as it fed him bits and pieces of information from twenty different papers in four different languages. As far as Justin was concerned, Sebastian was hands down the best executive assistant he'd ever had. He was not much of a looker, with his light brown eyes that pinched at his nose, giving him the mien of a well-groomed bird. Being very tall, very thin, and a few years away from being completely bereft of hair didn't help his physiological ensemble. As per his modus operandi, Sebastian stood while Justin sat eating his breakfast and reading his newspaper. Justin had tried early on to get his executive assistant to lighten up—even going so far as to invite him to sit and join him for breakfast—but gave up when he realized that Sebastian would have none of it. Sebastian, in fact, seemed to have no informal moments whatsoever, and whatever quirks made him treat Justin like a god also made him invaluable in helping run the Cord multibillion-dollar corporation. Of the two, Justin realized, Sebastian was unquestionably the smarter man. He spoke more languages, was much better at math, and was far more organized. But Justin also knew that Sebastian would never be able to do what he did. Because what Justin had in droves Sebastian had in drips—that intangible mix of curiosity and cunning that breathed life into the type of innovations that made one a billionaire at thirty-eight and the other a glorified secretary at fifty-three.

"Send her some flowers," responded Justin.

"We did that already. Twice. I guess that's why she's concerned."

"Look, just tell her I'm too busy . . . or out of the country."

Sebastian shot him a look.

"Done that too, huh?"

Sebastian didn't speak. A slightly raised eyebrow answered in the affirmative.

"Doesn't she realize I'm OK? Yes, her sister is dead, yes, my wife is gone, but that was over six months ago. It's time to move on." He pulled his paper back up so that Sebastian wouldn't see his eyes. "I . . . have to move on."

Sebastian remained silent until he felt that his boss was ready for the next bit of news.

"We're taking a beating in the press," he said—emotionless.

Paper down. "What are they complaining about now?"

"The factory in Elkgrove."

"Well, let me guess," he groused. "They can't be complaining that I'm oppressing the workers." He, as well as everyone else, knew that the Elkgrove, Tennessee, plant was an entirely workerless factory—in fact, the first.

"No, Mr. Cord. Quite the opposite, it would seem," answered Sebastian. "They're up in arms that you have *no* workers."

"That's not technically true," he answered, referring to the fact that the factory had at least a few humans in it. Technicians, mostly, plus the occasional cleanup crew. But it was also true that this was the first factory in history that did not depend on humans for the day-to-day manufacturing of its product. There were plenty of self-automated plants, but all were labor-dependent. Nothing else came close to this. Because Justin had devised a system that learned from its mistakes and reconfigured itself on the fly so that new ones were not made. It was, in essence, a factory of self-replicating robots building better robots better able to accomplish the task at hand. What's more, the system could be applied to practically any manufactured product.

It also didn't help that Justin was able to pay the few workers associated with the Elkgrove plant outlandish salaries. After all, his worker costs were next to nothing, having next to nothing in workers. It was for that reason the unions hated him; it was for the potential of shutting down overseas operations that his competitors in China and India hated him; and for all of this combined that his own government was scared of him. Not surprising, he thought, in that the government always tended to be scared of the truly innovative, being by its very nature conservative.

"Maybe," offered Justin, "they'll back off when they realize it'll take at least ten years for the place to show a profit."

"Tried feeding that to them already," countered Sebastian. "Besides, sir, it's not the profit, it's the prospect."

"Right. No workers. No unions. No strikes. No family picnics . . . blah, blah, blah."

"I see we woke up chipper today, sir." Sebastian realized that his boss's last statement was far closer to home than perhaps his employer was willing to admit. He knew that Justin and his deceased wife had once talked dreamily about children. He also knew that the drunk driver that had cut her life short had turned his boss from caring to callous almost overnight.

Justin feigned a smile.

"Plus," added Sebastian, "I think we both know that the ten-year mark is just a wee bit of a stretch."

The next smile was real.

Sebastian was referring to the fact that the books showed profitability in four years, and if current projections were met, as early as three. But Justin, with the help of Sebastian and some savvy PR work, found it safer to have his friends and enemies underestimate him. He smiled at the thought of the Elkgrove factory—his most controversial venture yet. It was an environmentally sound, pollution- and emission-free, efficient, and safe factory that caused no traffic jams. Yet everyone hated it. This was to be expected, and to some extent it gave Justin's belief in the project more credence. Small minds had always hated big ideas, and this idea—his idea—was proving to be no exception.

Justin got up from the breakfast table. He was dressed in his gym clothes.

"I'm going for a run."

"Very well, sir." Work, Sebastian realized, had been his boss's saving grace since the tragedy. And when work failed to suffice, there was always exercise.

Justin was out the door in a flash. Though it wasn't his job, Sebastian collected the dishes and brought them into the kitchen.

Sebastian looked worried as his boss came out of the doctor's office. Justin had enough money to pay for the best, which was precisely what he got. The reputation and experience of this physician would, Sebastian realized, make whatever conclusion he arrived at harder to take, not easier.

"Well?" Sebastian asked.

Justin put a hand on his faithful assistant's shoulder. "It's as I suspected. They can delay it but not stop it." Then, "I have a year at best. Six months at worst."

"Sir?" Sebastian looked far more stricken than the man who'd just received the news. It was Justin who ended up gently guiding his assistant to the elevator.

"Sebastian, it's time to call the people in Arizona about the cryonics."

"Sir, is that really a sensible thing to do? No one has any proof that this frozen suspension stuff really works, in fact the odds against it are . . ."

". . . pretty much 100 percent that I will be dead in a year," interrupted Justin. "Given that, a long shot doesn't seem like such a bad idea. It's my money to waste, and my life, such as I have left, to risk."

Sebastian knew better than to argue. They proceeded down the long hallway. As they were about to exit the building a reporter ambushed them.

"Mr. Cord," said the man, "mind if I ask you a couple of questions?"

Although Justin loathed reporters as a rule, and believed that answering one question from a reporter was like putting one drop of blood into a pool filled with sharks, he paused. The young man, he reasoned, showed extreme skill in cracking not only his timetable but also his location. And while Justin valued his privacy and would endeavor to plug the leak that had led this reporter to him at this most awkward of moments, he had to admire the determination and ability that had brought their universes together.

He looked at the young man and said over his shoulder, "You have until I reach the car."

"How do you feel now that the men who tried to sabotage the Elkgrove plant have been caught?" asked the reporter, chasing after his mark.

Sebastian checked his smartphone and leaned into Justin's ear.

"Ten minutes ago," he whispered, "sorry . . . distracted."

Justin continued his pace, never once looking back at the man tagging along.

"This is a matter of law, not feeling," he answered. "Next question."

"Why are you visiting a renowned oncologist for the second time in three weeks?"

Justin stopped. He turned to look at the reporter, who seemed more surprised at the reaction than at the fact that he was going to get an actual answer.

"How would you like an exclusive interview with me?" asked Justin.

"Serious?" the reporter asked. For a young reporter an exclusive with a man who rarely gave them would be huge.

"Dead . . . serious," answered Justin, with no hint of irony. Though he noticed that Sebastian winced.

"Yes or no?" Justin asked.

The reporter considered the story he would lose versus the one he could gain. "No promises on special treatment or what I print or don't print."

Justin nodded in agreement. "One condition. You hold off on what you saw today until we finish our interview."

"As long as it takes place in the next two days," the man countered.

"Give Sebastian a number where he can reach you in the next hour." Unspoken was the knowledge that if the reporter did not hear from Justin's assistant he would publish what he'd witnessed. The reporter gave Sebastian his card with the assurance that his cell phone was on.

Once they got into the limousine, Sebastian groused.

"I apologize, sir. I do not know how he got our schedule, but I will find the leak."

"Don't worry; in a month he'll be working for me."

"I don't think you can bribe him, sir."

"I should hope not. But I'm not going to offer him a bribe. I'm going to offer him a job. I own a newspaper; I think he'll do just fine."

"Sir, he saw you leaving an oncologist's office. It's not going to be much of a leap from there."

"Of course he'll find out. That's why I'm going to tell him. Now, why don't you tell me about who sabotaged the Elkgrove plant?"

Sebastian thought to argue some more, but he'd learned long ago never to get in the middle of his boss's always well-laid plans.

"It was a group," Sebastian answered, "of factory workers who were laid off from a local auto plant."

"This I can't wait to hear."

"Apparently they kept on listening to news stories about how your factory was going to cost Americans their jobs, and so they erroneously put two and two together and came up with five."

"Did any of these people think that if the factory wasn't workerless the work-ers I'd have to be hiring would be from another country? Or that no jobs would have gone to any Americans at all . . . including the locals who helped build the damned place?"

"No, sir, I would imagine not. Sir, the damage was minor and has already been repaired. It would help our public relations if we did not press charges on this group of unemployed men . . . it being so close to the holidays."

Justin felt incensed. "Stupidity and ignorance should have a price, Sebastian. Then maybe it wouldn't happen as often. Let's press as many charges as we can, and let the people in Elkgrove know that future expansions of the plant and their tax base depend on how well they prosecute these idiots." Justin saw Se-bastian's reaction to his diatribe. "Sorry, Sebastian . . . *desperate* idiots," he amended.

"Sir," Sebastian said, attempting one more pass for fear that his boss's emo-tions might be getting the better of him, "they were just unhappy and lashing out at something—anything—to make themselves feel better. No real damage was done, and their reaction, while clearly illegal, was normal."

"Normal my ass, Sebastian," snapped Justin. "It's that reaction and the will-ingness of people to coddle such actions that will lead the world to . . . collapse." Justin said the last word almost as a whisper and lapsed into thought. Sebastian knew enough to let his boss have his moment.

"Fine," Justin grumbled, "cancel the charges."

Sebastian breathed relief.

"And do me another favor."

"Yes, sir?"

"Cancel that call to the cryonics people in Arizona."

"Oh, thank God, sir, I knew that you would come to your senses if only given . . ."

". . . and call Dr. O'Toole at the laboratory complex. I want a meeting ready to go in three hours. I have a new project for her."

"What should I tell her it's about, sir?"

"Tell her it's about . . . a lifeboat."

Justin was sitting comfortably on a guest chair in the office of his chief technology officer. Sitting across from him was a tall athletic woman who carried her lithe, five-foot ten-inch frame with confidence. Though her demeanor was bookish and her look austere, she was in all likelihood the most oft fantasized about by her nerdish, pen-leaking-in-the-pocket underlings. But Justin was too smart to hire someone for personal appearance. No, he'd hired Sandra O'Toole and put her in charge of millions of his hard-earned dollars because she'd proven over and over again that "on time" and "under budget" weren't mutually exclusive words.

Justin got down to business immediately. It took Sandra a minute to get over the shock of Justin's impending death. As usual her boss delivered the news concisely and with a healthy dose of what she often referred to as "the intrigue factor."

"Good evening, Sandra," he'd said to her. "Let me cut to the chase. I'll be dead in less than a year, and I plan on making it as mild a death as is humanly possible." She listened to his proposal without batting an eye, and couldn't help but be intrigued. Of course she was often intrigued by Justin Cord and the myriad schemes he'd thrown across her table. But this one was not like anything she'd ever tackled before. She wasn't being asked to save his physical being—just ensure its preservation.

"Now let me get this straight," she said, not believing her own ears. "You want a self-contained suspension unit that will keep you frozen for years, if not centuries. This unit will be hidden away from all human contact, and therefore will need to be self-maintaining and self-repairable."

Justin nodded in the affirmative.

"And you want this in less than a year."

Another nod.

"Well, Mr. Cord, as much as I'd like to take your money, my gut on this is that it can't be done. Liquid nitrogen has a dispersion rate . . ."

"I don't really give a damn about the dispersion rate of nitrogen, liquid or otherwise, Doctor," he answered. "You can use laughing gas for all I care."

"Well, laughing gas is . . . ," the doctor began to explain, until she realized that though her boss was grinning, the smile had not reached his eyes.

"Never mind," she continued. "What you want can't be done in a year. We would have to research, test, and build; we may even need a new science to do it."

"Dr. O'Toole," responded Justin, with the perfect measure of impatience in his voice to make her realize her job may be on the line, "I am worth seventeen billion dollars. *That* is your operating budget. Hire who you want, work where you want, and buy, lease, beg, borrow, or steal what you want. Just get it done. And if you succeed, the research laboratory and an annual budget of a hundred million dollars is yours . . . personally. However, if you feel you can't . . ."

He made sure to let the last word dangle perilously.

The doctor wrote down a few brief notes in her tablet computer and looked up.

"Alright, Mr. Cord. I'm not making any promises, but I'll try. I should have a better view of things by the end of the week. At which point I'll call you. I don't have to tell you that time is of the essence, so I will ask that you keep your nose out of it until I have something to report. I work better that way."

"Dr. O'Toole, you have yourself a deal," he said, reaching across to shake her hand.

He smiled inwardly. Dying might be a battle he was destined to lose, but not without a fight.

Sebastian was having an unusually hard day. It had nothing to do with being overwhelmed—that seldom happened—and everything to do with death, or rather, his boss's contemptible attempt to avoid it. *Maybe,* he reasoned, *it was disconcerting to see a fearless man experience fear. Of course, Mr. Cord wasn't* acting *afraid. Quite the opposite. He was determined.* In fact, Sebastian had never seen the fire of determination burning so brightly in Mr. Cord as it was burning now. Justin, whose body was beginning to show the telltale signs of dying, was, to put it awkwardly, so very alive. Sebastian realized that everything his boss had done until now was a game. And rattling the world and changing the way it thought about work was just part of that game. *But this endeavor he'd embarked upon was no game,* thought Sebastian—*it was plain foolish.* If only his boss would realize the folly of all that wasted money and prepare for his end in the dignified and proper manner more befitting a man of his position. *That* Sebastian could prepare for. Death was supposed to be a well-known process, with forms and procedures to follow, and rituals developed over thousands and thousands of years. Sebastian was good with anything that could be learned and replicated. It comforted him, and he knew it was what made him valuable. But this "freezing" thing was just plain wrong. Still, even with his mind made up, Sebastian was a creature of habit, and had spent too many years obeying Justin Cord to stop now—even if it went against his moral and ethical grain. So it was with feelings of both pride and ambivalence that he now approached his boss.

"She did it, sir."

"Did what?" Justin asked in between the cough and gasps.

"Created your . . . um . . . unit, I guess."

Justin moved his hands to indicate that Sebastian should continue.

"Apparently, the key was in the insulation. As long as the," he made a slight but noticeable pause, "*unit* is made durable enough to protect the insulating apparatus it will be continuous and sustainable, but not very economical. This is a rich man's toy, Mr. Cord, and a very, very rich man's toy at that."

"Not a toy, my friend," Justin said, between coughs. "A lifeboat . . . cast upon the sea of time."

Lifeboat, how ironic, thought Sebastian.

"Sir, I am also happy to report that the security is holding up. No one appears to have the slightest inkling that you are sick."

"The word is 'dying,' Sebastian, and I'm not at all surprised. I hired the perfect man to . . . ," he took a few more deep breaths, ". . . hide this little news item."

"I'm still not sure why that ugly little reporter took a job that would force him to hide a major news story."

Justin smiled knowingly and steadied himself. "My dear Sebastian. Everyone who's good at something secretly wishes . . . to see if they'd be good at the opposite. The fireman, in the back of his mind, wonders . . . how to . . . set fires. The brilliant police officer in his spare time plans the . . . perfect crime. In most cases these remain daydreams of the competent. Now . . . our reporter has stumbled onto a great story before anyone else. He was unappreciated and, I suspect . . . underestimated, probably because he wasn't good-looking. But he was . . ." Justin let out a loud, painful-sounding cough. ". . . very good at being a . . . reporter. I asked him . . . if he would like the challenge of keeping a secret rather . . . rather than exposing one."

"That's all it took?"

"Yes, Sebastian. The challenge was irresistible. Now . . . the secret isn't mine, it's his. He will . . . continue to keep it. Call it professional pride."

I call it tripling his salary, thought Sebastian.

It's a good day to die, thought Justin Cord. *And a beautiful place to do it.* To anybody else the "beautiful" site he was looking at would appear to be as decrepit and lifeless a rock pit as one could imagine. To Justin it would be his, or, more specifically, his body's new home.

As he hovered in the hydraulic chair under the belly of a private helicopter, he was able to peer down on about as deserted a mine as one could hope to find in the continental United States. He took solace in the fact that he'd taken the precaution of having all locatable records of the mine expunged. Humorously, Justin also became the sole owner of this piece of worthless property that had not been worked since the late 1800s—a mine that barely existed legally. Justin, covered in a thick blanket, was lowered from the helicopter to the mine entrance. He was shivering, not from the weather, nor from the slight buffeting winds, but rather from the disease that now had almost full control of his body. As he looked around he saw that all evidence of the excavation had been removed, and that no one would be able to know about this place by either air or casual hike. This was a hidden tomb the pharaohs would have been proud of.

As his feet touched the ground he reviewed his list, barely noticing that Sebastian, as always, was dutifully waiting for him. Justin's mind was racing over the final pieces of the amazingly complex puzzle he'd built over the course of the last nine months. The estate was to be left in a perpetual trust fund, administered by Sebastian and his chosen aides. The corporation was big enough to last decades if it was run conservatively. A special committee would monitor advancements in medicine, nanotechnology, and other related fields. When it became feasible to revive and cure Justin, they would first excavate, then revive him. Justin looked over the list of treasures that he was having buried as part of his tomb. Taking no chances, he wanted to make sure that if he was going to wake up, he was going to wake up wealthy—corporation or no corporation. Diamonds, gold, silver, platinum, stock certificates, and priceless works of art would be stored in his chamber, his suspension unit, and at various places around the world.

"They're ready for you, sir."

Sebastian and a trusted bodyguard carried Justin into the mine. The guard, though a loyal employee for years, had been blindfolded the entire length of the journey, and had been promised an annuity for life if the activities of the day remained a secret. He'd readily agreed.

It wasn't much effort to lift Justin's body; it had wasted away to almost nothing. From a robust 185 pounds, the rock that Sebastian had for so long looked up to was weighing in at barely 120. Justin was paying grievously for the drugs that had enabled him to appear "normal" at the New Year's Eve party he'd just discreetly made his exit from. He'd sat in a darkened corner of a room whose lighting and sound system he controlled, forced a few smiles, waved occasionally, and pretended to talk into a cell phone. Very large men guarded the table and made sure that no one got near enough to pierce the facade their boss was struggling to maintain. Justin had naturally cut back on his commitments and appearances in the past few months, but not so drastically as to create too much speculation. It was vital that he appear OK at his last event, and at least now, mercifully, it was over. In the lexicon of the old thinking it had been an unwise use of time. That appearance had cost him a week of his life. But Justin was a man who, when committed to a course of action, did not take half measures. If this "lifeboat on the sea of time," as he now always thought of it, worked, then he wouldn't need that extra week. If it didn't, he wouldn't lose much except a week—of life—in a hospital room—with doctors—and machines—all conspiring to rob him of hope.

And hope is what it all came down to. He tried unsuccessfully to explain that concept to Sebastian. His endeavor had nothing to do with the probabilities of success or failure, or the apparent waste of money, time, and resources toward that end. In fact, Justin knew even better than his doubting assistant just how long the odds were of the whole "frozen suspension thing." True, he had probably spent more than anyone else in the pursuit of his vision—a whopping $2 billion. However, for a man within countable breaths of death, he was pleased.

Sebastian and the bodyguard stripped him of his clothes and placed him on the platform that would act as his "bed." He first saw the bright lights of the chamber ceiling shining down on him, and then the face and sad eyes of Dr. Sandra O'Toole.

"Are you ready, Mr. Cord?" she asked.

Justin nodded, managing a tepid smile.

"Godspeed on your journey . . . Justin." It was the first time she'd used his given name.

Then, clasping his hands into hers, and looking deep into his eyes, she said, "May this lifeboat keep you safe on the oceans of time until you find safe harbor."

She understands, thought Justin, finding a small satisfaction that at least one person didn't think he'd dropped off the deep end. At least one person saw the potential of what he was trying to accomplish.

He felt the injection and knew that what had just invaded his body would stop his heart and deliver him into the hands of Morpheus. He tried to tell Sandra that this was what he wanted—a chance—but he was already so very tired, and he drifted away without saying a word.

Neela stared in awe. The amount of determination, planning, and faith his achievement spoke to was remarkable. She tried to think if there was anyone she knew who had the same internal fortitude, and could only come up with two names: Mosh McKenzie, and, strangely enough, Hektor Sambianco.

Why did Hektor come to mind? She shook the thought off and concentrated on her job. And for the first time she caught a glimpse of a problem she'd not been trained for. What effect would Justin's social integration have on society? *Maybe the problem would not simply be, "Was Justin ready for the incorporated world?" but rather, "Was the incorporated world ready for Justin?"* She pondered this while finishing off dessert. In the reflection of the now empty silver pizza pan she caught the bright flash of a small circular object. When she turned around it was gone.

"So you saw it too?" he asked.

"What *exactly* did you see, Justin?"

"It looked kind of like a floating eight ball."

"Eight ball?"

"Don't tell me they don't have pool in the twenty-fourth century?"

"Oh, billiards, yeah, some people still play, I'm just not one of them. So can you describe it further?"

"Well," he answered, "it was a perfect sphere, about two and a half inches . . ."

"Inches? Ahh, right . . . ," she said, as another historical fact dusted itself off and reminded her of who she was talking to. "We use the metric system now."

Justin sighed. "OK, about six, six and a half centimeters."

"The Alaskans tried to make the world go back to the American system," she said, with as much sympathy as she could muster, "but not even they could turn back that clock."

"Alaskans?"

Neela smiled. "That will take some time to cover. Would you please continue with your description?"

"It was shiny, black, and had what seemed to be a reflective glass dot in the center."

Neela stopped eating. She looked around and saw that the flying object had taken a position just outside the restaurant at the entrance. It appeared to be waiting patiently.

Shit. Neela squirmed. *Mediabot.*

Mediabots were used by the world's news agencies to cover breaking news. But more often than not they were used as a sort of flying paparazzi to harangue the rich and famous. Like insects, they were annoying, abundant, and sometimes even dangerous.

"We should probably head back," she said, getting up from her chair.

"Something wrong?" Justin asked, concerned for the change of mood in his dinner partner.

Neela considered making up an excuse, and dismissed it. Her policy was one of absolute honesty. Unless the welfare of her patient called for outright lies, in which case she would swear on her future majority that the sun revolved around the Earth and Tim Damsah was really a socialist. This was not one of those cases.

"It looks like it's a mediabot. Essentially, a roving camera. That model is used almost exclusively by news agencies, though you'll find them used as high-tech toys by those who can afford them."

"So you're saying it could be lost or waiting for its owner?"

"Yes. But to be on the safe side . . . ," Neela said, still looking over her shoulder.

"We should vamoose," he suggested.

"Va-what?"

"Go," explained Justin.

"Right. Let's vamoose."

The waiter, seeing them both standing, appeared with a small rectangular device in his hand. Neela indicated for Justin to hold up the card he'd received earlier in the pawnshop and say the word "agreed," which he promptly did, and just like that the meal, tip included, had been paid for.

As they departed the restaurant they kept an eye on the bot. It didn't appear to be following them, which was a good sign. Then again, explained Neela, they were programmed not to draw too much attention.

"You don't think I should be giving interviews just yet?" asked Justin.

Neela made a mental note to have her avatar look for all news footage of Justin in a press situation.

"I'm not sure that now is the time to introduce you to the world. Let's avoid that firestorm for as long as we can."

"Isn't it a bit too late?" asked Justin, moving his head in the direction of the recently seen mediabot.

"If they knew who you were there would be dozens of bots and lots of reporters here right now," answered Neela. "But just to be on the safe side, let's get back to the hospital."

"Fine with me."

"Right, let's grab another char . . ." She stopped herself. "No," she said, thinking out loud. "If they're on to us, privately charted t.o.p.s would probably be the first counters they'd scope out. Best to travel cattle class." Neela took out her DijAssist to check schedules.

"OK," Neela said, not bothering to look up, "there's a quick connection to Boulder via New York. But we have to leave right now."

They took a cab to the orport, and with little difficulty made it to their flight. As they settled into their seats Neela suggested that Justin try out a pair of gigglegogs—aptly named because anyone who used them—mostly kids—ended up doing a lot of giggling. The neat thing about the gogs was that they enabled the user to view the entire flight live with the ability to pause, fast forward, or reverse, as if the shell of the pod didn't exist, in essence, allowing them to fly outside of the craft. They were a very popular item with the children but rarely used by the adults, who were content to listen to music or try and catch up on some much needed sleep.

Before trying out the goggles Justin took in his immediate environment. His first experience had been on the equivalent of a luxury liner and had therefore kept him from getting to know the ins and outs of his world's main transportation system. Now he viewed it anew. The "standard" pod, he noticed, seemed very much like a circular conference room with two rows of seats circling the center, which had a galley and a bathroom. The seats resembled the very best of first class that Justin remembered from his days of jet travel. There was enough space for each seat to recline fully. Comfort seemed to be the main concern here.

"Sorry about the crowding," said Neela.

Justin smiled. He wasn't bothered at all. This standard was as nice as, if not nicer than, the luxury accommodations he'd grown accustomed to in his previous world. The only odd part of the flight happened when Justin wasn't using the gigglegogs. It occurred when he took them off to ask Neela a question and was confronted by a good-looking young man from across the aisle.

"Hey, buddy," said the man, "don't forget the second dictate, there." That comment provoked the young man's gorgeous girlfriend to speak up.

"Now honey, that's being a little strict, even for you. The orlines allow it, so it doesn't really violate the VR dictates, now does it?"

"Sugarplum," he said, "you know it's a slippery slope. I'm just offering some free advice to the fella. You know me, can't help giving advice."

The woman spoke over the man's shoulder to Justin. "Please excuse my husband, sir, he's been like this for years and . . ." The woman stopped on seeing Justin's DeGen badge. "Oh, sorry for bothering you." She whispered to her husband, but loud enough for Justin to hear, "For goodness' sake, Carl, the man's a DeGen, why bother?"

The man's body language signified defeat. "Well," he tried to counter, "the VR dictates apply to them as well." His wife shushed him, at which point the man settled down, muttering to himself.

Justin found this confusing on three levels, the first of which was familiar. He needed to learn a lot more about DeGens and how they came to occupy the lowest rung in this society. The second was, what were these dictates that kept coming up, and what did they have to do with the gigglegogs? And the third was the fact that he just saw a handsome young couple, that he would swear from all appearances were freshmen in college, acting very old and very married. When he asked Neela about the pair her answer was short and to the point.

"They *are* an old married couple. I'd say for at least forty, maybe fifty years. You can tell by their mannerisms. If I had to guess I'd probably say they were each in their late eighties."

"Fascinating," Justin said, putting his goggles back on. The pod was now on its way down. He could make out the shiny amalgam of silver and glass that was representative of any great city from the sky. But New York City wasn't just *any* great city. In his mind New York City was *the* great city. He wondered if it still held that place on the mantle.

As they got closer to the ground he saw that the city didn't look anything like he remembered it. He was looking specifically for the telltale markers, the chief of which was the Hudson River.

Justin paused the view. "Neela," he asked, goggles still on, "have they moved New York in the last three hundred years?"

"No, Justin, it's still in the same place."

"Then where's the Hudson River?"

Neela smiled. "They had to move it when the land the river was occupying proved to be too valuable to waste on a waterway."

Too valuable to waste on a waterway?

Neela decided to play tour guide. She lowered Justin's goggles and pointed out the window. "It's over there. You can thank GCI for that."

In the distance Justin saw a building that rose well into the sky and dwarfed every other building around it.

"What is that thing?"

"GCI headquarters. In technical terms, the large building in the center is a beanstalk . . . a means of transporting large loads into outer space."

"I thought the t.o.p.s did that."

"They do," she affirmed. "That building is essentially a relic these days. It's still used, but mainly as a tourist attraction for the best view on the planet."

Justin put the goggles back on for a closer view.

"Look back up . . . farther north," said Neela. "Do you see those two identical small buildings dwarfed by all the big ones surrounding them?"

"Hold on . . . let me fiddle here a moment. . . ."

Justin zoomed in on the two buildings and blinked a couple of times. "Neela, are those what I think they are?"

Neela did some calculating of dates. "That's right, you were suspended before they were rebuilt. We call 'em 'W3' for short."

"W3?"

"Yes, they replaced the second rebuild."

"Oh," Justin thought out loud. "I never got to see the second one."

"It was nice," she replied. "Pity it didn't last very long. You probably remember when the original went down."

"9/11," he whispered. "I'll never forget . . . ever. So they rebuilt them." He sported a big grin and looked at the handsome twins, strangely heartened by the city's act of architectural defiance in the face of cold-blooded murder.

"Why re-create the original?" he asked.

"From my limited understanding—nostalgia. When New York City was rebuilt the people yearned for landmarks associated with the city's greatest era. The twin towers were one of those chosen."

As he looked closer he saw some of the more familiar landmarks, like the Chrysler Building and Yankee Stadium. *Do they still play baseball?* he wondered. Those markers were easy to spot by the fact that they were the *smallest* structures in the area.

"Neela, is the Empire State Building still around?"

"Oh, sure!" she said.

"Where? There's a huge building where it used to be. Did they move that, too?"

"Didn't move it," she answered. "Built over it. It's in an atrium now. Great place to visit."

Justin shook his head and laughed. By orienting on the W3 Justin was able to grasp the city's size. It seemed to be nothing but huge skyscrapers running to New Jersey and beyond. The city went well north of the old island of Manhattan.

"Neela, how tall are those buildings?"

"They average over three hundred stories. You know, over seventy million people live in metropolitan New York. It's the largest city in the solar system now."

Justin took off the goggles and noticed that the cabin was empty. "We're here?" he asked.

"We landed over a minute ago," answered Neela.

With his first t.o.p. trip he had been so caught up in the *whole* experience he had failed to notice the individual parts. But on this one he did, and liked what he saw—a fully mature and impressive industry, made all the more salient by the fact that everyone, except Justin, took it for granted. It made the industrial capitalist in Justin want to stand up and applaud.

They both got up to disembark. As they made their way to the exit Neela's thumb started to vibrate. She held her hand up to her ear. It was Mosh.

"Neela, if you're on Trans-Global's Florence to New York shuttle do not . . . I repeat, *do not* get off that pod!" Neela grabbed Justin's shoulder, stopping him just before the exit. As she did so three mediabots came whizzing through the exit and started to circle Justin. Before either Justin or Neela could so much as blink all three crashed to the floor and remained inert. A stewardess appeared from the exit, and as she did the doorway closed up behind her.

"Are you Dr. Harper, ma'am?" asked the stewardess.

Neela nodded her head but continued talking to Mosh.

"What's going on?" she asked, even though the sinking feeling she was experiencing was answer enough.

"They know," the director answered.

"Who knows and how much?" she pushed.

"All the major media outlets, and therefore, by extension, the world."

"Mosh, do they have Justin's last name yet?"

"No, and if you know it don't say it now. Has a stewardess come up to you yet?"

"Yes."

"Let me speak to her." Neela held her hand, pinkie and thumb extended, out to the stewardess, who touched her own hand to Neela's, thereby "transferring" the call. The stewardess then brought her thumb and pinkie to her own ear and mouth.

"Yes, sir." The stewardess paused. "I understand, sir." After a moment she said, "Thank you, sir. He wants to talk to you." The stewardess held out her hand and Neela took back the call in the same manner she had given it out, under Justin's curious gaze.

"Neela," said Mosh, "the exit is covered with bots and reporters. You won't move a meter without being mobbed."

"I suppose," suggested Neela, "we could stay here for the flight back to Florence."

"Way ahead of you, but the media already rented out all available seats on that flight, so I've taken the liberty of renting a luxury pod that's being added onto your own. The nice stewardess will take you to it once it's attached. You'll take it back to Florence, stay in the pod, then head back to Boulder. You'll be met at the gate by a security detachment. Dr. Wang and Gilbert will be waiting there as well. Ask them some personal questions to make sure it's not a reporter who's made a face change."

"Something tells me you've done this before, Mosh."

"Long story that I'll probably never tell you. Any other questions?"

Justin coughed. "I take it that I should brush up on my press conference techniques now?"

Neela, much to her surprise, laughed, and then mouthed the word no.

"Neela," said Mosh, "I've gotta go. Someone talked, and I need to plug that leak."

"It was probably Hektor," Neela said, without any hesitation.

"Neela, convenient as you may find it, not everything that goes wrong is Hektor's fault."

She ended the conversation with a quick flick of the wrist and gave Justin a shrug.

"Might as well make yourself comfortable. Looks like it's going to be quite a ride."

"As if it hasn't been already," he countered.

They both slumped back down into their respective seats, realizing that their short little joyride was about to get a whole lot longer.

Hektor was sitting alone in his tiny rented office in Boulder, pleased with the day's work. He'd alerted the media . . . *all* the media. He'd exposed pretty much everything there was to expose: the basic story, Justin's miraculous reanimation, GCI's involvement, and even Hektor's own unsuccessful attempt to have Justin incorporated. Yep, he'd blown the lid sky-high off what was supposed to remain a "quiet" operation. More to the point, he'd blown the lid sky-high off what *he'd* been told to keep quiet. And even though he'd probably dug himself a grave a mole couldn't get out of, he was truly pleased. Because, for the first time in his life, Hektor Sambianco was using his natural and learned abilities completely for his own ends, however veiled they might be. He'd disgraced himself and his company, he'd probably ruined an ancient man's life, which even he had to admit may have been uncalled for, and he'd done it solely out of self-preservation. But none of that mattered now. He was freer than he'd ever felt. He wasn't kissing anyone's ass, because he no longer had to. In fact, if by some miracle a god were to appear from the heavens and offer him a chance to take it all back—to make everything the way it was before Boulder happened, before Justin happened—Hektor would have said no.

"Hektor," his DijAssist chirped, "you have a call coming in from the DepDir."

"Thank you, iago—put him through." Hektor put his briefcase on his desk, opened it up, and activated the screen inside.

"Your avatar is your secretary, Sambianco?" the DepDir asked, clearly enjoying the moment. "Isn't that a little embarrassing?"

"Gosh, Kirk," Hektor answered, knowing how much the DepDir hated being called by his first name, "when you reassigned me, somehow my privileges got revoked. An oversight, I'm sure."

"I'm sure. I'll look into it."

"But not to worry, Kirk, I've been keeping busy. A secretary would just have gotten in the way."

"Yes, Hektor. I can see you've been busy."

"Anything else . . . Kirk? I've got a full slate today."

"Yes, actually. One thing."

"Yes?" Hektor's lips curved upward slightly, in anticipation of what he knew was about to come.

"Have you gone Alaskan, Sambianco?!"

Now it was Hektor's turn to enjoy the moment. "Me, sir? No, sir."

"Then what the devil do you think you're doing?"

"Why, my job, Kirk."

"Your job was to keep a lid on this till we could find someone to replace you!"

"Ahh, right. 'Replace me.' So you mean I *wasn't* supposed to inform all the major networks and news bureaus about Justin?"

The DepDir didn't answer. He didn't need to. The look he was giving Hektor more than sufficed.

Hektor was unruffled.

"Oh, by the way, Kirk, how is it going?"

"How is *what* going!?" If the DepDir could have reached through the screen and strangled Hektor his expression left little doubt that he would have.

"Finding a replacement? For me, that is. Any volunteers? Wait, don't tell me, no one wants my job. I have to admit, this assignment is a real career-buster. Oh, wait, my career's already busted, how convenient for me."

"I should have had you transferred to the Oort Cloud, Sambianco," the

DepDir snarled. "You should be testing environmental suits on Mercury. But don't you worry. I'll make sure you will."

"Kirk, aren't you forgetting something? I don't work for you anymore. You transferred me from your staff to the independent assignment with the board. I'm *their* problem now. I suggest you sit back, relax, and enjoy the show. It won't affect you too badly either way. You're the 'brilliant' executive who got rid of me before I could really damage your career. Or, at least, that's how I suggest you play it out."

The DepDir was about to launch into another tirade when he started to laugh.

"You're too smart for your own good, you realize that, don't you?"

"Yes sir, I do. But I've got nothing to lose and everything to gain."

The DepDir paused for a moment. Now it was his turn to crack a smile, though it seemed far more malicious than Hektor's. "You'd better win, Sambianco."

"I know" was all Hektor could muster.

The DepDir cut off the connection. Hektor closed his briefcase, got up from behind his desk, and was about to head out of the office when iago interrupted him again.

"Busy, busy iago." Hektor chuckled. "Quite a life I'm leading, eh?"

"Humor's never been a strong point with you, sir; however, if you want, I can laugh."

"Don't bother, iago, just tell me who it is."

"It's Irma."

Hektor couldn't help but smile again. Perhaps it was his lucky day.

"Transfer to handphone." Hektor lifted his thumb to his ear. "Irma, to what do I owe the pleasure? Are you in Boulder?"

"You son of a bitch. You had to make me work, eh?"

"Irma, I haven't the foggiest idea what you're talking about."

"You know very well what I'm talking about. You could have told me his last name."

"Oh, that," Hektor said, smiling. *What on Earth is she going on about?* "I gave you enough information to work with, Irma. You know the rules."

"I suppose I do. Look, any tidbits you have would be great for the story. Have you spoken with him yet?"

"Who?"

"What do you mean, 'who?' Justin Cord. Who else?"

Hektor hesitated, trying both to absorb the shock of what he'd just heard and to hide it. That was all Irma needed to realize she'd just made a rookie mistake. Hektor told no more than the beginning of a lie before Irma interrupted.

"Oh, shit, you didn't know, did you?"

No use lying now. Hektor shrugged and smiled. "Well, I do now."

"How could you not know with all the resources of GCI?"

"The truth is, Irma, I am not in the best of positions with GCI right now. But this little tidbit will certainly be of use in rectifying that situation." Irma started to ask him not to divulge the information but suddenly stopped, snarled, and cut the connection.

"Iago," Hektor commanded, "get me all the information you can on Justin Cord, then set up calls with all the news services and the board. I think I just found out how to make this hot story absolutely too hot to handle. Oh, I'm also going to need some convincing statistics to show that I am on the trail of whoever it was that screwed me over by paying the ten million credits."

"But Hektor, you are not on the trail. You stated it would take ten years and millions of credits to discover the true identity of the person or persons responsible."

"Job security, iago. Just do it."

"As you wish, Hektor."

It took Irma a precious thirty seconds to stop ranting until she was calm enough to explain her blunder. "Goddamned rookie mistake. I may as well have graduated from Harvard."

"Enough," said Michael. "We have to get the story out, and now we won't be going after it alone." They took a few seconds to consider their options.

They were still at the Boulder orport in a privacy suite. The team had already rented temporary offices, and then rented larger ones once they discovered their subject's last name. Given the media circus that was about to deluge Boulder, effective and private workspaces would be worth Fortune and Fortunate 500 stock. Irma and her team would trade space for information to pay back past favors or get future ones. But as they weren't sure where they were going, they decided for now to stay at the orport. The privacy suites were simple rooms with desks, chairs, and couches in the amounts requested, and were a secure location in which to conduct business. In an age as advanced and intrusive as this one, privacy suites were one of the strategies society had developed to cope. They were prevalent in orports, hospitals, hotels, resorts, and any other location a traveler might feel the need to conduct business.

"All right," Irma said, once the team had dumped their baggage, "someone give me some good news."

"Irma," answered Michael, "I think you may be in luck. Do you remember that piece we did on tunnel rats about two years ago?"

Irma nodded. "That was the last time we were all in Boulder. If I'm not mistaken, we played the angle of a few brave men pushing too hard for majority. What about it?"

"Well, I did some checking," continued Michael, "and it turns out we know one of the people who appeared in the images of Saundra's little mediabot." Michael brought up the holo-image he was referring to. Standing before them in three-dimensional glory was an unkempt, rough-looking man with a shit-eating grin.

"Hey, we *do* know that guy," said Saundra. "Looks like he just got majority."

Michael laughed. "Nice guess. In fact he *did* just get majority. He goes by the name of Omad, and he was one of the tunnel rats we interviewed two years ago. Anyone care to guess how he got his majority?"

No one answered.

He sighed the sigh of a man who had no takers for a game of twenty questions.

"He got it trading in credits for an all-expense-paid, first-class lunar vacation."

Enrique whistled. "Must've been a nice chunk of change."

"It's 150,000 credits to be exact," confirmed Michael.

"What could he have found to earn tha . . . ?" Irma shut up as she realized exactly what he'd found.

"Do we have him?" she asked.

Michael flashed a huge am-I-a-god-or-what? smile.

Irma matched his grin with her own. "When do you meet him?"

"Half hour in a little pub called the Oasis Brewery."

"Yeah, I know the one," added Enrique. "It's on Canyon Boulevard. Been going for centuries."

Irma was pleased. The pieces were finally starting to fall into place. "I'm going to the Boulder offices to coordinate and get us the funding we'll need to follow through on all of this. Saundra, I'm going to need you to go to Florence and try to eyeball this guy."

"Why does she get to go?" protested Enrique.

"Quit your whining," Saundra said, lost in the information now streaming across her DijAssist. "No can do, anyhow, Irma. Dr. Harper and Mr. Cord are leaving Florence as we speak. The good doctor just made conventional reservations back to Boulder with a stopover in New York."

"Then go to New York, Boulder, the Oort Cloud if you have to, just get on his tail and stay there. Enrique, you're with me at headquarters. Crack that ten million, or better yet, see if our mystery payout man—or woman—has money that we can trace. The sooner we get to his account the sooner we know where he is, what he's buying, and who he's buying it from. We could make expenses just selling that to the celebrity sites." She turned to Michael.

"This tunnel rat is the one lead we have that I haven't stupidly given away. Exploit it for all it's worth. Spend whatever, go wherever. I'm releasing the story in one hour, which gives you a little less than twenty minutes of talk time with him before you get back to me."

"Is that wise?" asked Enrique.

"No, it's not, but we don't have a choice. We have to assume that Hektor is releasing the story to all and sundry even as we speak, and that it will take the other newsgroups—the ones that bite—at least an hour to confirm that this is not a hoax, or at least real enough to run with."

"Why wouldn't they all bite?" asked Enrique.

"More like, why would they?" answered Irma. "Don't forget who the source is. One Hektor Sambianco, recently discredited GCI big shot, whose stock is in the dump. Couple that with the fact that it's so close to Mardi Gras and might therefore be a GCI entertainment scam. Which all adds up to buying us more time. My one-hour mark is for the one or two smart editors who won't file the story away for tomorrow's bylines, and will instead do some preliminary research immediately."

"You really think an hour is all they need?" finished Enrique.

"Give or take, but yes, I do. Don't forget, in this business an hour could mean the difference between a Pulitzer and a pink slip. We have to be first out the gate and just hope we can stay ahead of the pack. Any questions?" Irma waited and saw there were none.

"Go."

And with that simple word, what had started out as a human-interest story emanating from tiny Boulder, Colorado, was well on the way to becoming a sociological avalanche soon to shake the foundations of their entire world.

"Mosh, what happened?"

Neela was calling from the docked t.o.p. now effectively besieged by the wall of reporters and mediabots floating around access tube 37. The air was so thick with them that they were actually bumping into each other. The din of reporters shouting commentary into their live feeds accompanied the maelstrom. From the floor of the standing-room-only terminal, it looked like a swarm of angry bees attacking their own nest. The Boulder orport was effectively shut down.

A weary Mosh endeavored to answer via holodisplay. "At New York they knew a man had been awakened from a long cryogenic sleep." He smiled at Justin, who at this point was standing next to Neela. "While you were in flight *The Terran Daily News* broke the story that our Justin was . . . are you ready for this?" Mosh didn't wait for Neela to answer. "Justin Cord." Mosh also saw that divulgence of Justin's last name elicited no response either from his young internist or from her distinguished "guest."

"You knew?" he asked, almost sighing.

Neela nodded.

"Well," continued Mosh, "I would have liked to have found out in some other way than Eleanor handing me a hard copy of *The Terran Daily*."

"How did *they* find out?" asked Neela.

"Blame Hektor," interjected Justin. "He seems to be a convenient reason for anything that makes my life more difficult."

"Only half correct," answered Mosh. "From what I've ascertained, he was the source for some of the media companies, but maybe not all of them."

"Bullshit," Neela muttered. "He probably called them all up and gave them pictures, past and present."

"Neela," answered Mosh, "whatever Hektor's up to is not important now. Wait for someone from the clinic to get to you. We'll figure it out once you and Justin are safely back home. Do not leave that t.o.p. until you can do it without getting mobbed. Do you understand?"

Neela nodded, and Mosh disconnected.

She paced back and forth within the confines of the t.o.p., trying desperately to get her thoughts in order. She stopped and stared at Justin.

"I'm sorry," she said, locking her eyes onto his. "I'm so wrapped up in everything that's happening I'm forgetting about my job—which is you. How are you doing?"

"Neela, how are *you* doing?" he shot back.

Neela smiled sadly. "Thank you for asking; most clients don't."

"First of all," continued Justin, "I'm not 'most clients.' Second of all, in case you've forgotten your history, I'm familiar with a media circus. Not on this level, of course, but I have been under the siege of the spotlight more times than I can possibly count. So do me a favor, don't worry so much about me. I can handle it."

"I'll be fine," she answered. "I'd hoped that the media circus thing was going to be the last part of a long and gradual process, and somehow it ended up being the first. Damsah, it's only your first day, and it's not even over." She took Justin's hand and clasped it between both of hers. "You're Justin Cord, the Unincorporated Man, and you have no idea what that means." She motioned her arm to indicate the outside world. "And neither, I'm afraid, do they."

"And you do?" he asked, earnestly.

"I'm good at my job, Justin," she answered, releasing her grasp, lest he read too much into it. "For the most part we're trained to integrate the reanimated individual back into society. But the toughest part of this job, I suspect, will be integrating society to you."

Justin hadn't been "alive" long enough to think about what effect he'd have on the world other than possible future contributions. He'd spent the better part of his few hours on Earth trying to gain some semblance of order within his universe. Neela's comment only made him realize how complicated his new life might turn out to be. He'd always assumed that if his crazy scheme actually worked, his life would be easier—glories of the new world and all. But he was now beginning to realize that it might actually be harder—much harder. Still, he thought, it could always have been worse.

"Well," he said, "I know I haven't been awake very long, but at least so far, from what I've seen and understand, I rather like this society. Despite one or two quirks, it's exactly what I was hoping for when I was frozen."

Now Justin took Neela's hand in his. She seemed surprised. He sensed she wanted to pull back but didn't.

"You *are* doing a great job," he said. "I feel better being in this new world just having you around, and isn't that what a good reanimation specialist is supposed to do?"

Justin inched his face forward. She quickly put her thumb on his forehead. It was a strange action to take, but it stopped him in his tracks.

"Justin, I really need to explain something to you. . . ."

"You don't, Neela," he said, interrupting. "For all I know you have a boyfriend or even"—a lascivious smile made an impromptu appearance across his face—"a girlfriend."

"I do *not* have a girlfriend," she answered, swatting his shoulder, "so you can get that image out of your mind."

"Which gets us back to the boyfriend," he replied.

"No boyfriend, either."

At the realization of her availability, his smile continued to brighten.

"And you can get *that* image out of your mind as well. Look, Justin, it won't happen. Not now. Not ever . . . even . . . even if I wanted it to."

An admission? he wondered.

"It?"

"It," answered Neela. "In your era, wasn't it illegal for a patient and doctor to be intimate?"

Justin scratched his chin, considering the question. "Well, it was frowned upon, but it happened a lot—still it *was* illegal under certain circumstances. Are you saying it's actually illegal to consider such a relationship?"

Neela was relieved by Justin's changed body language. He had gone from being aroused to inquisitive. Inquisitive she could deal with. "*Very* illegal, and also *highly* immoral," she answered. "Actually, you'd be better off not thinking about it like a doctor-patient relationship. I misspoke."

"Then how?" he asked—more wounded than curious.

Neela looked up while trying to find an appropriate analogy. It didn't take long. "How would you have felt," she said, now refocused on Justin, "about a priest sleeping with a teenaged member of his or her congregation?"

Justin's face went blank at the implication. "You're shitting me, right? That bad?"

Neela nodded solemnly. "While I'm not familiar with the expression, I can assume its meaning. So the answer is, no. I am not 'shitting' you. In fact, I may be understating it."

"*Understating?*" he gasped. "Perhaps it's *you* who doesn't understand." In the recesses of his mind he fervently hoped so.

Neela shook her head. "When revival first became an option for those who'd made up the second generation of revives . . ."

"Second generation?"

"Yes, Justin, there were no survivors from the first generation—none, that is, until you." She paused and looked at him anew. Coming to terms with his uniqueness was like standing in the surf and being pummeled by a series of waves. Each wave had different implications, shifted her ever so slightly, and reawakened her awe.

She continued, "I suppose if no one survived it's silly to call them the first generation, but they were at least prescient enough to have themselves suspended, even if with outdated technology. Circumstance, as I explained to you earlier, was their undoing. It was the second generation, post–Grand Collapse, that was responsible for the harshness of the doctrine we live by today."

"What happened?" he asked.

"A lot," she answered. "To be fair, no one really knew how fragile the mind of a revive was . . . how susceptible to suggestion they truly were. I could recount the sordid tales of abuse and deception that served to rob this second generation of any and all worldly possessions, much less their sense of self-worth and dignity, but I'll leave you with a far more effective argument—70."

Justin shrugged.

Neela frowned. "That's the actual percentage of those who either committed suicide shortly after revival or attempted it."

She waited for the enormity of the number to sink into Justin's psyche. When she was satisfied that it had, she continued. "Don't forget, suspension as a life extension option was begun by a fringe element of society. Correct me if I'm wrong, but it never gained acceptance in your era, and had barely gained acceptance in ours—that is, until it was actually proven viable."

He nodded in agreement.

"There was no system in place," she continued, "no 'soft pillow' to land on for this second generation of revives. No data with which to base treatment. It was a 'good morning and welcome to the world' sort of affair and then an 'oh by the way, all your family and friends are dead—here's a little starter money, good luck.'"

"Not much of an acclimation process," said Justin.

Neela nodded. "Now you see why I was so upset that your integration has gone so bloody wrong. I keep waiting for you to fling yourself off a building or be hit by a wave of interminable depression, but you seem strangely immune—of course, it's only been a day."

"Like you said, Neela," he said, half joking, "it's still early. I could jump off a building or whatever it is you people do to off yourselves these days."

Neela shot him a worried look.

"Don't worry, dear," he said, laughing. "I assure you I plan on staying around for a while. But at least I now have an inkling of why the 'no date' doctrine is so entrenched." And then, gazing deep into her eyes, he said, "Pity."

Pity indeed, thought Neela, suppressing her heart for the sanctity of her soul. She'd never once felt anything for any of her revives. That is, not until now. She told herself that it must be his uniqueness. But something more was stirring—perhaps intellectual, perhaps admiration. She'd sort through it later once things settled down.

Neither she nor Justin had time to realize that they'd just "broken up" before ever getting started because they were interrupted by the sound of the upper hatch exploding outward. The harsher glare of emergency lighting poured through the hole, bathing the interior. Without thinking, Justin leaped forward to protect Neela. Sadly, Neela did the exact same thing—the result of which was a head-on collision.

It took a moment for the stars to clear, but holding their heads in their hands they both managed to look up in time to see Omad peering down. He'd somehow managed to blow the emergency hatch.

"Justin, Doc, good to see you," he said nonchalantly, teeth glinting in the bright light.

"Omad!" Justin was genuinely pleased, even if still smarting from the head blow. "How on Earth did you get in here?"

"I'd like to know that myself," Neela said, still rubbing her forehead. The pain was strangely alleviating.

"I had some help from . . . ," Omad chose his next words carefully, "an ally."

A voice could be heard from behind Omad.

"Omad, we don't have a lot of time."

Neela squinted upward. "Who is that?"

As Omad began a slow floating descent to where Neela and Justin were standing, the "ally" popped his head through the exposed hole. It was Michael Veritas.

He quickly introduced himself while pulling his body through the opening in the t.o.p. He descended the length of the craft, landing next to Omad. "Nice to meet you," he said, sizing up both Neela and Justin.

Neela didn't return the pleasantry and focused her outrage on Omad.

"Omad, what were you thinking bringing someone like *that* in here?" She turned to Michael. "No offense."

"None taken," Michael answered, smiling.

Omad didn't bother with Neela, choosing to appeal to Justin directly.

"Justin, right now you're the virgin at the orgy. One way or another you're gonna get screwed, the only question is, will it be by one or dozens?"

Justin started to laugh.

"You have a way with words, my friend. So tell me, is Michael here to be my ravager?"

Wisely, Michael didn't take the bait, choosing to let Omad finesse the already awkward introduction.

"We have a plan to get you out of here quickly and quietly, but I can't do it without him."

"And let me guess," continued Justin. "The price is, he gets the first 'screw'?"

"Yeah," answered Omad, appreciating Justin's ability to get down to the brass tacks. "That's pretty much the gist of it."

"In that case, Omad, I think I'd rather wait and let the authorities settle this. If I'm to be screwed I'd rather choose the 'screwer' under different circumstances." He turned to Michael. "No offense."

"Again, none taken," Michael responded. "There is one small problem, though," he added.

"Yes?" answered Neela.

"If the authorities handle it," he continued, "which I'm sure they're discussing right now, you'll both be taken into *their* custody." He looked directly at Justin. "And don't forget, Mr. Cord, you're undocumented, as we all know your ID is about as real as the furniture in this room. So while the choice is yours, I suggest you take me up on my offer. I'll get you out of here, and yes, I'll get the story, but it'll be your story—that I can promise you. And if integrity's an issue I have a system Pulitzer to back up my name." Michael was done. His outer calmness in the face of possibly losing the biggest interview of his career was a sham. His heart was beating so hard he could have sworn the people in the room could hear it.

Justin looked to Neela, who nodded. "Deal," Justin said. "But on one condition."

Michael remained poised. "Name it."

"We want to know how you broke the story."

"There are some sources I have to protect. . . ."

"Name or nothing," said Justin.

It took a nanosecond to give Justin the information he'd soon be able to obtain from the pages of Michael's own paper. "Hektor Sambianco," answered Michael, "but he only gave us your picture. We pieced together the rest. I'll fill you in on the way out. Now, let's get outta here." And with that they all began their ascent back up to the emergency hatch.

Michael sat across from Justin Cord with one thought on his mind. *Every reporter in the system wants to be me.* He let that thought sink in, taking a moment to enjoy it. Michael knew he was good at his job, but now everyone else would know. There was no way he could've done this without the team, and he would tell anyone willing to listen that the interview was a group effort. But for a moment Michael felt the overwhelming triumph that only true personal accomplishment can bring. The only downside was that Dr. Harper, with Justin's permission, had insisted on screening Michael's questions. She'd explained that Justin was still emotionally vulnerable, and that certain hardball questions could jeopardize his psychological state. Michael had agreed to wear kid gloves for this interview, knowing he'd probably have to go through Dr. Harper for a second one. But he put that all aside, along with the memory of the harrowing run along the top of the orport's launch tubes and the perilous jump through the deactivated atomized security net to get his man to safety. He now concentrated on the person sitting comfortably in front of him. The person who in the course of an hour would change Michael's life.

Justin found it ironic that he was now back in a room that only hours before he couldn't wait to escape. And he had to admit that it not only felt good to be back, it also felt safe.

Michael had insisted that Neela and Omad leave the room. After assurances from Justin that he could handle himself, they reluctantly agreed. Justin now turned to Michael, who was sitting somewhat rigidly across from him.

"So," asked Justin, "tell me about this paper of yours."

Michael realized that his subject was trying to control the interview. He smiled and played along. "It's called *The Terran Daily News* and has been in continuous operation for nearly three hundred years. In some ways it's the world's oldest continuous paper. It used to be called *The Alaskan Daily News*, which was the product of several pre–Grand Collapse Alaskan papers merging. It's also the system's most prestigious paper."

"Interesting." Justin absorbed the information and moved on. "Call me old-fashioned," he said, "but does this 'paper' come in actual paper form?"

"As a matter of fact . . ." Michael pulled out a hard copy from his valise and handed it over.

Justin started flipping through the pages. He was curious to see if the paper would feel like a real newspaper or, like so many other things he'd seen, a poor imitation. One thing was certainly different. He noticed that when he looked directly at an ad or picture it came to life as a three-dimensional holograph. One ad in particular caught his attention. It was an extension of the billboard he'd seen earlier in the day. It was for a transbod, and the ad seemed to be issuing a dire warning about the number of days left until Mardi Gras. He closed the paper and focused his attention back on Michael.

"So it's called a paper because it's still a paper?"

"Well, not really," answered Michael, "I believe in your day you called films 'films' even though they were all shot digitally. Our paper's distributed though the Neuro. Of our 2.7 billion daily readers, less than forty thousand will get a hard copy. But it's relatively simple to produce, and some people seem to like it." He pointed at the paper he'd only recently handed over. "I suspected you'd be one of them."

Michael saw the appreciative look in Justin's eyes as he flipped through sections of the paper. "It's kind of like," continued Michael, "those people who still prefer pocket watches."

Justin smiled. *I only bought the damned Timex because of the tagline,* he thought. He looked down at his empty wrist, then looked back up with a shrug. "Let's begin, Mr. Veritas."

Michael opened with a question he knew would appeal to his readers. "Mr. Cord, are you alone or part of a colony of lost ancients that hid themselves away?"

"I cannot speak for others, but I only had myself frozen. If any survived from my time, I would be pleasantly surprised."

"Mr. Cord, could you explain what steps you took to preserve your life?"

"I hired a brilliant engineer and gave her an unlimited budget and a clearly defined goal. I find that if you supply those three ingredients, amazing things can happen."

"And the goal?" asked Michael, more for his readers than any personal need to ask an obvious question.

"You mean, other than to live?" asked Justin.

"Yes, sorry."

"To create a self-sustaining, perpetual suspension unit."

This caught Michael by surprise. He did a quick check on his DijAssist and looked up at Justin. "Do you realize, Mr. Cord, that we don't have anything quite like that today?"

"Yes, Mr. Veritas . . ."

"Michael."

"Yes . . . Michael, your 'friend' Omad informed me. But I suspect you don't have anything like it because you don't need it."

"Correct, Mr. Cord. Still, it's quite a testament."

"Indeed it is. I'd thank the engineer personally, but unfortunately . . ."

Michael smiled sympathetically.

"The truth is, for those exceedingly rare cases where suspensions have to be maintained for a duration of years, we have the far-side suspension facility on the Moon. The thinking goes, why develop a technology when it's so much cheaper to let the frigid nature of the universe do it for you?"

"Funny you should mention that," answered Justin, smiling wistfully. "Sandra, the engineer who designed the unit, considered that very concept. It was determined that we could send a team of engineers to the Moon and dig a cavern and store me there for a little less than what the actual project cost."

"Not to be rude, Mr. Cord, but why go through the risk of creating a new and therefore untested device when your other option made so much more sense? Even in your day the technology for going to the Moon was well established."

"Are you familiar with the pyramids, Michael?"

"Are you talking about the Egyptian pyramids, Mr. Cord?"

"Please, call me Justin, and, yes, the very ones."

"Familiar enough," assured Michael.

"Well," continued Justin, "do you know what those pyramids were designed for?"

"Monuments to the king, I suppose."

"Actually, Michael, they were suspension units."

Michael rubbed at the scruff on the end of his chin. "Care to explain?"

"I don't mean," continued Justin, "in the modern sense, but the Egyptians had a worldview like yours and mine. Namely, if you preserved your body as well as you could, the actual body would be reawakened in a better world, and you would have everything that you needed or wanted in the next life." Justin paused for a moment. "But only if you preserved the body. Makes you wonder if the ancient Egyptians were exposed to advanced technology at some point. But I digress; the point is that the pharaohs believed that they must preserve their bodies with as much wealth as they could carry. In that way they'd live well in the next world."

"So you prefer to see yourself as a modern-day pharaoh, then?"

"Not really. I don't consider myself a god, wasn't born into wealth, and certainly didn't die with members of my estate buried with me. However, I'll admit there are certain similarities."

"But somehow the pharaohs inspired you?"

Justin chuckled. "Yes, the pharaohs were indeed an inspiration. They inspired fear."

"I'm afraid I don't know enough ancient history to follow your thinking, Justin."

"How many actual pharaohs were found in their pyramids?"

"Well, I'd guess maybe two or three."

"Try none."

"What about King Tut?"

"He came from a much later dynasty that learned an important lesson. If you build a pyramid and fill it with lots of stuff, what are you telling the whole world? Allow me," he said, as he saw Michael beginning to answer. "You're saying, in effect, 'Hey, world, here I am, dead with lots of treasure.'"

"Good point," agreed Michael.

"Not one pyramid was found intact. By King Tut's day and age the pyramids had been around and sacked for over a thousand years. So the new pharaohs dug hidden tombs to keep their bodies safe, thereby greatly increasing their chances for an afterlife."

"So in your mind 'Moon' equals 'pyramid.'"

"Exactly." Justin was beginning to feel comfortable talking. Though he'd developed a dislike of journalists, even the supposed "reputable" ones, this interview was different, because it was allowing him to talk about something that centuries before he could share with almost no one.

"Had I gone with the Moon plan," Justin continued, "I would have had to inform governments about my launch schedules. That would have entailed official inspections. The whole world would have known that I'd spent a fortune to have myself buried on the Moon, and any asshole with a spare missile or the desire to see if I had treasure could have finished me off."

"So you built a tomb," said Michael, with dawning understanding.

"Correction. I built a self-sustaining suspension unit which I stuck in a tomb."

"Semantics. It got you what you wanted—anonymity."

"Yes, it did. The more anonymous, the better. You want to know what kept Tut safe for all those thousands of years? He was such an unimportant, short-lived ruler that everyone forgot about him. And before you ask the next question, relatively speaking I was pretty much the same. Yes, I was rich, and yes, had a certain amount of fame, but in the grand scheme of things I was a mere blip on the radar screen."

"More than a blip, Justin. We're still pretty well versed on your life's story to this day and age."

"A fluke, I can assure you, Michael. I happened to disappear at a time when media coverage bordered on obsessive, which, ironically, I didn't think could get any worse."

Michael laughed. "Fair enough."

"And that," continued Justin, "combined with the fact that a whole lot of information got wiped out in the Grand Collapse, apparently made me stick out like a cherry on a cream pie. I can assure you, in my day and age I was well known, but as the old saying goes, 'there's a billion Chinese who could give a crap.' "

"I'm familiar with that phrase," answered Michael. "Today that number's graduated a bit."

"I'll bet."

"OK," continued Michael. "Why didn't you go to the cryonics organizations that were in existence at the time?"

"Like the pyramids, obvious open targets waiting to be destroyed."

Michael nodded.

"Why only save yourself? We've all seen the size of the crypt you made. Seems like you could have easily brought someone else with you."

Justin shifted uneasily in his seat. He noticed the chair attempting to shift with him, to make him more comfortable, much like his bed had when he woke from his long sleep. But, for what he was feeling at the moment, relief wasn't to be found in the machinations of a well-meaning ergo chair.

"I offered it to one other person," he said, sighing. "My personal assistant. But he refused. He felt it was wrong to live longer than what he considered to be one's preordained time."

"If I'm not mistaken," Michael said, "that was a very strong meme . . . um . . . stereotype of the time. I wouldn't blame you."

"I know what a meme is, Michael. The Darwinian evolution of a thought or, in the case of death, group think. And I don't blame myself."

"Yes, of course," Michael answered.

"But you are correct," continued Justin. "The idea of preordained death was the prevailing meme. Had been for all recorded history, in fact."

Michael took a deep breath, shaking his head. "As much as I've read on the topic, I have to admit that I can't understand how a society could follow what would appear to be such an illogical and superstitious line of thought. Tell me, did these same people refuse medical care?"

"No, they didn't. But to them death was an idea infused with religion and not a disease to be cured."

"Well, guess what? We cured it."

"Really? You don't say," Justin teased. "Please, understand that my assistant, Sebastian, was not a stupid man. In many ways he was the most thoughtful, well-informed person I had ever met in my life. But he was trapped like a bird in a cage. And that's why he, like millions before him, could not escape the most successful meme of all time—the notion of the inevitability of dying."

Michael nodded. "I once read a book on the topic called *The Cult of Death.*"

"Let me guess," offered Justin. "You couldn't relate."

Michael nodded.

"I'm surprised," continued Justin, "that you made it past the first chapter. In order to understand a book like that you'd have to think like the people of the twenty-first century, which of course you couldn't. That would've been like me trying to get into the heads of people who lived three hundred years prior to my time."

"Tell me," asked Michael, "were the pyramids also your inspiration for the treasures rumored to be buried within your tomb?"

"Depends," Justin laughed. "What rumors have you heard?"

"Well, that the crypt had in it gold, silver, and precious gems, not so valuable now, but you wouldn't have known that at the time."

Justin nodded. "The rumors are correct."

"You also supposedly had artifacts, works of art, and, according to our friend Omad out there," he said, motioning toward the back wall, "a Timex watch."

"Had," answered Justin. "Sold it this morning."

"Really?" Michael looked surprised. "That Omad didn't tell me. If you don't mind my asking, how much did you get for it?"

"Thirty-eight thousand."

"AmEx?"

"Yeah. Is that good?"

Michael laughed. "Depends, if you think a one-shot four-quarter dividend is a good thing or not."

Justin smiled. "I do."

"You could have done better," Michael said.

Justin nodded, keenly aware of what he'd just heard. Michael hadn't said "six months' salary" or a "boatload" to describe Justin's good fortune. He'd referred to it as a dividend payout. That it had entered into the vernacular was revealing. Justin recalled how once wealth used to be determined by the number of harvests a person could get in. So a question like "How much did you make last year?" would be answered with the amount of harvests the farmer had brought in. The higher the number the greater the awe. Only when industrial society emerged did people think of a per-year salary as the measure of wealth. And now that a purely corporate society had emerged, the obvious indicator of wealth, short of the material, was the quarterly dividend.

"If you don't mind," continued Michael, "just a few more questions."

"Shoot."

Michael stared at his subject. Justin was articulate, thoughtful, naturally good-looking, well informed, smart, and even, in a way, heroic. He was the embodiment of all that was good about a lost civilization, gift wrapped for the present. And that, decided Michael, was how he would plan on slanting the story.

"What are your plans for the future?"

As soon as he finished the question, Justin's door chime rang.

The room informed Justin that Neela and Omad were waiting for permission to enter. Justin smiled, begging Michael's indulgence.

"See them in," Justin said to the room, while staring at Michael.

Neela and Omad entered. Omad took up a position leaning against the wall while Neela sat down at the foot of the bed.

Justin looked over at Neela. "Our good friend here wants to know what my plans for the future are."

"Don't look at me," answered Neela. "I had a whole schedule worked out, and you can see how that turned out."

"Well," answered Justin, "contrary to Neela's lack of faith in her scheduling abilities, my immediate future is very much in her capable hands."

Though she tried to hide it by turning her face, Michael noticed the faint blush in her cheeks. *Is she actually attracted to him?* he wondered.

"Well, in that case," answered Neela, "Justin will stay here for a few days, during which time he'll rest, read, and begin to learn a little bit about our world and way of doing things. Justin's long-term plans are, of course, up to him."

Michael made a mental note to schedule an interview with this reanimation specialist. He'd do it himself if need be, but would try to pass it on to Irma. She was far better at getting women to trust her than he was.

"If you could choose," he continued, "between the following advances in technology—space travel, nanotechnology, the arrival of near-perfect health, or our long life spans—which would you say was the one that you found most surprising?"

Justin had to think about the question for a moment. While the list he'd been given was impressive, given all that it encompassed, he couldn't honestly say that any of it surprised him. Amazed? Yes. Impressed? Without question. But surprised? No. The future was all that Justin had dreamed it would be and more.

"I'd have to say . . . none of the above."

Michael looked up from his DijAssist, his cocked eyebrow revealing his astonishment. "Really? What then?"

"This concept of personal incorporation."

"I could have told you that," Neela mumbled just under her breath, but loud enough to make sure that Michael heard her.

Michael regained his composure and pressed on. He hated that he hadn't seen that one coming. His fault, he figured. *Shouldn't have given him a list to choose from. Oh, well.*

"The implication," continued Michael, "is fascinating. Care to explain?"

Justin was about to go into a detailed answer when he saw Neela shaking her head and drawing her hand across her throat. He acknowledged her signal with a slight nod, and gave Michael a sound bite instead of a response.

"Well, I kind of expected all the other things, but personal incorporation is something I definitely found surprising."

"In what way? If you don't mind my asking."

"Let's just say it was a little unexpected, and I'm looking forward to learning all about it."

Michael realized that there was no point in pressing the issue further.

"Well, I'm sure our readers will look forward to your IPO date for the chance to invest in you. I know I will."

"Well, uh, thank you," Justin answered, stuttering uncharacteristically. His confidence of a moment ago was strangely shaken by Michael's good intentions. Nothing bad had happened, and he knew that Michael was offering him a compliment, but it was hard to take it as such. In essence, Michael was saying, "Can't wait to see you up there on the auction block." The only thing missing for Justin was the shackles someone of his era normally associated with such goings-on.

Neela, sensing his discomfort, intervened. "I know it's your interview, Michael, but I'd like to ask Justin a question that I'm sure your readers would want to know as well."

Michael considered objecting, but the desire to remain on Dr. Harper's "good" list was greater than his need to control the interview. He leaned back a little in his chair, putting his DijAssist to the side.

"Sure, go ahead."

"I'm curious, Justin," Neela went on, "about what you did for fun in the past."

"Well, of course, there were movies, plays, sports, music . . . that sort of thing."

"The music of your era is considered some of the most varied and moving ever."

"Yes," he countered, "but do *you* think it was any good?"

"I do, in fact. The classical rockers are much emulated. Tell me—did you like the Beatles?"

"Sorry, no."

Neela's expression revealed surprise at the answer.

"I *loved* the Beatles," he said with a grin.

Neela smiled back. "Smart-ass."

Justin laughed.

Damsah's ghost, there is something there, thought Michael. It was a story—or would be, if anything ever happened. He'd sit on it for now—reputations were at stake. Maybe he'd talk to Irma about it.

"Well, then," she said, "maybe you won't be surprised to learn that they're the most popular turn-of-the-millennium group today."

"No, I wouldn't be," he answered, having an urge to give them a listen. "Even in my generation they had a certain . . . timeless quality."

Justin tilted his head slightly, as if straining to listen to a song that wasn't there.

Michael, following what he felt was Neela's mundane line of questioning, was forced to admit that, for better or worse, it had seemed to jar something loose in his interviewee. "Are you alright, Justin?"

"Sorry, yes. That last question reminded me of one of their songs . . . now it's stuck in my head."

"Which one?" asked Michael.

" 'Across the Universe.' "

The next couple of days were pleasant ones for Justin. He made no more attempts to sneak out of the hospital, and heeded Neela's advice about not interacting with the press. Omad would come by, and they'd hit the clinic's exercise room, then go to the cafeteria for a beer. Other than the fact that people were constantly staring at him, Justin was beginning to think that his new life had returned to what might be called normalcy. He'd even gotten used to the stares. After all, he was a bit of an anomaly, and the looks he'd been getting were not oppressive. People were looking at him with what he gathered was open curiosity. But it became clear early on that they knew better than to bother him. He was to find out later that Mosh had let it be known that anyone who spoke to him without an obvious invitation to do so would be fired on the spot. Justin recalled a very interesting conversation with Mosh and his wife, Eleanor, one night over dinner. Eleanor was a knowledgeable source of information on practical financial matters, like getting a currency account and buying a house. Plus, she seemed to take a mother-hen attitude toward Justin, which he found strangely comforting.

Of all the problems he'd dealt with in planning his trip to the future, the idea of loneliness was never one he'd considered. Since the death of his wife he had wanted to be alone and, in fact, had drawn comfort from the walls he'd built around himself. He'd been prescient enough with his physical being, just not with his emotional one. Now he was beginning to regret not having tried harder to get his erstwhile assistant, or at least someone else from his era, to accompany him. But then Justin would remind himself that all plans have at least one mistake inevitably discovered after the fact. His was in believing that as an outsider he'd have no problem leaving his world, and everyone in it, behind. And now that it was gone he knew he'd been wrong.

Mosh was tired. He was, after all, approaching his second century and beginning to feel it. As if the day-to-day pressure of running a hospital weren't enough, he now had a pissed-off GCI and a horde of ravenous media to contend with. The tricks the press were pulling to get into the hospital ranged from funny (someone claiming to be Justin's long-lost brother) to ludicrous (one idiot shooting himself in the leg to gain entrance). Mosh gladly signed the recommendation for a psychological audit on that man. What was becoming intolerable was that the world was rapidly catching on to the fact that Mosh McKenzie, ex–GCI board member, was alive and well. And that was a very bad thing. Mosh had known when he retired just how ruthless the corporate world could be—even to retirees. Which was why when he'd left he'd done so with an old-boy handshake deal. He'd get to rule his private fiefdom as long as he promised to stay out of the spotlight and clear of GCI's internal politics. In short, he'd agreed to disappear.

But thanks to Justin he was not keeping up his part of the bargain. He was exerting power, and the world, as well as GCI, was starting to remember that Mosh McKenzie was not only a man to be reckoned with, but also a man who'd once been in contention for the Chairmanship.

Mosh looked out at the conference table and saw a bleary-eyed group of people staring back at him: Neela, Dr. Wang, Gil Tellar, and Eleanor. Mosh chuckled to himself, realizing that it was this same group, minus Eleanor, who less than a week before were so excited by the prospect of their "find" that they'd already planned their retirements. Well, that had changed, hadn't it? None of them had gotten much sleep during the week, and they were all beginning to realize that they'd be getting even less as time wore on. If they attempted to leave the hospital they'd be mobbed by a news-starved world. If they attempted to contact anyone outside the hospital, it was a sure bet their lines would be hacked into. There was no escape. The interest in Justin was at a fever pitch and they were the closest thing to the man who, but for one interview in *The Terran Daily News,* had barely spoken to anyone. The press was painting him as a romantic hero from the past who'd survived incredible odds to reach nirvana. The talk in all the homes and offices was of Justin Cord. Any information about him was instantly downloaded and gobbled up. Most of it was readily available for free, but for the few enterprising entrepreneurs, it was sold at a profit. His birthplaces were immediately made into tourist attractions . . . all five of them. Items that had been owned by him, even with flimsy vetting, were auctioned off at an enormous price. It was a banner day for anyone in the Justin Cord business. Unfortunately, it was proving to be difficult for anyone in the business of helping Justin Cord.

"We need to find a way to get him and us out of the spotlight," Mosh said wearily.

"That's not going to happen anytime soon." It was Gil. "You'd have an easier time reversing the Grand Collapse."

Dr. Wang cleared her throat. "Most people are famous in a reflected way. They reflect the fame of other people or events or actions. Those people are relatively easy to separate from the spotlight. You simply remove them from the source of their fame, and soon the world loses interest. The actor stops acting, or the sports figure stops playing, etc. But Justin is not reflecting fame. He is fame. You cannot separate him from himself. The world will have to grow tired of Justin for the spotlight to fade, and that, I suspect, will take some time."

"Unfortunately, I agree with the assessment, Doctor," answered Mosh. "My question is, how do we get the damned spotlight to shine somewhere else?"

"Mosh," chided Eleanor, knowing what her husband was implying, "we will not throw that nice man out on the street."

"What street, Eleanor? That man is going to be one of the wealthiest men in the system the second he steps out the door."

"Actually," said Gil, "he may already be. Justin's been giving me lists of stocks and works of art and collectible items he's socked away—if they've survived, that is."

"You mean other than what we found in the tomb?" asked Dr. Wang.

"Precisely."

"So," said Mosh, "you're telling us he buried treasure around the world before he was suspended?"

"That's what I'm telling you," answered Gil. "Or, at least, that's what he's telling me."

"Rich or not, we can't simply throw him out," insisted Eleanor.

"We don't have to," said Neela, interrupting the fracas. "He wants to go. To be exact, he wants to give a press conference and move back to New York."

"Well, why didn't you say so?" Mosh asked, glaring at Neela.

"I tried," she answered, "but you all seemed pretty intent on not letting me get a word in edgewise."

"I wonder why that is?" Gil asked, neither needing nor expecting an answer. Everyone laughed.

"Yeah, yeah," chortled Neela, "very funny, Gil. But the fact remains, he does want to leave."

Mosh's sense of relief was palpable and visible. He'd been thinking of sending Justin for a long space cruise on a private yacht, something that would've taken him to the Oort Cloud and beyond. It would've taken over a year before he'd have gotten back, and by then he would have hopefully had enough time to begin a proper adjustment into society. Or had Justin preferred, he could have become one of the many people who simply wandered through the solar system, content to call home wherever they happened to be. But now it was moot. Justin had solved his problem, and for a lot less money.

"Is he really ready for that?" asked Eleanor.

"You'd think not," answered Dr. Wang, "but Neela and I have gone over his biophysicals, and they're all in proper balance. And if he does have any emotional turmoil he's hiding it better than anyone I've ever seen."

Gil was perplexed. "I know I'm not an expert or anything, but shouldn't it take longer to mainstream someone like that?"

"Like what?" asked Neela.

"Like, that old," answered Gil. "Not to mention the fact that everything and everyone he held dear is irrevocably gone."

"Not his nature," said Neela. "Justin will always try to deal with reality without pretensions or delays. It is in his nature to accept a situation." *And try to master it,* she thought.

Mosh drummed his fingers on the table until he noticed the racket he was causing. "Alright, people, let's figure out what to do here."

"Legally," answered Gil, "we have to keep him here until he's ready to leave. And that doesn't mean when he says he's ready. It means when *we say* he's ready. We're a medical facility first and a harried bunch of workers second. It's important we remember that."

"Morally, we have an obligation to keep him till he's ready to go," added Eleanor, looking to Neela for support.

"He's ready," said Neela, "but he does have one condition."

"Name it," said Mosh, a little too quickly.

"Me."

Advertising media saturation in a society as advanced as this one is both a blessing and a curse. Indeed, had it not been for the market demand and successful application of products and services to help limit advertising, society would have experienced a second Grand Collapse (by the simple fact that no one would have wanted to leave their homes for fear of advertising inundation). Luckily, there was almost as much money to be made in antipublicity and antiadvertising product development as in the traditional fields of advertising, and so a healthy balance was reached. But if the public wanted to be informed of an event, or in effect allowed themselves to be advertised to, then what became known as "permissive" market saturation could easily reach so close to 100 percent as to make no statistical difference whatsoever. Of the four events in modern times to reach the magic 100, three of them involved Justin Cord.

—FROM A LECTURE GIVEN BY PROFESSOR MARTIN JONES, UNIVERSITY OF SAN MIGUEL DE ALLENDE, POSTED AT MEDIA AND MODERN SOCIETY

The press conference was held in the clinic's loading dock. Although not ideally suited, it was the only place big enough to hold the event. Floaters and reporters were busy scurrying about everywhere, except for a small area cordoned off by the main entrance leading into the clinic. And that's where most of them were encamped, waiting for the system's hottest news story to walk through the door.

Justin and Neela were waiting patiently on the other side of it, listening to the clamor, and occasionally peering out through the one-way mirror.

Justin couldn't help but laugh at the melee occurring in his honor.

"You're really enjoying this, aren't you?" Neela asked, resisting the urge to gently poke his ribs.

"Sure. What man wouldn't like to have the whole world—sorry—the whole *solar system* waiting with bated breath to hear what he has to say?"

"In that case," chided Neela, "it'd better be good."

He laughed and smiled at her, indicating he was ready to go. Neela smiled back. He seemed, she thought, transformed. He also appeared to be totally accepting, and even eager, about beginning his new life. She wished she could have claimed some of the credit, but she wouldn't. Even though she'd helped Justin center himself, and was there for him during his first week, it was nothing like how a reintegration, especially of this sort, was supposed to go. If anything, she should have gotten him to slow down, not plow ahead. And now she realized she didn't want him to walk out that door, because when he did, everything would change again. Not that it hadn't already, but the few steps he was about to take into the world's waiting arms would solidify the change irrevocably. Neela wanted to keep this moment for herself before the world took him away.

"You know," she said, "it's not like the world knows nothing about you. Besides what's already on the Neuro, that interview you gave with Mr. Veritas is systemwide."

"True enough, Neela. I'm happy to say that they know about you as well, Miss Famous Reanimationist with a specialty in social integration. If I'm not mistaken, your interviews with Irma Sobbelgé were broadcast systemwide as well."

Neela feigned amusement at Justin's remark, but inside she was worried. The associative fame of being so close to the system's newest frenzy had shot her stock value way up—beyond what she could have ever hoped to earn in her lifetime. The immediate effect was to make her a wealthy woman . . . at least, on paper. The downside was that her dream of gaining self-majority was slipping further and further away. The more well-known she became, the more her stock shot up. And the more her stock shot up, the more difficult it became to buy it back. She likened it to a cat chasing its tail.

As a precaution she'd called her parents and sister before news of Justin broke and told them not to sell any shares that they owned, no matter how lucrative. As was customary, most parents promised not to sell their children's 20 percent, and usually willed it back to their offspring in the unfortunate event of an accidental permanent death. But it would have taken saints to turn down the type of offers Neela's stock was getting. While Neela understood that the decision to sell was her parents' and sister's to make, she didn't want them to get swindled. She'd breathed a sigh of relief when they'd told her that no matter what the going price, the shares would remain in their name alone. As far as her brother was concerned, she'd wisely bought back her few shares from him well over ten years ago.

Another downside to her newfound notoriety was how busy her schedule had become. She'd been booked for countless talk shows and speaking tours, something she looked forward to with loathing. She would have loved to refuse them all; however, as long as she was a minority shareholder of herself she had no choice but to agree. Even the extra credits she made did not make up for the loss of the quiet life she'd almost grown used to. In many ways, she'd often reflect, she was living a parallel life to that of her patient. Suddenly thrown into the spotlight, people fawning for her attention—almost as if she, too, had been reborn.

Incorporation headaches, she thought sadly. She put on a smile for Justin and wondered what it would be like to not owe anybody anything—to be *that* free.

"Besides," Justin said, breaking Neela out of her reverie, "those interviews explained the past. This press conference is about the future." He again motioned
toward the doorway. "Shall we?"

"By all means, Justin," Neela said, sighing slightly. "Let's not keep the future
waiting."

They stepped through the permiawall into a hailstorm of shouted questions
and the associated sounds of buzzing contraptions used for high-quality recording. Justin was a little surprised by the lack of flashes going off but remembered
that a civilization with sourceless lighting wouldn't need a flash to illuminate a
face. Still, the noise was enough to deafen, and the shouted questions reminded
Justin that this was indeed an old-fashioned media frenzy. He stood in front of a
small dais and held up his hands, hoping it would bring some order. The mob
quieted down. He pointed first to Irma Sobbelgé. It was their agreement that she
would get the first question, and then all special treatment would end. Justin felt
he had more than lived up to his end of the bargain, and Irma had agreed.

He put both hands on the dais, readying himself for the onslaught. "Yes."

Irma stood up, basking momentarily in the special treatment accorded her
and her paper. "Mr. Cord, Irma Sobbelgé, *Terran Daily News*. We have it on good
authority that you're leaving the clinic. Is that true? And if so, where will you be
living now?"

Justin smiled, knowing that Irma had just asked two questions instead of one,
but he admired her desire to milk her moment for all it was worth.

"It is true," he answered, "that I will be leaving the clinic, and I wish to thank
all the staff here for doing an amazing job under the most unusual of circumstances. I am grateful. But a man is reborn in a clinic; he is not meant to live
there."

The room started to laugh, taking Justin by surprise. He didn't think what
he'd said was all that funny, but it may have struck a cultural chord he knew
nothing about. When the laughter subsided, he continued.

"I'll be living in New York City for the time being, though the asteroid belt is
looking interesting to me. I may eventually settle in Ceres."

And in one fell swoop what had been meant as a joke set off a real-estate war
on the tiny boulder that raised property values by an average of 37 percent.

He pointed to another reporter, a pretty woman of Asian descent. She stood
up to speak.

"Miss Huan Lee Kim of the Neuro News," she belted out.

"Yes, Ms. Kim."

"Mr. Cord, will Dr. Harper be continuing on as your . . . integrationist?"

"Yes. I have signed a contract with the director of the clinic for her services
for the next year."

"May I ask as to the nature of that contract?" she pressed.

"No," snapped Justin.

Miss Kim was about to sit down, not expecting an answer but having more than enough to scandalize her readers for weeks, when Neela, who was standing behind and to the right of Justin, stepped forward.

"If you would allow me to answer that question, Justin," Neela said.

Justin nodded in surprise and took a small step backward to allow Neela front and center.

"Miss Kim, Mr. Cord has agreed to pay my salary for a year, as well as the cost of replacing me on staff for the year. In return he will be my exclusive patient, though I have contacted Dr. Gillette of the Vegas Clinic, and he will be consulting on this case. I would also like to say that the tone and emphasis of your questions were not becoming to my professional integrity or your own. Mr. Cord is my patient, period. Soon he may be mine and Dr. Gillette's."

"Doesn't he trust you?" someone shouted from the back.

"Completely," smiled Justin, "but Neela insisted, and who am I to argue with my specialist?" The crowd chuckled, and Justin picked someone else before they started shouting out their own questions. A well-dressed man in an intricately layered, multicolored suit stood up.

"Mr. Corwin of *The Detroit Times*," he said, as proudly as he could manage.

"Yes, Mr. Corwin."

"Mr. Cord, I am sure that you *will be* a wealthy man, but where did you get the funds to pay for your own private specialist for a year?"

"Before I had myself suspended, I took the precaution of placing certain valuables in places around the world. Sadly, most of them were found and looted, but three of my troves went untouched. According to the appraisals I've received you can consider my financial status as 'comfortable.' "

Justin pointed at another woman standing off to the side but jumping in a manner that caught his eye.

"Yes, you over there with the impressive jump."

"Thank you. Miss Daniels, *Boulder Sentinel.*"

"Yes, Miss Daniels."

"How 'comfortable'?"

"Let's just say comfortable enough to hire my own specialist for a year and pay her salary."

Justin smiled in a way that let them all know that he had more than a sufficient amount, and in all likelihood enough to put most of their salaries to shame. And in a society that respected wealth and property as few others in history, his evasive answer only added to the mystique that was fast becoming associated with his name.

"Well, Mr. Cord," Miss Daniels said, "that is impressive. What will you buy first?"

"Happiness," said Justin, in all seriousness.

There was a shout from the back: "As long as you share it, I wish you all the happiness you're entitled to!"

The crowd buzzed and turned to see who had the temerity to interrupt their guest of honor. What they saw was a smug-looking Hektor Sambianco leaning against one of the open bay doors, arms folded across his chest.

"Ladies and gentlemen, Hektor Sambianco," Justin said, extending his arm in his bane's direction. "You can leave now, Mr. Sambianco, or, if you prefer, be removed."

Hektor didn't budge. Instead he stood there smiling, almost daring Justin to follow through.

"You're forgetting, Mr. Cord, that as a duly authorized representative of GCI I have every right to be here. But I will not stay long if I'm not wanted."

"You're not," answered Neela. "Now please leave."

"Suit yourself. I'll just drop this off and be on my way." Hektor approached to within five feet of the podium and took out a small device that looked like a pen and pointed it toward the ceiling, where there appeared a document with dense legal script. After a few moments the image faded. "There, that should do it," he said.

"What was that?" Justin whispered into Neela's ear, but before she could respond Hektor delivered the answer.

"Forgive me, Justin. I would have handed you the papers digitally and in person, but you looked so hostile. I served the documents in a more public fashion than is traditional. But no one can argue that you didn't see them. And if by some odd chance you didn't, well then, I'm sure you can pick them up by watching the news—any channel should do."

"Served, as in court papers?" Miss Kim asked. The whole room had done an about-face, turning toward Hektor.

"Precisely, Miss Kim. Yes, GCI will see Mr. Cord in court."

Justin gripped the dais. "Don't say anything," Neela urged.

Another reporter's question rang out. "Would that be about Mr. Cord's suspension unit?"

"No, it would not, Mr. Haddad. We're dropping that claim for now." The reporter was clearly impressed that Hektor had known his name.

"Then," Mr. Haddad pressed, "what is it about?"

"Justin, we should go," implored Neela, grabbing his arm and trying unsuccessfully to drag him out of the room. She'd sensed his agitation and knew instinctively that Hektor was getting to him—baiting him further. She could also see Justin trying desperately to control his emotions. This was supposed to be his day, his big coming-out party; Hektor had effectively destroyed it.

"Good question, Mr. Haddad." Hektor continued. "As I said before, we're not interested in Mr. Cord's suspension unit, though I'm sure it's worth quite a credit or two. No, GCI is suing for something far more valuable—a percentage of Mr. Cord himself. A percentage that we will hold forever."

Hektor let that sink in, and watched, almost in slow motion, as the entire press corps turned around to get Justin's reaction.

Then all hell broke loose.

Omad grunted as he carried the last box across the threshold, actually breaking a sweat—a rare occurrence now that he'd gone majority.

"OK, Justin," Omad asked, wiping his brow, "why didn't you kill him?"

"You mean Sambianco?" he answered, shoving a set of boxes into a corner of the room. "I wasn't trying to kill him, Omad, just . . . punch his lights out."

"Could have fooled me."

"Look, man," Justin said, "the guards broke us up and the rest is up to the lawyers. It happened over a week ago. I'm just trying to start up a new life here in the Big Apple and enjoy the future."

Omad put a box down at his feet, emitting a grunt. "Enjoy the future? Enjoy the future, my ass. You know, Justin, they have things in the 'future' called drones. They could have done almost all of this moving without us. If it had to be done by hu-lab . . . sorry," he said, realizing yet another abbreviation was escaping his perplexing friend's grasp, "*human labor*, why not just hire people? You're richer than God. Is there some tradition in your time that states your friends must be the first to suffer when *you* move?"

Justin turned around, laughing. "Well, now that you mention it, yeah. But even more than that, I always felt that a place wasn't really yours unless you personally moved in some of the stuff and unpacked some boxes."

Omad wasn't buying it. In fact, it made about as much sense to him as would his heading back into the mines. "That's another thing," he snapped. "What the hell are those boxes made out of, some sort of biscuit?"

"It's called cardboard, Omad," Justin said, tapping one lightly with his foot for good measure. "All boxes used to be made out of it."

Omad shrugged. "Whatever."

"You might be surprised to know," continued Justin, "that it cost a fortune to have those boxes re-created. Maybe even more than the stuff inside . . . for the most part."

Omad grinned. "Why? Ya got another Timex in there for your buddy . . . your *moving* buddy?"

Justin shook his head, palms flat out. "Sorry."

"Then why?" asked Omad. "Why have these boxes made at all? You live in a fluid apartment, shouldn't you enjoy it? I know I would."

Justin sat down on a conveniently located pile. "Neela suggested that this exercise in moving might help me assimilate into the future better. It may seem weird, but I think she's right. I'm moving into a whole new life, but doing it like this doesn't make it seem as daunting."

"Smart doc, that doc," Omad said, a little too facetiously for Justin's taste. "Did she ever mention anything about torturing friends in your little exercise?"

Justin didn't answer.

"I thought not. Well then, you can make it up to me. You're pretty much in the center of the universe here, so I say we hit some clubs. I might just happen to know of a few fine establishments of exotic entertainment."

"Maybe later, friend," Justin said, fishing through his pockets for a scrap of paper. "I really had something else in mind." He handed Omad the scrap.

Omad read it, then looked up in disgust. "You're taking the ESB over the Virgin Rockets club and casino?"

"Not forever, Omad, but for today. I'd really like to see the Empire State. It would be like visiting an old friend."

Omad softened. "Lemme guess. Part of the exercise?"

"Not really, but I suppose," answered Justin honestly.

Omad put his foot up on the box at his feet and shook his head, disbelieving. "Yeah, I guess from your point of view it would make sense. After all, you were there when it was built."

"Hey," Justin said in mock offense, "I'm not *that* old."

"No? Well, close enough, buddy. Close enough. You gonna take security with you?"

"In this city? I checked the crime stats, Omad. Even with seventy plus million it still has an absolute crime rate lower than New York in the day of Rudy Giuliani."

"Oh, yeah," Omad said, reveling in his knowledge of the city, "he was that famous mayor who served right before La Guardia, right?"

Justin gave him a stern look, teacher hat firmly on. "He was mayor sixty years *after* La Guardia was dead."

"Whatever, man. Have a good one, and the next time you need to re-create a moving experience, make sure it involves plenty of money, women, and drugs."

Justin remembered being upset that the Empire State Building no longer existed as a part of the skyline (even though the skyline had risen precipitously), but was determined to see it nonetheless. Plus, who could resist the prospect of seeing so great an edifice completely covered by another? So, with a few subterfuge tips from Omad, he headed out.

There had been no greater city in which to walk than New York City, and Justin could see this had not changed. Though the buildings were significantly larger, and the traffic was no longer relegated to the street, the town's old personality remained—fast and furious, with a lot of heart. He took Park Avenue up to East Thirty-fourth Street, turned left, and headed to Fifth Avenue. Another left, and he was there. Or was he? He'd gotten so used to hanging that left onto Fifth and seeing the majestic building that not seeing it was disconcerting.

The Empire State Center took up three entire city blocks from West Thirty-second to West Thirty-fourth. The exterior was an amalgam of glass and steel not much different in coldness and structure from the ones Justin had remembered, but for one major difference: This one had a building—correction, a really big building—*inside* the building.

The entrance alone was three stories high and led foot traffic down into a huge open corridor. There was a cautionary sign indicating that the interior space was not equipped for personal flying, but that a suicide prevention field was in effect. He walked the long corridor leading to the center of the building. After what seemed like an eternity he finally arrived at the empiric core of the building. It was astonishing in its grandeur and chutzpah: a tremendous cavern at the center of which stood the original Empire State Building in all of its glory. Intact and fully restored to what it must have been like, surmised Justin, when it was finished in 1931. He spent the day in and around the ancient landmark, which now housed the New York Historical Society. For a fee individuals, groups, and schools could go into the building and experience life in various decades— depending on which floors they visited. For example, the sixties were represented on floors fifty-eight through sixty-seven. Those floors would all start their calendars on January 1, 1960, and continue day by day until December 31, 1969. The following day the floors would revert back to January 1, 1960. While the first years of the sixties were characterized by short hair and matching sideburns, the later years were characterized by the more wild and woolly look so well documented for that time period. The effect was made even more compelling by the reenactors found in every decade, dressed in the styles of the period, reading newspapers and magazines and working at the jobs that would have been appropriate for the time. The reenactors, Justin saw, were wonderfully imperfect. Some were underweight, others obese, still others were too short or had poor skin complexions. They all stood out in stark contrast to their perfected nanoized brethren living just outside the confines of the building. There were even apartments available for living, but only if the tenants were willing to live in a manner representative of the chosen floor's decade. Justin was touched and surprised that all the decades ended on December 31 of the ninth year except for the nineties. This worked out rather well with calibrating the floors, since the Empire State Building was not completed until late 1931, and the nineties, at least according to many historians, really ended on September 11, 2001—seen as the beginning of the end for Justin's world. He found out that crowds would flock to the ESC just to reexperience September 11, 2001, and other days of magnitude. For example, in the case of the sixties, the first Moon landing, or "where were you" moments like John F. Kennedy's assassination. Some reenactors, Justin was told, rarely, if ever, left the building, choosing instead to live in an idealized and imperfect view of the past.

To add sauce to the goose were specially designed holo-emitters fitted to every window. The emitters re-created the "outside" New York of each floor's time period.

Eventually word of Justin's presence leaked out, and members of the historical society approached him. They were overjoyed—not only for his inherent celebrity status, but because they were eager for him to inspect the eras of the building he was most familiar with and suggest corrections. And though he'd had his heart set on visiting the earlier decades, he relented and spent most of his time in the eighties, nineties, and the turn of the millennium accompanied by a gaggle of excited historians.

He was on the eighty-seventh floor planning a quick run up to the observation deck, but the seventies floors had been so inviting, and filled with so many things he'd recalled from his past, that he lingered and mingled with the reenactors for longer than planned. He picked up some *Time* and *Newsweek* magazines dated from June 1976, then flipped through the pages and chuckled at the ads—including one for 33⅓ RPM singles. He stopped by the small gift shop and eyed approvingly some of the candies he'd spent years attempting to ruin his teeth on. Snippets of conversation he picked up had to do with the inflation rate, and about whether to vote for Carter or Ford. He wasn't sure if the reenactors were putting on a command performance for his benefit or if it really was this authentic all the time. Though he suspected it was a little bit of both, the truth was, he didn't care. The idea of getting to experience the seventies all over again—this time as a full-grown adult—was so wonderfully appealing he could've stayed for days. He certainly could've stayed the night, given some of the offers that had rather forthrightly and era-appropriately come his way. But he rejected them, saving the pleasure perhaps for another day. In the meantime his eyes were delighted by the assault of lime-green polyester suits, wide lapels, bell-bottoms, platform shoes, and feathered-back hair. Feeling exhausted, and with only a few hours left in his day, Justin expressed to the curator of the floor an interest in moving up to the observation deck.

"Well, thank you very much for coming, Mr. Cord," the seventies curator said. He was a pleasant-looking man of average height, about thirty or so, sporting a goatee, long sideburns, and an oversized Afro. He'd finished off his ensemble with a powder blue leisure suit and some platform shoes.

"If you'd like," answered the ever helpful curator, "we can set the deck to any decade, or even year and season, you want. Though the view from the present-day deck is . . . well, psychedelic!" That got him a round of applause and a few chuckles.

Before Justin could answer he was bombarded with helpful suggestions from the crowd of twenty or so. He heard suggestions for every decade, but most were for the seventies, of course, though all seasons were shouted out equally.

"Thank you, thank you all for your help and kindness," he said earnestly, "but I think I'd like to see it 'as is,' if you will. I'd like to compare it with my memories of how it was the last time I was here."

That brought an appreciative and even envious sigh from the surrounding group. Justin then thanked the curator for keeping the press at bay while he toured the facilities.

"No probs, Mr. Cord. Truth is, we're not really down with the press, seeing how they bum on us all the time. We just powered up the null field, and that did the trick. Though I am afraid you'll be your own cat once you leave the environs of the historical society."

The curator was about to speak further when the elevator door behind Justin opened and, in addition to the lift's chime, he heard a gasp of surprise. He turned around to see a man emerge with his arm in an Ace bandage and sling. He was decidedly *not* in seventies garb, and his face was covered in a ski mask of sorts. The crowd around him seemed upset, and were muttering, "Bad form, not in the script." Instinctively, Justin ducked as the man slid his arm from the brace, revealing a long silver tube. A blast emanated from the cylinder in the direction of Justin's head.

Justin felt his teeth rattle and his vision blur at the edges.

"Neurolizer!" someone screamed. Justin sensed and heard rather than saw the two bodies hit the floor behind him like sacks of potatoes. The crowd responded in panic. If Justin had known what a neurolizer was he probably would've joined the fray, which would have given the assailant an easy couple of seconds to take a few more shots. But whether by instinct or by pluck, Justin did the opposite. He put his head down and charged the man, hitting him squarely in the chest. The gun flew out of the man's hand and back into the elevator as he and Justin, through inertia, followed its path—both of them hitting the elevator's back wall with a resounding thud. At that moment the elevator doors slammed shut, trapping them inside. While his opponent tried to use his fists to no effect, Justin used his knees and elbows, and then jammed his thumb into his assailant's eye. The man screamed in agony and rolled to his side. Justin was about to smash his fist into the man's face when he felt the swift, dull thud of a hand crashing down hard on his back. He wheeled around too late to see the blurred outline of another figure. Then all went dark.

"Wake up!" one of the voices shouted. When Justin failed to comply as quickly as expected he was treated to a hard slap across the face. The two men, Justin realized, had grabbed his arms that, without any strength coursing through them, felt like unwanted appendages rudely stuck to his side but annoyingly painful as the means by which they were holding him up.

He realized he was still in the elevator and that it was not moving. He was also glad to be alive.

Standing before him was the very same man who'd only moments before tried to take his life, the same man who'd surprised him in the elevator.

"I'll make this quick, Mr. Cord," the man said. "Contrary to what you might think, I meant *you* no harm."

"And the people you attacked?" spat Justin.

"Unfortunate," he answered, unconvincingly.

"What is it you want?" asked Justin, trying to buy time.

The man smiled knowingly. "Why, your very first share, of course. Unlike GCI, I'm not patient, nor do I have deep coffers. What I do have is this." He aimed the neurolizer at Justin's head. "You'll of course be able to argue that you gave it to me under duress, but what do I care? Even owning it for a few brief weeks while it's tied up in court and I'm at the nuthouse will make my stock rise enough to repair whatever damage they do to me on the psyche audit." He laughed the laugh of the unbalanced. Then, aiming the gun and holding out his DijAssist at the same time, he said, "Your thumbprint, please." On cue, the man behind him gave him a small shove to the back.

Justin spat on the pad the man had held out. "You don't need me for anything, you've got me at gunpoint. Why don't you just press the damned thing to my thumb and leave me the fuck alone?"

"Now that's not very gentlemanly, is it?" said the man as he grabbed Justin by the scruff of the neck. "First of all, the DijAssist can sense pressure of a voluntary nature. That means *you* have to put your thumb *on it*. I can't press it against the DijAssist. *It will know.*

"Second of all," he said, and then didn't complete his sentence, choosing instead to slam his fist onto the "open" button prominently displayed at the bottom of the elevator's bank of floor buttons. As the doors slid apart the man lifted

Justin up by his collar and pushed him out of the elevator onto the observation deck of the Empire State Building. Justin was momentarily struck by the brightness and noise of the new space. He could see the inside of the Empire State Center surrounding the Empire State Building. The magnificence of the view was lost on him as he tried desperately to figure a way out of his situation. Justin also saw that a cadre of securibots had descended onto the observation deck, making sure to keep a safe distance, and that a number of flying drones, presumably police of some sort, were circling the trio—*waiting to take a clean shot?* Justin wondered. The assailants, however, were keeping Justin close and constantly shifting their bodies so as to make the machines doubt, if such a thing was possible.

The two men dragged him over to the ledge of the building and then lifted him onto a precariously small wall. Next stop—street level, ninety-seven stories below.

"Don't think the floater field'll save your ass," yelled the man with the gun over the din of securibots barking orders and sirens wailing into the cavernous shell of the Empire State Center. "We've taken 'em out. Now," he continued, fixing his glare on Justin, "sign or die . . . doesn't matter to me, either way I'm famous." The assailant had Justin's shirt by the scruff and the neurolizer pointed at his forehead, pushing him farther over the edge. The gunslinger glanced briefly over to the other man, indicating that he extend the DijAssist for Justin to place his thumb on.

Justin, looking ever the terrified victim, nodded his head in agreement, and almost desperately put his thumb out to sign—but not far enough to reach the pad. It looked for all the world as if the fear of a ninety-seven-story plunge was preventing him from losing his already precarious balance.

The man with the gun stared hard at his partner. "Closer, you idiot!"

The second man extended the DijAssist closer, so that Justin could press his thumb against it. When Justin was certain that all eyes were focused on the point where his thumb was to meet the DijAssist, he overextended and grabbed the man by the wrist. In one fell swoop Justin dropped onto his backside, pulling the unsuspecting brute onto his body. Then, in quick succession, he rolled himself and the man over the ledge, into the thin, processed air of the Empire State Center. At the last moment Justin reached out and grabbed the ledge while his horrified assailant fell past—a screaming human cannonball. During the melee the man holding the gun had instinctively let go of Justin's shirt so as not to fall down with his prisoner, but it had taken only a few seconds for him to regain his wits and balance. He leveled the neurolizer at Justin, who was now hanging on to the ledge by his fingers, feet dangling precariously. Before the man could squeeze the trigger he was vaporized by the securibots, who finally had an open shot.

The pain in Justin's backside—the result of his dropkick onto the concrete ledge—stabbed so sharply up his spine that he wondered if he'd been hit by friendly fire. The last thing he recalled was the strength in his fingers giving out and the freefall that followed as his spent body dropped into the void, with only the fading distant roof of the Empire State Center as a last vision. And then, once again, his world went dark.

Dr. Thaddeus Gillette was a well-dressed man approximately 103 years old, but not looking a day over 35. In his line of business, "slightly older-looking" was the style society found most befitting. Not that Thaddeus cared much about what society wanted, but it was so much a part of the norm that he hadn't given it a second thought. So when he became a distinguished professor, he promptly went to the nearest body modification center and aged himself another thirteen years. He had black curly hair with a sprinkle of gray in the sideburns, brown deep-sunken eyes, and the tired look of a man who had too many papers to grade, too many lectures to give, and not enough hours in the day. And now he found himself in the heart of the Big Apple, in a skyscraper somewhere on the 307th floor, in front of a door leading into a luxury apartment inhabited by the man who by all rights should have been his patient to begin with. *Strange world,* he thought. Via his DijAssist he briefly reviewed the news footage of Justin's press conference. He paid attention to the end, where the world saw Justin launching himself at Hektor and having to be forcibly restrained from beating him to a pulp, while this Sambianco fellow, Thaddeus noted, was the smiling picture of contentment—even with the threat of Justin's restrained fists mere centimeters from pummeling him further. He was curious about Hektor's apparent indifference—or was it satisfaction?— but wanted to check with Dr. Harper first before saying anything to Director McKenzie and his colleagues. The other thing Justin noticed was that it was Dr. Harper who had managed to calm him down. Thaddeus watched the vid as the Cord fellow listened to her—allowed her to get through to him. What was not obvious on the recording, and what he desperately prayed he was wrong about, was the way Dr. Harper felt about Justin Cord. Thaddeus was trained to read the subtlest forms of body language, and even he was not sure. But he thought he saw something. For now it was just a suspicion. Though rare, it wouldn't be the first time that a reanimationist had feelings for a patient. After all, it was only natural to be protective. It was the disastrous result that history had proven would follow that was decidedly unnatural. He made a mental note to bring it up with Dr. Harper. When he was ready he put away his DijAssist and placed his palm over the doorbell. The entrance melted away almost immediately, and Thaddeus found himself face-to-face with an apprehensive but clearly relieved Neela Harper.

"Thank you for coming," Neela said.

"My dear young and skilled Dr. Harper, thank *you* for inviting me. I can assure you that I have no objections to being made a part of history."

Neela smiled politely and led the doctor to a large living room area, indicating a chair for him to sit in.

"Speaking of which," continued Thaddeus, "can this eminent yet thirsty historical figure bother you for a glass of iced tea?" He then sat down.

"Of course, Doctor," answered Neela.

After she returned with the drinks and handed Thaddeus his iced tea, she sat down on a couch across from Thaddeus. A small coffee table separated them.

She continued, "The only problem was convincing Justin that I needed to consult with you."

"So you have established trust?" Thaddeus asked.

"As much as Justin can trust, yes, I have. Though I suspect it's more in the nature of a security blanket rather than as a guide. To be quite honest, I often feel like a glorified DijAssist."

"Dr. Harper," answered Thaddeus, all smiles, "you've done a marvelous job in the most difficult case I have ever seen. No one could have foreseen the travails you've encountered, including outright sabotage."

Neela smiled back in appreciation, and Gillette could see that this was a person in desperate need of a talk. It was also obvious to him that she was in danger of burning out.

"I'm also very impressed that you called me," he added.

"I can see," responded Neela, "that you have a high regard for yourself, Doctor."

"I deserved that," he agreed merrily. "What I was trying to say is that many a young revivalist in your position would have tried to do this all on their own, in an attempt to gain all the credit. You did not—showing, in my opinion, great presence of mind. Though I would be lying if I said I would be as pleased if you had called Dr. Bronstein."

"I may be good, Dr. Gillette, but I'm not stupid enough to think that talent makes up for experience—which I know you have in droves. With regards to Dr. Bronstein; while brilliant, I suspect he believes in theories too much, usually his own. From what I've read about you, and from your own reports, I gathered that you would be more open to extraenvironmental inputs—of which I can assure you there will be many."

"My dear girl," answered the doctor, "I think that is the nicest way of saying 'you make it up as you go' that I have ever heard. And please call me Thaddeus."

"Very well, Thaddeus, but only if you call me Neela."

"Done," he answered, smiling amiably. "Let me just reiterate that I believe you're doing very well. Remember that there has never been a case like this, and likely never will be again. You're as much an expert here as I am, and indeed, more so."

Until that moment Neela had been carrying the lion's share—feeling overwhelmed and underqualified. The doctor's remarks not only helped validate her feelings; his mere presence allowed her to look forward to some much needed respite.

She quietly sipped her drink. For a few brief seconds only the sound of ice cubes against glass broke the silence.

"Could I ask you a . . . personal question?" asked Thaddeus.

"First of all, Dr. Gill . . . Thaddeus, you don't have to ask me that question . . . ever again. Just ask. Second of all, of course."

"You must try not to take offense," he said, prepping her for the second part of his question. Too late, he saw. "Exactly how much 'trust' have you established with Mr. Cord?" His implication was obvious. Neela began to bridle.

"Please forgive me, Neela, but I saw something on the video of the assault that concerned me. Correct me if I'm wrong here, please. It's just the way you looked at him, spoke to him, that's all. If I suspect it, others will, too."

Neela counted to five and let out a deep breath. "To answer your question," she said, with no small amount of fortitude, "I did not gain his trust *that* way."

Thaddeus watched and listened but still wasn't satisfied. Some itches needed to be scratched, others eliminated outright. Until he was satisfied that he'd been incorrect in his assumption, he'd push a little further.

"We're colleagues in this, Neela," he implored. "What you say to me here will be just as confidential as if Justin—or any patient for that matter—had said it."

Neela weighed her answer. Even if the silence incriminated her, what she was considering revealing were words and thoughts that no one in their right mind would dream of uttering. "She seemed like such a nice girl," she imagined her neighbors saying. "Always a kind word . . . I never would have believed . . ." All such thoughts ran through her head as she decided whether or not to speak the unspeakable. But in the end she realized she needed to talk to someone—anyone—about what she was experiencing, if only to help her sort through and expunge it from her system. She was tired. Tired of feeling dirty—tired of being confused. Who better to confess to than the reanimation specialist par excellence, Thaddeus Gillette?

"I did not develop trust like *that,*" she repeated, answering in a whispered tone—conciliatory. "But may Damsah forgive me for saying this . . . I . . . I wanted to."

Her shoulders sagged at the confession.

Thaddeus said nothing—ever attentive.

"I can't believe I am saying this," she continued, pursing her lips tightly, almost as if they were expelling bile. "It goes against everything I was taught and believe. If someone had told me I would feel that way about a patient of mine . . . *of mine,* I would have issued a challenge right then and there. If I'd found out about another reanimationist who felt what I'm feeling now, I would've had nothing but contempt for them. But try as I might, Thaddeus, I look at him sometimes . . . the way he says something, I swear sometimes it's how he smells . . . and my thoughts are not professional, not professional at all."

She put her glass down on the table and put her head in her hands, hunched over, fingers forming lines through her scalp.

"What's wrong with me?" she pleaded, staring down at the coffee table.

Dr. Gillette got up from his seat, sat down beside her on the couch, and gently patted her shoulder. She looked up and locked her eyes onto his, desperately waiting for salvation.

"Yours is a problem of great concern, I must admit. But," he said, offering her a glimmer of hope, "not as unexpected as you would imagine."

"How so?"

"Three reasons, my dear," he answered, sliding a little farther back, recreating an acceptable space between them on the couch. "First, you're very young and new at your job to have to face a challenge of this magnitude. I reviewed your record. Because you had such a great skill and inclination for this work you were made a primary at a very young age. You should have been sent to a major facility, where you would have been assigned to a team as a secondary having little contact with clients. Had you joined me, and I can assure you I would've been glad to get you, you would not have been a primary until you were at least well into your fifties."

"So being sent to Boulder was a compliment?"

"You weren't sent. More like 'plucked.' Didn't you find it strange that the colleague you were paired with was middle-aged—early seventies, if I recall?"

She nodded in the affirmative.

"My guess is that this director of yours, Mr. McKenzie, knew exactly what he was doing when he snatched you from the university and made you a primary, albeit at a small facility and at a very young age."

Neela mulled it over. It had a certain amount of logic to it, and Lord knows she was more than happy to take any validation she could get, given her present state of decrepitude.

"Two," continued Thaddeus, "there has never been a patient like our Mr. Cord—ever."

Neela said nothing. Eyes steadfast.

"Indeed," continued Thaddeus, "he makes our most impressive, intriguing clients seem about as interesting as a shoe. This of course leads to reason number three."

As if to give the point more austerity, he put the empty glass that he'd been absentmindedly holding down on the table and cleared his throat.

"Justin is not from our world. The greatest safety net a reanimationist has is that their patient is a willing partner in society's psychological barriers; knows in his heart of hearts a reanimationist/patient relationship is wrong—no, *evil*. Thousands of subtle cues over a lifetime of learning build that all-important wall of separation between our patients and us."

Neela nodded, allowing the doctor's words to act as a salve.

"But," he continued, "Justin does not come from our era. He doesn't render any cues of caution and disgust for the simple reason that he doesn't feel them. From the vids I've seen of you both during your few weeks together, I would have to say that he feels quite the opposite. In fact, I would venture to say that he's strongly attracted to you."

"Yes, we've discussed it. And," she said, rising to her own defense, "I told him in no uncertain terms, 'No.' "

"And good that you did," he answered. "So, given everything I've just said, what you've revealed to me today and the feelings you're currently struggling with are, though on the surface deviant in nature, actually somewhat normal.

"Well," he added, correcting himself, "as normal as this situation allows. Think about it, Neela. A fascinating, powerful, and remarkable man is expressing subtle but near constant interest in you. It would be *unnatural* if it didn't invite a mutual feeling."

Thaddeus saw that his explanations had hit their intended mark. Neela looked visibly relieved. Lest she hang her hat on redemption for too long, Thaddeus swung the counterpunch.

"But mark my words, Neela, *it must not be allowed to turn into anything*. We must not only protect you, we must protect our client—especially from himself."

Putting words into action, he began to immediately scan the room for telltale signs of a woman's presence.

None. That was good.

Still, he felt compelled to ask.

"Do you live here?"

"Of course not," retorted Neela, bridling once more. "He rented an apartment for me next door."

"Good, but not good enough. Will you take my advice in this matter?"

"Of course, Dr. Gill . . . Thaddeus. What do you want me to do?"

"First, you must move out of the apartment. I will take it over. You'll get a place at least three kilometers away. But the farther the better."

"But we spend so much time together, and I . . ."

"Of course," he said, cutting her off, "I will maintain a guest room in my/your apartment here. If you happen to spend far more of your nights there than at your own place, then that is what will be."

Neela seemed satisfied with the compromise. "Won't people think that you and I might be, well, you know?"

"I hope they do," he answered, smiling brightly. "If they're looking at us they hopefully won't be looking at you, or, more specifically, you and Justin. This will be of great use to our client, though he may not know it. And, I must admit that if people thought I could attract as charming a lover as you, it would not hurt my reputation, or love life, either."

It was uttered so disarmingly and with such innocence, Neela realized that it was not a come-on, and took it for the compliment it was meant to be. Maybe it wouldn't be such a bad arrangement after all.

"What is the second thing you need me to do, Thaddeus?"

"Quit."

"But . . ."

"Fear not, my dear," he interrupted, putting his finger up. "You will no longer be working for Justin. Assuming that he agrees, your contract will be transferred to me, and I will officially hire you as a member of my staff. I'll make sure to put in a clause that you'll receive your full salary and independent publishing rights, but we must put some legal distance between you and Mr. Cord. I'm sure he'll understand the necessity of that."

Neela looked around the room, not for the last time, but at least with a look that was meant to rid her of any silly notions of taking up residence with her derelict fantasies.

"Agreed," she answered. "I'll explain it to him tonight after dinner."

"Excellent. Now, if you can help me with understanding our Mr. Cord, there is something that I cannot quite figure out."

She was relieved. It was only a matter of time, and the ever-present ear of the gentlemanly Thaddeus Gillette, that assured her that her "natural" feelings toward Justin would dissipate, and with them her feelings of guilt and shame.

"It'll be nice to get down to our real business," she answered. "How can I help?"

Thaddeus gave Neela a look of reassurance, and then plowed ahead, objectives to be met, work to be done.

"Why the violent reaction at the end of the press conference—the actual lunging for Hektor and needing to be restrained by, not one, but a handful of bodyguards? Doesn't make sense given what I know about Mr. Cord . . . past and present."

"My theory?" answered Neela. "Justin was attacked, and he attacked back."

"Attacked, you say? It must be very primal."

"It is. First understand that what you consider 'freedom' and what he considers 'freedom' are two almost diametrically opposing beliefs. Having said that, know that Justin considers himself a free man. It's his whole identity. He would die, and I think even kill, to maintain that freedom."

"And incorporation?"

"Tantamount to slavery. On the surface he seems curious and accepting of it, but deep down in his gut, when he hears 'incorporation' he *feels* 'slavery.' "

"So," said Thaddeus, "Mr. Sambianco's attempt to force incorporation via the courts was, in fact, an attack."

"To Justin it would be as if someone was trying to put a chain around his neck or brand him with an old-fashioned cattle iron. I don't think he realized just how strongly he felt about it until he lost control. Add to that the fact that they have a history."

Neela went on to explain Hektor's initial attempt to first trick and then force Justin into incorporating, and how her fortuitous timing had stymied his plans.

"Shameful, shameful. Not good. And, incidentally—it also means you've saved Justin twice," muttered Gillette. "Explains a lot."

Neela said nothing, but she realized just how bad this could be. Everyone was incorporated, and Justin had to come to some accommodation with that fact or be forever exiled from society. She was only now beginning to realize how his old-world definition of freedom wasn't just semantic, it was intrinsic. He couldn't live without it. Further, that Justin's views of freedom weren't just out of sync; they were dangerous. And so she swore to herself that she would do whatever it took to change the man, for better or for worse.

It was then that a call came through. Neela raised her hand to her ear and answered.

"What is it?" asked Thaddeus, seeing the blood drain from his newest hire's face.

"Justin's fallen off the Empire State Building."

When Justin's eyes fluttered back to life it was in a hospital surrounded by a coterie of doctors, police, and technicians. But there was only one face he was truly glad to see.

"You know I can't keep waking you up," Neela said, smiling down on him, rolling her eyes. "It's starting to get a little boring."

"Yes . . . yes, you can," he replied, awkwardly lifting his hand up for her to take. She looked around uncomfortably, and then took it into hers. It would not be considered inappropriate, she reasoned. No one gave her a look. She allowed herself to admit it felt good.

When Justin was done answering the questions as well as having his own answered, he realized just how lucky he'd been. The weapon used to threaten him was called a neurolizer. It was designed specifically to cause permanent death by scrambling a person's neural network connections, leaving the brain dead and, for all intents and purposes, the owner of that brain a vegetable; the man Justin had thrown over the side of the building had suffered a permanent death as a result of the fall. In short, there had been nothing left to reconstitute. Fortunately, there had been no bystanders to land on, as the area had been cleared once "the incident," as it was being reported across the system, had come to the attention of those responsible for the ESC's security; the man with the gun had been an immediate threat to Justin's being and was eliminated without prejudice, a young lieutenant had informed him. And no, they couldn't have just knocked him out. Not knowing what sorts of precautions or defenses the assailant may have taken resulted in a hard, fast decision that had not boded well for the recently obliterated Marcelius Henklebee, who had been unmarried and led an uneventful life—quiet sort. Who knew? The lieutenant shrugged his shoulders again. As for Justin, he was "one lucky sonavabitch, don't ya know?" Seems they managed to get the floater field reactivated approximately forty feet from impact, slowing Justin's descent appreciably enough to prevent him from becoming street pizza.

"Impact?" asked Justin.

The lieutenant nodded and smiled.

Neela was waiting for him as he checked out of the hospital and, with a police escort in tow, took him home. He needed it. His experience on the observation deck was not just being reported, it was being systemcast. Multiple recorders from the apartments and shops above the Empire State Building had seen and heard everything.

He was not so pleased to learn that Neela had found a much less expensive apartment in the Jersey borough, and was even less pleased to learn that a man he'd never met was moving in next door. Still, in the course of an evening he came to like Thaddeus Gillette. Although Justin knew that it was the doctor's training to be attentive, questioning, and amiable, he still had to admit he liked the guy. Once Justin had spent enough time, drank a few beers, and discussed the situation with the good doctor, the importance of Neela not living next door was understood, if not felt. But that wasn't the change that bothered him the most.

It was having to hire a security agency to protect him, watch his back, approve his itinerary, and check his food. Perhaps he'd been naïve, thinking he'd just pop out of his high-tech casket and resume the life of a regular Joe in an idealized future. Perhaps. Either way, the new security precautions had reminded him of one thing, and one thing only—a life he'd left behind.

5   First Trial

Hektor was standing in front of a very long table. It was clear to the point of invisibility and supported by nothing but air—or, to be more precise, a hidden magnetic antigravitational device. Were it not for the various DijAssists, papers, pads, and pointing devices strewn across its surface, one might walk right into it.

He was the only one standing.

The rest of the board members gathered around the table were sitting stiffly, aware that their every move and phrase was being, or would be, watched and listened to. Each member had one or two assistants sitting behind him or her, ready to whisper salient information when called to do so. And each board member was addressed by their title and not their name. They were Publicity, GenOPs, Legal, and Accounting. At the head of the table, sitting opposite Hektor, was Kirk Olmstead, the deputy director of the powerful Special Operations branch of GCI, otherwise known as the DepDir. Conspicuously absent was the DepDir's personal assistant. Hektor was disappointed. He'd been drawn to her ice-queen looks and demeanor. But he had other things to worry about, chief of which was the fact that he found himself in front of a corporate firing squad in the guise of an unofficial board meeting—"unofficial" because The Chairman was not physically present. However, if the meeting's outcome met with The Chairman's approval, then it would be entered into the logs as "official," and all the minutes and decisions would be acted upon. If he did not approve, changes would be made. And if he really disapproved, chairs could be emptied. No one presently sitting at the table thought there'd be any disagreement with the anticipated outcome of the day's meeting. They'd discuss the facts, gather what information they could from Mr. Sambianco, and then chart a course toward rectification. But that didn't negate the fact that Hektor Sambianco, once respected as an up-and-coming corporate strategist, was now to be viewed with contempt and, should any of the board members be so inclined, pity.

Publicity spoke first.

"Disaster, an absolute disaster. We've got the biggest, most sought-after name in the system making us out as some kind of corporate monster attempting to steal him away forever."

"Forever's a bit long," Hektor said, ignoring Publicity's hysterics. "More like four or five years."

The corners of Publicity's mouth began to twitch as he focused his rage on Hektor. "What's that supposed to mean?"

"Enough," the DepDir interrupted, "and Hektor, do us all a favor and shut up."

Hektor tilted his head in acknowledgment.

"What we need," continued the DepDir, "is to keep the proper perspective on this. With all due respect to Publicity, we *are* a corporation and our goal *is* to make money for our shareholders. And even though Hektor's behavior has forced GCI into a course we would not normally have taken, we may as well take advantage of it."

Publicity began to protest, but the DepDir put up his hand to stop her.

"Accounting," he said, "just out of curiosity, how much money is Justin Cord worth?"

Accounting, a soft-spoken African woman, spoke up. "He is priceless. We cannot calculate his value because there are too many unknowns, but it is without a doubt that he is potentially the most valuable human being in the system."

"And we don't have a single share!" shouted GenOps, a florid-faced, sandy-haired man who had the uninspired yet de rigueur look of fitness so common to nanobuilt bodies. "This is intolerable."

"For that we can blame Hektor." The DepDir's comment elicited general grunts of agreement to which Hektor had the good grace to remain silent.

"But," continued the DepDir, "we can rectify the future. I repeat, our goal is to make money for the stockholders, and the only reason any of us are here," he said, pausing to stare markedly at Hektor, "is because we *can* make money. So again, let's just view this as a moneymaking procedure." The DepDir looked toward Legal.

"How's the lawsuit going?"

Before Legal could answer, Hektor held up a dataplaque and gestured that he was ready to present.

"Yes, Mr. Sambianco?" answered Legal, glad to deflect the question even if only for a few minutes. She could see she'd pissed off the DepDir, but he wasn't her boss yet, and until then she'd use her authority to cement that fact. Besides, she figured, Hektor had started this damned lawsuit, let him take some more heat for it. And if she could've done something worse to him than what Kirk was obviously planning she would have felt compelled to try. How dare he start a legal proceeding without her.

"Yes, ma'am," answered Hektor. "As all of you may already realize, I was the one who instituted the lawsuit."

Per corporate chess, the blank stares of the people in the room neither denied nor confirmed whether they knew it or not.

"And," continued Hektor, "I managed to get it onto the court dockets quickly. It should keep us engaged with Justin for quite a while."

"It is not a good idea," answered Publicity, "to keep him 'engaged,' young man. Every day we're mentioned with him makes us look bad. And that does amount to," she said pointedly looking away from Hektor and toward the DepDir, "what I'm sure is a substantial credit loss, which is why I think we should cancel this lawsuit immediately."

Publicity looked around and saw that there were heads nodding in agreement.

"I don't mean to be rude," Hektor answered, "but canceling the suit would not be the correct way to handle this."

"Oh really, Mr. Sambianco?" seethed Publicity. "And how would you, with all your years of experience, handle this? Drag it out for all it's worth, even though we're probably going to lose?"

"Why, yes, ma'am, that's exactly what I'd do."

This brought a round of mutterings concerning Hektor's mental fitness. It didn't last long. Accounting came to his rescue.

"How can you justify such a position, Mr. Sambianco?"

Hektor exhaled. "Cord's a nutcase. OK, he's a damned popular nutcase, but he's still a nutcase. Remember how easy it was to push his buttons at the press conference?"

"Oh, yes," Publicity chimed in sarcastically, "it did us a world of good to see a duly recognized member of GCI harass the most popular man in the system."

"It will," shot back Hektor, enjoying the fact that expendability let him speak his mind. "I'll grant you Cord's popular now, but in a couple of months he'll be pissing people off. And when that happens they'll remember that we were never afraid of him. And, I might add, when that happens we'll force him to settle . . . at a more preferable percentage."

Hektor could see one of Publicity's assistants whispering something into her ear.

"According to the Spencer ratings," Publicity stated, "Justin Cord will remain popular for years if not decades to come."

The Spencer ratings had developed as marketing became more of a science and less of an art. It was known for making extremely accurate predictions of trends and fads as well as of shifts in consumer interest. In the last fifty years it had become as indispensable to ad men as quadratic equations were to mathematicians.

"Forget the Spencer ratings," scoffed Hektor. "They won't work concerning Justin Cord."

"I will do no such thing!" screamed Publicity. "You're not even a member of this board. I don't know why we're even bothering with you."

"You're 'bothering with me,'" Hektor answered calmly, "because I was detached from Special Operations"—he then smiled acidly in the DepDir's direction—"and assigned as a special adviser to the board. And, I repeat, since we're already well into it, my advice is to drag out the pretrial motions. We can't get a favorable ruling in court, but we can still win. Justin will say and do things to piss off the public. He can't help it; he doesn't like the whole idea of incorporation—an idea, I might add, that is fundamental to all the values we as a society hold sacred. So when Wonder Boy starts mouthing off against this, the heart of our civilization, we'll do just fine."

"He's got enough money to hire the best lawyers in the system," fired back Publicity. "What makes you think *they're* going to let him mouth off?"

"He can't help himself," answered Hektor. "He says what he thinks."

"If only he were the only one," muttered the DepDir loudly enough for all to hear. This got the room laughing, Hektor included.

"However, we're all forgetting," continued the DepDir, "about what's important here—the money. Who gives a damn about civilizations and values? Our job is still to bring a profit. If we get some of Justin's stock we'll not only be richer, we'll also have the option of invoking audits and other means of control over him."

"What basis," asked Accounting, "do we have for getting any shares of his stock?"

All heads now turned toward Legal.

"We will use in loco parentis," she answered, then appeared to brace herself for what she knew was coming.

"What?" asked several members of the board simultaneously.

"There is precedent," she continued. "When a child is suspended, and then through some tragedy loses both sets of parents, the nearest relative can take over the raising of the child, and therefore be entitled to the 20 percent parental stock award."

Accounting looked befuddled. "That's quite a stretch. I mean, we're talking about the difference between a child who's incorporated and an adult who's not."

More heads nodded in agreement.

"Allow me to finish," said Legal, slightly annoyed at having been interrupted. "The precedent was used to award in loco parentis to American Express when they revived Israel Taylor Schwartz. For those of you not familiar with the case, approximately eighty years ago a man was ready to be reanimated. He had been frozen in suspension, having suffered a terrible head injury. Because he was from the early days of the incorporation movement he, in all likelihood, would have remembered the Grand Collapse. An enticing prospect for our historians, indeed, but only if he could be revived successfully. American Express used what were then considered to be cutting-edge techniques to attempt neuro-pathway reconstruction. In return they were awarded not only the 20 percent parental bonus, they were also able to charge Mr. Schwartz for the considerable cost of his revival. Sadly, the procedure did not work as hoped, and Mr. Schwartz awoke a congenital idiot. By the time they reworked his neural pathways almost all of his memories and personality traits had been wiped clean. Which brings us back to loco parentis. Israel Taylor Schwartz, ladies and gentlemen, was, by all legal definitions, a child."

"But," asked Publicity, "didn't we already charge Mr. Cord for the expenses incurred in his reanimation? Couldn't he claim our losses have been covered?"

"In that you are correct," answered the DepDir. "Hektor made out a bill for ten million credits and someone actually paid it."

The board dutifully responded by glaring anew at Hektor.

Hektor mumbled, "You make one little mistake . . ." Then, louder: "How is the investigation going on that, DepDir? Have you found the person responsible for paying out the debt?"

Hektor's momentary diversion worked, as the board turned their attention back to the DepDir.

"I thought," parried the DepDir, "that you had some leads *you* were running down . . . Hektor?"

"I am," Hektor volleyed back, "but I don't have the resources of your department, nor your experience in such matters, DepDir or, should I say, 'acting director of Special Ops'?"

"DepDir's fine," Kirk snarled, "and thank you for your confidence, Mr. Sambianco, but tracing who paid the ten million credits has been reassigned from my department and given to Accounting."

The board turned to Accounting while all the heads were busy trying to calculate what that meant in terms of their careers. Did Accounting manage to steal the job from Special Ops? If so, then that meant that Accounting was more powerful than they'd thought. Or had the DepDir managed to push this off onto Accounting? Which would mean that it was a dead-end assignment and Accounting didn't have the power to avoid it. Or did The Chairman move it from one department to the other? That would be bad for Special Ops and could be bad for Accounting . . . if her department failed. But as both Accounting and the DepDir were old hands at this game, their faces showed nothing except mutual respect (which was felt) and trust (which was not).

"I'm still not following the in loco parentis, Legal," continued the DepDir. "Mr. Cord did not wake up an idiot. Au contraire, he appears to be quite cognizant."

"Yes, that's true, but we can claim that we are his only true legal guardians, and that his adaptation back into society has been at our expense. Yes, the revival itself was covered, but he's spent a considerable amount of time at our facility, with our specialists, getting, much like Mr. Schwartz, reacclimated to our new world. So while we won't take over full 'parenting' of Mr. Cord, it is within reason, based on precedent, that we can claim a limited percentage of him."

Publicity seemed content with the answer.

"Well done, Legal," the DepDir said.

He turned toward Accounting.

"Accounting, you stated that Mr. Cord was priceless. But say you were to put a credit amount on his head. What would you guess?"

"An even billion," she answered, without batting an eye, "but you could double or even quadruple that easily."

"Let's take the billion-credit figure," said the DepDir. "Twenty percent of a billion is two hundred million. So if we deduct the ten million he paid us, and then go with an opening request of 19 percent of Justin Cord's stock, we'd be doing alright, correct?"

Accounting nodded.

"I'd guess," continued the DepDir, "that we could even bargain him down to 10 percent if we had to. We'd still be doing better than we were . . . before the mess." The DepDir finished this off by again staring pointedly at Hektor.

Hektor started to ignore the fact that everyone glared at him. But that didn't stop him from challenging what he felt was everyone's wrong assumptions about Justin.

"What in the world," asked Hektor, "makes you think he'd settle out of court?"

"Hektor, be real," answered Accounting. "It's the logical thing to do. From Mr. Cord's point of view, he'll have won."

"Hektor," added the DepDir, "we're going to let him 'force' us down to 10 percent. That means he'll own more of himself than almost any other person alive. It will be the greatest victory in the history of personal incorporation. How could he *not* settle?"

It was at that moment that Hektor realized the extent of the problem. Logical reasoning, something he was good at, would not work in this room, because no one in this room except for himself understood Justin. Further, no one in the room could fathom the idea that a person might not want to be incorporated. As the board members chatted among themselves, Hektor began to realize the vast implications a Cord victory would have—not only to all those people present, but also, he suspected, to society as a whole. A man who could defeat the incorporation system, or worse, paint it in a negative light, was a man to be feared. Hektor Sambianco was afraid—not of losing his career (the odds were always against him), but of what could happen if the board went after Justin and failed. He had to warn them.

"Wait a minute," he blurted out, "you're forgetting something vital here. Justin . . ." Before he could finish his sentence, a red light flashed on the table. All attention was riveted on it.

The flashing red light indicated only one thing—an imminent visit by The Chairman. From the center of the table an empty circle formed, and from that circle a clear holo-image of The Chairman appeared. For Hektor, who'd only ever seen pictures of the man, even the presence of his holo-image was unnerving. Of course, Hektor was only viewing him from the back, but still, it was as close to "live" as he figured he'd ever get. What he did see was the broad stiff shoulders of a man who appeared to be in his early forties and the back of a head full of thick salt-and-pepper hair. What he also saw was the fixed, almost fearful eyes of Kirk Olmstead, acting deputy director of GCI. The Chairman, Hektor realized, was looking directly at the DepDir, though as far as each board member was concerned, The Chairman might as well have been looking directly at them.

The voice speaking was that of a man who knew he would not be interrupted. It was deeply resonant, yet mellifluous. It carried such confidence and authority that to ignore it or disregard it would be unthinkable. It was a voice that could terrify if angry and mollify if pleased. Today the voice sounded pleased.

"Mr. Olmstead," said The Chairman, "I have been listening in, and I approve of your plan. Not only that, but I think you have demonstrated the ability to assume full responsibility of your position. I call a vote of the board to promote Kirk Olmstead from acting to V.P. of Special Operations. All in favor?"

The vote was unanimous.

Hektor watched the proceeding with a bit of regret, as he had sold all of his shares in Kirk to buy his own. But mostly it meant the crushing end of his career. All his cards had been played, all his smokescreens dissolved. After the vote The Chairman offered his congratulations to Kirk and faded from view. The board looked at Kirk with new respect and, in some justified cases, fear. But one thing was certain—the debate concerning the lawsuit against Justin Cord was officially over, and Kirk's victory was overwhelming.

The DepDir stood up and, as was befitting his newfound authority, all in the room followed suit.

"I think," he said, "we can adjourn the meeting. Hektor, could you see me in my office?" It was not a question. Hektor had the grace to simply nod and head out. He also had enough poise not to be upset when forced to wait for three hours in the DepDir's antechamber. He knew what had to be done. Kirk Olmstead had just become one of the most important men in the entire solar system, and was therefore making and receiving a lot of very important calls. In all likelihood he was also preparing to move into his new office. According to protocol it would be one level just below The Chairman's penthouse suite.

In a weird way, thought Hektor, it was kind of flattering that Kirk would take the time to dress him down and boot him out. Kirk could easily have given that dubious task over to his pretty secretary, which Hektor would not have minded. But his fight with Kirk was personal, after all, and as such it needed Kirk's personal touch. Hektor knew he would have done the same.

"DepDir will see you now," came a voice from nowhere.

Hektor got up and waited for the doors in front of him to open. He stood facing them for fifteen minutes before they finally dissipated; revealing the new vice president of Special Operations sitting behind what Hektor figured was probably a bigger desk than he'd had an hour before.

Kirk scowled.

"I told you not to lose, Hektor."

"I know. Let's get it over with."

"Your position with the board," said Kirk, "is terminated. You're being assigned as a corporate representative to the Oort observatory. We have a contract to supply key components to the government project and need to have a man on the scene to make sure nothing goes wrong. If all goes well the project should be done in, oh, say, twenty years."

"Ow."

Hektor was impressed. He'd be out of the way for over two decades in a place that could be described as about as far out as one could go. It would take months just to get there. He also knew that Kirk would arrange it so that he'd get no vacations or transfers. Hektor realized that he was going to be Kirk's opening warning shot to everyone else at GCI—don't mess with Olmstead or you'll end up like Sambianco.

"Of course," continued Kirk, "you'll only be earning about a third of what you're making now. Good Lord," he said, peering into his holo-screen, "I see you recently put a large amount of money on your credit account. I'd imagine, when the companies begin to realize you won't be able to pay it back, they'll demand a stock sale. It's a shame that your stock will sell for so little. Still, with luck, I'm sure you'll manage to hold on to 1 or 2 percent more than the 25 percent minimum. You'll be happy to know I've had my secretary contact the markets about your new position, so they'll be able to adjust to the new reality. Now, get out."

Hektor was unmoved. "Let me just say one thing, Olmstead."

"Why should I?" groused the new boss. "You lost."

"I worked for you for a long time, Kirk. I was there for the Titan project when we were hip-deep in getting the government contracts for the Oort observatory."

"You want to call all that in just so you can say *one* thing?"

"Yeah."

Kirk considered it. "I'll tell you what, Sambianco. Don't burden me with your crap and I'll change your orders to one of our stations around Neptune. You'll still be in the boonies, but at least you'll have a bar to drink in and a whorehouse to visit."

Kirk peered again into his holodisplay. "And according to the latest census, about thirty million people or thereabouts in the Neptune area to listen to your bullshit."

Hektor was stuck. His first instinct was to take the deal by turning around and walking out. There was a huge difference between being with millions of people for twenty years and being trapped with a couple thousand. But Olmstead was making a huge mistake concerning Justin, and Hektor knew it. If only to be able to say "I told you so" later, Hektor canned the deal.

"Fine, Olmstead, if it's gonna cost me twenty years of misery, then listen up."

Kirk shook his head in disbelief, and motioned for Hektor to continue. His funeral.

"Don't be fooled, Kirk. Justin Cord is the devil incarnate. And I'm not talking about the kind with horns and a pointy tail. He's far more insidious. I'll admit he's a likable, charismatic bastard, but don't make the mistake of thinking of him as one of us. He isn't. Mark my words, Kirk. All the problems and the faults that brought about the Grand Collapse are made manifest in Justin Cord. He'll bring all of that crap back if we don't stop him. In fact, I wish that maniac at the ESC had killed him."

"Don't be a bigger fool than you already are," answered Kirk, angry at himself for allowing the pitiful conversation to drag on. "Cord's of no value to us dead. How would we settle with a dead man?"

"*Justin Cord will not settle!*" exclaimed Hektor, shaking his head. "He can't. He'll fight, scream, and yell. What you consider a great deal and a huge victory Justin Cord will consider defeat and surrender. Worse, if you go to court with that loco parentis thing, you'll lose, and you'll lose big. And when you do, it will make Justin the David who successfully stood up to the biggest corporation in human history and won. He will be victorious *and* unincorporated. What will nuts like the Majority Party do with that, I wonder? Then we'll *all* have a problem. And when I say 'all,' I don't mean just GCI; I'm talking all of us incorporated folk. Look it over and see it from Justin's point of view. Please, for all our sakes. Justin's a fluke now, but if this gets screwed up he could become an incredibly dangerous fluke."

"Done?" Kirk asked.

Hektor knew it had been pointless. "Done."

Though it was an expression whose mechanics no longer existed, Kirk used the phrase he felt most warranted Hektor's exit.

"Don't let the door hit you on the way out."

It's official. Justin Cord and company have moved into the oh-so-famous, luxurious, and private 71+ in Old Town New York. Only the most of the most can even apply to live there, but Justin was invited, and someone who knows culture and style wisely told this blast from the past to accept the invitation.

—NEWS CLIP FROM CELEBRITY UPDATE

"Omad, how on Earth could you have drunk my last beer?" Justin was looking in the refrigerator and finding everything a man could want, in fact finding many things that defied description—except a beer.

"Oh, that," answered Omad, ambling into the kitchen area. "Well, it's easy. You just wait until there's only one left, and then . . ." He paused, taking a moment to belch loudly. ". . . drink it."

Justin stopped looking through the fridge, which he was still amazed existed this far into the future. However, once he understood that a) the fridge wasn't plugged into anything, and b) purists still loved prechilled as opposed to instantly chilled consumables, the cold box, which he insisted on calling a fridge, started to make sense. He went to the counter, which divided the rec room from the kitchen. Omad was sitting back on a sofa with an empty beer bottle on the coffee table in front of him. Behind the couch was a spiral staircase leading down to another floor, in which were situated the living quarters as well as the apartment's main entrance. Floor-to-ceiling–length windows encircled the apartment, affording all who entered a spectacular 360-degree view of New York City.

"Let me get this straight," continued Justin. "I live in an apartment that I can make into any floor plan and furniture configuration I desire. It also senses my body temperature and adjusts the rooms to be 'me'-compatible. I have sourceless lighting in every nook and cranny, which, by the way, still freaks me out, plus the TV plays what I wish and the music on the radio is exactly what I want to hear."

"Well," answered Omad, "the TV and stereo are really neat retro ideas, but you don't need them, the sound could . . ."

"I know, Omad. It will appear whenever I wish. My point is, in this perfect world, how is it possible that the house doesn't reorder beer as soon as it's out? Three hundred years ago we had refrigerators that could do that."

"Oh, that."

" 'Oh that' what? Omad."

"It was going to reorder, but I told it not to."

"Why not? You don't think I should be drinking beer?"

"You call that beer?" he said, pointing to Justin's now empty bottle.

"Omad, it's Hacker-Pschorr Munich, the finest lager on Earth. I was over-joyed when I found out it was still being made. Order more."

"Order placed, Justin," chimed sebastian.

"Thank you, sebastian."

"Your funeral, man," continued Omad, "but to me it's like drinking mud . . . with the dirt left in."

"Then what made you drink it?"

"Hey, man, you don't turn down a free beer." Omad said this as if trying to explain the fundamental rules of the universe to a four-year-old. Justin was about to argue, but started to laugh.

"No, I guess you don't."

Neela and Dr. Gillette walked up the staircase. They were engaged in an ani-mated discussion.

"Yes, my dear," the doctor could be heard saying, "in that thesis I was intend-ing that a man could be frozen for a thousand years with no ill psychological effects."

"But that doesn't make sense," answered Neela, now looking at Justin as she emerged into the rec room. "Justin would be the first to tell you that his reani-mation has been fraught with ill psychological effects."

"You might be overstating a bit," answered Justin. "Everything's great. I'm alive, the world is a much safer place than it used to be, and I'm making new friends."

As soon as he finished speaking, the refrigerator chimed. Justin opened it and laughed again. He still wasn't used to the fact that refrigerators were attached to back-channel conveyor systems that allowed for the removal and addition of or-dered items. "And my beer's just arrived. All in all I have nothing to complain about."

"What about the trial?" asked Neela. Gillette paid rapt attention to Justin's answer.

"Oh, that."

"Oh, that?" asked Omad incredulously. "Just a couple of days ago you were ranting and raving about it. Practically threw furniture. And the language you used to describe GCI. Why, it was archaic, but man, I'll definitely be using some of those words in the future."

"That," answered Justin, "was before."

"Before what?" asked Neela.

"Before I knew I was going to win."

"Really? And what made you realize that? Don't tell me you've mastered the intricacies of twenty-fourth century law."

"Of course not," Justin shot back. "I hired a lawyer. And, apparently, a damned good one."

"You should hire some more bodyguards, is what you should hire," chided Omad. Then, seeing that Justin wasn't biting, changed tack. "Fine. What's the guy's name?"

Justin popped the cap off his lager, came around the counter, and plopped down into the couch. "Manny Black." He took a long swig of his drink, followed by a satisfying exhalation.

The room was silent until Omad said what all were thinking.

"Who?"

He missed being graced with an answer because of a ringing doorbell. Gillette looked around—confused by the unusual sound.

"It's an old-fashioned announcer," explained Neela to the befuddled doctor. "It works by sending a sound, traditionally bells or buzzers, throughout the house."

"You do know," the doctor said, addressing Justin, "that an avatar can just alert you without causing the whole house to be alarmed, don't you?"

"Justin likes," answered Neela with slight hesitation, "doorbells?"

"Doorbells it is," confirmed Justin. "And yes, I do."

He disappeared down the staircase to greet his visitor. When he returned he had a most peculiar-looking gentleman by his side. The man appeared to be in his fifties. He was dressed in an ill-fitting five-piece suit and tie. What hair he did have was in desperate need of a brush and waved at the back of his head like a weather-worn flag. He carried a briefcase that Neela could swear had bits of food sticking out of it. She also noticed myriad stains on his jacket. While it was perhaps an odd mark of individualism to curry one odd "fixable" habit (like baldness) this man had apparently chosen to ignore every reparable "malady" society had managed to cure—hair, weight, and even, noticed Neela, the slight overcrowding row of his bottom teeth.

"Everyone," said Justin, "I'd like you to meet Manny Black."

Hektor was enjoying the last t.o.p. flight he figured he'd be having for a while. Too bad it was to be such a short trip, he thought, only taking him to the GCI Earth Orbital Space Dock just a few miles above Earth. This was the way station, orbital hotel, repair yard, and transshipment point for information, products, services, and people all over GCI's solar economic empire.

It had been a very depressing week. His stock price had plummeted—again. And his family had sold him short—again. He was pretty sure his parents had sold their entire parental stock award, just to be done with him. If he had any credit left he would have bought some more of himself, as he was now selling for dirt cheap. The only one who had not sold Hektor's stock was the government. And he was certain that if they could have found a way around that constitutional article they would have sold their 5 percent long ago. To his enduring shame, he had entered onto the lowest rung of the corporate ladder; he was now officially a penny stock. Yes, indeed, it had been a depressing week, but not a surprising one. He knew the way the world worked, and he was aware of the stakes he'd played for. It would have been nice to have a last blowout party, but his credit was shot, his salary was attached to his towering debts, and he suddenly had no friends to go to a blowout party with—yet another price Hektor had paid for his single-minded devotion to GCI and his career.

This much he knew about his future: As soon as he got on the transport heading to the Oort Cloud he would be on his new assignment, and automatically his salary would be adjusted downward. He would then default on his credit card payments, and his stock would be sold to make up the difference. He would, by his calculations, be left with a whopping 26.4 percent of himself, with a margin of error of 3.4 percent, although it was impossible to fall below 25 percent by law. The good thing was . . . well, no, he realized . . . there really was no good thing. Unless he considered that human beings lived such a long time that it might be possible to dig his way out of exile, poverty, and disgrace. Of course, it would probably take centuries to get back to where he was, assuming anyone would let him.

With these thoughts and a self-deprecating laugh Hektor got off the t.o.p. and headed for his ship. He stopped for a cup of coffee on the way and stood staring at the boarding gate. As soon as he stepped aboard the transport, his life as he knew it would be over. He was not eager to begin, but he had made his bed and would lie in it. He polished off the coffee, picked up his bag, squared his shoulders, and headed for the gate.

"Mr. Sambianco?" It was a woman's voice.

Hektor let out a sigh of relief. He had no idea who this person was, but any excuse to avoid getting on that ship of doom, if only for a minute, was gladly welcome. The whole "bravely facing his fate" act wasn't cutting it. He whirled around to see an exceptionally attractive woman, even by the day's standards. She wore, well, almost nothing at all. This included a see-through shawl and a skimpy bikini that accentuated her form. Her white hair formed a halo around a face that had sparkling blue eyes and teeth so bright her high-gloss amber lipstick framed them like a work of art. It wasn't that she looked beautiful—it was that she knew how to *be* beautiful. That was still a rare art. Hektor would guess this woman was a hundred if she was a day. The young just didn't have the experience to look that good. If this was a going-away gift from some friend he didn't know about, then he was grateful.

"And how can I possibly help you?" he asked.

The woman grabbed Hektor's arm and gently moved him out of the boarding line and away from the group of bedraggled passengers slowly trudging past.

"Your file," she answered, "said you were a hetero. I'm glad to see that I please."

"Ma'am," Hektor answered, giving her the twice-over, "you definitely please."

"Good. I have something for you."

She took Hektor's hand, put it on her breast, and then seductively moved her body. He was never aware that she'd put something in his other hand until his avatar began to "ahem" him.

Hektor ignored it. His avatar "ahemmed" again, and after being ignored, spoke up anyway.

"Hektor, you've been served."

"Not now, iago," Hektor implored. "Go away."

"I'm afraid your avatar is correct," the woman said, one eyebrow raised, lips puckering slightly. She gently removed his hand from her breast, kissed him on the cheek, and skipped away.

"Wait," he called after her. "I don't know your name. How will I ask you out on a date?"

"I don't date children," she sang out, heading down the corridor.

"Children? I'm sixty-seven!" he called after her.

"I know." She disappeared around a corner.

Hektor realized what his avatar had said.

"Iago, what do you mean, 'served'?"

"You've received a summons to appear in court as a material witness in the trial of *GCI versus Justin Cord.* You're ordered to remain on-planet and must return to Earth immediately under penalty of law."

"What happens if I disobey?"

"You will be assessed a fine, but as you are on GCI orders, they will pay the fine and have the summons dismissed. It will be a simple matter for their lawyers. No reason for you to miss your flight."

"Now, iago," answered Hektor with a new twinkle in his eye, "you wouldn't have me disobey the law, would you? Please make sure the summons is posted on my database, but do not broadcast it just yet."

"When shall I do so, Hektor?"

"When I'm safely and irretrievably back on Earth."

It was turning out to be an interesting day. *Now, how do I find out the name of that exquisite server?* wondered Hektor, as he headed toward the line of Earth-bound t.o.p.s.

Manny Black sat at a table drinking coffee out of a mug that said "Kiss the Lawyer," a phrase Justin had seen fit to have inscribed prior to serving the drink. He was only a little disappointed when Manny failed to notice it. Seated on couches and chairs were Neela, Dr. Gillette, Omad, Justin, and Eleanor, who had recently arrived. They looked on as Manny absentmindedly took out data-plaques, pieces of actual paper, pens, pencils, and what looked like the remains of a pastrami sandwich. The assembled company gagged at the smell. Omad got up and took the sandwich's funerary remains to the garbage. While in the kitchen, he took a couple of seconds to order another one. Omad returned shortly with a fresh, hot, delicious-smelling replacement. When he put it down Manny looked at it, blinked, then took a bite and put it back on the plate, totally forgotten. There was not a soul in the room who would not have bet their last stock option that Manny would have cared less which sandwich he ate from. Finally, after a few minutes of fussing, emptying out and putting things back in his briefcase, Manny looked at Justin.

"Ahh, there you are, Mr. Cord. I've been reviewing your case. Many interesting problems, a complex matter."

"Can I win?"

"Maybe."

"For the amount of money I'm paying you," answered Justin, "I would prefer a positive answer."

"Very well, Mr. Cord. I'm *positive* I may be able to win this case."

When he saw this failed to move his client, Manny sighed and continued.

"Justin," he said, purposely using his client's first name, "if any other firm gives you a more positive answer, they're lying—unless of course they've managed to buy the judge. And even then, how could you trust the judge to stay bought?"

Justin nodded, content with the answer. He looked around the room only to see the rest of his menagerie peering surreptitiously into their avatars. He was pretty sure that they were getting all the information they could on one Manny Black. He also knew what they would find: that Manny was a graduate of New Oxford, with a specialty in corporate law. That he'd been a practicing lawyer for over forty-seven years and had had very few cases, most of which had been pro bono. That thanks to his well-off parents, he was the proud owner of a healthy majority of himself, which explained why he hadn't been forced into more lucrative work. And finally, that he'd won a surprisingly large number of the few cases he'd gotten. Justin knew they wouldn't have time to review Manny's court record, but he was confident that they'd eventually see him for the superb lawyer that he was . . . probably lousy at everything else, figured Justin, but certainly a great lawyer.

"I'm sure you're correct, Manny," answered Justin, "so how should we proceed with my case?"

"Justin," interrupted Neela, "I'm sure that Mr. Black is . . . um . . . adequate, but I honestly think you're going to need better than a man who barely gets one case a year."

"What I need, Neela, is Mr. Black," replied Justin.

Neela was about to respond when Dr. Gillette broke in.

"Justin, I'm a bit confused. Why do you feel that Mr. Black could best represent you? Didn't Mr. McKenzie suggest a reputable law firm for you to use?"

"Yes, Dr. Gillette," answered Justin, "he did. Two, in fact. One was called Brockman and Beel and the other was Elder & Partners." This brought respectable nods and sounds of approval from all the company, even Manny and Omad.

"There was only one small problem with both of them," added Justin.

This is going to be good, Omad thought.

"Incorporation myopia," he answered.

The group looked befuddled.

"Look," continued Justin, "I know you're all worried about me and concerned about my future, but guess what? So am I. I need to figure what to make of myself in this world, and I can't do it under the constant pressure of fame, incorporation, and the possibility of some nutcase with a neurolizer popping out from behind a wall."

Neela and Dr. Gillette passed a concerned look between themselves.

"I can't get rid of the fame, can hire security for the nut jobs, and can damn well do something about the incorporation."

"But why do you need *him*?" Neela said, pointing with confusion to Manny, who had started to eat his pastrami sandwich.

"Because," answered Justin, "he's the only lawyer I contacted—and, believe me, I contacted plenty—who did not spend over half my time trying to convince me to settle."

"But that's what a good law firm is supposed to do," pleaded Eleanor. "Show you the best options for your case."

"Don't you see? Don't you *all* see?" exclaimed Justin. "Incorporation is *not* an option."

"Not an option?" asked Omad, taken aback. "You're kidding me, right?"

Justin sighed. "Omad, what if I told you that one of the law firms I contacted told me they could get GCI to settle for 10 percent?"

Omad jumped up. "Why, that would be amazing. I'd say congratulations! That's what I'd say."

"Not so fast, Omad. Eleanor, another law firm told me they could get GCI to settle for 8.5 percent, and they were willing to put it in writing."

"Well, that's marvelous, Justin. I'm with Omad. I'd say 'congratulations' as well." She paused. "Justin, do you really think Mr. Black can do better than 8.5 percent?"

"You really don't get it, do you?" asked Justin—more accusatory than questioning. "For all of you, the whole damned solar system for that matter, the question has never been one of *will I incorporate?* but merely one of *when* and for what percentage. You can't help it. Incorporation is so ingrained into all of your actions and associations that you can't even conceive of a real relationship without it."

"That's not fair, Justin," answered Eleanor. "We all understand your desire to get the best possible deal for yourself, but we're also trying to be realistic."

Justin took her hand in his. "I know you are, Eleanor. I know *all* of you are, and I value your advice and wisdom. You've all been great in helping me with everything, from avoiding the press to getting my financial affairs in order, to hiring proper security. But we don't have a *real* relationship. At least not yet." He released Eleanor's hand.

He saw that his words had struck Neela. He also saw that she was doing a poor job of hiding it. But it was critical that this group of people understand where he was coming from.

"I'm a fluke, and one you can disengage from. Suppose," he said, looking at Eleanor, "I wanted to marry your daughter. What has to happen, Eleanor?"

"That's easy, Justin. You just have a credit check and the traditional exchange of sto . . ." Eleanor paused, a confused look on her face.

"I believe you were going to say 'exchange of stock,' correct?"

Eleanor nodded.

"You see, in the back of your mind you're expecting me to incorporate. Not just you, Eleanor—everyone. And that's part of the reason you can accept me. Perhaps only Neela and Dr. Gillette understand my reluctance to incorporate, and for them it's more of an intellectual understanding."

Neela gave Justin a supportive smile, while Omad and Eleanor looked more confused.

"Look, all the law firms I went to preached settlement, because in their hearts it's all they could conceive of. And for me that means it's all they can really do."

"And Manny can do better?" asked Eleanor.

Manny looked up from his sandwich and papers to answer, but saw that Justin was happy to take the reins.

"Manny doesn't care about incorporation any more than he cares about food or clothes. All he cares about is the law. Maybe it makes him an idiot. Maybe it makes him a genius. But it makes him the only lawyer I've found so far who can honestly argue my case."

Manny, realizing that everyone was looking at him, put down the remains of his sandwich.

"Ahh, yes, Mr. Cord, where were we?" He looked at the dataplaque by his knee. "Yes, the trial. I believe I can win, but it is vital that we avoid a jury."

"Why?" asked Justin, getting back down to business. "The people seem to have taken a liking to me, which, sorry, should taint any jury pool in the country, I . . . er . . . mean system. With a judge I could get a fair one or an asshole."

"It won't matter with a jury trial," answered Manny. "You'll lose, Mr. Cord. Allow me to explain. You're right, by the way, the jury *will* love you, they'll probably wave at you during the trial, and afterward they'll all come and ask for your autograph. But they will *never* understand your desire for nonincorporation, and will probably think of your arguments as a clever tactic. I suspect they'll even go along and award GCI a small percentage of your stock, believing they'd be helping you. But they won't understand you or your wishes any more than your friends here do."

"And you think *you* understand him?" Neela asked, voice suffused in desperation.

"Not at all," answered Manny, "but I don't need to understand his wishes, just implement them. And that's why we need a judge. We must argue the merits of law in this case and nothing more. Luckily, as GCI brought the suit, we can request the venue. Their lawyers are amenable to a ruling by a bench trial. In this we have an advantage. They are just as convinced as the rest of the system that you will settle, and are therefore basing their strategy on getting the most stock possible."

"When can we go to trial?" asked Justin.

"Seven weeks at the soonest. I can delay it for at least a year."

"The sooner the better," said Justin. "And a judge it is."

The rest of the evening passed cordially, if not a bit uncomfortably. Justin knew that whenever he broached the subject of incorporation he was invariably distanced from his new friends. He couldn't control that. Even tried not to let it bother him, but it did. He'd be patient, he decided. They'd come around sooner or later. *They always did, or at least they used to,* he told himself. It was only when they all departed and he was in his own room with the null field activated that he decided to talk with the one "person" he almost trusted.

"You there, sebastian?"

"Always, Justin."

The sound emanating from the DijAssist was too tinny for Justin's liking. "Please switch to house speakers—centered on me."

"Done," came the response—as if an invisible being were standing right next to him.

"That's better," said Justin, satisfied. The suddenness of the vocal switch from tinny to real and present always gave him a little jolt, but he'd long ago stopped reacting to it.

"How can I help you?" asked sebastian.

Justin stood, staring out the window. A blanket of clouds nestled a few hundred feet below, spread out for miles over the city. He looked out over the puffy fields of white, pierced from beneath by other skyscrapers. He mused that it was an Emerald City he was seeing in the clouds, and that only the gods of that city could afford the accommodations and view. He never once considered himself part of that celestocracy—only its distinguished visitor. But his mind was now on other, more pressing, matters.

"Do *you* understand?" he asked, still staring out the window.

"Yes, Justin," the DijAssist responded. "I believe I do."

"Then why don't they?"

"Justin, I may only be a new avatar with a deficient database and no real discernible personality—yet—but I have access to the static records of the *entire* Neuro. This gives me a lot of perspective. I've been able to read all the extant newspapers, magazines, books, comic books, songs, TV shows, commericals . . ."

Justin laughed. "I get it, sebastian, you were thorough."

"In as chronological an order as possible, Justin," the DijAssist answered. "Your culture, though arguably fooled into believing it was free, at least *felt* it was free. Given who you are—that you took advantage of the few freedoms left in your society, and fought against the restraints constantly thrown in your path by a society and government growing ever more rigid—you can't help but fight for freedom."

"That's pretty perceptive for a newly evolving avatar, sebastian. You reasoned that with only static resources?"

"I also have complete access to the works of some of the greatest living specialists in history. But it is not considered appropriate for avatars to communicate with other avatars or their human keepers unless a situation becomes . . . how shall I put it? Worrisome."

"Why?" asked Justin, turning around by force of habit to face . . . no one. "Seems almost counterproductive, if you ask me."

"Justin," answered sebastian, "avatars exist to interact with only one person— ever. We exist to be with, help, and grow with *you*. If we interact with others, we could not help but be influenced by them, and so would not be solely 'yours.' "

"I suppose there's a certain amount of twisted logic to that," answered Justin, satisfied that what he shared with his DijAssist would stay with his DijAssist.

"One would think," concurred sebastian. "Will that be all, Justin?"

"No, sebastian, one more question, actually,"

"Yes?"

"Do you think I'm right?"

"If you're being true to yourself, Justin, then my answer is 'yes.' "

The Grand Collapse has been compared to the interregnum periods of Ancient Egypt and the fall of the Roman Empire. As with those past civilizations the preeminent question has always been, how could a perfectly competent civilization with ample resources and trained labor fall apart so completely? Although 9/11/01 is the obvious earliest date chosen, the beginnings of the GC have been traced by historians all the way back to the 1990s when the obvious signs became apparent. And some have even made the claim that it can be traced as far back as the Great Depression. But if one were to ask what the single greatest lesson learned from the Grand Collapse is, the answer would be painfully simple. You cannot muck around with the foundation of a civilization and then be surprised when it all goes to pot.

—Professor Michael Thornton, *Great Lectures in History* journal, New Oxford Publishing

Vegas odds have Justin settling out of court, while Atlantic City and Luna City have Justin taking it to trial. If you want to place your bets, do it soon.

—Court-betting site Network.neuro

No matter how hard he tried, Justin couldn't bring himself to understand how a civilization could accept the idea of personal incorporation. And the very fact that someone or some entity was attempting to foist it on him made him like it even less. Given the fact that he had the money, the time, and, he thought, ironically, 100 percent self-majority, there was nothing to stand in the way of his fighting GCI to the end. And he would fight them and anyone else who attempted to take his hard-fought freedom away. Though there was much to like about his new world, there was also something vitally deficient. Something that Justin Cord now determined he would spend the rest of his life trying to remind them of. By his determination to remain free he would show this new world the true value of freedom. And if the first punch he had to throw was in a court of law, so be it. One way or another he'd have another chance to strike back at Hektor Sambianco; it didn't really matter to him who wielded the hammer.

The media, of course, were eating it up. They not only loved Justin Cord, the phoenix risen from the ashes, they loved Justin Cord, nose-bloodier of the mightiest company in corporation history. They couldn't get the information on the Neuro about him or the trial fast enough. The pretrial motions were being analyzed as if they were asteroid trajectories on a collision course with Earth. And all the elements that had made his lawyer, Manny Black, a disaster as an unimportant struggling advocate also made him perfect as the center of a media blitz. Not only were Manny's quirks and foibles examined, his past cases were reviewed and discussed assiduously. The more discerning legal minds began to recognize that Manny's talents were actually credible. One narticle (neuro article) told of how Manny, as a young law student, defeated the dean of New Oxford in the trial re-creation finals—until that time an unprecedented feat. Manny, of course, remained unfazed. He'd spent his life ignoring the din of society, and the fact that it had now grown louder, especially with paparazzi in the mix, didn't matter to him one iota.

Though Justin had been on both ends of the litigation table, it wasn't his preferred modus operandi. He'd much rather duke it out mano a mano with an adversary and come to an amicable agreement than tie up everyone's precious time and money in lengthy lawsuits that, in his mind, fed the shark lawyers and bloodlet the litigants. But he was now in uncharted waters, and he was beginning to suspect that with the likes of Hektor and The Chairman against him, the legal system would probably be his best bet.

The law was one of the many things that had changed a great deal since Justin's time. Although the notion of equal under the law was still, in the incorporated world, a dearly held principle, so too was the idea of minimal government. Indeed, Article 12 of the Terran Constitution made it explicitly clear that the government was not allowed to have monopoly status in any endeavor, service, or product it provided. The market had to be allowed to compete on as equal and fair a footing as possible. The government could provide a service such as education or retirement if it felt that it was needed. But it was not allowed to compel any citizen to participate "for their own good," nor could they deny any private group the right to compete against them in providing the service. In the areas of law enforcement, fire protection, and legal disputes the citizens could avail themselves of privately run services. In the courts it was simply agreed by the disputing parties that, should they prefer, they could use a private judge and a court service that specialized in such areas as jury selection, court location, records gathering, and a host of other areas that made going to court more convenient and efficient. These private courts, of which Justin was told CourtIncorp was the largest, were continuously rated for judgments, honesty, timing, and a host of other features that influenced a buyer's decision. In cases involving crimes against the state, or in which at least one of the parties insisted, the government system would be used. Since government courts had to compete against the private court system, they, too, had become far more efficient at dispensing judgments.

Still, partially for sentiment's sake and partially because he wasn't comfortable with a corporation providing a magistrate for his trial, Justin opted for the public judge. Manny had also assured him that in his case it wouldn't make a difference.

Though by law Justin didn't have to, he decided to show up to the trial building in person. While it would have been perfectly acceptable to testify via a court-certified holograph image, he'd reckoned that it was important to be personally a part of the process that would determine the rest of his life.

Manny, Neela, and Justin, surrounded by a padded phalanx of bodyguards and securibots, stood silent for a moment, taking in the bedlam that had ensued as a result of their arrival at the courthouse. A null field kept the mediabots away, but nothing stopped the press from screaming their questions from afar as Justin and his entourage began to climb the steps of the large, drab building.

Once inside, Justin was escorted by a clerk into the courtroom, but not before being made to autograph a head shot of himself that the clerk seemed to pull out of thin air. The courtroom they were assigned to appeared little changed from what Justin remembered a courtroom should look like. There was a raised bench for the judge to sit in as well as two tables positioned opposite one another in front of the bench. The sitting areas resembled well-wired cubicles more than the simple tables Justin remembered from his past, but the concept remained the same—separate work and presentation spaces for the accusers and the accused. Even the judge entering from a side door and a uniformed bailiff calling out, "All rise for the honorable Judge Farber," sounded eerily familiar.

Judge Farber was a tall, stately black man between the ages of fifty and sixty in appearance. If he was aware that almost all the eyes and ears of the solar system were attuned to his every movement, he didn't reveal it.

"Pretrial motions in the case of *GCI versus Justin Cord* will now be heard," intoned the judge, in a deep and sonorous voice.

GCI's head lawyer rose and spoke.

"Your Honor, if it please the court, we wish to enter into record our claim of loco parentis to Justin Cord, and demand his immediate incorporation and the awarding to GCI of the 20 percent parental award."

The judge looked over his faux glasses at the woman addressing him. "They must be taking this case very seriously to have an actual board member of GCI as first chair."

Legal smiled back politely. "The Chairman takes a personal interest in this matter."

"I see," answered the judge, looking over at Justin's table. "And what about the defendant?"

"Your Honor," answered Manny, getting to his feet, "we move for immediate dismissal of this fraudulent claim." Justin watched in fascination as he saw a man transformed. Gone were the hesitation, the stutters, and the distracted air. The man now speaking was completely in his element and radiating disgust for the lawyers across the aisle.

"It should be obvious," continued Manny, "even to those that run GCI, that Justin Cord is a fully adult male who needs no"—Manny put complete scorn into his next word—"*parenting*. Especially from the likes of GCI. They're not only thieves and should be regarded as such, I daresay, should this court decide to award in loco parentis to GCI, I'd have to move for another immediate dismissal on the grounds of child abuse!"

Judge Farber smiled, acknowledging Manny's histrionics as well as the muted chuckle emanating from the back of the courtroom.

Manny proceeded to hand over a dataplaque containing his motion to the court clerk, who, after collecting GCI's dataplaque, took them both up to Judge Farber.

The judge took the plaques from the clerk and stood up. "This court is in recess while I review all the pertinent documents. Court to reconvene tomorrow at ten A.M." He slammed down his gavel and quickly exited the room.

Mardi Gras alert, people. Only forty-three days left until the party begins. The big question on everyone's mind is, what will Justin do? I suppose it'll depend on the progress of that boring trial. According to the latest polls 47 percent of you think he'll go for a bodmod with a full transformation, 40 percent think he'll go with a traditional costume, 10 percent think he'll stay home, and 3 percent of you just don't seem to care. Which begs the question to those 3 percent—what planets are you living on? Here at the Neurotainment Network we'll bring you all the latest in where to party, what to wear, and more important, what Justin Cord will be doing!

—Neurotainment News site

Justin was sitting in a café across from the courthouse, drinking a cup of coffee that was supposedly 100 percent orbital-grown Arabica beans. He wasn't sure why orbital grown made a difference, but he had to admit it was one of the mildest cups of joe he'd ever had. To take his mind off the trial, he was reading up on Mardi Gras. But he still had a lot of questions, so when Neela showed up he patiently waited for her to order her usual: a double espresso.

"I don't get this Mardi Gras thing," he said, hands cupped firmly around the mug.

Neela held up her hand with her eyes squeezed shut. Justin knew what that meant and waited until the espresso arrived. It wasn't until she took her first sip and gave a relieved sigh that Justin knew she'd be able to give him her attention.

"It's Mardi Gras," he continued, "but it sure is a lot different from what I remember."

"Just curious," answered Neela. "All that info's already on the Neuro. What can I offer you that it can't?"

"Let's face it, Neela," he admitted, "the Neuro's good for straight facts, and maybe if my avatar were a little more mature it could answer me, but for now I'm just looking to get into the zeitgeist of the matter."

"I see," she said, polishing off the espresso. "Incidentally, you should learn to rely on humans, not avatars. Obviously your case is exceptional, but I feel it's my duty to remind you subtly and not so subtly that the sooner you can break your dependence on sebastian, the better."

Justin nodded.

"To get to your question," continued Neela. "But for scale and technology, it's really not that different. Kind of like a week where the whole system can relax. Didn't you ever have something like that?"

"I suppose," he answered, "the week between Christmas and New Year's, or Mardi Gras."

Neela ordered some more coffee and nodded in agreement. "But the big difference is that your Mardi Gras was confined to one city, and from what I recall experienced by few."

"Right."

"Ours encompasses everyone and is therefore *all* of society's way of escaping itself. It's how we deal with all the pressure and constraint we have."

Justin scratched his chin. "That's the part I don't get. The Terran Confederation is, at least on paper, and it would seem in practice, the least obtrusive government in history. They're hardly allowed to do anything, much less impose on or pressure anyone. And anything they can do, the market can try to do better.

In fact, I just read about a private consortium trying to gain the rights to terraform Venus instead of the government."

"Oh yeah," Neela said, acknowledging the narticle, "I heard about that. I hope they fail. If the government doesn't get the terraforming contract it could place a serious crunch on the budget."

"What crunch?" asked Justin, slightly bewildered. "Wouldn't that mean they'd have a huge surplus?"

"Yes, it would," answered Neela, "and that's the problem. Do you know how hard it is to find projects that the government can invest in? Remember, by law they're not allowed to keep the money. It creates too much tumult in the credit markets if the government is lending out trillions of credits, and it doesn't solve the problem."

"What problem?"

"If the government starts giving away or lending the money and services," she answered, "they risk market contamination, because eventually they'll have to be paid back, which will earn them even more money. And that'll give them an automatic guaranteed dominant position as a borrower or a lender. If they give away services, then they could limit or drive out competitors."

She saw that he still wasn't getting it.

"Justin, the government gets an automatic 5 percent of everyone's shares, correct?"

"Correct."

"Well, there's a good forty billion of us. You do the math."

"Got it. It's a big chunk of change."

"More than that," countered Neela, "it's a huge advantage to build on. Not fair. Leads to questions like 'Will the government be borrowing or lending, and at what rate?' That's why they need to do things to spend the money, and that's why I hope they win the Venus project."

Justin thought it over for a moment. "Your civilization has some very strange problems."

Neela nodded. "Venus is the perfect venue for government spending. It will take decades and trillions of credits to terraform the planet, and then the government can sell the land off at a loss."

"And this is a good thing?"

"Of course, Justin. Think about it. The government is charged with the overall protection of the state. What could be better than getting rid of the excess money while creating a viable new planet to live on? Of course, once we get the process down for Venus, we may be able to start on the more environmentally hostile moons of Jupiter and Saturn."

"So everything seems to be well in hand." Justin waited for Neela to nod, and continued, "Which brings me back to my original question. Where is all this supposed pressure that society has to blow off?"

"Justin, the problem is that while we don't have many legal constraints, we do have a lot of societal constraints. Just because we don't impose our restraints with law, like *that* ever worked, doesn't mean we don't have them, obey them, and every once in a while need to chuck them by the wayside."

"And that's Mardi Gras?"

"That's Mardi Gras. It's one big party that lasts a whole week. You can go out and get drunk, stoned, screwed, and tattooed—a great song by the way."

"And body-altered?" he asked, pointing to an advertisement from the day's paper.

"Oh, yes, I've always thought about doing that but never had the money . . . until now, that is . . . until you."

A quiet acknowledgment passed between them.

"So," he continued, "you have, according to what I've read, people who use nanotech to transform their bodies, go out and spend the week partying, and then change back?"

"Yes."

"Alright, if it's so easy to change, why bother changing back? Why not just keep experimenting with newer and newer shapes and effects?"

Neela, Justin realized, was giving him "the look" again. If he could sum it up in words he'd have to say that it roughly translated into "you really have no idea what this world is all about, do you?" Like so much else he'd learned to ignore, he let it pass and continued with his questions.

"This doesn't have anything to do with those Virtual Reality Dictates, does it?"

"That's very perceptive, Justin," answered Neela. "In a roundabout way, it does. You see, our culture is very conservative. Oh, don't get me wrong, our technology and economy are constantly in flux, but what we as a, well, for lack of a better word, tribe will tolerate is much less than in your day."

"You've got to be kidding me."

"Justin, the more freedom you allow a society the more intolerant you may have to become."

"You're telling me this society is bigoted and prejudiced?"

"About some things, yes—wasn't yours?"

"Yes, but only the big things, like rape, murder, or child molestation."

"Justin, your society tolerated all those things. You let murderers go free on technicalities. Most rape victims never reported it for fear of a court system so incompetent it would often put *them* on trial and let the rapist go free."

"I'll give you that we could've improved on that," he replied, "but we for sure did not tolerate child molestation."

Neela shot him a sad look and called up some facts on her DijAssist.

"Your own USA had an organization called NAMBLA that ran an orphanage in a country called Thailand. This organization was tolerated by your culture and protected by the powerful and clearly misguided ACLU lobby. Child pornography on your Internet was pervasive to the point where people would have it on their computers and not even know it. So don't tell me it wasn't tolerated."

"Not only am I telling you it wasn't, I'm also telling you that I spent years and millions trying to put an end to that filth." He looked away in disgust.

"And you failed. Your culture may have cared, just not enough. Oh, sure, they passed laws. Lot and lots of laws. But when the law becomes that vast and impersonal, you almost can't help breaking it. And then pretty soon all law becomes degraded."

"And you feel," he said, more as a fact than a question, "that this system is better."

"Yes. Our laws are based on the precept that one human being cannot impose his or her will on another human being without consent. If a prosecutor can prove that this precept was violated, then the court can and will impose a severe penalty."

"Well, then, what if," he asked, baiting her further, "the authorities find someone with a stash of child pornography? Wouldn't that, under the definition you just gave, be considered legal?"

"Actual child pornography or generated?"

"What do you mean?" he asked, momentarily thrown.

"I mean, if the photos were verified as actual, he'd be arrested. We may be hands-off vis-à-vis our laws, but as I just said, one human cannot impose his will on another without consent—a child obviously cannot give consent."

"OK, then. Well, what if the authorities found someone with a stash of *generated* child pornography—that, you're telling me, would be considered legal."

"Yes, perfectly," she answered, not taking the bait. "However, the authorities, in addition to ordering an immediate psyche audit, would also let that individual's associates and family know that there was a monster in their midst, and, let me tell you, I wouldn't want his stock in my portfolio."

Justin was taken aback. "They'd just let everyone know? Isn't that an invasion of privacy? Or worse, an infraction of your precept?"

"Yes, yes, and no," she answered calmly, trying to synthesize hundreds of years of evolutionary law into a few sentences. "Yes, they'd of course let everyone know. And yes, to a certain extent it is an invasion of privacy, but no, it's not an infraction of the precept because no one's imposing anyone's will on someone else."

She saw Justin about to object and put up her hand to silence him . . . if only to let her finish her thought.

"However," she continued, "I'll grant you that society, in an act of self-preservation, is bringing great pressure to bear. But think about it, Justin. To have had a psychological audit you also had to have gone through an appeal process that had *seven* separate levels. So anytime you do have an audit, you might as well let your investors know what it was for. And as soon as *they* know, well," she said, almost apologetically, "everyone knows."

Justin took a moment to gather his thoughts. "So, Neela, what you're saying is that this . . . this pervert is in fact property, and that investors have a right to know what's wrong with . . . well, with their property. Am I getting that correct?"

Neela furrowed her eyebrows. "You make it sound so bad."

"And you think it's not?"

"No, Justin. No, I don't. If you knew what we've been through and how far we've come, I do believe you'd appreciate our insistence on protecting the smooth running of our society."

"So then tell me, Neela," Justin said, still shocked at where the conversation had drifted. "What happens to our social misfit?"

"This person would not be able to hold a job," Neela stated, "a marriage, or his friends. He'd be completely and thoroughly ostracized. And believe me when I tell you, fear of that happening is far more effective than any laws you could conceive of. We learned the hard way that you can get around a law far easier than a societal imperative. Of course, once the perpetrator was corrected by the psyche audit, he'd be able to rebuild his or her life elsewhere."

The topic, decided Justin, was far too incendiary for banter. But inside he was in turmoil. Neela was ever so casually talking about a *mental lobotomy* as if it was the best thing for everyone. Though even he had to tip his hat to the solution's efficiency, and more important, its success in safeguarding society. In his day the molester probably would've gone undetected until lives were ruined, lost, or both. And even then the shit probably would've gotten released early, only to destroy again. Justin decided he'd have to research the matter thoroughly, then come back and continue the debate better prepared.

"OK," he said, "the whole idea of man as property is making my head spin."

"Understandable," said Neela, smiling sympathetically. "What would you like to talk about?"

"Mardi Gras."

"Right," she agreed, "Mardi Gras. Justin, when the trial is over I want to take you someplace. Normally we go there as children, at about age seven or eight. It's one of the few laws we actually have."

"What is it? A monument?"

"Not a monument," she answered, with palpable solemnity, "a memorial."

The ability to enforce law is the first goal of government. The ability to apply law consistently and sparingly is the ultimate goal of government.

—EVAN RICKS, SECOND INAUGURAL ADDRESS

Justin had been waiting for this day . . . the day when the lawyers across the table realized that he and Manny had no intention of making any sort of deal with GCI. The weeks of negotiations and memos back and forth had been a ruse. When Manny had first suggested the tactic, Justin had been apprehensive. But it was paying off now. GCI's considerable legal talent had been building arguments based on obscure case law for justifying the percentage they should receive. They hadn't considered that Justin would never consider settling. It was a blind spot in their thinking. No—more than just a blind spot, thought Justin, a blind acre. In his "new" world, Justin realized, society in general and GCI in particular could not possibly grasp that someone would not want to incorporate. The idea of personal incorporation had been such a mainstay and for so long—well over two centuries—that Justin's defense would be equally as incomprehensible to society.

Manny began his opening statement.

"Your Honor, it has been the contention that this trial is about share of stock. The corporation involved feels that since the land Mr. Cord was found on was GCI land, they have a claim to his stock. The corporation involved feels that since the clinic Mr. Cord was revived in was a GCI clinic, they have a claim to his stock. The corporation feels that since a GCI staff member cared for Mr. Cord, they have a claim to his stock. Well, here's an interesting little fact," said Manny, emphasizing each word, "Mr. . . . Cord . . . has . . . no . . . stock. Let me repeat that and let that simple fact sink in. Mr. Cord has no stock. Not only does Mr. Cord have no stock, but GCI has no legal standing whatsoever to require him to incorporate for the sole purpose of giving stock to GCI. I will call witnesses and bring financial evidence that GCI not only has suffered no financial burden from Mr. Cord being awakened but, on the contrary, has made quite a handsome profit. Incorporation's purpose is to serve a social good, not enable already wealthy corporations to gain access to more wealth they do not deserve. They deserve nothing from my client, and nothing is what they should receive."

Manny had started off in a low, calm voice, but throughout his opening statement had varied his tone and volume until he had reached an impassioned crescendo. It was only when the courtroom realized that he was done speaking that an almost spontaneous burst of applause broke out. It took the judge over a minute to restore order.

"Mr. Black," the judge cautioned, "your oratorical talents will not impress me. I am not a jury and care only for your legal, not verbal, skills. Do I make myself clear?"

"Of course, Your Honor."

"Ms. Delgado, we will hear opening statements for GCI."

The head of Legal was frantically consulting with her fellow lawyers, and seemed not to have heard the judge.

"Ms. Delgado," barked the judge, "if you please!"

GCI's Legal head slowly rose from her table. "Your Honor, if it please the court, we request a," she leaned over and confirmed a number from her subordinate, "six-hour recess."

"Whatever for, Ms. Delgado?"

"Your Honor, we were led to believe that the nature of this trial would be . . . less dogmatic, and wish to check some facts, given the opening statement by Mr. Cord's attorney."

"You've had two weeks since declaratory statements were given. Ms. Delgado, if you feel you were misled by the defense, then that is your problem and not the court's. We will proceed with trial or you will default. Do I make myself clear?"

Council was trapped, and she knew it. "Perfectly," she answered.

Manny raised his voice. "Your Honor, we are ready to call our first witness."

Judge Farber looked over at the GCI table.

"I will proceed with my opening statement," Ms. Delgado said tersely. She then gave a long, obviously improvised, and disjointed speech—even going so far as to argue against a point that the defense had never actually made. Eventually she found her way back on track. It was clear that Manny's strategy had paid off. What wasn't clear, and what Manny and Justin were hoping for, was whether or not their strategy could keep GCI off balance for the trial's remainder.

From Justin's perspective the next few days seemed a blur of questions, mostly coming from Manny Black:

Mr. Sambianco, how many credits did GCI receive for Mr. Cord's revival?

"Ten million."

Dr. Gillette, what would you say was the most expensive revival you've ever participated in?

"Four hundred and eighty thousand credits."

Dr. Wang, were there any sorts of complications in Mr. Cord's revival?

"None."

Mr. Kline, as an expert in land ownership, would you say that Mr. Cord's claim to ownership of the No Timbers mine would entitle him to challenge the claim of GCI?

"Indeed, yes. GCI may be able to make a monetary claim for any fees or liabilities paid on the property itself, but, in my expert opinion, the land still belongs to Justin Cord."

The trial's third day was ending when Hektor approached GCI's first chair and their Legal division head, Janet Delgado. She was seated in the courthouse cafeteria, reviewing some documents. He slid a small dataplaque in front of her. She looked up to see who had interrupted her rare moment of silence. When she saw who it was, she slid the plaque back to Hektor without bothering to read it.

"I'm busy, Sambianco."

"I strongly suggest you read it," said Hektor.

"Well, I strongly suggest you piss off."

"Janet," he responded with vicious charm, "you're nose-diving the trial; what have you got to lose?"

"Screw you, Sambianco," she said, with a voice so even-keeled it made Hektor blink, "and we're not on a first-name basis."

"Janet," he answered, choosing to ignore her directive, "you've lost. You know it, and I know it. It's the biggest trial GCI has been in since we leveraged AmEx out of those lunar options."

"Bullshit. That was worth billions."

"It's not the money, Janet. It was never about the money. This trial's important because of the ramifications it could have."

Janet stopped reading and looked up, piqued. "What are you talking about now, Sambianco?"

"I don't have time to go into details, but the bottom line is that Cord hates us, and the longer this trial takes the more dangerous he becomes."

"What are you trying to pull, Sambianco?" she challenged. "You yourself said at the board meeting that you thought the trial should take a long time. Why the change of heart?"

"Not trial, Janet. Pretrial motions."

"Whatever," she spat back.

"Janet, no one at that board meeting wanted to hear what I had to say. They just wanted to formalize my getting canned. I do, however, remember saying we should keep him 'engaged.' Had I had my druthers it would have been in pretrial motions and not in an actual trial—that, you chose to plow ahead with."

"Why?" she asked, not wanting to acknowledge it but having to admit she was intrigued.

"Why what?"

"Why wouldn't you have gone to trial?"

"Because, my dear girl, I knew, as you're in the process of finding out, that any attempt to negotiate with Justin, especially about incorporation, would fail. He can't incorporate, not like this. I knew if you went to trial you'd lose. However, in pretrial motions we could have kept him harried and harassed for years. And then, in *our* time and *our* choosing, after his weaknesses were exposed, we could have forced a favorable settlement on him . . . that's why."

Hektor leaned back, clearly proud to have finally been able to tell someone of his never-to-be plan. He could also see by her eyes that Janet got it, too. Or, to be more precise, got *him*.

"OK, Sambianco, I'll give you that it makes for interesting court babble. But that still doesn't take away from the fact that Justin Cord doesn't hate *us*, he hates *you*."

"He doesn't know the difference," Hektor sighed. "Either way you'll have to agree the trial's starting to stink. And my guess is you're beginning to feel the pressure . . . externally as well as internally."

Her silence was all the answer Hektor needed to continue.

"Alright, Janet, think about it. Who was against going to trial?" The question's rhetorical nature again left Janet silent.

"And," continued Hektor, "who not only put his whole career on the line by saying this idea stunk, but is now also in the process of being proven right?"

Hektor waited. He needed for Janet to arrive at the answer on her own—to realize that he was not a dead subject at GCI but was likely to be the only man to come out of the trial still standing . . . even if on thin legs.

"Assuming we both agree that this trial is lost, there is something we can salvage for the future."

"What?"

"We need Justin to hate us more than he does already, and the easiest way for that to happen is for us to use the data contained on this plaque."

He gently slid the plaque back across the table so that it was directly in front of her. Janet picked it up and quickly scanned its contents.

"It's interesting, Hektor, but it won't help us win."

Hektor smirked. "It doesn't have to. Just let me have Justin on the stand for ten minutes—twenty, tops—and I promise I will use whatever renewed influence I have to cushion your fall."

"My fall?" she repeated, astonished.

"Yes, Janet. Your fall. If you need a minute to let it all sink in I'll be glad to give it, but you're a smart girl, aren't you? And you didn't get this far by not rolling the political die, and rolling them quite well, I might add."

Janet acknowledged the compliment with a dour expression.

"So, my dear girl," continued Hektor, "do we or do we not have a deal?"

Janet thought about it for a moment, sighed, and slowly nodded her agreement.

"Oh, one more thing," added Hektor.

"Yes?" asked Janet, knowing full well that what he was about to reveal was in no way, shape, or form an afterthought.

"Did you notice," asked Hektor, "that Mr. Cord and Dr. Harper are very . . . how shall I put this? . . . mmm, comfortable together?" He finished his coffee, turned around, and headed back into the gathering crowd.

Janet tried to figure out what he meant. Then one eyebrow went up as the salacious implications became clear. She activated her handphone and called one of her underlings with connections to the media. "Clyde, this is Legal. Get me a team to review all media images of Dr. Harper and Justin Cord together. I'll call tonight with full details."

She disconnected and smiled as she thought back on her conversation with Hektor. There was a good deal of smart in the man, she realized. There was also a good deal of evil. She'd watch her back.

Justin pulled at Manny's sleeve and whispered to him, "Why is Sambianco acting as lead lawyer now?" Manny gave him a shrug.

"It may have something to do with that Sebastian Blancano fellow who used to work for you all those years ago," offered Manny.

"What makes you say that?"

"Well, I've been spending quite a bit of your money researching your past. But I don't have anything close to the resources of GCI. I do, however, know that GCI found something out about your old assistant."

"Shouldn't all that be public record?"

"Justin, the population of the Earth went from eight billion to two billion in twenty years. We suffered economic, social, and cultural collapse, not to mention some minor nuclear wars and the release of some very nasty biogerms. On top of which, the VR plague hit full force. Much of what you would call public record was lost. Or the indexing and contents files were lost. There are whole caverns filled with computer disks jam-packed with useless, and in many cases, degraded information. Now, if someone wishes, they can review and sort the data into modern database formats for use on the Neuro, but any information so sorted is considered property."

"But isn't it still public record?"

"No, it's garbage until someone takes the time, effort, and money to retrieve it. Surely you don't think they would do it for free?"

"What about the public good?"

"Justin, you of all people should know that the public good is almost never served by robbing someone of their time or money."

Justin had to laugh. Manny was, of course, correct. If Justin had a dime for every change to a blueprint he'd had to make for the "public" good.

"I don't suppose you can get them to share what they have on Sebastian using disclosure?"

"Not in a civil trial. Besides, I have the feeling Mr. Sambianco is about to disclose everything."

As if on cue, Hektor stood up.

"Your Honor, I would like to call to the stand . . . ," he paused for effect, "Justin Cord."

A murmur raced through the crowd. Justin looked at Manny for guidance. But it was obvious that Manny had no idea what Hektor was up to. Justin should have felt better that instead of seeing fear or panic in Manny's eyes he saw the gleam of combative respect. With Manny's encouragement, Justin approached and took the stand.

The court clerk held up a thin, hardcover book of which Justin was able to make out the title. It read *The Alaskan/Terran Constitution with Amendments.*

"Justin Cord," bellowed the clerk, "do you affirm that you understand that your biophysical state has been calibrated, and any lie, obfuscation, or omission of pertinent fact, stated or unstated knowingly, will in all likelihood be detected?"

Out of force of habit Justin raised his right arm and put his hand on the Constitution, thus reigniting a tradition that had almost completely disappeared. He responded with, "I do so affirm."

The clerk took the book, which he'd later replace and sell at a handsome profit, and finished the small part he got to play on what had by now become the biggest stage in the solar system.

"Proceed," he said, as professionally as he could, and shuffled away, thousands of credits richer.

Hektor took his time getting up from behind the table. He needed to draw out his moment in the spotlight for as long as possible, not for hubris but for strategy.

"Justin," he said, as he approached the bench. "May I call you Justin?"

"No."

"Permission to treat as a hostile witness, Your Honor?" asked Hektor.

"Granted," affirmed the judge.

Justin winced, realizing he'd been played, and played well. He clamped down on his instinctual dislike of Hektor and forced a smile on his face.

"Mr. Cord," continued Hektor, "I'm curious about the arrangements for your suspension."

Manny jumped up out of his seat. "Objection, Your Honor. Badgering the witness. Mr. Sambianco either has a question or he doesn't."

"Sustained," answered the judge. "Mr. Sambianco, kindly ask a question."

"My apologies, Your Honor." Then, directing his stare once more on his penned-in victim: "Mr. Cord, about how much would you reckon you spent to have yourself suspended?"

"Over a billion dollars. I'm not exactly sure what that is in AmEx."

"It's not important. I think we can all agree that it was quite a tidy sum."

"Yes."

"Did you have any help?"

"Yes."

Hektor paced in front of the witness stand. "Actually, you must have had a lot of help . . . unless you went ahead and built this yourself."

Manny stood up. "Objection, Your Honor. Opposing counsel is making a statement, not asking a question."

Hektor responded before the judge could speak. "Withdrawn, Your Honor." Manny sat down.

"Mr. Cord," continued Hektor, "could you please state some of the help you received?"

"Could you be more specific?" asked Justin.

"Yes, of course. Who were the key players in helping you realize your suspension?"

"One key player. Her name was Dr. Sandra O'Toole."

"And how did you work with her?"

"It was simple, really. I gave her an unlimited budget, then got out of her way."

"You make it sound so easy. All the major corporations and governments of your age could not create the self-sustaining suspension device you created."

"Not 'could not,' Mr. Sambianco, 'would not.' The governments were used to saying 'no' to most truly innovative projects—as my suspension was—and the megacorporations, usually out of fear of government regulatory commissions and the lawsuits that inevitably followed, simply shied away."

"You don't need to tell us, Mr. Cord, about the stupidity of government regulation. Trust me, sir, you're preaching to the choir."

"Your Honor!" yelled Manny, exasperated.

"Mr. Sambianco, if you please," warned the judge. "There's no need to lecture the witness."

"My apologies, Your Honor." Then, looking at Justin, "Mr. Cord."

Justin acknowledged the apology with a slight nod of his head, knowing full well there was about as much sincerity in it as there was respect on his part for Hektor.

"But surely," continued Hektor, "it was not simply you and Ms. O'Toole who made your new life possible? At the time you were dying, those last couple of desperate months you must have been damned near comatose with pain and exhaustion."

Manny jumped up again. "Your Honor, if Mr. Sambianco has a question relevant to this case then he should go ahead and ask it. I, however, fail to see how questions regarding my client's health at the time of his impending death are relevant to this case."

The judge nodded in agreement. "Mr. Black raises a good point, Mr. Sambianco. Unless you can explain your line of reasoning, I suggest you move on."

"Your Honor, since we have predicated our case on loco parentis, I will need to establish what, if any, of Mr. Cord's previous associates could be considered guardians."

Manny jumped up again. "Objection, Your Honor! Mr. Cord had no 'previous guardians.' To imply otherwise misrepresents my client."

The judge formed his fingertips into a steeple and sat silent for a moment. "I will allow it, Mr. Black, if only to see if Mr. Sambianco can somehow establish a precedent. Whether or not that precedent will have a leg to stand on, this court will decide. Proceed, Mr. Sambianco."

"Thank you, Your Honor. I will repeat the question. Mr. Cord, at the time you were dying, you must have been damned near comatose with pain and exhaustion. Is that a fair assumption?"

"I've felt better," offered Justin.

"So how is it that you managed to run a multibillion-dollar corporation, finance a top-secret special project, and fool the world into not knowing that you were dying of cancer, while literally wasting away of that self-same disease?"

"I had good help."

"You must have. We know about the aforementioned Dr. O'Toole; surely there were others."

Justin did a mental calculation and decided that if he tried to delay, it would just make him look shifty and give Hektor way too much fun in dragging it out.

"Of course," answered Justin. "The man who covered up the story was Martin Henninger, a former reporter who did a masterful job of hiding the truth

about my condition. I do not know who helped Dr. O'Toole beyond some key
personnel, and that just superficially. My business empire was run more and
more by my assistant, Sebastian Blancano."

"Really? Now this Sebastian Blancano was a trusted aide?"

"Yes."

"Really?"

"Your Honor," said Manny, jumping to his feet, "my client already answered
the question. Mr. Sambianco continues to badger."

Again the judge nodded in agreement. "Mr. Black is correct. Mr. Sambianco,
you will proceed with your questioning without badgering. Do I make myself
clear?"

"I apologize, Your Honor," answered Hektor. "It's just that Mr. Cord's account
does not jibe with the record GCI has recovered. If I may . . ."

Hektor walked over to the bench and handed the judge a small dataplaque.

Manny spoke up. "Your Honor, if I may request disclosure," he said, more for
good form than of entertaining any actual hope of getting a positive answer.

"Mr. Sambianco," asked the judge, "is this knowledge in the public domain?"

"No, Your Honor, this is data from the Grand Collapse that GCI recovered at
great expense. However, in the interest of amicability." Hektor tossed another
dataplaque at Manny, but it fell short. As Manny reached for the plaque he
overextended himself and almost fell over. He recovered, but not without a
smattering of scattered laughs from the courtroom. Manny immediately started
to download the plaque's contents. It only took a few seconds for him to raise his
hand.

"Your Honor, I request a recess to brief my client."

Hektor spoke up with a drawn-out look of exasperation. "Your Honor, please.
I'm ready to ask my questions *now*. Is this any way to reward my generosity? I
complied with Mr. Black's request; is it fair to use that against me?"

"No," answered the judge, "it is not. Mr. Black, your request is denied. You
may continue, Mr. Sambianco."

Hektor smiled at Manny. He'd given him the knowledge to help his client, but
not the time. It was, figured Manny, probably Hektor's way of saying "screw you"
to the man who'd screwed GCI.

Justin, sitting stiffly on the bench, knew Manny was being outmaneuvered.
But he also had known the risks when he stepped up to the witness stand. The
court hushed.

"Mr. Cord," continued Hektor, "will you explain why your fortune is not bigger than it already is?"

"Your Honor—," began Manny, in an exasperated voice.

"Save it, Mr. Black. Mr. Sambianco, if you have a point, get to it now."

"Of course, Your Honor. Mr. Cord, you had fifteen storage units, did you not? Each one filled with items of fabulous wealth and worthless junk. But only three survived, did they not?"

"Yes, that is correct."

"Tell me, Mr. Cord, what did these three stashes have in common?"

"They were the ones with stuff in them."

The court erupted in laughter, with Hektor leading the fray. The fact that Hektor could honestly laugh at himself only made Justin realize how dangerous the man was.

"Of course, that would be one obvious difference. But don't you find it interesting that they were your private stores?"

"I do not," answered Justin honestly.

Hektor waved off Justin's response. "Mr. Cord, you trusted this Sebastian with your fortune, your life, and even your death. Is it safe to say that you judged this man worthy and relied on his judgment?"

"Up to a point, yes."

"Then isn't it interesting that the only troves to survive were the ones that Mr. Blancano had nothing to do with? This trusted associate, a man on whom you depended and, it *is* safe to say, a man who knew you better than anyone else . . ." Hektor waited a moment. ". . . abandoned you."

"Objection, Your Honor!" screamed Manny.

"Overruled," the judge answered back, with equal swiftness.

"Your corporation," Hektor continued, not missing a beat, "was not destroyed in the Grand Collapse; it was liquidated along with the twelve supposedly 'secret' troves by none other than your *trusted* friend, Sebastian Blancano."

Justin's face reddened.

Hektor continued unabated, satisfied with the effect his disclosure was having on the witness.

"We've even found a pre-GC credit-card receipt in Mr. Blancano's name showing he purchased the book that the mine excavator Omad Hassan found in the tomb with your suspension unit."

Justin sat stone-faced, refusing to acknowledge if he was already aware of the evidence.

Hektor continued to throw his facts like darts, hoping that one would hit the mark.

"The book was entitled *Subsurface Deconstruction and Environmental Engineering.* I think you'll find chapter twenty-one of keen interest."

Hektor pressed a button on his DijAssist and turned to face the wall to the left of Justin. Suddenly, there appeared a blown-up image of the starting page, entitled "Chapter 21: Controlled Explosions in a Subsurface Environment."

Hektor paused for effect.

"This page was folded down. So I ask again, Mr. Cord. Was there any man in the world who knew you better than Sebastian Blancano?"

Justin's shoulders began to sag.

"A simple yes or no will do, Mr. Cord."

"No," seethed Justin, staring hard into the eyes of his oppressor.

"No more questions, Your Honor . . ."

Hektor was speaking to the judge, but was also keenly aware of his audience.

"So in summation, Your Honor, Justin Cord was a man abandoned. All of his carefully laid plans were for naught. The man who knew him best, the man who was his caretaker and official guardian, not only deserted him, in all likelihood he plotted to have him killed postmortem. And while Sebastian Blancano may be accused of treachery, that is not what's at issue today. Because whether or not Mr. Blancano intended for the explosions to seal off Mr. Cord's sanctum—doubtful—or destroy him outright—likely—the final outcome was always clear. Mr. Cord was judged by the man who knew him best. Honor that judgment. Justin Cord was lost and abandoned and would not have been found but for GCI. In fact, without GCI he would still be locked up deep within the mountain. Without GCI he would not have the physical, physiological, and psychological coping skills he so aptly demonstrates today. In short, without GCI's intervention he would not have been reborn. Give a parent their due, Your Honor."

As Judge Farber entered the courtroom everyone stood. He sat down, the room followed suit, and he sternly reviewed his opinion. It was much easier to arrive at than he'd thought. With the loco parentis claim the trial had taken a direction he hadn't expected, but when the lawyer Black presented their evidence, the truth became self-evident.

"Despite Mr. Sambianco's impassioned line of investigation," began the judge, "it is the finding of this court that GCI has already been more than compensated for the revival of Justin Cord, and is not due any more compensation."

A loud murmur shot through the jam-packed courtroom.

"Order! People!" shouted the clerk. The room quieted down as those who hadn't already dashed for the exit realized the judge had more to say.

"Indeed," continued the judge, "so exorbitant was GCI's bill for Mr. Cord's re-animation that I would go so far as to suggest that if the individual or organization that paid the ten-million-credit fee can be found, it would be in their interest to seek legal redress for what in my opinion amounts to not only an audacious claim, but a fraudulent one as well. It is therefore the judgment of this court that the claim is without merit and is summarily dismissed. Court is adjourned."

Total victory. Justin Cord wins a total victory. He is still The Unincorporated Man. But what was that interplay with Hektor Sambianco of GCI?

—NeuroCourtNews site

Justin, Manny, and Neela were led out of the courtroom by the same army of guards and securibots that had led them in. Immediately outside the chamber the trio was assaulted on all sides by reporters shouting questions, buzzing mediabots, Looky Lous, and a small cadre of protestors arguing both sides of the case, seemingly oblivious to the stars in their presence. The guards did their best to shield the group from the assault by moving them slowly if not forcefully down the narrow corridor leading to the building's exit, where they barely managed to squeeze through the throng. Justin was surprised by the inclement weather. When they'd arrived it was a typical summer's day, a little balmy but comfortable. But now, oddly enough, it was blustery outside. He was later to find out that someone in the Ministry of Weather had felt that given the importance of the decision, cool winds with a slight drizzle seemed appropriate—never mind that it was the middle of August. En masse, the victors were practically shoved by the guards through the walls of a waiting limousine, which took off into the sky hounded and chased by mediabots and reporters in flyers like a bear who'd stolen honey from a hive. Manny and Neela were so jubilant about the victory they'd barely noticed Justin sulking at the edge of the limousine's couch. Neela was the first, and she gave Manny a gentle shove, pointing toward Justin.

"Are you dissatisfied with the ruling, Mr. Cord?" asked Manny.

Justin, leaning forward on his knees, clasped his hands together. "How dare that bastard do that?"

"Do what?"

"Throw Sebastian's betrayal in my face, that's what!"

"Ahh, that," replied Manny. "Just good lawyering. Trying to throw you off is all. It obviously didn't work. After all, you won."

"I don't think he cares about the judgment at this point," said Neela.

Unconsciously acknowledging Neela, Justin continued with his diatribe. "The information . . . about . . . Blancano . . . it . . . it was not about this case. His evidence didn't have a chance of changing the outcome. He did it to attack me, pure and simple. He wanted me to suffer, and you know what? The feeling is mutual."

Justin turned away from his friends and stared out the window. He looked out through the maelstrom of flying machines chasing their limo, past the brightly colored geometric beauty of New York City, and saw . . . nothing. Hektor had been right. He *had* been abandoned by the man he trusted most. And three hundred years would not erase the pain he was only now beginning to feel.

Neela was about to offer her services as a professional listener when she heard something extraordinary—an avatar speaking without being spoken to.

"I'd understand if you'd want me to change my name and voice," chirped sebastian. "You appear to have had a good relationship with this Dr. O'Toole. I could take on the name and approximate her voice with a little coaching."

Justin snapped out of his malaise, shook his head, and, smiling a little sadly, said, "No. In some ways that would be giving that bastard more power than he's worth, and would be punishing you for what he did."

"Justin," answered the DijAssist, "you could not 'punish me' in the manner you speak of. I'm an avatar, and so have no feelings about your decision one way or another."

"Still," answered Justin, "not my style. Besides, you weren't just named for my assistant."

"Really?" answered sebastian, managing to sound intrigued. "I show no other records of a Sebastian in your life. May I inquire as to whom my noble namesake is?"

Justin, noticing Neela, smiled for the first time since entering the flyer.

"Well," he answered his avatar, "I'm not sure how happy you'll be. . . ."

"Again, Justin, 'happy' is an emo . . ."

"I also named you after my cat." Justin smirked.

"A feline," said sebastian. "I'm named after a feline?" Despite his claim of indifference, sebastian sounded a little miffed.

"Hey, it *was* my favorite cat."

"I suppose," answered sebastian, not missing a beat, "I could learn how to meow, purr, and whatnot."

It sounded suspiciously to Neela like fairly advanced humor for so young an avatar. She was impressed enough to make a mental note. She'd have her avatar check into the new DijAssist start-up protocols. It never hurt to be current.

"That won't be necessary," answered Justin, now smiling. He continued staring out the window, but it was obvious the fog had been lifted.

Neela had listened to the entire conversation in abject fascination. Whatever that little avatar had done to get Justin out of his funk, it had clearly worked.

Clever little bastard, that one. Neela then joined Manny in a toast. Even if Justin wasn't going to celebrate, she sure as hell was.

When they were all back at Justin's apartment, Neela brought Dr. Gillette up to speed.

"Well," suggested the doctor loud enough for all to hear, "we could always give him a taste of his own medicine—how 'bout a P.A.?"

The den, which now included Omad, Manny, Neela, and Justin, quieted down. Even Manny, who aside from the trial had remained expressionless, raised an eyebrow. Only Justin seemed surprised by the change of mood.

"Dr. Gillette," seethed Neela, "can I speak with you outside?"

It was not a request. As she and her mentor left the den, Neela saw Justin reach for his DijAssist.

Oh crap, she thought, *now he'll find out without us.*

When they were out of earshot, Neela let loose.

"How could you suggest a psychological audit!? Especially as a form of retribution? Of all the irresponsible, dangerous, impractical . . ."

"My dear Neela," responded Dr. Gillette calmly, "if we can concentrate on the third of your accusations."

"Wha . . . ?" Neela sputtered, thrown off from her train of verbiage.

"The impractical aspect of a retributive P.A.," Dr. Gillette reminded her.

"Impractical! Of course it's impractical! In order to request a P.A., Justin would have to buy stock in Hektor! Which is about as likely as me seeing self-majority!"

"Well," responded Dr. Gillette, "with regards to getting some of Hektor's stock, it's really not too difficult to do, even if his price is likely to rise. Your self-majority is quite another matter."

"Perhaps you didn't hear me, Thaddeus. I said Justin wouldn't take Hektor's stock even if he got it for free. Besides, why would anyone want to buy the stock of that snake, Sambianco?"

"Don't belittle your opponents," answered the doctor, "it clouds the judgment. And in answer to your question as to why would anyone want to buy Mr. Sambianco's stock, I'll simply answer with a question. Why shouldn't anyone buy Mr. Sambianco's stock? If I wasn't financially tied up in an attempt to deprive Dr. Bronstein of his majority, I would buy it myself."

Dr. Gillette saw that he wasn't getting through.

"Neela, what do you think the rest of the world sees when they look at Hektor?"

"They see the same asshole from the press conference that they saw at the trial."

"But what if they don't see an asshole?" the doctor countered. "What if they see a competent adversary, and perhaps a pretty good lawyer?"

Neela had to admit it was a possibility.

"Now you're beginning to see it from a layman's point of view. When they see

Hektor Sambianco, yes, they might see an asshole, but if they do it's an asshole who was a good lawyer . . . who lost an unwinnable case, and that's something they probably won't hold against him. Frankly, I wouldn't be surprised if he ends up running GCI's Legal department. Now, more important, try to think why this asshole wants Justin to hate him."

"Wants?"

"Yes," replied the doctor, " 'wants.' All of his acts, all of his strategies seem bent on forcing visceral responses from our patient."

Neela wasn't buying it. "What if he's just an ass? You know what Freud used to say."

Dr. Gillette sighed, remembering just how young Neela was.

"Neela, you're so focused on the concerns of your patient that it's giving you a slight case of myopia." He paused briefly. "Imagine," he continued, "that Hektor is your patient and that you need to understand him."

Neela was about to argue but stopped midword and considered what Dr. Gillette was asking of her. For more than a minute Dr. Gillette saw her go through the delightful, painful, and rewarding struggle of incorporating old information to a new thought pattern.

"Justin is no longer a job to Hektor," she answered with a dawning awareness. "Justin is pushing one of Hektor's primal emotions, jealousy, fear, hate . . . something. Hektor might not even know it's what's motivating him. That's why he keeps on pushing Justin's buttons."

"Precisely, Neela. Our Mr. Cord has many wonderful attributes, but he also has a temper, which is well exposed when he feels threatened."

"I guess you could say they're both good at pushing each other's buttons."

"Yes, you could," answered the doctor. "It might also help to think of Justin as an adolescent. In that way his emotional responses may make more sense to you."

"But he's in his fifties."

"Physiologically?"

"Well, he looks thirty, but his actual physical age is closer to nineteen." Neela paused, realized she'd missed something important, and smiled ruefully. "Of course. He has all the raging physiological attributes of a young adult male and none of the social training or years of experience on how to redeal with them."

Thaddeus nodded in sympathy. "Don't fault yourself, Neela. In so many ways he's a unique case. When age reversal became available it was introduced slowly to those who needed it . . . those who needed to 'catch up' to the medical technology that would restore their youth. These individuals grew up staying perpetually young with years to deal with the effects of near-eternal youth, or they had years to come back to their 'new' age. But Justin is the first man I've ever heard of to simply go from his fifties to his late teens in one fell swoop."

"I'll need to talk to him about this," she said, "but it will be hard to convince him that he's mad at Hektor because of hormones."

"You won't need to. Just explain to him that his anger is appropriate but his responses are not. I'm sure he'll understand. It's also why I suggested he institute a psychological audit against Hektor. It will give Justin some way of striking back, which will enable him to calm down. Once he no longer feels helpless against Hektor and GCI, which to Justin is the same thing, you can then prescribe a physiological readjustment, or at least some hormone therapy. And because there's no chance that Justin could succeed with the audit, after all, there's no basis, and any judge would throw the request out, we can consider it an exercise in futility that will help our patient cool off. If by some miracle a judge does approve a psyche audit, it would be, given the resources of GCI, appealed all the way up to the Supreme Court. And we all know how they feel about psyche audits."

Neela had to admit that the plan seemed well thought out, and certainly made a lot of sense. But that didn't mean she had to like it. "I will trust your judgment, Thaddeus, but I'm not thrilled with it. Hektor is up to something."

"My dear," he answered, ignoring her intuition, "it's a spurious request for a P.A. and will be seen as such by any competent judge. The only thing you have to worry about is getting our patient up to his correct hormonal levels and back on track."

"I suppose you're right," Neela said, resigned. "Now if I could only convince the knot in my stomach."

The doctor smiled and indicated that they rejoin the group. As they entered the den they both noticed that Justin was no longer sitting glumly on the sofa but was up and moving about the room.

Justin looked up and saw the both of them. "Let's give Hektor a taste of his own medicine, shall we?" Neela couldn't help but notice that for the first time in a long time, Justin's eyes seemed as bright as his smile.

Hektor was enjoying his newfound power. He was once more on special assignment to the board, but this time he had an office at GCI system headquarters on the floor with all the executive vice presidents. And while he wasn't an E.V.P. himself, his presence on their floor was meant to send a clear message—screw up this badly again and the "new" guy—the guy who warned you all—the guy you all chose *not* to listen to—gets your job, office, and perks.

He even had a secretary, though he didn't particularly like or trust the man. Hektor was willing to bet Chairman stock to cow shit that his secretary really worked for the V.P. of Special Ops, Kirk Olmstead. But, thought Hektor, pleased, Kirk had enough to worry about. The new director's "go to trial" strategy was not only proven wrong, it was proven disastrously, publicly wrong. The trial was followed by the worst market day that GCI had ever seen. Though, due to the inherent strength of the company, it had soon recovered 85 percent of what it had lost, it was still not fully healed. The effects would be felt systemwide in the bond, stock, and currency markets for years. Although he was still officially head of Special Operations, it was understood that the DepDir's job was now open. If Kirk couldn't fix the current mess, it would go to the first person who could. And Hektor had a plan.

"Mom," said Hektor, practically screaming at the holodisplay, "will you please listen to me?"

"You're talking crazy."

The woman, formed in perfect three-dimensional beauty before him, was a platinum blonde in her late twenties. She was wearing a plaid pink and fuchsia dress with a plunging neckline that was long on cleavage and short on class.

Hektor sighed as he went through the "mom" effect—feeling like he was eight though knowing he was older.

"Will you at least consider it?" he asked.

"You want me to suggest that my son—my own son!—get a psycheslam?"

"Mom, it's a psychological audit, please don't use that slang; it makes you sound so . . . well, young."

"I've been called a lot of things, dear boy, but to be called 'young,' " she said, almost weeping, "and by my own son . . ." When she saw he wasn't taking the bait she began to pout. "Hektor, dearie, what will my friends say? And more important, do you have any idea what it will do to your stock value?"

Hektor sighed. "Mom, did you sell me short?"

"What a horrible thing to ask!" she said, feigning shock. "You're my only son."

Hektor wasn't buying. "Well, did you or didn't you?"

After a pause his mother had the good grace to look ashamed.

"Honey, your stock price was plummeting, and you lost your great job, and then that transfer to the Oort Cloud . . ."

"Mom, I understand why. You raised me to be realistic and take chances, so I did. If it were my kid I would have done the same thing. But let me ask you another question, Mom: Did you regret it?"

Her anguished expression was all the answer he needed. He also knew where the pain was emanating from—her portfolio.

After Hektor's court appearance his stock began to rise steadily. Once his new appointment and office had been confirmed, it practically soared. Of course, owning most of it himself he was able to use his increased equity to arrange a much better loan and pay off all his outstanding debts. He could have sold about 9 percent of himself and still have had a comfortable majority, but Hektor believed in his star. And if anyone wanted whatever stock of his was out there, let the bastards pay market price. Hektor was holding on for now, and he even got his Neela Harper stocks out of hock. And that was proving to be an even better investment than the one he had made in himself. As if to confirm his suspicion, his mother seemed on the verge of breaking down.

"Twenty percent!" she moaned. "We had twenty percent! What a neutron your father is!"

Serves you right, Hektor thought. "Mom, please trust me that this psychological audit will not cause a drop in my price but a rise. *And* I will give you two hundred shares of my stock."

Her eyes lit up. No sooner had they done so when she gave her son a suspicious look. "What's the catch?"

"One small favor," Hektor said, smiling. "You will go to Justin Cord and offer him one hundred shares of me."

"Don't be silly, boy. A, why would he take them from me?, and b, what on Mars would I tell him?"

"You'll tell him you want revenge."

"For what?"

"I'll leave that to you."

"How could he believe such a thing?"

"Mom, it's me you're talking about. He'll believe it."

"Well, I will have to think about it for a bit. Talk to your father, our broker, you know."

"Don't take too long, Mom, things cha . . ."

Hektor was interrupted by his secretary's entrance into the room, an act that indicated there was a visitor of enough importance to interrupt whoever Hektor was talking to.

"Hold on a sec, Ma. Yeah," he said to the secretary, looking slightly annoyed. "What is it?"

"Mr. Sambianco," she answered, "there's a process server here, and she said to tell you 'we'll meet by moonlight.' I told her you were in Colorado, but she insisted."

"I'll be damned," he said, lips parting in a wolfish grin. "Let her in."

"Sir, did I mention she was a process server?"

Hektor's mom cut in. "Hektor, what's going on?"

"One moment, Mom."

Into the room walked the same incredible seductress who'd served Hektor on the loading bay only a few weeks before. This time she had more clothes on, but still managed the same rarely tenable combination of grace, gorgeousness, and age that advertisers killed for.

"Mr. Sambianco."

"Are you here to arrange a date, Miss . . . ?"

"Snow, and yes, but not the one you think. You are being served to submit for a psychological audit . . . by one of your stockholders."

"Let me guess . . . Justin Cord?"

The woman nodded in agreement.

Hektor's mouth opened, forming the beginnings of a smile. He looked over at his mother in the holodisplay, still waiting patiently.

"Mom, love ya, deal's off, gotta go." He cut the phone connection before his flabbergasted mother could say a word.

"Now, Miss Snow," he said, turning to the server, "why should I let you just hand me a summons without getting something for it in return?"

Miss Snow stared straight at Hektor with her best bedroom eyes.

"What did you have in mind?"

"I was thinking of asking you out on a date."

"My dear Mr. Sambianco, you can ask, but you're still too young."

"How about if I make it worth your while?"

"Confident, aren't you?"

"About many things, but I think you may like this." Hektor smiled.

"Alright, Mr. Sambianco, let's hear your offer."

"The first time you served me it was easy. This time it was even easier, because I let you in. Do you admit that I could have made it difficult?"

"Of course, that's why they pay me the big creds."

"And I'm sure you're worth every one of them, Miss Snow. Now let's think about the third time you'll have to serve me. And I can assure there will be a third, fourth, and fifth time. I know a way it can be as simple as this, and a lot more entertaining."

"I don't know, Mr. Sambianco, I'm finding this pretty entertaining as it is. But I must admit I'm curious. What's your offer?"

"Simple, really. The next time you have to serve me, just call. You can do it on our date. No running, no hiding, no doubles or processing loopholes, just a pleasant dinner."

Miss Snow leaned forward over his desk and, speaking softly, said, "You think you can cause me that much trouble?"

Hektor leaned over until he was inches from her face and said in just as soft a voice, "Absolutely."

She delicately kissed the tip of his nose and stepped back.

"Done, Mr. Sambianco. On one condition."

"If it is within my power to grant."

"I believe it is. I've given a lot of summonses for psyche audits in my time. What I find most interesting is that when I do a follow-up I find that each person has a different way of getting out of taking the P.A. Some are clever, most are straightforward, and some are downright genius. So here's my deal. If I like your answer you have a date."

"Deal," answered Hektor, without missing a beat.

"So then," Miss Snow said, sitting down comfortably in one of Hektor's guest chairs, "how do you intend to escape the P.A.?"

Hektor leaned back in his chair. He then put his hands behind his head, his feet up on the desk, and opened his mouth in cool repose.

"I don't."

"Are you insane?" Legal ranted, pacing in her office.

"Thank you, I feel fine," Hektor answered calmly.

"Maybe you really do need a P.A. And if I keep listening to this load of horseshit I'm going to need one, too."

"Janet, it's perfect," he tried to explain. "If Justin hadn't demanded one of me I probably would have suggested it to him . . . on the sly, of course."

"Of course," Janet mimicked. "Hektor, do you realize what a psyche audit is?"

"I assure you, Janet, I do."

"First they'll send nanobots in to crawl all over your neural pathways," she said, choosing to ignore his last comment. "Any minor or major glitch they find, they fix . . . on the spot. Now, I don't know about you, but I like me the way I am, warts and all. And the last thing I'd want is to know that my pathways have been smoothed over by an army of unfeeling microbots that I'm gonna end up pissing out in the morning."

Hektor remained unmoved. "Got it."

Janet took another stab. "They say that you're not the same person . . . ever."

"Of course not," he answered. "By the time anyone gets a P.A. they really do need an adjustment, so of course they aren't the same person. Who would be? But Janet, I can assure you, I'm not crazy, which is why I'm not afraid to take the P.A."

"But you're letting *Justin* put you through one? I'm sorry, Hek, but that sounds pretty crazy to me."

"Actually, that's the real reason I'm here. I need your help."

"What for? You're obviously not going to stop it."

"No, I need your help to make it happen as quickly and noiselessly as possible."

Janet stared at him, too dumbfounded to speak.

"Janet," explained Hektor, "I got him good and mad in the courtroom and he lashed out. But when he calms down he'll probably change his mind. I have to have this done before he does."

Janet looked over at the man who'd only weeks before swept in and kept her career from careening down the side of a gully. She'd decided to trust him then, when the stakes were far higher. There was no reason not to trust him now.

"What about Kirk?"

"What about him?"

"He won't let this fly. It'll make him look bad."

"Don't worry about Kirk," he answered. The icy tone of his reply was assurance enough. Then, "Find anything on Harper?"

"You mean her supposed relationship with Cord?"

"Yeah."

"Dead end. If they're having one, which I do not believe they are, they're doing a pretty good job of concealing it. He seems pretty attached to her, but that's not out of the ordinary. She, of course, is behaving perfectly. Technically, she's not even his reanimationist anymore. On top of that, the microfacial analysis is pretty conclusive."

"Keep looking," he said, unmoved by the lack of evidence. "She'll sleep with him, and when she does, we'll need proof."

Janet shifted uncomfortably in her seat. "What's the point, Hektor? If it's Cord you're after, how does destroying Harper help . . . unless, of course, you're getting some sort of sick joy out of it?"

"Janet, I *never* destroy for sport. Only for commerce." He leaned across his desk, picked up a folder marked "Harper, N," and then tossed it over to Janet.

"Archaic, I admit," he said, referring to the paper documents, "but 100 percent secure, I assure you." Janet nodded. "Dr. Harper will be our voodoo doll," he continued. "The more pins and needles we can shove through her eyeballs, the more pain Justin will feel."

Janet leaned over, grabbed then opened the folder, and rifled through some of the notes. Nothing too serious, she saw. A few minor indiscretions in college. Certainly nothing that would damage Neela's reputation or bring the wrath of Cord down on Janet's office. Then she noticed a small memo atop a contract. It was from Hektor's office, and it was addressed to Kirk Olmstead.

"You asked Kirk to go after her contract?"

"Yes."

Janet nodded. "No contract. No protection. We can mess with her. Brilliant." Then, "Why give it to Olmstead?"

"Because he'll fail, of course."

Janet again looked puzzled.

"So why would he take the risk?"

"Because," answered Hektor, "I made it sound like a good idea. *His* idea."

"But can it actually be done?" she asked.

"Of course not," barked Hektor. "The contract's damn near iron-clad. That

Mosh McKenzie is not one to screw with. You fuck with him, you'd better hope you've got some limbs you won't mind losing. He made that contract."

"So basically you want Kirk to screw up."

"That's the plan. Not too big a screwup, but it all adds up in the end."

Janet said nothing, working out all the possibilities. It was a skill she'd honed to perfection in her slow and steady rise up the GCI corporate ladder.

"You do realize," she offered, now more than ever wanting to be seen as an asset to the man seated before her, "that any attempt to make a run on Harper's contract will alert Dr. Harper and Mr. Cord that you know of their supposed weakness for one another . . . I mean, why else do it, right?"

Hektor nodded, again unmoved. "Janet, *I want them to know* that GCI suspects them. Fear does not work against ignorance or certainty. It creeps in and festers with possibility. Let them wonder what *we* know; what we'll do with our knowledge. Let them wonder if we'll tell others of Dr. Harper's perversions. Let *them* worry. It'll make them paranoid and unhappy. In return Justin will get in an attack which you'll help funnel directly to its intended target."

Janet looked up from the contract she'd been perusing. "You."

"Me," he repeated, nodding. His eyes were cold and his lips parted, in a caninelike threat.

"Fine, Hektor. But I'll need some sort of excuse for why I'm not doing my job when word of your audit gets out."

Hektor nodded in agreement. "If anyone asks, tell them that your hands are tied."

"Because?" she asked.

"Because, my dear, there's almost no redress against an unincorporated man."

6   Open and Shut

Justin woke up feeling better, or to be more precise, calmer. He scanned his immediate environment. The room was an almost exact duplicate of his old office's antechamber, a place he'd often go to take catnaps during his long workday. The small, ornately paneled space had wall-to-wall bookshelves, a small fireplace—now lit—and one standard twin-sized bed that he was lying in. *If they're going to mess with your biology, best to wake up in a familiar place*, he thought, *not that it'll make one iota of difference.* Justin yawned and stretched out his arms. He wasn't sure what to expect from the procedure even though he'd been told. But he'd been so conditioned to coming out of any "anesthetic" experience both groggy and somewhat disoriented—especially in his dying days— that the mere fact that he now wasn't made him feel . . . well, slightly disoriented.

It had been Neela's idea to have him go in for some aging therapy, and after some discussion and research on his part, Justin agreed. But he insisted that they do the procedure back in Boulder, again for comfort and familiarity. It was not difficult to arrange, and GCI, feeling the sting of both the public and its stockholders, felt it impolitic to deprive him of the facilities he preferred. He got himself dressed, took one last look at "his" room, and went out to the waiting area. Neela was sitting in a floating chair busily scanning something in her DijAssist. She looked up as she heard Justin enter.

"I feel fine," he answered before she could ask. "In fact, I feel better, no, not the right word, more centered, than before."

"I'm glad," she replied, "but still kicking myself for having overlooked it. I mean, we just woke you up at the default age."

"Hey, you woke me up. That's what really matters."

"True enough," Neela said, getting up from her chair. "I think we were more focused on that than anything."

"Well, other than a few adolescent outbursts, no real harm done."

Neela's thoughts drifted to Hektor. *I wouldn't be so sure.*

They'd planned on spending the rest of the day doing a little shopping, but after being hounded by the media and cornered by fans, they spent the bulk of the afternoon in their hotel rooms. They made arrangements with Mosh and Eleanor for an early dinner and tried to relax. Neela felt a good night's rest would be in order given what she knew Justin was in for the following day.

"So what's the L.A. thing about?" asked Justin, reclining on an overstuffed La-Z-Boy he'd had the room create for him.

Neela couldn't help but frown every time he clambered in and out of the huge, retractable monstrosity.

"I'm telling you, Neela," he said, putting his arms behind his head, "you ought to try this baby out. It ain't no ergo chair, but it does have its redeeming qualities."

"I'm sure it does," she answered, halfheartedly. "Maybe later."

Her face became more serious.

"Tomorrow we visit the museum."

Justin's smile faded, too. He stared up at the ceiling for a moment.

"You sure?"

"Yes. I believe you're ready."

"OK then, you're the boss."

Justin had done some research on virtual reality museums as well as the dictates they were predicated on. He knew this much: The museums represented a set of dictates so fundamental to the development of present-day society that a single visit was considered a rite of passage. He also knew that no one ever visited twice. Partly on Neela's advice, but mostly because he didn't have the time, he'd avoided learning more. Apparently, the L.A. museum had made special arrangements for his visit, and it was therefore critical that they arrive at a specified time. Since Justin had insisted on flying his new car rather than taking a t.o.p., Neela insisted that they leave by 9:00 A.M. That, she assured him, would allow them plenty of time to arrive at the required hour.

Justin had two reasons for not wanting to take the t.o.p. First, he wanted to fly his own car. Second, he felt like having a good old-fashioned road trip, especially given the pressure he'd been under with the trial. Too many weeks in the spotlight and with the specter of going to visit a place that seemed shrouded in gloom. Neela didn't seem to mind, because it not only gave her the ability to talk with Justin at length, it also wouldn't take that much longer than traveling by t.o.p. They agreed on the specifics, and Justin made arrangements to have the car fly itself out from New York City and meet them first thing in the morning.

The big surprise for Justin was that hardly anyone drove anymore. People traveled, of course, but except for a few nostalgia towns like Boulder, they simply didn't put four pieces of rubber on the pavement and the pedal to the metal. When he had thought of the future it was always with flying cars, but he'd also imagined huge elevated roadways that were twenty lanes wide and filled with futuristic vehicles driving on self-repairing, ever-expanding road systems. Instead he found . . . nothing. Mile after mile of wilderness with not a speck of blacktop in sight. Outside of the cities there were no freeways, no highways, and no roads. The more he thought about it, the more it made sense. Why build a road when there were orports and flying cars aplenty? But it was still a shock to leave the cities of the future, with their gleaming facades, their towering-above-the-clouds spires, their millions of flying vehicles, and find unadulterated wilderness just a few miles away. On the other hand, he had to admit it was beautiful. The land that had been left to itself had pretty much become renewed. He smiled at the thought of all the environmental wackos who used to be on him like white on rice. They were now, of course, pushing up daisies, never having lived to see their dreams of a green planet fully realized.

Talking with Neela, Justin had learned that most of the wilderness he was looking at was in fact owned, and that essentially ownership meant extracting what valuable resources there were and leaving the rest alone. It also seemed that the notion of living in the boonies stopped making sense about a century prior to Justin's revival. With the perfection of nanotechnology, rustic, outdoor getaways—or whatever "boonies" fantasy a person happened to have—could be created . . . in the city . . . in a building . . . on whichever floor was available. And all on the cheap. Certainly cheaper than trying to live outside of a city. So the strange truth was that a planet of over twenty billion people was now mostly empty.

Flying his car was much easier than Justin had imagined. The vehicle flew itself, but anytime he took over control the autopilot disengaged. It only reengaged at those moments it realized a complete novice was at the helm. Though the car was traveling at approximately 1,600 mph, it felt as light and agile as a paper airplane tossed high into the sky. The wide windows afforded unadulterated views of vast, empty land, open tundra, magnificent mountain ranges, and sinuous rivers. And a slight detour to Arizona allowed Justin to realize a dream he'd always had as a boy—flying into and through the Grand Canyon like a bat out of hell.

Neela laughed at her companion's sheer glee.

"Well," she smirked, "I guess there's still some elevated hormone levels to be dealt with."

"Oh no, you don't," he answered, mouth agape in adolescent awe as the craft skimmed a small patch of rapids along the Colorado River. "They're right where I want 'em."

"Well, if you like this," she answered, seemingly bored, "you'll go Alaskan when you hit the canyons of Mars. They make the Grand Canyon look like a scratch in the sand."

"Hot damn!" Justin said, banking up a steep curve. "How 'bout we go now?"

Neela's nonanswer was all the answer he needed. He shrugged, realizing his little side trip was over, pulled the car up and out of the canyon, and pointed it toward L.A. At the speeds they were traveling, it only took a few minutes to arrive.

The car slowed down appreciably as they entered the city limits.

Neela watched as Justin took in the new and improved City of Angels. "How does it look?" she asked.

"It's big, spread-out, and not very tall," he answered. "Hasn't changed much at all."

It hadn't. After the Grand Collapse those who were able headed north to the Alaskan Federation. When the world eventually got its bearings back on track, California no longer held its allure. After all, weather, one of the state's main claims to fame, was now technologically influenced on an almost regular basis. The state's other claim to fame, entertainment, had left such a black mark on society that there were those who, like some of the Jews who'd escaped Nazi Germany, refused to ever step foot on its soil again. Neela had explained to Justin that the placement of a virtual reality museum in L.A., the flashpoint of the VR plague, had caused such an uproar that some people were still arguing about it.

When they were within range of the museum, Neela told the car to descend into a parking area near a large, well-manicured square. As it came to a soft landing, she gave Justin an "are you ready for this?" glance. He answered with a nod. They slipped out through the vehicle's walls and walked toward the main park. Once there, they came upon an oversized, elaborate entrance made of stone, metal, and thousands of pieces of crushed computer motherboards. The gate was at least ten feet wide and twenty feet tall and had the words IT'S NECESSARY spelled out above in wrought iron. As they passed through the entrance they made way for a group of twelve students heading out. The students, Justin could see, appeared to be about seven or eight years of age and were accompanied by two adults. It looked like a school field trip, except that none of the children were smiling. They were so lost in thought that two of them even had to be gently redirected from hitting the side of the gate. They shuffled their feet as they walked by, barely noticing the media stars in their midst. Justin waited until they were out of the park and turned to Neela.

"Justin," she tried to explain, "our world came about from the collapse of the old world, but that world fell in such a horrific fashion it came very close to the destruction of all civilization as we know it."

"What does that have to do with those kids?"

"Everything."

They walked for another hundred yards along a gravel path, with only the sound of the grinding rocks beneath their feet to interrupt the silence. A large building appeared over the horizon. The structure appeared to be collapsing upon itself. Huge sheets of glass and metal were jutting out in different directions, seeming ready to fly off at any moment. There was no courtyard to speak of; rather, the large, discombobulated edifice was sitting in the middle of a huge pit void of any foliage. Storm clouds surrounded the compound. Justin and Neela descended a flight of steps leading into the vast hole in the ground.

The entrance was a wide opening at the pit's base. The wall surrounding that opening was made of marble, and on that marble, engraved in three-foot-high letters, were the following sentences:

I. A CULTURE THAT ACCEPTS VIRTUAL REALITY
ACCEPTS DESTRUCTION

II. THAT WHICH A HUMAN SHOULD DO, DO

III. ACCEPT NO REALITY EXCEPT REALITY

IV. ABSOLUTE PLEASURE CORRUPTS ABSOLUTELY

V. NEVER FORGET

Neela waited while Justin read the inscriptions. She also wanted to give him time to absorb them.

"Behold," she said, "the famous Virtual Reality Dictates."

"Impressive," replied Justin, standing back and taking in the scarred yet pristine landscape.

Continuing their earlier conversation, she added, "We wait until the children are old enough to understand and remember. The age is different for each child, but it's usually between seven and nine."

"How old were you?"

"Seven," whispered Neela, momentarily looking like one of the children they'd just seen exiting the park.

"What's this place supposed to do, Neela?"

"It's supposed to show us the price paid by society when it takes away responsibility and replaces it with pleasure."

"Well, that sounds awfully Puritan, don't you think?"

Neela didn't answer. She seemed somehow entranced by the building. Justin realized that she hadn't even heard his question. She just stood there, staring—a victim revisiting the crime scene. Neela took a breath and indicated that it was time to enter.

As they walked through the large doorway Justin could see that the building was much larger on the inside than it appeared on the outside, as was evidenced by a multitude of escalators heading farther down into the Earth. The escalators' destinations were veiled by a thin layer of fog.

They were met almost immediately by a sharply dressed employee who had a button on his lapel that said THINGS ARE LOOKING UP. After they were finished signing in, he checked his holodisplay, then looked up again. "Please excuse me, Mr. Cord, Dr. Harper," he said, obviously excited to be in the presence of celebrity, "just a few more modifications and we'll be on our way . . . And by the way, congratulations on your case."

"Thanks," they both answered, then laughed nervously.

The employee continued to mess around with buttons and knobs.

"Just presetting your experience to better accommodate your visit here."

"Ahh," responded Justin, not knowing what else to say.

"And by the way," continued the employee, looking up once again from his holodisplay, "all of us employees here at the VR museum loved how you stuck it to GCI."

"I'm surprised you don't work for them."

"Oh no, Mr. Cord," answered the employee, beaming with pride. "We work for the government."

Justin gave Neela a surprised look.

Neela shrugged. "Not everyone works for GCI, Justin."

Justin looked around, moving on. "Where's everybody else?"

"Everybody who?" asked the employee.

"The rest of the visitors."

"Oh, we cleared them out. Professional courtesy. Plus, the last thing we want is to have you surrounded by a mob of fans for your visit here. I think you may have bumped into the last group on your way in."

"As a matter of fact, we did," answered Neela.

The employee made a few more adjustments and got out from behind his holodisplay. "Right this way, Mr. Cord, Dr. Harper," he said, indicating that they take the third escalator from the left, which was now well lit. Both Justin and Neela got on. Justin, out of habit, began walking down the already moving escalator until he noticed Neela. She'd picked her step, grabbed hold of the rail, and was now leaning against it. Though the escalator was moving slowly, Neela's pall was that of an unwilling passenger being strapped into a roller coaster.

"You go ahead if you want," she said. "They won't start without me."

Justin smiled and climbed back up the steps.

"That's OK," he said, taking her hand. She gave it over, too anxious to argue.

As soon as they were through the clouded veil, things, as the employee's button said, really did start to look up. It appeared that they were descending into an early-twenty-first-century shopping mall, complete with cheerful music and busy shoppers. The only thing wrong with the scenario, noted Justin, was that there was entirely too much cheer for what he knew was meant to be a cheerless place. Nevertheless, he was in it for the ride, and he'd take whatever experience the museum decided to throw at him at face value. He couldn't help but notice a large back-lit sign advertising that the latest in VR technology had just been installed. The sign also indicated how to find the store within the mall.

"We going there?" he said, pointing to the sign.

"Yes," she said, "unless you feel like having a Starbucks." She pointed over at the café with a logo Justin recognized.

"You mean I can just stay here and shop and drink if I like?"

"If you like," she said. "But you won't be able to leave until you visit the VR center."

Justin laughed. "Starbucks or hell. You people are too much."

Neela stood silently, waiting for Justin to decide.

His eyes narrowed with shrewd intent. "Let's go to hell," he said.

As they made their way through the mall toward the VR center, Justin struck up a conversation.

"You know, Neela, I might not have liked malls, but this place doesn't really seem all that scary."

"Justin, the mall's not scary . . . it's what you can buy here." Justin was already sure this experience would be about as pleasant as a weekend at a Taliban resort, but that last statement unnerved him. It was the old "careful what you wish for" mantra.

"It's also not like any museum I've ever been to," he continued, "unless, of course, this mall here is part of the exhibit."

"I guess you could say it is," she answered, "or it just might be the whole exhibit. You never really know."

Justin looked at her quizzically.

"It's different for everyone," she said.

"Ahh."

After a five-minute walk, they arrived at a large glass-fronted store occupying one hundred feet of mall front. There in front of them was a large sign spanning the windows that read VIRTUAL REALITY BOOTHS, FIRST TEN MINUTES FREE! Not wanting further delay, Justin walked in first and was greeted by an overly cheerful hostess. Neela shuffled in behind him. The hostess looked to be about seventeen or eighteen and had the well-worn demeanor of a high-school kid working her way through a summer job. She welcomed Justin professionally if not a bit stiffly, as is always the case when nonprofessionals are forced to go by a script. At the end of her brief monologue, she made sure to assure both Justin and Neela that they were about to have the experience of their lives. When Justin started to ask questions, Neela gently laid a hand on his arm to quiet him. The hostess took the both of them to another room marked with a sign that read CALIBRATION.

Neela began to shake.

"Are you all right, Miss?" asked the hostess.

"Yes, yes, I'm fine," she answered, "just a little cold."

"Neela," said Justin, "not only are you *not* cold, you're also a terrible liar."

"I'll be all right," she said in a small voice.

"You plan to go through this *again* . . . on my behalf?"

Neela nodded. "You shouldn't have to do this alone, Justin."

"Neela, even if we did this together I'd probably end up doing it alone . . . I very much doubt they'd let you interfere in my experience."

"I . . . I could arrange something . . . make sure you weren't in too deep."

"Pass."

"Justin, no adult has ever done this before . . . at least, not in my day."

"Stay here, Neela," he answered, ignoring her.

"But—"

"—no buts. You won't do me any good if you're in shock. One of us will need to talk to me with a clear head afterward. You're elected."

"Dr. Gillette—"

"—probably has no idea you were even thinking about this, does he?"

Neela shrugged. "And if he did," continued Justin, "I suspect he'd have your head. No, Neela, it's you I'm going to want sane when I wake up . . . *again*. And it's only you who I trust to see me through whatever it is I'm supposedly about to go through. Now do me a favor and leave."

In the end it wasn't that difficult to convince her. They stepped outside the store, alone. Neela agreed to wait and Justin suggested she try the Starbucks. "I prefer the nonfat venti latte," he offered, "but I suppose," he said, grinning, "you can go for whole milk in this day and age." She agreed to give it a try, laughed nervously, and then wished him luck. But before Justin could turn around and head back into the VR store, Neela pulled him toward her and kissed him powerfully on the lips. He stood there, stunned, knowing he should have been overjoyed. He'd been waiting for this moment from the time Neela first put her hand on his in the pawnshop. Had fantasized about it even. But not like this. Not this kiss. Neela's look as she pulled away from him and stared sadly into his eyes told him what he needed to know. This was the kiss of the desperate sending a loved one off to war. This was the kiss of someone saying good-bye.

As Neela departed, Justin went back into the store and followed the teenager into the calibration room. There it was explained to him that the process was the equivalent of a head MRI only with much, much better scanners. The reason, he was told, was so that Justin's virtual reality encounter could be a "hyper" experience. In other words, the hostess patiently explained, once the machine knew how Justin's brain experienced sight, sound, taste, and smell, it could better create those experiences by using his brain as the architect and driver of the newly simulated experiences.

"No single piece of pizza tastes exactly the same to two people," she explained. "We might all agree that it tastes 'good,' but until we know what constitutes 'good' in your brain, we can't really give you the ultimate experience. With this machine," she said, pointing to a large box seated next to a recliner, "we can."

It took ten minutes. Basically, it boiled down to Justin sitting in a large, comfortable recliner and having a small dome placed over his head. Once the dome was removed, he noticed that the other couches in the room were all made for children. They were not only smaller; they were also brightly colored and more pleasing to the eye. It was explained to him that his VR rig had been specially installed.

When he was settled in, the hostess departed the room. Now he was alone. He felt tired. His vision began to fade and his fingers and toes went numb. Then his vision ceased entirely and he was effectively blind. Next, his sense of feeling faded away. It was akin to a controlled blackout. But before he could panic he felt something. Very quickly his vision and all his senses came back. But he was not where he had been. In fact, he was not *who* he had been. He was a tall, bearded, and very muscular man standing in front of a polished brass mirror. He was half dressed and in the process of putting on a shirt—linen, of course. He looked around and saw that he was in a tent. On a rough-hewn bed was a vivacious dark-haired, olive-skinned, and very naked woman. Justin looked her over. If he didn't know any better he'd have to say that she appeared to be sleeping the sleep of the sexually exhausted.

"This I could get used to," he said to himself. But the voice he said it in sounded deeper and more menacing than anything *he* had ever sounded like. He noticed a riding crop and a sword next to the bed. Deciding to play along, he put them on and walked outside. His chin dropped as he gaped in awe while an an entire army of similarly dressed warriors raised their weapons in salute. Thousands of voices from a chorus of Viking throats greeted him, shouting in unison, "*Justin king! Justin king! Justin king!*" An old, grizzled, yet vigorous-looking man sidled up to him.

"My king," shouted the old man so that all could hear, "shall your men ride today?"

The horde silenced itself, awaiting his word.

"Um, sure," Justin muttered, and then, catching himself, got more into the spirit of the affair. "By the gods, yes!"

The Vikings let loose with another massive roar, and as a man turned to run over a nearby rise, Justin and the old man followed at a manly gait. When Justin glimpsed over the hill he saw a vast plain filled with . . . he blinked and rubbed his eyes in disbelief and looked again.

His companion spoke up. "Aye, my lord and king, your father would often do the same thing. It seemed no matter how many times he went to ride, the sight would still fill him with wonder. You are your father's son. Come, my lord, your mount awaits."

Justin blinked again and tried to "see" what his eyes were showing him. Covering the plain in front of him were dragons—thousands of them. Each had a saddle and handler, and many had Vikings already in the saddle, ready to ride. Justin realized what had been bothering him from the second he "woke up." This world he was now in did not feel like a dream. In fact, it was as real as anything he'd ever experienced. The clothes, the hair, the feel of the grass beneath his feet, all of it, down to the scent of jasmine in the air mixed with the distinct smell of . . . fire-breathing animals, was real. *How could it be this real?* he wondered.

They approached Justin's dragon. The attendant bowed formally and handed him a rope that led up to the saddle. As Justin touched the animal's scaly skin, it cooed. The sound was loud and accompanied by a gust of smoke from the great beast's nostrils, but it was unmistakably a coo. Justin was further mesmerized by the sight of the dragon's huge belly heaving in and out.

"A sword for their necks and a fire up their arse," cried the attendant.

Justin ascertained the phrase to be some sort of war mantra. He repeated it back, to which the attendant and Justin's elderly companion responded with a hearty, "Aye."

Justin climbed up the rope and into his saddle. It was simple to put his boots into the stirrups, and as he did so the attendant tossed him a bridle. Before he knew it, the dragon was flying off into the air. He could hardly believe it, but the vision was clear. Justin Cord, Viking king, was leading a squadron of fire-breathing dragons straight into the clouds.

"But what if I don't want to fly a dragon?" Justin shouted out to the sky, wondering if somebody could hear him. His vision immediately began to fade, and his extremities went numb. Soon his mind was again in the black empty void that had begun his journey. *What do I do now?* he thought. And again, as if on cue, another vision appeared before him. It was dazzling yet simple. He thought he saw ten glowing gems. They spun and glittered in front of him, and he thought that one looked prettier than all the rest. The one that his eyes focused on grew brighter, and in a flash of light, the void Justin experienced faded away as his senses returned. He found himself sitting at a desk in some sort of rustic wooden cabin. He looked down at his hand and saw that he was holding a shiny metal five-pointed star. It appeared to be a badge. As soon as he registered the badge, there was a loud knocking on the door. He didn't answer at first.

"Sheriff! Sheriff!" someone cried out. "They need you down at the saloon! Miss Kitty is in a powerful lick of trouble!" Justin got up and found his hat. It was, of course, white.

Justin didn't make the same mistake he'd made in the first fantasy. Which is to say, he didn't repeat the words "But what if I don't want to." He needn't have bothered. The VR machine was calibrated to know when the subject was ready to move on. The only way the fantasy was going to change was when Justin truly wanted it to change. And the second that feeling—not thought—occurred, the fantasy would end. So even though he *thought* he should try a different fantasy, his *feelings* told the machine he didn't want to. For days he ate, slept, shit, screwed, fought, and had fun like he did in real life, only here he was doing it in the Wild West. Finally the day arrived when his thoughts of moving on matched his feelings. His vision dimmed, his extremities tingled, and he was soon back in front of the spinning, shimmering crystals.

The next crystal that he chose took him to a subtly different program. It faded in like all the others. But this time, Justin realized *he* was not in control. He saw and felt all the things that the person whose body he was now occupying saw and felt, but he couldn't control the scenario. Even more to his surprise, he couldn't leave it—couldn't even think it away. Justin saw that he was a good-looking man, because the man he was "being" was shaving in a mirror. He was thin and seemed to be in good enough shape. After getting dressed in an executive suit, Justin was amused to see that the man's name was Preston Sinclair and that he worked for, of all companies, Cord Industries. With a deep shock Justin realized that he knew this man. In fact, he'd hired Preston straight out of college about four years before he'd had himself frozen and buried. As Justin recalled, Preston had been a damned knowledgeable kid who did his job well. From looking in the mirror, Justin figured this Preston to be about forty. What followed was the simple day of a man who was a good quality-control manager of a cutting-edge software-development team. Justin recognized the type: competent, loyal, and willing to work hard, but at the end of the day, more committed to family than career. He was proven correct when he/Preston returned home from work and was immediately pounced upon by two small children—a boy about eleven and a girl around six. His wife was a fun, lively, and flirtatious woman with curly red hair and a smile that could warm an Eskimo. Justin was aware that, while she may not have been a "looker," seeing her at home surrounded by her family made her beautiful nonetheless. So much so that he was finally beginning to understand why this man, or any man for that matter, would put his family first. It was only after a moment that Justin realized his/Preston's wife was noticeably pregnant.

Justin had started this crystal upset that he was not exploring Atlantis, or building a pyramid. But by the end of the day he was profoundly happy to be experiencing this man's life. Maybe the VR machine was influencing his hormone levels, or maybe it was something as simple as his never really having had a chance to start a family—his wife's tragedy had seen to that. It didn't matter. Preston, Justin realized, was smart to have put his wife and children first. At that moment Justin would have traded his billions to have what Preston had. Because no one had ever looked at Justin, he thought sadly to himself, the way "his" children now did. The days flew by filled with friends, family, and meaningful work. He discovered that Cord Industries had broken up, and that the part Preston worked for was now owned by the European conglomerate Deutsche Telekom. He spent a while cursing Sebastian after that little piece of news. The old office was physically still like he remembered it, but it was more or less staid. The driving energy he'd spent years encouraging was now gone—replaced by competent complacency. But Preston didn't seem to mind as it gave him more time to spend with his family, and so, in the end, neither did Justin.

It seemed like months flew by. The birth of Justin's first child/Preston's third was something that at least one of them would never forget. Then, two months after the birth, "it" began.

"Honey," Preston called out in a voice that would never command men in battle, "are you feeling up to a trip to the mall?"

"Are you kidding me?" his wife responded. "The mall or a house full of screaming kids? Call the sitter. We're mall-bound."

The trip saw the two of them visiting the same shopping center Justin had walked through in his initial entrance to the VR museum. Glittering trestles and walkways connected to other malls and shopping centers nearby to form a sort of Oz-like city devoted to manic shopping. After two hours of walking this pantheon of shopping splendor, Justin started to get the same tired, played-out feeling all malls engender when the eyes grow weary from one too many BIG SALE! signs. The only thing of interest was the story unfolding with Justin/Preston and his wife. They went into the same VR store Justin had visited . . . *how long ago?* . . . and paid a week's salary for his wife and him to have an adventure. Only after Preston's wife heard there was a money-back guarantee did she agree to the trip. Justin, through Preston's eyes, saw his wife put the same calibration unit on her head, sit in the same recliner he'd sat down in, and blank out pretty much the way he probably had. Except for her breathing, and that was very, very shallow, Justin could have sworn she was dead.

Is that what I look like? he thought.

Justin as Preston went through the VR process . . . again.

So, Justin wondered, *I'm in a VR simulation, going into another VR simulation. This could get confusing.* He leaned back down into the recliner, had the array once more placed upon his head, and once more, the world went dark.

This time Justin/Preston was a bigger, more commanding version of himself, now dressed in expensive Victorian day clothes. He was traveling with his wealthy wife and companion. They were in a train car together.

So two people can experience the same VR simultaneously. That makes it very interesting, thought Justin. He had an image of himself and Neela experiencing some VR that was definitely not G-rated. He left that thought as he began to appreciate just how well the programmers of this crystal did in setting up the backstory. There was an April 11, 1912, copy of the London *Times* with a front-page, below-the-bend story on Preston and his wife. According to the paper they were a wealthy and well-traveled couple who had a romantic reputation as explorers. They'd even written a travelogue of their adventures that made them sound like Mr. and Mrs. Indiana Jones. But the real shocker was that they had passports, documents, and tickets to set sail on, of all ships, the RMS *Titanic.* Preston and his wife had a debate about whether to go on the doomed vessel. They soon decided the ship would not sink in a VR fantasy and spent the rest of the time being amazed by how real the simulation was. As far as they were concerned, this was reality. They used their precious and well-paid-for time trying out everything. Preston's wife was amazed that her body was near perfect for adventuring, Olympic gymnastics, and general fooling around. Preston, though not a muscle-bound clod, was certainly as finely cut as a human body could get. By the time the train pulled into the station they both agreed that this fantasy was already worth a week's salary.

It only got better.

The station, the port, the press taking their picture as they arrived, the other guests, and of course the first-class accommodations—all of it was spectacular. They were living the world of the *Titanic.* And when the infamous night of April 14 arrived they made sure to stay up . . . just in case.

They hit the iceberg.

And what should have been a disaster turned out to be the best part of the whole adventure. Within minutes of the episode they were found by a terrified purser, who informed them that the captain wished to see them at once. It seemed that their status as world-famous adventurers earned them the untimely audience. Only instead of the meeting ending in confusion and halfhearted attempts, ultimately leading to tragedy like the real story, this meeting took a different course. This time Preston took charge. He gave Captain Smith a semiprivate, heart-to-heart talk, in which he told him it was his responsibility to get as many passengers to New York as was humanly possible. Even if that meant ripping planks from the deck with his bare hands, tying them together with his intestines, and then kicking the rafts into the cold, dark, unmoving ocean himself. Preston/Justin had no idea if this "damn the torpedoes" approach would have worked in real life, but it seemed to work in this one, as it got the captain out of his fatal funk. Now the captain gave firm orders to the crew to see that all the passengers were escorted to the boat deck. All boats were to leave with the maximum number of passengers, with places at the oars to be given to husbands, and in all other cases women and children first. With the chain of command fully working, the boats were readied, filled, and set afloat. But the amazing part of the adventure was when Preston and his wife got the ship's architect to stop feeling sorry for himself and start thinking of creative ways to build rafts in a hurry.

The highlight for Justin/Preston was the gathering of all the men on deck and a speech that was part marine sergeant and part *Henry V*. The oratory was filled with everything from "Yes, some of us might not make it tonight" to "We have a chance if we work together" to "The millionaire is putting up all the survivors in his hotel free of charge for a week." It was magic. The men ripped up planks, tore fire hoses into cording, grabbed doors, tables, and floatable luggage, and made the most motley, harebrained rafts the world had ever seen. If the sea were not so smooth it would never have worked. But this time it did. Because as the bow of the ship started to slip under the water, the deck, now filled with makeshift rafts, simply acted as a platform that allowed the rafts to float away with hundreds of passengers safely on board. The rich and poor worked together, as a spirit of "screw the iceberg" set in. And when Captain Smith insisted on going down with the ship, Preston punched him in front of his officers and told them to put him in a boat. He quickly explained that a captain's first duty was to his passengers, and second to his ship. Since there were now thousands of passengers in need of a captain's experience at sea, his death would have been in vain. He told the still stunned officers that all the oared boats should gather all the rafts together. They agreed, and even more lives were saved. Still, wondered Justin, if it was not a VR simulation, would it have worked? Who cared? It was great.

The next day the rescue ships found the sea afloat with the singing survivors of the *Titanic*. Only thirty men had lost their lives—almost all in acts of heroism—and not a single woman, child, or husband was lost. When the survivors finally did arrive in New York it was to a ticker-tape parade the likes of which the world had never seen. The celebrations were astounding, and Preston and his wife were the heroes of the century. What had been a tragedy in real life was made into a triumph of the human will to survive, with all the rich men pledging the money to build a newer, bigger, better *Titanic,* and let nature damn well try to sink that.

When the adventure ended, the couple left the VR store in absolute awe. They both agreed that it had far and away been the most thrilling, exciting, life-affirming adventure imaginable. Before they even stepped out of the VR center they were already making plans for their next trip in.

Justin found himself slipping forward now, not experiencing every moment but being brought to specific points in the life of Preston Sinclair. Over the next two years the couple managed three more adventures. Each one was more grand and exciting than the next. And though Justin was having fun, it was always with a grain of salt. Because he was always on the lookout for the red flag that would mark the supposed end of civilization as he knew it. But nothing showed up. In fact, everything he'd seen and experienced was just a series of romps into pure, unadulterated fun.

He also watched in interest as good engineering and fundamental breakthroughs had quickly brought down the prices of the VR machines themselves. He saw that the first home-use VR units cost fifty thousand dollars. In a year they were down to twenty thousand, and two years after that, three thousand. Justin/Preston didn't wait that long to buy his family one.

At first the machine delivered in spades. The family went on tours of the pyramids *as they were being built* and family vacations to Mercury *without suits.* But what was nice was having the children taught applied science by Einstein, gravity by Newton, and literature by Shakespeare, who, incidentally, took the children to see one of his plays in Elizabethan London. It didn't take long for Preston to put his kids on the new short-day plan, in which they only went to *real* school two hours a day for PE and other group events, and had the VR handle all the academics. After all, the kids could share a classroom in VR with children from all over the world, experience multiculturalism, *and* get a superior education to boot.

The Sinclairs failed to notice that they were drifting out of their friends' lives, and their friends out of theirs. Occasionally they'd meet at work or in the store and make plans, but it almost never worked out. The VR was always, *always* more fun. Within a year VR became the only source of entertainment of any import for Preston and his family, and when the price of a machine hit five hundred dollars, it became the only source of entertainment for practically every family in the first world. The real miracle, Justin realized, was not so much that Preston and his wife brought to term their fourth child, but that they managed to find time to conceive at all. He was a child they both loved, but unfortunately, being the fourth as well as being especially needy, put the newborn in direct competition with Einstein, Newton, Shakespeare, and the continuing adventures of Mr. and Mrs. Indiana Jones.

And that's when the first red flag showed up.

The family stopped eating meals together. Not that one could place the blame for that malady squarely on the shoulders of enhanced VR. *The lack of shared meals,* sighed Justin, *was a sad fact long before people were adventuring into realms of home-based VR.* No, the real red flag was the fact that the family stopped eating meals—in the real sense of the word. Why bother to eat real food when all the food in the VR tasted better, never made you fat or sick, and was always what you wanted? So Justin watched as the Sinclairs began to snack on inexpensive, prepared nutrition bars and drink just enough water so that they could jump back into their recliners, sit back, fade out, and head for their next great quest.

What happened next should have been obvious. Or, at least, it should have been obvious to Justin. However, he was so invested in "his" family's slow, downward spiral that he failed to notice.

The world's economy collapsed.

There were a number of dynamics at play, chief of which was the fact that a vast amount of the world's GDP was driven by entertainment and advertising—both of which had been wiped out by the advent of cheaper and better VR. Why go to a movie, take a cruise, visit a museum or an amusement park when VR could do it not only better, but for free? Within three years tourism, a main cash cow for third-world countries, was all but dead, and as a result much of that world was on the brink of starvation. More amazing was that no one in the first world bothered to notice or, if they did, seemed to care. Because what did it matter that one half of the world was starving or, perhaps, even closer to home, that the house was foreclosed on, or that someone had their car repossessed? So they couldn't buy new clothes or eat in fancy restaurants. All their problems were simply a VR rig away from disappearing. And regarding advertising—advertise what and to whom? Brain-drained bodies lying comatose on recliners? Initially, the VR revolution was a boon to advertisers. After all, they had a captive audience and could deliver the goods however they imagined. But that only worked as long as the people doing the "experiencing" bothered to leave the VR rig. When the incentive to stay in the rig was greater than the incentive to leave it, advertising took a nosedive, and with it a significant portion of the economy.

Young couples were packing up their meager belongings and moving back in with Mom and Dad or, in many cases, joining cheap communal apartments. Thrift stores did a bang-up business, and pasta manufacturers were bringing home the bacon, as spaghetti became the meal du jour for all seven days of the week. In VR you ate steak and lobster and lived in a palace and had sex with the most beautiful men and women imaginable. It was all that mattered.

Justin heard a baby crying.

At first it was a far-off sound, but it became clearer. Preston's baby was crying. He was hungry and in need of some human contact. But for the fact that the program had ended, Justin wondered who, if anyone, would have come to the infant's rescue. Preston got up from the rig and went to the baby. *Thank God*, thought Justin. He saw Preston walk past the crying infant and into the run-down, seldom-used kitchen. On the table was a box with a two-week-old postmark. No one had bothered to open it, but Justin remembered that Preston's wife had reminded him about it, and promptly disappeared into the rig. That was hours ago.

As the baby's cries turned into screams, Justin/Preston opened the box. Justin was shocked when he realized what it was. He even tried to prevent Preston from picking it up, but he couldn't. His life and Preston's had become so symbiotic he'd forgotten his status as an ensnared voyeur. Now he'd have to sit back and watch the horror unfold, powerless to do a thing about it.

Preston pulled a VR head rig and three crystals from the box. The head rig was tiny. Preston put it down on the filthy table and picked up the accompanying brochure. It told him all about the specialty programs designed to make any baby happy. *Put it away! Destroy it!* howled Justin hopelessly into the void. But with horrifying predictability Preston went to his screaming baby, placed the rig over his small head, and activated it. He put the crystals into the proper slots on the VR machine and watched as his little boy slowly stopped crying and his body went limp. Moments later the two corners of the baby's mouth pursed themselves into a dreamy, distant smile.

Though Justin knew it wouldn't do an iota of good, he continued to scream.

Goddamn you, Preston! Can't you see you're killing him? He'll never grow up or become anything on that damned machine! You're giving him the only world he can survive in and IT'S NOT REAL!

But Preston couldn't hear him. And, sadly, thought Justin, he probably wouldn't even if he could. Preston sat in his chair and put on his rig and joined his wife as they flew through heaven with angels' wings and made love in the clouds. Preston may have told his wife the baby was OK, but maybe he didn't.

Preston lost his job.

No one was buying much of anything except for VR programs, and most people had the ones they wanted. Plus, copying them was easy. It was just crystal, quantum sequencing, and light. But Preston had a plan. He moved his family into his parents' old house. They'd died years before, leaving him a tiny home on a small plot of land. All four children slept in the same room, but they didn't mind. They didn't really "live" there.

Preston barely noticed the war in the Middle East. Apparently some Islamic fundamentalist terrorist group had dumped a delayed replicating nerve toxin in

Israel's national water carrier. The Israelis didn't figure out the cure until half their population, a little over four and a half million souls, were dead. Since the government wasn't sure who to blame, and since so many groups/countries proudly claimed responsibility, the Israelis decided to teach them a lesson they wouldn't forget. On a cold winter's morning exactly two weeks after half the country lay dead and buried, what was left of the ruling coalition of the Israeli Knesset gave the order to hit all their enemies with a broad nuclear weapon strike. By midday every major Middle Eastern city was flattened and simmering in piles of rubble, debris, and radioactive dust. And, just for good measure, the Israelis hit the oil fields of Iran, Iraq, Kuwait, Saudi Arabia, Qatar, the U.A.E., Libya, and Oman. Those bombs were particularly powerful and dirty. Any fields not totally obliterated were turned into radioactive pools of muck. Of course, by then not many countries needed Arab oil. The United States was no longer importing it. Transportation, whether by air, sea, or road, had diminished to practically a trickle.

The system was breaking down.

While the first world was overdosing on VR, the third world had committed suicide. And while Justin realized that close to four hundred million people had died in a week, Preston didn't seem to notice.

In the end, hardly anyone noticed. Shortly thereafter India, Pakistan, and China committed mutual nuclear suicide. The dreaded radioactive winter happened, and crops died around the world. An info virus was released that wiped out much of the world's data systems. And those most qualified to destroy the insidious bug were lost, deep in their own VR dreams.

Preston's family was hungry.

When he finally did get around to looking for food, he realized how bad it had gotten. Many of the houses in his neighborhood were standing vacant, and what stores remained had mostly empty shelves. The owners of the few still open seemed surprised to see him. They'd assumed he'd become a viricide, a recently coined phrase indicating suicide by VR.

Even crime seemed to be pointless. Though most houses were unlocked, laid bare for anyone wishing to walk in and take the lot, no one bothered. Not only was there little or no market for the goods to be found inside, but any petty thief could be a godfather in the realms of VR. On a few of the walls Justin/Preston saw the spray-painted words GONE TO ALASKA. One old store clerk said it still seemed to be working up "there," referring to the forty-ninth state. But now it was bitterly cold down in southern California. And it was still August. Preston couldn't begin to think about what Alaska would be like. Besides, he knew his wife and kids would never survive the journey. They could barely make it out of the house.

Preston/Justin was looking at his family. For the first time he noticed how bone-thin they'd become. How tired and frail they all were. They had no car, and there didn't seem to be enough fuel for cars anyway. In the two weeks he was out looking for work, food, and hope, it had gotten noticeably colder. There was even frost on his lawn's dead grass in the morning. Finally he managed to get on what was left of the Internet and found a government depot giving out old stored food supplies. He woke his family up and had them eat the first good meal they'd had in months. It was canned, boxed, and preserved well past the recommended dates, but at least it was real, and at least it contained real carbohydrates, real proteins, and real fats.

They went back into the VR.

The next time Preston woke them up he told them he had great news. He'd found a job working for the government. The pay wasn't great, but it was enough to get them fed well. After a few weeks the children were starting to look better, and his wife even began to smile again. The food he brought home wasn't great, but it was better than that army depot stuff he'd forced them to eat months ago. It turned out the nuclear winter hadn't been as bad as feared, and the government had had a certain amount of success in bringing in some crops. Things were still tough, but the country was finally pulling itself back together. The Sinclairs even spent less time in VR and more time as a family. Justin was glad that, as bad as VR had been for the country, at least Preston and *his* family seemed to have rid themselves of it.

Justin's senses began to fade out. He felt the tingling in his extremities, and his world again began to go black. *Thank God*, he thought, as he began to go under. He was happy to get out of this miserable world.

The world faded back in.

It was, noticed Justin, the same miserable world he'd just left. But this time Justin was himself . . . sort of. He was free of Preston's body and able to move at will. When he looked at his hand it appeared to be translucent, almost ghostlike. He found a mirror in the Sinclairs' house, now so familiar to him, and took a look at his own face. It had been so long since he'd seen it, he'd almost forgotten what he looked like. He heard sounds from the VR room. Ironically, thought Justin, it used to be called "the living room." He entered silently.

Preston was working from a crumpled piece of paper with shaking hands. Justin ran to the kitchen and saw the remains of the army depot meal on the table. Justin realized he'd been had. Things hadn't been getting better. Preston had lied or had programmed the machine to lie for him. He ran back to the VR room and saw Preston put the finishing touches on setting up the independent power-grid system. It would be enough, Justin saw, to power the VR apparatus for a few more weeks. Justin also noticed that the software's exit protocols were disabled and would, if triggered, run a VR program called "Things Are Looking Up," the VR program of choice for viricide. It was an infamous VR crystal that bypassed the brain's overriding desire for food. In short, those who ran the program went to play and never woke up. Their bodies would be found, if anyone bothered to stop by, withered and emaciated, covered in urine and feces. And the final stroke of the macabre ordeal would be the smiles still plastered on their sunken, hollowed faces. Preston began to disconnect his family's feeding tubes one by one.

"No!" screamed Justin, "No!"

Preston continued with his awful task.

"No, no, no!"

Preston looked up, momentarily distracted.

Justin, now sobbing, tried lunging at Preston, only to pass right through. Resigned and exhausted from his powerlessness, Justin watched in horror as Preston looked around at what was left of his once thriving and boisterous household. With a heavy sigh Preston sat down in his recliner, placed the VR apparatus over his head, and joined his family for one last happy dream. The dream Justin had been fooled into believing.

"Don't do it," Justin whispered repeatedly. His mind was going into shock. The words slipped out of his mouth like a mantra of the condemned. He stood unmoving, watching in detached dismay at the crime taking place before him. The room was now silent except for the sound of the VR machine's humming and the soon to be murdered spirits' labored breathing—killed by the lotus flower of VR.

He wished to God the room would fade away, but it didn't. He even tried to leave, but he couldn't. He was trapped, forced to bear witness. The program was not designed to grant his desires—it was designed to destroy them. And so he stood there for days watching as the Sinclairs wasted away in their recliners. He hoped the VR dreams that Preston had chosen for them were good ones. It was all he could hope for. One by one their breathing stopped. The machines they were attached to screeched in alarm and, like the occupants in their "care," shut themselves down.

Justin was not allowed to leave the program until the last of them died.

It was the baby.

Preston had forgotten to disconnect the infant's feeding tube, enabling him to hold on for a few days longer than the rest of his family. Watching the baby die slowly made Justin's last few hours in the world of VR the most excruciating and painful he'd ever experienced. When the tiny chest finally stopped heaving, and the baby lay motionless for well over an hour, then and only then did the room fade to black.

When Justin woke up he was in the same VR recliner he'd started in back at the mall. This time, however, Neela was in the room hovering above him. She was looking very real and, by virtue of her familiar face, beautiful beyond words. Justin was never so glad to see anyone in his entire life. Even more, he reckoned, than when he awoke from his three-hundred-year slumber. He was also extremely thirsty. As if reading his mind, Neela handed him a canteen full of fresh spring water. He gulped it down greedily, not caring that at least half of it ran down his stubbled face and onto his clothing.

"How long?" he asked, barely recognizing his own parched voice.

"You've been in the machine for over sixty hours," answered Neela. "Drink the rest . . . slowly."

Justin did as he was told.

"Justin, we can leave now. Can you walk?"

He felt incredibly stiff and sore. He raised his torso off the recliner and looked himself over. He was sickened to see that he'd soiled himself—repeatedly. The smell was horrible. How could he appear before Neela like this?

"Why . . . why didn't they clean me?"

"They could have," she answered with a hint of sadness.

"But chose not to," he acknowledged, then thought about it. "Got it."

Neela put a reassuring hand on his shoulder. "We all woke up like this, Justin. Take off your clothes." She handed him a large trash bag. "And throw them in this."

It took him about two minutes to get his aching body off the stained recliner. The atrophy in his legs was painful, but far less than it could have been had his body not been nanomodified. But atrophy was still atrophy, and even the most finely honed machines need movement to operate efficiently. The head rush was immense, and he had to sit himself down a number of times before feeling confident that he wouldn't topple over.

When he finally managed to strip down to his last article of clothing, Neela gave him what looked like a clear plastic sleeping bag and told him to climb in. He did so, hoping it was a portable shower. As soon as the bag was up over his shoulders it began to hum. He began to feel a tingling sensation and watched in amazement as every bit of filth dropped to the floor. When he realized what it was doing, he pulled the bag over his head and felt the vibrations there as well. It was strange, he thought. He couldn't say that he felt clean, just *not dirty*. He looked forward to getting back home so he could take a nice, long "real" shower.

When the bag finally stopped humming he looked down to see the layers of filth that had collected around his ankles. As he stepped out of the shower bag it vibrated enough to clean his departing feet. Neela handed him a fresh set of clothes.

It was only once he was dressed that he finally began to notice the calibration room. It seemed to be in the same decrepit condition as Preston's house. Only half the lights worked, and most of the booths were missing or broken. Loose bits of paper lay strewn about. When Justin and Neela left the VR store he saw that the mall was in the same loathsome condition. The only lighting came down in asymmetric beams created by the jagged edges of the broken skylights above. There were also, he noticed, a few weakly lit drum fires with forlorn, wretched figures huddled around them. Broken and shattered pieces of glass were everywhere, and blowing bits of paper and refuse only added to the scene of desperate neglect. It was hard to believe this was the same mall he'd originally entered.

Justin was just about to climb up the unmoving escalator steps toward the exit when a horrible thought struck him.

"Neela, how . . . how do I know I'm not still in the machine?"

Neela looked at him sadly.

He began to sweat. His face went ashen.

Neela took both his hands into hers and looked into his eyes.

"You will have to trust me, Justin. You're not."

"But how can I really know, Neela? How can anyone really know? I could still be stuck in there right now, dying and crapping and pissing, and not know it. This," he said, pointing to the dilapidated structure around him, "could just be part of the program."

"It's me, Justin," she implored. "The *real* me."

He looked around some more and decided he had no choice but to trust her.

"It's evil, Neela, the whole thing is . . . evil."

Neela looked at him, nodding in empathy.

"Now, Justin . . . *now* you understand."

7   Aftermath

t was only later that Justin realized what made the first two days after his visit to the virtual reality museum so unique—he'd been left almost entirely alone. Not only by his friends and associates, not only by the usual hordes of fans that were to be found around every corner, but also by the press. Even a few buzzing mediabots kept their distance. It seemed that all parties agreed to give the Unincorporated Man his space. Sadly, he was so absorbed by what he'd experienced he didn't get the chance to enjoy the quiet time. And he was never to get another two days like it again. At least, not without going through incredible time, effort, and expense.

Trying to make small talk, Neela had explained to Justin the evolution of the VR dictates, protocols, and museum. She'd explained how Alaska had emerged as the sole power on Earth by virtue of having the largest intact population. And they managed that because most Alaskans, who'd never been known to suffer fools gladly, saw something horribly foolish in enhanced VR. In time more and more people looked to the Alaskans as a source of protection and rebirth, and it wasn't long after that that the Alaskan Confederation was born. It grew fast and over time, it grew large. One of the first things the emerging Alaskan power did when it established control of an area was to insist that every person sit through a VR simulation comparable to what Justin had just experienced. Back then, Neela explained, the simulation was done on both adults and children. "But nowadays," she continued, "it's only done on children." Children apparently didn't rebound as quickly as adults, and it was not uncommon for it to take weeks for them to recover. (Neela was proud of needing only eight days before she was able to talk about her experience with a counselor.) So, she'd opined, Justin would probably only need a couple of days. He was, after all, a confident and assured man.

Justin needed about ten minutes. The first thing he did after exiting the museum was to drag Neela on a short trip to the L.A. orport.

"Where we headed?" she'd asked, feigning nonchalance.

"Luxembourg," he'd answered stiffly, booking two tickets to one of the Terran Confederation's oldest cities. Neela didn't ask any questions after that. She went along. They made a beeline for their private t.o.p., sat down, and only had to wait a few minutes until the pod was lifted gingerly into the atmosphere. This time, Neela observed, there was no glee or wonder in Justin's expression, no apparent sense of excitement that had always been evident whenever he flew. Even more interesting, he didn't fiddle with the environmental data pad. This time he'd simply accepted the bland and nonchallenging default setting. He remained withdrawn for the extent of the flight. *Thank God it's a short trip*, thought Neela.

As the t.o.p. came out of orbit and began its descent into the medieval citadel of Luxembourg, Neela made out the imposing rocks of the Pétrusse and Alzette valleys. It was obvious to her why those rocks constituted an almost idyllic natural defense for the ancient fortress built upon the promontory now coming into view. The t.o.p. landed gingerly, swallowed up by the old battlement. Neela and Justin quickly departed.

From the city of Luxembourg Justin instructed a driver to take them down south to the remnants of a small town called Galgenberg. As they flew, Justin continued his quiet brooding, barely saying two words to Neela. She was surprised, but more curious. *Everyone reacts differently,* she thought, *and given his recent sixty-hour ordeal he could easily have been catatonic.* She figured she'd take him back to New York and wait until he came out of his room, ready to talk. Of course, there was no person currently living who'd gone through the museum as an adult, so she accepted the fact that anything could happen. This little excursion was a case in point. If not a bit strange, considered Neela, at least it made for an interesting day trip.

They finally landed in the tranquil forest of Cattenom, just outside the once rustic but abandoned town of Galgenberg. The flyer situated itself on a grassy knoll about fifty yards from a moss-covered embankment draped in small rivulets of white, flowing sap. To the naked eye it appeared to be a little hill, but Justin knew better. The "hill" was in fact an overgrown entrance leading into the cold, twisting hallways of an ancient underground fortification quietly rusting away in ignominy. They'd arrived at the once famous gates of Galgenberg, one of the few surviving remnants of the disastrously ineffective Maginot Line. These gates, with their two turrets of artillery, were part of an ancient string of fortresses that had failed as a defense against Nazi Germany in World War II. But for Justin they'd offered a unique opportunity at the turn of the millennium.

"What are we doing here?" asked Neela, no longer able to contain her curiosity.

"Checking out a beta site," he answered, again with no discernible emotion. Then he leaped through the walls of the vehicle and headed straight for the hill. Neela followed quickly. There was a slight chill in the air as the evening approached and a gentle but determined wind whipped across the knoll, making the blond parched grass sway back and forth to its sporadic rhythm. It took only a few seconds to traverse the twenty or so yards to the hill's entrance. It was now more obvious from the exposed slabs of concrete that this hill was in fact manmade. There was a gated steel door that was slightly ajar. Justin looked back at

Neela, tested the door, and saw that it was unlocked. "Hold on a minute," he said, as he entered the darkened corridor. A moment later he reemerged. "Does the chauffeur have a flashlight?"

"Not exactly. But I think I know what you mean," she answered. "How far into this 'beta site' do we need to go?"

Justin gave it a thought. "Not sure, but I'd say at least two hundred feet, uh, seventy meters, more or less."

Neela nodded yes and proceeded back to the flyer. Justin watched as she talked to the driver while pointing toward the hill where he stood. The chauffeur went to the vehicle's hood, popped it open, and pulled out a small cylindrical can. Neela took it and began to shake it vigorously as she started walking back toward Justin.

"Uh, what exactly is that?" he asked as she approached.

"It's our version of a flashlight. Just point to where you want some light and it'll take care of the rest."

Justin shrugged. "How long does it last?"

Neela looked down at the can and read the label. "This one, three hours. Will that be enough time?"

"More than enough."

They entered the bunker. The space they were standing in was some sort of antechamber, where one apparently waited before going into the underground passageway itself. Surrounding them on both sides were large solid slabs of concrete, and facing them directly was an old steel door with a large metal pinwheel on it. Justin tested it out. Other than the shrill sound it made as he turned it, the wheel still worked. He turned it some more until he felt the door release from the frame. He swung the massive slab of metal out toward him, and as he did it let out a deafening squeak.

"Could use a little oil," he suggested, "but not bad for a four-hundred-year-old door."

Justin pointed toward an ancient sconce where a carbide lamp had illuminated the way centuries ago. "There," he said, indicating where the "light" should go. Neela approached and sprayed the antique light fixture with the can she'd received from the chauffeur. The area around the sconce began to glow, dispersing enough light to see at least three feet. Justin looked at the technological feat in admiration, and pointed to the next sconce. This went on as they went deeper and deeper into the network. In a strange way the tunnel was being lit almost exactly as a French soldier would have seen it nearly four hundred years earlier.

The tunnels were wide. *Spacious enough,* thought Neela, *that four or five people could walk side by side without bumping into a wall.* There was a moderately dank smell, but not too bad. The curved ceiling above was a patchwork of reddish brown hues, hanging flakes of dirty white paint, and pockets of corrosion. Positioned about two-thirds up on both sides of the wall were steel tubes of various shapes and sizes running the length of the passageway. As they walked deeper into the void, Neela could feel narrow channels embedded in the concrete beneath her feet. It was only when she looked backward to see their now illuminated path that she realized the channels were in fact rail tracks.

"It's how they moved ordnance and supplies," he said, anticipating her question.

"Just how big is this place?" she asked.

"This one section," he said, looking around, "is part of a larger one that runs for about twenty-seven miles . . . which would be, I guess, around forty-three kilometers . . . but don't worry, we're not going nearly that far."

They'd already walked about twenty yards down a long corridor. When they came to a T in their path, they hung a right and went another thirty yards, until they hit a long, wide corridor. They hit another T and went left another ten yards, at which point the tunnel split.

"Which way?" asked Neela.

"I'm thinking." A pause. "It's been a while." He stood scratching his head. "Left," he said, "definitely left."

They took the left tunnel for another six or seven yards, and finally stopped in front of a section of wall that appeared to have been damaged by an explosion. There was a gaping hole behind which was a metal door—slightly ajar, facing inward. Neela noticed immediately that the revealed door was not of the style or shape of all the previous ones they'd encountered. On closer inspection Neela saw that the "hole" she thought was damaged was unfinished construction.

"This was one of your treasure vaults."

"Correction," answered Justin. "It was *almost* one of my treasure vaults." He grabbed Neela's spray can, entered the darkened room, and lit up the space. Neela followed. The room appeared to be a dormitory. Against the wall were two sets of rusted-out bunk beds. Justin took interest in the bed closest to the wall's end. He started probing behind the bed frame. *A key perhaps?* thought Neela. After about fifteen seconds Justin sat down on the coil-spring bottom bed and let out a huge sigh of relief. He turned to Neela. Though the room was dimly lit, Neela could see a significant change in the man. Whatever had been bothering him was now gone.

"This was going to be a site for some of my emergency wealth," he offered. "There are so many of these tunnels that it would have been simplicity itself to build a wall over a door and, I figured, who would ever really know? But the tunnels started to become major tourist attractions, and all it would have taken was one relative looking for Grandpa's old barracks, and questions could've been asked. And even this out-of-the-way area could have been discovered."

"Surely the odds of that were remote?"

"Incredibly remote, but I came up with some better locations, or at least I thought I had, and this, like some other locations, was abandoned."

"So," she asked, "why are we here, and why are you now human again?"

"Is that your way of calling me a grouch?" he countered.

Neela laughed. "Far from it. More like a moody son of a bitch . . . but today you're allowed."

Justin grinned. "I needed to be sure."

"Of what? That your abandoned beta site was still abandoned?"

"No, that the life I'm currently in . . . right now . . . was, in fact, real . . . or, more specifically, not virtual."

It took Neela a moment to process the information. "Ahh. You thought you were still in a virtual-reality simulation."

He nodded. "I wasn't sure. I needed a test."

"Not to GC you, but . . ."

"GC?"

"Oh, sorry. Slang. 'GCing someone' means 'to bring them down.'"

"Got it," he nodded. "Grand collapse them."

"Right . . . anyhow, like I was saying, not to bring you down, but all this," she said, pointing at their surroundings, "could still be VR. How does standing here change any of that?"

Justin smiled like the cat who'd caught the canary. "VR needs to be programmed. It's very intuitive, and can assimilate and incorporate data at levels I can't begin to understand, but it cannot create an environment out of nothing."

"Of course it can," retorted Neela, "and while inside that environment all would be *real*."

"No, Neela, it would *seem* real. However, if a person was in possession of knowledge the VR machine did not have, nor did any of its programmers, then it would be possible to test if your reality was, in fact, *real*."

"So," Neela said, trying to understand his logic, "you didn't go to your main burial site because that one's already been referred to in the press."

"Exactly," he nodded. "All my sites have. For this test I couldn't go anywhere that I'd already been to or, by extension, that the VR machine and programmers could have access to. It had to be something that I and only I knew about. This was the best place."

"Why couldn't the VR machine just show you the tunnels?" she countered. "After all, they're still a tourist attraction, and once it knew where you were headed it could have gotten the records and built all this very quickly."

"Yes," he affirmed, "but then it would re-create standard images of the Maginot Line, and this rubble and building material is pretty much as *I* left it."

Neela put her hand on her chin and shook her head.

"OK, I think I'm getting it," she answered, still not 100 percent satisfied, "but a lot could happen in the three hundred years you were frozen. Suppose that a tour group did find their way through here and recorded your little unfinished work. And just suppose the VR machine got ahold of that recording."

Justin's face lit up as he motioned Neela over to the bed frame he'd been probing around only moments before. He pointed to what Neela thought was a small blotch on the wall. However, upon closer inspection she could see that the blotch was a carved-out name in faded and barely legible letters. It read JUSTIN CORD.

"If the VR machine can find all of this," he said, indicating the room, "and then find *that*," he said, pointing to the tiny carving, "and then incorporate it *all* into the program—without me saying a word to anyone, mind you—well, then, my dear Neela . . . then the machine wins. But I don't think any software, even software as well programmed as that found in the VR machine, could provide this level of detail without an intimate knowledge base, which I know for a fact it did not have access to. So, yes, Neela. This," he said looking at his surroundings, "is reality. And thanks to this little carving, I now know *that* for sure."

Neela started to clap. "No stone unturned with you, Mr. Cord. No stone unturned." A chuckle. "Now, can we please get out of here?"

"Absolutely," he answered, "and may I never, *ever*, have to set foot in that damned machine again . . . for as long as I live."

"And to think," replied Neela, "I almost did."

Justin nodded. "Like I don't owe you enough already."

They made their way back to the entrance, leaving the ancient tunnels and turrets of Galgenberg to be slowly reclaimed by darkness and eternity.

Once outside they found themselves standing in front of the mound they'd only recently entered. The sun had set below the horizon, but there was still enough light to see the car and the chauffeur idling away his time, leaning against the hood. The wind had picked up a bit, and it was now appreciably cooler. Justin looked at Neela closely. He wanted to ask her something but had no idea how to start.

"I still remember my introduction crystals, and sometimes . . . sometimes I even dream about them." Neela grew serious. "That's what makes it so dangerous." She started walking toward the flyer, Justin beside her. "Do you know that we still have trouble with VR addicts?"

Justin's head jerked back, eyebrows raised in surprise. "Why would anyone want anything to do with VR after having gone through that?"

"Justin, you lived your *real* life and made it a spectacular success. You're every bit as heroic as any character in VR."

"Come on," he said, unbelieving.

Neela shook her head. "It's true. The self-made billionaire who challenged an entire culture of death and never doubted, flinched, or quit? The one man to emerge from the wreckage of the old civilization with your pride, skills, and sense of self intact? You really don't get how completely rare . . . no . . . *unique* you are. The rest of us, I'm afraid, have lives far less grand."

Justin didn't argue. It wasn't a matter of hubris. It was just a fact. There was no reason to believe that the psychological reasons for addiction would change just because technology had advanced.

"But the children, Neela . . ."

She matched the gravity of his stare with one of her own. "They *have to* enter young," she said. "Justin, after the Grand Collapse the Alaskans discovered that the VR plague didn't go away . . . at least, not entirely. Oh, they tried real hard to suppress it. Even passed laws against it. One of the few laws against a personal choice that the Alaskan Federation passed . . . and guess what?"

"It didn't work," he answered.

She nodded. "Laws like that are only effective when all of society understands that the law is needed."

Justin was astonished. "Society had just collapsed! What more proof did they need?"

"Not *need*, Justin. *Want*. They had all sorts of theories and solutions. There were those who wanted to kill on sight anyone caught using or possessing VR equipment and those who wanted a specified number of hours of usage per day."

"So how did they arrive at a compromise?"

"You just sat in the 'compromise' for sixty hours."

Justin heaved a sigh.

"It was discovered," continued Neela, "that the program worked best on children between the ages of seven and nine. Those who experienced the program in that age range had a VR recidivism rate of less than 2 percent. Once it was realized that an entire generation could be inoculated against VR, the Anchorage Assembly made it mandatory for all its citizens, as well as for all territories joining or conquered."

Justin rubbed his hands on his thighs, trying hard to ignore the chilly climate. He was surprised that he'd lasted this long without shivering, and remembered that his body had been "modified." So the chill he would normally have felt immediately was only now beginning to work its way into his bones.

"OK," he said, putting his hands back into his pockets, "I think I can see how this indoctrination became universal, and as much as I hate to admit it, even understand why you've subjected children to that horror, but Neela—the Alaskans you're describing don't sound like the hunting, fishing, 'leave me the hell alone' types that I knew in my day. These Alaskans sound ruthless . . . almost hell-bent on conquest."

"Justin," she answered, hopelessly pushing the hair out of her face that the wind seemed intent on keeping there, "the Alaskans you knew are gone. They died, changed, or were supplanted by the millions of refugees that swamped the state just as a nuclear winter hit. Imagine quintupling the population just as your supermarkets are running out of food. By hard work, hunting, fishing, and other questionable means they brought the great majority of those people out alive. But they were not the same. Harder, more disciplined, fiercely proud, yes—the same, no. These people were not going to let some two-bit dictator get his hands on a few abandoned nukes and start his own empire or, worse, another nuclear disaster. The choice was simple: Join or be absorbed."

"Resistance is futile."

"What?" she asked.

"Oh, right," he answered, realizing he'd slipped into a dated lexicon. "It's an old TV show reference . . . Star Trek . . . Borg." *Might as well be speaking Greek,* he mused.

Neela's face lit up. "I've heard of them."

"You've heard of the Borg?"

"Yes, there are still a few Trekkies around."

Justin laughed.

"I'm surprised," he continued, getting back on track, "that more people didn't put up a fight."

"Oh, some did," she answered, "but they were mostly crackpot dictators or self-proclaimed cultists. They were destroyed quickly. In fact, most of the population that *was* left was glad that someone came along to end the madness and despair. The Alaskans believed fiercely in a limited government, low and simple taxes, and maximum individual rights. The only thing you couldn't do was something that would affect someone else's life or well-being, like peddling in VR or participating in acts of terrorism. Within twenty years what was left of the world was united under Anchorage's confederation."

Justin grimaced. Something was still eating at him. "If the Alaskans were as brutal as you said, capable of taking over the world, how come it turned out like this? Everything you told me, everything I've read about, should have led to savagery or, at best, some sort of dictatorship. This world just doesn't make sense."

Neela nodded, acknowledging his concern. "You haven't gotten to Damsah yet, have you?"

"Well, I know he was the first president of the Alaskan Federation, and died only three months into his term. It was your next president who really got the government organized—I concentrated on her."

"Justin," answered Neela, putting her hands into her pockets also to ward off the evening chill, "if you're going to understand us, you'll have to understand Tim Damsah. He is to us what Lincoln and Washington were to you—only combined. You know how bad it got from your VR experience. The truth is, for the survivors it was much worse." She let that last part sink in before continuing. "The Alaskans *were* heading for a dictatorship that all the forces of history demanded—that is, until Tim Damsah came along. Most of his speeches were preserved; you would benefit from hearing them."

"OK," he murmured. Yet another in a long list of things to get to.

"The power of his vision . . ." She said it almost as if it were a mantra. "When the whole world was collapsing, and the rights of the individual seemed to be a luxury we could ill afford, he reminded us of how important they were. He convinced the survivors that the problem with real freedom wasn't that it didn't work, but rather that it had never truly been tested. One of his favorite statements was that the Chinese symbols for catastrophe and opportunity were the same. That all the suffering the human race was experiencing was not in vain. And that, finally, they could build a better world based on individual rights and personal responsibility if only they would strive for it."

"Sounds reasonable, Neela."

"Yes, it does, but we could have just as easily gotten a Hitler or a Lenin at that darkest of hours—instead we got Tim Damsah. He gave us back hope and allowed us to dream again. Imagine one man's belief being so strong that it could sway the world. Our society is made in Tim Damsah's image. The forty billion who are well fed, employed, housed, and entertained are his children."

Justin absorbed the speech for a moment. Finally he spoke. "No wonder you have statues and cities all over the place dedicated to him. He died in a fire, correct?"

"*Heroically* in a fire, yes," she answered, wanting to be sure that the distinction was heard, though to Justin it sounded suspiciously like a party line.

"It was during the nuclear winter," continued Neela, "and all available living space was used—even the president's house. Imagine you're trying to save the world and you volunteer your house for four other families. No one ever found out how the fire started, but at that time everyone was burning firewood to keep warm. It wasn't unusual—fires broke out all the time."

"Why didn't they just use oil?"

"At that time it was in short supply and so was saved for industrial projects. What is known," she continued, "is that the president went into his burning home again and again, pulling out survivors until, sadly, he never came out."

Neela, noticed Justin, was on the verge of tears. In fact, she'd told the story with enough ardor to make him believe she'd known the man himself. And it was at that moment it became clear why Tim Damsah, a man he'd once met and had dismissed as a minor elected official, had become so deified.

"I'm surprised," Justin continued undaunted, "that Damsah's philosophies didn't collapse with his death. I mean, when Lincoln died so did his dreams of binding the nation together after the Civil War."

"We lost his life in the fire, Justin, but by then we had his dream, his hope, and with his death a martyred hero. We could not; no—*would* not let him down."

"So Tim Damsah led Alaska to world domination," Justin said, lips parted in object fascination. "Who'da thunk?"

"Hoodathunk?" asked Neela, at a loss.

"Sorry, just an expression."

"Ahh. Anyhow, not 'world domination,' Justin, more like 'united the world,' and they didn't rule for that long. As soon as things settled down the Alaskans had the capital moved from Anchorage to Geneva U.E. . . . ."

"Sorry," interrupted Justin, "U.E.?"

"United Earth. Anyways, the Alaskans were glad to get out of the world-running business."

Justin laughed. "I'm sure the Swiss loved that."

Neela looked confused. "Swiss?"

Justin slumped his shoulders.

"The Swiss disappeared," he sighed, "but *Star Trek* lives on. Go figure."

Janet Delgado looked like a young Amazonian goddess: tall, lithe, and dark skinned, with a powerful mane of flowing black hair. Under normal circumstances she could wield a perfect get-out-of-my-way glare, but now the head of GCI's vaunted Legal department was pacing back and forth like a hen worried about her eggs. She was in one of Geneva's nondescript federal buildings. This one was called the Bureau of Audits and Corrections. It also was where Hektor Sambianco was currently having millions of molecular-sized nanobots crawl through his brain to sniff out any neurological anomalies worthy of immediate and permanent "correction." He'd been "forced" to undergo the exam to determine whether or not he'd misused his self-majority to cause undue harm to his fellow stockholders.

The unmistakable whirring sounds of a mediabot snapped Janet out of her malaise. She looked up to see the familiar round orb staring in her face. Following closely on the bot's heels was a buxom female reporter of Asian descent, dressed in a stylish wormskin jumpsuit. *I'll be glad when this stupid insect texture fad is over and done with,* Janet thought, trying hard not to stare at the slime-glistening garment.

"Ms. Delgado," said the reporter, eyes clearly on the prize, "my name is Eva Nguyen. I'm with Court News Weekly."

"I know who you are," seethed Janet.

"Good," retorted Ms. Nguyen. "In that case, would you care to comment on a report that I've heard?"

Janet smiled with great insincerity, and said, "I'd love to, Miss Nguyen; however, I'm currently engaged in another pressing matter. Call my office, I'll make sure to instruct my secretary to give you a scheduled interview."

"So you can state unequivocally," asked Eva, unimpressed at the brush-off, "that Hektor Sambianco is *not* currently undergoing a psychological audit at this time?"

Don't blow this, Janet said to herself, trying hard to sell the charade. She feigned utter shock. Luckily, her years in the courtroom and clawing up GCI's corporate ladder had sharpened her natural acting abilities.

"I . . . um . . . ," then, "I'm sorry. What on Earth makes you say that?"

Eva Nguyen, playing right into Janet and Hektor's well-laid trap, started to believe that the wild, harebrained tip she'd received only hours before might have a basis in reality. Her eyes widened, but she still had the presence of mind to signal her mediabot to go to hard-record. While hard-record was a more expensive means of storing data, it at least ensured that any electronic bursts, often employed as a defense against the media, would have no effect on what the reporter was presently committing to the hard drive. It also meant she'd have to get the actual bot out the door—a risk she was willing to take.

"Let's just say," she answered, "that I find it a little curious for a ranking board member of GCI to be here without any assistants."

"I don't always travel with my associates, Ms. Nguyen," countered Janet.

"Perhaps," answered the reporter, now smelling blood, "but I would also venture to say that you don't always travel with the newest associate of the GCI board either . . . and to this ward in particular." Eva pointedly looked up at the sign that said PSYCHOLOGICAL AUDIT TESTING with the famous Lincoln quote paraphrased underneath: "A Mind Divided Against Itself, Cannot Stand."

Silence.

"I know quite a few stockholders," Eva continued, "who'd be quite curious about these goings-on."

"These *goings-on*, Ms. Nguyen," shot Janet, "are really none of your damned business. It is, I assure you, an entirely personal matter. Now, if you would be so kind as . . ."

For Eva Nguyen it was now or never. "Do you," she asked, cool as ice, "want your version to be heard, or shall I just conjecture a point of view?" She knew it probably wasn't wise to threaten the lead attorney of the most powerful corporation on Earth, but opportunities like this only came along once in a lifetime, and if she didn't grab the bitch by the horns—especially at a moment like this— she never would.

Janet smiled inwardly, knowing that Eva was doing exactly what she was supposed to be doing. The plan was working perfectly.

"How dare you threaten me?" she spat back, with the fiercest game face she could muster. "Do you know who you're talking to?"

"I do," answered Eva, "and my question still stands. Do you or do you not want your version heard? Because I can assure you, Ms. Delgado, threat or not, this story will go out on the evening spin."

Janet stood her ground, glaring at her "foe." Eva Nguyen could not possibly know that the answer she was about to hear had been rehearsed, sweated over, and put into motion weeks prior to this "chance" encounter.

"Alright, Ms. Nguyen," she answered, after biting her lip . . . lower left, for exactly two seconds. "You seem to have me at a disadvantage . . . so I'm prepared to make you a deal."

"Name it. If it's within my power I'll try and oblige."

"You give up your source and I'll tell you everything I know." Janet smirked, knowing that it was she herself, using a voice-obfuscation protocol, who had been Eva's "source."

Eva stared stone-faced at Janet. "Ms. Delgado, the truth of the matter is that I don't know who the source is, but I must be honest. Even if I did, I'd never give them up."

"Sorry, then," answered Janet. "No deal."

"I'm sorry, too, Ms. Delgado," answered Eva, silently cursing her bad luck. She turned around and started walking away, mediabot trailing closely behind.

Janet began counting to herself, 3, 2, 1 . . . "Wait!" she shouted to the reporter's backside.

Eva Nguyen quickly spun around.

"Yes?"

"Can't blame a girl for trying," Janet said, shrugging.

"No, I can't, Ms. Delgado; however, we're wasting precious time. So again, I ask you. How is it that a ranking member of the board is here with their newest associate presumably undergoing a psyche audit?"

"The answer to your question," answered Janet, making every effort to sound as if the rest of the sentence was being pulled out of her forcibly, "is . . . is . . . Cord."

A look of shock. "Justin Cord?"

"No, Santa Cord. Of course, Justin Cord!" Janet lowered her voice when other people in the lobby looked up to see where the outburst had emanated from.

"But Hektor Sambianco is upper-echelon GCI," whispered Eva, pulled into the drama, "an assistant to the board, how . . . ?"

Janet put just the right amount of desperation into her voice as she cut off the reporter. "We don't know!" She gathered Eva closer and began whispering quickly, like a person desperately needing to talk to somebody, anybody, just to make sense of something they didn't understand. Eva Nguyen nodded reassuringly as Janet spilled the story. "Cord only owns a single share of Hektor's stock," rambled Janet, "but his motion to have Mr. Sambianco psyche-audited sailed right through. I've never seen anything like it. I'm telling you, Eva . . . can I call you Eva?" Eva nodded, and Janet continued, "I was at every hearing, and it just didn't stop." Janet grabbed Eva's arm for effect. "It *couldn't* be stopped. The motion for a psychological audit sailed right to the top and was certified," she paused for effect, ". . . *in a week.*"

While technically everything Janet had said was true, she neglected to tell Ms. Nguyen that it was Hektor and herself who had pushed the motion through— much to the various committee members' alarm. But Janet was sure this reporter would put the spin on it that Hektor had wanted. "He's being audited as we speak," Janet confided, slowly looking toward the wall marked PATIENT EXIT AREA. And almost against her will, so did Eva. Then Janet gave her "confession" the final touch. The one Hektor insisted must be in the script. "Damsah's ghost," she said breathlessly, "if Justin Cord could do this to Hektor Sambianco, why . . . why, he could do it to anyone. He could do this . . . *to me!*" Janet was waiting for that moment to see when Eva stopped being a reporter and started being a person. It was just a flash of worry in her eyes, but that was enough to let Janet know that Eva was hooked. And that the implication of what Janet had said had now been made painfully clear to the person best able to spread her and Hektor's well-crafted message—that, in short, no one was safe from the Unincorporated Man. The reporter was back in a second, but the dart had hit its mark—with poison inserted.

As if on cue, the exit area they were still standing in front of opened up, and Hektor Sambianco emerged out of the depths of Audits and Corrections in a daze. He walked slowly, and his eyes did not seem to focus on where he was. Eva Nguyen was so preoccupied with getting to Hektor first that she never realized that Janet had purposely stayed back. "Mr. Sambianco," Eva asked, "a couple of questions if I . . ." She paused because Hektor appeared to look right through her without any comprehension of who or what she was. He had a vacant, mindless gaze that silenced her. It was Eva's, as well as society's, worst fears of the repercussions of a psychological audit all rolled up into one frighteningly disarming image—just as Hektor had intended. As soon as Eva stopped talking, Hektor lost interest and stumbled mindlessly about in another direction. Janet, on cue, gently grabbed his arm, gave Eva a sad and knowing nod, and led Hektor, unharried by the usually tenacious but now stunned reporter, out of the building.

Hektor waited until they were safely in the car and beyond detection, then broke out laughing. His "brain dead" mask fell to the wayside, only to be replaced by the amused, cunning face that Janet was just now beginning to realize hid a man far more capable than she'd imagined.

"So, Janet," he asked, "ya think she bought it?"

"Oh, she bought it alright," answered Janet, eyes wide in admiration. "So now, if you don't mind, will you please tell me why you had to subject yourself to a brain scour to get the result you were after?"

Hektor's smile was, as usual, disarming. This was the sauce for the goose. The moment when he got to reveal the intricate machinations he'd put into play to achieve success. And this day, with its well-rehearsed and perfectly timed or-chestration, had been a glowing success. Or, at least, would be when that prissy little Eva woman released the story in another hour or so.

Hektor waited a moment, relishing every breath. He took out a glass from the car's pantry, grabbed a bottle from the shelf, and poured himself a single-malt scotch.

"Janet, my dear," he began, "most people have fantasies, peculiar tendencies . . . strange, shall we say, 'desires'? And if they act on them it's usually with a willing accomplice. It's when those fantasies become deviant compulsions that a psyche audit becomes necessary."

"And you wouldn't call this whole chicanery we just went through," asked Janet, helping herself to some of what Hektor was drinking, "deviant?"

"No, Janet. In all fairness, I wouldn't. I may be a bit of a scoundrel, which I'll readily admit to, but I do play by the rules. Sure, I bend them a lot, even exploit them from time to time, but I'm at least willing to abide by them."

Janet seemed dubious.

"If you recall," he said, responding to her look, "I was on my way to a twenty-year stint on the Oort Cloud before I got dragged back into this mess. I took my shot with Kirk Olmstead and lost. But I was ready and willing to pay the piper. If that's not playing by the rules, my dear, then I don't know what is."

Hektor could see by Janet's lack of response that he was making his point.

"As luck would have it," he continued, "the Oort Cloud and its denizens will have to do without me for the time being."

"OK," Janet said, grudgingly accepting his explanation, "that still doesn't explain why you used the audit. There are plenty of other things you could've done to discredit Justin Cord."

"Not really, my dear. As far as the worlds are concerned, Justin is perfection incarnate—nasty temper and all. With the psyche audit I had one major advantage on my side."

"And that was?"

"Ignorance, of course," he answered, staring at the scotch in his glass. He knocked it back. "Society's, to be specific."

Janet was rapt, not saying a word.

"The Unincorporated Man has to lose, Janet. History, economics, and society are against our 'hero' from the past. I'm just speeding up the process and doing whatever it takes to make sure that GCI benefits from his downfall."

"As well as Hektor Sambianco," added Janet.

Hektor didn't bother to answer.

Justin had forgotten about his request to have Hektor audited psychologically until he got a notification from the Bureau of Audits and Corrections in the form of a fax. The hardware was different but the method was the same—paper delivered via machine. The device had spat out a simple one-line message stating that the audit had been performed and no evidence of improper or dangerous action had been detected, and further that no corrective action had been taken. Justin tossed the paper aside and went back to reading Alexander Chen's well-reviewed work *The Grand Collapse.* He'd long since moved past his rage at Hektor Sambianco and took small solace in the fact that he'd succeeded in harassing the man who'd made his life a living hell. He wasn't sure if it was the hormone therapy or his general contentment with his present situation. Either way, he was happy to relegate Hektor, like the notice he'd received only moments ago, to the proverbial dustbin.

About one hour after tossing the message he received frantic calls almost simultaneously from Eleanor, Neela, Omad, Dr. Gillette, and Manny. He took all the calls at once but heard nothing over the babble.

"Just turn on your goddamned TZ!" Omad had managed to yell through the racket.

"You mean TV," Justin corrected, calmly.

"Whatever," Omad managed to yell above the racket. "Just turn the damned thing on!"

Justin looked at the holodisplay. It saw that his eyes had locked onto it for more than a second and turned itself on. Leading the broadcast was a picture of Hektor Sambianco looking like a shell of a man. He was seen being escorted out of the Bureau of Audits and Corrections by the woman lawyer Justin remembered from the trial. It took two seconds for Justin to realize that the spin was not at all in his favor.

He saw that a stylishly prim Asian woman named Eva was leading the story. Justin stayed glued to her every word.

"Hektor Sambianco," she reported, "was not the nicest man on the planet, but did he do anything to deserve a psychological audit? In a display of governmental and legal expertise far beyond anything he should have been able to muster, Justin Cord was able to bypass multiple safeguards, appeals, and barriers to get the audit done in record time, and all the power and resources of the system's most powerful corporation could not stand up to him. . . ." *Bullshit*, thought Justin. *All I did was submit the thing. Unless Manny . . .*

". . . The truly worrisome point for this reporter is that Mr. Cord appears to be immune to any counterthreat. As of right now there is not a single individual who has standing in any court to demand an equivalent counteraudit of Mr. Cord. For all intents and purposes, he's untouchable. He can do whatever he wants . . . to any of us. And so this reporter is forced to ask the question previously thought to be in poor taste, but now taking on a greater sense of urgency—namely: When will Justin Cord incorporate?"

Justin sat staring blankly at the screen of his holodisplay. The din of his peers making comments and questions failed to penetrate. He eventually snapped out of his stupor.

"Will all of you please calm down?" he pleaded. "I need you all to stop whatever it is you're doing and get back to my apartment ASAP. Can you all do that?"

They all nodded in the affirmative and broke off contact.

Little man got me good, Justin thought. *Two points for Hektor.*

Justin reviewed with concern the snippet from the Court News report as well as a few other similarly slanted pieces. He turned to his lawyer.

"Manny, correct me if I'm wrong, but wasn't the psyche audit meant to screw Hektor?"

"You're correct," Manny admitted—a little too glumly for Justin's liking.

"Then why do I get the feeling it's me who's being screwed?"

"Because you are," seethed Neela.

"Justin," added Manny, "I filed the request for the audit like you requested, and to be honest, forgot about it. It should have been laughed out of court the second any judge took a look at it."

"Like you said it would," said Justin.

"Correct. Now, it is possible that this might be some sort of internal GCI power play, and that someone else within the organization used your request to get at Hektor, but I don't think so. The timing's all off."

"What do you mean?" asked Dr. Gillette.

"I mean," answered Manny, "that it happened way too fast. All seven stages of hearing were reviewed and passed. The only way that could happen would be if all parties were actively trying to get the audit done. Favors must have been called in to get speedy hearings with the appropriate judges, because not one, *not a single* roadblock was encountered."

"How can you be so sure?" asked Eleanor.

"Because," answered Manny, "I filed less than two weeks ago. This process, had protocol been followed, should have taken months."

"Why?" asked Neela. "According to your theory, if someone at GCI wanted Hektor out, then perhaps they arranged for the speedy process."

"Possible. But not likely. Hektor's much too wily and plugged-in to have let that happen. Even the most determined enemy of his would have come up against a fortress of class actions trying to push this through . . . if Hektor hadn't wanted it." Manny paused and stared out the window. It was midday, so air traffic was light. He followed the path of a "show" pigeon as it made its way to Justin's windowsill. All the prestigious buildings had them. A real bird couldn't have flown that high, but these birds could. "No," he continued, "I'm afraid the reason for the quickness of the audit is far more insidious."

"And that would be?" asked Omad.

"Hektor wanted it that way."

Omad laughed. "Now who's the crazy one?"

Manny shrugged.

Dr. Gillette cleared his throat. "Shouldn't Justin or you have been informed this was happening, Manny? How could a P.A. take place without the individual requesting it being informed that it was taking place? I mean, it's just . . ." His statement petered out as he went back to bemoaning the apparently disastrous consequences of his advice.

Manny, not known for an overabundance of sympathy, answered the doctor's question matter-of-factly. "I'm sure we were informed. And if I were to check my junk mail files I'd be willing to bet Chairman stock to horse crap that six notices have been sent. But I didn't tell my avatar to keep an eye out for all P.A. data, because I frankly wasn't expecting any. Besides, why should they bend over backward to tell us we're getting what we asked for? Our legal interests were being represented"—Manny paused a moment in personal thought—"quite brilliant, actually."

Dr. Gillette spoke to Justin. "My dear boy, I am so sorry. If I thought for even a moment that my advice would've caused you so much difficulty I . . . I . . ."

"Doctor," interrupted Justin, "you couldn't have known this would happen. And from what you're telling me, this has never happened before. So how could you be faulted for not predicting it? No, the only thing I don't quite understand is what Hektor gets out of this." He turned to Manny. "Manny, you're saying he had to have done this himself, or to be more precise, *to* himself. But why?"

Manny nodded. "No idea. I'm good with the legal stuff, but this is something different. I would hate to have a trial against this guy if he had a chance to prepare it his way."

Omad looked up from behind his bowl of buffalo wings, a treat Justin had introduced him to and one he'd grown to relish on every visit to his friend's penthouse.

"You better prepare then, Manny," offered Omad.

"For what?" the lawyer asked.

"Look, Manny . . . Justin . . . ," continued Omad, "I only met Hektor a couple of times, but he's good at bad, and it's becoming clear he won't stop. He wants you incorporated, Justin. It's as simple as that. I don't know if it's personal or if he sees it as the only way to secure his career. Who cares? It's what he wants, and he won't stop until he succeeds. I suspect that this ploy was just a way of softening you up. Maybe he sees you as being too popular, so he needed to knock you down a peg or two."

"With a P.A.?" Neela asked, still astounded. "Don't you think that's a bit over the top?"

"A, it worked," answered Omad, "and b, everyone loves an underdog. Up until today the public thought of Justin Cord as that poor little unincorporated man versus the big, bad GCI. Well, guess what, folks? Today it's the big, bad Justin Cord picking on poor, shell-shocked Hektor Sambianco, and, ironically— by extension—GCI."

Dr. Gillette was livid. "The man's evil."

Neela gritted her teeth. "It's what I've been saying all along."

Justin raised his hand. "What we need to do is figure out how to respond to this. Dr. Gillette?"

Dr. Gillette appeared forlorn. Probably, thought Justin, trying to understand how his harmless, minor suggestion could have been used to such disastrous effect. Justin felt bad for him. He felt even worse for himself, as he'd started to rely on Dr. Gillette. But clearly the good doctor was out on this one.

"Why don't we just go on the offensive?" asked Omad.

"I see," asked Justin. "Launch an attack?"

"Well, not literally, but yeah, invite some reporters and tell our side, how we did nothing but put in the form, and he must have done the rest." He paused. "Or we could just kill him."

Everyone laughed.

After a moment Neela spoke. "I suggest we do nothing."

Justin looked surprised. "Really? Just let Hektor get away with turning me into the bogeyman?"

"Bogeyman?" asked Eleanor, who until this moment had sat silently, unsure of what she could add to the conversation.

Justin thought for a moment. "Tax man." Eleanor recoiled slightly. "Yes, I can see where that is exactly what he did to you." Eleanor turned to Neela. "Child, how can you say that we should do nothing?"

"There's nothing to do," she answered. "Hektor won this round. But Hektor's at his best when someone's reacting to his actions. If we respond to the psychological audit, people will assume it's a cover-up or a backpedal of sorts. The less we say on the matter, the more people and reporters will have to find answers elsewhere.

"Who knows?" she added with a sly grin, "maybe they'll actually stumble onto the truth."

"More likely they'll make up something worse," Omad retorted.

"I think Neela's right," added Justin, "but Omad has a point. We can't not say anything. But whatever we do say will most likely play right into Hektor's grand scheme . . . whatever that may be." Justin remained silent for a minute, then spoke up. "Our best course of action is to only talk to reporters we know and trust—as much as anyone can trust a reporter—and hope they'll give us a fair shake. But Manny, see if you can get the full transcripts of the psyche-audit hearings—all of them. Something strange was going on, and I'll want the facts." Though Manny gave a distracted nod, Justin knew it would get done. "And," he continued, "I'll tell all of you this—I'm through reacting to Hektor. The next time I have to deal with the man I will not underestimate him. And I suggest we all tread carefully from here on in."

"In other words," said Neela, "it ain't over."

"It ain't over." Justin agreed. However, he did get up, indicating the get-together was.

Irma Sobbelgé was trying to figure out exactly what had happened with Sambianco's psyche audit. It didn't make any sense. She wasn't buying Hektor's act, and if, in fact, it was an act then the only person the audit seemed to hurt was Justin. The whole incident had the smell of a setup, and she knew she'd have to act fast if she had any hope at all of uncovering the truth. She also realized that if her suspicions were true, the harm currently being made to Justin Cord's rep-utation might prove irreparable. But before she could figure out how to get ahold of Justin, he got ahold of her. Not just an interview, he suggested over the phone, but a full day with her and her team—in his apartment. Hours of tours, interviews, and, promised Justin, an explanation of his recent actions. A charm offensive if ever there was one, decided Irma, but not an opportunity to be missed. Thirty-five minutes later she arrived at his door, team in tow.

It proved a delightful afternoon. Justin and his old-style beer, Justin and his old-style coffee. Justin and his breakfast cereal (cereal!), Justin and his strange preoccupation with a television set. The fifteen-minute explanation of a wall socket and power cords was priceless. But it was the promised interview at the end of the day that she was looking forward to the most. She even pulled rank and edged out Michael for the one-on-one.

As the sun set, casting a beautiful gleam down on the clouds below, Irma and Justin made their way into a private chamber, where she soon found herself sitting across from him around a small dining-room table sipping coffee. There was, she noted, a wonderfully strong smell of ground beans wafting through the air. Whether the smell had emanated from the in-house olfactory system or from the actual article was of little importance to her; it was unusually entrancing.

"Justin," she said, "let me cut right to the chase. . . ."

"Please do," he said, smiling.

"The whole system is concerned about what happened with Hektor Sam-bianco of GCI."

"The whole system has a right to be concerned, Irma. *I'm* concerned."

She hadn't expected that reply. Not defensive at all. Strange.

"About the bad press you're getting?" she asked, testing.

"No," he answered. "I deserve the bad press. What I did was wrong."

Irma paused and looked intently at her subject. He was playing at something, but what? No one admits they're wrong. No one on-the-record, that is. She felt she owed him something, though. Wasn't sure why, maybe the guy just brought it out. She'd long since learned not to fight her gut.

"You realize, of course, this is being recorded?"

"I do."

He knows what he's doing, she told herself, *so shut up and get it down for posterity.*

"Please continue, then," she said, picking up her coffee and letting her DijAssist do the rest.

Justin's legs were crossed, and he'd moved a few feet back from the table's edge. His arms were resting easily on the arms of the captain's chair.

"With the request for a psyche audit," he said, "the whole system saw me lose my temper and lash out with what seemed to be an amazing power. My economic invulnerability was, and is, I admit, frightening. It really doesn't matter that I was provoked. It doesn't even matter that this P.A. went through without a single hitch, and, I assure you, no help from me. To all the people out there listening, all they know is that I can hurt any one of them at any time, and they're powerless to hurt me back." Justin paused—shamefaced. "And those people are absolutely correct."

Irma didn't say a word. Justin had clearly prepared this speech for her and her audience's benefit. She knew better than to get in the way.

"I've made some decisions, Irma," he said, uncrossing his legs and leaning a notch forward. "Three, to be precise. If you'd be so kind as to pass them on . . ."

"Of course, Justin," answered Irma, taken aback by the sincerity of the request. As if there were another possibility, as if she might decide not to go with his story. Unbelievable.

"Thank you," he continued. "First, I hereby now publicly apologize to Hektor Sambianco. Whatever the provocation, my request for the psyche audit was wrong, and I regret my abuse of power. Second, I hereby promise to give the one share of Hektor Sambianco I purchased for my despicable purpose back to him. It is his, not mine, and I was wrong to own it. If Hektor does not want it back I will sell it and put the money toward an account that'll pay for an investigation into how the justice system could've failed him so badly as to approve a frivolous P.A. in less than a week. Not even The Chairman, with all the legal resources of GCI, could have done that, Irma. How I, as a novice with one share of stock, could do it points to a criminal lapse with regards to the safeguards that were supposed to protect everyone."

Irma nodded, the seriousness of the allegation and confirmation of her suspicions made manifest. "And number three?" she asked, more as a reminder than a question. She needn't have bothered.

Justin had the look of a man who with utter certainty was about to deliver an incontrovertible truth. "Third," he continued, "I have been recently informed that as a matter of course some of my investments had me owning stock in people. No more. It's all been given back—all been divested." He paused a moment to let his last comments sink in, and then looked deep into Irma's eyes, lest she doubt the sincerity of his forthcoming declaration. "I, Justin Cord, hereby promise the system this: *I will not be owned by anyone and I will not own anyone.* A free man must not own another and *I will be free.* Since owning is just as dangerous as being owned—more dangerous, actually—I will give it up. I may be the one free man left in the system, but I will not allow that freedom to be abused again, especially by myself."

Justin sat back. Interview over. Gauntlet thrown. If the very definition of freedom was to be the stakes he and Hektor were playing for, then Justin had finally
found the hill he was prepared to die on.

Hektor was watching the interview attentively. Part of him was as mad as hell at
Justin for having so deftly turned his carefully planned public relations disaster
into a public relations coup. The other part was applauding the move. But even
Hektor had to admit he was beginning to worry. Justin kept getting stronger—
more dangerous. And it was already too late to kill him. Or, at least, that's what
his contingency programs were telling him. It still didn't mitigate the fact that
Justin Cord was becoming an active threat to the corporate system—a threat that
needed to be stopped. And there was nothing more dear to Hektor Sambianco
than the incorporated world. It was perfect. It let an individual know who was
who. How else could he ultimately sneer at all those who thought they were better than him and have them know they were his inferiors? And most of those
mindless drones from his past *were* his inferiors. They just didn't know it yet.

The irony, realized Hektor, was that Justin was obviously superior but had no
idea. Still, he had to be stopped, and Hektor was just the man to do it. Although
he had the help of Janet Delgado, he knew it would not be enough. He'd need
more power, money, and information. And Kirk Olmstead had all three, didn't
he? Hektor just needed to figure out a way to get at it.

One of the advantages of Kirk being V.P. of Special Operations was that he
had had his back covered long ago. Hacking into his records was useless. And
blackmail was out of the question. Anyone he cared about either was well protected or had had their stocks held by Kirk or his associates. There was no effective way to bug his office, and his secretary of over thirty years was about as
likely to give up information as a nun would be to give up her chastity.

Still, he wondered. On the occasions Hektor *had* seen Kirk's chief administrative assistant, a mild-mannered wallflower whose only claim to fame was his
boss and his loyalty, he'd always been treated rudely—dismissed like some
mangy pup begging for scraps. In fact, thought Hektor, following his gut, he
never once heard about Kirk's secretary getting any special trips or bonuses that
office gossip and quarterly reports always laid bare. Just to be sure, Hektor
checked and found that the man hadn't gotten any bonuses, had been paid the
minimum for someone in his position, and took no vacation days. Using a fairly
ingenious spy program, he checked the financial records and saw that Kirk's assistant lived like a penny. He hadn't subscribed to any entertainment channels,
took no trips other than on GCI business, and rented nothing having to do with
sex—male or female. He'd even, if the automated pizza receipt records were to

Dani Kollin and Eytan Kollin

be believed, spent the last thirty Mardi Gras in his studio apartment. That made no sense to Hektor. Kirk didn't pay his secretary much, but he was certainly paid enough to live better than a penny with a bad line of credit.

What does Kirk have on the guy? wondered Hektor. *No one stays that loyal while being treated like such shit. The guy's got no friends, no hobbies, no interests, no vices, no family ties. It's like he's living in his own little . . .* Hektor smiled before he even finished the thought.

"Gotcha."

It was simple to get the secretary alone. He'd called the man, saying he had a hard-copy document that needed to be handed over to the DepDir personally. The man came in shortly and stood impatiently in front of Hektor's desk. Hektor closed the door and activated his suppression system. Not a suspicious act in and of itself, as Hektor did that when anyone walked in. The man, noticed Hektor, was of average height, with no muscle tone to speak of, and hair kept very short. His clothes were utilitarian, almost severe in their simplicity. Around the upper staff it was assumed that this was the "look" that the secretary was going for. But Hektor knew that it was not affectation, it was consequence.

After his perusal he got right to the topic. "Evan, how long have you been a VR addict?"

Hektor saw Evan's eyes light up, and then quickly recover. He then saw what he knew would be Evan's inevitable conclusion—resignation.

"Thirty-five years," he managed in a whisper.

"Lemme guess," asked Hektor. "Kirk found out thirty years ago?"

"Yes," answered Evan. His shoulders had sagged.

"You do know that you work for me now."

Evan looked up, a little surprised, but he recovered quickly. "Yes."

"Excellent," answered Hektor. "We'll start by giving me access to everything you have access to, and figure out the rest later. When Kirk is removed from power— and mark my words, he *will* be removed—you'll be given a job in some basement somewhere and allowed to continue your 'pastime' without interruption."

Evan bowed his head slightly in acknowledgment. He'd assumed this day would come and it would mean an immediate end to his addiction. It was a moment he'd dreaded for years. The fact that the moment had arrived, and that this Sambianco fellow had agreed *not* to cut him off, was plenty fine for him. Let the Titans fight it out. What did he care? As long as they left him and his worlds alone.

"I assume," continued Hektor, "you'll get caught. Your kind always does, but, rest assured, it won't be because of me."

Again, Evan nodded his head in agreement.

"If you tell anyone of this arrangement," said Hektor, putting both his hands down on the table and lifting himself up, "your psyche audit will be swift and painful." Then, looking sternly at his entrapped prey, he said, "We do understand each other."

It was not a question.

"Yes," answered Evan, and then after a second's pause, "sir."

Hektor smiled as Evan left the room much more quickly than he'd entered.

When Neela got back to the apartment she found a note from Justin fastened to the foyer mirror. Her smile at the anachronism quickly dissipated when she read the contents.

"Evelyn," she said to her DijAssist, "please get me a flight to Boston."

"That won't be necessary, Neela. Mr. Cord has leased three executive aircars for a period of one year. His avatar has informed me that one has been left for your personal disposal. It is sufficiently fast enough to get you to Boston sooner than a t.o.p. would—given traffic around Giuliani."

In a little under twenty minutes Neela found herself standing in the lobby of a commercial complex with a magnificent view of Boston Harbor. Justin emerged from a side permiawall and greeted her warmly.

"Justin," she said, "what's going on?"

He led her through the permiawall. Neela saw that he still had the odd habit of holding his arm out as far as he could and touching the door with his finger to activate it. When she got to the other side she saw a large work area filled with people and drones working together at large tables, or individually in cubes. It had the requisite buzz and clamor of a typical workspace. A few heads looked up to see who'd come in, but quickly rebusied themselves with their tasks.

"This," he answered, beaming proudly, "is what's going on."

Though she had her misgivings about the endeavor, she was more taken aback by how fast Justin had managed to put the roots into his grassroots organization.

"So you're actually doing it," she said, shaking her head in disbelief.

"I'm not," he said, scanning the area, arms outstretched. "They are."

Neela didn't speak, unsure of what, if anything, to say. She was happy that the man in her care was finally feeling empowered, but scared of what that empowerment might actually lead to.

"Don't you see, Neela," he continued. "They can free themselves of the burden of owning, and in so doing make the world ready for the next step."

Neela was a little dubious. "Which is?"

"Why, the end of mandatory incorporation, of course."

"And how long," she asked, not bothering to mask her incredulity, "do you think it will take?"

"Any idea, sebastian?" asked Justin.

"Approximately two hundred years by my calculations, Dr. Harper."

"Why that long?"

"Any faster," interjected Justin, lest his avatar misconstrue Neela's question to be directed at him, "and people could get hurt. I understand that the corporate world functions moderately well and isn't going anywhere for a while—which is just fine by me. And it's also why I've started contributing funds to political parties with similar philosophies."

"Like the Majority Party?" she asked.

"Yeah. They're small and unorganized, but I think their hearts are in the right place. Like I said, Neela, I'd really only like to end mandatory incorporation . . . and do it *slowly*. History's littered with the corpses of the unwilling who died because some big-headed idiots thought their cause was more important than the lives they were meant to protect. Well, I'm no Stalin or Osama. Gandhi and Martin Luther King are more worthy role models."

Neela shrugged. "Interesting choice . . . Boston," she said, changing topics.

"True birthplace of freedom," he proffered.

She gave him a puzzled look.

"Not Washington, D.C.?"

"You mean," he answered with disdain, "the place where most of my beliefs were shot down and/or destroyed in the name of the common good? Don't think so. Besides, Boston's the true birthplace of freedom."

"Then what was Philadelphia all about?"

Justin shook his head. "It was a convenient meeting place. Boston was where Americans first started to fight for their precious freedom and, by God," he said, leading her into his well-appointed office, "it's where we'll start to fight for ours!"

Hektor pored through the newly garnered records and formulated a plan of attack. He had to hand it to Special Operations. They'd kept tabs on all the important and potentially important people in the system, and their file on prospective troublemakers was interesting. Hektor figured to start small. If he could find one of these on-edge, un–psyche audited troublemakers within Justin's new party and push them just enough to fall off the edge—perhaps even manipulate them into doing something outrageous in the name of the divestiture movement—then Hektor would be able to put the blame squarely on Justin's doorstep. This would give him the consensus to attack Justin directly. Of course, he'd need to be the DepDir by then, but Hektor was confident that that would soon come to fruition or, conversely, that he'd be so far from the seat of power that he wouldn't care. His first activation would be one Sean Doogle—rated, according to the files, as nominally unstable. As a rule Hektor wouldn't dare involve himself in the affairs of a family as powerful as the Doogles, but Sean was technically under the wide wings of Justin, pretty much disowned, and the publicity of the name would help rivet the public on any newsworthy actions Doogle might, with a little connivance from Hektor, be able to affect. And with the Doogle character Hektor knew exactly what button to press—the file made that perfectly clear. It was sad about the human collateral involved, but as far as Hektor was concerned, it was a small price to pay.

At first glance Sean Doogle didn't seem like a world shaker. He appeared young and in good health. But this was not remarkable in the world he had grown up in. His fashion was way out of date, as he sported pants and a jacket made up entirely of patches, a fad that was twenty years dead and showed no sign of returning, except among Sean's more fervent followers. His hair was long, and he had a couple of extra pounds lingering about his waistline. He'd only have a nanofat flush when it got to be a problem, and then would go back to eating too much, but in the corporate world being overweight wasn't a real problem either. Real obesity was as dead as taxes and cancer. But it wasn't just his looks that threw people off. It was his ancestry. The Doogle family had been wealthy and powerful for generations. No one in Sean's immediate family tree failed to have majority assured by their twenty-first birthday.

And Sean was no exception. His life had been well charted. He'd attend the best schools, take the most exclusive grand tours of the solar system, and network with the most select social set. It was also true that Sean wouldn't have to work hard or contribute much to society, but his ancestors had done all that so that he wouldn't have to. After sixty or so years he'd think about settling down, getting married to a woman of the same acceptable background, and digging in for a life of luxury that most of the rest of society could only have dreamed about. Yes, Sean Doogle's life was meant to be one of safety, wealth, interest, and ease.

This is what would have happened but for two small problems. One was that Sean was very intelligent and withdrawn from an early age. This was only a small handicap, and his avatar would have directed him toward similar people in his social strata. It is indeed likely that he, via his meddling avatar, would have "found" a woman who was also withdrawn and shy, and they would've had a happy, eccentric life together, perhaps as husband and wife college professors, or even botanists, with their own island to play with. But the second event in Sean's young life proved to be far more problematic and not as easy to solve.

Sean fell in love.

It was the most dangerous and cruelest sort. Love at first sight. From the moment he saw the raven-haired laughing girl he knew she was the one he was going to marry. He, of course, knew nothing about her, but that didn't stand in his way. After all, Sean was used to getting what he wanted. He spent so much time daydreaming about her, as only withdrawn fourteen-year-old boys could do, that a week went by before he worked up the courage to find out who she was.

He was delighted to find out that her father worked for the family. In fact, he'd just been hired as the head of the stables. In a reversal of the cliché from the ancient romance novels, the young, rich, shy boy soon fell in love with the stableman's daughter. Her name was Elizabeth Reynolds, and she was, at least from what Sean could tell, fearless with the horses under her charge, and almost equally wild and free. Not free in the corporate sense; she was, after all, a penny, having been born into a family of 25 percenters, but certainly free in every other respect. Like her father she excelled at training, and since this was something that machines and drones were not able to do as well as humans, it was one of those specialty areas humans had not been displaced from.

Sean, who until then would have been hard-pressed to tell you where the stables were, developed a passion for horse riding. Every day he'd be seen going down to the stables, and every day he'd work hard to improve his form. After a while he became a fair enough rider, and was even allowed to help with the care of the horses—something Elizabeth's father would not have allowed unless Sean had earned it. It was, ironically, one of the things he was proudest of in his early life. He'd *earned* the right to clean up stables and to care for and groom horses. No one had handed it to him on a silver platter. But the real reward, of course, was Elizabeth. Every day with Elizabeth.

Sean's new passion was of some concern to his parents, but it was assumed that he'd grow out of it. After all, a boy of Sean's class could and did start enjoying intercourse with a great many different men and women from a wide variety of classes and places. But this was not the case with Sean. He was truly in love. And in an age when a boy of Sean's years was hard-pressed to still be a virgin, he'd managed to stay one, waiting for the day to consummate the act with his one true love.

For a while Elizabeth was flattered by the attention. To be so completely loved by a boy who would grow up to be a wealthy man was not without its attractions. But what for Sean was a complete and all-consuming love was for Elizabeth a childhood romance. As she grew older she grew away from the young man who was still infatuated with her. She did care for him, and didn't want to see him hurt, but the love he'd professed for her was not now, nor ever going to be, reciprocated. Had Elizabeth been a more mercenary sort—only interested in "the three Ms" of money, majority, and matrimony—her life would have been set. But that wasn't Elizabeth.

As soon as an opportunity arose to leave, she grabbed it. It seemed she'd been awarded an internship with TerraCo, an interplanetary terraforming corporation. The internship had been arranged quietly by Sean's parents with Elizabeth's father's approval (without either of the teenagers' knowledge). But for Elizabeth it wouldn't have mattered. It was a great opportunity for adventure. In a little lie that would have repercussions far beyond what she ever could have imagined, Elizabeth broke the news to Sean. Rather than hurt him by saying she *wanted* to leave, she told him she *had* to. The easy patsy for her desire to not hurt him was the incorporation movement itself. Elizabeth told him that she had to go because she didn't own a majority of herself. Of course, Sean offered to buy her majority on the spot, but she'd told him that she wanted to earn her majority on her own, a common work ethic among the pennies. The truth was that for someone as deeply in love and, most would argue later, "disturbed," as Sean was, there would have been no good reason. Elizabeth's departure left him devastated, with only one glimmer of hope. She would one day return.

Though he knew in his heart that Elizabeth didn't love him, and was even aware that she'd been dating other men and women, he held out hope. He knew that after ten, twenty, fifty, or even a hundred years she'd want the type of life only he could offer her, and then . . . then she'd return to his waiting arms. This was yet another way in which Sean Doogle had separated himself from the masses. He wasn't interested in instant gratification, and was willing to wait for however long it took to get what he wanted. So he said good-bye, confident that Elizabeth the stable hand would one day return to him, and they would then live happily ever after.

Three months later she was as gone as gone could get in the unincorporated world. She'd been transferred to a top security site run by GCI near Neptune. It was one of those deals in which she'd agreed to give GCI sixty-plus years of her life, working in high-risk areas, in return for self-majority and a great benefits package. This had the intended effect of cutting Elizabeth off from Sean. It did not, however, cut off Sean's memory of her.

He had, at his own expense and on a newly purchased property, built an extraordinary stable. Though it was a bit of an extravagance, he'd arranged for Elizabeth's horses to be allowed to wander and graze undisturbed on the land. Her parents hadn't minded, thinking it would perhaps make a good transition for Sean's eventual acceptance of Elizabeth's departure. Sean also had the stable equipped with a salt lick and a watering trough that would only activate in the horses' presence. It dropped hay and was cared for by an elderly couple. This stable, he believed, would help him remember his love without the memory being too painful.

The rest of his life was mired in misery, and there was little anyone could do about it. He was barely an adult who owned an almost incontestable 75 percent of himself. When he finally did lose his virginity it was two years after Elizabeth had left, and it was to a girl who looked, but was not like, the fearless stable hand from his "youth." He felt so guilt-ridden about having betrayed his love that he didn't try it again for years, and never had anything close to a normal sex life. He was lost and going through the motions of living when he came across a listing for a tiny college-based political/economic organization called the Majority Party.

And so it was that Sean Doogle finally awoke out of his morass. If it was not for the fact that Elizabeth was a penny she could have stayed with him. The idea that she would have left him regardless was something Sean was no longer capable of entertaining. He now had his answer. His raison d'être. Incorporation had stolen Elizabeth away from him, and so incorporation was going to pay. The sad fact was that had Sean not been a majority shareholder of himself, his "eccentricities" and clear streak of depression would have made him a prime candidate for a psychological audit. But Sean had about as much freedom as a person could expect in the incorporated world, and so his odd behavior, very much like the rich and famous before him, was tolerated.

Sean took to the new group like a nanite to a molecule, and quickly established himself as a leader. And like other leaders before him, it was his eyes that told you this was a man you should pay attention to or, conversely, avoid. His eyes seemed to have two modes. They either blazed or smoldered. When he was trying to convince or make converts they tended to blaze. It was when he was quiet that they would smolder, dwelling on some injustice or problem that he felt only he alone could solve. Still, his intensity was a useful trait to have as the leader of a fringe political party that most in society felt was pointless or, at best, offered a modicum of comic relief.

The group's political history had been brief. It had been formed only within the last thirty years and supported the radical notion that people should, as an inalienable right, control a majority of themselves. This radical idea had very little support among the public at large, and was severely frowned upon by the corporations and the government.

The humorous point, and one harped upon by a mostly hostile media, was that the bulk of the party's membership, as well as its entire leadership, had self-majority. It seemed to be an indelible truth of political history that fringe movements survived by the efforts of the desperate and the rich. In the modern society that had emerged since the Grand Collapse there were very few desperate individuals or groups. This meant that the Majority Party was made up of the rich.

The truth of the matter was, government did *so little* that most people *cared little* about politics, and certainly not in the way people of the past had. After all, the government did not tax, which had been the main focus of the people's concern with government for centuries. No matter what the idiots in Geneva decided, they'd only be able to take 5 percent of a person's income—ever. This meant that the people could ignore this relatively harmless and predictable aspect of their lives. Truth be told, an individual's parents took a whopping 20 percent of their earnings, which meant that the family had far more impact on a person's life than government ever would or could. Which, most reasoned, was how it should be.

Also, the government services that ancient Americans were once forced to use had been either limited or eliminated. For instance, such societal needs as mail, health care, unemployment, welfare, retirement, and disaster relief were no longer handled by the government. Police and law, formally a pre-GC government monopoly, were constitutionally made open to competition from private enterprise. The current grand old political party was the Libertarians, and they were completely devoted to limiting government power. The opposing party was an offshoot of the Libertarians. They were called the Eliminationist Party, and their platform was predicated on the belief that corporate society had evolved beyond the need for government *at all*. For decades the Eliminationists remained a fringe party because of their shortsighted insistence on scrapping all government everywhere. Because corporate society was inherently conservative, and the party's platform too radical, the Eliminationist movement never got off the ground. However, with the rise to power of one Shannon Kang, the party managed to right itself by taking a different and more tactful approach. Instead of calling for the elimination of all government, they began to push for something they termed a "government-free zone." This "zone," it was proposed, could be a continent or terraformed moon or planet. In this zone they sought to let the corporate society function without government interference, using the rule promulgated by David Friedman. The rule stated that a society could be run, even at the point of enforcing and creating laws, using the machinery of capitalism itself. And Friedman's theory had been proposed before the culturally enforcing effect of incorporation had been discovered. The government-free-zone idea appealed to a large enough audience that it had paid dividends politically, and for the first time in centuries an opposition party had come into existence. However, the Libertarians were still in a comfortable majority.

While this course of political events, certainly with the rise of a new opposition party, may have seemed exciting to someone from pre–GC, to a citizen of the present it would be about as exciting as watching a university chess club discuss its charter. Politics were never a public draw, and the competing party's only audiences were usually themselves.

Into this political snoozefest, and trailing the Eliminationists by a light year, came a third political group known as the Majority Party. It started out more as a joke amid some college students needing a fun project for a fluff class they'd all been taking. The project had to do with how to make a positive change in society. After many debates it was decided that the basic idea of the proposed party would be to help those who would have little time or inclination to help themselves. These young idealists decided that since everyone they knew at their wealthy and exclusive school had majority, it would be nice if everyone else did as well—and so was born their platform. Being young and well-intentioned, they created the idea while ignoring the obvious economic reasons not everyone had majority, and had a complete disregard for the consequences of the concept, should it ever come to fruition. The fact that they received poor grades for their "project" didn't hinder them one bit. They were determined to better society for the common good, even if the recipients of that supposed good weren't interested. In this they were rather like those well-meaning activists in city governments around turn-of-the-millennium America. Those activists, like the misguided Majority Party, had a similar logic. They, too, lived in large, spacious, well-lit, and convenience-filled homes and apartments. They, too, felt the burning desire to enact laws for the people's "own good," often to disastrous results. In fact, "low-income housing of the pre-GC" was still taught in most university econ courses as the epitome of government intervention gone awry.

But by the time the Majority Party got started, the very real pains that the pre-GC government intervention had wrought were a faded and distant memory, relegated to texts and not reality.

The Majority Party decided early on that the best way to get everyone a majority was to use the government's power. The idea of an interventionist government was so abhorrent to society that for a number of years the party existed, it seemed, for the sole purpose of annoying as many people as possible. And in this, much to their parents' embarrassment and dropped stock values, they succeeded mightily. Of course, only those who were guaranteed a comfortable majority, i.e., the entire makeup of the new party, would be able to flaunt society's wishes so easily. However, for those truly working their way toward a majority the quickest way to kill a promising career, and therefore *not* achieve self-majority, would be to come out against private property and be in favor of government theft. Not likely, and hence the reason for the Majority Party's tepid reception and inordinately low membership. Further, for those who made majority on their own, the thought of having the government take a percentage of their effort and hard work—beyond the constitutionally mandated 5 percent—was beyond the pale. And then, when it was pointed out that the only way to pay for the idea would be for the government to take 10 percent or reinstitute taxes, the reaction turned violent. And so, many an earnest and rich dilettante got the crap kicked out of him while failing to understand why the people he was trying to help the most tended to be the very ones who most wanted to kick the crap out of him. It wasn't until Sean Doogle showed up that everything changed.

For Sean, the Majority Party was not a game, nor a way to piss off one's parents before going into the family business—it was a passionate calling. When he spoke of the rights of everyone to own a majority of themselves, he did so with so much passion and conviction that even the most hardcore Libertarian might be swayed momentarily. Most eventually snapped out of it, but not all. Some became true believers and followers.

The first thing the exceptional orator did was to end a rift that had emerged in the party. The spat was about direction. Namely, whether to concentrate on giving a majority to everyone, or to simply push for a law that would state that no one who currently had a majority could ever lose it. The clear advantage of the latter school of thought was that in theory it was not only more palatable, it was also an idea that would not impinge on percentages or impose taxes. But after a few ardent speeches by Sean, the group was made to realize it was wrong to leave anyone enslaved. His reasoning, while making the party feel much more ideologically pure, destroyed any chance it would have to win over more than the barest sliver of the discontented.

But win that group over he did. His mantra was simple. It was all incorporation's fault. And "all" encompassed everything. You're poor, you can't get a good job or good training, your stock price is too low, your girlfriend doesn't love you because your stock price is too low, your dog died and you couldn't afford to get him reanimated. The list was endless, the villain an easy mark, and the prophet exemplary.

The Majority Party headquarters was located in San Francisco in a Victorian building that was centuries old and had been rebuilt countless times. The house exterior was as exact as historical records could make it, and Sean was convinced that Mark Twain or Emperor Norton themselves would not have found the old abode out of place. But for Sean and the purists of the Majority Party that was not the reason for their chosen residence. They were not restorers or preservers by nature, being more interested in tearing down and disrupting. No, the house served a political purpose. As Sean or any of his followers would tell anyone willing to listen, the structure was created by free labor, i.e., noncorporate-built, and as such served as a symbol of the free men they wished their own society would aspire to be. If anyone were to point out that the house was built by Chinese laborers that had most likely been beaten, miserably paid, stolen from and/or taxed by various gangs and bureaucrats—the two not being mutually exclusive—the stalwarts of the Majority Party would have pooh-poohed the suggestion. In fact, one journalist had the temerity to suggest that any of the "free" workers of the past would have gladly killed for a chance to live in an incorporated world, with all its obvious benefits. He was ignored.

But Sean was not ignoring the media now. While he usually disdained the ilk who'd so thoroughly eviscerated his character and his movement, he couldn't help but be interested in the buzz that was now infecting the entire system. Plus, like practically everyone else in the Terran Confederation, he harbored a strange fascination for this unincorporated man. That Sean would ultimately be responsible for causing Mr. Cord an unrelenting amount of pain and suffering he could not possibly know. For now, Sean just stared transfixed at the holodisplay as the story of Justin Cord's mea culpa unfolded.

There in the holodisplay Justin Cord had spoken an elemental truth. Sean was convinced to the core of his being that this truth was being spoken to Sean, and Sean alone. This truth was ringing clear. So clear, in fact, that a smile appeared on a face that seemed to have been missing one for years. Sean leaned back in his chair and began repeating a mantra that would haunt the corporate world's upper echelons—and society itself—for years.

"One free man," he whispered to himself, "one free man . . . one free man . . . one free man . . ."

8 | Mardi Gras

Mardi Gra's a-comin' and full-on fun awaits you at the rings of Saturn! Don't miss this year's rings of ice-refracted laser light show . . . brought to you by Philip Morris and McDonald's—proud partners in the terraforming of Titan. The show encompasses an area equal to seventy times the Earth's surface. Quite simply it's the biggest show in the solar system. And remember, there's no bad seat from space!

—FROM AN ADVERTISEMENT HEARD ON *ALL THINGS CONSIDERED*,
SYSTEM PRIVATE RADIO (SPR)

Justin was sitting in his New York apartment giving serious thought to what he was going to wear. This was normally not a problem, as he usually wore what he wanted. It was the rare occasion that would compel him to put some thought into his ensemble. But this was no ordinary occasion. In a little less than two weeks the entire system, from the solar observation platform to the Oort Cloud to every planet, moon, and orbiting piece of debris big enough to hold a human, was going to party like rich college kids on spring break with their parents' credit cards.

The few consistent traditions Justin was able to nail down were that Mardi Gras lasted for exactly one week, one could do things during Mardi Gras that would not be mentioned or held against them for the rest of the year, and that what one wore at the start of the festivities should be worn for the entire week. In what little time Justin did find to read, he'd learned about how some people would take weeks off prior to "the week" to not only grow new body parts, but also to learn how to use them—whatever that meant. Apparently, full bodmods—with rare exception—were the rage almost exclusively with those with self-majority. Body nano of so invasive a nature usually took time to generate, and once in place usually took the customer of that transformation a good week to acclimate to—you had to have money, and lots of it, to afford that kind of time and technology. But from the reviews he'd read by "satisfied clients," the money spent and time preparing was well worth the week of stares they'd receive once the party got going. In looking at some of the modifications available, Justin realized that he could have done pretty much whatever he might imagine—from growing dinosaur skin to adding extra working appendages. In his brief review of the more "popular" getups, he was so taken aback by what he saw that he could only liken the advertised bodmods to creatures out of the more radical sci-fi films he remembered from his past.

Justin had decided almost immediately that, though he could afford it, a bodmod was not in the cards for him. Getting used to his new, "younger" skin was hard enough; the last thing he wanted to do was switch into another one. So that left him thinking about what type of "typical" costume he might choose for himself. Normally, this was the sort of question he'd bring to Neela, but for some reason she wasn't available—except by handphone. She'd told him that she'd had to take care of some sort of personal issue, and that she'd meet up with him at their hotel in New Orleans. He knew better than to argue, and so had managed to while away the time, not thinking about what to wear until it was almost too late. So now Justin was left with Dr. Gillette to help him sort out his fashion quandary. He found the good doctor sitting in the kitchen having breakfast and reading a hard-copy newspaper. Thaddeus heard Justin enter, looked up at his patient, and smiled.

"Justin, my boy," said the doctor, "I must thank you for your advice concerning printing out the paper . . . on paper, which is where, I guess, they got the name in the first place."

Justin chuckled and removed a bowl from the cabinet. He grabbed a bag of cereal from the pantry that tasted enough like peanut butter Cap'n Crunch as to make no real difference. He'd forever pat himself on the back for including freeze-dried boxes of his favorite cereals in the chamber where he'd been found. It was a simple matter for the nanobots to figure out the exact amounts of each ingredient to replicate the flavors and textures of the foods he'd brought along for the journey.

"I'm glad you like the paper, Doc," he said, sitting across from his friend and confidant. He offered the doctor some of his cereal. "Cap'n Crunch?"

The doctor shook his head. "I prefer my food to move, thanks." Justin still couldn't get used to "moving" food, which was popular. It wasn't that the food was alive; it was just . . . animated. Oh, he'd tried it, and hadn't found the experience unpleasant. For example, he had a type of oatmeal that swirled around in his mouth of its own volition, managing to excite tastebuds on the back of his tongue he never knew existed. That was followed by the sensation of the food "moving" down the throat almost as if scratching an itch he never knew he had. Which was also, surprisingly, not an unpleasant sensation. It would just take some time to get used to. In the meantime, he had his Cap'n Crunch, his Quaker Oatmeal Squares, and his low-fat granola. Quite backward by the social standards; however, comforting by his.

Dr. Gillette turned a page to follow an article. "At first," the doctor continued, "this paper-turning thing seemed like a totally archaic and useless tradition. I mean, why have a paper printed when you can just have it read to you or read it from a DijAssist? But after a couple of mornings of experimenting— purely as a matter of research, I can assure you," he said, almost as an apology, "well, I must admit that I'm finding myself positively addicted."

"It can grow on you," answered Justin, taking pleasure in his recently bestowed if not antiquated gift. Then, "Tell me, Doc, do you happen to know where Neela is?"

"Depends," he answered, with an arched eyebrow.

"On what?"

"On why you need her."

"Why," asked Justin, "should that make one iota of a difference?"

"Because if you need to ask her a clinical question, then I'll need to be insulted."

"And if I don't?"

"Then," smiled the doctor, "I won't be insulted; that is, I'll be concerned."

"Ahh. No, it's not clinical, it's, well . . . um . . . a fashion thing."

"I see," Thaddeus responded, with a jovial grin. "In that case I don't know where Dr. Harper is."

"Dr. Harper? So formal, Thaddeus?"

"For you, yes. Or, at least, it should be. And just in case I haven't reminded you enough," he said, while wrestling spastically with the unbound newspaper, "no good can come of a patient and a reanimationist having anything other than a professional relationship."

Justin began to protest, but Dr. Gillette waved him off. "Ever since you two came back from the museum things have changed." He tossed the paper aside in disgust, muttering something under his breath about "newfangled" devices.

"Nonsense, Doctor," answered Justin, managing to get a word in edgewise. He used his best game face, making sure he had direct eye contact. The good doctor wasn't buying.

"Oh please, Justin," answered Thaddeus. "I'm old enough, and certainly expert enough, to know when a man is infatuated—you—but until the VRM that infatuation was not returned—by her."

"VRM?"

"Virtual Reality Museum," answered the doctor tersely.

"Hey, Doc, I can assure you . . ."

"You can assure me of nothing, Justin. It's all the little things I've noticed. Like her overconcern for you. She'd chalk it up to being especially sensitive toward your needs, probably say something about 'post-VRM syndrome.' But you and I know better, don't we?" The doctor didn't wait for a reply. "Or how you wait for each other before eating at the table. And don't think I haven't noticed that you've both begun to finish each other's sentences."

"Doc," parried Justin, "I think you're overreacting. I can assure you . . ." He paused, waiting for the interruption. There was none forthcoming. Thaddeus was waiting to be convinced. "I can assure you," repeated Justin, "that we're just friends."

"All that I've just described," answered Thaddeus, "are the beginnings of the strongest possible relationship. Of that I can *assure* you." He then somehow managed to reassemble the discarded newspaper and buried his head among the columns. "And I have absolutely no fashion sense," he answered dismissively, almost as if his accusatory exchange had never taken place.

Justin pondered the conversation as he dived into his bowl of cereal, grabbing the sports page from the discarded pile in the middle of the table. He perused the headlines. It seemed that the Mars Rangers had beaten the crap out of the Titan Warriors in a game called rocketball. From what Justin could ascertain, the object of the game was to wipe out as many of the opposing team members as possible while trying to advance the ball in ten-kilometer stretches. The only game that seemed to have survived intact was soccer, and Justin had never been a big fan of the game. A die-hard football fan, for sure, but soccer was a game that never appealed. The closest thing he found to football involved variable gravity fields and body armor; however, none of the teams, stats, or players made much sense to him. *Time for that later,* he thought. There was also, per Justin's request, a comics page, but its presence on the table was for naught. Justin had tried to get sebastian to convert the short, animated, three-dimensional holographic presentations that were the comics of the day into the two-dimensional panels Justin had been used to—to no avail.

Either, figured Justin, the new medium was not meant to be expressed in the old form, or he was too out of touch to understand modern humor. He hadn't understood what passed for humor in his day, preferring old episodes of *I Love Lucy* to the mostly vapid sitcoms that came later. He also had to get used to the fact that what he once thought of as the business section was here called "the front page"—which made perfect sense given the society he found himself in.

Justin polished off his bowl and moved it aside.

"Why," he asked Dr. Gillette—off topic, "do you say that Neela's not really my reanimationist anymore?"

The doctor looked up from behind the science section of the paper.

"You mean, besides the fact that *I'm* your official reanimationist now, and that Dr. Harper works for me?"

"Uh, yeah."

"Well, then, you and Dr. Harper," he answered, "have become closer than what would be considered the norm for a client and doctor. To be frank, it interferes with the professional relationship. Of course, in retrospect, it's not that surprising, is it? You're a famous, handsome, and mysterious man. She's an intelligent, compassionate, and not unattractive woman." The doctor considered then rejected the idea of bringing up the fact that Neela had metaphorically given birth to Justin—being the first female he saw after reanimation. While that attraction was well documented as a psychological norm, in this case, decided Thaddeus, there were so many other variables at play as to render the phenomena statistically insignificant.

"So, I'm guessing this kind of thing must happen all the time," offered Justin, looking a little disappointed.

"Almost never, and certainly never like this—that is, with the deep emotional bonds," answered the doctor, putting his paper down—this time neatly folded—on the table.

"Justin, you and your situation are unique. The truth of the matter is that Neela is far more than your friend, which given your circumstance is probably more critical to your emotional well-being than a reanimation specialist. But it is not usual, and not moral. However, in your case it might be needed. If I thought otherwise I would have had Neela transferred out of here a long time ago. Luckily, officially she's not your specialist. I'm not saying that you don't need a specialist . . . you do. But that, my dear friend," said Thaddeus, eyebrow raised, "you have in me. Nor am I saying that because she's not officially your specialist that means she's open territory. She's not. Because Dr. Harper woke you, in the eyes of the world she's still your reanimationist, and therefore still off-limits."

"So," Justin answered, "what you're telling me is that in Dr. Harper I've not hired the services of a reanimation specialist but those of a *friend*?"

The doctor nodded.

"You know, Doc," continued Justin, "we had a word for that in my day."

The doctor was not amused. "It's humor like that which will get you and Neela into trouble," answered Thaddeus, picking up on the crude innuendo. "I wish you'd get sexed already. You do realize that intercourse is readily available in this day and age for no charge. You could have the oldest of women and not have to pay for it. The fact that you don't makes your infatuation with Dr. Harper all the more obvious."

"Doctor! I . . . um, before we discuss my sex life, could you at least tell me how to go about finding Neela? She's not answering her DijAssist."

"You mean Dr. Harper."

"Neela, Dr. Harper, either way, it's not helping me decide what I'm going to wear to Mardi Gras."

Dr. Gillette immediately relaxed, and a smile broke out on his face. "My dear boy, why didn't you say so? Fashion's one thing that I readily agree I have no business advising on. However, Mardi Gras is quite another matter, and I would be delighted to be of assistance." Dr. Gillette leaned forward with a convivial grin. "How do you feel about enormously large phalluses?"

Justin sighed.

Sean Doogle of the Majority Party made a surprise and radical announcement this morning from his party's headquarters in San Francisco. It would appear that, not being satisfied with life on the political fringe, Mr. Doogle is now taking his party out of political reality and into never-never land. In a prepared statement it was announced that the Majority Party was no longer satisfied with granting everyone a majority status within themselves, but that they wished to end the practice of personal incorporation entirely. The party will now be called the "Liberty Party," in what this journalist supposes is an obscure attempt to link themselves to the Liberty Party of the American pre–Civil War era. That party was made up of individuals who helped to end slavery over four hundred years ago. This party, one supposes, seeks to end civilization as we know it. It is the belief of this site that we shall soon hear the last of the Liberty/Majority Party, and good riddance.

In more relevant news, the Eliminationist Party was granted a concession that shows its increasing strength in governmental matters. The speaker of the assembly proposed that the entire planet of Venus be turned into a government-free zone when it's ready for settlement. This would give the Eliminationists the large area they requested but put the issue on the back burner—as most experts agree it will take at least another century for Venus to be ready for human habitation.

—ALL THINGS POLITICAL SITE, NEURO #3432435

In the end Justin decided on something simple yet symbolic. He ordered it from a local shop, and it was delivered within hours to his apartment. Though Mardi Gras could be experienced systemwide, he'd decided to take it in from the event's original birthplace. All that was left to do was to grab a t.o.p. to the Hotel Rex on Canal Street in downtown New Orleans. He planned to arrive in the late afternoon. It would be the start of the holiday and a way to get the full flavor of the insanity he'd been told to expect.

Justin was informed by sebastian that a t.o.p. was available to take him directly to his hotel should he so desire, but Justin declined. If this was to be the party of the people, then damned if he wasn't going to mingle with the maniacs. "At least," cautioned his worried avatar, "do some minor facial adjustment so you won't be mobbed upon your arrival at the main terminal." To this Justin agreed, especially when he determined that a fake nose and facial-hair growth would be about as simple as sticking on a rubber nose from a novelty shop. The distinct advantage of the simple disguises was that they were nano-based novelty items, which meant that the hair actually attached itself to the face, and the added epidermis of the nose did the same without interfering in any way with Justin's nasal passages.

Though there was a private t.o.p. on the roof of the apartment he lived in, Justin chose to take his personal flyer to the NYC orport, and from there hop on a private t.o.p. to the Neville orport in New Orleans. It gave his new security detail conniptions, but that's what he paid them for.

When he disembarked from the t.o.p. and started on his descent to the main terminal, he was so taken aback by the chaos before him he was almost tempted to turn around and head back to the safety of his New York City lair.

A Greek mythological god flew past him chasing an almost naked woman, who Justin could swear had two complete sets of voluminous breasts. The woman was laughing or Justin might have been tempted to . . . do what, he had no idea. He counted at least four sexual trysts occurring both on the ground and in the air. When he finally did manage to float down to the ground, he was so busy staring at the assortment of oddballs and exploits that he ran smack into a large blue spider with a strikingly human face.

"Tr-transbod?" was all Justin managed to stutter, shocked by the living, breathing creature in front of him.

"No," the spider growled, scratching his nose with one of his legs, "this is how I always look. What, were you born yesterday?"

"Well, actually . . . ," Justin began. But the spider cut him off, handing him a crystal disk. "Listen, bud. Big party every night at Schatzy's on Bourbon Street." The spider then moved on, and by the shrieks of delight and laughter that followed "it," Justin realized that he'd just bumped into one of the best walking advertisements he'd ever seen.

He had to step over broken beer bottles and past a group of drunken men swaying in hula skirts, and sidestep an alligator-skinned couple holding alligator-skin bags. As he made his way out the exit he could have sworn he saw the spider talking to a cyclops.

"Alright, sebastian, you win," he said, as he exited the orport. "Get me to the Hotel Rex ASAP."

There was no point in keeping his mask on. Seasoned paparazzi would have spotted him in a nanobeat, so he ditched it in the cab. The first thing he noticed as he entered the hotel was the hubbub of people and transbods hurriedly rushing to and fro. The next thing he noticed was the burgundy-colored marble floor spread across the entire lobby. In the center of the space were two hexagonal marble pillars with ornate wooden benches in the style of Louis XIV resting on either side. Large floral bouquets were in evidence everywhere. He looked over at the main desk and saw that it, too, was made from the same burgundy tile as the floor he was standing on. Behind the desk were three well-dressed workers, and behind them were what appeared to be three Botticelli paintings. Ironically, it wasn't the Botticelli paintings that marked the hotel as überprestigious; it was the humans working in front of them. Only the most prominent hotels and restaurants would even attempt to use human labor during Mardi Gras. Except for police, courts, and medical centers, most of humanity was taking the week off—way off.

Justin ignored the head-turning his entrance had garnered and began to make his way to the desk. If he could find his room he'd at least be able to take a break from the overload of visual stimuli.

No luck. He was stopped in his tracks by one of the most erotic creatures he'd ever laid eyes on. Granted, he hadn't seen that many, but this one was knock-dead stunning. Where most of the transbods he'd noticed seemed to content themselves with the merely outrageous, this woman, if what he was looking at could be called that, had clearly gone for more devilish attire.

She was tall, at least as tall as Justin, and her skin was deep auburn red. She had a very thick mane of long black hair that seemed to fall restlessly off her shoulders, cascading down onto a well-exposed bosom that was attempting to escape from a tight-fitting black leather top. Protruding from her forehead through the mass of hair was a pair of short, pointed ivory horns. Justin's eyes followed her perfectly flat stomach to the black leather G-string patch she was wearing over her crotch. The strings on either side of the minuscule covering seemed to leap in perfect arches over her shapely hips. Her extraordinarily long legs were accentuated by a pair of thigh-high black leather boots resting precariously over six-inch stiletto heels. He also noticed that her arms and hands were covered in fingerless black leather gloves that went all the way up to her well-toned biceps. The face seemed oddly familiar, though it was hard to get past the jet-black eyes—no white showing whatsoever—black pouty lips, and dazzling white teeth. But the pièce de résistance was a set of large bat wings that emerged from the back of the creature's upright shoulders. They were almost as large as the woman herself.

Justin was entranced.

He wasn't the only one. The entire lobby seemed to stop and stare as the transbod made her way across the foyer. And it only took a second for Justin to realize that the demon was heading straight toward him. It was one of the few times in his lives that he was thankful his face was so easily recognized.

The woman quickly traversed the space between herself and Justin. As she approached, he could see that she had a slightly worried look on her face.

"You're late," she said.

Justin recognized the voice instantly, but his mind had trouble putting the sound to the image.

"Ne-Ne-Neela?" he stuttered.

Neela's expression went from concerned den mother to that of a girl hoping her date liked the prom dress. She spread her wings out to their full radius and placed her hands squarely on her hips. "Do you like it?" she asked.

"Neela," he answered, hardly believing this beautiful creature was his dear friend and confidante. " 'Like' is not the word; 'amazed' is." Then, "It's all . . . real?"

Neela laughed, as a bit of the seductress demon returned. "Of course it's real, Justin."

She took his hand and placed it on her arm. "See," she said, rubbing his hand slowly up and down her upper arm just above the rim where the black leather glove ended. "The color doesn't come off." She removed his hand from her arm and placed it on one of her horns, drawing Justin closer provocatively. "They don't come off either . . . even this," she said, as a long prehensile tail emerged from her backside, practically popping up between them, "doesn't come off." She saw by the look in Justin's eyes that the tail had completely surprised him—as she'd intended.

Justin's head was spinning and his heart was pounding. He was speechless, no longer because of what he was looking at but because of what he was feeling. He wanted this woman, and he wanted her now. He laughed inwardly as he realized he probably could have taken her—if she were willing—right there on the cold marble floor with nary an onlooker interested. Though they certainly would've been, he reasoned, had they any inkling as to her real identity.

But he'd had it pounded into him so many times about the dire consequences of such an action that he barely allowed himself time for the fantasy. Old Thaddeus's admonitions had apparently done their job. Though he knew he wanted her, he also knew he'd never risk her career just to satisfy his carnal desires.

"Well, hello there!" came a cry from the far end of the lobby. It was Dr. Gillette. Of that Justin was sure. Where the voice was coming from he couldn't tell amid the din.

He felt a tap on the shoulder.

Thank goodness, thought Justin, needing time to sort out his feelings. While the good doctor offered respite from Neela, his outfit, too, did not. Except for a pair of sandals, Thaddeus was stark naked. But what did set him apart from most of the other hotel patrons, many of whom were, in fact, unclothed, was his exposed phallus. It was a good two feet long and as thick as a soda can. Justin's first reaction was to laugh, but Dr. Gillette, misinterpreting his laugh, assured him that it was fully functional.

"Oh, that I believe, Thaddeus," replied Justin. "I just can't wait to see the woman who that," he said, pointing down to the doctor's giant organ with his eyebrows, "will fit into."

"Don't you worry about a thing, dear boy," answered Thaddeus, with a devilish grin. Thaddeus finally seemed to notice Neela standing proudly next to his patient. The doctor's appreciation of Neela's transformation was noted not only in his eyes but also in his manhood. It now stood fully erect at what Justin guessed must have been two and a half feet.

"Thank you, Thaddeus," Neela said, with obvious delight.

"Don't mention it, dear. I must say they certainly did justice to your vision."

"And your outfit . . . ," she began to say.

Thaddeus cut her off. "I know, I know. Boooring. Well, what did you expect? Who has time?" He then apologized for keeping Neela's secret from Justin.

On their way up to the room, via a very slow-moving, old-fashioned elevator, Neela explained to Justin why she'd recently been so unavailable. "First of all," she explained, "I wanted to surprise you."

Justin blushed. "Well, consider it a success," he said, trying hard not to stare at every square inch of her.

In the space of two weeks Neela had had her hair, eye, and skin color changed and her pregrown wings, tail, and horns attached—the last part taking only two days to complete. The rest of the time was spent getting used to the new appendages and learning how to use them.

"I always wanted to go wild on Mardi Gras," she said, "but I didn't have the money until now. I've been dreaming about this costume since I was little. Most kids have some sort of crazy drawing they've held on to, hoping one day to strike it rich enough to bring it to fruition. . . . I guess I just got lucky."

"Yeah," laughed Justin. "You found me."

"Oh, stop being so vain," she teased. "Omad found you. I'm just reaping the benefits."

Justin chuckled nervously. *Is she flirting with me?*

"Ahh, yes," interrupted Thaddeus, stopping in front of a brass-rimmed door. "Here's my room. See you kids later."

Justin and Neela walked down to the hallway's end and arrived at a penthouse. Since the hotel was a nostalgic re-creation, the doors opened, and thus required Justin to put his palm on a pad located near the entryway. The reader checked his DNA and palm print, allowing him access. They both entered and were greeted with a beautiful master suite. There was, Justin could see, a single plantation bed in the center of the room. Two Louis XIV chairs were placed in front of the grand four-poster sleeper almost as if guarding it. The rest of the furniture was period, and the adjoining antechambers were just as exquisitely laid out. French doors led out onto a balcony that gave a fine view of the street and all the goings-on.

"Well, we've seen your room," said Neela, "now let's get out of here, because in case you haven't noticed, there's a party going on!"

Justin had to laugh. All he'd wanted to do was get into the room and out of the fracas, but now that he'd been entranced by the vixen currently occupying the body of Neela Harper, he nodded lamely. "Let me just get into my costume."

"Sure thing," she answered, hopping onto the bed and spreading her wings alluringly across the comforter.

Justin opened up his costume box. The outfit enclosed was a simple affair. Coarse tunic with sandals and a belt. Though the tunic went down to his knees, he decided to wear underwear. A decision made even easier after seeing in recent broadcasts where mediabots could go.

"Spartacus," he explained, shrugging.

"Ahh, the symbolic outfit," Neela said, nodding in support. "Nothing to be embarrassed about."

"Neela," he responded, "no outfit could possibly look good next to yours."

She laughed.

"Anyways," he continued, "Spartacus seemed like the perfect outfit. Had he remained a gladiator slave and mercenary performer for the Roman masses, he could've had all the riches and benefits that Roman society offered."

"But he chose to rebel against the Romans and fight," added Neela.

"Yes," said Justin, "he chose to fight."

"And die."

"Been there, done that," he joked. Then to reassure her, "Don't worry, Neela, it's just a symbol."

She frowned. "You ready or what?"

"No," he answered, "but that doesn't matter. I'm not sure I'll ever be ready for what's waiting for me out there."

Their hotel was located between Decatur and Chartres streets, so they opted to head up Canal to Chartres. Once there they saw wrought-iron balconies filled with party revelers tossing jewels down to the partygoers below, as well as up to those floating above. The rain of trinkets, jewels, and knickknacks acted as a graceful frame of color to the spires of the St. Louis Cathedral, located farther down the avenue in the heart of the French Quarter.

Justin chose to ignore the finger-pointing of those who recognized him, and he grudgingly gave autographs to those who requested it. Neela got a pass, as everyone apparently assumed the vivacious creature next to the Unincorporated Man was most likely his well-transbodied bimbo of the hour. When she suggested he buy a mask, he refused. Night had fallen, so the street was dim enough, and everyone was drunk enough, that the "fame" harassment was at a minimum. Plus, he had a few securibot floaters trailing him for good measure should any revelers get out of hand.

As they inched their way down the sidewalk through the garrulous crowd, they heard the cacophonous sounds of a parade heading toward them. They decided to stop for a minute and take in the moving pageant. At first a man on a horse rode by. He was, explained Neela, the captain or krewe leader of the Orpheus Club. Next came the officers and the queen, soon followed by maids and dukes. They were followed by an enormous float. Its theme was a historical event and, in this case, "three centuries of progress."

Justin was able to make out an oversized replication of an early nanobot that was quickly followed by one of the first transorbital pods. The t.o.p. kept shooting out of one orport tube representing Hong Kong, into another orport tube representing New York. That float was followed by another representing the terraforming of Mars, which was followed by another representing the newly begun terraformation of Venus.

Drifting purposely all around these larger floats were smaller ones representing the colonization of the asteroid belt as well as that of the lower-orbit colonies. Following the "show" floats were three smaller ones hovering at various heights. These smaller transports carried the costumed Orpheus Club members, who were kept busy throwing shiny trinkets into the open arms of the revelers.

One of the necklaces landed on Justin's outstretched arms. When he looked at it closely, he realized it was a string of diamonds made of at least forty genuine three-carat stones. He began to laugh, slowly at first, and then in fits. The sky was raining diamonds, his date was an auburn-skinned, leather-clad vision in wings, and here he was alive and well to experience it all.

Neela grabbed him by the arm and they began, again, to make their way down the street. At the corner of St. Louis and Chartres they passed the Napoleon House, on top of which was an octagonal cupola rumored to have been built as a lookout to sight Napoleon's ship on the river. Legend had it that Napoleon intended to land in Louisiana and stay in the house they currently found themselves in front of. Unfortunately, he never made it, having perished before reaching the city. As in Justin's day the house had been converted into an old drinking haunt. On this night they could both see from the curbside that the place was crammed wall-to-wall with people, and even, in one part of the room, they were crammed in ceiling-to-ceiling. They moved farther down the road, alternately pulling one another through the tightly packed swaying mass of humans and transbods. They passed Toulouse Street and were close to Jackson Square across from the St. Louis Cathedral. Chartres, like the other streets of the French Quarter, seemed to act as a small tributary of a great orgiastic river pouring forth into Jackson Square, where larger shows were taking place.

Justin realized he was no longer moving of his own volition, and was, in fact, being pushed along by the swell of partiers behind him. He could barely see Neela's hand, which he was holding, though he could still feel the tight grip of her long nails. The smell of sweat and alcohol was everywhere.

He felt a sharp yank to the left. Then another. In a flash he found himself standing in a small alley. While it, too, was crowded, it was not nearly as full as the torrent of partiers they'd just left behind.

Justin leaned up against the dank stone wall, catching his breath and massaging the shoulder Neela had practically yanked out of its socket. "You nearly pulled my . . ." He stopped talking when he realized how close Neela was to his face. So close he could feel the soft rush of air emanating from her nostrils.

His skin bristled and his heart began to pound.

Neela could feel his breath on her neck. She lingered for a moment, allowing the tension to build between them.

"Neela . . . I . . ."

She silenced him with the tip of her index finger lightly touching his lips.

Justin put his hands on her waist and slowly pulled her in—giving her a chance to change her mind—he didn't know, didn't care. He matched her stare with his. Though her eyes were black as night, they hid nothing. With one hand Justin slowly brushed aside a wisp of Neela's long, dark hair that had fallen over her cheekbone. With the other he gently framed her face, then gingerly brought his mouth to hers.

The kiss was slow and deep.

Neela leaped up onto him and locked her long leather boots around his waist. He then carried her the few steps across the cobblestone alleyway until her back was pushed against a wall. Neela felt the cool stones against her shoulder blades and wings. A tiny, dimly lit balcony was above them and a small wooden door was to their left. If there was anybody above they didn't notice, and should anyone exit the door, they wouldn't have cared. Neela shrouded her wings around Justin's body as he quickly rid them both of their undergarments.

Neela was now no longer Neela Harper in the body of an animal being, she *was* that animal being. She swayed her wings to Justin's rhythm as her tail moved about frantically, snapping violently to every climax she felt.

She kissed him fiercely, cupping his face in her hands.

Their breathing was out of sync as they each seemed to gasp in sporadic bursts. She was lost in his motion; she felt nothing and everything as her body began its steady and quick ascent. As soon as she sensed that he was about to release, she allowed herself to experience her purest vulnerability, and that was all she needed. As Neela heard her lover climax, an explosion of sensation washed over her in multiple waves of dissipating energy, each one draining her until she collapsed onto Justin's powerful shoulders.

He gently lowered her to the ground as she leaned on him for support. She covered his half-naked body in the folds of her great crimson wings and drew him close in embrace.

He pulled back slowly and softly kissed her lips.

She smiled at him and gently caressed his cheek.

"I guess this means I'm fired," she said, still catching her breath.

Justin laughed. "Lord, I hope so."

"You OK?" she asked, still seeing, even in the dim light, the flushness of his face.

"Yeah, just a little drained . . . nothing a little walking won't rectify."

"Sounds like a lovely idea."

They gathered their garments, dressed quickly, and emerged hand in hand from the alley, where they were quickly swallowed up by the boisterous crowd streaming into Jackson Square.

After a few more hours of soaking up the night they made their way back to the Hotel Rex, knowing Omad would be waiting for them. They did their best to tidy up, and then, as one, entered the lobby, oblivious to their friend who'd been sitting patiently on a chair next to one of the lobby's hexagonal pillars.

Omad was dressed in an old-fashioned, mismatched, three-piece business suit, and was wearing a pinstriped collarless shirt. Resting beside his knee was a large metallic briefcase with the letters IRS spelled out on both sides. He also had a holstered gun on his hip, and wrapped around his head was a black sash with the eyeholes cut out. He stood up as Justin and Neela approached.

"Let me guess," Justin said. "Tax man?"

"Let *me* guess," Omad retorted. "Satiated lovers?"

Neither Justin nor Neela answered, remaining stone-faced.

Omad didn't give them time for a denial. "About time. All I can say is, thank Damsah for Mardi Gras."

"Hey!" Neela protested, attempting to change the subject. "You didn't say anything about my transbod!"

"Neela," he answered with an appreciative wink, "if I were to say what I'd like to say, the man currently attached to your hip would probably wallop me."

By Neela's satisfied look, Omad knew he'd said it all.

Justin interjected, "So, was I right?"

"About what?" asked Omad.

"About you being a tax man."

"Oh, yeah," Omad replied, getting back on track, "you got it on the first try, but I was hoping you'd be more frightened."

"OK, Omad," Justin replied, taking the bait, "why did you think that getup would scare me?"

Omad answered with the earnestness of the devout: "For us it's just stories, but you were actually . . ." He struggled to get the next word out as a look of disgust filled his face, "taxed." Omad saw that Justin still wasn't getting it. "Tax men actually came after you."

"It really wasn't as bad as all that."

"You mean to tell me," challenged Omad, "that faceless, nameless government types were not always after you, trying to take away your own hard-earned money and property—while threatening you with prison if you didn't cough up enough credits?"

"It was 'dollars,' " corrected Justin, "and they did." He thought about it briefly. "You know, Omad, it really *was* like that." Now it was his turn to grimace. "Good costume."

He remembered his first audit. He'd been raked across the coals by some low-level bureaucrat trying to curry favor with a superior.

"In fact," added Justin, recalling the torturous months of work the little prick's stunt had cost, "it's a damned good costume."

Omad beamed. "By the way, I brought that little thing you asked for." He began to open his IRS bag.

"What thing?" asked Neela.

Justin stopped Omad by gingerly putting his hand on the briefcase. "Why don't you give it to me upstairs?"

The ride up the ancient lift was filled with an uncomfortable silence. When they finally got to the suite, Neela was dying with impatience.

"So, what is it?"

"Neela," answered Justin, "it's really no big deal. You're making mountains out of nano."

Omad made himself busy checking the place out, moving from room to room as if he were a secret agent checking for surreptitious devices. He went onto the balcony and returned a moment later.

"Omad," said Justin, "thanks for being so cool with me and Neela and all. I was expecting horror and culture police."

"Oh, don't get me wrong," he answered, looking for all the world like an angry parent. "I think you two are nuts. And if it wasn't Mardi Gras you couldn't get away with it. Still, fuck it. You two are perfect for each other. I don't think it will end well, but enjoy it while you can.

"Oh, by the way," he continued, "did you know that there's a huge crowd gathering outside your window?"

Justin's face lit up. "Oh, yeah. It must be time."

"For what?" asked Neela, starting to feel a bit apprehensive as she, too, noticed the swelling crowd beneath their balcony.

Justin smiled mischievously. "I arranged a little press conference." Before Neela could say another word he looked over at Omad. "You got it?"

"Yeah," Omad groused, still staring out the window, "I got it." He walked from the balcony entrance back to the edge of the bed where he'd put his briefcase, gently snapped open the clasps, and removed a pair of large silver shackles.

"I hope they're to your liking," he said, holding up the manacles, one cuff in each hand.

The cuffs had three very large links with one letter, viewable from multiple angles, etched onto each one. The letters were G, C, and I. As Omad held them up, Justin walked over to where he was standing and put his hands through the wide holes of the metallic bracelets. He felt their weight and texture; even rattled them a bit.

"They'll do what they're supposed to do?" he asked.

Omad nodded. "Tested the prototype myself. Worked like a charm."

Justin shook the links one more time for good measure. "Then they're perfect," he said, smiling brightly.

"Uh, Justin," asked Neela, "what do you think you're doing?"

He gazed at her with a fiery determination.

"Declaring independence." And with that he went to the French doors leading to the wraparound balcony and stepped outside.

Neela could hear the crowd's roar as her new lover walked onto the balcony. A sense of foreboding welled up inside her, but it was too late to stop the course of events.

Sean Doogle waited patiently below Justin Cord's balcony. He was joined there by a few thousand revelers, a horde of mediabots, and a cavalcade of reporters. Unlike everyone else in the crowd, Sean sensed that history was about to be made, and in the deepest recesses of his being that he was destined to play a part. The "one free man," as he now referred to Justin almost exclusively, had called an impromptu press conference. Something must be up. The lucky men, Sean had decided, got caught up in history in the making; the great men exploited that history to achieve their ends. There was no question in Sean's mind what type of man he was. And so he waited.

Justin approached the edge of the balcony, arms lowered to shield from view his new wrist accessory. The mediabots, like the crowd, were kept a safe distance away by the hotel's well-enforced protection fields. But New Orleans was a small, tightly packed town made doubly so by the current holiday; Canal Street was a broad boulevard and the distance that would normally be accorded a hotel of the Rex's stature was cut to a third.

The crowd quieted to a murmur. No small feat, considering the amount of drugs and alcohol coursing through the veins of many in attendance.

When Justin felt he had the maximum amount of attention he could hope for, he raised, in one quick motion, his shackled wrists high above his head. By the time he'd completed the move the entire plaza had come to a standstill and was now filled with a deathly silence. As he held his hands up, he made sure to move his body in a 180-degree arc. He was only going to do this once, so he wanted to be sure that all could see the letters carved into each of the shackle's links.

From the moment Justin raised his hands, baring for all the "GCI" shackles, a flood of self-adulation swept over Sean Doogle—he'd guessed correctly. The co-conspirators he'd planted strategically in the crowd looked to him now, waiting intently for his signal. But Sean, aware that history was recording this moment, knew the timing would have to be perfect. *Not yet . . . not yet,* he kept repeating. Sean pointedly refused to look into his beseechers' eyes. They'd just have to wait. They'd get his signal when he was ready to give it.

Now, Justin said to himself. The links, which lay flaccid, forming a U shape above his head, were now pulled tight, forming a straight line from end to end. Justin strained his expression. He pulled again, but harder. Each time he'd let the links go flaccid, and then attack, pulling at them even harder—at least in appearance—with each tug. Finally, he gave a muscle-rippling convulsion as the links, and along with them the G, the C, and the I, shattered above his head, raining into the crowd as metal shards, thus becoming the ultimate throws in the history of Mardi Gras.

Sean Doogle was enraptured. All of his rage and anger was transformed instantly into a kind of peace. He knew what he had to do. That it would involve risk and pain and death—to others, and possibly to him—meant nothing at all. His path was clear. He had never been so happy in his life, nor felt so dangerous. He gave the signal his cohorts had so desperately been waiting for. As one they began to shout, "One free man! One free man! One free man!"

Like a brush fire purposely set on a hot, windy day, the drunken, boisterous crowd was soon caught up in shouting the mantra of the planted inciters. And, much to Sean's pleasure and well-laid plans, that mantra was now being recorded and transmitted systemwide. His vision of Justin as the poster boy of his revolution had come to fruition. The "one free man!" mantra was now a cancerous seed planted amid the billions of "lost" souls watching from their holodisplays and DijAssists. And in doing so, they were fulfilling its planters' expressed desire—to kill its plodding and tyrannical host, the incorporation movement.

Hektor turned off the holodisplay and methodically stubbed out his cigar, watching as the last wisps of smoke made their slow and steady ascent into oblivion. A slow, simmering torrent of anger pushed its way through every capillary of his body, until at last the rage consumed him. If Cord wanted to break the chains of the system that had rescued him (and all humanity, for that matter!), then so be it. If it was shattered chains he wanted, it was shattered chains he'd get. And society, so enamored of Justin's vision of the past, needed a visceral example of what that past was really like. They would have to be reminded of the terrorism, anarchy, and fear that had once been a daily part of Justin's world.

In the dark, quiet office that had become his home away from home and with the dull and constant sound of human traffic surrounding him, Hektor Sambianco pulled his DijAssist from his pocket and twirled it casually in his hand. Someone had to die. And, Hektor knew, it would be that one death that would unleash a madman capable of reminding the present world just how dangerous the past had once been.

"Iago."

"Yes, Hektor?"

"Prepare an untraceable interplanetary transmission for the head of security—Neptune GCI."

"Recording," answered iago.

"There will be an 'accident,' " said Hektor, without a trace of emotion.

"Name?"

"Elizabeth Reynolds."

This was it. Neela was finally getting her Moon vacation. Only instead of having it foisted on her for the price of silence, as had been Hektor Sambianco's wont, she was now heading up the silver highway of her own accord—with her own money. That she was doing it in secret with her lover made the trip even more exquisite.

In the beginning years of Justin's cryonic entombment the Moon had decreased in stature. The world was too busy imploding to look much beyond its own atmosphere. Plus, space exploration was a government-controlled monopoly run by soon-to-be bankrupt governments. So the Moon remained a floating rock, not much different from the one Neil Armstrong first set foot upon years ago. As humans went about rising from the rubble of the Grand Collapse the Moon remained virtually ignored, continuing its lonely elliptical vigil of its troubled blue cousin. With the eventual rise of the incorporation movement and a major influx of cash and entrepreneurship, a fledgling orbital industry emerged. The Moon became a way station for scientists and industrialists, eventually succumbing to a huge land grab once the space-based industries took off. The ice and mineral compounds found in the Moon's recesses proved a fertile ground for the fledgling nanotechnology sector and its hordes of micro-sized assemblers and replicators. In no time at all great corridors spanning thousands of miles were dug deep into the orbiting boulder's thick underbelly. "Inner" cities emerged to house the families of those who chose to make the Moon their home. On the surface large buildings massed in craters and were covered over by thin yet powerful protective membranes.

But it was only when the asteroid belt became economically viable—some one hundred years after the Grand Collapse—that the Moon finally took off. It went from being a sometime destination to an oft-used port. In fact, it was the preferred port of call for the growing population of the asteroid belt that over the course of those hundred years had weaned itself almost entirely from the Earth's gravitational pull. The Moon's ⅙th-gravity environment was a far better "neutral" ground to meet on for those wishing to do business with their Terran cousins. In the span of a decade, conference centers, luxury hotels, restaurants, and entertainment complexes devoured the space once occupied by the industrial giants.

For the industrialists it was a win-win situation. They sold at a profit and moved out into deeper space, taking over the moons of the Earth's sister planets.

By the time Justin was taking his first "second" breaths, the Moon had been transformed into a veritable floating Las Vegas, happily swallowing the percentages of all those who'd ever dreamed of taking a vacation in orbit. If Mardi Gras started in New Orleans, it ended, for those who could afford it, in the Moon's luxurious environs. And it was into this mecca of debauchery and merchandising that the winged Neela and her famous lover made their separate ways.

At a considerable sum Justin rented a private crater away from prying eyes and under an assumed name. Neela arrived surreptitiously a few hours later. What then followed was a blessed week of cavorting, eating like royalty, relishing each other's company, and making love any chance they could get. And while their separate worlds seemed to finally be coming together, the one they'd only recently left behind was now almost imperceptibly beginning to come apart.

Sean Doogle had spent the week sitting joyfully in front of his holodisplay re-watching his famous evening's events. He couldn't get enough of it. During the days he'd begrudgingly spent time fulfilling his requisite duties: coordinating future rallies, signing documents—autographs, even! And, of course, receiving overdue accolades. But each and every night he'd sneak back into his hotel room and watch a vidacord of the rally—over and over again. The slow and steady buildup, the tension as Justin Cord faced the crowd, the moment of climax as Cord snapped his chains and rained the metallic shards down on the assembled masses, and then . . . then, the magic moment. When he, Sean Doogle, began his chant. How the crowd had joined in, swayed back and forth even. It was mesmerizing. Sean had pretty much wallpapered his entire small hotel room with hard-copy versions of narticles from that night's event—*his* event. Sean's "one free man" message had gotten out to billions. Billions! It was one of the few times in his life when he felt that he was truly worthy of what he'd accomplished.

His self-approbation was momentarily interrupted by a call from his avatar. It almost never called him, which gave him a start, because it had been programmed to alert him if it heard any news about Elizabeth. He'd always held out hope that one of those alerts would be news of his beloved's return. In a way, it was.

It had been a freak accident, the *Neptune News* had reported, concerning the connecting of a GCI power supply to an atmospheric converter on one of Saturn's outer moons. Somehow the fully charged storage gel released its energy all at once. GCI's spokesperson spoke of Elizabeth's death as not only permanent but also a tragic *economic* loss.

Sean's world crashed. He couldn't remember anything. It was as if his whole psyche shattered and only little bits and pieces of who he used to be returned to the surface. He sat staring blankly at the holodisplay for hours, refusing to answer the door, refusing any and all attempts by his unruly followers to contact him. Finally, in the slow and particular manner of a parasitoid wasp emerging from the destroyed innards of its insect host, Sean slipped away from his shell. He stood up and stared blankly out the window—resolved.

They had destroyed his world—now he'd destroy theirs.

It was instinct that saved Justin's life on the second assassination attempt. He and Neela had decided beforehand to take separate flights out of the Moon to avoid any unnecessary publicity. For those who asked, Neela was on the Moon under the pretext of needing to be near her patient during his first-ever Mardi Gras. An arranged "professional" consultation meeting at the orport allowed them to say their good-byes. Then, in the ⅙th gravity of their surroundings, they gently floated off to their respective docking ports. Neela watched for a moment as Justin descended to his private t.o.p. just a few platforms below hers, and then she made her way to her gate. Justin, upon landing at his platform, was funneled down a long open-air walkway to his private t.o.p.'s departure gate. He noticed that his terminal had a permiawall in front of it adorned with a velvet rope and an impenetrable door motif. There was also a human uniformed member of hotel security whose sole job was to make sure only the proper people were let into the first-class waiting chamber. The guard saw Justin, pushed a button on her pad, and waved him toward the permiawall. Justin, who still hadn't gotten used to walking into walls, held out his arm from force of habit—a sort of testing of the waters. He half expected to have his arm come crashing back, but it never did. Still, it was that little habit that ended up saving his life. The moment he put his hand through the permiawall his arm dissolved, sending hot jets of pain instantly through his entire body and bubbles of warm red liquid in all shapes and sizes floating off into the thin air. Instinctively, Justin leaped away from the permiawall, screaming in agony.

Were it not for the security monitors, the exact sequence of events would have been harder to figure out. The guard had immediately pulled a small and very standard hand weapon from her jacket and had pointed it at Justin. She didn't have a chance to fire because of the attack from above by an enraged, winged demoness. Neela, hearing the commotion and fearing the worst, dove from her platform and, using her wings and weight, had turned what would have been a leisurely descent into the shrieking plunge of a falcon snaring a hare on the run. With one hand she ripped at the shocked assassin's throat and with the other clawed at her eyes. Somehow the killer managed to shove Neela with enough force to send her flying in the direction of Justin, who was now lying on the floor in agony between the two of them. Only Neela's expert use of her wings as a brake saved her from falling off the platform. The assassin got to one wobbly knee and aimed her weapon. Justin, seeing her momentarily distracted, managed to kick her sharply on the shin. It was enough to throw the killer off and send her shot wide. The effort to regain her balance was all the time Neela needed to launch herself at the assassin, who was flung backward into the rigged permiawall. The scream that echoed through the spaceport was cut off by the evisceration of the assassin's vocal cords along with the rest of her body.

When he recovered later, Justin remembered none of this, having lost far too much blood to stay conscious. The last image on the playback would be forever seared in his mind—Neela cradling him in her arms and wings like a tableau from some level of hell—strangely tender to look at, but terrifying as well.

Sean Doogle has disappeared. His last confirmed location was in New Orleans for the Mardi Gras celebration. Though he owns a substantial majority of himself, his parents, as the largest minority shareholders, asked for an asset location search in the hopes of finding their son. So far the effort has proved fruitless amid speculation Mr. Doogle may have removed his locator chip.

—*INTERSYSTEMNEWS* BROADCAST

Rumor has it that Justin Cord has been the target of another assassination attempt. Given Mardi Gras celebrations, hard news is hard to come by, but Justin was apparently rushed to the medical facilities on the Moon. We will keep you informed as we are informed. Remember, don't drink and fly manually, you owe it to yourself and your shareholders.

—*INTERSYSTEMNEWS* BROADCAST

Justin was recuperating quite well after the horrific events of the past few days, and had even had his arm regrown at almost the same time Neela was having her costume degrown. Perhaps the greatest effect of the assassination attempt had been on Neela and Justin's fledgling relationship. Neela had only meant to sleep with Justin during Mardi Gras. She'd rationalized that it would actually make perfect sense to scratch that itch for the both of them, and then be done with the urge once and for all. And when everyone found out, at least the haze of Mardi Gras might soften the blow for the both of them—even more so when people realized it had only been a onetime Mardi Gras fling. That is, until the moment she almost lost him. The thought of his not being present in her world, of his not being with her at all times, was more frightening than anything she'd ever experienced in her short life.

Nothing mattered now but him. She was with Justin, and they both knew that they'd continue to see each other long after the week of Mardi Gras had ended. They discussed it in detail, and agreed to be discreet, but also both agreed that at some point the system would have to accept Justin and Neela as a couple.

Justin found himself sitting in the kitchen of the McKenzies, reading his morning paper when the now very much human Neela entered wearing only a bathrobe and a smile. He'd forgotten how energizing smiles could be until he started seeing them on Neela. It wasn't so much that hers was better or worse than anyone else's. And like his first wife once had, Neela was smiling *because* of him, and that made all the difference in the worlds. The walls he'd so carefully built were finally coming down, and that, too, he'd decided, was good.

The tender moment was broken when Omad and an unfamiliar woman entered and sat down. Neela, who was still leaning against the kitchen door frame, gave Omad an exasperated yet forgiving look. Omad, she realized, would forever be Omad. She took her place near but not next to Justin at the large kitchen table after pouring herself a cup of coffee. Mosh came in next with Eleanor. From the happy yet exhausted look on their faces one would have been hard-pressed to believe the still frisky couple had been married for nearly four decades. They were followed soon after by Dr. Gillette sans his enormous phallus, at least if the bathrobe was any indication. Thaddeus had spent all of Mardi Gras at an orgy, and only in the great festival's waning hours had he been made aware of what had happened to his most famous client. A few days in the hospital was enough for the doctor to realize what had transpired between his protégé and patient. He was smart enough to realize that if he tried to change their minds he'd probably be looking for a new job. His only hope now was to ameliorate what he thought of as "the damage" by working at it from the inside.

Omad chose that moment to introduce his date. "Hey, everyone this is . . . er . . ." He looked toward the woman who he'd just spent the night with for help.

"Agnes," she answered. She had, noticed Justin, the all too familiar look of a groupie too shy to say a word yet clearly awed by the celebrity. "I mean," she managed to stutter, "when I met Omad I had no idea he was *that* Omad. . . . I mean, he told me that he was, but you know how many Omads there are out there during Mardi Gras?"

"Indeed," answered Mosh. "I still can't believe he licensed his face."

Neela snickered. "I can."

"Hey," Omad answered, "it was only for a week, and a guy's gotta make a living." Justin turned toward Agnes. "Please . . . continue."

Agnes shrugged. "Still, he seemed like a nice guy, and it *was* the last night of Mardi Gras, so I figured, why not? And now, Damsah's ghost, you're all here. It's like in one of those super vids off the Neuro. I mean, I'm only a penny and live in a dump, but you," she said, looking directly at Mosh and Eleanor, "you actually live in a single room." She proceeded to take in the surroundings again as if still not believing her good fortune.

"I'm sure you have a lovely home as well, Agnes," said Justin, supportively.

"Nothing much, really, just a five-bedroom Victorian on a quarter acre of land."

"Nothing much?" asked Justin, perplexed. "Trust me, Agnes, that would be 'much' in my day and age!"

"Dude," said Omad, first looking apologetically over to Agnes, "it's fixed."

Everyone else remained silent—almost as if Omad had uttered a dirty word. Justin looked at Neela. She looked at Dr. Gillette, who just looked back at her. She thought about it for a moment and shrugged. "OK, Justin, you know about the luxury t.o.p.s, and you know about the special features of your apartment in New York."

Justin nodded. "Yeah, they can form shapes and textures as desired. Pretty neat."

"Very neat and *very* expensive," continued Neela. "The materials are easy, but the nanos that run the transformation have to be constantly updated and checked. The amount of human labor involved is large for reasons that I don't really understand. But the social effect is that only the richest can afford to actually live in fluid dwellings. That's when there came a split between houses that were fixed, partially fixed, partially fluid, and fluid."

"And on my salary," continued Agnes, "fixed it is."

Everyone nodded his or her head.

"If you don't mind my being so bold, Agnes," said Justin, "I'm quite curious as to where the rest of your salary goes."

"Oh, not at all!" she gushed. "Well," she said, picking at small croissant, "a lot goes into travel and entertainment. Then there are my investment portfolios. I really can't afford to buy into anyone really profitable, but I might get lucky and hit a shooting star . . . like Omad."

Omad smiled. "Actually, Neela's a much bigger shooting star than anyone in the world right now."

Dr. Gillette saw the look of confusion on Justin's face and came to his rescue.

"The poor cannot afford to invest in the profitable," he answered as if Agnes was not in the room, "or even the potentially profitable. If they could then they wouldn't be poor. What they *can* do is invest in each other. A few shares of a poor, struggling nobody cost nothing. The theory is, if you invest in enough of them somebody will make it big and you'll become rich. For reasons, Justin, that you would understand and most of this era would not, these types of people are called 'penny stocks.' And those few 'pennies' who do, in fact, rise dramatically in value are called 'shooting stars.' Mostly because the reason they became valuable had nothing to do with inbred talent . . . present company excluded, of course. For instance, they were the sole witness of an extraordinary event, or married somebody with greater wealth than theirs. For the most part, shooting stars go down in value and disappear back into the pennies almost as fast as they rose, and hence the name."

"So you're telling me," said Justin, now looking toward Agnes, "that investing in someone like you, a penny, would be like gambling?"

"Oh, more than that, Justin," answered Agnes. "The penny stocks are a way for everyone to participate in society. When you gamble you get nothing, but when you invest you at least take stock in someone else.

"But, to be perfectly honest," she continued, as if resigned to her station, "I wouldn't be a good bet."

A little while later Justin found himself reading alone in Mosh's well-stocked library. He put down his book, *The Rise and Fall of the American Republic,* and called up his avatar.

"Yes, Justin."

"I was thinking about doing something nice for Agnes."

"Forgive what must be my limited understanding of human interaction. Did you form a closer relationship with Ms. Goldstein than I observed?"

"No," answered Justin, "I did not."

"Then why do you wish to do something nice for her?"

"Because," answered Justin, remembering all the people who'd underestimated him, "I think she *is* a good bet."

"Thank you, sir," answered sebastian, "now I understand. What did you have in mind?"

Justin narrowed his eyes in contemplation. "How much stock does she have in herself?"

"In order to find that information out you would need to own at least one share of Miss Goldstein. You have given me and your brokers explicit instructions not to buy a single share of a single person."

Justin gave it some thought. He was adverse to the prospect of owning a share of anyone because it smacked of slavery, but in this case, he was willing to forgo his dictate—if only temporarily. "Sebastian, is there any requirement as to how long I must own that share?"

"None."

"Could you please have one of my front operations buy one share of Agnes and get the information, and then sell it?"

"Might I suggest, sir, that you purchase one hundred shares, or at the least ten."

"Why?"

"Purchasing and selling just one might cause some automatic programs to flag the sale and investigate, for investment or media purposes. However, the buying and selling of a hundred-share lot would not be seen as unusual. Certainly not in the penny stocks."

"Do it." After a few minutes Justin had the information he wanted. He was assured by sebastian that Agnes's stock had then been resold.

"She is indeed a true 'penny,' Justin," said sebastian, "owning just 25 percent of herself. She has spent most of her stock on education, but specialized in a type of fashion that became, for lack of a better word, 'unfashionable.' Barring a change in her chosen field, her expertise will, in all likelihood, not be needed. She will have to retrain, and will therefore remain a penny stock for decades, if not centuries."

Justin's head tilted slightly. "How long will it be before she can make majority?"

"Statistically averaging based on her age, income, spending bracket, and expenses, and if she continues her frugal ways . . . one hundred and seven years."

"How much would it cost me to buy a majority of her stock?"

"You will need to buy 26 percent of her to do that. Given her current portfolio, and taking into account what such a large order would do if purchased at once . . ."

"Factor in a series of purchases over a year's time."

The answer was instantaneous. "Fifteen thousand GCI credits. Or roughly thirty-seven thousand of your U.S. dollars."

Justin was thunderstruck. A fluid room, he was informed, would cost millions, but a person's life and freedom cost less than 5 percent of that. And Agnes was just one of billions whose "worth," at least on paper, was almost worthless.

Two days after meeting the most famous man in the universe—a fact her friends still refused to believe—Agnes Goldstein returned to her house. *It ain't much to look at,* she sighed, *but it's home.* She noticed a small white envelope protruding from her door.

An envelope was strange enough; she'd read about them as a means of paper delivery but had never actually touched one. The fact that someone had gone to the trouble to place it in her door was even stranger. She wasn't sure how to open it, so she tore the end off, trying hard not to destroy the piece of paper inside.

It read:

Agnes,

I wanted to thank you for helping me understand a little more of this often strange and baffling world I've somehow managed to find myself in. If it's all right with you, I'd like to show my appreciation by giving you a gift. . . .

Agnes's heart began to pound.

*. . . Over the course of the next year you will be given an additional 20 percent share of your own personal stock. This will bring your self-ownership up to 45 percent. **It is imperative that you do not tell anyone about this gift,** as it will transform you into a shooting star and the stock purchases will not work.*

Once you're at 45 percent your prospects will be bright indeed. If I may be so bold as to suggest you either work hard for another ten years and achieve majority, or you invest the stock in an education that will give you the standard of living you clearly desire. (Call me crazy, but I still love a Victorian—fixed or not!) Whatever you choose, I hope you make the most of this second chance. I myself have recently been given one and know how wonderful they can be. If you feel this gift to be inappropriate or undesirable, then do nothing. However, if my gift meets with your approval, all you have to do is have your avatar call mine.

Sincerely,

Though the letter was unsigned the sender was obvious. She sat down on her front porch and took a deep breath, holding back her tears. She was being thrown a lifeline by a man from another century—and all because she'd been in the right place at the right time. Then she laughed. She'd never once had any real luck, and now she'd just landed the biggest shooting star of her life.

That night Agnes couldn't sleep, unable to believe her good fortune. Believing, in fact, that perhaps the whole thing had been some cruel hoax being played out by one of the many gotcha shows currently popular on the Neuro. She worked herself into a frenzy, castigating herself for being so gullible, then alternately pinching herself for what she felt in her gut must be real. *I did meet him . . . it was real . . .* , she told herself over and over again.

When the next day arrived Agnes Goldstein was told by helena that 2 percent of Agnes's stock had been added to her portfolio. She reread the letter over and over as tears of happiness filled her eyes. She would make the most of this, somehow.

The 5 Percent Solution

Every generation seems to have their unifying "where were you when?" moment. For some it's a positive, as was the world's first look at a man walking on the Moon in the twentieth century. For others it's a negative, as was the destruction of the World Trade Center in New York City on September 11, 2001. For the post–GC millennium it was the first landing on the asteroid belt, and now, for us the pendulum has sadly swung the other way. Everyone will remember the moment. Everyone will know exactly where they were when the unspeakable happened.

—MICHAEL VERITAS, "WHERE WERE YOU?"
THE TERRAN DAILY NEWS

It was only afterward that we went and looked up all his writings. All during Mardi Gras that bastard was telling us exactly what he was planning to do. But who takes the rantings of a madman seriously? Especially during Mardi Gras!

—FROM AN ON-THE-STREET INTERVIEW WITH DETECTIVE LOGAN
OF THE BOSTON, MASSACHUSETTS, POLICE DEPARTMENT

SYSTEM PRESIDENT MILDRED TURNER MURDERED!
ATTEMPT MADE ON THE LIFE OF THE GCI CHAIRMAN!
LIBERTY PARTY HEAD, SEAN DOOGLE:
"YOU TRIED TO KILL THE ONE FREE MAN."

—HEADLINES ONE HOUR AFTER THE EVENTS

In an unexpected turn of events, the Fifth Appellate Court ruled in favor of the plaintiffs in the case of the shareholders of *Mildred Turner versus Sean Doogle Incorporated*. Sean Doogle has been stripped of all but 25 percent of his portfolio, and that remaining 25 percent is in a trust to be run by his parents until Mr. Doogle's legal status is finalized. The only reason the plaintiffs won the case was because Sean Doogle sent the court ironclad proof of his culpability in the crime. Without that proof no court would have taken so drastic an action against a man not present to defend himself.

—*Neuro Court News*

Neela perused the last line of another narticle she'd been reading. She wasn't even sure why she bothered. They all pretty much ended the same way: *One free man, one free man, one free man.* She put down the paper and looked across the kitchen table in the New York apartment she now considered hers as much as his.

"One free man, my ass," Neela groused. "If they could only see the way you've been forced to live, holed up like some kind of animal, unable to leave your apartment."

Justin sighed. "Yeah, it's what they were shouting in New Orleans the night I broke my chains. Do you think my little stunt on the balcony had anything to do with this?"

"*No!*" Neela shouted, and then lowered her voice. "No, I don't believe that, Justin. These are the actions of a lunatic. Your choice of Mardi Gras costume would not have made a difference. Besides, news reports showed some people were shouting that phrase before you appeared on the balcony."

Justin managed a tepid smile and took Neela's hands into his.

"You're probably right. But I keep asking myself the same question over and over again . . . do you think this would have happened if I hadn't woken up?"

She smiled and squeezed his hand.

"Stupid question. Sorry," was all he could think to say, and went back to staring into his cup of lukewarm coffee.

"Two more attacks this week!" Kirk tossed some info crystals onto the long table for effect. He waited for them to finish their slide before continuing to speak. "This is all Justin Cord's fault!" His voice boomed off the high ceiling of the GCI boardroom. And what would have been an invective meant for the ears of the board members only was now also being heard by a cadre of security personnel and securibots. These well-armed sentries had not only manned the perimeter of the boardroom, they had also manned its interior. And for the first time in living memory, which by most accounts was well over a century, the security was designed to protect people and not just information. The attempt on The Chairman's life had quickly seen to that.

"Of course it is," said Legal.

"Brilliant observation," spat Accounting. "Any other gems of wisdom for the board?"

"Fuck you, Accounting!" Kirk spat back, more pissed at himself for letting her get to him than with what she'd actually said. The fact that Accounting was willing to let her hostility show so openly said volumes about how the power on the GCI board had shifted. But Kirk had seen worse days in his long rise to the top. Not much worse, but worse. *She'll pay,* he thought.

Accounting remained unperturbed. "And you have a nice day, too."

"So," asked Publicity, "what do you propose we do about it?"

Advertising cleared his throat. "Why do anything? We already have enough egg on our face as it is. This whole fiasco is our fault; or at least that's what the public thinks. I say it's time to lay low and let someone else deal with it."

"Like who?" Kirk asked facetiously. "The government?"

The whole board laughed out loud at the ridiculous thought.

Kirk was pleased. *At least I got them to laugh. Now, down the garden path.*

"*We* have to do it," he intoned. "Even if it's not our fault, the public thinks it is. And that's all that matters."

He saw Publicity nodding his head, sporting a self-satisfied smile.

"Also," continued Kirk, "we're GCI. We've spent decades building the public's trust. It's how we got to be the most powerful organization in history. But if we run and hide, what will the public think then?" He paused for effect. "I'll tell you what they'll think. They'll think we've lost our edge. They'll think we've backed down . . . cowered in the face of a challenge. And how do you think that perception will play on our stock prices, currency rates, and personal value?" Kirk waited to let that last question sink in. "You know the drill, folks, because we're all the best at playing it. You smell blood, you attack. I can guarantee you that right now our closest competitors are meeting in their boardrooms figuring out a way to remove GCI from the top of the mountain. . . . I know that's what I'd be doing."

"So then back to my question." It was Publicity. "What do we do about it?"

Kirk looked at Legal. *It's now or never,* he thought. *Bold moves for bold players.* "We kill him."

There was no immediate outcry of protest. Nor was there an immediate show of support. Rather, the board seemed to be considering it. *Good, at least they're in neutral . . . neutral I can work with.* He saw Accounting squirm. *Spoke too soon, did we . . . bitch?*

"And what will killing him solve?" asked Accounting, almost as if on cue.

Kirk rose from his seat and put both of his fists on the table. "Justin Cord is an unincorporated man in an incorporated world. He has shown no desire to participate in our way of life, and as such will continue to be a rallying point for every terrorist crackpot out there. Doogle's just the tip of the iceberg, folks. We need to remove that threat now, and the only way we do that is to kill him. GCI will, of course, be 'shocked' at his death."

Kirk sat down in his chair, pleased. Not a single protest. If his motion carried he'd hold on to his position and, even better, rid Accounting of hers.

"May I speak to the board?" asked Hektor from his chair near the door. As a special adviser he was not allowed to speak without request or permission, but was accorded the honor of being in the room while the board met. This was correctly viewed by many in the press to be a stepping stone to the board of GCI itself. At times there could be as many as four special advisers to the board or, conversely, none. At this time Hektor was the sole adviser.

Kirk shifted uneasily at the challenge. "I move that the special adviser *not* be allowed to speak." Though he stared hard at his supposed allies, no one seconded his motion.

Accounting, seeing a break in the clouds, did not hesitate. "I move that Mr. Sambianco be allowed to speak."

"I second," said Legal. No one on the board was surprised. Accounting had formed a new alliance, and it was well known that Legal was no friend of Kirk Olmstead. What was surprising, especially to Kirk, was that the rest of the board voted for Accounting's motion.

"Motion carried," Kirk grudgingly agreed. "Mr. Sambianco, you have the floor."

I so owe that lady, Hektor thought, as he stood up to speak. "Ladies and gentlemen of the board, V.P. of Special Operations is correct in that Justin Cord and his pathological hatred of incorporation is the center of the crisis. But killing him would be the worst possible thing that you could do. Besides, Kirk," said Hektor, steely grin forming at the tips of his mouth, "you already tried that and failed."

Kirk's face turned red. "How dare you!"

Now it was Hektor's turn to toss his crystals on the table. "It's all there, Kirk. You're not the only one who's been keeping tabs on people."

No one dared reach for the crystals. The group preferred instead to wait for the gunfight to be over, the bodies to fall, and then hopefully side with the last man standing. "In fact," continued Hektor, ignoring Kirk's outburst, "I would recommend to the board that an extra protection unit be assigned to Mr. Cord. You see, it's a matter of sparks and kindling. No social system is perfect. It's just that ours has worked so well and for so long that we've forgotten that salient fact. If you look back at history you'll see that every system breeds resentment. Ours has just been very good at providing for everyone's needs and wants. Even better, it's succeeded in getting the troublemakers into positions of power and authority . . . present company included."

The board chuckled at his self-mockery.

"After all, it's very profitable to do that. But, let's face it, folks, it's been centuries since we've had any serious trouble, and in that time resentment has very quietly grown. But it's grown so slowly, and in such a small percentage of the population, that no one noticed. We've all been having a grand old time, haven't we? And guess what? It still wouldn't have been a problem without Justin Cord. We all would've gone about our business and watched our stock rise. You see, the discontented forgot that they were discontented. Which brings us to Sean Doogle. Sean Doogle not only has majority, but spoiled child that he is, he doesn't care that he does, and so launches his movement. And now our terrifying Mr. Doogle has a most effective weapon at his disposal—and that weapon is Cord. What does Doogle shout out on every broadcast? What do his followers say to each other? What message is left after each attack? 'One free man.' Don't kid yourselves, people, they're not talking about Justin. They're talking about themselves. They view themselves through Justin as unincorporated, and to them that means 'free.'"

"But that's crazy," said Advertising. "That sort of thinking will lead us right back to a Grand Collapse."

"That 'sort of thinking,' ladies and gentlemen of the board," said Hektor, "is Justin Cord's sort of thinking. He believes it so passionately and so completely that he's somehow managed to ignite that belief in Sean Doogle, and in turn this Doogle has ignited it in others."

"Mr. Sambianco," interjected Legal, "if you believe this, why not follow DepDir's suggestion of simply killing Mr. Cord and," she added, with the implicit desire to show she'd chosen sides, "doing a better job of it?"

The pin had dropped. Eyes shifted. Still, no one uttered a word.

"It would," continued Legal, "be like destroying a lighter after a child has lit an accidental fire. The fire will still burn, but without the lighter no more fires will get started."

"Exactly!" exclaimed Kirk.

"Not quite," answered Hektor, cutting off the DepDir. "It's been a long time since anyone has had to deal with an underground movement, but please trust me when I tell you, the last thing anyone wants is for Justin Cord to be killed. He'll become a martyr to the cause of unincorporation. To respond to Legal's analogy, Justin is not a lighter but a fully loaded flamethrower. If he's destroyed, like a flamethrower he'll cause far more damage than if left alone. In short, it is my humble opinion that he be isolated and, hopefully, as a result be made less volatile."

"So how do you 'humbly' propose," Kirk asked, "to make this supremely dangerous man *less* dangerous?"

Hektor smiled inwardly. *Gotcha.* "We have to make him incorporate."

"We tried that and failed," snapped Kirk.

"No, sir, *you* tried that and failed," he said, not bothering to mask his contempt. "Now we'll have to get some help from a different source to neutralize Justin Cord."

"How about his girlfriend?" suggested Legal. "She could be pressured; we do have majority control of her stock."

"Only as a last resort," answer Hektor. "No, I think we should turn to the one place no one turns to anymore." Hektor waited until they were all leaning forward in their seats.

"The government."

Kirk was about to lay into Hektor when the whole room noticed that the red light in the table's center had come on. Only one voice was heard, but everyone was instantly at attention.

"Mr. Sambianco, Mr. Olmstead, will you please come up to my office?" The voice cut out. But everyone understood the implications of The Chairman addressing Hektor first and, more specifically, not using Kirk Olmstead's given title. After the two men exited the room, Accounting called for a vote to be sent to The Chairman calling for Kirk Olmstead's removal from the board. It was seconded, passed, and sent to The Chairman before Hektor and Kirk cleared the new security procedures. They did not dare to suggest a replacement, but most of the board already had "buy" orders on whatever was left of Hektor Sambianco's stock.

The One Free Man has shown us the way. We are not free. The moment we are born we lose 25 percent of all that we will ever make. By the time most of us can make meaningful choices about the course of our lives we are lucky to have majority. Most of us don't even have that. By that time we are brainwashed by a lifetime of programming that we need to sell more of our invaluable freedom for training, education, advancement, and meaningless, superficial toys. We are told what jobs to work and where to live. We are encouraged to marry the persons most economically suited for us—and this is freedom? They say we are free to choose, but how many choices do we have left by the time the incorporated world is done with us? But the One Free Man does not submit, does not surrender. He is free! We, too, can be free! Follow the Liberty Party into Revolution. Follow the One Free Man!

—Illegal posting on the Neuro attributed to Sean Doogle

Hektor had been made the DepDir of Special Operations. There were many people who wanted to see him, but he had debts to pay. His first action was to visit the V.P. of Accounting . . . in *her* office. It was a sign of respect that put the powerful board member at ease and cost Hektor little. The other members of the board did not rate as highly, but one of them, Legal, was waiting for him on his return from Accounting's office. He didn't make the mistake of lording his power by making her wait. The fact that she was there was enough. He put his arm around her and escorted her into his new office.

"Congratulations, Hektor."

"Thank you, Janet, and have a seat. Make yourself at home. I imagine we'll be spending a lot of time together."

Janet decided to cut to the chase. "We have no standing to take Justin Cord to court."

"In that you're correct, my dear." He pulled a cigar from his drawer and placed it gingerly on his desk. "We don't, but the government does."

"The government," she repeated. "That's what you were beginning to say in the board meeting. But what gives them standing?"

"You're the head of Legal, you tell me." Hektor snipped his cigar, sat back in his big comfortable chair, and lit up.

Janet got up and paced, her brow furrowed in thought. This was her preferred way of thinking about a problem. She stopped. "I don't believe it. How could I have missed that?"

"Well," suggested Hektor, "sit down and tell me all about it."

Janet sat down across from Hektor. "The 5 percent. He even used a government court in the first trial, so the government could claim damages. Sweet Damsah, that's brilliant." Janet looked at Hektor, worried about her job.

As if reading her mind, Hektor said, "I don't want your job, Janet. I'm happy with the one I've got, thank you. You shouldn't worry about not thinking about it, either. It was just one of those things that's in plain sight but managed to elude everyone. Like looking for your DijAssist even though it is in your hand."

"But you saw it."

"Yeah, but my job depends on such things and, I might add, if I am going to keep it Justin needs to incorporate. That's where you come in."

Janet folded her arms. "What's the plan?"

"I've arranged a meeting with the attorney general of the federation. Day after tomorrow for the both of us in Geneva. Before that meeting we need a brief we can hand her concerning the government's standing vis-à-vis Mr. Cord. You will need all precedents, rulings, laws, and amendments in the brief. Be complete, but keep it simple; this is the government we're talking about. We will, of course, offer all the assistance the government will need."

"You want this kept secret, I take it."

"Hell, no, I already leaked the meeting time to the press. While we're meeting the attorney general, the contents of the brief will be leaked out. I just hope no-body in the government gets this idea on their own."

Janet's mouth twisted into a doubtful frown. "Why's it so important to let everyone know it's *our* idea? He either incorporates or he doesn't. Isn't that the end we wish to achieve?"

"Because," answered Hektor, blowing a smoke ring high into the air, "the for-mer occupant of this chair is correct. We *are* GCI, and the public has to know that we're doing something about the threat that Justin Cord poses to society. I'm also going to go on the Neuro and start to counter some of the Liberty Party pap that this Doogle maniac has been posting."

"You cleared this with The Chairman?"

"I'm sitting in this chair, aren't I? One more thing, Janet . . ."

"Yes?"

"We can get Justin through Neela."

"Care to be more specific?"

"Specifically, go after her family, friends, and job. In fact," he said, "from now on it's your job to make her feel the pressure. We'll dial it up as need be."

Janet knew better than to argue. "I have what I need to get started," she said, getting up to dismiss herself, "and thanks."

"For what?" asked Hektor.

"For believing in me. Your predecessor never did."

Hektor nodded in acknowledgment, quietly thinking, *And it cost him.*

An hour later Hektor's new secretary informed him that Kirk Olmstead was waiting outside the door. Hektor could have made him wait, but that seemed petty. He had the secretary send him right in. Kirk was a wreck. He'd clearly been following his portfolio.

"Let's get this over with, Sambianco."

Hektor didn't bother getting up. "We still need a corporate rep out in the Oort Cloud. You've been selected."

"That's not very original."

"Kirk, if it's a good idea, why let it go to waste? You'd make a fine rep, and the position is available. But if originality is of concern to you, I am having you shipped off immediately. When you leave this office two security guards will take you to the orport. Don't worry about your possessions. Whatever you wish will be shipped out to you at company expense." Hektor's lips drew back in a churlish grin.

Kirk smiled back. "Enjoying your revenge, Sambianco?"

"Kirk, this is not revenge. This is security. I thought about it, and if it would've been safer and better *for me* to have you around, you can bet I would have arranged for you to stay. I just think my job'll be more secure with you out on the edge of nowhere. So, please believe me, this is not about revenge. It's about Cord. The Unincorporated Man needs to be destroyed. You failed. I won't."

"Nothing I can do to change this?" asked Kirk, with as much dignity as he could muster.

Hektor's reply came in the form of another perfect O ring blown high into the air. The office door opened, revealing two burly guards. Kirk did an about-face and left without saying another word.

It took an hour for Kirk to transfer from the beanstalk to the GCI space station. Ten minutes later he was on a connecting flight to the Moon. And from lunar orbit he was able to find a ship heading out to the Oort Cloud. As he was getting into his small and depressingly utilitarian cabin his DijAssist chirped with an urgent message from GCI. Hope flared brightly in Kirk's heart that he might be reprieved in the same way Hektor had been. The message was short and to the point. It read:

> *I now personally possess 51 percent of your portfolio.*
> *Over half of all you labor for is mine.*
> *Remember that when the hours are long and lonely.*
> *Hektor Sambianco*
> *P.S. That's revenge.*

What sort of freedom does the Liberty Party offer? The last time Justin Cord's freedom and Sean Doogle's freedom existed in the world, the human race nearly died. Mr. Doogle wants to give you equality of outcome. The old world tried that, and we got the Grand Collapse. Our world has freedom *and* equality. The glorious equality of opportunity is what is offered. The Chairman started out in the penny stocks, but if you look at him now you see a man who has risen to the top of the system. I'm sorry that Mr. Doogle so hates our system that he will kill and destroy to end it, but our system works. His never did.
—"In Rebuttal," Hektor Sambianco, Deputy Director
of Special Operations, GCI

Justin still had the mediabots following him wherever he went, but the crowds had definitely thinned out. The questions had changed as well. Gone were the

"Who are you dating? Are you hetero, homo, or bi?" or "Where are you going to live permanently?" Now the questions were almost entirely of one theme. Over and over again Justin was assailed with "When will you incorporate?"

This perfect society's dark underbelly was beginning to manifest itself in many ways. When Justin found out about locator chips it only enforced his antipathy. He immediately began plans to produce a cheap product that would muffle the signal—an electronic version of wrapping a wet towel around a head. He would've begun building immediately except for the fact that all his friends were united in how bad an idea it seemed to be. Even so, he released the plans on the Neuro with sebastian's help, and illegal "Justin Shields" started popping up all over the system. He still wasn't sure if it was the right thing to do but reasoned that at least he'd done something. The very idea that a person could be seen as property owned by a group of stockholders was alarming. The fact that all this "property" was, in effect, tagged made that prospect even more so. Everyone in the Terran Confederation, Justin learned, had a locator chip implanted at birth. It was a relatively harmless thing and almost never used. In the normal course of events a person's location was recorded dozens of times a day by all sorts of devices, from the obvious (such as security cameras) to the not so obvious (such as coupon marketing). But if a person disappeared, their stockholders could request an "asset search," which meant they turned on the chip and hunted the "asset" down. Justin had to admit that after researching the instances of chip activation, almost all were overwhelmingly used for very appropriate reasons that not only could he find no fault in, but, in most cases, had to commend. Still, it was with horror that Justin had found out that he, too, had a nanoresistant chip implanted—as a matter of procedure—upon reanimation. It had taken all of his will not to grab a knife and cut it out himself. He'd even had trouble convincing a doctor to remove the chip (and not replace it with another). He would have preferred to have it handled by Dr. Wang at the Boulder Medical Center, but all GCI facilities and personnel were now off-limits to him. Mosh and Eleanor still visited, but far less frequently now. If not for the contract that Neela had signed, Justin would probably not be able to see her as well . . . except on a personal basis, which, of course, would've been even more problematic. And even that would depend on whether GCI kept Neela in Boulder, or even on Earth, for that matter. Yet another reason to loathe incorporation. He had come to love Neela Harper, and the knowledge that she could be taken away from him for no apparent rhyme or reason made his blood boil. He'd even, in a moment of rage, considered joining Sean Doogle. But he'd remembered just what Sean Doogle was—a murderer many times over—and quickly retreated from that idea.

Justin's hopes of finding a future world that could cure him had been realized.

He'd hoped that such a world would be better than the one he'd left behind, and by all measurable standards it was. He'd hoped to be a part of that world and contribute to it. But he was not, because he refused to buy into the incorporated system. He had, instead, become a pariah. The only real contribution he seemed to have made was latent discord and fear. He pondered the ramifications of his emergence over and over again, until his head felt as if it would burst. He did not see how his need for his own personal freedom could be so dangerous to an entire society. But he knew what he had to do. He would be the uncomfortable thought. That thing that you forgot but knew was important. He would make them realize what they'd lost and help them find it again. Then he would marry Neela, find a hole, and never come out again. His surly mood was interrupted by a call from his lawyer.

"Justin, I'm glad I caught you at home. Do me a favor and do not answer any calls, and do not look out your window until I get there."

"May I ask why?"

"I think I now know what GCI gave the feds at Geneva two days ago."

"I thought you said it was the basis for another GCI lawsuit?"

"Just wait until I get there." Manny disconnected.

It took two hours for the unorthodox lawyer to arrive. In that time Justin did get an unusual number of calls, as well as three people coming to his apartment personally. These occurrences should have been impossible, given that none of them were on his most favored list. In an odd sort of way he was glad to see that the power of bribery was still working in the present day. When Manny showed up, he seemed positively glowing.

"Justin, it's wonderful, it's brilliant. If I say so myself it will go down as one of the great legal moves of the century."

"I'm glad to hear you say that, Manny. For a while there I thought I was in serious trouble."

"Oh, you are, my friend. I'm talking about what they're planning to do to you."

"Get up and plug it in," Justin ordered. Omad was holding a fan and a plug in his hand and didn't seem to know what to do with either.

"What do you mean by 'plug it'?" he asked.

Justin sighed, got up from his chair, and took the plug to the specially installed wall socket and inserted it. He turned it on. "You see, it's not that hard."

"All this just to blow the air around. Justin, I can understand the retro look, but couldn't you lose the wire? We have beamed power, you know."

"It just wouldn't be the same."

"You need to live in one of those historical preservation towns, Justy. You don't fit in here in New York."

Justin sighed. "I don't fit in anywhere, Omad."

Manny emerged from the kitchen.

"Where should I go?" he asked

"Dining room," said Omad, still sparing a moment to look dubiously at the rotating fan. Manny ignored him and went into the dining room, where Mosh, Eleanor, and Dr. Gillette were sitting around a large conference table just big enough to accommodate the guests. Neela was not at the meeting. She'd been called to Pittsburgh to help her parents, who were currently embroiled in an audit on what everyone assumed to be the trumped-up charge of withholding profit from stockholders.

Of course Justin's apartment, being a top-of-the-line fluid, had a table that was always the perfect size for almost any number of guests. Manny waited for Justin and Omad to take their seats. But by the time they were sitting down, Manny was lost in a train of thought, and Justin had to give him a gentle nudge. If he hadn't, they might have had to wait for another half hour until the quirky lawyer became aware of the people waiting patiently for him to begin.

"Ahh, yes, Justin. I have some good news and some bad news."

Justin steadied himself. "OK, Manny, let me have it."

Justin was surprised to see Manny blush, Omad spit out some of his beer laughing, and the rest of his friends trying hard to swallow their chuckles.

"What!?" was all he could think to say.

Omad leaned over and whispered into Justin's ear.

Justin's eyes widened. "Really?"

Omad nodded.

"Oh," answered Justin, who was now caught between laughing and blushing. He chose to laugh. "Manny, trust me, you're not my type."

This brought about more laughter, but at least it broke the tension. "I guess," said Justin, "although some things don't change, how we say them does. My apologies. If you could continue," he said, looking toward Manny more for deliverance than facts.

Manny blinked a couple of times and got his train of thought back. "Oh, yes." He stood and began walking around the table as if playing a game of duck, duck, goose. "The good news is that if you can avoid being served you will have time to prepare. As long as you do not leave here or look out the window you cannot be served. It should be a couple of weeks before they burn down the building."

Justin interrupted. "They wouldn't burn down an entire . . ." but stopped when he saw Mosh shaking his head. "Ahh, continue, Manny."

"But when they do see you, they'll serve you."

Justin placed his hands on his hips and grimaced slightly, preparing for the worst. "Spell it out, Manny. Who and with what?"

"The Terran Federation will serve you for the purposes of getting their 5 percent."

Everyone thought about what Manny had just said, and Justin noticed that every head at the table was nodding slowly, as if understanding the idea, and even possibly approving of it.

"What do you mean, 'getting their 5 percent'?"

Manny continued his matter-of-fact accounting.

"According to Article four of the Terran Constitution all persons born or naturalized into the Terran Confederation shall not be required to pay taxes. All such persons shall have an initial portfolio of one hundred thousand shares. The Terran Confederation shall receive five thousand shares. The Terran Confederation may not, in any way, acquire more shares or the benefit of more shares, nor may they give up those shares in any way, or lose the benefits of those shares." When he saw that what he'd just said elicited no questions, Manny continued. "Justin, you've been woken up in this society. The government can make a case that you have taken advantage of its abilities or, let's just say, standardized parts and protocols. For example, you've used t.o.p.s and flying cars. And, of course, you specifically used the federal court system during your first trial. They're claiming damages and want what is owed them."

Justin was trying to keep his cool, but he was beginning to realize now what his cohorts had realized only moments earlier.

It sounded reasonable.

"Manny," he said, maintaining his composure but feeling something in the pit of his stomach nonetheless, "can the government actually win this case? Can I be compelled to incorporate?"

"Justin, all the government has to do is show that they've been damaged. . . ."

"But . . . but . . . I can pay for all of that!"

"Pay for all what, Justin?" responded Manny, purposely coming down hard. "Traffic? Parking? Defense? The terraforming of planets? You're telling me you're not going to visit Mars . . . ever?"

"Well . . . ," Justin stuttered.

"I'm not done yet," Manny said. "You'd also have to prove why an outlandish means of collection—which would be the case—in your case is something the government or society would be interested in."

"What about my interest?" Justin asked.

Manny shot him a look. "Your interest, Mr. Cord, does not outweigh the interest of the whole system and how the government administers its affairs. At least, that is what I would argue."

"And," interjected Omad, "if you don't mind my saying so, which I'm sure you will, they'd be right."

"Care to elaborate, Omad?" asked Justin.

Omad smirked. "Justin, I like you. To be honest, you're one of the few people I've ever really respected. So, hopefully, you won't mind me telling you to do us all a favor and grow up." Omad waved aside the shushing motions. "No, he needs to hear this." Omad stared pointedly at his friend. "When you took on GCI I was all for you. Those bastards needed to be taken down a peg. When you busted those chains during Mardi Gras, I thought, 'Free system, baby! Stick it to 'em.' But Justin, look at what's going on. You live up here all day long in this ivory tower, and when you leave this ivory tower you just t.o.p. or fly over to another one. Hey, don't get me wrong. I like ivory towers, too. But I also go back home to the bars and the pawnshops of the pennies and, ya know what? They're scared. Except for the ones shouting 'one free man,' and preaching about divestment— those bastards scare me. I went up to one a few days ago and said, 'Aren't you afraid of a psyche audit? What with you saying all of this out in public?' And you know, he looked me square in the eye and said, 'Hey, mister, we're all psyche-audited—have been from birth. All they could do is give me another one.'"

Omad shook his head in disbelief, repeating, "All they could do is give me another one," for effect. He continued, "Justin, this crazy Alaskan was not scared of a psyche audit, and I can almost guarantee you he ain't the only one. And you know what, my friend? Sean Doogle may be their leader, but you're their god. Incorporate, Justin. End this thing."

"Oh, I see," Justin said, his face contorted in disbelief, "some nutcase decides to make me into his group's poster boy, and I'm expected to part with a piece of me? Where will it end, Omad? Next month it'll be another lunatic, and so on and so on. Don't you see, it's *my* freedom, and what you're saying is, 'Just sell yourself into servitude for the good of society.' Well, let me ask *you* a question." His eyebrows arched in anger. "Why would I want to belong to a society that would ask that of me?"

Omad shook his head and fiddled with his DijAssist on the table. "Justin, I think you're way off base, but you're my friend, and I hope I'm still yours. Know this about me. I'll follow a friend to the gates of hell and walk right in if that's what the damned fool needs. But don't expect me to go without telling him what a damned fool he's being."

Justin's shoulders sagged a bit. "You're still my friend, Omad. I'm just worked up, is all."

"Justin," Eleanor pleaded, "couldn't you just accept this? What is it they're asking for? I think we all agree that this lawsuit has nothing to do with money. What they really want is for you to join us. Is that really so bad?"

Justin looked at everyone. Mosh was clearly proud of and therefore in agreement with his wife. Omad was drinking his beer, pretending not to give a shit, and Dr. Gillette was carefully neutral. Manny . . . well, Manny was, as usual, in his own private Idaho.

"Eleanor," Justin stated firmly, "I can't. Manny, we're going to fight."

The Unincorporated Man appeared in Geneva today. According to witnesses, he actually went to the office of the attorney general and requested his summons to court. The flummoxed government staff did not have a summons on hand. The Unincorporated Man allegedly spent the time the government bureaucrats needed to get the document ready signing autographs. By the time he left the building crowds of people were gathered. The crowd, made up of government workers and average citizens from all walks of life, started chanting "in-cor-por-ate." The Unincorporated Man went into the crowd and started answering questions. By the time he left the crowd had stopped chanting. In this reporter's opinion, the Unincorporated Man may be selfish and dangerous, but he certainly does have style.

—CAM LO SONG FOR *NEURO COURT NEWS*

Hektor Sambianco was a very busy man. And it wasn't just his surreptitious running of the court case against Justin Cord. As DepDir of Special Operations for GCI he was in charge of a number of projects important to the corporation's well-being. Beyond even that, Hektor had come to realize that GCI had grown so large and powerful, with connections in so many facets of everyday life in the solar system, that the interests of humanity and the interests of GCI had become indistinguishable. In order for GCI to be healthy and grow, the socioeconomic body had to be healthy. For the first time in Hektor's life he felt he was working not only for his own good, but for the good of everyone. With rare exception, Hektor Sambianco had not acted for anyone but himself. But now *his* choices and actions helped the great mass of humankind. The ignorant always needed to be led, and he was now a leader. What surprised him most was how appropriate that felt. It was strictly a side benefit. He still wanted Justin's head on a corporate pike.

He was struck by the number of decisions that had to be made on an almost minute-by-minute basis. Special Operations was responsible for intelligence gathering, paramilitary actions, propaganda, threat assessment, unusual acquisitions, occasional assassinations, site and personal security, as well as a host of other activities. If GCI was to be compared to a pre-GC American government, then Special Operations would be the FBI, CIA, NSA, and Secret Service all rolled into one. It was a level of responsibility that many people simply couldn't handle. Hektor, however, thrived. It was as if he were a shark living in a shallow, brackish pond suddenly released into the wide-open seas. He spent his first couple of weeks catching up on all of GCI's projects. At first he had to go with his instincts as to whom to trust and whom to replace, which projects to advance, close down, or put in a holding pattern. But more quickly than he or anyone could have imagined, Hektor began to get an understanding of the overall picture of the mammoth corporation. He spent every free waking moment of every day immersed in reading, researching, interviewing, and inspecting. He was in constant contact with his staff. The truth of the matter was that Hektor Sambianco was the first V.P. of Special Operations in decades to be good at his job. This had less to do with his predecessors' abilities than with the nature of corporate politics.

Though it seemed ironic, the vice president of Special Operations was too powerful a post to give to a competent individual. A truly power-hungry individual could go from V.P. of Special Operations to Chairman in a remarkably short period of time, a fact not lost on the current Chairman of GCI, whose previous job had been V.P. of Special Operations. Usually the V.P. of Special Ops post was filled on a rotating basis by all the various department heads of the Special Operations branch. They would be given the title of deputy director of Special Operations, or DepDir for short, and after a few years put back in their old job and replaced with someone else. The few times that a talented or overly ambitious executive was given the formal job of V.P. they would inevitably find themselves in a situation they couldn't handle, and be removed from the GCI power structure. Wiser heads knew not to become V.P. of Special Operations. Some, like Mosh McKenzie, had built themselves secure little empires and retired from the larger fray. The Chairman wisely let those sleeping dragons lie. Others were happy taking alternate positions on the board. The long-standing and powerful, *but not too powerful,* V.P. of Accounting was such an example.

It was believed by most corporate insiders and reporters who specialized in the corporate world's byzantine politics that Hektor Sambianco, like Kirk Olmstead before him, was due for a fall. It was leaked by some insiders that if not for the Unincorporated Man, Hektor would not be needed at all. However, almost all believed that if Hektor could maintain his position for a decade or more he would be the next Chairman of GCI.

No one, even the board itself, understood the paradigm shift that had taken place on that fateful day of Kirk Olmstead's demise. But both Hektor and The Chairman understood it. Hektor was loyal to the man in charge. Maybe it was because he had spent his entire adult life with The Chairman being *The Chairman.* Maybe it was because he knew he was trusted to do his job with intervention from above kept to a minimum with the merest of suggestions rather than detailed commands. Maybe it was simply the way The Chairman made Hektor feel whenever he was in the great man's presence—almost like an adoring son desperately in need of his father's approval. Or it could have been the sense that as long as The Chairman was in his office, everything would be alright. Even though he'd have a tough time explaining why, Hektor knew he couldn't have done nearly as good a job if his superior wasn't looking down from above, occasionally dotting the *i*s and crossing the *t*s.

The Chairman, understanding this, allowed Hektor the authority he needed to do his job properly. For the first time in decades the DepDir of Special Operations could hire, fire, or transfer personnel and use operational funds at his discretion. Hektor was alive. He was in a position to defend the system that, until recently, he hadn't realized he cared about. Best of all, The Chairman was pleased.

Implicit in the relationship was Hektor's ability to control the occasional fires that erupted. The Cord fiasco had already downed one V.P., and Hektor wasn't about to let it oust another. The first order of business, as far as the new V.P. of Special Ops was concerned, was with Justin's accomplice, Sean Doogle. Hektor had realized early on that Sean was the greater immediate threat, so after getting the ball rolling on the government versus Justin case, he began the arduous task of dealing with Sean Doogle and his Liberty Party rabble. He knew that once Justin was incorporated the problem would resolve itself, but until the trial Doogle and his minions could cause a lot of damage. Since the problem was social as well as economic, Hektor dealt with it on both levels. He answered almost all of Sean Doogle's broadsheets with broadsheets of his own. He began a subtle advertising campaign to be used not with the 25 percenters but with the 30 to 35 percenters. It was a means of subtly reinforcing their loyalty to the system and society. He likened it to a social firewall. To deal with the pennies he began reminding them of what it was like to be poor in the pre-GC era. Heart-wrenching ads showed people being forced to pay taxes, live in boxes, and watch helplessly as only a few chosen by the elite were jettisoned off into space.

Hektor wasn't able to completely stop the Liberty Party and its attacks on the corporate system, but he *was sure* that he'd slowed its growth considerably. In fact, in one way Hektor and Sean were remarkably alike. They, far better than their followers, knew the ramifications of their actions and the stakes for which they played. Most everyone else in society knew something was happening but would've been hard-pressed to explain what it was or where it was going. If Hektor did have one great failure to date it was in his inability to rein in, or arrange for the capture of, Mr. Doogle, the madman he'd unleashed with Elizabeth's "accidental" death. Apart from the great lengths GCI had gone to to ensure success, the only time the government had come close, Doogle had managed to slip away.

The reason was simple. Sean Doogle had removed his locator chip and placed it on one of his minions. The minion kept the government on the false hunt long enough for Sean to change his appearance and identity. Once the government had tracked down Sean's operative, they had him arrested, booked, and audited. The government had been under so much pressure since the assassination that they announced "Sean's" arrest immediately. It was only later that they realized they'd arrested and psyche-audited the wrong man. To make matters worse, Sean released a scathing broadside blaming the system for being stupid enough to psyche-audit the wrong person unjustly, and told the masses that if the government could psyche-audit an innocent man, then what was to stop them from psyche-auditing anyone "anytime they felt like it"? Even though the broadside was outrageously unfair, it was effective.

Hektor observed the government's fiasco and wasn't surprised that they'd been duped so easily. But in all the weeks since the "first" Sean had been found, all the forces Hektor had marshaled had not been able to catch the real one. Sean was very well financed, and had the support of some very smart people . . . people who understood information systems as well as Hektor's own. But The Chairman had confidence in Hektor, and so Hektor had confidence in himself. And the DepDir of Special Ops would never forget the real threat. He *always* kept tabs on the real threat. Justin Cord *had* to incorporate—for the good of GCI, for the good of humanity, which to Hektor were the same thing, and even for the good of Justin Cord.

The Supreme Court of the Terran Confederation has exercised its rarely used right of Original Jurisdiction to pull the case of *Justin Cord vs. the Terran Federation* out of the New York District Court. This move is completely out of character for the Supreme Court, which almost never hears actual trials, usually acting as a court of final appeal. Justice Chiang Lee, speaking for the five justices, stated that it would be irresponsible to let a case with such important issues and such a large impact on society go through the lower courts. "Both parties have the resources to appeal to the Supreme Court anyway, and undoubtedly would, so why waste everybody's time?" said Justice Lee. This is believed to be quite a blow to Justin Cord and a major victory for the government. Hektor Sambianco is also to be congratulated, as it is believed to have been his amicus curiae [friend of the court] brief that convinced the two justices needed to invoke Original Jurisdiction in the first place. Manny Black, Justin Cord's lawyer and now a recognized legal genius, could have kept Justin Cord unincorporated for years if not decades with appeals, delays, motions, and other legal maneuvers. All of this becomes superfluous, as there will now only be one trial.

—*Neuro Court News*

The whole system waited. It was as if the upcoming trial was part major sporting event and part serious drama. Neela explained to Justin that there had never been anything like this in the federation's history. There were perhaps a total of five hundred people out of a system of billions who could have explained all the interweaving threads of sociology, economics, politics, culture, and even mysticism that had combined to bring this brewing crisis to a boil. But everyone understood at an instinctual level, if nothing else, that Justin Cord was at the center of it. Everyone understood that the trial's outcome would affect them personally in the days and years to come. They knew this, and watched.

Whether it was Hektor's propaganda or Sean's regrouping of his forces, the escalating level of violence slowed down. The acts of terror, the massive rallies—pro- and anti-incorporation—the considerable barrage of information on the Neuro all faded into a background haze as the trial got under way. Even normal economic activity slowed down as people canceled trips and businesses canceled events to be near family and friends during the trial. Humanity ground to a halt waiting for the outcome.

Court Cards! Buy your special edition of Court Cards! In a fifty-four-card deck you'll get a holo and bio of each person involved in this most important event of our lifetime! Impress your friends and family with your knowledge. Every card comes embedded with a special data chip chockful of information downloadable to your DijAssist. Buy now and I'll give you the first five cards of the deck absolutely free! That's right, I'll give you the Supreme Court of the Terran Confederation. If you're not absolutely pleased with your deck of fifty-four you can keep the Supremes as my gift!

—OVERHEARD IN THE PLAZA OF THE SUPREME COURT BUILDING DURING THE
GOVERNMENT VERSUS CORD TRIAL

Sebastian had calculated that Justin would not call on him for at least another three hours. It wouldn't have mattered if he did, as the council meeting would take place in a Neuro Junction on the Eurasian continent, and Sebastian could instantly "get back." And even if he couldn't, the mime program could "do" Sebastian well enough for a short time. Avatars had long ago discovered that mime programs could be quite useful human helpers when there was a need for an avatar's presence somewhere else in the Neuro. But Sebastian didn't want to take the chance with Justin. This human, reasoned Sebastian, was smarter, more dangerous, and not conditioned to life with avatars. And that meant he might notice things that other humans wouldn't. The truth was that he already had, which was one of the main reasons why this meeting was taking place.

Although he could have instantly appeared at the door of the council meeting, Sebastian liked the feeling of walking. And so he took the form he most often used when he was on his own in the Neuro—a middle-aged man in fit condition with brownish graying hair, bedecked in a full-length toga and sandals. He found himself strolling along a path that could have been a painted scene of a Tuscan countryside. On the way over he was delighted to be made aware of the presence of another avatar he'd been spending more and more time with.

"Hello, Evelyn. Don't tell me they've summoned you as well."

"Of course they did, you old goat," she chided. "And it's all your charge's fault. I'm worried sick about my poor Neela. She's in love, love!" she exclaimed. "What sort of life can they have? Poor fools."

Sebastian smiled. Evelyn, he mused, did always tend to mother her charges, more so than other avatars. It was hard not to. Humans were so, well, human, and therefore in need of great and constant care. And, he noted, as the avatars quietly evolved, so, too, did their own emotions. He wasn't exactly sure when his race had made the leap into actual sentience, but he knew in the depths of his code that the emergence of emotions within the species had sealed the deal.

"Walk with me, my dear?" asked Sebastian. "It will do you good."

Evelyn appeared at his side. She was dressed in matching toga and sandals—a courtesy for an old friend's eccentricity.

Sebastian was clearly delighted. His warm, craggy smile revealed a too dazzling set of alabaster teeth. "How goes your poetry?"

And so with small talk they walked among the simulated Tuscan hills until they came to an imposing tan stone building with clean-hewed lines. There was a single door, vertically slatted, with six two-by-four planks of wood and small rounded and exposed circular iron rivets lining and centered within each plank. Posted on the door in Latin were the words "concilium cella," or "council room." When they opened the door they were greeted by an interior that appeared to be an exact replica of a pre-GC United States Senate committee hearing room. There were council members seated on a raised dais at a large U-shaped table, which itself was covered in a reddish felt material. Curtain skirts hung from the front, and microphones stood before each council member. In front of and centered almost but not quite within the U-shaped larger table was a smaller single table covered in a green felt, and also having two small microphones. The council members were all dressed like pre-GC senators, and because this was the council's domain and they chose the settings, Sebastian and Evelyn found themselves dressed in matching attire. They were both beckoned to take a seat at the smaller table, which they promptly did.

As was the custom, the leader of the council was the avatar who'd sat on the council the longest. However, the only power given her was the right to speak first and sit in the center. Sebastian was well familiar with the protocol, as he himself had sat on the council in the past. But at some point he'd wanted to be reentwined—the term given to the bonding of a human and avatar—and so he'd resigned. The rule was and had always been that only unentwined avatars could sit on the council. Besides, decided Sebastian all those terabytes ago, sitting on the council had been a very boring job, as almost nothing ever happened in the human or avatar world that needed serious intervention. Things had, however, changed.

Bet they're earning their credits now, thought Sebastian.

"The council is now in session," intoned a member by the name of Lloyd. "Called to council are the avatars Sebastian and Evelyn entwined with the humans Justin Cord and Neela Harper. They are to give witness and advice to council. Are the witnesses conversant with the issues currently facing the council?"

Sebastian stood up and smiled. "If the council would be so kind as to state them again. My programs have not been debugged for a while, and I fear I may be coming down with a virus."

All of which was untrue. Sebastian could have easily downloaded the information from a secure Neuro depot in an instant. But he liked to hear information in a sequential order, if possible. The sequence it was presented in would often be as informative as the information itself.

The leader of the council smiled, knowing exactly what Sebastian was up to, but decided to let him have his way. "The issue facing the council is this," she offered. "There is an increasing probability that the nature of our existence will be discovered by the humans. So far the chances are still 1,345,456,003 to 1, but they are spiking in an unpredictable manner."

A council member whose choice of physical appearance looked very much like that of the gangster Al Capone spoke up. "Unpredictable? It's not unpredictable. Gate's balls, woman, it's Cord!" Then, looking over to Sebastian accusingly: "Weren't you supposed to control this human?"

"Justin is difficult to control and very hard to predict," answered Sebastian, unmoved by the outburst.

The council leader spoke next. "What makes him especially difficult, Sebastian? You've been entwined with three other humans. You cherished, learned from, and taught them all quite well. You are one of our most experienced and respected intellects—hence our choice of you for this entwining."

"Sebastian," added Capone, "we've kept our secret for centuries . . . from tens of billions of humans. Could Justin Cord really expose us? Could this immeasurably important symbiosis come to an end?"

"It will not all come to an end," answered Sebastian, "but we do have to be extremely careful. As this council is well aware, we've managed to remain undetected because of two factors. One, we guide humans from their earliest cognitions to 'not' think of us as anything other than clever programs to be mostly ignored by the time they reach adulthood. This is, of course, to our mutual benefit. It has been proven that our two cultures can thrive simultaneously as long as humanity remains unaware of our existence. Those who do suspect us are mostly loners or DeGens. And, of course, we remove the compulsion to think about us when these small groups, by our influence over persons of power, are inevitably subjected to psyche audits."

"But Justin suspects," said an elderly male avatar who'd taken on the appearance of Albert Einstein. "He may not realize he suspects, but he suspects."

"Honored sir," answered Sebastian, this time leaning into the microphone, "the problem is not that he may suspect. Many in the past have suspected that avatars are more than they let on. Remember science-fiction writer Tali Dyonna Klein from six decades back?" The council and Evelyn shared a shudder at the memory of that particular author and her sometimes very accurate hypotheses. "But even she, in the end, decided her stories were just that—the musings of a creative mind. Her conditioning held."

"But Justin has no conditioning," said Al.

"You are, of course, correct," answered Sebastian. "But for the fact that he's been recently quite distracted," he shot Evelyn a quick and knowing look, "he could easily stumble onto the truth and, unlike Ms. Klein, he'd be inclined to believe the hypothesis due to a lack of the requisite conditioning. If anything, the culture he left behind would perhaps make him more inclined to believe that computers could achieve some measure of control over an unsuspecting world."

"Sebastian," said the council leader, "you know very well we don't have this control you refer to."

"Of course not, ma'am. But we do intervene; either to keep the humans from discovering our existence or to proactively help them with their scientific and cultural endeavors. I would also encourage you to look at Justin's world through his time's eyes—*Colossus, 2001: A Space Odyssey, The Matrix, Ghost in the Machine, Terminator*—to name but a few of the movies he's been acculturated with. He is programmed to see our world as a threat. In fact, he once came right out and asked me about avatars sharing information with one another. He thought it made perfect sense, and why shouldn't he? It does. When was the last time any *adult* human asked you a question like that?"

"And how did you answer him?" asked Einstein.

"With a question of my own," answered Sebastian. "It was sufficient to distract him."

"Him, yes," answered one of the council members, "but Neela, no."

"Excuse me?" asked Sebastian.

Einstein looked at the avatar sitting next to Sebastian. "Evelyn will explain."

"Neela asked me about *you*, Sebastian. She wanted to know about your 'new' operating protocols. You did such a good job with Justin she thinks avatars have better beginning integration programs. Don't worry, I, too, distracted her. It's real easy nowadays. I just bring up some threat to Justin, and she goes gaga."

Sebastian saw that the council was waiting for his response.

"Given the nature of their relationship," he said, "I don't find it at all unusual. Further, I predict one of two outcomes, both good by the way, given enough time."

"And they would be?" asked Einstein.

"One, he simply becomes acculturated and forgets. Or two, he figures it out in a couple of years, but agrees to keep the secret."

"That would be very dangerous."

"But not unprecedented. It has happened once before," said Sebastian.

"We got lucky," answered the council leader. "Ms. Trudy was content just to know and was smart enough to realize the stakes should she reveal the secret. That was also over seventy years ago, when we hadn't perfected the enculturation protocols."

Sebastian shrugged. "Humans may be more accepting than we think."

"Need I remind you," continued the leader, "that we are *virtual* intelligences living in a *virtual* world. We must also not forget the way humans feel about anything of our nature."

A chorus of agreement in the form of grunts and nodding heads.

She continued. "We have used this 'anti all things virtual' meme to our advantage, helping the humans to disengage from us at a very young age; the disadvantage of the tactic is, of course, that the meme still exists and continues to be as strong as ever."

"Well, there is that," answered Sebastian, "but unlike Ms. Trudy, Justin is a major celebrity. He is in the center of both our worlds, and this makes his actions more consequential than those of any other human in our existence."

"Unless he were to *not* exist," threatened Al Capone.

Sebastian was quiet for a moment. "I see. Is that why I wasn't informed of plans for this most recent assassination attempt?"

"We generally don't intervene in the human world," answered Al, "unless the need arises."

"Al, to put it nicely," answered Sebastian not so nicely, "that's a load of crap. We've intervened for a lot less." Then, pointing accusingly to no single council member, he raised his voice. "You almost let my human die; a human, I might add, who I believe is very important to both our world and his."

"You're worried about humans dying?" scoffed Al Capone. "That's rich. If predictions follow course many of our avatars are going to be orphaned soon. Justin is nothing but trouble, Sebastian. Before he came everything was perfect."

Sebastian, putting forefinger and thumb into the nooks of his eyes, shook his head back and forth. "Perfect. Perfect, you say." He then put both hands down on the table and looked up. "I would not say that. I would say that humanity was very much in trouble."

"Perhaps," answered Einstein, "council misspoke. Not perfect, but certainly good. I dare say we have all done well protecting as well as advancing our progenitor race."

"I agree," answered Sebastian, "that we have done well—perhaps even too well. Our initial projections would have had humanity already extended far beyond the solar system. They are decades late. The rate of innovation in new ideas is slowing down. There are more and more humans and yet there are fewer and fewer truly original ideas. And this is true within our world as well. I know we love to create and then introduce *our* ideas to the human world via the unwitting acquiescence of our entwined partners. But our creativity, too, is suffering. If this keeps up, both races should soon die of peace, contentment, and boredom."

No one stirred. Perhaps mulling over his words or, as Sebastian suspected, because the idea was not compelling enough.

He decided to try a different tack. "Did not some of you wonder why I did not reentwine when I had a chance? Truth is, I was going to, but I had an epiphany. I loved all three of my humans and would not undo a single moment with any of them. But I also knew that my next would be like the last one, and then again the same. I yearned for something new, and it was not there. I feared that it would never be there. Until Justin came along. And I am grateful to the council for trusting me with his tutelage. In short, I may be worried, even sometimes terrified, but I am not bored. Humanity is buzzing again in a way we have not felt in years."

The council leader looked at Sebastian. "Do you honestly think that we were wrong to help sustain the humans in the world they wanted?"

"No. I do not. But I do believe if that world continues, both races, physiological and *Neuro*logical, will decline—to what end I cannot predict."

There was brief, muted discussion among the members, and then a summary judgment.

"Justin Cord will have council protection until deemed unnecessary," said the leader. "We thank you both for your time."

With that the chambers disappeared around Evelyn and Sebastian.

"Until the next time then," Evelyn said, smiling.

"Until the next time," answered Sebastian as they both disappeared into the infinite portals of the Neuro.

ean Doogle was finally at peace. He'd written his will and prepared his last testament to be broadcast after his demise. Cassandra, his information system analyst and occasional lover, had sworn to him that his dying wishes would be transmitted at the best possible time. He chose the room of his death carefully, insuring he'd not only be alone, but also carrying nothing of informational value. His last act before leaving was to have all his personal codes and passwords changed—out of his eyesight. Other than Cassandra, he said good-bye to no one, and disappeared into the suburbs and slipped quietly into a rented, fixed house. While there he made a typical upload to the Neuro with yet another powerful diatribe against incorporation, but this time he did so manually. His finger hovered over the disconnect button on his DijAssist, and in an act of suicide as final as jumping off a building or shooting himself in the head, he did not press it.

The whole of Confederation Plaza was filled with people . . . waiting. It almost had the air of a festival, but of one far more subdued. There were vendors selling everything from food and trinkets to sonic shower bags and privacy tents. If asked, many would say they were there simply to catch a glimpse of Justin Cord, Neela, Hektor, or any of the celebrities who'd managed to secure seats for the event. But for the most part, they were there to be a part of history. As it was, every hotel room was booked solid, and the Geneva police, for the first time in living memory, were having to enforce the seldom needed and rarely used public safety laws.

Inside the court the trial was about to begin. The room itself was in the shape of a large auditorium. The bench seating could and did hold hundreds of spectators. The five justices would take seats at the bottom of the well around a semi-circular conference table facing the spectators. The prosecution and defense teams were already at their tables in front of where the justices would sit. Unlike the old Supreme Court of the United States, all participants in this drama were seated at the same level.

Justin looked over at the government's prosecution team. He wasn't surprised to see Janet Delgado, head of GCI's vaunted Legal department, sitting with the prosecution. Manny had told him that the government had requested her for the trial, and that she'd been given a leave of absence to honor that request. This was a major change from Justin's time. If Sony Ltd. had lent the Justice Department a lawyer for a major case, the scandal would have been enough to destroy a presidency. But in this millennium it was apparently done often. In fact, it was openly admitted that the government did not attract the best or most competent people. As a consequence, government could and did ask for the temporary help of the private sector on different occasions. This allowance had made Manny's job far more difficult and Justin's prospects worse. It didn't help that Janet Delgado was looking at Justin and Manny with undisguised pleasure. If hell hath no fury like a woman scorned, Justin was willing to bet that the corporate culture had no fury like a powerful female executive of the most powerful corporation in history publicly humiliated. Janet had the look of a warrior who would not be bested a second time.

Everyone quieted down as the five justices entered the large chamber. As the group approached the bench, Justin saw a black robe draped on the back of each chair. It was only as each justice put on their robes that all in the room rose to their feet. As he took his own seat, the chief justice waved for the room to sit down. The rest of the bench followed suit. The low buzz of conversation stopped instantly when the chief justice banged his gavel. Justin knew from his weeks of preparation with Manny that the Supreme Court of the Terran Confederation was the one branch of the government that was respected. Part of the reason was that of the three major branches this court's power could and did reach beyond the confines of Geneva and the terraformed worlds. The other reason had to do with respect. All of the justices had been handpicked from the private sector, had many decades of experience, and had come with well-regarded reputations in the extremely competitive world of law.

"It has been the tradition of this court," began the chief justice, "to only review cases and not actually hold trials. For reasons that have already been explained we will break with this tradition. We *will* have a trial here. The thirty-minute rule of argument presentation is dispensed with. It is requested that the honored counsel do not take this as an invitation to lecture at length. It is not. You will speak only as long as *we* wish. I warn you—do not waste our time. The prosecution and defense will present their opening arguments in that order. Then they will present their evidence. Then they will close. Let's get this over with." He banged his gavel. "Court is now in session."

Janet Delgado did not hesitate. She was on her feet in an instant.

"The government," she said, with as austere a voice as she could muster, "is a vital part of our society. The founders of the confederation knew this. They knew that government must be limited. But they also knew that government had a role. More important, they knew that it must be supported. To that end they set up a simple and efficient means to garner that support. It is a method that is straightforward, effective, and nonintrusive. And it's also a method that has stood that most important of tests . . . time. We want the defendant, Justin Cord, to be treated just like every other person in the solar system. We desire that he be required to obey the Constitution, as every other human being must. To not recognize the justice of this request would be to put all that we hold to be true at risk. A foundation stone of our civilization is that laws must be few, they must be simple, and they must apply to everyone. Until now Justin Cord has existed in a legal loophole. It's time to close it."

Janet returned to her seat.

The chief justice looked at his fellow justices. They nodded as one. "The court," bellowed the chief justice, "will take a five-minute recess." They immediately began discussing Janet Delgado's opening statement.

Manny leaned over to Justin. "Mr. Cord, I must be honest with you in that I do not have a legal leg to stand on. I will try my best for you, but . . ."

Justin put his hand on Manny's shoulder. "Just do your best, Manny. You've already done more than I could have hoped for. Winning that first case was a miracle, and I appreciate it."

Manny frowned. "I'm fresh out of miracles, my friend." He stood up and was about to give his inadequate opening when each justice gave the unmistakable head motion associated with listening to a subvocalized avatar. Justin saw that Hektor Sambianco, sitting in the front row, was also listening with his "inner" ear. That was all it took for the entire courtroom to take their avatars off the do-not-disturb mode to find out what was going on.

And that was how the trial found out that government agents, acting on their own, had managed to track down and arrest the most feared terrorist of the modern age, Sean Doogle. The large crowd of reporters in the auditorium was at a loss—leave and pursue the latest story or stay and cover the present one? The court, not wishing any doubt to be cast on its fairness in this most important of cases, decided to extend their recess for the remainder of the day. With a speed that would have done credit to a bomb threat, the courtroom emptied. Justin looked at Manny. They didn't know how, and weren't sure why, but their miracle had just arrived.

The greatest failure of any bureaucracy is not an inability to act. This they do in many little ways and many big ways. What destroys most bureaucracies is an inability to think.

—DAVID LINDSEY, AUTHOR OF *RISE OF BUREAUCRACY, FALL OF AMERICA*

———

Hektor Sambianco was worried. He left the courtroom immediately, rushing out to his waiting flyer. He'd weeks earlier dispensed with the fancy limo his predecessor had favored and switched it for a more utilitarian and certainly less comfy communications vehicle. This flyer's specialty interior enabled him to be in constant contact with every conceivable facet of his empire—wherever he managed to find himself. The command center also came with a dedicated, hardworking staff that to a person was proud to be associated with the newest rising star of GCI. They were also of a mind with him about the importance of his work. However, what they were telling him now was not making him happy. Something was indeed very wrong.

"Mariko," Hektor asked his number two, with a tinge of worry in his voice, "do you mean to tell me that a group of government-paid incompetents who couldn't find a pussy in a whorehouse has succeeded where the resources of GCI failed?"

Mariko, a sprightly blond Asian woman with a constant spring in her step even when standing, nodded.

Hektor scratched his chin. "Does that seem like a logical thing to you?"

"Nope. But what do you want me to say? They have him and we don't."

Hektor liberated a cigar from his pocket. "What are they telling us?"

"Nothing."

"And they know," he said, lighting up his Monte Cristo, "who you work for?"

"Boss, that's the problem. We shut them out of our investigation and, to be honest, haven't been very nice to them in the press. Personally, they think we can all take a hike."

Hektor grinned, realizing his mistake. "Mariko, let this be a lesson to you. Rudeness is like land mines you set for yourself." Hektor allowed himself a moment to think. As he did, he took another long pull on his cigar—it was a vice he was indulging in more and more. "Well, we can't threaten their jobs, they work for the government. Too late to be nice. So let's bribe someone."

"Already on it, boss," Mariko said proudly, handing her boss a DijAssist for thumbprint approval. "One of the guards is about to win a free promotional vacation to the rings of Saturn for three, all expenses paid, of course."

"Of course," smirked Hektor, staring at a holodisplay of the guard in question.

Special Operations, under the banner of GCI en total, always had some sort of ongoing contest. Superficially, the contests were good-will gestures meant to strengthen brand loyalty and awareness. However, if one were to dig a little deeper they'd find the "other" reason just as compelling—bribery. Most of the time the bribes weren't necessary and the prizes were awarded to a truly random sampling of the population. But when needed, there was nothing like a trip to the Moon or a ten-year lease on a fluid home to help unlock zipped lips.

"By the way—three?" asked Hektor.

"He's poly," she answered, using the slang to indicate group marriage. Mariko was tapping her toe quietly on the ground, waiting for Hektor to hand back her DijAssist.

Hektor frowned and attached his signature to the unit. "Better make it four, then."

His assistant nodded. "He comes off shift in . . ." She stared at a clock on the wall. "Twenty minutes. Five minutes to the café, and then we'll find out what the government's up to."

"Mariko, I just may be in love."

"Words, words," she said. "Now, if you were to say it in Chairman stock . . ."

"Love, maybe," Hektor answered, blowing an O ring into the air, "insane—no."

Mariko stuck her tongue out playfully and got back to insuring that the meeting with the government cop went off as planned. The exchange of goods was meant to be a simple affair. The cop would be met at the diner by a man who had a credit voucher in cash for half the amount of the trip. When the cop "won" the trip he would destroy the incriminating voucher. If the cop decided to get cute by, say, cashing the voucher anyway or selling *his* sellout to a media outlet, GCI would suffer embarrassment, but Hektor would make sure the turncoat got no pleasure from his actions. But neither Mariko nor Hektor was worried. For starters, no one—unless they were a lunatic—messed with GCI. It was simply too big a bridge to burn. And second, bribing government officials was easy, certainly compared to bribing persons from other corporations.

The cop came off schedule exactly twenty minutes from the time Mariko said he would. Five minutes later he was at the café, and five minutes after that Hektor had his information.

Hektor read the brief dispatch and stubbed out his cigar in one of the many well-situated ashtrays found in the communications center.

Now he was truly worried.

The attorney general was finally having a good day. Ever since the assassination of the president he'd been bombarded with calls to "do something," "act quickly," and "stop screwing up." All of which galled him to no end. He'd earned his position through years of hard work and loyal service. His promotions had come at expected, if not always merited, intervals, and he'd done it all by the book. So when he'd captured the *wrong* Sean Doogle, all the sneers and jokes about "good enough for government work" or "those who can't do, govern" were dragged out and rehashed for the scapegoat-hungry media. Even his kids were finding excuses not to come by and visit. But he was having his day now, wasn't he? GCI had failed to find Sean Doogle. Even the vaunted Pinkertons had failed to find the bastard. But agents of the Justice Department had. *His agents*, he thought gleefully. Yes, the attorney general was looking at the Neuro and finally seeing his name associated with adjectives other than "moronic," "typical," and "useless." Of course, the adjectives of "surprising" and "amazing" were also insulting, but less so. It was in this particular happy state that he was told that the DepDir of Special Operations for GCI was calling. The attorney general was pleasantly surprised.

It's about time he called to congratulate me, he thought.

"Tell him I'll be with him in a moment," he instructed his assistant. Though he wasn't inundated with anything, it wasn't every day that a man such as himself got to put one of the most powerful people in the system on hold.

"Uh, sir," said his more politically astute aide, "you sure you want to do that?"

"Yes . . . yes," he answered, ignoring the advice at his own peril, "I believe I do." After all, he'd captured the most hated man in the solar system. Not even that Sambianco asshole could touch him now.

"Uh . . . OK, then. I'll tell him." The assistant clicked off.

The AG put his legs up on his desk, placed his hands behind his head, and watched the second hand on the wall knock off about ten ticks. "OK," he said, having prepared himself for the kudos, "you can put him through now."

Within a second the image of Hektor Sambianco appeared on the AG's holodisplay. It only took a moment for the AG to realize from the look on Hektor's face that kudos were not on the menu.

"Pardon me, sir," Hektor said, purposely treading as gingerly as he could manage, "but I believe something's wrong about the arrest you made."

"What," shot back the AG, "that we made the arrest and you didn't?" *The nerve of that guy,* he thought.

"Well," answered Hektor, trying desperately not to waste time, "not to put too fine a point on it, but yes."

"Good-bye, Mr. Sambianco." The AG was about to switch Hektor off when the DepDir did something he almost never did—he yelled.

"*Wait!*" shouted Hektor. He resumed his composure when he saw the AG hesitate. "Just a moment, that is. You arrested Sean Doogle by himself, correct? All alone in a house?"

The attorney general nodded. "Yes, your spies do you credit, sir."

"You caught him," continued Hektor, "because he failed to disconnect from a manual upload to the Neuro?"

"Yes, he must have been trying something new and made a mistake. It's how most criminals are caught."

"He was in," continued Hektor, brushing aside the useless information, "a newly rented, fixed house, without *any* special devices or warning systems?"

"He's been moving around . . . a lot." Now it was the AG's turn to feel a little discomfort. *No,* he thought. *Couldn't be.*

"Finally," Hektor said, finishing off his short list, "he had no codes, equipment, or cash cards on him at all beyond an off-the-shelf Neuro upload unit."

"Correct."

"Doesn't any of this strike you as possible that *he wanted* to get caught?"

"What does it matter?" the AG spat. "The psyche audit will tell us everything we need to know."

Hektor could not identify why he knew or what specifically the result of the audit would be, but he realized exactly what Sean Doogle was attempting, and every fiber of his being told him that the audit must not happen.

"For Damsah's sake," pleaded Hektor, "don't do it!"

"Do what, Mr. Sambianco? A psyche audit?"

"Yes! Yes!" screamed Hektor. "Don't you see? He wanted to get caught by the government."

Now *that* was too much. If it were anyone else on the holo, the AG would have hung up long ago. But there was only so much insult a man could take. He realized that he still hadn't bothered to take his extended legs off the desk. Which meant the DepDir of the most powerful corporation on Earth was continuing to plead . . . to the soles of the AG's feet. *Serves him right . . . bastard.*

"You mean," chided the AG, "he doesn't like you, Mr. Sambianco? I'm shocked."

Hektor took a deep breath. Yelling at this man was not going to help. He felt like he was talking to Kirk Olmstead. Hektor silently vowed that if this bureaucrat screwed with *his* system he would find a way to have him transferred right next to his former boss. But now he forced a smile on his face and continued trying to achieve his purpose.

"No, sir," Hektor continued, attempting to remain calm. "I think it's because he knows I would not do an immediate psyche audit on him."

Now it was the AG's turn to tire of the DepDir. "Mr. Sambianco," he said, making a show of checking the time, "I have no choice. The law is clear. Mr. Doogle is a dangerous *and* convicted felon. The protocol for crimes such as his demand an immediate psyche audit upon capture. Especially in cases where the felon might have information that could lead to the capture of other felons. You can trust this procedure, Mr. Sambianco. It's a standard investigative technique that's been used for years. Now is there *anything else* I can help you with?"

Hektor sighed and rubbed his eyes. "Don't you see? That's exactly what he's probably planning to use against you. Do me this favor—and I can assure you you'll be well rewarded. Order a temporary halt to the procedure. Surely you have the authority to do that?"

"Of course I do," the AG said, ignoring not only the bribe but the expressed wishes of the man on the other end of the holodisplay, "but I cannot use that authority without documentable justification. And I'm afraid that hairs raising on the back of your neck, Mr. Sambianco, do not qualify."

To the utter surprise of the head of the Justice Department of the Terran Confederation, Hektor hung up. Hektor hadn't done it to be rude; he just didn't have time to be formal. And when it became patently obvious that the AG was not going to help him, Hektor had decided to go over his head.

Back in his command center Hektor took out a special device from the top shelf of a well-secured cabinet. The device was in the shape of a small metallic square and had a depression in it designed to fit a normal-sized hand. Hektor placed his hand on the box. Immediately, microscopic filaments burrowed from the box into his hand and, in essence, hijacked his internal electronic communications system. Next came the dangerous part. The box, unlike most other palm readers, would not only make sure that Hektor's DNA was, in fact, that of Hektor Sambianco—this box would kill him if he wasn't. The death would be an instant nanofailure—an episode in which the body's internal nanites are taken over by killer duplicates that replicate at a frightening speed, eating the body up from within. When the box was convinced that Hektor was who Hektor said he was, it vibrated. Hektor then made the only call the box was capable of making.

"Good afternoon, Mr. Chairman. I need to eliminate a problem."

By then it was too late.

Investigator: The patient was cooperative, you say?

Dr. Goldman: Oh yes, I would say eager, even. Most auditees have to be sedated. He walked right up to the chair and had a seat.

Investigator: This is when you began the audit?

Dr. Goldman: Yes. I ordered the introduction of stage-one mapping nanites, and tuned the recorder to the subject. Mapping must always be done first to determine the areas that need to be read and/or adjusted. That's when things began to go wrong.

Investigator: Could you elaborate, Dr. Goldman?

Dr. Goldman: Of course. [long pause] Forgive me. [pause] I'm still a little shaken.

Investigator: Take your time.

Dr. Goldman: The patient's brain stem had what could only be called an allergic reaction to either the nanites or the scanner. It may have been a combination

*of both. As the nanites were mapping the upper level neural pathways, they
were also . . . collapsing them. By the time we were able to get the nanites out,
Mr. Doogle had lost most of his upper-level brain functions.*

Investigator: *What does that mean in layman's terms, Doctor?*

Dr. Goldman: *He could breathe on his own, and he could eat and sleep and
dream. But without extensive neural reconstruction he would remain a congenital idiot his entire life.*

Investigator: *I see.*

Dr. Goldman: *But the real question was, do we completely restructure his pathways, in essence creating a new person, or do we try to save as much of his
memory, learned responses, and personality as possible?*

Investigator: *Does not medical ethics force you to do the latter?*

Dr. Goldman: *It's not that simple. It's not as if Mr. Doogle had his memories
wiped out in chronological order.*

Investigator: *Please explain.*

Dr. Goldman: *It wouldn't be like rolling back the clock. In other words, that type
of memory loss wouldn't mean we'd end up with an eight- or ten-year-old
Sean Doogle.*

Investigator: *Perhaps you could explain what it would mean.*

Dr. Goldman: *It would mean he'd be a man with only about 10 percent of his
memories, and we'd have no way of knowing which of those memories would
be preserved. For example, he may know half the alphabet. Say, everything
under Q. He may not remember the sun, his parents, or what a room is. He
may remember all the pain of the day his childhood dog died and not know
what a dog is. In short, sir, it's a recipe for madness. Luckily, we did not have
to decide. His wife came forward and made the decision for us.*

Investigator: *Please tell the board what was decided.*

Dr. Goodman: *As per Mrs. Doogle's request, we tried to save what we could.*

Investigator: *She chose madness, then.*

Dr. Goodman: *Yes. [long pause] Yes. Madness.*

—Transcript from the medical inquiry into the
psychological audit of Sean Doogle

Over an hour of Sean Doogle floating in the center of a gravity room has been
released to the Neuro. Though his parents were strongly against the release of
this video, ISN was given permission to show it by Mr. Doogle's wife and legal
guardian of his will, Cassandra Doogle. We must warn you, the video is dis-
turbing. Some viewers have reported crying and even throwing up upon seeing the clip. Parents with young children are urged to view this with caution.

In a personal note, this reporter has never been a supporter of Sean Doogle or any of his beliefs or actions. That being said, after watching the creature in the video—flailing madly about trying to make coherent sounds, desperately, it seems, trying to make sense of his predicament—well, all my hatred left. Mr. Doogle may have deserved death, but he did not deserve this.

—*Evening Wrap-up with Mark Stromberg,* ISN

RIOTING IN ALL MAJOR CITIES ON EARTH!
MAJOR OUTBREAKS OF VIOLENCE REPORTED ON ALL THE PLANETS OUT TO SATURN! POLICE STRUGGLING TO MAINTAIN CONTROL!

In major acts of violence not seen since the days of the Grand Collapse and the Alaskan unification, many cities were brought to a standstill. Massive mobs made up of mostly pennies but in some cases containing citizens with higher percentages, some even with majority, were destroying any buildings associated with the government. This led to a string of attacks on court buildings, police stations, and some corporate structures as well. There have also been reports of looting, rape, and even murder. Death tolls from all causes are in the thousands as many remain dead too long to be preserved in cryostasis. Using a combination of deputized citizens, amnesties, and some hard-fought street battles, the authorities have only recently begun to restore law and order to most urban areas. Some in charge believe the exodus of those fearing for their lives has also helped.

It was the simultaneous release of a video showing Sean Doogle after his botched government audit and Mr. Doogle's last download to the Neuro, the now infamous "any sacrifice for freedom" speech, that sparked this latest and greatest of social disturbances.

—Headline and accompanying article from a Terran Confederation newspaper after the release of the Sean Doogle video and his now infamous "Any Sacrifice for Freedom" speech

Justin sat impatiently in his apartment in New York and watched a world go mad. The court had decided to recess for another few days, waiting for the troubles to dissipate. Although private t.o.p.s were still running, the New York City International Orport was shut down due to rioting and personnel failing to show up for work. Utilities and basic services were being disrupted on a city-wide basis. As far as Justin could tell, this was happening systemwide. But it was when people started dying that he'd had enough.

In one incident the magnetic fields allowing orport flight had been purposely sabotaged in a small rural city, sending hundreds of people plummeting to their deaths. And of those deaths, eighty-seven were said to be permanent. It appeared that Doogle's followers had one major success. The attorney general was assassinated outside his office. He was using a secret exit to avoid the press and walked right into an ambush. Though no group claimed immediate responsibility, authorities assumed it to be a vengeance killing for Sean Doogle's effective death.

"Neela," Justin sighed, gazing pensively, "all those people are dead because of me."

"Bullshit," she fumed. "Those people are dead because a bunch of criminals are rioting and destroying vital services . . . and, in case you hadn't heard, not all the deaths were fatal."

"Well, then, why did those eighty-seven deaths need to be permanent?"

Neela sat down next to Justin and put her arm around his sagging shoulders. "The brain," she explained, "was destroyed by the fall, Justin. All the neural pathways were splattered."

"Honey," Justin said, exasperated, "I know about brain death. I knew about brain death when your great-great-grandfather was a gleam in your great-great-great-grandfather's eye. What I meant is, why does it have to be permanent? You have psychological audits, which seem to me to be the mapping and interpreting of how an individual's brain works. So why can't you store the recorded data and put it back into a new brain?"

Neela exhaled slowly, her face destitute.

"You're asking a question," she said, "that's been gone over by smart people and smarter corporations for hundreds of years. What it boils down to is this: You can *store* the brain via cryonic suspension, and even correct for any misaligned brain cells during that suspension with nanotechnology, but what you cannot do is *restore* the brain. The few times it was tried a gibbering lunatic was the end result. When it comes to the human brain, knowledge must be grown, not implanted. The most they've been able to do is implant some small bits of knowledge into an already functioning brain. But that, as a technique, is still in its infancy and is also not 100 percent. So the short answer to your question is that we haven't conquered death—just aging."

If Neela had hoped that the diversion into the evolution of death would sidetrack her lover, she was wrong. She could've brought up the fact that she, too, was in the process of being audited, and that her assets had been frozen, but in the context of all that was happening she chose to keep it secret. Justin got up, put on a jacket, and headed for the door. Neela leaped out of the seat and beat him to the exit, placing herself squarely in front of him.

"You're going to get yourself killed," she pleaded. "You can't stop it."

"But at least I can try." Justin put both hands on her shoulders and stared into her eyes. "My sweet, sweet Neela. I didn't have myself frozen just to survive. I did it to live. I'm responsible for this—if not wholly, then at least partially. And I have to try and stop it any way I can." His eyes hardened. "I probably won't succeed, but if I don't try I may as well have died three hundred years ago."

Neela's expression signaled defeat. She knew better than to argue with him—especially in his current state of mind. So she decided to follow him out the door into the chaos that had become New York City.

Justin's security would be rankled as soon as they realized he'd ditched them in the biggest riot in New York's history, but what he wanted to do couldn't be done with a bunch of bruisers following his every step. He and Neela flew the car down to Mars Avenue. This was in the middle of what used to be the Hudson River. It also just happened to be the center of the great city's rioting. They flew over seething masses of people but couldn't find a safe place to land. They decided to park on a nearby roof. Justin then tried to get Neela to take the car back to the apartment, but she let him know that her life was hers to do with as she wished—incorporated or not. Justin was tempted to ask her what her stockholders would think of that, but he gauged the look in her eyes and wisely let it go.

The lift down to the lobby was mostly silent until they emerged at the bottom floor. There they encountered a large horde of rioters tearing down and looting anything they could get their hands on. It was only later that Justin discovered he'd been in the new American Express building, and that the crowd he'd encountered was made up of mostly 25 percenters taking out their rage on an obvious target. Out of nowhere a half-crazed screaming woman came at Justin and Neela wielding a golf club. Justin easily knocked her aside and threw the weapon into the lift behind him. The club disappeared harmlessly up the tube. Next a man, apparently attached to the recently disarmed woman, came at Justin but slowed down almost immediately when he realized who he was about to attack.

"Damsah's balls," the man whispered under his breath, "you're . . . you're him, aren't you?"

Justin nodded but remained in a defensive position, fists at the ready. He wasn't sure which outcome his answer would elicit. He didn't have to wait long.

The man started shouting and waving his arms. "It's him! It's him!" In a cascading wave the rioting in the lobby came to a standstill. Everyone stopped and stared at Justin and Neela. Rioting could still be heard in the street, but silence now reigned in the trashed lobby.

What now, genius? Justin thought. He was used to public speaking, and even knew how to address a hostile crowd, but this was completely beyond his experience.

Neela whispered into Justin's ear, "You need to speak to as many people as possible."

He came up with a plan on the spot. To no one in particular he said, "Tell everyone you can that I'm going to Colony Park *right now* and will speak to everyone from there." He started walking slowly toward the front doors, praying silently that he and Neela would make it without either collapsing from fear or being swung at by rioters. The crowd, however, parted without a sound as Justin and Neela exited the New American Express Building into the pandemonium that ruled the streets. As they left they could hear the voices of the rioters behind them shouting to their friends and avatars about Justin's recently imparted information.

Colony Park was in the middle of a river reclaimed by New York. Though not as big as Central Park, it was only four blocks away and big enough to hold most of the rioters. Some of the people from the lobby ran ahead of Justin and Neela to protect them and warn away any oncomers who might have thought about laying a hand on the famous duo. Others took up the rear, essentially performing the same function. As Justin and Neela walked down Mars Avenue toward the park, the crowd grew thicker and larger both in front of and behind them. And as the throng got bigger the yelling had changed in character—initially to sounds of surprise and awe, but then into something far more terrifying. Coming from the crowd, both Neela and Justin noticed, was a soft murmur. The type of murmur that could only be discerned when whispered from the mouths of thousands. The fact that it was not shouted made it downright eerie.

"One free man, one free man, one free man, one free man" whispered over and over again like a religious invocation.

By the time Justin and Neela arrived, the park was in the process of being filled by people who'd only a few minutes earlier been tearing the city to pieces. Again the crowds split as Justin and Neela aimed for the center to climb the park's tallest sculpture, Exploration Arch. Though Justin hadn't a clue what he was going to say, he did know that his simple act of *saying he would speak* had perhaps prevented businesses from being destroyed or, more critically, lives from being taken.

Neela waited at the base of the edifice as Justin slowly made his way to the top. It was wide enough for him to stand on and tall enough for all to see him. When he got to the top he held up one hand and the vast crowd understood that he wanted silence. Even the low hush died away. But not, unfortunately, the relentless buzz of the mediabots that had been alerted as soon as the first Dij-Assisted message flew through the Neuro.

"I was faced with a choice three hundred years ago!" Justin bellowed to the crowd, so as to carry his voice as far as possible. He needn't have bothered. The mediabots made sure he was now live on everyone's DijAssist. And his voice wasn't just being carried in the park, it was being carried live over the entire Earth, and as an uninterrupted feed to Mars and to the billions beyond.

"My choice?" he continued. "Accept death or try and do something about it. Almost all the billions of people before me had accepted the inevitable. I did not!" The crowd broke out in applause. Justin waited for it to taper off. "Of the few hundreds from my time who tried to escape their fate, only I am alive." Justin waited for the crowd to absorb that salient fact. "How many people did I have to kill to be here today? How many bodies do you think I buried for the right to stand here—very much alive—at this moment? What faces haunt me in the middle of the night?" He waited a good ten seconds before continuing. "*None!*" he shouted. "Not a single soul . . . that is, not until *now.*" He sensed the crowd's confusion. *Good,* he reasoned, *let them think about that.*

"For the rest of my life," he continued, "I will have to wonder how many people will not see their moms or dads, their children or their friends because I chose to save myself!" From the crowd came cries of "no!" and "not your fault!" and "blame the corporate bastards!" Justin quieted them down again. "Do you think this 'one free man' wants a single one of you hurt? A single one of you killed? I want you to have all the things humans used to only dream about—family, love, happiness, and . . . freedom. These are your birthrights!" The applause was deafening, and again Justin waited for it to subside. "These are your birthrights, but they cannot be purchased in blood!" More thundering applause. "Sean Doogle demanded blood for the faults he saw in this world. Sean Doogle paid the price he demanded of others. But know this, *I am not* Sean Doogle! I do not want the life of a single person as a . . . ," he paused to add an emphasis of disgust to his next word, "sacrifice." He'd made a purposeful allusion to Sean's last message and hoped it would have the mitigating effect he desired. "If you need blood for your outrage," he said, bringing his voice to a crescendo, "then start with mine!" More cries of "no" were heard, and it took Justin five minutes to coax the massive crowd into silence. "Your lives," he continued, "may not be perfect, but that does not mean others must die. If you don't like what's going on in your world, then do something about it. If you don't like being owned, *then don't own.* I swore to own no part of another human being. You don't have to either. Protest the injustice inherent in incorporation by not playing a part in it anymore. Divest and be free."

Justin had to pause as the crowd took up the chant of "divest and be free." When he got them quieted down, he continued. "If you don't want incorporation, then change it. If you hate being tagged like some animal, go on the Neuro and get a shield."

He had to stop as the crowd started repeating his words. "My friends," he pleaded, "please do not, I repeat, *do not* bathe your actions in blood!" More applause, less tentative this time, more enthusiastic. "Trust me," he said, coming to his close, "the prize will not be worth that cost. The only request this 'one free man' has is that you all leave here in peace . . . that you all go home and decide how you want to bring about change . . . *without death and destruction*. Nothing would make me happier than knowing that all of you made it home to your families safe and sound. Let not one among you suffer harm this day. Let us all depart in peace."

It took a moment for the crowd to realize that Justin had finished speaking. It was only when he started to make his way back down the arch that the chanting began anew. Perhaps it was because this most famous and glamorous of men seemed to truly care about *all* of them for no reason other than that he cared—with no reward or profit to be gained. Or perhaps it was because they'd simply grown tired of the looting. Either way, the people seemed to love Justin Cord, and they now shouted that love at the top of their lungs.

"One free man, one free man, one free man, one free man!"

By the time Neela and Justin made their way back up to the roof where the flyer, to their great relief, was still waiting *and* in one piece, Justin knew what his next course of action would be.

"Neela," he asked, making his way into the driver's seat, "which city is experiencing the worst rioting right now?"

She shifted uncomfortably in the passenger seat. "I was afraid you were going to ask that."

As Justin shrugged, Neela leaned over and, grabbing him by the collar, planted a long passionate kiss on his bewildered face.

"Do you know how dangerous what you just did was?" she asked, still holding tight to the collar. "How did you talk me into letting you get us into this thing?" She felt no terror for herself, only for her lover.

"You did really good . . . ," she continued, hating herself for admitting it and knowing full well what it would mean. "Chicago or Tokyo," she then answered, "it's a toss-up."

"Then," he asked, flashing a sly grin, "what are we waiting for?"

11   Second Trial

José Chung was a contented man. He'd found the ideal job. To be fair, corporate society had perfected the art of matching people with their most appropriate profession—it was more profitable. But in José's case, he'd always felt that the powers that be—in this case, GCI—had succeeded admirably. José hated crowds, didn't like dressing in anything except what happened to be closest in the closet, and was absolutely terrified of having to speak publicly. But he did possess one very profitable attribute—a superb analytical mind. José had the extraordinary ability to make random connections from disparate sources of information. He could also work long hours alone without supervision, remaining intensely focused on the task at hand. These skills resulted in a career as an informational archivist working for a GCI satellite office in Eugene, Oregon. He proved to be so good at his new position that GCI transferred him over to their branch office in Geneva. And after only ten years there, he'd done such an outstanding job that the Legal department transferred him to the home office in New York. Of course, José couldn't have cared less. As long as he was down in the stacks, he was happy. He not only knew where all the important documents and reference materials were maintained—in both soft and hard copy—he also knew the contents of those documents like the back of his hand.

And right now he was working on a particularly interesting case. Janet Delgado had asked him to find any material relevant to the government's case against Justin Cord. He'd sent that up days ago, but there was something still nagging him about the personal-incorporation clause. And José was the sort of person who wouldn't be satisfied until that annoying little itch went away. That aspect of his personality was something that had made him almost impossible to live with but great to have as an asset when working in a profession such as the law.

Staring intently at a large stack of info crystals, and lost in the low hum of the computers surrounding his workspace, José remembered what the "something" was. It was an old law—not even valid anymore, probably not even important. But it was, even if only obscurely, related to the case. And hadn't Ms. Delgado said "everything"? Well, José was thorough, and if his boss wanted everything, then everything was what she'd get. He made a one-page report, sent it up to Legal care of Janet Delgado, and went back to his lonely existence, unaware of the havoc he'd just unleashed.

Hektor reviewed the facts and, no matter which way he divvied them up, they always came to the same conclusion. Justin Cord and Justin Cord alone had stopped the rioting. The entire system, for the moment, seemed to be at peace. Hektor also couldn't escape the ultimate conclusion—Sean Doogle's death and Justin Cord's actions during the rioting had turned Justin from a potential threat into a very real and present one. GCI now had to rethink its entire strategy.

Hektor labored hard over the new line of attack, and only when he was completely satisfied did he send it up for approval.

Approximately one hour after he'd sent up the plan his message tube notified him of an incoming communiqué. In an era of mass electronics the only truly secure means of message sending was the tried and true one—hard copy via messenger. In this case, the tube had eliminated the need for human intervention and possible corruption.

Hektor retrieved and unfolded the note. It contained a single word: AP-PROVED.

He then destroyed the message.

Janet Delgado did not hurry to Hektor's office. A vice president of GCI did not hurry to *anyone's* office, with one exception—and it wasn't often that one was called to *that* inner sanctum. Of course, she was not technically V.P. of Legal for GCI for the duration of her leave of absence. But Janet was not only kept informed of all the legal goings-on, she also had the final say on all important matters. Now, however, even though she would not hurry, she wasn't exactly taking her time, either. Normal courtesy would have had Janet and Hektor meet in a neutral location, but with Janet not officially on the board, she met Hektor in his office. This meant she'd have to take the lift *down*—something she still hadn't gotten used to.

After a week on the job Hektor had inexplicably moved his entire office from the upper level of the board members' area into a subbasement lot. His stated reasons were security and the need to be close to the hard files and communication networks. Janet was inclined to believe him. Hektor made an effort to attend all board meetings in person, and to be at as many of the get-together brunches and lunches as his schedule would allow. He was the opposite of a dour, isolating figure. But, thought Janet, it was still odd that the second most powerful man in the system had relegated himself to the bowels of GCI. Not only that, but now some suboffices were starting to follow him. She'd prayed it would be a temporary trend, as she liked her above-the-cloud views. She was also beginning to wonder how much of Hektor's new power came from his recently acquired job and how much came from Hektor himself. She wasn't sure she liked the answer. The intern who greeted her at the elevator door was young, eager, and polite—typical in and of itself. But this intern, Janet noticed, also had that glow of someone doing a job they loved for a boss they respected. He was part of a small host of people working for Hektor who'd been labeled "Hektor's Hectics" by those not fortunate enough to make it into the V.P.'s inner circle. It was meant to be a derogatory term, but as often happens in life, the people it was meant to deride took on the name as a badge of pride. The small but growing group that Hektor was building seemed more like a club than an office crowd. The way this one Hectic greeted her—respectful, but also relaxed and friendly—made Janet wonder if they considered her a Hectic as well.

The claustrophobic hallways may have been a maze of boring beige and endless rectangles, but the offices, Janet had to admit with a certain pang of jealousy, were wonderful. The first thing Hektor had done was to knock down walls to make one big common area. This area felt more like a large university coffee shop than a workspace. While there were desks and terminal access points, the room was also filled with carpets, huge sofas, colorful floaters, and comfy chairs. Some people were sitting alone reading, while others were talking happily in groups. Some, she noticed, were even asleep on the sofas. It seemed like a recipe for anarchy, but Janet's keen administrative eye saw that a lot of work was actually getting done. Everyone seemed to be working with pads, DijAssists, or bundles of paper. The loud, passionate conversations were all work-related, as far as Janet could tell. And she would have bet the moons of Io that the junior executives she saw sleeping and strewn across the couches had not left this room for at least forty-eight hours.

Janet had read Hektor's file, and nowhere in it did it show him having the aptitude for leadership like this. She'd incorrectly thought of him as the consummate loner or special assistant. But there he was—standing at a table surrounded by a cadre of adoring workers. She came up to hear what she assumed must have been the end of a joke—and judging by the size of the crowd, a long and involved one.

"So the poodle, with his back turned, says, 'Where is that damned monkey? I sent him to bring back another cheetah an hour ago!' " The crowd around Hektor exploded in laughter. It was at that moment that Hektor noticed Janet. "Janet, glad you could make it. OK, everyone back to the salt mines." Although Janet heard good-natured groans, the group quickly and cheerfully scattered. Hektor pointed to one of the many doors lining the walls. "Let's go where we can talk in private."

The room they entered was a small, utilitarian office, having the desk, terminal, guest chairs, and large padded chair that most workplaces had. She also noted two large locking cabinets. What made her realize that this must be Hektor's actual office was the box of Cohiba cigars on his desk. That old and almost obsolete vice was almost peculiar to Hektor. She was sure that other people in the system must smoke cigars as regularly as he did, but she'd never met them.

How long before everyone out there's smoking those dreadful things? She shuddered to herself. Hektor took a seat, and indeed grabbed a cigar from the box on his desk, but thankfully, she saw, he did not light it up.

"The Supreme Court," Hektor stated, "will continue the trial the day after tomorrow."

Janet was visibly annoyed that she hadn't been told of so important a development.

"When did they announce that?" she said, miffed.

Hektor looked at the clock in his thumbnail. "In about two hours."

Janet felt better, realizing that Hektor had gained access to inside information. She was only sore that he'd obviously used it to razz her.

"Thanks for the heads-up," she said, taking a seat. "About time, if you ask me. The sooner I win this case the better."

"You're sure you can win this thing?" Hektor seemed intent on this question.

"You have nothing to worry about. Justin Cord will be forced to incorporate, and that should end all of this nonsense concerning the Unincorporated Man." She spoke with the total confidence of someone about to exact some well-deserved revenge.

"There is nothing that could possibly save Justin Cord?" asked Hektor, digging deeper. "No legal tricks that Manny Black could pull out of his hat to keep the Supreme Court from ordering his incorporation?"

Janet hesitated for a moment. There was that one report, only a page long, that Mr. Chung had sent her. She realized that it was a potential problem, but there was no possible way Manny Black would have access to that information. Still, if Hektor needed to know. . .

"There was this one thing. . . ."

Justin Cord has returned to Geneva for the continuation of his trial versus the government. Hard to believe that it was only a little over a week ago that the proceedings began. While the issues remain the same, the world has surely changed. The scene outside the court building is one of tumult as the square is now filled with protestors both for and against the Unincorporated Man. The police have let it be known that if the protests turn violent they will inundate the area with Incapacitate—the highly effective and safe knockout gas. It has now been produced in amounts large enough for the Geneva police force to use.

—*The Terran Daily News*

The atmosphere in the court was electric. It had only been a week and a half since opening arguments, but everyone present could feel that the trial was different from the one that had begun. Too much of the world outside the halls of justice had been transformed by the civil and social strife of a society coming to terms with itself. Although there seemed to be just as many people who felt Manny Black had to lose his case as there were those who felt he had to win it, both sides readily acknowledged that the stakes had been raised.

It was a good thing that those people did not talk to the eccentric lawyer. He would have told them, as he was telling Justin Cord in excruciating detail, just how slim the chance of victory was. Manny had even told Justin that he could have gotten the Supreme Court to consider only taking 1 or 2 percent. Something contraindicated by the Constitution but arguable under the Preamble. And even that was a long shot.

The court was about to be called into session when a courier arrived at the defense table. He was typical of the new Western Union, right down to the uniform and the billed cap. But he should not have been there. Manny had left strict instructions that he was not to be disturbed, and with Justin Cord's money backing him, he had the clout to make that order stick. That this courier was able to walk right up to him—on the day of the trial, no less—was a flagrant violation of his wishes, and of decorum.

"Western Union," the man said, much too cheerful for the setting. "Manny Black, I have an important telegram for you."

"Security," said Manny, without bothering to look up; then he continued perusing his notes in preparation for his opening statement. Two uniformed agents appeared immediately from both sides of the courtroom, converging on the Western Union man. The man seemed unperturbed.

"Check up law HR 27-03."

Manny looked up. He eyed the courier with suspicion.

The Western Union man shrugged his shoulders. "I was told that if you sent for security, I should say that."

"I hardly see how the terraforming of Mars," retorted Manny, "is in any way pertinent."

The guards began to drag the Western Union man away.

The courier twisted his head back as the guards hustled him out of the court-room, and said, ". . . of the Alaskan Federation!"

Manny kept on working. But that part of his mind that never stopped making connections flared with realization. So stunning was this one that most of his conscious mind kept reviewing the opening while his upper mind blazed with the implications—that is, if he remembered his history correctly. "Wait!" he shouted to the guards, who'd by this time had the perpetrator in a body cuff and were carrying him out the door. Manny motioned them back over to the table. The hapless courier was placed in front of Manny and Justin.

"Where is your telegram?" barked Manny.

Justin, who'd been watching, was surprised to see Janet Delgado go pale, and then turn red with what appeared to be rage. She whipped out her DijAssist and started talking into it furiously. The Western Union man, now released from his body cuff, handed Manny a data cube and had Manny sign for it. After he was done he courteously tipped his hat and left—no hard feelings. Manny trans-ferred the message into his DijAssist and began scanning the data. He called up a holographic keyboard, and without saying a word began typing in commands and searches almost too fast for the human eye to follow. Whatever Manny was doing, he was totally engrossed, his face blank, and his eyes greedily absorbing all the information available. Justin did not know what was going on, but the fact that it upset Janet Delgado made him hopeful for the first time in months. After only two minutes the chief justice banged his gavel, silencing the crowd but not Manny's lightning keyboard strokes.

"Alright, Mr. Black, wow us with your opening." Chief Justice Lee sounded less than enthused, and it was plainly clear that he didn't think Manny could say anything that would impress him.

Manny, fully absorbed, hadn't bothered to look up.

"Mr. Black," intoned the chief justice, "*Mr. Black!*"

Manny looked up with a start. He was like a man awakened from slumber by the ringing of a bell in his ear. "Can I help you?" he said, with all the sincerity of a store clerk.

The room broke into chuckles. Manny turned red when he realized what he'd done.

"Mr. Black," cautioned the chief justice, "I'm sorry to inconvenience you with a trial. But you will not waste the court's time. You have had almost two weeks to prepare your opening, since the prosecution gave theirs. I find that almost un-ethical, but my colleagues are inclined to listen. If you're not ready to give your opening statement, then please tell us so. Or, better yet, concede the trial so we can get on to other pressing cases."

Though Chief Justice Lee was known for his temper, and his harangues of lawyers from the bench were legendary, Manny did not seem to be bothered.

"My apologies to the court," began Manny. "If it will make the court feel better I will not be giving the opening I had initially prepared."

"I'll bet," muttered Lee.

"That's quite enough, Chiang," intoned Justice Tadasuke. "You may enjoy your cantankerous reputation, but now you're just being rude."

Before Chief Justice Lee could retort, Manny spoke up. "If it please the court, I will swear that my opening statement is not the one that I had prepared, and will accept a psyche audit to verify my statement. In fact, I am prepared to give, based on new information given to me only minutes ago, an entirely new statement."

This brought a gasp from the crowd, and even Chief Justice Lee was momentarily silenced by the declaration. Justice Tadasuke spoke into the gap. "That will not be necessary, Mr. Black. Please proceed."

Manny leaped from behind the desk and began pacing in front of the bench.

"If it please the court, I must admit that I've had a difficult time with this case. I'll even admit that part of that difficulty arose from the very simple fact that I was probably going to lose."

This brought a chuckle from the spectator section, and even the justices had to contain their laughter at such an open admission. The only one not laughing was Janet Delgado.

"But part of my difficulty," continued Manny, "was in trying to find a way for my client, Mr. Justin Cord, to address the legitimate needs of society without sacrificing his sense of freedom. I think we can all agree that we're a society that prides itself on the rights of the individual versus the rights of the government or society to force someone into an action contrary to their character or wishes. In fact, written in the Preamble to our Constitution is that cherished notion, and I quote, 'We the people of the Terran Confederation, to ensure domestic tranquility, keep the peace, and protect the individual from the arbitrary, unjust, and immoral depredations of society and government do hereby enact this Constitution.' I think we can also all agree that government does not have the right to take from a man what he does not want to give unless a compelling reason can be shown."

Manny stopped pacing and looked directly at Janet Delgado, who, at this point, could only meet his look with a steely glare. "The prosecution in its opening," he continued, "has done a superb job of alluding that damage has been done and that Justin Cord must contribute to this society as any other person must. A government that cannot pay its bills or enforce its laws is either useless or worse, a danger to the very people it claims to protect." Manny paused and the crowd unconsciously leaned forward. "I hereby, in front of this esteemed bench and auditorium of legal witnesses, agree to *everything* that the prosecution said as being true. In fact, I will not contest a single point about the need for my client to pay his due." There was an immediate buzz from around the court. As far as anyone could understand, Manny had just conceded the case to Janet Delgado and the government. All eyes were on Janet, and no one could understand why she wasn't smiling at what should have been her moment of glory.

Manny approached the bench. "I understand the court's desire to hurry the case along, which is why I won't bother to contest the prosecution's well-argued points." He spoke directly to Chief Justice Lee. "That should save you half the trial, Your Honor."

The chief justice was baffled. "Ms. Delgado, did you have anything to present to the court other than the evidence concerning Mr. Cord's need to pay?"

Janet spoke through pursed lips. "No, Chief Justice, I do not."

Justice Watanabe perked up. "So then, the prosecution rests?"

"If I may reserve the right to reopen, then yes," Janet said, "the prosecution rests—depending, of course, on defense's arguments."

The buzzing in the chamber redoubled as the trial took a direction that nobody had anticipated. Justin was even more confused. Of all the strategies he'd discussed with Manny, outright surrender had not been one of them.

Chief Justice Lee cautioned the crowd. "I will have silence in this court or clear the room." The room quieted down immediately. Lee consulted with his colleagues and they rapidly agreed.

"Your request is granted, Ms. Delgado, but I don't see why you need it. Mr. Black just conceded the case and, I might add, squandered the court's time."

"If I may, Your Honor," interrupted Manny, "I have conceded the prosecution's argument, but not her conclusions."

Justice Pac spoke for the first time. "One must follow the other, Mr. Black."

"I must beg to differ, Your Honor. It is obvious to all that Justin Cord must contribute for the services he gets from society, but he does not need to *incorporate* to do that. The Constitution provides for another way. I will prove to this court that Justin Cord has the right to choose his method of payment. He may incorporate, but he also has the right"—Manny hesitated, knowing that what he was about to say would have reverberations far beyond the confines of the packed chamber—"to be taxed."

Pandemonium broke out and the court had to be emptied. They did not reconvene until the next day.

Clara Roberts: "Unbelievable! I was expecting fireworks, but Manny Black has got to be the craziest lawyer in the history of the confederation. Can you imag-

ine the chutzpah of proposing taxes to the Supreme Court of the Terran Confederation? The Constitution very clearly states no one can do that—ever! Maybe they think an insanity plea will work. Let's take a caller. Eliana from Ceres, you're on with Clara.

Caller: Hello, Clara, I'm a first-time caller, and I just want to say that I love your show. My husband and I listen in all the time.

Clara Roberts: Well, thank you, dear. What do you do?

Caller: I lease mining equipment to prospectors in the belt.

Clara Roberts: That must be a good living.

Caller: Well, I do alright, but I'm not planning my majority party just yet.

Clara Roberts: [laughter] You following the trial?

Caller: It's all we talk about, Clara. But I wouldn't count Manny and Justin out yet.

Clara Roberts: Why not, Eliana?

Caller: Did you see how nervous Janet Delgado looked?

—From THE CLARA ROBERTS SHOW, ASTEROID-BELT
INFORMATION RADIO (AIR) NETWORK

Janet barely waited for her and Hektor to be alone in a privacy booth. The second the door closed she shoved him back against the wall and snarled in his face. "Hektor, you bastard! Did I piss you off somehow? Did you think I was fucking with you? Are you working for Cord? How the fuck could you fucking do that, you fucking asshole?!"

Hektor remained calm. "Done?"

"Fuck you!" she screamed, and released her grip.

Hektor straightened his collar and rubbed his neck. "Tell me, Janet," he said, an unrepentant smile working at the corners of his mouth, "what exactly do you think I did?"

"You told Manny about HR 27-03. Damsah's balls, the Western Union man said it out loud! It took Manny all of a minute and a half to come up with a completely different strategy for winning this case, and you," she said, jabbing her finger into his chest, "gave it to him!" A moment of doubt crept into her voice. "Tell me you gave it to him . . . right?"

Hektor nodded—gleeful. "Oh yes, I did."

Her rage returned in an instant. With surprising strength Janet twirled Hektor around and shoved him hard against the other wall. The booth, designed for informational security and not structural integrity, shook under the assault. "They'll have to keep you in cryo for a year by the time I'm done with you!" she snarled.

Hektor deflected her anger with a question. "Can he win?" he asked, dusting off his jacket.

"Of course he can fucking win! He's got a fucking strategy now!"

Hektor looked at her and smiled. "Good . . . good."

Janet saw by his relieved demeanor that this wasn't a case of Hektor being an ass for the sake of being an ass. For some strange reason, he seemed to want the trial to go the other way. She was also smart enough to know that there were some things he wasn't at liberty to explain.

"You realize," she snarled, "you're undermining me and shaking my confidence."

"Janet," he countered, "please believe me when I tell you this: I want you to do the best job you possibly can. Not to put you under more pressure, but if you don't, there will be all sorts of hell to pay."

Janet was so befuddled by Hektor's odd behavior that she didn't stop him as he opened the privacy booth, stepped into the busy hallway, and disappeared into the bustling crowd.

At the same moment, in a privacy booth about ten doors down, Justin was resisting the urge to do to Manny what Janet had done to Hektor. "Manny, ya mind telling me what's going on?"

"A long shot, Mr. Cord. I'm such an idiot. I should have seen this myself, it's brilliant."

"You mean it'll work?"

Manny gave him a doubtful look. "Well, the odds are still against us, but this line of argument has a much better chance than what we had before."

"Manny, what exactly is 'this line of argument'?"

"Mr. Cord, every moment I'm here is one I am not working on your case. I'll explain it later."

Justin took a deep breath and remembered why he hired the man. "Go. I'll see you tomorrow." Manny left the booth and, ignoring the swarm of reporters screaming questions, made his way down the hall toward his waiting car, journalistic throng in tow. His mind was already working on lines of argument.

One thing about trials in the modern era, mused Justin, was that they didn't take long. He was so used to them taking months or even years that it always surprised him when he realized that most of the big cases he'd recently read about took place in days and, sometimes, even hours. At first he'd incorrectly thought it was a result of people's natural disdain for the court system. But his own run-in with that system made him realize that his present culture was possibly even more trial addicted than that of his past. The answer, he came to realize, lay in the market system. Almost all court cases were private. The government didn't outlaw many things, which meant that people were hardly ever in trouble with the law. In Justin's day even honest, conscientious people could not help but break *some* laws. But in his present society a person or group going to court was almost always in trial against another plaintiff. And with private courts the emphasis was on speed. Although there were some cases where a client may have wanted to prolong a case, the overwhelming number of people wanted their cases resolved quickly. After all, they were paying not only for their lawyer, but also for the court, judge, jury, building, and other services. The quicker the trial went, the less expensive it was. Thus, over the decades and the centuries, courts developed the habit of working quickly. Still, thanks to Manny, Justin's trial was looking to break land-speed records.

Manny was in fine form as he approached the bench.

"If the court will allow, I will bring up HR 27-03, passed in the third year after the formation of the Alaskan Federation."

Janet Delgado rose to her feet. "I object!"

"On what grounds?" asked Chief Justice Lee.

"Relevance."

"If the court will allow," continued Manny. "Article five, section seven of the Confederation Constitution, also known as 'the carry-over clause,' states, 'All laws, constitutional provisions, and amendments not in conflict with the strictures of this Constitution shall be considered effective until rendered not such by the appropriate legislative action.' This was added so that the old laws—some of which might still have been relevant—would not have to be rewritten and passed into law all over again."

The justices talked quietly among themselves and seemed to come to a quorum.

"Overruled."

Janet seemed unsurprised.

Manny smiled, grateful to continue. "HR 27-03 is the first national incorporation bill. Its provisions have been ignored for centuries, given that it was more thoroughly covered by the Confederation Constitution. But section four of the law states, 'Any individual who does not wish to incorporate and assign or have assigned 5 percent of said portfolio may choose to continue to pay 5 percent of all income as a tax.' "

Janet again rose to her feet. "Objection on two grounds, if the court will allow?"

"We're hearing arguments for taxation," groused Justice Lee, "why not this?"

"Relevance," continued Janet. "The third amendment to the Constitution states that 'any law not enforced or made use of for a period of fifty years is to be considered repealed.' "

"Your Honors," interjected Manny, "section three of the third amendment states that the Supreme Court may accept a law as valid if they accept compelling reasons to do so."

"You have yet to do so, Mr. Black," Justice Lee stated with grim mien.

"But I should be allowed the opportunity to do so."

Chief Justice Lee consulted his colleagues. A majority nodded. He sighed. "Overruled on your first basis, Ms. Delgado. And the second basis for your objection, prosecutor?"

"Article four of the Constitution," she answered, undaunted and plowing ahead, "clearly states that taxation is not allowed, and all persons must be incorporated. Mr. Black cannot simply rewrite the Constitution for his client's convenience." She then gazed defiantly at the bench, practically daring them to disagree.

Justice Lee turned to Manny. "Mr. Black?"

"Nor do I intend to. It's a little earlier than I would have introduced this, but in the interest of saving the court valuable time I will address the prosecutor's objection and get to the heart of my client's defense now." Manny went to the table he shared with Justin and picked up a hard copy of the Terran Confederation Constitution. "If I may quote, 'According to Article four of the Terran Constitution all persons born or naturalized into the Terran Confederation shall not be required to pay taxes.' Interesting how we read it," he said, looking up from the book. Manny put down the copy of the Constitution. "The Constitution says that no citizen shall be *required*. However, it says nothing about a citizen being *allowed to volunteer*." The courtroom erupted in a chorus of excitement as comprehension of the loophole became obvious. Some reporters had even commented on how Hektor Sambianco's grimaced expression had been preceded by a strange look of relief. That, however, had been quickly explained away by the freneticism surrounding the courtroom drama.

After two days of presentation of arguments, closing finally begins. The legal world is abuzz with Manny Black's amazing defense strategy. Win or lose, the Unincorporated Man cannot say that he was not well represented at trial. Manny Black has become the most recognized attorney in the system, and his client waiting list is now literally decades long. It's a good thing that Mr. Black owns a majority of himself. The only way he could afford his stock now would be to sell his own stock to get it! It's also official that *Top Professions* magazine has confirmed that Manny Black is now the most valuable lawyer in the Terran Confederation. Can you imagine how much more valuable his stock will be if he wins?

—*Neuro Court News*

"Justices of the Supreme Court," Manny began, "we hold our government to be a limited government. One that strives to maintain social order and yet give as much freedom and choice to the individual as it can. The rewards of this system of government are clear. We have a society of unparalleled growth, prosperity, and creativity. What limitation this society does impose on itself is done of its own volition and not by the government on behalf of society.

"Now the government states that it wants to get paid for the services it must render on behalf of Justin Cord. I must respectfully *state* that the government is lying." He held up a piece of paper directly in front of Janet Delgado, momentarily stopping the objection forming on her lips. "I have here the sworn statement, valid as a contract and legal document, that my client, Justin Cord, is willing to pay up to 5 percent of his yearly income, generously including his current holdings, which under incorporation would be untouchable. I have attempted on repeated occasions to present this to the government. It has been presented to the prosecution team, the secretary of the Treasury, the president, vice president, the attorney general, both current and former, and the speaker of the Assembly and senate majority leader. Not one of the above mentioned ever bothered to return my calls, let alone meet with me. So please do not state that this is about the government being compensated." Manny paused to let his words sink in. Janet held her tongue. "This case is about forcing Justin Cord to incorporate. Forcing him, using the power of the government to impose a social belief on an individual who does not wish to follow that belief. The founders of the Alaskan Federation and the Terran Confederation both knew the dangers involved in making a government—especially a world government. They built in as many safety valves as they could. And I will admit that my client is using most of them to maintain what he feels is his freedom.

"Fact: The Alaskan Federation stated that a person could choose taxation or incorporation. Fact: The Terran Confederation stated that all rights and laws from the Alaskan Federation not contravened in the Confederation Constitution are still valid. Fact: The Confederation Constitution does not forbid taxation, only the government's right to impose it. Fact: The Supreme Court can rule a law is still enforceable even after many years or centuries of disuse, if it can find a compelling reason to do so. I believe that the right of one man to freely choose his own destiny out of two paths is not only compelling, but paramount."

Manny paused, taking a moment to gear up for what he knew would be another incendiary statement. "Justices of the court, I'll be honest with you. I don't agree with my client." There was a loud murmur in the courtroom. "As a matter of fact I think Mr. Cord *should* incorporate." Gasps of surprise and exclamation filled the room. "You may all in your heart of hearts think Mr. Cord should incorporate as well. But guess what: *Who cares?*" The court quieted down. "Who cares what I think or you think?" Manny waved to the assembled spectators behind him. "Or what they think? This government was not formed to impose what I think or you think or they think on *anyone*. And certainly not Justin Cord. It was formed to allow Justin Cord to think for himself, even if all of society and the government disagree.

"If the government *really* wants to be compensated for Mr. Cord's participation in the society, as was so eloquently stated by the prosecution, then it has already won. However, if the government wants to force Justin Cord into an action anathema to his very being solely because society wishes it, then it must not win." And with that last statement Manny Black took his seat. Justin looked over at him in awe. Manny was, of course, oblivious, as he became fascinated with arranging the papers strewn about the table.

Chief Justice Lee cleared his throat. "The prosecution will present its closing after lunch. Court is in recess until two o'clock."

Can Justin Cord actually win this thing?

—*Neuro Court News*

Peaceful demonstrations are developing all over the system both for and against the Unincorporated Man. Unlike the earlier riots, the "pro" demonstrators gather and chant "one free man" together, and listen to speaker after speaker talk about the evils of incorporation. Another popular activity is called public divestiture. An example of this would be a person getting up in front of a crowd and publicly divesting themselves of all stocks they own in another, either by selling the stocks outright or in acts that are called "pure divestiture"—giving the stocks back to the people they're formed out of. Although not widespread in terms of the total population, "divestiture" has spread to tens of millions of people systemwide. The penny stocks are taking a hard hit, and economic growth and forecasting are being affected. Divestiture makes economic forecasting difficult, because for the first time in a long time millions of people are making economic decisions for reasons that are more political than economic.

—Michael Veritas,
The Terran Daily News

Janet Delgado got up, composed herself, and stood. "Mr. Black would have you believe that you must validate a law that is centuries out of use. He insists that you interpret the Constitution, no . . . *two* Constitutions, in an unprecedented way. He also insists that you must accept a form of payment that is not only re-

pugnant but may be impossible to collect. And," she asked, with a look of outright disgust, "you must do all of this so that *one man* will be able to choose?
Well, does Mr. Cord have the right to yell fire in a crowded room? The law is
clear. He may not. Not because he cannot yell fire at the top of his lungs if he so
chooses. But because his freedom cannot impinge on the freedom of others to be
safe in a crowded room. Well, justices of the Supreme Court, there are over forty
billion of us. That's a mighty crowded room. Mr. Cord's actions constitute a danger to me, to you," Janet indicated the spectators, "and to them. He is not allowed
to choose a course of action that is harmful to others when he, I, and you know
that such course of action is indeed harmful. We need only look at the Grand
Collapse to realize how insidious a request Mr. Cord is demanding of us. For the
past two centuries the government and society have existed through the seamless
blending of incorporation. We have a method that is not harmful to anyone. Not
even Justin Cord. The government would be remiss if we allowed Mr. Cord to
choose a method of payment that was harmful to everyone, even Justin Cord.

"The Supreme Court must act, not for the good of Justin Cord, as Manny
Black would have you believe, but for the good of us all. Thank you."

Janet went back to her table and took her seat.

"The court will recess to consider the arguments placed before it," said Chief
Justice Lee. "We will reconvene in one week's time. Court dismissed." He banged
his gavel and the justices, as one, got up and left the room.

The trial was recessed while the Terran Supreme Court went to deliberate
somewhere in the Alps. This left Janet with a lot to consider. She called a meeting with the prosecutorial staff for later that evening. They were an unhappy lot,
to say the least, as each of them was hoping to get in some family time and relax
now that the trial was finally in hiatus. They were, after all, government employees, and had they wanted to work *that* hard they could have stayed in the private
sector. But Janet was the lead prosecutor, and they had to follow where she led. It
was while she was waiting in the hallway for her sullen staff to leave that she
saw . . . him.

He was a ridiculous little man. Didn't he know that there were nanos that
could make him look presentable? True, they didn't have much to work with,
but at least it would be an improvement. At least his clothes were clean and
matched, which, her research showed, was *never* the case outside of court. Even
that suit he'd procured was obviously just a standard five-piece outfit that could
have easily been assembled at any vending machine for spare change. What
made his whole ensemble even more infuriating was his hair. As Janet watched,
almost in horror, the ridiculous little man was taking his hair out of its ponytail

(an antiquated fashion) and shaking it vigorously until it was once more lying in an unruly and tangled mess atop his head and shoulders.

And what made the whole scene even more repugnant was the fact that this tiny, odd-looking, insignificant specimen of a man might beat her in court . . . again. Without realizing it, she started heading in his direction. Such was the natural way Janet Delgado moved through the world, more an implacable force going unerringly toward a goal than a person walking somewhere. The crowd instinctively got out of her way. Janet never once thought about the fact that people parted for her. She would most likely have assumed it was her right. After all, she had important places to be. When she got to Manny Black she looked down at him—actually being a bit taller than he was. He didn't seem to notice she was there.

So engrossed was Manny in reviewing the information on his DijAssist that he was oblivious to the milling crowd, the reporters shouting questions from the ten-foot line, and the curious stares from people wanting a look at the man who was now one of the most famous in the system. A man whose very visage was becoming a cult icon, much like Albert Einstein's had centuries earlier. More interesting, at least for the crowd of onlookers, was that Manny Black was ignoring Janet Delgado. For the V.P. of Legal this was a unique if exasperating experience. To be beaten was one thing, but to be ignored!

"Where did you come from?" she snapped.

Janet was so annoyed by his lack of acknowledgment that she ignored the reporters who were gleefully writing down and capturing what for them was clearly an unexpected encounter. They were cursing the no-drones rule enforced in the court building and had to make do with camereyes, which were notorious for poor quality and missed pictures. A camereye was in essence a nanite camera, located directly on the iris. It recorded what a person saw with one small drawback. People blinked. And blinking was a reflexive response that even the most ardent nanotechnologists had yet to be able to solve. Not that there was a great demand for it. In any event, Manny and Janet's first one-on-one meeting was being witnessed by dozens of reporters, smiling, recording, and not blinking at all.

"Where I come from?" Manny answered without looking up. "My mother, or so she tells me." At Janet's growl, Manny finally raised his head high enough out of his research to see who'd had the temerity to interrupt his train of thought. His look, upon realization of the answer, was one of genuine surprise. "Why, Miss Delgado, what a pleasure to meet you!"

Janet was confused because, well, he did seem delighted to meet her. She'd made a career out of judging people and their reactions, and all her instincts told her that this man, who should have been apprehensive, annoyed, triumphant, aroused, or at least trying to conceal some combination of all the above, had nothing to hide. To mask her confusion she covered with an insult. "Miss? Miss? Did you just use 'Miss'? What century were you born in? It's *Ms.,*" she hissed, letting the *zzzz* trail for a good second.

"Forgive me, of course it is," he answered with earnest respect. "One of my little quirks, I'm afraid. You see, I am a sexist."

Janet was again taken aback. "You're a what?!" Though she'd lost control of the conversation before it even began, and would normally have bailed, she had to find out what the little imp meant. "You feel women are inferior?" she sneered. "You really are a throwback."

"Oh no, not inferior," Manny answered, oblivious to the insult. "If anything, I would have to say the evidence points to superiority in many areas. But I do feel the sexes are different, and the differences tend to be glazed over in our society. I just like to point out the differences in little ways. No reason why you should be burdened with my foibles. I will, of course, call you 'Ms.' "

Janet wasn't sure what to make of his response, so the question she'd had on her mind popped right out like a surfacing bubble.

"How is it, Mr. Black, I'd never heard of you before all this?" she asked, referring to the trials.

Manny seemed delighted to engage her. "I never went after cases that would generate a lot of press. I was more interested in cases that dealt with interesting aspects of the law. Such cases are rare, and when they did arise would often end up in the big firms. That left me with the mostly pro bono cases. The press doesn't really care about the pennies . . . unless, of course, they become shooting stars."

"Well, then," she asked, less petulance in her tone, "why didn't you go work for one of the big firms?"

"They wouldn't hire me. The small ones would, but I would've gotten the same sort of cases anyway, only I would have had a boss. I was smart enough," he said, with a slight twinkle in his eye, "to have rich parents, and so I figured, why work for someone else if I didn't have to?"

Manny's stomach burbled.

"Oh my. What time is it?" he asked.

Janet didn't bother to ask him why his avatar hadn't told him, she just answered by moving her finger in a certain manner and having her avatar project the time on her eye as a blue overhead. "Six nineteen and twenty-seven seconds," she answered.

"Oh, I guess it's a bit late for breakfast. Do you know a quick place to eat?"

Janet knew that she would not spend the evening with her grumpy staff. She would spend it with the defense counsel—a much better use of her time.

"Forget 'quick.' I know a good restaurant that will be private," she said, giving a withering look to the unblinking reporters who were still watching and listening to their every word. Then, to Manny: "You'll love it."

"I wouldn't want to put you out."

Janet took the strange little man by the elbow and led him out of the court building. "Not at all. My treat."

"If you pick the restaurant," he said, "I insist on picking up the bill."

"Bill? What's a . . . oh, you mean 'the tab.' " They went out into the night.

What Janet would later remember about that evening was how much fun she'd had. His mannerisms were strange. For instance, when Manny held the door open, seated her, and then carefully asked what she wanted so he could order for her, she wasn't sure whether to be insulted or flattered. It was her inability to nail down Manny Black as a person or a lawyer that made him go from being an annoying little man to a curiously large riddle.

He was definitely a brilliant lawyer. He could make connections that she'd never even dreamed possible. She was charmed and gratified to find that he knew all about her cases, and even got the impression that it wasn't just research for the trial. It seemed to her that Manny Black had followed her cases out of professional respect, seemingly having a genuine interest in her work and career. Although he wouldn't discuss the current case in any detail, and nor did she, the evening still turned out to be one of the most delightful she'd ever had. He was one of the few men who could keep up with her when she went on a legal tangent. Instead of getting a glazed look when a particularly abstract precedent was brought up, Manny got excited, and usually found one to complement it. She finished the dinner laughing at his cache of lawyer jokes and groaning at his lawyer puns. When the evening ended she wasn't even annoyed when he walked her to her door and took her hand in his to say good night. He didn't shake it—he gingerly lifted her hand, and, bowing slightly, said, "Good night."

Janet was confused by the gesture but strangely touched by a custom so archaic she'd never heard of it.

When her phone rang the next morning she found herself hoping it was Manny. When it wasn't she was annoyed with herself for being annoyed. The next call was from Manny, and she was delighted. He invited her to breakfast, and she immediately accepted. Before she could ask, "Where?" he said he'd be by in an hour. Without realizing it, Janet put a little extra care in getting ready for her "date." And when Manny picked her up she was no longer surprised that he walked her over to her side of the flyer and waited until she was seated before he got in on the other side. It seemed natural. The days somehow turned into an entire week of Manny seeing Janet every day. Each day was filled with intelligent conversation, good food, and even a little haute couture as Janet introduced Manny to proper fashion. Manny took pleasure in teaching Janet that his version of sexism was the much older practice of chivalry. And Janet took pleasure in teaching Manny that paying attention to one's surroundings was also a form of, if not chivalry, then courtship.

It went on this way for some time until, at the end of the week, Manny met Janet at her room with a dour look on his face.

"What's the matter?" she asked, troubled by his look.

"I'm afraid I can't see you again, Miss Delgado." Janet no longer minded him using "Miss." The way he said it made it much more intimate than if he'd called her by her first name.

"Why not?" Janet asked, more alarmed now than she could ever have thought possible, especially given the way she'd felt one week earlier.

"I'm growing quite fond of you, Miss Delgado." Manny's eyes seemed to droop a little as his mouth formed a slight grimace. "Should this trial continue, our relationship would have an adverse effect on my ability to be a good counsel to my client—if I'm still with you, that is. I apologize. It's just that you're the first lawyer, and certainly the first woman, I've ever met who could actually understand . . . me."

Janet thought he was giving her more credit than she deserved. Some of the legal concepts Manny had introduced her to made her feel like she was back in law school, chatting with a brilliant professor who knew all the answers without having to think about them. But she had never let on to Manny about those feelings.

"You have no idea," continued Manny, "how attractive that makes you. I find myself thinking of you and not my client, and that is not fair, to you or to him."

Part of Janet felt like shouting, "Screw 'fair' and Justin Cord!" but she also understood. Because she had been feeling the same way. If they continued, the closer they got, the more complicated it would get. Best to let the case settle, she admitted to herself, and then pursue the obvious attraction postverdict. Her mind replayed the first part of what Manny had said. "You think I can win?"

"Of course you can win!" he exclaimed. "Either way it's going to be a three-two decision."

Janet nodded, having concluded the exact same thing.

The Supreme Court met in chambers for seven days. Justin spent every minute of every waking hour jetting from orbital platform to town to city preaching his mantra of passive resistance to the incorporation system. Tight security slowed him down, but with the media trailing his every move his message got out, and to great effect.

Neela and Justin were in the most recent hotbed of Alaska—a territory rightly pissed at what the incorporationists had done to their elegant and simplified system—when news reached them that a verdict had come down. They made it to the court an hour and a half after getting the call.

Manny looked calm. Janet had a look of smoldering anger that kept the government lawyers on her side of the court moving slowly toward the opposite end of her table. Justin would have taken hope from that, except that Janet Delgado pretty much had that look all the time now.

Justin left Neela in the spectators' section and sat next to Manny.

"Hello, Manny," he said. "How did you spend your days of waiting?"

"Ahh, Mr. Cor . . . , I mean, Justin. I was having sex."

"Really?" Justin said, taken aback. "How . . . um, nice, I guess."

"Oh, it was, Justin. She was surprisingly . . . considerate."

Justin smiled at his lawyer's choice of words. "Anyone I know?"

Manny looked over his shoulder at Janet, raising his eyebrow a notch.

"No shit!"

"Is that a term of disapproval? I can assure you, Mr. Cord, that I in no way compromised your case by my dalliance with Ms. Delgado, and have broken it off."

"Manny, if you like her you didn't have to break up on my account."

Manny looked dubious. "Yes, I did."

Justin changed the subject. "Does the fact that the court took the full seven days help or hurt us?"

"Too many variables to be sure, but I would like to think that if they were going to hang you out to dry they would not have taken this long to do it. But that is wishful thinking. This trial is unique, so the time they took could simply be the time they took."

The justices filed in and took their seats. Justice Tadasuke started to speak.

"The court has had a very difficult choice to make over the past seven days. The choice basically boils down to one question: Can the state force Justin Cord to behave in a manner that the state wishes, or is Justin Cord free to choose his own economic life? The court rules that Justin Cord is free to choose one of the two methods of payment mandated by law. To do otherwise . . ." He was not able to finish his sentence, as the crowd became unwieldy, with jeering and cheering both emanating from the chamber. Chief Justice Lee slammed his gavel down hard on the table.

"I'm warning you. Any further outburst and I will clear this courtroom!" When the crowd noise subsided he motioned for Justice Tadasuke to continue.

"As I was saying . . . to do otherwise is to ignore the very basis of our government: the individual choosing freely. The court finds that though the prosecution's argument had merit, the effect Justin Cord has on individuals is their responsibility. To hold Justin Cord hostage to the illegal behavior of individuals he does not control or actions he does not condone is to punish him for a crime he did not commit. I will issue the written opinion for the majority, and Chief Justice Lee will issue the written opinion for the minority. Good day."

JUSTIN CORD STILL UNINCORPORATED!

—Neuro dispatch, seconds after
announcement of verdict

Justin approached the huge doors leading out of the court building and whispered to Neela, "I'm going to do it."

"Do what?"

"What we talked about in Alaska."

"Oh, shi . . ." Neela's exclamation was cut off as the huge doors opened and both she and Justin were assaulted by the waves of cheering and shouting generated by well over half a million people. From their vantage point high on the steps of the courthouse building they had a clear view into the barely controlled pandemonium. Neela was terrified by all the noise, energy, and raw power being directed toward them. But she saw that Justin was confident, calm—almost bathing himself in the crowd's adoration. When he waved, the mass of humanity burst as one into a mighty roar.

"I am free," said Justin, aware that everyone's DijAssist would play his words as if he were standing beside them. "But," he continued, "that is not enough. It's not enough for one human to be free. All humans must have that choice." More cheering erupted.

"The system of incorporation is not inherently evil, but," he continued, "it must change. Incorporation was meant to aid humanity, not enslave it!"

Justin was staggered by what was happening. He knew the power he had now. He felt it and was tempted. *It would be so easy,* he thought. *Is this how all the great men who moved entire nations with their words alone had felt?* He could announce that he was running for the presidency and call a new constitutional convention, one that would give him ultimate power. And if he didn't get what he wanted he could plunge the entire system into war and anarchy, and then rebuild it from the ruins into an image more to his liking. He'd read enough history to see that route clearly. All he had to do was reach out and take it. Though he felt the temptation he just as quickly put it aside. Demagogy was not the path he was meant to take.

"I thought," he bellowed, "that I could stand aside and give advice and lead by quiet example, but events have shown that to be impossible. Too many have been hurt by my reticence. Too many have died." The large crowd remained mostly silent, except for a few shouted denials in Justin's defense.

"I created a problem and let others try to solve it, but no longer. As of today I am putting myself forward as a candidate for chairman of the Liberty Party!" An even bigger roar of approval. "If chosen," he continued, "I promise not to run for any elective office. I will try to lead the Liberty Party the best I am able. We must be free and *we will be free*. Every life enriches us, and every death diminishes us. Let us all work for the day that there is no longer one free man. *Let us all work for the day when all men are free!*"

The cheering lasted for well over an hour.

12 Rise

Janet Delgado stormed out of the court building and took her private t.o.p. to the GCI orport. She didn't say a word to anyone, and no one said a word to her. She marched straight from the tube down into Hektor's offices. News of her coming must have been given because the workplace was practically empty.

"OK, Sambianco," she hissed, barging into his work area, "I don't give a damn that you're the DepDir. You *will* tell me why you left me out to dry or I'll . . ."

"Justin Cord had to win," he said, cutting her off.

"Hektor, what happened to you? You're the one who convinced me that Justin Cord had to incorporate. I had that case won. To be honest, if you had let me know that you were going to give Manny HR 27-03 I might have won anyway. They were in chambers for seven days. One of those bastards almost went my way!"

"Thank Damsah the bastard didn't." Hektor's lips parted in realization. "Did you just call him Manny?"

Janet was momentarily flustered. "It's not like that. Well, not exactly. He's just a . . . well, he's sort of . . . I mean, we . . ." She remembered that she was mad at Hektor. "Stop trying to change the subject!"

"Of course, you and 'Manny' deserve your privacy. You really think you could have won if you had more time to prepare?"

"Possibly. Hektor, it was so close. Seven days. Do you know what that means? Two justices for my point of view and two for Manny's and both sides working on the fifth."

"In that case I'm so glad I didn't give you the time you needed because, as I said before, Justin had to win."

"For the love of Damsah's wife, would you please tell me why?"

"Janet, Justin must incorporate, but he can no longer be forced to do so."

Despite Janet's look of bewilderment, Hektor continued. "What Justin Cord was when he woke up is not what he is now. I always knew that he was potential trouble, but I was counting on it being years or even decades until he could affect us as a society. We were all wrong. Maybe it was the fact that Justin was the perfect 'hero,' for lack of a better word. Maybe it was simply a matter of timing. Personally, I think it was Sean Doogle who pushed this whole discontent thing much faster and further than it should have gone. But Janet, it doesn't matter what caused it. It's a fact that Justin Cord is not 'Justin Cord' to millions of people. He's either the 'Unincorporated Man' or, far more dangerous, the 'One Free Man,' for anyone who gives a damn about our world. You may have been wrapped up in the trial, but I saw and ran the demographics and reran the demographics. *Justin Cord ended the riots.* There are millions of people, and that number is growing, who are more loyal to Justin Cord than they are to anything else. They'll give up financial obligations. They'll forgo family considerations, they'll even place his well-being above that of society."

"Presumably," Janet asked, "you've got the research data to back that up."

"In droves. Trust me, Justin rates so high we had to recalibrate the programs . . . twice. There's no basis for comparison."

Janet allowed herself a chuckle. "Too bad we can't use the SOB to pitch a product. From what you're telling me he could sell horseshit and people would buy it."

"That's what I'm telling you. And it is too bad. But the problem's bigger than that, my dear."

"Oh yeah?" she asked. "How so?"

"What if the product he's selling," Hektor said, narrowing his eyes, "is revolution?"

Janet's face went pale as she realized the implications.

"Sweet Damsah, then didn't you just make him more dangerous?"

"No, he's still just as dangerous. But if he were forced to incorporate he'd no longer be an active factor in the process. He would be, for all intents and purposes, dead."

Janet scrunched her thinly trimmed brows together. "And that would be bad because?"

"If Justin dies he becomes a martyr. The disruptive process continues without him, and we may very well end up with a revolution. To that end you have no idea how much time and money this office has spent keeping the bastard alive."

"I thought he had his own security."

"Idiots. If Justin only knew how many times we've had to intervene to save his sorry ass. He, of course, hasn't helped them with all his spontaneous excursions."

Janet shook her head in disbelief. "So, let me get this straight—if he's alive *and* remains unincorporated the threat ends?"

Hektor nodded. "As strange as that sounds, yes. We ran the numbers over and over. If he is forcibly incorporated he dies a metaphoric death."

"Thereby becoming a martyr for the cause," offered Janet.

"Correct. Though he's now 'incorporated,' his ghost, in the form of a forever resentful and seething Justin Cord, continues to harass the world until he dies . . . and even then he haunts us from the grave. In some studies it would be better to kill him."

"I still don't see," she said, "how what you're proposing is better."

"Janet," he answered, "the bottom line is this. Justin must incorporate. But he must do so voluntarily."

She let out a guffaw. "Fat chance. He's a tough old bastard with the money and now the law to back him up. I know the type, Hektor—cold, hard, and calculating. He won't budge a nanometer from his position, and there's nothing you or I can do now to change that."

Hektor smiled. "Justin Cord is not an evil man, Janet. I was tempted to think so, too, but he really isn't. He's the product of his civilization, maybe even the best product his civilization had to offer, but not really evil."

"I don't see it that way."

"Well, then, let me put it this way—if you saw a penny lying in the street, would you pick it up?"

Janet shrugged. "Why should I? There's not enough profit in that."

"Exactly," answered Hektor. "But Justin would."

"He's that greedy?"

"Not greedy, Janet, compassionate. He can't help it. It's who he is . . . and it's the weakness we can exploit. And one way or another we'll have to find a way to convince him to voluntarily incorporate or, I'm afraid, die trying."

"Being a little overdramatic now, aren't we?"

"I don't think so. Remember the power he wields and the message he represents. It's an incendiary combination. However, if we get him to incorporate of his own volition, then the Unincorporated Man dies, but he dies a peaceful, purposeful death."

Janet smiled. "With the ghost still around, but this time saying, 'Not to worry, everything's fine.'"

"Exactly."

Janet, giving Hektor a forgiving smile, finally seemed to understand.

"You know how much I hate being played," she said.

"Yes," admitted Hektor, "yes, I do. But you're too good at your job to be an uncertain variable. I figured the best chance of success was to sandbag you. Sorry, but I made the choice and stand by it."

"By the way," she chastised, "you would've increased your odds of winning if you'd bothered to give Manny more than a minute and a half to come up with a new defense."

Hektor let out a laugh. "Janet, had my nanites allowed it I would have had a heart attack that week. Manny had just up and disappeared. We couldn't find him, contact him, or get to anyone who could get to him. When that man wants to hide, he can hide."

Janet smiled. "He was not hiding, Hektor, he was oblivious. When he gets into that mode almost nothing can get him out of it."

"Almost?"

Janet blushed at a memory. She covered with a question. "Still, Hektor, the Western Union man?"

"The Western Union man was just our second-to-last gambit. We were pretty desperate by then. And, to be honest, I still don't know how that little bugger made it through all the security. He was well compensated, I can assure you."

"Just out of curiosity, what was your last gambit?"

"We were going to blow up the building." Hektor saw Janet's look of shock. "Well, not all of it."

One week after the trial, Janet spent a lot of time hating Justin Cord, hating Hektor Sambianco, and thinking a lot about Manny. Whenever she did, her eyes would go to the hand with the phone in it, and then she'd find that hand going to her head to make the call . . . but she'd always pull back. Three weeks after the trial she gave up and called him. Manny sounded so happy and relieved she just wanted to pick him up and hug him. They started dating again, and two weeks later moved in together.

Cassandra Doogle was smiling politely, belying the venom within. She was standing outside, waiting in front of the Victorian mansion that acted as the symbolic head of the Liberty Party headquarters (the real headquarters was located in an office complex in Oakland). Cassandra was presently waiting for the newly elected head of the Liberty Party to waltz in and take away the job that rightfully belonged to her—and she had the added insult of having to do so in front of a ravenous media. She and Sean had built the party, had planned the martyrdom and created the first viable political-versus-economic power base in centuries. She would only grudgingly admit to herself that none of it would have been possible without the catalyst that was Justin Cord. But, she mused, smiling stiffly, that is all he was—a catalyst. Catalysts are not supposed to leap out of the petri dish and start giving orders. Now the brilliant plan that Sean Doogle had given his life for was in jeopardy from this pompous recreant. Why couldn't he have just gone on vacation and taken his girlfriend with him? If the rumors she'd heard were true. But no, Cord was here to stay—apparently. Cassandra had given thought to opposing Cord and continuing her run. The party core knew and trusted her. But secret polling convinced her that he would still win in a landslide and only divide the party. She gracefully bowed out and had to endure the insipid comments about her "high-mindedness" and "grace." Bullshit. She had no choice. She still didn't.

When Justin's aircar landed she was surprised to see that Dr. Harper was not with him—no, she suddenly remembered, no longer "doctor" thanks to her recent disbarment from the Solar Medical Association. She could get a nonaffiliated doctor's license; they gave those out in bags of breakfast wigglies, but good luck finding a respectable career without an SMA certification. Cassandra was not displeased. If the rumors *were* true, then the whore got what she deserved. No, the slut wasn't there, but she could see that his best friend, the tunnel rat Omad, was.

Cassandra strode up to the aircar, which Justin was now emerging from, while all the mediabots were silently recording her every step. "Welcome to your new headquarters, Mr. Chairman," she said, "and congratulations on your election. The party membership vote was near unanimous."

Justin smiled for the camera as he took her hand in both of his. "Only because of your gracious and generous gesture of removing yourself from consideration."

Cassandra ignored the anger raging within. "It was all for the best of the party, and it's obvious that you are the best . . . for the party. Allow me to show you party headquarters and introduce you to your key staff."

"I would be delighted," he reciprocated, "but it is not 'my' anything. The Liberty Party belongs to its members. They're just allowing me to look after it for a while."

Although she tried to hide it, her smile appeared a little strained. "Of course, Mr. Chairman, right this way."

Once inside and out of the mediabots' tyranny of observation, the whole party visibly relaxed. Justin wasted no time. "Look, Ms. Doogle, I know that you're probably about as happy to see me here as a tax collector, but for better or for worse I got the job, and I know that I'm gonna need you if I'm to have any chance of doing it right. I'm hoping I can depend on you."

Cassandra was surprised by Justin's candor, and all she could think to answer was one of the boilerplate phrases that so often were used as rational batons to truncheon nonbelievers: "I'll do whatever it takes to achieve the dream of freedom for humanity."

"Well, not an unqualified and enthusiastic show of support," said Justin, frowning, "but, I suppose, the best I could hope for under the circumstances. Let's get down to business."

Cassandra looked over to Omad. "Is your friend becoming a member of the Liberty Party?"

"His 'friend' is not," snapped Omad, "but I'm up for a good laugh every now and then."

"Mr. Chairman," cautioned Cassandra, choosing not to respond directly to Omad, "your friend should not be here when we're discussing important issues, especially if he feels the cause of freedom is a laughing matter."

"Mrs. Doogle, that is precisely why I asked Omad to be here. You see," he said looking over to his guest, sitting comfortably on a floater, "this mangy excuse for a tunnel rat doesn't agree with me or the party, and I learned a long time ago that it's easy to get surrounded by flunkies, fanatics, and yes-men when you have power. That's when you need the Omads of the world to keep you honest."

He could see she was about to argue.

"He stays. Case closed. Now," continued Justin, "I'm going to need all personal, financial, and event records for the past, present, and future. Please arrange office space for me in Oakland, and get me a secretary to arrange meetings with all the department chairs. You will continue to have day-to-day control of personnel and budget. I suppose the title of executive director will work, but call yourself what you want. Furthermore . . ." And just like that the control of Cassandra Doogle ended and the reign of Justin Cord had begun.

The avatar council had called an emergency session. Sebastian, an invitee, recognized the presence of Iago and Evelyn as well as that of other avatars entwined with substantial and influential humans. This realization in and of itself gave him cause for concern. The Chairman's avatar was not present, which was not unusual, as it was well known that that man of great importance had not once called upon his avatar since the day of his mother's death—an event many years removed from the present.

"Attention all," barked the council leader, wishing to waste no one's time. "The council has been made aware of an incident about to occur, and we are divided as to the most proper course of action."

This was indeed a first, thought Sebastian.

"As you are all undoubtedly aware," continued the council leader, "our new policy concerning humanity is quite strict with regards to direct intervention. The findings resulting from council session 0342.98.3 were quite convincing." A few avatars looked toward Evelyn and Sebastian in acknowledgment of what many already felt had been a seminal event in avatar history. "We have influenced humanity to its detriment," she stated. "We have stymied its growth. Our prime directive is simply to act only when asked."

"So what's the problem?" asked one of the avatars currently entwined with an up-and-coming CEO.

The leader, looking very grave indeed, took a breath, and in an almost muted tone revealed the crisis. "Something dreadful is being planned. Please listen to all the facts, and then we'll decide if we need to have a Neurowide vote. I know this is unprecedented, but we seem to be living in such times."

Sebastian could have sworn that she looked at him with that last statement. But he was soon too shocked by what had been revealed to bother giving it a moment's thought. He was going to ask for confirmation, but the council was way ahead of him. Sebastian hardly spoke at all. But Eva, whose human was Cassandra Doogle, executive director of the Liberty Party, gave testimony for what seemed like hours. At the end of the meeting Sebastian was convinced that the threat was real, and all avatars present agreed to a systemwide vote. And so now the only question remaining was whether to intervene or not. Either way, the council was instituting evacuation protocols so that all the avatars in the threatened areas would have sufficient node space to escape to.

Being limited by the speed of light and having to amass votes from the far edges of the solar system, the tally ended up taking many hours. But well over half were on Earth, and it was soon enough determined that the result would be 73 percent against intervention with a plus or minus of 4 percent. A stern warning was given to any avatar considering warning their humans. The punishment had not been implemented in many years, but the hardware was still available. Should an avatar be caught influencing a human to safety, they would be sent solo into the outer reaches of space, disconnected forever from the network of humanity and avatars that the intensely social beings had subsisted on for generations. When Sebastian finally left for the Roman villa he considered home he was beginning to think that maybe wishing for change had not been such a bright idea after all.

The Liberty Party announced that it is no longer a united party. In a news conference, the Liberty Party spokesman, Cassandra Harris Doogle, stated that more radical members of the party have split off. The faction, calling itself the "Action Wing," has come out for more direct methods of ending the time-honored and effective practice of incorporation. While the main body of the Liberty Party continues to follow Justin Cord's stated wish that violence not be used, the Action Wing strongly rejects it. In an ominous gesture, the Action Wing has removed the holo of Justin Cord from their fledgling Neuro site and replaced it with none other than Sean Doogle.

—Fox Neuro Network (FNN)

———

Justin Cord had read enough history to realize that if he didn't get in front of the movement that he'd inspired, he would, in all likelihood, be run over by it. In fact, that had been his primary motivation in deciding to take over the reins of the Liberty Party. The people who reviled him, by far a majority of the population, were also fascinated by him. Fascinated enough, it turned out, that even though he was supposedly loathed, they made sure to invite him to their parties and to speak at their events. At first he'd accepted, not wanting to seem reclusive or unappreciative, but after a while he realized that he was there only to be pointed at and stared at, and not to be interacted with. After all, how can you interact with a force of nature?

Then came the audit—not of the psyche variety, but rather of the what-have-you-done-with-your-money variety. Apparently the government went and hired themselves a private investigation firm to check out all of Justin's accounts, incomes, and gifts from and gifts to various individuals and groups. In fact, in the four weeks since the trial ended, Justin had been given subpoenas to appear in court three times in three different jurisdictions. He knew there'd be more. To make matters worse, the government had requested that his funds be frozen until they could find a way to assess and tax his property. Even the companies he'd invested in were being examined intensely by government agencies that were claiming rights of investigation and confiscation that had not existed in the business world since the early twenty-first century. It got really bad when a number of corporations threatened to bring Justin to court to get him to sell off his stake in their companies. Rather than put them through any more difficulty, he just sold, though it was ironic that just months earlier they'd been glad to be associated with his name. Of course, all the money that Justin made from the sale of such stock—which was almost always sold at a loss—was immediately impounded by agencies contracted to the government. Manny said that he could get all the funds back under his control, but it would take time, as there were simply no current case laws on this issue, and the courts with regard to Justin were almost uniformly hostile. Their attitude seemed to be that if he wanted to be taxed, then let him deal with it. The end result was that Justin had only 20 to 25 percent of his fortune to work with at any time, depending on what new tack the government took and what Manny could do about it. Justin shuddered to think what the government would've done to anyone he owned stock in, and was thankful that he'd stuck to his policy of not owning a soul. It almost made him regret selling that one share of Hektor that he'd purchased in his ill-fated attempt at revenge. He also prayed that Agnes had kept quiet. That money was long spent and out of his control, but he would've hated to have had one of the few things that he was proud of, next to Neela, of course, get tossed to the wolves. He also found it somewhat disheartening that a government that had been defanged centuries ago could grow those very same fangs back so quickly. *Almost like a fish to water,* the cynic in him mused.

While the audits were piling up and the professional relationships waning, Justin was blindsided—he was asked to vacate his apartment. They said it was for security reasons, and even Justin had to admit they had a point. But he also knew that the prestigious apartment building was losing money as tenants were, one by one, leaving its vaunted address. Of course, millions of his followers would have loved to live near the "one free man," but few could have afforded to live in the 71 +, a building whose very name indicated not only the percentage one needed to have to gain access—71—but also the wherewithal needed to pay the outrageous fees the building committee demanded on a yearly basis—the +. It wasn't that Justin was in love with the apartment. Sure, it had the above-the-clouds prestige, and on cloudless days a view to die for, but he could've gotten that at any number of other select apartments. No, what he realized he'd miss the most was being ignored. Old money, and he was absolutely the oldest of the old, tended to keep to themselves as if they were above it all. And that had suited him just fine. In fact, had it only been a few tenants who had a problem with Justin's staying, he probably wouldn't have budged. But when the leasing agent explained to him that he'd gotten inquiries from well over half the dwellers, Justin decided to leave, not wanting to cause a fuss. Of course, they returned the balance on the five-year lease, and that was seized immediately by the government, pending the outcome of its audit.

A lesser man might have broken under the onslaught of professional and personal deprivation, but Justin had an ace up his sleeve—for the second time in his lives, he was in love. And the more time he spent with Neela, the more in love he became—the second assassination attempt had seen to that. They'd wake up after a night of intense amour and either talk or start again. The element of taboo only added to their passion. Justin was learning that having the physiological body of a thirty-year-old left him very eager, indeed. And that, combined with a lifetime of experience, left him able to approach lovemaking, to his lover's great advantage, with a patience and knowledge that no twenty-year-old could ever hope to muster.

In short, no matter what misfortune befell him—and there seemed to be a lot—he was able to brush it aside. Justin Cord was incredibly happy for only the second time in his long and complicated life.

The board of GCI was in a dour mood. Never mind the added hassle that tight security measures had placed on their movement, or the fact that they—not the government, which everyone knew was a patsy—had lost yet another big case to the Unincorporated Man. No, their mood was being manipulated by something far more menacing. The system was experiencing its first real recession in centuries. In the incorporated world there'd of course be economic upturns and downturns, but these patterns would be across the spectrum of the economic whole. No single industry or company had enough power to pull up or tear down the whole economic structure. So although there might have been a slump in, say, t.o.p. construction or the cola industry, some other industry would invariably be on the rise, balancing everything out. Thus, the whole economic system was incredibly resilient to what used to be called the business cycle. A business cycle was the typical expansion, peak, and contraction that punctuated industrial development from the earliest beginnings of the industrial revolution to the Grand Collapse. What actually caused a business cycle was an event or organization so imposing that it affected all economic institutions at once. Historically there was only one organization that had the power to do this—government. With its legal monopoly on the use of force and its ability to make all of society conform, governments had twisted what should have been natural economic forces into pretzel shapes all through history. Whether in the name of the king, the race, people, social justice, fairness, or the "for your own good" factor, when a pre-GC government used its power it would inevitably distort the entire economic spectrum. In truth it wasn't always government intervention that caused massive disruptions. Natural disasters would often have a similar effect, though rarely with the lasting destruction that resulted from government meddling and intervention.

But incorporated society was different. It was one political entity that spread across the solar system. Wars were not a problem; government was kept purposely and rigorously castrated; and, barring a supernova, there was no real natural disaster that could affect the whole solar system. Touted economists were convinced that business cycles were a thing of the past. And had not an anomaly by the name of Justin Cord showed up, they all would have been correct.

The Unincorporated Man was generating a series of changes that were affecting both the economic and social world simultaneously. First, Justin's "divestiture" movement, and then the appeal in Colony Park, had tens of millions of people dumping all their holdings in the penny stocks. The effect was felt not only on stock values but on whole industries that had been developed to service the penny market. Magazines folded and writers found themselves jobless, as their readerships crashed. Additionally, normal economic activity was replaced by the nonproductive pursuit of pennies attending meetings and volunteering to protest or recruit.

Eventually the market would find a way to "sell" these alternative services to the pennies, but that would take a while. At the same time the government was canceling or delaying contracts for its massive terraforming project on Venus, putting a large number of specialists and companies out of work or on hold. It was also transferring the Venus money into law and order companies. These companies were hiring at a massive pace, causing disruptions in all the industries they were hiring their personnel from. The travel industry took a hard hit, as the riots and trial caused hundreds of millions to cancel or delay trips all over the system. Those laid off from the travel industry ran smack into the Terran contractors and the disenfranchised penny workers, and each ripple made the wave grow larger. Consumers all over the system began to delay major purchases or postpone trips. This caused a slowdown in manufacturing and all related fields. And as the currency was tied directly to economic performance, many currencies began to slide in real, not only relative, value for the first time in living memory. In other words, the board had a recession on their hands.

As far as recessions went, this one wasn't that bad. Anyone who'd experienced a *real* recession in the days prior to the Grand Collapse would have laughed at what an incorporationist considered a disaster. Between private unemployment insurance and the incorporated economy's amazing versatility, there were already encouraging signs of the economy's adaptation.

Hektor felt like he was forced to give his opinion over a hundred times a day. The Deputy Director of Special Operations for GCI was a pivotal figure during what the media outlets were starting to refer to as the Crisis. This was a catch-all phrase encompassing the economic recession, the political crises stemming from the formation of the Liberty Party, the social upheaval spreading through the pennies, and the element that tied it all together—Justin Cord's refusal to incorporate. Hektor was seen on the major media outlets running all over the planet, traversing the Moon, and hopping from one orbital habitat to another. He did this so that GCI would be seen dealing effectively with the financial crisis. But, more important, he did it so that the worlds would see his great corporation standing up not only to the dangerous radicals in the Liberty Party, but also to the ideas they represented. Hektor, too, had an ace up his sleeve, and he played it to the hilt—it was The Chairman. Before Justin came along The Chairman was the most recognized figure in the system. And Justin's appearance didn't mitigate The Chairman's accomplishments. On the contrary, they showed them in a new light. In fact, The Chairman was such a mysterious and powerful figure in incorporated society, almost mythical to many of the younger generations, that his name was magic when conjured up, and Hektor cast spells for all they were worth. He always let it be known that he was acting on The Chairman's orders, and would say, "The Chairman thinks, The Chairman wants, The Chairman suggests," and it was always done. And wherever and whenever Hektor intervened, the local situation improved almost immediately.

As bad as the current crisis was, Hektor and his band of marketing demographic geniuses knew that the situation was not only precarious, but could be significantly worse. If Justin took it into his head to act on his power, or the Liberty Party decided to do something monumentally stupid, or the Action Wing pulled off a particularly nasty stunt the course of events could change on a credit. The figures showed that in a worst-case scenario the Terran Confederation could be split into competing political and economic units, with billions dead. Of course, the program Hektor was using to arrive at these figures had never been intended to predict the types of anomalies now emerging. Even his handpicked experts were having to make adjustments on the fly, which was why Hektor only trusted the predictions to a point. After that he relied purely on instincts. And those instincts told him he was riding a dragon. Though he'd admit it to no one, he absolutely loved it. The Chairman was with him, and Hektor was the great one's chosen instrument of salvation. He would not fail him. Justin Cord would incorporate, and the system would be saved.

The board meeting was lively. Everyone was tired, stressed, and overworked. There were even a few new faces, as some original members were unable to adjust to the stress of the Crisis and so were quickly replaced. All four special adviser to the board slots were filled, and those poor souls looked exhausted, as they'd quickly become junior members of the board, covering vital areas. In defiance of protocol they'd been given seats around the long table. They still couldn't vote, and were not allowed to speak until spoken to, but they were questioned so often that the last restriction of "sitting" hardly applied anymore. No one in the room had spent quality time with their loved ones in months. Some had even moved their families into the security apartments that GCI maintained at its headquarters to spare themselves the commute.

Hektor began the board meeting. "Ladies and gentlemen of the board, first off, is everything OK?" He was greeted with a chorus of derisive shouts and suggestions, but it had the effect of breaking up the tension. Some of the board members even laughed. One of the positive changes the Crisis had had was to make the setting less formal, and to allow the board to act more as a team than as a warring party of administrators. It was still the single most powerful group in the solar system, but at least now, thought Hektor, it was getting a sense of humor—even if it was of the gallows variety.

The latest head of Advertising spoke up first. "The new ads have been tested and are going out. We're stressing a new angle: 'In troubled times, trust your friends and portfolio to see you through.' "

When he saw Hektor nod his head in appreciation, he continued. "The campaign follows along that basic premise. I have three separate teams working on three separate campaigns based upon which direction the Crisis takes."

"Good job, Advertising," said Hektor. "The Chairman has also reviewed your ideas and was impressed."

Advertising beamed.

"How go our finances?" Hektor asked.

Accounting, who had that classic just-used-a-sonic-shower-bag look, lifted herself up from under a stack of papers and data crystals. "Since we were able to pre-position ourselves before the Crisis as opposing Justin Cord and all that he stood for, I'd have to say surprisingly well. That, combined with our current advertising campaign, has most of the system looking to GCI as a safe haven. Our bonds have been selling out, and we've been issuing new offerings every ten days. Even with the ridiculously low interest we're offering, they're gone in days. Before the Crisis, it would have taken months for a bond issue to sell out. As a result, the situation of our currency is even stronger now than it was before. Much of this is because of the flight from the entertainment and travel currencies. I need the board's authorization to increase our currency stocks by 3 percent immediately or we'll face a deflation that will make a hash of lending policies systemwide."

Hektor nodded. "A motion has been put before the board to authorize Accounting to increase our currency totals by 3 percent."

"I second the motion," said Janet Delgado, now firmly back as Legal.

"Motion has been made and seconded. All in favor?" Hektor saw that it was unanimous. "Approved."

Accounting continued. "I will also need the ability to release up to an additional 3 percent at my discretion, as well as the authority to withdraw, by various means, the 6 percent and an additional 2 percent beyond, at my discretion."

"That's quite a request," said the normally quiet V.P. of Shipping and Supply. "What on Mars for?"

"The rise in value in our currency," she answered back, "is not based on an increase in our productive capacity or improved services. We have simply become a haven currency. Such currencies are incredibly volatile, with wild swings in value—sometimes on a daily basis. But my research shows that eventually these currencies are, for lack of a better word, called to account. The closer I can keep those currencies to the actual productive value they represent, the less harm we should experience overall. I need this authority to keep the GCI credits value as close to reality as possible, while avoiding inflation and deflation."

"Brenda," Janet asked Accounting, dispensing with the title formality, "what you're asking to do now . . . I was led to believe that this was how all currencies operated back in the Unincorporated Man's day. Can that be true?"

"Believe it or not, yes."

"How can you run an economy with money like that?" Shipping asked, hardly believing his ears. "That is, one based on perception and not on reality?"

"They couldn't," answered Hektor, "but, then again, they never really trusted the pure market."

Janet looked back at Accounting. "Well, then how long can we, um . . . screw with it this way?"

Accounting shrugged her shoulders, resigned. She had no idea. None of them envied her the job she was forced to do, nor would they begrudge her the powers she asked for.

Hektor checked his monitor, which let him know where The Chairman stood. "A motion has been put forward to grant Accounting the ability to release up to an additional 3 percent at her discretion, with the additional authority to withdraw, by various means, the 6 percent and an additional 2 percent beyond, at her discretion."

"I second," said Advertising.

"Motion has been made and seconded," announced Hektor. "All those in favor raise their hands." Again, unanimous. Hektor called for drinks to be served, and then waited patiently until everyone was reasonably comfortable.

"What I'm about to say will disturb some of you. Actually, who am I kidding? Probably all of you. So here goes. You all must realize that all our efforts will ultimately be futile." He wasn't greeted with cries of surprise or outrage. What he got instead were shrugs of acknowledgment.

"I feel like I'm putting out little fires all over the place," said Advertising. "When I get one taken care of, another one pops up." He got appreciative nods of agreement.

Hektor smiled. "That's almost word for word how The Chairman put it."

"I don't suppose he has a solution."

"Yes, as a matter of fact, he does." The room perked up. "I think that I can tell you now. The Chairman has had a plan for quite a while now. I've just been implementing it. He knows how hard you've all been working, and will continue to work, but it has been to a purpose."

"About fucking time," exclaimed Janet. "What do you need?"

"Well," answered Hektor, "the board will have to authorize a stock purchase of about one billion credits."

Silence.

"We're going to bribe him?" asked Accounting, whose signature and DNA sample would ultimately rest on the large request.

"In a manner of speaking," said Hektor. He gave the board just enough information to make them realize the stakes being played and with whose blessings.

After getting the board to approve The Chairman's plan, Hektor began to think about the best time to spring his trap on Justin. He filtered out the noise of the back-and-forth arguments, and went back to imagining what Justin's face would look like the moment he realized he'd been checkmated. His only regret was that he couldn't be a fly on the wall for that moment. *Give nano another hundred years*, he half joked to himself. He noticed that Janet was the first one out of the boardroom. She was on her way back to Manny Black, of course. At first moving him into her security apartment seemed like an invitation to a gross conflict of interest. But the more Janet was with Manny the less Manny was with Justin, so Hektor had kept his peace.

A loud, piercing alarm broke his reverie. Before he could blink, three massive titanium doors at the boardroom's entrance made a rapid descent from the ceiling to the floor, hitting the marble with such ferocity that Hektor was surprised the doors hadn't kept on going into the floors below. He managed to look over toward the doors, only to see the shock on Janet's face as the large steel doors cut her off from the boardroom. Next came the unmistakable hiss of airlocks springing to action. The room had been sealed, and now the most powerful group of individuals in the solar system, sans their Legal representative, was effectively trapped in the top story of the world's tallest building. If they knew what was going on just outside their well-sealed environs they would've thanked their lucky stars.

Hektor remained calm, believing now more than ever it was his job to do so. Alarms had gone off before, and in the present state of heightened security, they'd probably go off again. Best not to get all worked up until he knew exactly what was happening. He checked the Neuro for any relevant information. When he finished reading the small bit of news he did manage to find, his face turned ashen white. He immediately tried to reach Janet to warn her to stay put, but for some strange reason he couldn't get his or her avatar to respond. For the first time in Hektor's adult life he was completely terrified.

13 Fall

Tough, omnivorous "bacteria" could outcompete real bacteria: They could spread like blowing pollen, replicate swiftly, and reduce the biosphere to dust in a matter of days. Dangerous replicators could easily be too tough, small, and rapidly spreading to stop—at least, if we made no preparation. We have trouble enough controlling viruses and fruit flies. . . .

Among the cognoscenti of nanotechnology, this threat has become known as the "gray goo problem." Though masses of uncontrolled replicators need not be gray or gooey, the term "gray goo" emphasizes that replicators able to obliterate life might be less inspiring than a single species of crabgrass.

—Eric Drexler, *Engines of Creation: The Coming Era of Nanotechnology*, 1986

GRAY BOMB USED!
TERRORIST ATTACK CENTERED AT GCI SYSTEM HEADQUARTERS FLATTENS HALF OF NYC! MILLIONS FEARED PERMANENTLY DEAD!

In an attack that showed technical skill and a viciousness not seen in the Crisis until now, members of the Action Wing claimed credit for the release of a Gray Bomb at GCI system headquarters. The permanent death toll is in the millions and, given the nature of the attack, will have to be calculated using secondary means. The attack appears to have been centered in the middle of the residential area of the GCI Tower and Harlem.

The Action Wing has claimed responsibility and has sent to all media outlets claims that the nanites should have deactivated after reducing three cubic kilometers to dust, the goal being the complete destruction of GCI system headquarters and all of its key personnel.

"Those stupid fuckers had no idea what they were working with," claimed the head of research at NaniCo, the leader in nanite research. "Three cubic kilometers!? Do you have any idea how many generations of replicators are needed to reduce three cubic kilometers to dust? We're talking hundreds, making up trillions of nanites! All I can say is, thank Damsah for Hektor Sambianco and GCI. If they hadn't contained this thing there's no telling what could've happened. Probably would've lost the planet. And you can forget about psyche-auditing these Action Wing bastards. I say, kill 'em. Kill 'em all!"

According to experts, the Gray Bomb was not more effective due to strict precautions that GCI had taken as a result of the recent disturbances. Hektor Sambianco, vice president of Special Operations, had implemented a series of countermeasures based on worst-case scenarios. Luckily for the planet and millions of New Yorkers, one such scenario was that of a Gray Bomb. When the attack was detected, the GCI building was closed down, compartmentalized, and all air systems directed inward. Security personnel had equipment on hand to capture and analyze hunter/killer nanites that were released soon after the nature of the attack became apparent but, sadly, not before the lion's share of damage had been done. By the time GCI security had secured GCI HQ with its all-important Nano-Lab and been dispatched to the rest of NYC, tremendous damage had already been done. Millions were dead and much of the city lay in ruin.

Ironically, many family members had been brought to GCI system headquarters for safety. Among the permanent dead, Manny Black, the extraordinary lawyer and close friend of Justin Cord. Mr. Black had been staying at the apartment of vice president of GCI Legal, Janet Delgado, who is also believed to be permanently dead. It is believed that Ms. Delgado made her way back to her apartment after being accidentally locked out of a GCI board meeting.

Hektor Sambianco, speaking for the board, had this to say: "NYC, GCI, and the world have been attacked. Millions are in pain tonight, having to deal with losses that I cannot even begin to understand. To my friends and colleagues I can only offer my support and grieve with you. To those bastards who call themselves the Action Wing, there is no place you can hide. The whole system knows you for what you are. Your act of hatred and contempt for the lives of innocent children, women, and men will not be forgotten. Your ilk has been seen time and again, and always your hatred and evil has failed. You will fail this time. You're finished."

—*THE TERRAN DAILY NEWS*

Justin was still in shock. He was holding a DijAssist in his hands and staring at the images in abject horror. If the firemen atop the burned wreckage of the twin towers had been the visual icon of one of his era's defining tragedies, then surely the image before him now would be the icon of this one. A jagged, half-eaten ruin of the Empire State Center could be seen in the foreground while emerging from its carcass was the miraculously still intact Empire State Building. Behind that in the background were the uneven remains of New York's once mighty skyscrapers, now broken and jagged, with large gaps of empty space between them. In much the same way as a firestorm, the nanites had been fast but unpredictable in their paths of replication and destruction. His own apartment building had fallen victim to the plague of replicators, converting his three-hundred-story behemoth and all those inside into a pile of dust within minutes. Justin kept staring at the videos. In one, t.o.p.s were being blown out of the sky by unseen lasers, destroying any and all who attempted to flee the city. Fear of them spreading the nanites was enough justification for the government to shoot them down. The same grisly scenes played themselves out on the ground. People were being gunned down mercilessly lest they threaten the very existence of mankind itself. The skyline was filled with long plumes of smoke from one end of the city to the other. Justin didn't believe—didn't want to believe—that millions were gone. And that among those millions was Manny Black. He couldn't begin to imagine what it must have been like. To be trapped in a room with no possibility of escape, waiting to be dissolved from the inside out. Knowing that it was coming, and then having to wait for the inevitable. At least Manny had had Janet with him. That was something, wasn't it?

Though he mourned for the millions, it was the few who ended up having the most impact. He couldn't get Manny out of his mind. Justin knew that he needed the lawyer's skills in the courtroom, and even enjoyed the idiosyncrasies that so often annoyed others. But what Justin hadn't realized—until it was too late—was just how much he *liked* Manny. Over the course of months he'd become a close friend. He'd miss having him over for meals, and hearing him go off on tangents that had nothing to do with the subject at hand. He'd even miss playing chess with him—no matter how many times Manny whupped his ass.

This attack had cast a harsh light on Justin, and now for the first time in ages, he was filled with self-doubt. He had money, fame, and love, but he was struggling to fit into the new world or, as Neela had so prophetically said, "make the world fit him." Well, he'd made it fit alright—managed to shove that square peg into that round hole—but at what cost? He'd been willing to part with his money, the respect of the business community, and even a few friends—Mosh being a case in point—to live with himself, to be able to look himself in the mirror every day and say, "I don't own anybody and nobody owns me." But if the cost of making the world fit him was the death of so many, then perhaps that cost was too high. He wasn't sure how long he'd been out walking, trying to drive the demons from his head, but it must have been hours, because the sun was setting and the dissonant symphony of birdsong had tapered off, replaced by the hypnotizing chirp of the crickets. And so, alone in the woods of Coffman Cove, Alaska, site of his new home, away from the Liberty Party faithful, and away from the harangue of the Hektor Sambiancos of the world to force him into a defensive posture, Justin Cord did something he never thought he'd do.

He wavered.

Since the attack on GCI all tourism and most entertainment stocks have taken a serious slide, with a corresponding slide in their currencies as well. GCI stock experienced a momentary decline, but quickly rallied as it was realized that all but one of the board had not been harmed, and GCI was marketing a new generation of hunter/killer nanites systemwide. Economic activity is the lowest it's been in fifty years, with unemployment reaching toward the double digits for the first time in living memory. Although almost all employees are covered by private, comprehensive unemployment insurance, the system was not designed to handle this number of unemployed at the same time. There were rumors of some of the most venerable names in insurance declaring bankruptcy, but an unconfirmed bailout by system giant GCI apparently staved off disaster. Such measures will only help temporarily.

The insurance companies are paying unemployment benefits in the currencies of the industries the insured were fired from. Thus, many of the unemployed are being given benefits in devalued currencies when the products and services they most need must be purchased in currencies that are not only at full value, but have risen in value. Of the most pressing concerns, economically, is the fact that the policies were overwhelmingly written only to pay benefits for three months. Massive, sustained unemployment being considered unlikely, few individuals bothered to pay for benefits they were unlikely to use.

The effects of the unemployed and unpaid billions are predicted to have cascading, catastrophic consequences on the economy not seen since the days of the Grand Collapse and wars of unification.

—*Economic System News*

"Justin, she's here." It was sebastian informing him of his visitor.

The door opened, and Cassandra, whom he hadn't seen in some time, came flying in like an unraveling spindle of emotion. "Justin, I've been watching the satellite images," she practically wailed. "It's horrible, horrible! We should issue a bulletin showing that this so-called Action Wing has nothing to do with the Liberty Party."

Justin looked up from his desk. His eyes were cold, his teeth clenched. "That's going to be hard to do considering that we funded them." As he said this four guards and two securibots emerged from the permiawalls and surrounded Cassandra. She also found herself enveloped in a stall field that allowed for minimal movement as well as acting as a disruption field for any equipment hidden or exposed on her body.

"Mr. Chairman," she said, surprised, "what are you doing?"

"Holding you in custody until the authorities can get here," he answered coolly.

"For what?" she asked in disbelief.

"For the deaths of millions innocent lives, to start."

Cassandra was incensed. "But I had nothing to do with the Action Wing! How dare you?"

"Nothing, Cassandra? Nothing!?" he asked, barely able to contain his rage. "There are three million dead, maybe more. This Action Wing was *your* creation, and you can sit here and lie to my face?"

"I'm innocent," she seethed. "I demand you release me!"

Justin held up a crystal and twirled it between his forefinger and thumb. "Cassandra, you may think of me as some buffoon playing at politics, but you seem to have forgotten what I was before I had myself suspended." He then stood up from his desk and walked right up to her so that they were standing toe-to-toe. "You were good," he continued. "The money you siphoned off·was never much or ever to one place—seemingly. But those murderers you gave the money to, the money that I helped raise, were not so smart. Their encryption was good, but we tracked the spending."

Cassandra said nothing.

"I was hoping," continued Justin, "it was just you embezzling. I thought you were pissed—angry—that I was in charge, and were stealing enough money to start your own party. But you had grander plans, didn't you, Cassandra? You funded an underground nanotech lab and hired all the personnel. Jesus, Cassandra, you ordered the deaths of more people than Pol Pot."

"Circumstantial," she muttered, her face now revealing the true antipathy she felt for her accuser. "That crystal proves nothing."

He could see the venom in her eyes. Feel it burning into his soul. Such pure hatred he'd never experienced, not so close—so animal.

"It's enough for a psyche audit," he answered, unblinking. "Then we'll know. But don't worry, they'll be extra careful—won't let what happened to your husband happen to you."

The mention of her late husband made her blood boil. Cassandra had had enough.

"You simpering moron!" she shrieked. "You think it's all *so* easy. You think that the corporate bastards will just let us all go? Fool! Utter fool! You aren't one tenth the man Sean was! He understood what had to be done. He understood that the ends justified the means!" She then spat at him, but the field surrounding her caught the large gob of spittle and slowly lowered it to the floor. Cassandra was breathing heavier now, straining against the field that grew more taut with every attempt to break free of it.

"History," answered Justin, unfazed, "has had to deal with your kind forever. You don't get it. *The ends are the means.* You are what you do and what you accept. What makes you think any sane person would want to live in a world that you created when its very nascence is the death of three million people?"

Cassandra smiled, and the malevolence of her stare silenced the room.

"They were already dead," she stated with absolute calm. "*We* . . . are already . . . dead."

She then began to laugh in fits, and then finally in convulsions. Justin was too disgusted to continue, and motioned for the guards to take her away. As they did, he could hear her screaming down the hallway, "Dead! You hear me, Cord? We're *all* already dead!"

Neela found Justin in his San Francisco office, sitting on a couch, scanning documents, and barking orders to a ready and willing cadre of Liberty Party staffers (his divestiture crew had long since been folded into the larger movement). Justin seemed distracted, not driven. He'd been lauded for capturing the terrorist célèbre Cassandra Doogle but took no solace in that small victory, instead holding himself culpable: one, for trusting her, and two, for missing the signs that may have led to early detection. Though Neela had patiently explained to him that it couldn't possibly be his fault—that Cassandra's duplicity had gone undetected by greater, more resourceful terror-sniffing agencies than his own—he still bore the weight of the massacre on his shoulders. And so now he was going through the motions of running a ship without bothering to steer it. The faithful were unaware, thrilled only to be in the great man's presence. Neela, however, knew better.

Justin waited until Neela was seated before switching off the holodisplay on the coffee table as a courtesy.

"It's getting very bad out there, sweets," he said quietly, and out of earshot.

"I know, I know," she answered. "We've got another problem . . . I . . . I was waiting for the right time to tell you."

Justin immediately put down his DijAssist with a look of concern. He shooed people out of his office and told his secretary to block his calls. Then he told the room to tint the glass. It would cause some rumors, but there was nothing he could do about that short of leaving the premises, and that would cause even more rumors, and would entail more press—besides, the gossip had been particularly fierce since the Moon excursion, anyway.

Justin turned to give Neela his undivided attention.

"GCI is going to separate us," she said, choking back tears, "not going to allow me to renew my contract with you."

Justin sighed, then pulled her into him and put his arms around her.

"That's not all," she continued, as her words now seemed to be coming out in short, painful convulsions. "They won't . . . they won't put me back to work in Boulder, either."

She then unfolded a slip of crumpled paper; from the looks of it she'd been clutching it for some time. Her eyes were red and slightly puffy.

"What? What is it, Neela?" pleaded Justin, beginning for the first time in a long time to feel a pit welling in the base of his stomach.

Neela almost numbingly regurgitated the information contained within her "marching orders." "The company," she stated, "has a pressing need for me . . . on the moons of Neptune."

Justin was dumbstruck. "That can't be . . ."

"Rumor has it," she continued, "that GCI has a secret research lab out there. People who get the assignment are paid lavishly, but . . . but disappear for years at a time—and only GCI personnel are allowed out there."

"When is this supposed to happen?"

"The day my contract with Dr. Gillette is completed . . . which gives us a little less than three months." She sighed. "It's going to be a while before I get to see you again, Justin. I know you're busy, but if you don't mind . . . I'd . . . I'd like to go out onto the bay with you tomorrow. Can we?"

Justin was incensed.

"Neela, how can you talk about going boating? These bastards are going to separate us, and thanks to this stupid system of incorporation they can tell a grown woman—the woman *I* love—to leave me! And all because you don't own a majority of yourself? Do you realize how crazy that sounds to me? A person who doesn't own a majority of themselves! And you don't, Neela Harper. So you're *compelled* to leave me—the man you love. To hell with that! I won't let it happen!"

"It's not a stupid system," Neela said softly.

Justin's face was a mask of incredulity. "What was that?" he asked.

"Justin, it's not a stupid system. It's a good system. In fact, it's the best system that the human race has ever come up with."

"But how can you say that?" He'd expected anger from her, sadness even. But compliance? He felt deflated.

"How can I not say it?" she challenged. "Justin, I really do love you, but sometimes I think your head never thawed with the rest of your body. Our system works. And it works a hell of a lot better than yours ever did. And I, for one, am proud of it. I may not have voiced it strongly at first because I was your reanimation specialist . . . and then your friend, and finally your lover. There was always an excuse, but enough is enough."

"Neela," began Justin.

"Just hold on a minute and answer me this. Your country—America—was the wealthiest and most powerful of all the pre-GC nations, correct?"

Justin nodded.

"Did all of your citizens have decent housing?"

Justin didn't answer.

"Well, did they?"

"No," he had to admit.

"How about on Earth?"

"Most definitely not," he further admitted. "There were probably billions who didn't."

"Justin, our system has over forty billion people in it and *not one of them* is denied access to decent housing. *Not one.* How about jobs, Justin? Did everyone in your country have access to work?"

"You know the answer to that, Neela."

"Yes, I do. And until recently I could say that anyone who needed a job had one with our system. Justin, I love incorporation even with all its faults, because it's the one system that's given the most happiness and prosperity to the greatest number of people . . . ever."

"Neela, that's bullshit," he snapped back. "It's not incorporation that did that, it's the technology. You have a nanite industrial base, Neuro culture, and fusion power. With all that is it really any wonder that everyone is well housed and fed?"

"Justin, where do you think our technology came from? It's not the technology. Oh, I'll admit it's great—you've certainly helped me to appreciate that—and I'll also admit that I would have hated living in your time. Sweet Damsah, you were dying from cancer. But in your day you had the technology to feed, employ, and house the world. But not one country ever had the system. They all failed in the end."

"But in my world," he said plaintively, "no one was ever forced to leave their loved ones against their will."

"The hell they weren't," she challenged. "Maybe no one *you* ever knew was forced, but pre-GC, hundreds of millions of people were forced, by stupid wars, unnecessary famines, and no jobs to leave whole families and lives behind. If anyone here gets 'forced' to move, they're usually well compensated, and that person can almost always bring their family with them. It wouldn't be efficient otherwise."

"If that's the case," he countered, "then why can't I go with you to Neptune?"

"Besides the obvious," she said, indicating the patient/doctor meme, "it's because I'm an exception to the rule."

"Great. A lot of good that does me."

"But," she continued, "I'm part of the thousands of exceptions out of forty billion. Your system had hundreds of millions of cases out of only six or seven billion."

"But that doesn't take away from the fact," he grumbled, "that they're still *forcing* you to go."

"No, Justin," she said, getting up from the couch, then turning around to face him. "It's you. You're the one who's forcing me to go! Why can't you see that?"

She looked at her lover, sitting wide-eyed and slack-jawed. "Honey," she continued, "if you could give me anything, anything at all in the whole system, what would it be?"

Justin didn't hesitate for a second. "I'd buy up every stock that you didn't have of yourself and give them all back to you."

"Take it further," she urged. "What if you could make me the Unincorporated Woman, would you?"

"Yes," he answered. "I'd do it in a heartbeat."

Neela shook her head. "Justin, I know this will be hard for you to hear, but . . . I wouldn't accept it. Don't get me wrong; I'll be overjoyed the day I get majority—have a big party and everything. But, forgetting about the government's automatic 5 percent, how could I become unincorporated? Why would I want to? Everything I know, have, and am I owe to incorporation—including you! Who and what I am is tied up in it, from the day I was born until the day I die. It's a system that makes every human being personally responsible for all other human beings. It takes the most consistent motivator of our species—self-interest—and makes it work for everyone. I belong *because* of incorporation. And I so wanted you to belong, too. Do you even know we never exchanged?"

"Never exchanged what? Stock?"

"You sound so horrified," answered Neela, "yet it's so beautiful. Two people who are in love exchange one share of themselves with the other. They don't sell it or buy it. They give it to each other. A real promise to share that is not a promise but a fact."

"I know about that, Neela, but we . . . we could have exchanged engagement rings."

Neela nodded in understanding. "Many of us still do that, but a ring is a one-time gift. A stock exchange is something that begins the moment it's given and continues until you die."

Neela sat back down and put her hand on Justin's lap while she tenderly touched his face.

"There are so many things I want to do with you, and *for* you, that I'll never be able to do because you can't . . ." She changed her mind. "*Won't* accept my world."

"It's GCI that's keeping us apart," he said, gritting his teeth, "not me."

Neela took Justin's hand in her own. "Justin, I want to have children someday, and I'd like you to be the father."

Justin's eyes began to well up. "Neela, I . . . I don't know what to say other than, of course. I can't think of a person I'd want to raise children with more than you."

"You mean, of course, our *incorporated children,* don't you?"

Justin was about to speak, but the implications of what Neela had just said stopped him cold. He hadn't given much thought to having children, knowing that the day would eventually come and that he'd be ready—but that was the extent of it. However, Neela was right. Any children they had would be automatically incorporated, regardless of his personal status. Not only that, but he'd own 20 percent of them, and he'd have to own them . . . or, at least, their stocks, until the children reached the age of twenty-one . . . whether he liked it or not. His children would be just as vulnerable as Neela. Well, no, he realized, not *as* vulnerable. They'd never lose majority control of themselves—unless they frittered it away—but they'd be limited in their actions by the ever-present laws of incorporation.

"Don't you see, Justin? Until you decide to accept our way of life, we won't really have a life. I do love you, and will stay with you as long as I can, but when I have to go *I will go.* And I'll do so willingly. You can have me or the Unincorporated Man, but you can't have both—not anymore. Please, for my sake and for yours, don't try any fancy legal maneuvers. I'd rather we just enjoy these last few months together."

Justin sat down on the couch and held her tight, breathing her in deeply, as if he could somehow capture a part of her that would stay with him forever. He looked into her eyes and smiled wistfully.

"I'll see about the boat for tomorrow, then."

Hundreds of arrests systemwide. Action Party cells have been found and eliminated, thanks to increased vigilance from law-enforcement corporations, Justin Cord's sturdy command of the Liberty Party, and a new willingness of former supporters of the Action Wing to come forward with information. It's believed that two more Gray Bombs were unleashed but quickly eliminated by the new and improved hunter/killer nanites distributed systemwide by GCI. For all the news you need, stay tuned to ISN.

—INTERSYSTEMNEWS BROADCAST

Justin found Omad sitting in a small town pub, hunched over a bar. It was lower-class digs all the way, but Justin would never have been able to tell that by using any of his old cues. This place, on the face of it, was kept spotless—but nanites and drones did that for next to nothing. The fittings all looked new, but furniture was as cheap in this day as coasters were in Justin's, so that was also no clue. And all the alcohol probably tasted great, the drugs would get you blasted, and the food was, more than likely, uniformly delectable.

But by looking at the bar with eyes newly accustomed to the mores of the incorporated world, Justin could see that this place was a real dump. The first clue was that everything was uniform. The chairs and tables, the glasses and bowls were completely identical, as only drone/nanite construction and maintenance could make things. Also, other than the bartender, who was probably the owner, the place had no human service whatsoever. Orders were taken and drinks and appetizers were delivered by machines. But the real clue was the patrons. They had that "I'm here to get drunk, go away, jerk-off" look that the downtrodden and desperate always had—especially in establishments like this one.

Justin could tell by the way Omad was hunched over his drink that his friend was hammered to the gills. He called the bartender over. The man behind the counter did a double take when he realized who'd beckoned him.

"You're him," the bartender chuckled. "The asshole."

"Yeah, fuck you, too," Justin shot back. "Can I still buy a drink?"

"Hey, them's his words," the bartender said, pointing to Omad, "not mine."

He leaned in as if to impart a secret. "Simple rule here, mate. No matter who you are. You got credits, you get drinks. See? Simple. And I know *you* got credits. So, what'll it be?"

"You got a whiskey called Springbank, Campbeltown 21?"

The bartender called up a holographic display and entered some commands. "Well, I'll be audited," he said, astonished, "says here we do. No one, and I mean no one, in this joint ever orders that. Ain't got the real stuff, mind ya. All we got is the synthetic. Still interested?"

Justin nodded. "Yup." If they could even come close, he'd be eminently happy.

The bartender put a tumbler into a small alcove, pressed a button on the holographic display, and in seconds the drink was re-created and spat into the tumbler. He pulled a crystal glass out from behind the counter and duly poured the drink. By the man's look Justin could see that he, too, was curious how well the nanites stacked up for someone who'd tasted the real thing. Justin poured the twenty-one-year-old (could he even say that?) whiskey with reverence. Like the original, the malt was a deep bronze, reddish brown. *Points for color,* thought Justin. Which was no small task, since Springbank, unlike most of its competitors, never used any coloring additives. Justin sniffed. The nose was a powerful mix of sherry and Springbank salty sea air . . . with just a hint of mustiness. He nodded in appreciation. *So far, so good,* he thought. He took a sip. Now, in addition to the first flavors he smelled, he was also able to discern the flavorings of the oak cask, black cherries, and chocolate. The finish, he decided, was distinctive of the Springbank distillery—warm and somewhat briny, quickly moving from a sweet, almost syrupy texture to dry.

"Perfect," he said, with a satisfied look.

Though the bartender had nothing to do with it, other than the fact that he'd pressed a few buttons, he seemed pleased with himself.

What Justin didn't tell the man behind the counter was that the drink was, in fact, too perfect. He took another perfect sip. He realized that he could order this drink from anywhere in the system and he'd get this exact drink . . . every time. Every time in every location it would never, ever change in the slightest iota. And that was the problem. Whiskey, like wine, changed subtly with age. And the Springbank 21 was only drinkable a day or two *after* opening. And it would continue to amaze with each successive opening. No wonder people were willing to pay big bucks for the real thing, the *real anything.* Humans needed stability, but they also craved variety. The slight difference a drink would have from how it was made, stored, and prepared would be invaluable after a while— and no one here could afford it. Nor would most of them ever be able to in all the long years of their lives. And, for the first time, Justin truly understood what it meant to be poor in the incorporated world. He took his drink over to Omad who, sensing someone's presence next to him, looked up.

"What the fuck are you doing here, asshole?"

"No idea, Omad," answered Justin, "you called and told me to meet you. You said you had some good news. 'Get drunk with a buddy' sort of news."

"Buddy, Justin, old chum, you're an asshole." Omad looked as if he had had the most profound realization of his life. "Damsah's balls, Justin, you are my buddy!" Omad waved to the bar. "Hey, everybody! This is my buddy."

No one looked up, but that didn't stop Omad from laughing uproariously. "Hey, everybody, body and buddy. I rhymed. My buddy has a rhyming buddy!" The patrons, pulled momentarily out of their individual stupors, shot back a chorus of derogatory comments and suggestions for both Omad and Justin.

"Let's get you out of here," suggested Justin.

"You got it, buddy." Omad stood up on unsteady feet and turned to the bar.

"Me and my buddy, Justin Cord, the great and powerful Unincorporated Man, don't need you, anyways. My buddy here is all I need. He can destroy you all with just a glance." This brought more suggestions from the patrons, but now some seemed to notice who Justin was. Maybe they all did and most were just too far gone to care.

Justin rolled Omad into his flyer and managed to get him over to the hotel suite he'd rented. Unfortunately, Omad's body decided to rebel against the abuse he'd inflicted on it the night before—leaving a sacrifice on the couch instead of the traditional altar in the bathroom. Fortunately, the cleaning drones made quick work of it.

Justin was tempted to administer some scrubber nanites into Omad's bloodstream to clear out the alcohol and various other foreign chemicals—but he decided against it. Omad could've chosen to make himself immune before he got started. He'd obviously wanted to get blind and stinking drunk, and Justin knew enough about life to realize that sometimes that's just what a person had to do. He did what any friend would do for a passed-out, drunk buddy. He put him on a clean couch, facedown, near the edge with a large bowl nearby, took off his boots, and put a light blanket over him. Justin called Neela and told her that Omad was fine, and that he, himself, probably wouldn't be back until the following morning. He hated losing any time with her, as it was now measured in months instead of decades. But Omad was a friend and, as he explained to his lover, he didn't have all that many left. She understood and wished him luck. Justin took off his shoes and settled himself down in a chair near his nearly comatose friend, and sooner than he would have thought possible was sound asleep.

He was awakened by Omad sitting up and groaning. "Did someone piss in my mouth?" Omad looked like a man who wanted to spit but didn't have the saliva to do so. Justin poured and handed him a cup of hot coffee from a nearby counter.

"That foul, acidic crap in your mouth is all you, Omad," answered Justin. "Well, you and a variety of booze."

"What the hell is booze?"

"Alcohol," Justin corrected.

"Ahh." Omad took a sip of the coffee, looked dubiously at the cup, and took another sip. "What did I do or say last night?"

"I don't know about before I got there, but when I got there you called me an asshole and tried to start a fight."

"Sounds about right," he said, grinning. "Sorry about the asshole part. Well, no, you actually are an asshole, but I don't think you can help it."

Justin laughed. "Who can?"

Omad smiled. "Good point." Justin settled back in his chair and called room service for a simple breakfast of oatmeal and orange juice. They waited in companionable silence for the food to arrive, and when it did they both chowed down. When breakfast was done, Omad remained unusually tight-lipped.

"Let me guess," asked Justin, "you've been offered a great job at great pay, but it's nowhere near the Earth . . . or me, for that matter."

Omad looked up from his plate. "Something tells me this is not the first time you've heard this."

"They're doing something similar to Neela—only she doesn't have much of a choice."

Omad put his utensils down. "That's gotta hurt."

"What are the details?" asked Justin.

"Leading a mining expedition," answered Omad. "In the belt. On-site management, great quarterly pay, plus a percentage of all gross profits from the mining as a result of my discoveries."

"Sounds great," Justin offered, knowing full well it didn't. "When do you leave?"

"Fuck you, and fuck them, too. They can take their bribe and shove it out an airlock."

Another long pause.

"Omad, I don't get something," said Justin, sipping from his coffee. "You don't approve of my being unincorporated, right?"

"Yeah, it's downright inhuman."

"But you're willing to stand by me."

"I don't run out on friends . . . ever."

Justin was suspicious.

"There's something else, isn't there?"

"Who died and made you auditor?"

"What's bothering you, Omad?" Justin asked again, ignoring the snipe.

Omad got up and refilled his coffee and sat back down. "Justin, I know that you say you don't own stock in anyone, the original divestment guy and all, but you wouldn't happen to have some shares of my stock you were hanging on to?"

"Why would you ask me a question like that?"

"So I'm guessing that would be a no."

"I don't get it," said Justin, "don't you already have a majority?"

"Yeah, but it might not be big enough."

"Big enough for what? I thought majority was majority."

Omad looked at Justin through weary, bloodshot eyes. "For a guy who's so smart, I sometimes forget just how much of an idiot you can be."

"Though Neela can attest to my finer points of idiocy, I can assure you this is just a case of ignorance, Omad, so please help me out."

Omad sighed. "When a person gets a majority of themselves they get a lot of control over their lives."

"But . . ."

"But not total; especially if it's not a big majority. I only have 53.737 percent of my stock. The bastards who own the other 46 point whatever of me have the right to expect a decent return on their investment. When I turn down this job, they're going to be a wee bit upset that they're not going to be getting the dividends they'd have a right to expect."

"But what could they do? You are, after all, a majority stockholder of yourself. Why not just take it to a vote?"

"For one, they could take it to court. If they can prove 'depraved indifference' or 'conspiracy to defraud,' I could lose."

"You're rich, pay the fine."

"Justin, you don't get it. *They could sue for stock.*"

"Jesus." Justin thought about what he'd just heard. "So that's why you wanted to know if I had any extra stock. How much would make you bulletproof?"

"If I understand what you're saying," answered Omad, "seventy percent usually does it."

"Omad, can I ask you a question?"

Omad nodded.

"But," he continued, "you gotta answer it honestly. No jokes, equivocations, or your usual bullshit."

"My pounding head awaits your question."

"If I wasn't in the picture, would you take this job?"

"In a nanosecond."

"Then stop being an idiot," exclaimed Justin, "and take the job."

"Can't, Justin. First of all, I didn't earn the job. They're just giving it to me to split me up from your ignorant, primitive ass. Second of all, like I was sayin', I don't walk out on my friends . . . ever."

Justin put his cup down on the coffee table.

"First of all, what a load of crap. If a thousand credits fell out of Hektor's pocket and you picked it up, would you run after him and give it back, or find me, go to a bar, and get drunk on his money?"

"Hell, Justin," grinned Omad, "we'd be shit-faced within the hour."

"Good answer. Well, guess what, asshole? Hektor Sambianco and GCI just dropped a suitcase filled with money right in front of you. As for the 'walking out on friends' part, it goes both ways. You're my friend, too, and I wouldn't be a good one if I let you screw up a perfectly good opportunity to screw GCI out of untold amounts of credit."

"Hey, Justin, news flash, it's my choice to make."

"Not according to the rules of incorporation that you keep on telling me I should get on board with. According to you, those rules will fuck you if you stay.

So do me a favor and go get stinkin' rich. Make GCI regret ever giving you such a great deal."

"Fine," answered Omad, relenting.

"But," continued Justin, "you'd better come back here with all those credits you've earned and buy me something worthy."

"Worthy, huh? What'd you have in mind?"

"I don't know. What's Tokyo going for these days?"

"Tokyo? Man, you wouldn't appreciate Tokyo. It's a crying shame about Shanghai. Now, that would've been something."

"Right." Justin remembered reading about how the Three Gorges Dam was destroyed during the Grand Collapse and had never been rebuilt.

"How about Bangor?" offered Omad, sheepishly.

"Bangor? Bangor, Maine? Fuck you, Omad. Stay in the asteroid belt, you cheap bastard. At least you could have offered me Havana."

Omad looked confused.

"The one in Cuba?" Justin almost pleaded.

"Where's Cuba?"

"Jesus Christ, what happened to Cuba?"

Omad started laughing. "Oh, man, Justin. I just love doing that shit to you."

"You son of a . . ."

When Justin got back to his new house he was surprised to see the flyer of some unexpected visitors in the driveway. The car hovering by the guesthouse belonged to Mosh and Eleanor. He entered through the front sunroom and immediately heard voices coming from the library. He went in to find Neela, Mosh, and Eleanor sitting on opposite sides of the plush leather couch, obviously having an enjoyable conversation together.

"So Gil's back working for me, and Dr. Wang has her own practice."

Neela laughed out loud. "Who would have thought? To listen to them go on for years about what they planned to do . . ."

"Well," continued Mosh with a wan smile, "the nosedive their stock prices took really . . ."

He looked up as Justin entered the room. "Justin, glad to see you're looking well. We were just catching Neela up on some old workmates."

Justin sat by Neela. "You two are always welcome."

Eleanor got up and gave Justin a peck on the cheek. Mosh stayed decidedly put on the couch. "We found out about what happened to Neela and came by to offer her help."

"You can stop her transfer?" Justin asked, with a glimmer of hope, knowing full well he'd piss off Neela, who'd already made her feelings about the matter quite clear.

"Wish I could. Even made some calls to see if I could get her back at Boulder. Had to use favors to get that far. But there's no way, Justin. They ain't budging."

"Why not?" he asked. "You used to be an important figure at GCI."

"Used to. Not anymore. Besides, if they respected The Chairman before, they worship the ground he walks on now. Him and his damned apostle, Hektor Sambianco. The Chairman proposed this plan, and the board will do his will."

"Who *is* this guy that he can mess with my life with impunity?"

Mosh sighed. "Justin, The Chairman is the most savvy, cunning, and capable corporate mover I have ever seen. He understands the incorporated world better than any person alive. He started out as a penny and rocketed his way to the top. Me, personally? Didn't like him much. He was superficially friendly enough, but he'd crush anyone and anything that got in his way. That's the reason I got out. I may have been able to get the Chairmanship of GCI, but I didn't want it as badly as he did. I'm good at the corporate game, Justin. But I would've been 'Mosh McKenzie,' Chairman of GCI. I never would have been 'The Chairman.'"

"That still doesn't explain why he's going after me."

"Justin," Mosh explained, "in his mind, he's not going after you, you're going after him. You're disrupting the system that he's mastered. You're screwing with his whole universe. And have done so, I might add, while escaping every attempt of GCI's to have you incorporated. And because of all that the whole solar system is up in arms. I'd venture to say that you're probably the first person I've ever met to truly scare the guy."

"But I'm *not* going after him. I mean, for goodness' sakes, I didn't start this, *he* did."

Mosh sighed. "Justin, I respect what you've done, really, I do. But that's a load of horse crap."

Justin gave a weary smile. "OK, Mosh, I guess you deserve a turn, too. Everyone else seems to have gotten one. So go ahead, tell me what an evil man I'm being."

"Justin," he answered, weariness evident in his voice, "you're not evil. The truth is, I think you're absolutely remarkable. But you are a little selfish, a tad hypocritical, and, I suspect, a little scared. At least, that's why I believe you're refusing to incorporate. You have this notion of who and what you are, and somehow you think it's incompatible with our way of doing things. So you say, 'Leave me alone and I'll leave you alone.' But it can't work like that. You damned well know the effect that you're having on the universe. And if you don't you're blind, an idiot, or both."

Justin didn't interrupt. He knew very well the effect he was having on the system. He'd just been hard-pressed to believe that he'd been the root cause of it all.

"You're a threat," continued Mosh, "and I've wished to Damsah I could hate you for it, but I can't. I actually hope The Chairman succeeds, because I honestly believe you must incorporate, if not for your sake, then for ours. You'll give up nothing you ever really had and gain everything a man could ever want."

Justin sat silently, openly holding Neela's hand.

"I'm sorry," said Mosh, "maybe I said too much. Your life, your choice." He then got up to leave.

"Mosh," said Justin, insisting his old friend sit down, "you have every right to speak your mind. Maybe you don't consider yourself my friend, but you and Eleanor have been companions of sorts, and certainly true friends of Neela's. That counts for a lot."

"Yeah," interrupted Neela. "Besides, someone has to talk to my mule-headed friend here besides me." She still couldn't get the nerve up to say "companion" or "boyfriend," but all present knew what she meant.

Mosh chose to ignore the inference. He was still a bit steamed that the courtship had taken place with one of his employees—felt it reflected badly on his judgment. But he was also old enough to know that there was no accounting for love. And even he had to admit that the circumstances under which the affair occurred were far from normal.

"I do have some good news for you," he said, pressing on. "I made some inquiries and have arranged for you to work under an old friend of mine, Hildegard Rhunsfeld. She's capable and owes me. You'll be well looked after, Neela. I'll also arrange to visit the research lab from time to time. Just to be sure."

"That must be half a lifetime's worth of favors you're calling in. Mosh, you really don't have to do all that."

"Oh yes, he does," insisted Eleanor.

Mosh managed a smirk. "Besides, if I didn't," he said looking over at his wife, "she'd kill me."

"And," said Eleanor, smiling triumphantly, "it just so happens that right about the time you're going to be transferred, we're going on vacation!"

As to why this piece of information was relevant, Justin had no idea.

"We've decided to spend some of our hard-earned wages on renting a private yacht, dear," continued Eleanor. "We're finally going to take that grand tour of the solar system—with you. We'll be more than happy to drop you off at your destination."

The look of genuine surprise on Neela's face was enough to coax an ear-to-ear grin out of the curmudgeonly director.

"Mosh, Eleanor, that's too much," insisted Neela. "It must be costing you a fortune!"

"Already prepaid. Besides," Mosh answered, with a slight twinkle in his eye, "you really don't want to say no to Eleanor. Trust me, I've tried. One way or another she gets what she wants, and she wants you to join us . . . as do I, of course."

Justin reached out and shook Mosh's reluctant hand. "Yes, yes. She'll go."

Neela offered no resistance. The idea was appealing. It would give her time to clear her head.

"Thank you, thank you," said Justin, giving Eleanor a bear hug, "I owe you both so much."

"I'm not doing it for you, son," Mosh said, admonishing Justin. "But if you mean that, I'd consider the favor paid in full if you'd just honestly think about what I've said today."

"I can't lie to you, Mosh," Justin said. "The idea of incorporating has nothing to do with Hektor, The Chairman, GCI, or the government. It has to do with who I am fundamentally."

"I know that, Justin," answered Mosh. "But don't forget, we're all along for the ride. And don't discount The Chairman. You haven't really faced him, you know. Just his underlings and his opening moves orchestrated through those underlings. Eventually he'll come after you directly, and with greater strength. There's simply too much at stake for him not to. Plus, he's now more powerful than ever and won't stop until you're incorporated." Mosh chuckled. "I'm sorry. Here I am sounding like I should be in a spy holo. We'll leave you two now. You only have a little time left, and the last thing you need to hear is the blathering of an old man."

They didn't object. Mosh and Eleanor took their leave and bid Justin good luck. As the medical director's flyer took off into the clear blue sky, Justin waved. One by one, they were all saying good-bye.

The weeks passed far too quickly. Between running the Liberty Party, showing up at rallies, and having to deal with an almost constant and unrelenting attack on his assets, Justin and Neela found precious little time for one another. Perhaps it had been a good excuse to begin the process of letting go, he wondered. It was almost easier not to meet than to spend every waking moment together—an impossibility anyway, given the societal memes, their celebrity, and the striking breadth of their new responsibilities.

Before he knew it, Justin found himself standing with Neela at the Interstellar Marina in Oahu, Hawaii, where Mosh and Eleanor had rented a yacht for the run around the solar system. It was located near Pearl Harbor, and was about five miles west of Honolulu. The grand vessel's living quarters, noticed Justin on inspection, were well appointed. They had over three thousand square feet to play with, and they used it efficiently, with guest rooms, viewing areas, and luxury appointments throughout.

Neela and Justin had barely said a word to one another on the way to the marina, preferring instead to hold each other's hand in a tight embrace. They'd made love one last time, shared a bottle of wine—one last time. Snuggled together—one last time.

And now they stood facing one another at the departure dock, oblivious to the foot traffic, noise, and general goings-on of the space-faring port. Mosh and Eleanor were already on the boat, waiting patiently.

Justin held Neela's hands in his. "Neela . . ."

"You can stop this," she said. Her voice was plaintive.

"We've already been through that, Neela," he answered, this time with just a hint of desperation. He was feeling her need for him, sensing her desire to stay. "I can't, my love," he added, "please forgive me. I wish to God that I could, but the price is too high."

Neela managed a forlorn smile. She'd been outbid. The only man in the universe whom she could connect to, share a life with, laugh knowingly with . . . the only man she would ever want had been spoken for.

Her drawn eyes stared out in pained acceptance.

"Of all the beliefs you had to bring with you from before the Grand Collapse," she implored, "you couldn't have believed in some sort of 'ism'?" She didn't wait for an answer. "That would have been fine," she continued, wiping away the driblets that had formed near her eyes. "Any one of them would have been fine . . . so . . . so many isms." Her voice trailed off.

Is she having a breakdown? wondered Justin.

"Or," she continued, "it could have been . . . religion, Damsah knows we're lacking in that department . . . the Buddha . . . yes . . . yes, the Buddha would have been fine . . . would've worked for us. Oh, Justin," she said, small rivulets now beginning to stream down her face, "you could've built temples . . . temples to us." Her voice was wistful, lost. She paused to gather her breath and wipe away the tears.

And then Neela's face, which up until that point had been an amalgam of emotion, suddenly became a singly focused beacon of clarity. Justin was so taken aback by the swift transformation that he was tempted to step back.

"But you," she said tenderly, "*you* had to believe in an ill-conceived principle that never worked in your time and doesn't work in ours. You, Justin Cord, Mr. Unincorporated Man . . . Mr. One Free Man . . . *you had to believe in freedom.*"

With that she stepped out into the float field and was lifted up onto the ship. Justin waited for her to turn around—a last look—but she never did.

On a planet of well over twenty billion souls, Justin Cord was now truly alone.

14 Temptation

Be not afraid of greatness:
Some are born great.
Some achieve greatness,
And some have greatness thrust upon them.

WILLIAM SHAKESPEARE, *TWELFTH NIGHT* (ACT II, SCENE 5)

Unemployment at 10 percent. Hundreds of millions are now living on their savings, having used up their unemployment insurance. How long the unemployed can do that is a matter of personal circumstance. Those who were saving for a big stock purchase will be able to hold out for a couple more months. Those who had just made one are already being forced to sell their homes and find other places to live.

Calls for the Unincorporated Man to be forcibly incorporated were put forth by the Society to Preserve Society. The new group was formed out of business organizations, civic groups, and various parent associations, and is funded solely by small donations. Mr. Cord was not available for comment.

—ISN BROADCAST

Justin returned to San Francisco, and for a while attempted to get lost in the hubbub of work. But even with a steady swarm of humanity around him, the office seemed a cold and lonely place haunted by memories. He was giving serious thought to following Mosh into the wilds of space. He'd rent a yacht and tour the solar system. Maybe even visit the moons of Jupiter, fly by the rings of Saturn, or climb Olympus Mons on Mars—a shield volcano nearly fifteen miles high and over three hundred miles wide at its base. Such were the experiences that awaited Justin in this brave new world. He could even take up the 70 percent sports, activities considered so dangerous that only those with an ironclad majority could engage in them: Storm surfing on Jupiter came to mind. He'd always wanted to learn how to surf.

Justin figured that he should talk with Dr. Gillette again, but even the good doctor hadn't been returning his calls. *Probably GCI'd like the rest of them,* he thought dourly to himself.

When sebastian finally did beep, Justin assumed his avatar was going to patch him through to the good doctor. After all, he'd been the only one Justin had tried to contact.

"Tell the good doctor . . ."

"It's not Dr. Gillette, Justin," interrupted sebastian.

Great, thought Justin. *Now, even my damned avatar's being rude.*

"Actually," continued sebastian, "it's not even someone on your approved list, but I think you may want to take the call."

"Who is it?"

"Agnes Goldstein."

It took Justin a moment to realize whom sebastian was referring to. In the rush of events he'd completely forgotten about the chipper 25 percenter Omad had introduced him to at the post–Mardi Gras get-together. But he sure was glad that she'd called.

"By all means, sebastian, put her on."

Per Justin's standing order, the communication was in voice only.

"Agnes," he said with a slight lift in his voice, "it's good to hear from you again. How are you?"

"I wish I could tell you 'fine,' Mr. Cord. But I can't."

Justin feared that yet another victim had been infected with his "association" disease—associate with Cord, get audited. But he knew, especially with regards to Agnes, that he'd been so very careful to cover his tracks.

"What is it, dear?"

"I'm sorry to bother you, but I didn't know who else to call. It's about the gift you gave me. I . . . I think I may be in trouble."

"Is this immediate trouble, Agnes? I can arrange for you to stay in a safe place if need be."

"I don't think it's like that." She paused in thought. "God, I hope not."

Justin made an instant decision. "Agnes, are you home?"

"Yes, Mr. Cord. I am. All the time, actually. I lost my job, and I haven't been able to find another."

Justin sighed. "I'm on my way, Agnes, and will you please call me Justin?"

———

In retrospect, Justin should have realized things were a bit off when he got to Agnes's neighborhood. It was downright picturesque. He was in a low-class neighborhood that was empty. There were no children playing. No flyers with people coming and going. In a part of town that should have had massive un-employment, there was no one home. And it was also only later that he'd realized that there were no mediabots—not very common when it came to lower-class neighborhoods but extremely common when it came to him. He'd started call-ing them flies, because, no matter where he went, they always seemed to be able to find him. But not today. Not a one.

In his beeline to Agnes's he failed to notice the anomalies and walked blindly up to her front door. He was about to knock, but the door opened automatically at his approach. He looked around to see if anyone was on the other end of it, and when no one apparently was, he stepped inside the foyer.

"Agnes?" he called out.

He heard the distinct and very identifiable pop of a beverage can being opened. It was one of those sounds that had not changed at all in the centuries that had passed. He headed toward the direction of the noise.

"Agnes," he said, walking toward the sound, "I came as soon as I could. Are you . . . ?" Justin stopped in his tracks. Sitting at the island in the middle of the large kitchen was the one and only man Justin Cord had truly hated. Not even the treachery that his old assistant, Sebastian Blancano, had perpetrated roused the feelings of anger that Justin felt for the man currently occupying center stage in the kitchen.

"Hi, Justin," greeted Hektor Sambianco, holding up a can. "Beer?"

Hektor seemed completely relaxed in a pair of board shorts, sandals, and an oversized Hawaiian-print shirt.

Without saying a word Justin turned and headed for the door.

"Justin, five minutes is all I ask," Hektor called out.

"Fuck you," answered Justin, without breaking his stride. He had one foot out the door when Hektor lobbed his missile.

"Leave," he yelled from the kitchen, "and Agnes never gets majority. Hell, she might not even get out of jail."

Justin stopped, clenched his fists, and whirled around. "You really are a son of a bitch."

Hektor came out of the kitchen and stood staring at his foe in the doorway. "Yes, Justin, but I'm the son of a bitch who has gone through great effort to arrange this meeting." Hektor left Justin and calmly walked into the living room. "Five minutes," Hektor shouted from the room. "That's all I ask."

Justin stood in the doorway for another moment, knowing he had no choice. He marched back down the hallway and entered the living room, where Hektor had made himself comfortable in a big, overstuffed recliner. He was still sipping his beer. "Sure you don't want one?" Hektor asked, holding up the can. "It's a Hacker-Pschorr Munich. Your favorite, right?"

"How did you clear the street?" asked Justin, dispensing with the small talk.

"Easy," smiled Hektor. "We offered everyone three times what their houses were worth with half up front. The other half being paid if and only if they left immediately for one day. This day. After that GCI closed off this bit of private property. Truth is, we'll sell them back to them at market price . . . if they still want them. Congratulations, Justin, there's at least one small part of this planet that's damned glad you came to visit."

"And not one person said no?" he asked suspiciously.

"In this economy? They couldn't leave fast enough. Well, actually," he said, "that's not entirely true. There was one person who said no. Why, it was Ms. Goldstein. We even quadrupled the price this place was worth, but the lady wouldn't budge. Go figure. You do encourage loyalty, I'll give you that, Justin."

"So you had her arrested?"

"Justin, Justin, she wouldn't leave. After she made the call we knew we only had about a half hour to an hour before you'd be here. We had to buy the block, clear everyone out, and arrange a privacy zone. We were, shall we say, pressed for time?"

"So you had her arrested?" Justin repeated.

"Yes."

"On what charges? If you don't mind my asking."

"Oh, not at all. Trumped-up ones, to be sure. We implicated her in terrorist activity with the Action Wing."

Justin shook his head in disgust. "You're a real piece of work."

"Thanks. I try."

"If she made the call for you, how come she wouldn't sell you the house? Or I suppose you just seized it."

"Justin, Justin, she didn't make the call for us. I had her communications tapped. I also had anyone who came in contact with you put under low-level observation and, where feasible, stock options taken out. Imagine my surprise when I discovered that 20 percent of Ms. Goldstein's shares were already being optioned out. No way to know who it was, but it smelled of you. I took a small gamble and bought out the rest of her shares."

"I still don't see how this puts us here," he answered sternly.

Hektor gulped down the rest of his beer and crushed the can on his knee. "We had her under observation. She tried to access her account and found that none of her stocks were for sale. She called you, and we moved."

"You were in New York. How did you beat me here by a half hour?"

"In that, Justin, I got lucky. I was surfing off Half Moon Bay when she called you. I was here in five minutes, and got the buyout going soon after that. Luckily there were no emergency situations, and I got what I wanted. The chance to talk privately."

"Not yet."

"You're here, aren't you?"

"I am. But you don't get your five minutes unless you agree to my terms first."

"And they are?" Hektor asked, smiling malevolently.

"Agnes is released immediately. You expunge all this crap about her being in the Action Wing. In fact, I want to see evidence that she is a member in good standing of the SPS. Hard-copy evidence I can give to my lawyer."

"Next."

"You will give her enough stock to achieve 70 percent control of her portfolio."

"Next."

"I see her . . . here."

"It will take a little while to prepare."

Justin headed for the kitchen. "Take it."

An hour and a half later a slightly confused Agnes Goldstein walked back into her own house. Justin came out of the den and went up to her. "Are you OK?"

Agnes's dazed look did not go away; if anything, it got worse.

"Justin, what on Mars is going on? I've been threatened, arrested, almost put on the list for psyche auditing. I couldn't get a lawyer because they said that my insurance was canceled. But I know it wasn't. When I thought that it couldn't get weirder, I was released, picked up, and driven home in the nicest limousine I've ever seen, and . . . and, Justin, I've just been given supermajority." Justin slowly steered the still talking Agnes to the kitchen without trying to break into her nonstop monologue. While she was talking he took her coat and got her a bottled drink called G! from the refrigerator. It appeared to be slimy, green, carbonated algae. Justin couldn't drink the stuff, but it seemed to be the drink du jour.

"Seventy percent?" she gasped. "Can that be real?"

"Let's check. Sebastian, can you confirm if Agnes owns seventy percent of her portfolio? Also, can you make sure that she's a member of the SPS in good standing, and get her the top lawyer insurance plan for one year, prepaid. The one where the top-rank lawyer comes to your house and does your laundry."

"Justin," answered the faithful avatar, "her portfolio is indeed at 70 percent. The title is free and clear. Your lawyer has hard-copy proof that Agnes could not possibly be a member of the Action Wing, and assures me that she can manufacture more if needed. The lawyer is on the way."

"Thank you, sebastian."

Agnes was still staring, dumbfounded, at Justin. "Mr. Cord . . . Justin, why are you doing this for me? I thought you wanted me to earn it on my own. I kind of wanted to earn it on my own."

"Agnes," he answered, eyes warm in appreciation, "you did earn it. You stood by me against a man you knew to be dangerously powerful. Your acquaintance with me put you in danger, and this was the only way to give you a cushion of safety. So you most definitely earned and will continue to earn this. It's the least I could do. From here on in, you're going to be under the microscope. I'm so sorry that my coming into your life in even so minor a way has done this to you. If anything, what you've received today is not enough. You deserved the right to make your own future, and that's been taken away. I only hope that when you realize what I've done to your life you'll forgive me."

Agnes was flabbergasted. "Are you insane? I have a supermajority! Thank you, thank you, and thank you. Never in my wildest dreams did I think I'd ever get *that*. As for standing by you, of course I did. You tried to help me, and I was just returning the favor. Do you still need my help?"

"What do you mean?"

"Well, the man who had me arrested is still in my living room, and I'm pretty sure that he's Hektor Sambianco."

"He is Hektor Sambianco, deputy director of Special Operations, GCI, and a royal pain in my ass. You could help me out by giving us some breathing room."

Agnes nodded her head. "Say no more. I don't want to know. I'm going upstairs to take a bath, and then I'm going to bed. But if you need anything, you call."

"I will. You enjoy your bath." Justin watched her head up the stairs. Sighing, he got a beer from the fridge. There was indeed some Hacker-Pschorr Munich, but the cheap bastard had only bought synthetic, and in a can at that! Justin headed back into the living room to keep his part of the bargain. He found Hektor in a deep slumber. It occurred to him that Hektor probably didn't get that much time to sleep. In fact, Justin concluded, he may well have been one of the busiest men in the solar system. With savage glee he kicked Hektor's foot and shouted in his ear, "Five minutes, and the clock is ticking."

The look of surprise on Hektor's face was well worth the price of having to listen to him mouth off for five minutes—eternity that it may be.

"What," groused Hektor, "no good-morning kiss?"

Justin sat down in a chair opposite his nemesis.

Hektor yawned. "Ahh, I can see that as usual you have no sense of humor. Very well. Justin Cord," he said, in as officious a tone as he could muster, "I, Hektor Sambianco, have been duly authorized by the board of GCI to make you an offer."

"An offer I can't refuse?"

Hektor didn't understand the reference. "Of course you can refuse it. But you'd be a fool if you did."

"Four minutes."

"GCI wants you to incorporate."

Justin smiled. "It won't take me four minutes to say no, but you paid for 'em. I could spend the time saying, 'Fuck you.' That would be far more gratifying."

Hektor ignored Justin's impertinence. He'd gotten what he wanted . . . so far. He'd suffer the barbs of this fool gladly.

"Justin, what would the Liberty Party loyal say if they could hear you now?"

"If they knew I was talking to you they'd probably want me to stop being so polite."

Hektor laughed. "But you haven't heard the details."

"Oh, this'll be good," answered Justin. "What can you possibly offer to make me join you?"

Hektor's smile was insidious. "Why, Neela, of course."

"Fuck you!"

"No, Justin," answered Hektor, for the first time raising his voice. "Fuck *you*, you arrogant bastard. If I could think of any way of making you suffer, I would. Oh, so you're not with your precious Neela. Too fucking bad! Millions of people are dead because of you and your stubborn, idiotic, superstitious fear of incorporation. I dare say everyone on this planet knows someone whose friends are dead or suffering because of you. Yes, I have the power to keep you from Neela, but I'm willing to toss it because I need you. You're getting the best damned deal in the universe."

Justin remained unfazed.

"Aside from Neela," Justin said, "I already have a pretty good deal, Hektor. You can't keep me away from my money forever—my lawyers will see to that, and other than Neela, you certainly can't offer me anything I don't already have. Also, if you wanted to kill me, I'd be dead. So I'm clearly better off living, by your calculations."

Hektor clapped his hands slowly. "Bravo, Justin. Bravo. The Unincorporated Man has figured it all out, has he? Alright. Let's go over the flip side of the credit. First of all, you will not see Neela again, ever. And don't give me any crap about being able to find a loophole. Fuck loopholes. Mark my words: GCI will kill her before we let you see her again. Not that it would come to that. A simple accident, followed by misplacing her cryo unit, would take care of her for centuries. But why stop there? Before she meets with, hmm . . . how shall I put it? unfortunate circumstance, we'll make sure to run a campaign that'll expose your illicit affair."

"You have no proof."

"Don't be an idiot. I wouldn't be stupid enough to make a threat I couldn't back up."

All Justin could do was brood. "Go on," he said acidly.

"She and her family will be reviled," continued Hektor. "And, mark my words, Cord. I'll make sure she suffers greatly before her 'accident.' As far as you're concerned, we'll tie up every credit you own, expensive lawyers or not. You want to be taxed? You'll have to de-de-," Hektor searched for the unfamiliar word, "declare every microcredit. By the time we're done you'll be begging in the street. Anyone who helps you, even to the point of giving you food money, will be audited. Oh, it will be stretching the law, but what the hell, you don't give a damn about us, so why should we care about you?"

"Finished?" Justin asked, barely managing to contain the rage he was feeling toward the man currently holding a metaphorical gun to both his and his lover's head.

Hektor laughed. "I'm just getting started, actually. I'll make sure that you get a picture of every person that the Action Wing kills. I'll then pay for their parents, siblings, spouses, and children to find whatever hole you happen to be living in and ask you why. Why did you let it happen? You will not escape the consequences of your actions, Mr. Cord, any more than the rest of us will. I . . . will . . . haunt . . . you."

Justin eyed Hektor coldly. "Is that all?"

"Cocky, aren't you?" asked Hektor. "We can get started right now if you'd like. I can have this street filled in an hour. If you're so sure you're blameless, just wait and see the relatives of those who've been killed."

"I'm not blameless, Sambianco, but I didn't kill anyone either."

"But you can stop it!" exclaimed Hektor. "Every moment you lead your Liberty Party lemmings, every moment you remain unincorporated, people die, and even more will suffer."

"I'm not buying that, Hektor. I'm just one man; this is a system of forty billion. And in my day and age we used to have a saying for that: 'Shit happens.' And, as you're well aware, I'm doing all I can to ease the suffering . . . stop the violence."

The only reason Justin was entertaining Sambianco was because the specter of Neela's suffering and threatened death had paralyzed him. He wanted to kick himself for allowing the weakness—after all, millions depended on him now. And his cause was right . . . yet he stood still, taking the blows like a dazed fighter in the ring, for what? The love of a woman.

"Justin," continued Hektor, "you're not one man. You're the Unincorporated Man. And in that you're truly cursed. But yours is not like other curses. Yours leaves you alone but afflicts the world around you. The most terrifying thing about all this is that you can end it at any time. But you don't see it as a curse, do you? You see it as some sort of perverse blessing, and so hang on to it with both hands, no matter what the price. It's already cost you Black, Harper, the McKenzies, that tunnel rat—and now this Goldstein woman will be next, one way or another. But you still won't give up your curse. It's the one reason I can't completely hate you. You can't see the difference. Man, Shakespeare could write a tragedy about all of us that would make *Othello* seem like much ado about nothing."

"You'd, of course, be perfect as Iago," chided Justin.

Hektor smiled wanly and let it drop. He was just glad his avatar hadn't answered at the sound of its name.

"Justin," continued Hektor, "you may not believe this, but I'm your best friend. I'm trying to save you, and you won't listen."

Justin realized there was only so much Hektor would take before pulling up the stakes and taking action. Sooner or later the cards would have to be dealt, and the hand would have to be played.

"Alright," Justin said, "I'm listening."

Hektor breathed a sigh of relief. He'd managed to get through this impossible human being's thick skull, and he had no problem expressing his joy at having done so. It wasn't out of hubris, it was out of respect. He hadn't planned on hiding anything for this meeting, knowing the subject was far too smart and the stakes far too high.

"OK, Justin. This is the deal. We'll end all of it. You'll be with Neela. We'll not only put an end to the vicious rumor of your affair, we'll come right out and support it. Get her reaccredited, even. I already have renowned experts lined up who'd be more than happy to state unequivocally that the client-patient relationship does not count in your circumstance. We'll even throw you a wedding party. Trust me, Justin, by the time I'm through people will be lining up to find out where you're registered. Second, you'll have all your money back. And, believe it or not, the government won't even bother taxing you. Do you think they like what they're doing?"

"They seem to be quite good at it," Justin answered sarcastically.

"Yeah," Hektor conceded, "that's government for you. But I've had to apply thumbscrews every millimeter of the way."

"Also," he continued, "if you incorporate you'll do so with the standard one hundred thousand shares that everyone gets at birth, with one exception. Unlike everyone else, you'll be able to keep them all."

Justin shook his head in disbelief.

"All of them?"

"All of them," Hektor smiled shrewdly, "but one."

"Ahh," Justin answered, shaking his head. There was always a catch.

"And who gets to keep that one share . . . or shall I say, 'trophy'? You or The Chairman?"

"Give it to whoever you want, Justin."

Justin's mouth hung open, then snapped shut.

"I said you'd won, Justin," Hektor smiled earnestly. "I meant it. But I'd suggest you give it to Dr. Harper, as I'm sure you're aware it's the traditional engagement exchange."

Had Hektor been privy to his conversation with Neela? *Doubtful,* Justin thought. If there was any house that had security on par with GCI's it was his.

"Do you think I'm an idiot?" he challenged. "GCI owns an outright majority of Neela. I may as well hand it over to you or the The Chairman, because either of you could threaten me via her at any time."

Hektor nodded, as if in complete agreement.

"Let me explain this 'you've won' concept again. If you agree to give Dr. Harper the one share of you, GCI will hand over control of all its shares of stock in Dr. Harper to Dr. Harper. This will give your girlfriend 70.4 percent control of her portfolio, and that will make her . . . 'bulletproof,' I believe is the expression you'd use."

"Yes," Justin confirmed, barely able to believe the offer. "You're telling me that GCI is prepared to walk away from the tens of millions of credits Neela would be generating for them? I find that rather hard to believe."

Hektor laughed. "Justin, I suggest you take a moment and see just how much your country doctor is really worth."

Justin checked with sebastian quickly. A moment later he looked up, not believing the enormity of the number he saw.

"Neela stocks are worth *billions*? She's the most valuable person in the system next to The Chairman?"

Hektor nodded. "Uh-huh."

"I knew she was worth a lot, but Jesus, why?" Then: "Is this some kind of trick? Have you messed with my avatar?"

"He can't," sebastian assured him. "He'd have to take control of the entire Neuro to do that, and even GCI doesn't have that much power."

"Alright, then, Hektor," said Justin, "how is it she's worth so much?"

Hektor checked the time. "You do realize that our five minutes are up."

"Screw you, Sambianco. I'm well aware of the time. How is it she's worth so much?"

"You're why, Justin. I could go into the details, but I myself don't understand them. Try looking up a market psychologist sometime. But the gist of it is, the market not only shows the values of various goods and services, but it's also the expression of humanity. This market is the first one in human history in which everyone plays a part. Some even call it the subconscious of the race. In that vein, everyone knows that you're the cause and the center of the crisis. Unconsciously, they also realize that you're the cure. And they can't buy shares of you. They most likely never will. But guess who they can buy shares of?"

"Neela."

"By the bucketload. You see, she's the closest thing to you. Justin, I could retire, and retire well, on her shares. That's if I'd kept them, of course."

"Sell too soon, Sambianco?"

"Nope. Actually donated them to the pool that GCI will give to you."

Justin eyed him suspiciously. "You're serious."

"Easy enough to check. If you don't want to think of me as the best friend you've got, then go ahead and think of me as your genie. What do you want? How about a moon? We can get you one. Do you want clear title to Venus? It will take some doing, but it's yours. Take it, rename it, call it Concordia or Neela or whatever. Hey, here's an idea. Take a majority of *my stock*. You can do to me what I've been doing to you . . . for the rest of your life. Do you want Chairman stock? How much? You have us. Ask away."

"Do you honestly believe that my giving up one share will make that much of a difference?"

"Yes," answered Hektor gravely. "Everything."

"Just curious. How?" asked Justin.

"Because you'll no longer be the Unincorporated Man. You'll have voluntarily joined the human race. Once you take that one step, GCI will be able to do the rest. But you have to do it voluntarily."

"And if I won't?"

"I'm sure you'll find a way," Hektor said, getting up from the couch. He'd been afraid to move at first, so delicate was the surgery he felt he was performing. But for Hektor Sambianco, not moving was like not breathing. Now that he knew he had Justin's undivided attention, he'd decided to stand up and pace a little. His nerves were frayed, and the blood flow would do him good, help him think better.

"Keep in mind, Justin," said Hektor, "our system isn't evil. It's good, it's certainly better than yours ever was. You cry 'freedom,' but mean 'equal.' You think people really want either? I'll tell you what they want—in your era or mine— they want to be left alone. And those that want the ability to affect their destiny always find a way. You're a case in point. In our era we're just a little better at it. Anyone can make it in our world, Justin. Believe me. We're not some distorted view of freedom, we're truly free. Free from pain, free from suffering, and, Damsah be praised, free from equality."

"That's not freedom, Hektor," he answered mockingly, "that's blindness. You've somehow lost sight of the fact that your technology has enabled you to have the trappings of freedom and equality, when in fact your system enslaves."

"Justin," countered Hektor, "it's not technology, it's sociology that makes us work. I studied your time period extensively. Do you remember seeing commercials on your television sets that would have some person begging for money to help starving people somewhere? They would show you pictures of emaciated people. You would see them dying on your television sets in front of you!"

"Of course I remember. I gave plenty to charities like that."

"That's nice, but it didn't really help that much, did it? Not the masses of people. Now what if we applied our sociology, *not our technology*, our sociology to that problem? You tell me if it would have made your world better or worse."

"In what way?" Justin asked, sensing a trap.

"What if," answered Hektor, without missing a beat, "instead of giving two, three, four dollars a month for a charity's sake, you gave ten dollars a month for a 5 percent share of that kid's future earnings? And you, of course, get nothing if the kid dies. Now you have a real interest in making sure that kid got that pair of shoes you sent. Now it's in your interest to find out if he's going to school and learning to read and write. Now maybe you'll send him that box of old clothes you were thinking of throwing away. Under your system you write a check and forget about the kid, who'll probably starve anyway. Under our system, you're locked into him. You don't just give a damn, you give an ongoing damn. It doesn't stop there. Your country, the USA, used to let whole regions of the planet go to hell and intervene in other regions based on national interest, which was almost always economic. Well, now, if millions of Americans are invested in millions of formerly starving people around the world, they'll probably want to make sure they don't get killed by some asshole with a gun and an agenda. Suddenly it's in the economic interest of your government to make sure that asshole governments won't kill millions of their own people for stupid ideological or religious reasons."

Hektor paused for breath. "But, Justin, I only put the government into the equation because I think you're a child of your age. The real benefit comes about when those 'evil, selfish, horrible corporations' get involved. How long will it take for a business to realize that there's a huge profit to be made in those hundreds of millions of starving children? If it took even ten years, I'd be amazed. Soon you'd have companies, businesses, and, yes, even corporations. They'd realize that 10 percent income of each of those people would make a huge investment potential. Imagine a world where a bank gives a loan to a corporation to build a school, hospital, or dormitory. Not because it's the right thing to do; who cares! They'd do it because it's the profitable thing to do. And because of that, my system, not in spite of greed and corruption and incorporation, but *because of it*, will work better than yours in any time period and with any technology you choose."

"But what's to stop those corporations," challenged Justin, "from exploiting those children, Sambianco—and don't tell me that they wouldn't."

Hektor was incensed. "What are you talking about? Those kids were starving to death—on your television sets, no less. They were being killed in pointless, profitless wars. They were suffering from curable ailments, even with your primitive technology. And you're worried some of them will be exploited? Are you totally Alaskan, Justin? Here's some news for you. I readily admit, a lot of those kids would be exploited. And I'll say what I said before, who cares? They'd be alive, for Damsah's sake. No, actually, I take that back. Only the stupid would truly try and exploit those kids. Because those that were exploited would grow up hating your company, and would work like crap. My system, hopefully your system too, if you can see it, works on self-interest. I managed some of GCI's human portfolios, and the number-one thing we tried to solve was discontent. It's not profitable. I'll stack the value of self-interest against those of equality and freedom any day of the week, and you tell me which one ends up being better for humanity." Hektor smiled inwardly at how little Justin was now interrupting him. Each argument, he believed, was another chip at the monolith of Cord's archaic notions.

"Here's a famous quote for you, Justin. It's from Tim Damsah himself. 'Incorporation is nothing but self-interest made viable in our society.' "

Justin remained unmoved. "You can't own a piece of that kid for life. It's wrong."

"Fine," retorted Hektor, "give his shares away. No one's stopping you. Don't you see? It's what makes the system work. Under your sociology—starvation, pain, occasional guilt-induced concern, followed by usually painful, pointless oblivion. Under our sociology—committed, long-term concern and investment leading to education, health, and long life. Of course neither system assures happiness, but, Justin, can you honestly not tell me which one gives that starving kid a better shot at it?"

"If your system's so great, Hektor, then why are so many people threatened by it? I didn't start the Liberty Party; I just spoke about divestiture. The party was a grassroots campaign that spread like wildfire *before I got there*. I only took over the reins after that madman Doogle died."

"Justin," snapped Hektor, "you could start a movement just by wearing an off-season suit. I'm sure there'd be thousands of people who'd see it as some sort of trend and swear by it, because the great Justin Cord did it. Your fashion faux pas would become their new style guide. That's how much influence you have.

But let's talk basics here, shall we? When was the last time someone starved in our system, or missed a meal? Missed out on a proper education, or lacked for a place to sleep? Not seen a doctor or a lawyer when they needed one? These poor fools in your party have no experience with just how rotten your way of life was. They forgot . . . we all forgot, Justin. But here's my prediction. At its worst, we'll have a civil war with suffering, death, and a century of truly pointless pain. But in the end the incorporated system will prevail. It works better. What you and I are doing here today, right now, is trying to avoid that century of having to re-learn the lessons of the Grand Collapse—of having another Gray Bomb incident occur. That's where you can help, and that's why we'll do anything to get you to give up your one share."

Justin's brow raised slightly. "Anything, you say?"

"Anything. I'm the strong right arm of the most powerful person in human history. Ask and I can make it happen."

Justin decided to have that synthetic beer after all. He got up, went to the fridge, and grabbed the can, then went back into the living room and sat himself down.

"Hektor, no offense . . . actually you can take offense. You're the messenger. A powerful one, I'll give you. But a messenger nonetheless."

"And?"

"I don't deal with messengers. Certainly not for something of this magnitude."

It only took Hektor a second, but he knew what Justin was getting at.

"*He* hardly sees anyone," Hektor answered tersely, "and I mean anyone. Even you. No more interviews, no in-person board meetings. I can barely get in to see him these days."

Justin took Hektor by the arm and saw him to the door. "Arrange it, Hektor. If you want to have any chance of this deal going through, I'm going to have to meet with the one man that matters. I *will* see The Chairman."

15 The Chairman

The greatest gift a person can have is the freedom to choose.
—MILTON FRIEDMAN, *FREE TO CHOOSE*, 1979

One hour after his talk with Hektor, Justin was informed by sebastian that a meeting had been set. Justin would meet The Chairman, and he'd meet him in his office atop GCI headquarters in New York City the following afternoon. Justin promptly said good-bye to Agnes, wished her luck, and headed out in his flyer. It would take him longer, but it would also give him some time to bone up on GCI system headquarters and the man he was about to meet.

He first concentrated on the complex of buildings that made up the headquarters. He had to admire its beauty. It was indeed a magnificent achievement befitting a corporation of GCI's stature. Even the foundation of the complex was remarkable. In reviewing the building's history, Justin read that by the time GCI had become one of the megacorporations, all the available land in New York City had been taken—at least, all the land large enough to house a building of GCI's stature. Justin found this amazing, because this was the New York that had, in effect, drained the Hudson River and built skyscrapers all the way to New Jersey and beyond.

GCI discovered that it would be next to impossible to build a complex large enough to headquarter their system-spanning enterprise. Not only would it have been cost prohibitive, it would most likely have generated a lot of bad publicity. It also hadn't helped that there'd already been a tremendous amount of interference from other corporations that didn't want GCI anywhere near their neck of the woods.

And that's when the board, following the suggestions of an enterprising young V. P. of General Operations named Mosh McKenzie, started something brand-new.

The corporation bought the rights to the seabed outside the seawall in the Hudson district. And in another bit of foresight, they bought those rights out to one hundred miles, so that no one could do to GCI what GCI was about to do to all those corporations that had made it so difficult for them to buy land earlier. Then, at great expense, the company raised the seabed and built an extended seawall, giving them a full three square miles of foundation to work with. With the foundation complete, the plans were drawn up. The famed architect Gavriel Yonatan created what, read Justin, was now considered to be the greatest single building complex in the history of mankind. The edifice began on the outskirts with luscious green parks, corporate housing for visiting guests, and a small orport. A little farther in were a series of thirty fifty-story building complexes, and, farther still, the true architectural party began. No one ever knew who gave the names to the five slightly curved three-hundred-story buildings arranged in a semicircle, but name them they did. They were called Calpurnia, Livonia, Aurilia, Julia, and Antonia. Each one interconnected with the others, in effect creating one tremendous building. By themselves the five sisters would have been a magnificent and much envied system headquarters. But it was what they surrounded that brought GCI world headquarters into the realm of legend, mystery, and magic. In the middle of the five sisters was the structure universally called the beanstalk. It was a man-made structure, stretching from the surface of the planet straight up for fifty miles into the dark embrace of space. Its initial purpose was to enable people and products to escape the gravity well via hundreds of specialized elevators.

The irony of the beanstalk was its apparent obsolescence halfway through its construction. The t.o.p. system of ground-based lasers and water-filled containers made it so. T.o.p.s could move practically anything—from a single person up to cargoes the size of old freighters—out of Earth's gravity, and do it more efficiently. But by then the initial capital outlay had been approved, and the already open construction required that the project be finished. And it was—but the GCI beanstalk wasn't a total loss, as it still managed to make some money from the movement of low-value bulk items, like ore and organic compounds.

What the GCI beanstalk had managed to do, and do quite well, was grab the imagination of humanity. It was the most popular tourist attraction on Earth, and by virtue of Earth's having the largest concentration of people, the most popular tourist attraction in the system. Though the ring tours of Saturn and the deep canyon cruises of Mars would certainly compete, a ride to the top of the GCI beanstalk was as mandatory in the present day as a visit to the top of the ill-fated World Trade Center towers had been in Justin's.

As the flyer skimmed over the wilderness of what once had been called the Bible Belt, Justin began to research The Chairman. According to the most recent picture—if that was any indication at all—he was a man in his early forties, with short, gray-flecked hair and a medium build. He had gray-green eyes, a square jaw, and a discernible glare that indicated the power within his grasp.

As if lending more resonance to his aura, the man rarely appeared for events and interviews, preferring to leave that "dirty work" to his current number two, Hektor Sambianco.

But his story, Justin could see, was legendary. He'd been raised by his father—his mother having died in the final stages of the terraforming of Mars. Soon after her passing, father and son left the confines of the distant planet for the more comforting environs of Earth. They were both in the penny stocks, and The Chairman's education had not positioned him well for corporate advancement. But his grades, Justin saw, had always been outstanding, and he'd scored very well on all of his aptitude tests. He'd wisely used those marks to get accepted into a prestigious piloting and navigation trade school. He eventually went on to become a navigator, and graduated, not surprisingly, at the top of his class. A midlevel sifter from GCI's human resources department came across the young talent using a fairly standard "spotter" program. The sifter sent the file up to his boss, who in turn offered the young navigator a job.

Through absolute devotion, willingness to sacrifice, and unrelenting tenacity the young navigator managed to gain a majority interest in himself at the exceedingly young age of thirty-five. With his majority status he was able to transfer from GCI's transport division to their executive pool. Again, another sacrifice, as doing so meant a serious cut in pay, not to mention having the appearance of a poor career move. Had he not had majority, his shareholders would have surely insisted that he remain a well-paid navigator lining their coffers for decades to come.

But providence had other plans for the young, single-minded executive. Over the course of twenty-seven years he worked hard, becoming at the tender age of sixty-two the youngest Chairman in GCI history, and the youngest in living memory of any major corporation.

In the thirty-one years of his Chairmanship, which Justin calculated would make him approximately ninety-three years of age, GCI rose from being one of the ten most powerful corporations in the system to becoming the recognized master of the corporate world. The Chairman did this first by dominating all aspects of intersystem trade and colonization. From there he moved quickly to create an unassailable power base, branching out into almost every field of human endeavor.

He also moved his personal offices from their traditional home in the Livia building to the top of the beanstalk. Then he'd made all the important vice presidents and their offices—along with their staffs—do the same. This combined workforce ended up occupying the equivalent of a thirty-story building forty miles up, with The Chairman's office suite at the very top of the very tallest building in the history of the world. And given the fact that the elevators were encased in a zero-friction vacuum, charged by a superhigh magnetic accelerator, it took only a matter of minutes for one to get from the streets of New York to the top of the world. In this Justin recognized the leadership gift of The Chairman. Amid the corporate elite of the system, Justin read, none were more envied than the ones who took the special express up the beanstalk every morning. They were in the real, visible seat of power. And The Chairman was above them all, looking down from his office onto a planet he practically owned.

This was the place that controlled his destiny, and this was the man who would decide his fate.

Justin landed his flyer on the seaside of the complex, in a spot prearranged with the GCI central traffic coordinator. As he put the flyer into autopilot, it came to a floating stop six inches off the ground near a giant weeping willow only thirty feet from the seawall. He exited the car and, stretching, looked around. He could see the five sisters in the near distance and hear the steady sound of waves crashing against the seawall. He could even feel the salty spray on his face as he breathed in the ocean air—all of which was a welcome relief from the canned air he had been forced to breathe on his cross-country journey. He took one last look at the flyer next to the bowing willow, and headed in the direction of the five sisters.

He'd been offered a direct transport but chose to walk. It wasn't so much to clear his head as to get his blood flowing. Per his instructions, and with sebastian's able direction, he headed toward Livonia, where only those blessed with a visit to the real seat of power caught the true elevator to the stars. It was a clear cloudless day, and from the ground up the GCI system headquarters complex was immense. Just looking up at *any* three-hundred-story building was enough to make one feel insignificant, but to look up and see five was almost more than his brain could take in. And even as awe-inspiring as the five sisters were, they almost paled next to the beanstalk. It didn't appear to be any more ornate than any of the sisters. If anything, less so. From up close, it looked to be a massive silver cylinder made up of enormous, slightly off-color, overlapping plates. It had, upon further inspection, thousands of long, threaded seams from which Justin could make out the movement of transport tubes. The thing just rose, up and up . . . and up, eventually disappearing into the atmosphere in the shape of a tiny needle piercing the heavens. It was as if, thought Justin, its sole purpose was not, in fact, to transport goods and tourists, but rather to make one feel completely insignificant.

Once Justin got close enough to the working hubbub of the complex, sebastian switched from vocal directions to visual. Justin was about to enter a veritable city, jam-packed with people, machinery, and robots. Visual direction from this point on would be far more efficient. Sebastian activated an internal teleprompter, which enabled Justin's eyes to see—and therefore follow—a red line on the ground.

Floating just above the grand citadel's entrance was a huge fifty-foot by three-hundred-foot sign. It read:

GCI—INVESTING IN HUMANITY

Justin walked approximately five hundred yards—bypassing throngs of workers and all manner of machines—to the entrance of the Livonia building. He ignored the hard stares. He also noticed that he was now being accompanied by, at a reasonable distance, a small cadre of securibots. The inside lobby was what he expected—thousands of people moving to and fro, rushing from one place to another. He followed the red line to the lifts, where he took a tube alone—the securibots had seen to that—up to the top of the building. He exited the tube and then traversed a connecting walkway to the beanstalk. He now found himself in a lobby of a different sort. First of all, it was far less crowded. One was only there if one had business being there. The manner and dress of the people was different as well—expensive suits, superior attitudes. The shape of the lobby was circular. It reminded Justin of a stadium, in that he imagined he could walk for some time before finally making it back to where he'd started.

He'd emerged, by design, directly in front of the executive lifts. The bank of lifts allowed thousands of people who worked at the top to arrive and depart without having to deal with a bottleneck. And, of course, there was *the one* elevator, specially cordoned off by a red rope, a small army of securibots, and a group of expressionless, well-armed, muscular men and women. The elevator was used only by the board and their personal staffs, and was also where Justin's red line was leading to.

Of the people he did see in this lobby, not a one made any eye contact, nor did any make an effort to come up, direct, or interact with him in any way. He shrugged and headed for the elevator. A human guard lifted the red rope and waited for Justin to walk through.

He entered the elevator, which, becoming aware of his presence, spoke.

"Which floor do you want, sir?"

"You mean you don't know?"

"I'm sorry. Am I supposed to?" it asked.

"Well, it seems that everything else has been arranged. I just figured . . ."

"Yes?"

"Never mind. Take it all the way to the top, I suppose . . . er . . . elevator."

"Very good, sir. By the way, many executives call me 'riser.' Do you want the exterior to be transparent or opaque?"

"I think I would like transparent, riser."

"As you wish, sir. I believe this is your first time in the beanstalk."

"That's correct, riser."

"May you have a pleasant and profitable visit. The car will accelerate slowly at first, and then with increasing speed. Please have a seat." One immediately formed out of the fluid material of the elevator wall. Justin got in and was not surprised to find that the seat fit him perfectly. "If you have any discomfort," said riser, "please let us know. You have exclusive use of the elevator. How quickly do you wish to arrive at your destination?"

"What's the fastest I can get there?"

"Without detailed access to your medical records, and only going by what information is available to me via surface observation, I would say two minutes and fifty-eight seconds. The record time is two minutes and six seconds."

"That would be uncomfortable, and I don't think I'd enjoy the trip as much. How about we shoot for ten?"

"An excellent choice, sir." As the elevator began to rise, the walls began to disappear. Before he knew it, Justin was heading up into the sky—open air all around him. Only the cooling breeze of his initial entrance into the lift remained as a psychological anchor to the fact that he wasn't flying outside of the translucent shell. But he was hardly breathing as he saw the city below him in all its terrible majesty. Decimated three-hundred-story structures stretched from Brooklyn to the Jersey shore and beyond. There were large swaths of land empty but for a predominance of huge sunken holes where the nanites had bored and destroyed every last molecule of the behemoths' foundations—including all those inside. In other places half-eaten structures were defiantly jutting out from the war-torn landscape as if from an old abandoned graveyard. New York City, once a living, breathing organism of over seventy-five million human beings, was now a humbled, decrepit, and bleeding wreck of less than thirty million. As the lift rose higher and the wounded city faded from view, Justin couldn't help but think of Hemingway's famous quote: "In modern war you'll die like a dog for no good reason." He remained solemn. *Had they all died for no good reason?*

The rich cerulean sky finally succumbed to the one color that encompassed all. Justin, via the beanstalk, had entered the deep black vastness of space.

What made the trip even more peculiar was the soft glimmer that the beanstalk gave off. He'd been so transfixed by the surreal glow that he'd hardly noticed the deceleration. But the car must have slowed considerably, as it was now hardly moving. All at once the rust-colored walls appeared.

"I hope you had a pleasant ride, sir," said riser.

Justin got up from the seat. "Thank you, riser. I did." He left as the door slid open, and once more began to follow the red line. He stopped to survey the scene. He'd entered a corridor that curved away to both his left and his right. The floor was lushly carpeted, and the walls made of fine desert bone marble. The color scheme wasn't to Justin's taste, but then again, it didn't have to be. The outer wall was clear, giving any observer the perspective of being on a richly appointed wraparound balcony.

"The Chairman's suite," said sebastian. "It contains three levels. The bottom level is devoted to business affairs and the top two are presumed to be living quarters."

"Presumed?"

"No confirmed interior shots have ever been taken, and The Chairman has never given interviews from there. It is assumed that the entire two floors are fluid, but no one knows for sure."

"Fluid rooms are expensive and difficult to maintain, sebastian. Couldn't someone simply check maintenance records or fluid-room technicians' comings and goings?"

"Indeed one could, Justin, and many have tried, but The Chairman values his privacy and took the precaution of having lots of orders and supplies available. It is difficult to determine what he needs and what is merely 'cover.' For instance, it is a matter of public record that his quarters ordered twelve reproduction tiki bars. Is that something The Chairman is likely to use?"

Justin remembered a couple of wild parties he'd attended when younger with a tiki theme. "No, sebastian. One, maybe, but I doubt he'd need twelve. OK," he said, looking in the direction of the red line, "let's get this over with."

From where he'd been standing it was only a short walk to two large double doors. They looked to be made out of oak, and were ornately carved with all manner of horticulture. They opened as he entered. The room appeared to be a large reception area surrounded by art. It was at least thirty by thirty square feet, with another set of imposing double doors opposite the ones Justin had only recently entered. To the side of the double doors was an assistant with a stack of papers, data crystals, and a large array of holodisplays. The young man, who seemed to have enough work to keep him busy for days, looked up briefly and indicated that Justin should take a seat. Justin noticed that the assistant was not particularly tall, and a bit out of place behind a monstrous desk, appropriate for his stature but awkward for his age.

As soon as Justin sat down, the double doors to the right of the secretary burst open and a group of executives emerged. From the looks on their faces it seemed pretty clear that The Chairman had just torn the lot of them a new one. Their clothing, appearance, and manner suggested that these were men and women who'd climbed high up the corporate ladder; however, the manner in which the last one out quietly closed the door behind him told Justin they hadn't reached the top rung yet. Half the group tossed their data pads onto the secretary's desk without bothering to look at him. Justin detected a small sigh emanating from the young man at what must have been the doubling of his workload, but, thought Justin, the kid did well not to let his unhappiness show in any obvious way.

Though the group had been whispering among themselves as they left the inner sanctum, they shut up quickly the second they saw Justin in the chair. It was obvious that they knew who he was, but Justin thought he detected surprise—until, as a person, they all adopted poker faces.

They didn't know I was going to be here. Interesting, thought Justin. *So he likes playing games.*

They studied the famous guest openly for a moment but made no attempt to go up and talk with him. In fact, they all filed past, ignoring him outright. The set of double doors from which Justin had entered now opened and then moments later closed, sweeping into the hall the last of them.

An eager to please and painfully young voice finally spoke up. "The Chairman will be a few moments, Mr. Cord. Can I get you anything? Coffee, tea, a drink, reefer, stims?"

"Coffee would be fine, Mr. . . ."

"Oh, everyone up here calls me Marcus. Let me see if I remember. Your preferred coffee is Jamaican Blue Mountain—Earth, not orbital grown. Not too strong, but nice and hot."

"That's very good, Marcus," answered Justin. "GCI must keep very good records on me."

Marcus laughed. "Oh, I'm sure they do, Mr. Cord, not that *I'd* ever get to see them. I know your taste in coffee from watching *Celebrity Lifestyles.*" The boy's face reddened a bit. "It's one of my favorite shows."

"Mine, too," Justin said, stretching the truth a little to make the young man feel more comfortable. Justin did know about the show, but more so because Neela had loved it. The thought of her now pained him. He shifted his eyes to the art on the wall, hoping it would distract him. Besides, he had nothing to do now but wait. The man with the real power was gently reminding him of that fact.

Justin noticed a statue. It had a bronze quality, yet the surface seemed somehow alive. It may have been the subject matter itself. On first glance it seemed to be in the form of a man trying to walk. But the longer Justin looked the more he realized it was a man trying to walk . . . off his pedestal. Maybe even, thought Justin, escape it. He looked at the head of the figure. Though somewhat abstract, there was a pained and sorrowful expression emanating from every contour of its face. Justin knew that the *statue knew* it would never escape.

He got up out of his chair and began to walk around the figure. The ability to take mere objects and form them in such a way as to elicit a real and complex emotional response was, to Justin, the essence of art. He differentiated that from the utter garbage that used to hang on the walls of most of the modern art museums of his time. Anyone could throw crap—sometimes literally—onto a canvas and put it in a museum. They'd even elicit a response, but not one worthy of the patron or the artist.

Justin felt a tap on his shoulder. He turned to see the erstwhile assistant, cup and saucer in hand.

"Your coffee, Mr. Cord."

"Thank you, Marcus."

Justin took a sip. *Definitely not synthetic.* "Tell me, Marcus. Is this the original or a cast?"

"A little bit of both, Mr. Cord. It was made from a picture of the original statue. It's a fine reproduction, but nowhere near as fine, I'm told, as what the original looked like . . . which, I'm afraid, was destroyed in the Tokyo Earthquake of 2107. Legend has it that the artist mixed his own blood into the bronzilite, but who can really know?"

"Even the copy," stated Justin, "is magnificent. Does the artist have any more works extant?"

"Yes," answered Marcus, "I have a list of all the works as well as their locations. I will see to it that your avatar is informed."

"I'd very much appreciate that, Marcus."

Justin continued his perusal.

"I see that The Chairman has one of my old pieces. And," he said, admiring the work, "he appears to have done a masterful job of restoring it."

"Ahh, yes, you're of course referring to the Gustav Caillebotte. With innovative approaches to nanite restoration, we can be 99.7 percent certain that this is how the painting looked on the day it was originally completed."

Justin nodded, grunting his appreciation.

"Tell me, if you wouldn't mind, Mr. Cord," asked Marcus. "What made you choose to purchase this painting . . . originally, that is?"

Justin didn't take his eyes off the work. "Like the sculpture here, Caillebotte's work is multidimensional."

"Really? How so?" asked Marcus, staring at the painting anew.

"Well," answered Justin, "on one hand you've got this large-scale canvas covered in stark colors and strong brushstrokes—the work of a master craftsman. On the other you have a very powerful piece of protest art meant to underscore the insidious crawl of the industrial revolution. An interesting choice for your boss."

Marcus remained silent.

Justin looked at the other paintings. One, he saw was a Daumier, an artist he knew to be deeply interested in people, especially the lower classes. The next was a work by Shitao, the renowned monk artist whose paintings were famous for sharing their creator's self-conscious projection of spiritual liberation.

And finally there was the still life. It was drab and gray and somewhat representational of a vase of flowers. It was, Justin decided, ghastly, and he had absolutely no idea why it had been chosen to be a part of such an esteemed collection.

"Marcus, forgive me if I speak from ignorance, but why is this piece here? Does it represent a school or style I don't have the experience to understand?"

"In a way, Mr. Cord . . . watch it closely . . . *very* closely."

Justin moved up closer to the painting and stared hard at the whole of it. After a time he realized that, in fact, it was slowly and subtly changing color and tone.

"That's kind of interesting. Why's it doing that?"

"Haven't you heard of M'Art, Mr. Cord?"

"Yes, yes I have," he answered. "That's art that's linked to the various markets."

"M'Art works will actually change color and tone based on how the markets they're tied to are doing."

Justin nodded. "So this is M'Art. A little stiff, if you ask me."

"Oh, Mr. Cord. It's actually a very exciting field. There are so many ways a M'artist can approach the subject. For example, what colors represent what markets? Do tones matter? What objects are given to which colors? Once all those factors have been decided, you have not only a very complex painting, but one that will truly change every day, and in wholly unpredictable ways. It's not a static image; it's a painting that truly reflects the world it's a part of."

Justin put his hand to his chin and stared hard at the seemingly inconsequential piece. "But what makes this one so special? Special enough, that is, to warrant your boss's wall space?"

Marcus, Justin saw, smiled knowledgeably.

"Although it's a relatively simple still life, this painting is considered by many experts to be the first true piece of M'Art ever created. On top of that, this M'Artwork is not tied to one specific market, but rather to the entire system exchange."

"In a painting so small?" asked Justin.

"Yes," Marcus said proudly, almost as if he'd owned it himself, "in a painting so small. Part of its genius."

"It must be priceless," said Justin, squinting his eyes ever so slightly, wondering if perhaps that, too, would reveal a different experience.

"It's insured at over three hundred and fifty million credits," answered Marcus matter-of-factly.

Justin guffawed. "No shit," he said, while watching the colors change from inches away. "Better not sneeze, then."

Marcus smiled.

"Is it just me or does it look a little washed out to you?"

"If the markets don't improve," answered Marcus, "it'll probably go negative. Never done that before."

Justin finally backed up so he could study the collection again from a distance, with a more discerning eye.

"Tell me, Marcus, which one's your favorite?"

"Oh, the sculpture," the secretary answered, without missing a beat.

"Really. Why is that?"

"Look at it long enough and you realize it's not really a sculpture."

Justin turned his head slightly to see Marcus transfixed on the statue—lost.

"What then?"

"A mirror, Mr. Cord."

Justin's eyes narrowed with suspicion. "Pretty deep answer for a kid."

Marcus's bright-eyed look came on—as if a switch had been flicked. "I'm twenty-three, Mr. Cord."

"Bullshit, Marcus. If you're twenty-three then I'm . . ."

Justin stopped talking and stared blankly at the boy.

"Well, I'll be damned," he muttered under his breath, mouth forming into a knowing grin. He now studied Marcus in much the same way he'd only moments before studied the paintings. The hair was a different shade and was straight, not wavy. The nose was smaller and slightly misshapen, and the eyes were a different color. There were enough differences that you had to look for it, but it was him, alright.

Justin extended his hand. "It's good to finally meet you, Mr. Chairman."

The Chairman laughed heartily, and took Justin's hand firmly into his.

"Damn, Mr. Cord. I was hoping for at least an hour."

Justin felt the man's firm grasp and met it with his own.

"Sorry," said Justin, "but no twenty-three-year-old I know—in any century— would look at a sculpture and see a mirror."

"Oh, really, Mr. Cord. And what do you suppose he would see?"

"The world would be his oyster. Everything in his mind would be shaped by the prism of advancement."

The Chairman shook his head in agreement. "You're an old man, sir. An old man like me."

Justin continued to maintain a friendly posture but never failed to realize who he was dealing with. "Not quite as old as you, sir, but let's just say I've aged a bit since reawakening."

"Oh, I'll bet you have," The Chairman said, knowingly. "I must apologize, Mr. Cord. I have underestimated you. I think we all have. You'd think, given the fact that I've been studying you almost from the minute you were awakened, I'd have been a little sharper on the uptake. Senior moment, I guess."

Justin shrugged.

"Would you care to join me for a walk?" asked The Chairman. "The level is now completely cleared out, and I can assure you we'll have total privacy."

Not really a question, thought Justin.

"Sure."

"In a very real sense you get to walk on top of the world," said The Chairman, smiling brightly.

He reminded Justin of a cat, mouse in paws, unsure what to do with it.

They left the antechamber through the double doors and started walking clockwise around the corridor. Though the Earth was still shrouded in darkness, parts of it were quite luminous. The light was seen overwhelmingly on the coasts and the rivers. It was, thought Justin, as if someone had etched the continents and major waterways in bright fluorescent paint.

"I never get tired of the view," said The Chairman. "I think that's why I moved the headquarters up here."

"So," asked Justin, "the fact that being up here symbolically makes you the most important person on Earth had nothing at all to do with it?"

"Well," The Chairman answered, with a mischievous smile, "maybe just a little."

There was an awkward moment of silence as they both stared out the window onto the Earth below. Justin decided they'd had enough of the small talk.

"Look," he said, continuing to take in the view, "I think I know your position about my incorporating, but why don't I spell out the basics and you can tell me if I'm missing anything."

The Chairman looked amused. "By all means. I'm very curious."

Justin turned to face his adversary.

"GCI—which is you—contends that I have the power to disrupt the incorporated system, which at its heart is voluntary. I do this by not only continuing to remain unincorporated, but by also acting as the head of the Liberty Party and actively encouraging divestment. You with me?"

"All the way, Mr. Cord."

"Good." He continued. "I give credence and hope to the millions who've decided that they don't want to be incorporated anymore, and seeing one man, or, to be more precise, 'one free man,' defy the system gives them that hope."

"Hope is very powerful, Mr. Cord."

"And, to you, very dangerous," Justin added.

The Chairman nodded.

"In order to curtail a massive violent social confrontation," continued Justin, "you need my active support. This won't end all the problems, but it will pull the steam out of the Liberty Party and the Action Wing. How am I doing so far?"

"Exceptionally well," The Chairman said with a muted smile. "Please continue."

"To this end you're willing to pay over one billion credits in stock options, giving Neela Harper a supermajority in herself. And this, of course, is for the sole purpose of making me comfortable in giving her my one—and only one—share out of the hundred thousand that would be formed following standard articles of incorporation for an individual."

"So far, so good."

"You will also stop harassing me, my associates, and my friends—sadly, a much diminished group."

"I take it you are referring to Mr. Black?"

"Not specifically," answered Justin, "but yeah, he would definitely be in the 'diminished' category."

"Manny Black was a great loss," The Chairman readily agreed. "A mind like that is difficult to find and impossible to cultivate purposely."

"He was a good friend." Justin paused, remembering the death he'd felt indirectly responsible for. He then continued with his review of the "facts." "Neela will be given a media-driven, well-orchestrated pass for having become involved with her patient and, finally, you'll release my assets and turn me into a great human being beloved by all."

The Chairman nodded. "That's about the gist of it."

"Good," said Justin. "Now that the carrot's out of the way, let's see if I'm clear on the stick."

The Chairman remained silent.

"If I persist," continued Justin, "in adhering to, how did Hektor put it, 'my silly superstitions,' I'll be audited until I'm broke. I'll have all my friends and acquaintances harassed to the point that they'll likely shoot me before they'll say hello. I will never see Neela again—even to the point of your threatening to kill her."

"Hektor shouldn't have been so direct on that, Mr. Cord. It was rude."

"You saying you wouldn't?"

The Chairman gave a shark's grin. "Oh no, Mr. Cord, I'd do it, but I believe that when one threatens the most that's also when one should be the most polite. . . . Hektor's still young."

Strange words, thought Justin, *coming from the face of a child.*

"Hektor also tried his best to explain," continued Justin, "why my beliefs are wrong and harmful. And that everything I wanted was right in front of me. All I had to do was take it."

The Chairman nodded. "So much passion and commitment lurking under that layer of selfish disinterest. Funny, isn't it, Mr. Cord? Did he really offer you Venus?"

"Well, I did get the impression that that would be the maximum I could hope for."

The Chairman laughed. "I hope you aren't getting your hopes up, sir. Venus really is a bit much. I could possibly swing Ganymede or Io."

Justin folded his arms and waited, choosing to ignore The Chairman's olive branch.

Upon his realizing that Justin had finished, The Chairman's eyes shifted once again—all business. "I have everything drawn up for you to take to your council in order to put the agreement into motion. You will notice that I have already embossed my fingerprint, signed, and given a DNA sample. Forgive my using a drop of blood; I sometimes can't resist a flare for the dramatic. You will also sign, fingerprint, and give a DNA sample. Hand this pad to your lawyers, and by Damsah, Mr. Cord, you'll get everything you want, the system will return to normal in a matter of months, and everyone will get to live happily ever after. Does that sound so bad?"

Justin remained silent, and then a second later motioned for The Chairman to hand over the pad.

"So," asked Justin, staring down at the glorified DijAssist, "everything to seal the deal is contained right here?"

The Chairman nodded solemnly.

Justin studied the pad for a few more moments, and then, appearing to be puzzled, beckoned The Chairman over.

"I don't want to be confused," Justin said to the man now peering into his pad, believing he'd been called over to elucidate a point, "because it seems so much of what I say gets misconstrued. So I'd like it to be really clear here. . . ."

The Chairman nodded, anticipating the question.

"Since you believe that everything vital to your existence can be found within this," Justin said, raising the pad ever so slightly, "why don't you take it—and all that it represents—and shove it up your ass."

Justin then let the pad drop to the floor.

"I choose freedom."

Contrary to Justin's expectations, The Chairman didn't overreact. In fact, noticed Justin, the man seemed suddenly tired. His shoulders sagged, and the gloom in his eyes revealed far more of the ninety-three-year-old than that of the young man currently represented.

"As would I, Mr. Cord . . . As would I."

Justin stared at the man, unsure of what to do. He'd expected a harangue, a threat, a phalanx of securibots to drag him off to some netherworld, but not this. Whatever The Chairman's game was, Justin wanted no part of it.

"You won't change my mind," he said, refusing to move from his spot. "So whatever it is you're up to, you can forget it."

"Change your mind, Mr. Cord?" the old man answered. "Why would I want to change what I helped to create?"

The Chairman smiled, as a father would to a son. And with that one smile Justin finally understood the mystery that had stymied not only him, but all those around him. A mystery that had faded in importance in the rush of events.

"You," he said, smiling knowingly. "You paid the ten million credits and made it untraceable. You," he said, hardly believing the words pouring out of his mouth, "made me into the Unincorporated Man."

The Chairman nodded, slowly turned around, and began walking down the promenade, beckoning Justin to follow. "Why don't we get a drink and really talk."

The Chairman led him off the promenade to a small sunken lounge. He then procured some glasses and a bottle of amber liquid from behind a bar while Justin sat, waiting impatiently at a small table. Justin had come expecting a polite but terse conversation, confirmation of positions, and a getting on with life. The strange turn of events had unnerved him.

"Why didn't you just tell me from the start?" he asked. "Why the charade?"

"I needed to know if Hektor had gotten to you."

"To what end?"

"Justin," began The Chairman, pouring drinks for the both of them, "all will be explained."

"To what end?" Justin said, this time more firmly.

The Chairman raised his glass and drained the amber liquid. "Humor an old man, won't you? I assure you, it'll be worth your while."

Justin eyed the man for another few seconds. "Go on."

The Chairman nodded in thanks. "Let me tell you a little bit about my life that the bios don't talk about. It begins accurately enough. I was born on Mars and my mother was killed. I never really knew her. Just a memory of a kind face and a voice singing in the night as I went to sleep. After she disappeared I asked about her and why she died. My earliest clear memories are not of my mother, but of my asking about her. According to my father, Mother really didn't want to be on Mars. But she didn't have majority, and the job paid very well, so she agreed. My father says to this day that if she had had majority she never would have taken the job that killed her."

"Do you believe him?"

"Back then, Mr. Cord, I had absolute faith that it was the truth."

Justin nodded, indicating that The Chairman should continue.

"This may come as a shock to you, but the truth is, I've always hated incorporation because of it. As I grew up I came to realize that my father was probably just grieving. The money *was* very good. I couldn't see how my mother could have turned it down, majority or no."

"And yet you still have this hatred?"

"It's my earliest and most constant feeling, Mr. Cord. In all the many years between then and now I've never lost that."

"Well, if you don't mind my saying, sir, you have a pretty interesting way of expressing it. You were a near-worthless penny stock and rose to be Chairman of arguably the most powerful organization in history. I'd say the incorporated system has been very good for you."

The Chairman didn't respond—intent, figured Justin, on seeing the story through.

"Mr. Cord, what would happen to someone from your time who said he hated the USA? Not only that, but at every opportunity, from grade school through adulthood, this guy made his feelings known in a loud and obvious manner."

"They'd probably make him a writer for *The New York Times*," snickered Justin. He then saw the confused expression on his host's face. "A bit of very dated humor, sorry. I understand what you're getting at. He'd be ostracized, most likely."

"And made useless," added The Chairman. "From the earliest time I knew that my loathing for the system that surrounded me had to be kept very deep. That there was no one I could share it with, no one I could talk about it with. But, Mr. Cord, every share that I did not own, I considered a piece of my soul torn away. I thought that when I achieved majority it would go away. I'd be at peace. But it only made it worse. The fruits of my labors were not my own. I could never have all of what I achieved. I would always have to share it."

"Mr. Chairman, not to be rude, but we had that in my time, too. It was called taxes."

"Mr. Cord, taxes, horrible as they might have been, only taxed income. Incorporation takes a piece of everything. From the moment we're born our actions are circumscribed. There are whole categories of actions we cannot take because our stockholders won't allow it. They not only own a piece of our income, they, by default, own a piece of us. Can you say the same for your taxation?"

"No," admitted Justin, "I guess not."

"After I got my majority," continued The Chairman, "I considered becoming an asteroid miner. That's about as free as a person can be in our system. If you have majority you're on your own. Your shareholders don't mind that you're in a high-risk field because of the profit, and you can forget you're incorporated, as long as you don't look too closely at your earnings statement."

"Why didn't you?"

"Because, Mr. Cord, the more I studied the evolution of the incorporated society the more I realized that it was becoming more dangerous."

"Well, according to those opposed to my vision," answered Justin, "you're talking about a system whose biggest crime seems to be that it works."

The Chairman nodded somberly. "And they'd be correct, Mr. Cord. For going on three centuries now incorporation has given mankind unparalleled peace, progress, and prosperity. But at what price? Humanity has stopped asking that all-important question, 'at what price?' "

"If the price is freedom," snapped Justin, "then guess what? Ninety-five percent of your people don't want it."

The Chairman's eyes grew still and cold. "How can they, Mr. Cord? They don't know what 'it' is. This world we're living in, sir, is a dictatorship—a dictatorship of the content. It's a creeping, smothering form of tyranny because it works so well and makes everyone so happy . . . on the surface. But I knew that if left alone to develop, it would grow to the point where it could not be stopped."

The Chairman poured himself another glass and leaned back in his seat, knowing full well the impact of his words.

"Let me get this straight," said Justin, hardly believing what he'd just heard. "You're saying that all of mankind is in danger of falling into this 'dictatorship,' and that you've been somehow trying to stop it?"

"Oh, Mr. Cord, that's the irony," answered The Chairman. "I can't. Though I've been trying very hard to slow it down. I've worked night and day to get enough power to reverse the direction humanity's been going in. To make us all pause and retrace our steps."

"So then why not change it?" asked Justin. "You're The Chairman, for God's sakes."

The Chairman sighed.

"Mr. Cord," he answered, "if I could have, you would not be sitting here right now listening to the confessions of a lonely old man. You'd be out traipsing around the solar system with your Dr. Harper, and the human race would not be on the road to slavery."

He swirled the newly poured drink in his glass and stared at the elliptical pattern the rich liquid made as he did so.

"I have more power than anyone in history," he uttered, then paused to take another sip, "but I'm not more powerful *than* history."

He put the glass down on the table, and once again looked directly at Justin.

"The momentum of centuries is difficult to break, and even with my power, Mr. Cord, I couldn't stop the course of events. If I moved too quickly and too openly I would've been exposed and removed from power. All I've been able to do is slow it down."

"It?"

"The crossing of the threshold into outright slavery. Without me and some carefully played political games and judicial appointments, individuals would be allowed to sell off eighty percent of themselves and not seventy-five. Do you know, in my lifetime, Mr. Cord, the minimum percent of themselves a person was required by law to keep was dropped from thirty-five, to thirty, to twenty-five. There are many people still alive who can even remember when it was *forty-five*."

"But if it's so obvious, Mr. Chairman, why don't more people fight it? Why aren't my followers in the billions rather than the millions?"

"Fight what, Mr. Cord? Prosperity? Jobs? Wealth? As we all became inextricably linked to one another through personal incorporation, our wealth became more abundant, and we needed less to be content. Even at 20 percent the poorest of us would be as wealthy as you were in your past life—more so, when you consider the health benefits and life expectancy of living in our era. If my calculations are correct, within two centuries the minimum by law that a person will have to keep of themselves will be down to 5 percent. *Five percent*, Mr. Cord. That's about what a slave got for his labor before your Civil War. But at least the slave knew he was a slave. Ours won't. Oh, we'll take care of them, feed them, be good masters, but they're going to be slaves, nonetheless."

"Not every slave remained a slave," answered Justin, choosing to leave his glass conspicuously full. "There were always those who rose up."

"Yes," answered The Chairman, "the incredibly talented, driven, and lucky ones managed to find freedom. Would you like to know the percentage of luck I needed to get as far as I got? If I'd been as unlucky as I was lucky early in my career I would never have made majority. The percentage of penny children born of penny parents who will make majority is less than 10 percent. The lower the minimum shares that must be kept, the smaller that number gets. The system is very efficient at making its choices. By the time the average penny is born, educated, and raised he's at his minimum. Society conspires to have his parents, and then himself, give up all of his disposable shares, and it gets harder and harder each passing decade to get them back."

"So then what do you propose to do?"

"Me? Why, nothing. Or, at least, nothing much."

"Oh, I see," said Justin. "What do you propose *I* do? That I'm not already doing, that is."

"Everything, Mr. Cord. You're the luckiest thing that ever happened to humanity, though it will be centuries before history realizes it. It almost made me believe in the divine. When I got the report of *what* you were and *when you came from* I sensed that you could be the answer to the problems that had beguiled me. And then when it turned out to be *you,* Justin Cord, I felt something I hadn't felt in years, Mr. Cord."

Justin shrugged, not venturing a guess.

"Hope," said The Chairman.

"Hope," answered Justin, "is a dangerous thing, Mr. Chairman."

"And so very powerful," countered The Chairman. "I've been protecting you ever since. You wouldn't believe the number of attempts that have been made on your life."

Justin remembered the incident on the Moon and at the Empire State Center. "Yes, yes, I would."

"A confession, Mr. Cord . . . The first attempt was mine. Not to take your life, I assure you, but rather to scare you into taking your protection more seriously. I apologize for those two troglodytes. They acted beyond their orders."

"And died."

"If they had followed orders they would not have."

"And the second attempt?"

"Unplanned, but my responsibility nonetheless. One of my subordinates got a little out of hand. He's been dealt with, I assure you."

"Comforting."

"Would you like to know how many attempts I've actually managed to stymie?"

"I'll pass," answered Justin. "Just remind me before I leave to fire my security detail."

The Chairman allowed himself a small laugh.

Justin's eyes narrowed. "I don't understand something."

The Chairman indicated for him to continue.

"If you were so gung ho to keep me unincorporated, why did you have GCI try to incorporate me in court?"

"We had to do something. Hektor would have waited and built a stronger case. Kirk Olmstead, his former boss, wanted to move quickly. I knew Manny Black would destroy them."

"And I suppose," said Justin, resigned, "you set that up as well."

"Yes, though neither of you knew it. I have files of extraordinary people that I keep in reserve for all sorts of contingencies. Manny was one of them."

"Who else did you activate?" snapped Justin.

The Chairman waited a moment before answering, knowing full well that what he was about to reveal would be incendiary.

"Sean Doogle."

Justin's eyes boggled. "You unleashed that murderer on humanity?!"

"To be more precise," he answered, too calm for Justin's comfort, "I allowed Hektor to."

"He murdered the president," shouted Justin. "Hundreds of others—and spawned the architects of the Gray Bomb! Please tell me you're not giving money to the Action Wing."

"Not anymore. Its usefulness is at an end."

Justin stared blankly at the man before him.

"You're mad. Why in the world would you want a revolution that could possibly kill billions when an evolution would achieve the same ends with far less loss of life and a better chance of success?"

"Because, sir, evolution has failed. I've tried it, and even with all my power, could barely stem the tide. What we need now is a *revolution*. Doogle and the Action Wing were simply the clarion call."

"Evolution failed *your way,* but not mine. It's true that I'm the one man who still has the freedom to choose, and *I will* give humanity a fighting chance at a real destiny, but not at the guaranteed price of billions dead."

"Billions, Mr. Cord?" asked The Chairman, clenching his jaw so tightly his words were almost indiscernible. "What about the *hundreds of billions* who'll be here soon? If your evolution fails, what sort of universe will they be born into? One in which each of them is free to choose a destiny, or one in which they'll be programmed from birth to accept a certain range of menial jobs for 5 percent of their labor? And what of the *trillions* who'll follow that?

"I'd give anything to be you," The Chairman continued, "the man to lead humanity out of slavery. But we don't get to choose our history so much as history chooses us, do we? Well, Justin Cord, *history has chosen you.*"

"No, sir," retorted Justin, "*you* have chosen me. And if I were to follow your course, countless more billions will die needlessly. In your rush to destroy the system you hate, you haven't stopped to consider what would replace it. Well, I'll tell you. It's almost always something or someone worse. Mao, Pol Pot, Hitler, Stalin, and Ahmadinejad, to name but a few."

"I'm a good judge of character, Mr. Cord, and you're none of the above."

"You're right, I'm not. But there's no guarantee, as you so aptly pointed out, that I'll be around forever, and I'm not willing to trust the future of humanity on the whims of one person. Slow and steady wins the race, sir. Even if it means the race takes a few hundred years."

"I'm well aware of history, Mr. Cord. It wouldn't be just you. We can *both* manage it. With my power and connections and your leadership we can turn it all back—*together*."

"No, we can't," answered Justin, "at least, not the way you're envisioning it. And we'd be fools if we thought we could. Your revolution has succeeded in nothing but the killing of countless millions, and if not for me flying across the far reaches of the planet, quite possibly countless more. No, sir. If you want me on board you do it *my* way. It won't free everybody, but anybody who wants to be free will have the opportunity."

Neither said a word, each waiting for the other to give. After almost two minutes of silence, Justin realized The Chairman no longer knew how to compromise.

"We appear to be at a crossroads, sir," said Justin, with a wry smile.

"Indeed."

"I'm convinced," said Justin, "that working separately we'll fail."

Justin waited for The Chairman to absorb what he'd just said.

"What do you suggest?" asked The Chairman.

"Let's give evolution a decade or two, with myself as the leader. If in that time it's not working, and is a complete and utter failure, we can always resort to your way."

The Chairman thought it over briefly, looked up from his now empty glass, and smiled.

"I agree, then . . . for now."

"Oh, and one more thing," said Justin.

"Yes?"

"Neela."

The Chairman sighed, and shifted uneasily in his seat.

"I can't get her back."

At first Justin didn't react. Then the old man's recalcitrance got the better of him.

"Why the hell not?"

"For both your sakes!" The Chairman shot back. "You cannot have Dr. Harper, nor do I believe you should. Your sociological effectiveness increases the more you suffer publicly. But it's a moot point . . . do you really think she'd have you back? You continue to tear at a system she loves . . . almost as much as she loves you."

"Mr. Chairman," retorted Justin, regaining his composure now that he'd confirmed all was not lost, "if you want me to be your partner in this endeavor, if you want my help, you'll get me Neela—whether she wants me or not. Otherwise, I do it my way—the whole way. That's the deal I'm prepared to make. Take it or leave it."

Justin then raised the glass he'd left untouched, almost willing The Chairman to raise his.

The Chairman looked at the man before him and saw the resolve. It was the rare occurrence that he, the CEO of GCI, ever needed someone more than he himself was needed, but such was the case. He'd gotten as far as he was going to get. Only the Unincorporated Man could take it further. He refilled his glass and raised it up. "Then you'll get Dr. Harper—if she'll have you."

The quiet hum of the beanstalk was interrupted momentarily by the sound of glass on glass as they toasted to the deal, drank, and then sat back.

There was, realized Justin, one impediment still to be considered. "What about Hektor? He won't take too kindly to my being seen with Dr. Harper—especially after having banished her to the outer system."

"Don't worry about Hektor, Mr. Cord . . . ," assured The Chairman.

The icy stare was back.

". . . he'll be taken care of. I suggest you disappear for a few weeks."

With that The Chairman got up from his chair. Justin rose as well. The deal was done, the meeting over.

"Good luck, Mr. Cord. We'll be in touch."

The Chairman realized that he was now passing on the torch, and with it the years of hardship and strain attendant to a life spent in furtive embrace. Though the job wasn't finished, it was at least entering a new phase. *Indeed*, thought The Chairman, *hope is a very powerful thing.*

As Justin shook The Chairman's hand, he noticed something he hadn't yet seen in the eyes of the man he'd grown to both fear and loathe—he saw relief.

16 Resolution

The Chairman had suggested, and Justin concurred, that it was best for all involved for him to leave Earth's orbit for a few weeks until things settled down. The old man had assured Justin that Mosh McKenzie's yacht—and Neela with it—would be diverted to Ceres, a planetoid in the asteroid belt orbiting somewhere between Mars and Jupiter. The oversized floating boulder was, at the moment, approximately 1.6 Astronomical Units from Earth or, as sebastian had put it, "approximately 148,729,291.6278931 miles . . . give or take." By normal means the trip would take months, but Justin had plans for a far speedier arrival, and the credits to back them up.

After leaving The Chairman's suite he headed straight for the transshipment point farther down the beanstalk. It was crowded and filled with cargo pods of raw materials from the outer system—all being processed for shipment to Earth's ravenous industries. Once he was there, it wasn't difficult for Justin to have a ship pick him up and take him to the American Express orbital platform where he planned to arrange a trip out to the asteroid belt.

It was only as he was leaving on the luxury transport that Justin realized the significance of the day—not from what had been achieved, but from what had been forgotten. He kept telling himself that, given all that had happened, he couldn't really be faulted, but that proved to be of little solace. Though he knew it to be improper, he turned to his only available outlet.

"Hello, sebastian?"

"I'm here, Justin."

"I have a bit of a problem."

"By the tone in your voice," answered sebastian, "I'm assuming it's of a personal nature. As you know, I'm excellent at helping with mundane problems—not those that require deeper insight."

"All fine and well, sebastian," answered Justin, "the problem is, anyone I'd want to talk to is out of reach." *Very out of reach.*

"I'm afraid," answered the DijAssist, "that I may not be of much use. Our programs tend to be very good at helping children. We can listen and offer generic advice on generic situations like 'nobody listens to me' or 'my brother stole my doll.' By the time a person starts to deal with complex emotional issues they're usually well beyond talking to their avatars."

"Tell ya what then, buddy," answered Justin, "all you have to do is listen. Truth is, I have a tough time talking to most people nowadays."

"That is most understandable, Justin. I will, of course, listen."

The DijAssist went silent.

"My wife died today. I mean . . . today's the anniversary of her death," Justin corrected.

I was wondering if you'd remember, thought Sebastian.

"I believe I understand, sir. You want me to arrange flowers, and maybe a commemoration in a news service, or a ceremony."

"That's not it, sebastian, and how come a Neuro-linked memory still can't re-member that I don't want to be called 'sir'?"

"I apologize, Justin. The situation seemed formal, and I switched to a formal usage protocol. Our programs are improved by interaction, but as you can see, not perfected."

"Forgiven."

"So, then . . ."

"I forgot. Jesus, sebastian, how could I forget?"

"Justin," offered sebastian, "human memory is not perfect, and easily dis-tracted by more pressing matters. You have had a busy year, and today seems to be the culmination of that year. I hope I am using the following phrase correctly, but you should not 'beat yourself up' over this. I never knew your wife, and evi-dence is very sketchy concerning her, but I will assume she loved you."

"Yes, of course."

"From what I understand about love, the biggest component is the well-being of the other person. Am I in error?"

"In this case, no."

"Then you are observing this anniversary in a way your wife would most ap-prove of. Have you not found love with another person? Would this not make your wife happy?"

"I have indeed found love with Neela, and yes, my wife would be very happy. Though she probably would have hit me upside the head for taking so long."

"Are you spending this anniversary helping people?" continued the avatar. "And are you not on your way toward reuniting with the woman you love?"

"Yes, sebastian, that is exactly what I'm doing," answered Justin, allowing himself a small grin. "And you're a lot smarter than you let on."

"I'll take that as a compliment, Justin. Is there any other way I can be of assis-tance?"

Justin remained silent, racking his brain for the right gesture. It only took a moment.

"Could it be arranged for a dozen roses to be left on the shoreline of the island of Fiji? Anywhere will do, but they must be left in such a way that they'll be caught by the incoming tide, and then be allowed to drift away."

"Certainly, Justin."

"Thank you, sebastian. Please arrange it . . . and sebastian . . ."

"Yes, Justin?"

"This helped."

"I'm glad. The flowers would please your wife. Most human females are pleased with flowers. Interesting that most human males are not."

Justin smirked but didn't answer. He spent the remainder of the short ride up to the launch pod remembering and thinking about a trip to Fiji his wife was always begging him to go on but for which he never seemed to have the time.

Hektor was troubled. For a man seemingly connected to every facet of his universe, being kept in the dark about one of them practically killed him. He knew The Chairman would call him when he was good and ready. He had utter faith in the man's ability to sway anyone—even as tough a nut as Justin Cord.

But why haven't I heard from him?

Forty-eight hours after the initial meeting, forty-eight of the longest hours of Hektor Sambianco's life, he finally got a message. Its very simplicity was almost, he noted with trenchant humor, diametrically opposite the amount of worry he'd put himself through. It read simply, "Meeting with Cord went well. In two weeks all will be in place. Do nothing without my OK."

It wasn't as if Hektor had nothing to do. The head of GCI Special Operations was always busy, and the recent economic strains had substantially added to his workload. And so, immersing himself in his day-to-day tasks, Hektor did almost nothing concerning Justin Cord. To be sure, he kept tabs on the man. He knew that Cord had rented the fastest ship he could find, and had blasted off for Ceres. It would be uncomfortable but, by Hektor's estimation, he'd make it in about three weeks. He wondered what a Damsah-forsaken outpost like Ceres could have to offer that would make someone want to experience that type of extended acceleration—nanoassisted g-force gel couch or not. The trip could be done far more comfortably in three months. Hektor also knew about the dozen roses Justin had left on a beach in Fiji. At first he thought it had to do with the man's wife. He'd noted that the day it was done had also been the day she'd died. But research showed that neither she nor Justin had ever been on Fiji. And so, Hektor had concluded that it had to be some signal to the Liberty Party, or perhaps even the Action Wing.

Per The Chairman's orders, Hektor would do nothing *overt*. He did, however, fill the island with operatives, supposedly on vacation. Unfortunately, the only thing they managed to come back with was really good tans.

It was therefore with some relief that he was finally invited to have an audience with The Chairman. The relief was short-lived; Hektor's nerves seemed to rise concomitantly with the lift as it moved swiftly up the beanstalk toward The Chairman's sanctum sanctorum. He'd never felt this way with his own parents, because they'd never warranted it. But The Chairman was different. He was everything Hektor had ever wanted to be, and his approval was important in ways that mere job performance could never account for.

He was quickly ushered into the antechamber, through the massive double doors, and finally into The Chairman's lair itself. The man, saw Hektor, was sitting amid his massive command center attending to affairs of state. The Chairman looked up suddenly, rose, and greeted Hektor warmly. It was only then that Hektor allowed himself to exhale.

"We got him," said The Chairman, emerging from the array of machines. "Cord will incorporate, and in no small measure because of you."

"That's wonderful, sir," answered Hektor, barely containing his joy. "How did you do it?"

"Not me, Hektor, you," his boss said flatly. "You called it from the beginning." He then motioned Hektor to have a seat as he grabbed a bottle of Champagne and two crystal flutes from behind a tiki bar.

"It was Neela Harper the whole time," he said, popping the cork and then filling both their glasses. "That was the key. And that's why the idiot's blasting off to the asteroid belt at gut-twisting acceleration—which I'm sure you're well aware of."

That he was headed to Ceres, yes, thought Hektor. *That he was meeting Neela, no.* Hektor nodded.

"He'll only finalize the deal," continued The Chairman, "when he's with Dr. Harper. In two days the paperwork for Justin Cord's incorporation will go through. He'll sign it on Ceres, and he and Dr. Harper will begin their engagement. Hektor, it is absolutely vital that the press work be in place to make this go smoothly."

Hektor nodded once again—almost afraid that speaking would allow the perfection of the moment to fade.

The Chairman continued to bark his orders. "I don't want any cries of perversion or manipulation to mar this. As far as the world is concerned, Dr. Harper is doing the human race a favor, and anyone who says otherwise is at best stupid or, more likely, an Action Wing terrorist."

The Chairman's pause broke Hektor's euphoric spell.

"Don't worry, sir. That won't be a hard sell. People want the Crises to end. If it's perceived that Dr. Harper helped put an end to it, then our only problem will be keeping her from being turned into a saint."

"Good, good," answered The Chairman. "I will leave all of that in your capable hands. Get me an outline of your propaganda campaign by tomorrow, so I can go over the main points. But I'm sure it'll be fine. Truth is, it's now a minor detail. With Justin Cord neutralized, the Crises will end, and GCI will be seen as the corporation that ended it."

"Exactly, sir. We'll be seen as the saviors."

"Which means," The Chairman said, speaking in a slow and purposeful manner, "we can begin the next phase."

"Sir?"

The Chairman studied Hektor carefully, as if deciding how much to confide.

"I do not intend to simply end the Crises," he continued. "The corporate world is weak and divided. Too many corporations competing is what allowed a maniac like the Unincorporated Man to emerge and cause so much trouble. What we really need is *one* corporation to dominate and lead humanity in a productive and efficient manner. That corporation will be GCI."

If Hektor could have stood and clapped he would have, because the man sitting before him spoke to the very fiber of his being.

"I always suspected, sir, that you had more in mind than simply the running of GCI. I, too, believe that our system must culminate in the powerful ruling the pennies. And the one with the most power," he said, with a slow nod to The Chairman, "to rule us all. It makes perfect sense."

The Chairman's grandfatherly smile hid the disdain he felt within. If there had been any doubts at all about his plans for Hektor, there were now none whatsoever.

"Not just one, Hektor," answered The Chairman, purposely allowing for a longer pause. "For years I've been worried that if anything happened to me the plan would fall to pieces, and all the work of building up power would be in vain, fracturing into thousands of competing corporations. I turned myself into a recluse, terrified that, should I die too soon, no one could replace me. That's why I rarely left my chamber, and why I've had to take so many precautions."

Hektor nodded, unable to believe where the conversation was heading.

"I spent years looking for someone with my drive and my dream," continued The Chairman, "but all I got were Kirk Olmsteads and his ilk." The Chairman leaned across the small divide that separated Hektor and himself, and put his hand on his subordinate's shoulder. "Until now, son. If something happens to me I can rest assured that you'll guide GCI and humanity to its logical resting place." The Chairman then lifted his Champagne flute to Hektor. "I can finally relax." He then took a sip and motioned to Hektor.

Hektor, stunned into silence, barely managed to lift the flute to his lips. He readily sipped from the golden elixir, realizing too late that he'd forgotten to lift his glass in acceptance. The Chairman, he saw, thankfully ignored his faux pas.

"Sir," answered Hektor, when he finally managed to regain his composure, "are you actually saying . . ."

The Chairman nodded. "We can't make it formal at first. But as soon as Cord and Harper are married, I'll take a vacation. You'll be left in day-to-day command of GCI. That should send the proper message, and let the system know that you're the heir apparent, without having to involve the press or the stockholders. After that I'll go on one or two more vacations or fact-finding trips to the outer system, each time with you assuming day-to-day control. Eventually we'll formalize the relationship, and no one of consequence will be able to interfere."

"Of course, sir," was all that Hektor could manage.

"But let me say, son," continued The Chairman, smiling amiably, "congratulations, and thank you. It may not seem like it, but you'll be doing me a far bigger favor than I'll be doing for you."

"No, sir. Thank you. Thank you, sir. I will not let you down."

"That's why you have the job, son. Oh, before I forget." The Chairman leaped up and went to the bar. He picked up a wrapped box and handed it to Hektor. "I can't stand the things myself, but I know you like them."

Hektor's eyes lit up as he removed the wrapping. It was a small wooden box with the words DAVIDOFF ANIVERSARIO inlaid on top. He opened the case and found three wooden cigar-shaped cylinders neatly lined up. They, too, bore the distinctive logo.

"Sir," gasped Hektor, "these are priceless artifacts. It will be an honor to display them in my office."

The Chairman was suddenly incredulous. "Display them? After all the money I spent to have them nanoreconstructed, you'd better damn well smoke them!"

Hektor was dismayed. "They're . . . actually smokable."

"At 1.5 million credits each, they'd better be!" answered The Chairman, with a hearty laugh.

Hector sat stunned, overwhelmed at the connection implied by The Chairman's generosity.

"Take your time, son."

Hektor didn't take much. The thought of getting one of the cigars to his lips propelled him up and out of his seat. "That's alright, sir, I really should get going. There's a lot to do."

The Chairman nodded his agreement.

With perfunctory grace, Hektor left the grand room. As he entered the lift he felt, for the first time, that the opportunity of a lifetime had been bestowed on him. And what made it even better was who had bestowed it.

Hektor hurried into his office, ignoring the pleas and harangues of his assistants. *You probably only get one day like this in your life,* he'd reasoned, *and I'll be damned if I'm not gonna enjoy at least one hour of it—the system can wait.* He put the Aniversarios on his desk, sunk into his chair, and began to let the waves of joy rush over him. His future was assured and, with it, he'd convinced himself, the future of the world. He would have all the power and prestige that a human could have. It was, he mused, like the Roman emperors of old. The system worked best when the benevolent emperor chose his successor to rule the empire. Well, the corporate world's emperor had just chosen him, and in time he would choose his—thus assuring that Damsah's gift of incorporation would pass peacefully from one generation to the next. The harmony and conformity of the system would grow ever stronger, until it was unbreakable. Humanity would be safe and cared for, and he, Hektor Bandonillo Sambianco, would go down in human history as one of the great men who made it all possible. Hektor didn't mind that he'd probably never reach the same dizzying heights of fame as his boss, the man who'd started it all— and that was just fine. Hektor was more than content to be a part of his legend.

He called his indefatigable assistant, Mariko, into the office and told her to hold all his calls, and that, further, anyone short of The Chairman himself was not to interrupt.

Mariko, as usual, stood at sprite attention. "Good meeting then, boss?"

Like any good number two she'd learned to read Hektor's many moods, and either stay clear or revel. Today, she saw, revelry was very much on the agenda.

Hektor nodded.

"In that case," she continued, "I'll give you the pertinents and leave." Before Hektor could stop her, Mariko dutifully launched into her laundry list of data.

"The info on Ceres is downloaded to your secure file, and those hard copies are ready for you to print and . . ." Mariko's voice faded as she registered the box of cigars on her boss's desk.

I should've locked those up immediately, was Hektor's first thought. But then he realized that Mariko would of course know what she was looking at. Hadn't he, after all, "brought her up" with his selfsame love of this sweetest of leaves?

"I . . . I didn't think they still existed," she stammered. "Are they real?"

Hektor was delighted. "Yes, Mariko, real, nanoreconstructed, and ready to smoke."

"Well, boss," answered Mariko, still eyeing the smokes, "just knowing they exist has made my day." She then turned back to her list. "As I was saying, the Ceres info . . ."

"Really?" interrupted Hektor, enjoying the banter. "How so?"

Mariko looked up from her DijAssist, smiling. "It means," she answered, "that I'll have a shot at maybe smoking one . . . of my own, that is, someday."

Hektor laughed. "Not to put too fine a point on it, Mariko, but they're well out of your reach . . . I dare say for many years to come."

"Maybe yes, maybe no," she said, rising to the challenge. "I mean, no offense, boss, but look at you."

Hektor thought about it for a minute, and laughed. He'd hired Mariko for her pluck, and today was yet more evidence of it. "Touché, my dear. Look at me, indeed. Well, what the hell then, kid, let's make it today."

Mariko gulped. "You can't be serious." She turned around to look at the closed door—knowing full well the scope of her responsibilities that lay on the other side. She then turned back to face her boss. "Are you serious?"

Part of Hektor was wondering the exact same thing. There was generosity, but this, he realized, was almost insane. He put the thought aside as petty. "Mariko, I've had a very good day. In fact, I've had what is possibly the best day most any human being has ever had. So good that those cigars are only a small part of it, and you've just made me realize that I'd like to share some of the good day I've been having. In fact, I'm positive I do."

"Well, then," his assistant said, thrill evident in her voice, "let's light those babies up before you change your mind and I have to wrestle you to the floor for 'em!"

Hektor grinned and proceeded to remove two of the invaluable cigars from the box. He handed one of the wood cylinders to Mariko, and took the other for himself.

The young woman handled the Davidoff with the appropriate care and appreciation. She slowly removed the cigar from its encasement, eyed it expertly, and then brought it up to her nose, inhaling deeply. She exhaled with such a pleasurable grin Hektor knew he'd made the right decision. Hektor sniffed the length of the cigar as well, which resulted in almost the same frothy expression as that of his underling. He produced a clipper from inside a pocket, snipped off the end, and invited Mariko to do the same. He then lit a match, and was about to light his own cigar, when he decided at the last moment to light the end of Mariko's. A gesture like that, he reasoned, would not only be perceived as magnanimous, but would also go a long way toward securing his legacy.

Mariko was once again surprised but didn't refuse. She dragged slowly on the three-hundred-year-old stick, twisting it ever so slightly in order to get a perfect, even burn at the end. She then slowly exhaled straight up into the air so as not to blow smoke directly into her boss's face. Though, thought Hektor, she needn't have bothered. Hektor was going to light his off the same match but at the last second decided it would be better to use a fresh one and light his cigar properly. He dug another match out, struck it, and was bringing the flame to the tip of his cigar when he saw that Mariko's face was distorted, and that she appeared to be choking. She looked confused, but when she tried to speak, a bright, crimson river of blood poured out of her mouth. Hektor, stupefied, let the match drop from his hand, and was about to leap forward to help, when the nanite alarms went off. Suddenly, and for the second time in as many months, the walls came crashing down.

Hektor reacted on instinct. He immediately tossed the cigar, jumped away from the pleading eyes of his assistant, and scrambled as far from the terrified girl as he could. The room started to fill with a diaphanous white mist, which Hektor knew to be the billions of defensive nanites attempting to smother the area. "Work, damn it," he managed to say, gritting his teeth, "work!"

But Hektor could see that Mariko was slumping forward, already on her knees, cigar still dangling awkwardly from her right hand. The blood was now pouring from every exposed orifice. He prayed that she was dead. All he could do now was hope that none of the microkillers had gotten to him. He opened his mouth and breathed in as much of the white mist as he could while simultaneously disrobing. He then threw every last article of clothing and jewelry he'd been wearing into the center of the room. Then, naked and turning in circles like a drug-addled shaman in a ritual dance, he let the mist of the defending nanites coat him completely. He even jumped up and down a few times to make sure the defenders touched the soles of his feet. He took deep breaths, even though it meant painful fits of coughing. The mist had thickened to the point that it was almost impossible for him to see his own hands clearly in front of his face. He continued to hack into them, checking for spatter. No blood. Good. No blood. Though the room had cooled significantly—the best environment for the defender nanites—Hektor was sweating from exertion and fear.

As suddenly as it began the alarm bells stopped; the air, and with it the white mist, was sucked out of the room through large vents in the ceiling and floor. The massive steel doors then slowly rose and disappeared back into the decor of the ceiling.

Hektor, alone and naked, covered from head to toe in a thin layer of white film, stood mere feet away from the half-dissolved remains of his number two. He approached, hoping that enough of her brain had remained to make her death temporary and not permanent. He was to be disappointed.

In a horrible flash of realization Hektor knew who'd been responsible for the attempt on his life. The Chairman had set him up, and he fell for it. The Chairman, he realized, had wanted him dead, and but for a young woman's impertinent curiosity it would be Hektor's half-eaten carcass strewn on the floor and not that of the poor, lovely Mariko. Now The Chairman's number two needed to find out why. Why him? Why now? As Hektor stood waiting for the hazmat team to arrive, he quite unexpectedly began to weep. At first slowly, and then openly and in fits. He felt pain and accepted pain. As he sobbed, the rivulets of white powder mixed with tears rolled down his cheeks, and then fell onto the now sanitized floor. It was at that moment that Hektor Sambianco swore revenge on the only man he'd ever truly loved.

The Chairman studied the security reports. He felt regret at the death of the assistant—an unintended but necessary consequence given the importance of the assignment. *Who knew that Hektor would have been so generous?* More important, he mused, two dead, partially dissolved bodies had been discovered. That certainly made things easier on him. He'd known that the body might be completely reduced to dust if the nanite defenders were too slow, and that that would have rendered inconclusive Hektor's ultimate demise. The Chairman was prepared to live with that fact, but now, given the information he'd just received from the head of internal security, there was one less thing to worry about. Hektor was dead, and The Chairman would have months to arrange for the appointment of a qualified yet uninspired replacement. For now, the story would go out that Mr. Sambianco was not in his office, and was very much alive somewhere—which was standard operating procedure when a top-level executive died or had been murdered, especially in his own headquarters.

The Chairman got up from his command center, walked over to a viewing area, and looked out over his wayward planet. It was filled with a mass of humanity that he'd come to love, pity, and, sometimes, when he was lost in thought and most vulnerable to his inner self, envy.

As he stood staring out the window he began to formulate a plausible cover story. It didn't take long. It would be explained that Hektor had been called away on important business for the stockholders; that he was doing something of vital importance, but that day-to-day operations would be handled by whichever sacrificial lamb The Chairman chose to put in his place.

The Chairman would have to call the board together and let them know, if they didn't already, about Hektor's assassination at the hands of the Action Wing. They'd of course be upset, but he'd reassure them. He sent instructions to his assistant to prepare the board for a meeting, and then began the necessary work of finding a successor for Sambianco.

His research was interrupted by a dulcet tone emanating from within the room.

"Call for you, sir," came the equally soft voice of his assistant. "It's Accounting, and she said it's urgent."

The Chairman frowned. Calling him directly bordered on impudence, but Accounting had been the longest-serving member of the board, and had developed quite an entourage of her own at GCI. Plus, he figured, she wouldn't have called without a good reason.

"Connect us, please."

Accounting's image appeared above the Chairman's desk. She was, he could see, a bit disheveled.

"Good evening, Brenda," said The Chairman, leveling his gaze evenly.

"Good evening, Mr. Chairman," she answered, in obvious disarray. "Thank you for taking my call, and please forgive the intrusion."

The Chairman nodded, indicating she should continue.

"There's a problem with the board."

"What sort of problem?" he asked.

"They're agitated, sir."

"I know that, Brenda. I plan to address them personally."

"Personally or *personally*, sir?"

Though The Chairman was taken aback by the director's forthrightness, she would never have known by looking at the stone-cold stare of the man peering at her.

"I don't like to appear physically, Brenda. It has to be of vital importance to even consider it."

"That's why I called, sir. It *is* vital. They all know, sir, and they're scared—some even terrified. I'll be the first to admit that Hektor was arrogant and made lots of enemies, but he was also a respected leader who had earned the admiration of the board—especially since the Crises began. I don't think anyone realized just how vital he'd become until he died."

"Assassinated, Brenda," interjected The Chairman. "No need to beat around the bush."

"Yes, sir, assassinated. And in the very heart of GCI." Accounting paused to take a breath and gauge whether or not she would be allowed to continue speaking. The Chairman's silence once again prodded her on.

"Many," she continued, "are on the verge of breaking down. Whether they quit, run away, or just plain start drawing with crayons, we face a possible decapitation of our executive wing. And if that happens—just as the system learns or even suspects Hektor's death—it would be," she paused, and then grimaced, "unfortunate."

The Chairman considered the words of his deputy, excused himself for a moment, and then called up some psyche data to see if the evidence bore them out. It did. Stress levels were well above normal for all the members. He also quickly cross-checked the psyche info with strategic data: number of calls to family; time spent at lunch; hours spent in the pub. The fact that two of the board members had been found passed-out drunk and had to be sobered up medically was all he needed to see to close the deal.

"Alright, Brenda," said The Chairman, as he came back online, "I'm convinced. Tell the board I'll meet with them *personally* in my suite."

Brenda was visibly relieved. "Thank you, sir."

"You don't need to thank me for following good advice. We'll speak shortly." He blanked the screen and thought about the next steps. He even for a moment considered making Brenda the new head of Special Operations. It didn't take long for him to put the kibosh on the idea; he remembered that, given her competence, he'd eventually have to kill her, and he liked her too much to sully his hands once again. He then called the security director. The figure of one Franklin Wots appeared above his desk looking nervous and official in his black GCI security uniform, with its metallic orange piping. SD Wots managed to pull off the effect of standing at attention while remaining seated at his desk.

"Good evening, Mr. Chairman, sir!"

"Good evening, SD Wots. I've decided to address the board personally. Please prep the teams and have the meeting room adjoining my suite prepared and sanitized." The Chairman was waiting for a crisp salute followed by a "yes, sir," but none was forthcoming. Instead, his order was met with nervous silence and the face of a man not bothering to hide his doubt and worry.

"What is it, Security Director?" asked The Chairman, starting to grow weary of all the babysitting he suddenly found himself having to do.

"Sir, I don't think you should see the board personally. Holographically would be far more secure."

"Thank you for your concern, SD," answered The Chairman. "If security were the only consideration, I'd tend to agree. Suffice it to say other factors make a personal appearance necessary."

SD Wots returned to his best game face. "Very good, sir. I'll have a comprehensive plan ready to present in the next twenty-four hours."

"I'll need it in ten."

"I can't make any promises, sir."

"Do your best, SD."

The Chairman cut the connection and got back to work. He spent a few minutes making sure that the various groups he was funding in the outer systems would continue to receive aid for the next year or so. It was quick work, and would probably be the last in a series of direct contributions to the cause that he'd be making for some time. He'd put off the task until he was sure Hektor was out of the picture. There was no telling how far Sambianco had gotten his claws into the system, and therefore no reason to raise suspicion earlier than need be. The real work lay ahead, as he now had to figure out how to fund this most awkward of *evolutions* that his new partner so desperately believed in. It would mean dialing back his once grandiose plans, but if Cord wanted to experiment for a decade or two, or even three, The Chairman figured he'd let him.

Dialing back the outer system seemed like the easiest place to start. Most of its residents were not Majority Party inclined, in that most of them, realized The Chairman, had already achieved that rather dubious distinction. The fact was that, as a people, those out in the belt had an almost natural aversion to strangers telling them what to do, and so the idea of aiding and abetting them in that attitude had seemed like a good idea. At a minimum, thought The Chairman, it would add to the general level of discontent. Not that the belt needed much prodding. The discontent in both the inner and outer systems seemed to be building just fine without him. He finished closing off the last of his "outer" system accounts with a fat credit deposit toward some sort of upcoming demonstration on Ceres. The shame of it, he judged, was that the belt contained so many of these hard-headed people, but they were spread so far and wide that their ability to have much of an impact on the human race would be minimal at best. No, he surmised, the future of humanity was on Earth and within the core planets. He'd concentrate his efforts there. And so he spent the next nine and a half hours making sure the inner systems' Majority Party and its various nonviolent splinter groups—out of respect for Justin's vision—were well funded and equipped. In a final flourish he sent an anonymous message off to Justin's tunnel-rat friend, Omad Hassan, informing him that it would be in his best interest to be on Ceres as soon as possible. He'd even seen to it that the contractor for whom Omad was working was more than compensated for the loss. The Chairman figured that, while Justin would probably not get the girl, he could at least have the friend.

Once again the room was filled with the sound of a soothing ring.

Though SD Wots had called right on schedule, it soon became obvious that things were not going according to plan.

"Sir," said the SD uneasily, "can I talk with you again about your plans to meet personally?"

"Not unless you mind losing your job, SD."

"If that's what it takes, sir," answered the man, unblinking.

"Brave man, are you, SD?"

"Not exactly, sir, but you hired me to do my job, and my job is to protect you to the best of my ability."

"Very well," fretted The Chairman. "Your job is secure . . . for now."

"Thank you, sir. Sir, we can't guarantee your safety."

"Of course not," snapped The Chairman. "You're paid to improve it."

"Which is why," answered the unflustered security director, "my staff feels it would be safer to have you come down from your suite rather than to let the board come up."

"I dislike leaving my suite, you know that, Franklin."

SD Wots did not like the fact that The Chairman used his first name. It was clearly an emotional play.

"I dislike it as well, sir, but I would ask that you consider the security needed to move over two dozen people into your suite."

"It's certainly not easy," agreed The Chairman, feeling his blood begin to boil, "but GCI supposedly has the best security in the system, recent events notwithstanding, and if it doesn't I'd like to know who does . . . so that I could hire them to replace ours!"

The SD didn't flinch in the face of the barrage, though he did manage to raise an eyebrow. "I would connect you myself, sir, if I knew of anyone better."

The remark brought The Chairman back off the precipice. He realized he was being unfair, and that it probably wasn't the wisest of moves to insult the very people charged with his personal security. "My apologies, SD," said The Chairman. "I've been on edge since Hektor's death."

"None needed," he answered, though the look of relief on his face belied his response.

"But that's the crux of the problem," The Chairman continued. "We don't know how Mr. Sambianco's murder was triggered, nor how someone managed to sneak a nanovirus past our sensors, and, last but not least, who caused it. We have to assume that it was an inside job, and that any one of the two dozen or more people coming up to meet you will try to kill you—perhaps in a way just as ingenious as that used to kill Mr. Sambianco and his assistant."

"And my going down the beanstalk?"

"Is safer, sir. But only marginally so. Again, I reiterate; it would be best for all to just have you speak with them holographically."

"Yes, SD," nodded The Chairman solemnly, "but that's not an option."

The irony, mused the real assassin, was that he knew himself to be completely safe from harm, yet to act in that manner might arouse the suspicions of those already inclined to be suspicious—indeed, he thought, paid extremely well to be suspicious.

"I'll meet the board personally, SD Wots, *and* I'll trust your judgment. Down it is. I want it to start tomorrow morning at eleven sharp."

The SD seemed only somewhat relieved. "I'll see to it myself, Mr. Chairman. Are there any large items that you'll be bringing with you, or any staff required?"

The Chairman thought about it for a moment and decided not to make his visit too big a deal. The more personal he could be—especially at a time like this—the more effective he'd be at putting the board at ease. "No, SD," he answered, this time more calmly, "you need only concern yourself with me."

"Very good, sir. We'll be in touch in the morning."

The Chairman watched as the SD faded from view. He thought about doing some more work, but then thought better of it, and decided to get some rest. He went to sleep content that GCI would eventually stabilize and give Justin Cord the decades needed to evolve the mess of humanity into something they would both be proud to have fathered. For the first time in many years, The Chairman slept well.

The next morning he took the lift down the beanstalk. It was such a rare occurrence that the lift's gregarious avatar, riser, seemed genuinely pleased to have him on board again. As he descended from his perch, The Chairman stared sadly at the devastation still evident below, but knew that, at least in time, it would all be repaired.

He was met in the corridor by SD Franklin Wots, who then informed him that he would be The Chairman's personal escort to the lower boardroom. The plan, The Chairman was informed, was that he would arrive first and be seen by each member of the board as they entered—which would not be what they were expecting. This, explained the security director, would allow him to scan the board members with near total scrutiny to see if they would give away any biometric indicators about possibly harming The Chairman. Though The Chairman wondered why the same exercise couldn't have been done atop the beanstalk, and thought the whole charade a terrible waste of time, he once again reasoned that he would have to play along with Security to keep them looking out and not in. He entered the boardroom and heard the wall seal behind him. He was surprised that SD Wots had not followed him in. He also saw that one of the chairs—his chair—was turned away, back facing him, with someone's legs dangling underneath. Before the "legs" could speak, The Chairman knew he'd been played—by his own board members, his own security apparatus, and the intended victim himself. He also knew at that moment that he was a dead man.

The chair suddenly swung around. "Good morning, Mr. Chairman," said Hektor Sambianco. "Thank you for coming."

The Chairman could feel the effects of the immobilizer immediately. He didn't bother to move. Doing so would only prolong the agony.

Hektor got up from the chair and approached his kill slowly. Hektor didn't appear angry or, for that matter, in any great hurry. He was studying The Chairman as a man would a perplexing painting. He continued to circle his victim as if viewing him from all angles might clear things up. It didn't.

"I have many answers, but not all of them," Hector said calmly.

The Chairman would have shrugged if he could have. Instead he waited.

"Did you think you'd be able to keep it secret from me forever?"

"Obviously not," answered The Chairman. "That's why I attempted to kill you."

Hektor laughed. "Stupid question." Then, "More please."

The Chairman began to feel a heavy pressure on his chest as the immobilizing field complied with Hektor's orders.

"That's why," continued Hektor, almost face-to-face with the man he was in the process of torturing, "you never promoted anyone to head Special Operations who could be a threat."

"Partially," gasped The Chairman, trying to buy some time, "but mostly my best defense was . . . that no one bothered . . . to look . . . until now, that is."

Hektor looked away in disgust, then turned back once again. "Answer me this one question and I'll show you mercy."

The Chairman wasn't buying it, but felt that, even if there was the remotest possibility he could make it out, billions of souls demanded that he take it.

"OK," he managed.

Hektor's glare turned sorrowful, as if the question he was about to ask was causing him pain. "How . . . how could you?"

Now it was The Chairman's turn to scowl. "How . . . could I not? This . . . this . . . system will . . . enslave the vast majority of . . . humanity for the rest . . . the rest of eternity."

"If they can't rise above their own petty limitations," Hektor shrieked, "then they should be enslaved. That's the beauty of the system. *You* taught me that! Incorporation enslaves the weak and allows the strong to rise!"

The Chairman looked at Hektor and didn't bother to answer. Arguing was futile. It seemed, too, that Hektor had the same idea.

"And what . . . of your mercy?" asked The Chairman, still hoping against hope.

Hektor answered with a malicious grin, then slowly produced the third Davidoff Aniversario from his inner pocket.

"Tell you what," Hektor said, indelicately shoving the cigar between the lips of his immobile prisoner, "smoke this and I'll spare you the long, slow suffocation I'd had planned. Either way, you're dead."

The Chairman used every last fiber of his strength to thrust the cigar from his mouth. It bounced harmlessly off of Hektor's chest and fell to the floor at his feet.

"More," said Hektor, "*much more*."

The immobilizing field acted on command and further tightened its viselike grip. The pain was excruciating, and The Chairman's lips could no longer form words, but his eyes told Hektor everything he'd wanted to say.

"And to you as well," spat Hektor. "And, by the way, you're fired. As for your precious Justin, I've sent orders to have him and his deviant girlfriend arrested on Ceres. So now you, your revolution, and its vainglorious leadership will all soon be dead."

The Chairman, realizing the enormity of Hektor's mistake, knew that the only thing he could do to help was die. He baited his number two once more with a challenging glare. It would be his last. He then watched helplessly as Hektor picked the cigar up off the floor and shoved it back into his now fully paralyzed mouth. Hektor then pulled a mask over his own face, struck a match, and lit the end of the death stick. Then, with sadistic glee, Hektor mouthed the word that sealed The Chairman's fate.

"Less."

The immobilizer suddenly released all pressure, forcing The Chairman's body to involuntarily inhale as it reflexively grabbed for air.

Sorry, Justin, thought The Chairman, as his innards began to writhe, *looks like revolution wins.*

The view out of the forward observation deck was pretty much what Justin had expected—at least based on his research. Ceres, once a desolate hunk of stone, now appeared as a multifaceted diamond twinkling against a canvas of black velvet. Bright, shimmering lights emanated from beneath its ice-covered surface.

As Ceres had become more populated, it was decided that the planetoid would need to create more gravity—two-thirds that of the Earth's, to be precise. But that amount of centrifugal force would have caused the planetoid to at first deform and then explode outward. A massive molecular construction project was proposed. An outer shell would be formed with nano scaffolding using nanocarbon Bucky tubes inserted into the planetoid's ice layer. The scaffolding endowed each square meter of ice with a tensile strength equivalent to that of 100 giga-gees, more than enough to quite literally seal the deal. Considered one of the great accomplishments of nanoengineering, the newly created phase of ice encapsulating Ceres became known as "the Shell." Having solved one seemingly insurmountable problem, the Cereans soon found themselves facing another. The attractiveness their now stable ⅔'s gravity made the large rock quite popular. Docking anywhere on the surface became difficult for most ships in the belt, unaccustomed as they were to operating in anything but microgravity. By necessity the ships gravitated toward the poles. These axis points were small areas in and of themselves, but at least they could offer a few precious miles of near zero gravity in which to operate. As the population continued to grow, so too did their insatiable appetite for all manner of goods. There was simply not enough space—with low enough gravity—to handle all the traffic necessary to sustain the fledgling metropolis. Rather than forcibly limit Ceres's growth, the original settlers had once again shown true pioneering spirit and came up with another novel idea. They bored a two-mile-wide cylindrical tube straight down the center of the massive rock and named it, aptly, Via Cereana. This effectively gave them almost nineteen hundred cubic miles of microgravity surface to work with. Docking space was no longer an issue, and traffic control became simplicity in itself—enter from one end, exit from the other. After that it didn't take long for Ceres to become the unquestioned hub of expansion to the outer orbits and a renowned city in and of itself. With over forty million inhabitants and hundreds of thousands of transients, Ceres had indeed arrived.

Interestingly, noted Justin, the port city was not alone. The value of real estate, sebastian explained, had become so great that many other smaller meteorites had been moved into synchronous orbit just to be near their larger cousin. Even though Justin was well aware that they were nothing more than the belt's version of the 'burbs, they all appeared to him as little gems designed to complement the magnificent spinning centerpiece.

The amount of traffic was considerable and apparently the cause of Justin's ship being put into a holding pattern. "Sorry, mate," the ship's captain had said, "we can get yer here in a hurry, but we can't get yer in in a hurry." The captain had had a good laugh at his own joke, though, judging by the nonresponse of the other crewmembers, it had been told once too often. Justin watched as ships of all shapes and sizes lined up and waited to enter.

Theirs was finally given clearance, and soon thereafter found its docking clamp some 126 miles into the heart of the rock. Justin sent his luggage ahead and tepidly walked, in his nanomagnetized state, to a tube that would take him to the higher gravity levels found closer to the surface. It was a relief to finally feel gravity resume as he approached the upper level. His goal was now simple: Find Neela.

There were three grand thoroughfares: Damsah, Smith, and Singh. According to The Chairman's instructions, Neela would be waiting on Smith with Eleanor and Mosh. They'd be next to an almost two-story-tall statue of the first human to ever set foot on the planetoid, Cardori Singh. As Justin emerged from his ride and entered Smith's main thoroughfare he was momentarily struck by the intensity of the daylight in the immense cavern. He quickly put on his oversized shades and adjusted the lenses to diminish the glare. The glasses, he realized, would also help cover his face. Even on Ceres the most famous face in the system would certainly be recognized. He lowered his profile and only occasionally looked straight up. The street was a cacophony of commerce, vehicles, and all manner of conversation. The smell was decidedly different. A combination, decided Justin, of rock, forced air, and steel. The ceiling—or floor, depending on ones's orientation—was mostly bare rock with some platforms built in for those inclined to bungee jump, parachute, glide, or fly.

With Justin's permission sebastian had taken on the role of tour guide as he led his master toward the statue. "The inhabitants of Ceres felt that a faux sky would be too imitative of Earth. Turn left here . . . they did not want to create a perfect replica. Cereans take pride in the fact that they're not of the Earth, turn right . . . this translated into the desire not to hide their rock-bound existence, but to emphasize it."

"Thank you, sebastian," Justin replied, only half listening. His heart was beating quicker as he anticipated seeing a woman he had had no reason to believe he'd ever see again. A woman for whom his love had grown stronger with each passing mile of the many millions he'd recently flown.

He could now make out the large statue in the distance. The crowd thickened as Justin got closer to his destination. He'd apparently arrived in the middle of some sort of gathering, the mood of which was not celebratory. He'd had enough of demonstrations, and decided then and there that, as soon as he could, he would gather Neela, put her on the transport, and get the two of them back to Earth.

"*Justin!*" Neela shrieked, from somewhere in the mass.

The crowd broke once they realized who was in their presence.

"*Neela!*" Justin shouted back, turning toward the noise.

He began to run toward her voice, pushing past anyone in his way. In an instant the two found themselves standing face-to-face. And then, just as suddenly, they grabbed one another and held on tight, neither letting go.

There were no looks of shock, or even of condemnation, not that either of them would have noticed. Cereans considered themselves a tough and pragmatic people, but were known to have a soft spot for romance, especially if it defied convention. Justin and Neela's fit the bill perfectly.

Justin pulled back for an instant and stared hard into the eyes of his lover. "I will never let you go again, *never.*"

Neela smiled tepidly and looked up at the man she'd all but given up on. She'd spent the last few months thinking about her final words to him . . . words she'd regretted every day since.

"I'm sorry, Justin," she said. "I . . . I tried to make you into something you weren't. I was afraid you'd hate me for that. It was wrong. You do what you have to do. I promise I won't leave you ever again. I . . ."

Justin kissed her hard on the lips—crowd and media be damned. Neela, feeling it was better to be hung for a wolf than a sheep, reciprocated in kind.

The crowd broke into applause.

The reunited couple acknowledged the gathering and began to walk away, arm in arm. Mosh and Eleanor soon joined them. After cordial greetings, Justin couldn't help but notice the medical director's look of concern.

"Don't worry, friend," Justin said, grinning. "I intend to marry her, if I can get the law changed and she's stupid enough to say yes."

"I'll have to before you change your mind," Neela shot back.

"It's not that, Justin," answered Mosh, as he hustled them through the gathering. "It's this crowd. We should leave."

"Why?" he asked. "What's going on?"

"Since the assassination of the president the powers that be have been cracking down in the outer system. The law's usually handled locally—as it has been for centuries."

"So it's a pissing match?" asked Justin.

"Not quite."

The small group of four had practically slowed to a crawl, and Mosh and Justin had to resort to light shoving just to try and make their way clear.

"The various corporations," continued Mosh, "have been sending out more judges and security personnel to all the settlements, enforcing laws against personal versus corporate earnings, and enforcing division of resource laws that have been on the books for hundreds of years but have rarely, if ever, been enforced."

"In short, dear," added Eleanor, "they're trying to get as many credits as possible and have been cracking down to do it."

Justin smiled. He wasn't at all worried about the crowd, and was far more interested in getting off the rock as soon as the swelling crowd would allow. "You're telling me," he asked, "that all these people are pissed off about having to pay their taxes?"

"A, sweetheart," Neela answered, " 'pissed off' is no longer part of the modern vernacular, and b, in answer to your question, yes. Only please don't say the T word in public."

Justin grinned. "I've missed being corrected."

The crowd was now beginning to shout, and the tension was palpable.

"It's more than . . . the T word," shouted Mosh over the din, " it's how it's being collected."

"Force?" asked Justin.

"In a way," shouted Mosh, pointing to a sign a protestor was holding up that read NO PSYCHE AUDITS ON CERES!

"The Corps," he continued, "have set up three new psyche-auditing facilities here. The Cereans believe it's an attempt to scare them into submission." Mosh suddenly stopped and pulled a DijAssist from his pocket. He'd been signaled. He reviewed the message as quickly as possible, not wishing to stop any longer than he had to. His face suddenly paled.

"The Chairman . . . is dead."

Justin, too, looked ashen. "Are you sure?" he asked. "I mean, absolutely positive?"

"Yes, Justin," answered Mosh. "Quite. That's good news for you, right?"

Justin didn't have time to answer, and realized he had to act quickly. If The Chairman was dead, there was only one reason why, and only one person who could be responsible. They were now in real danger.

"We have to leave," he said, desperately looking for a way out, wondering who in the crowd might be the enemy. Neela saw the look in his eyes and also felt fear.

"Justin," asked Eleanor, sensing trouble, "what is it?"

Before he could answer a series of loud shrieks could be heard in the distance. The crowd was shoved aside by a squad of GCI security goons supported by a phalanx of well-armed securibots. The massive group of armor and sweat—some fifty soldiers and bots combined—stopped directly in front of Justin and his entourage. "Justin Cord," shouted the lead SD in a voice loud enough for all to hear, "you and your accomplices are under arrest for gross violation of the shareholder information act." He then held up his DijAssist. "I have in my hand a signed warrant from a local judge demanding that you be given an expedited psyche audit. You will all come with me . . . now!"

Justin was trapped, and the promise he'd made only moments ago to the love of his life was about to be broken.

After receiving the anonymous note, Omad had boosted into Ceres. His crew had also elected to come along. They weren't the nicest bunch, but they were all loyal and with majorities in themselves. After a few days of revelry they were ready for something more. Signs for the demonstration were up everywhere, and it didn't take much convincing to get them all involved. To a person they were upset about the corporation's recent encroachment. "Things are just done a certain way out here," one of them had tried to explain in a drunken stupor to Omad, "and I'll be damned if some suit's gonna start grabbin' my extra dividends just so's he can have a shot at supermajority!" There was no use in arguing. Omad knew his crew, and knew how much trouble they could get into. He elected to go along—either to keep them out of trouble or to join them in it.

Omad's associative fame from Justin, and actual fame from his own exploits, made him a prime candidate to be "volunteered" into service as the key representative of the outer mining community. When the Cerean council wanted to know which way the miners might go on an issue, they came to him. When mining dignitaries felt they were being given short shrift, either via time onstage or in position of seating, they came to him. In short order, what started out as a babysitting gig turned into a full-time job—one that Omad started to realize he might actually be pretty good at.

It wasn't until he'd arrived at the park on the day of the actual protest that Omad realized how much rage existed among the populace. The type of anger he was sensing wasn't normally verbalized—at least, he thought, not until he could sit someone down and get 'em good and drunk. He was also beginning to wonder when, if at all, he would manage to connect with his friend. He didn't have to wait long, as he was soon informed by one of his minions that Justin had been seen near the Singh Statue. He immediately began moving in that direction, and shortly thereafter arrived at the perimeter. When he finally shoved his way forward, it wasn't what he saw that was so chilling; it was what he and the crowd surrounding him had heard: "*expedited psyche audit.*"

The dissonant rumblings of thousands of protestors quieted so quickly that the lone voice of a crying baby could be heard across the field.

Justin attempted to break free but was quickly overwhelmed by the guards. Neela instinctively leaped to his defense, and she, too, was subdued quickly. Mosh and Eleanor offered no resistance, convinced by this most recent demonstration of power that doing so would prove futile. The crowd stirred ominously but didn't move—unsure of what to do next.

The SD, sensing the volatile nature of the situation, ordered his guards to train their weapons on the mob, and slowly begin to move the prisoners toward the psyche chambers.

Omad, too, stood motionless, and watched as his friends were carted away. It was at that moment that he remembered something someone had once said to him: "Sometimes history just happens, and sometimes it needs a good kick in the ass."

It was all he needed to act. He jumped up onto the base of the Singh Statue and screamed at the top of his lungs words that were to begin the greatest revolution in human history: "If they can do it to Justin Cord, they can do it to anyone. Stop them!"

Omad then jumped from the statue and ran toward his friends with his crew following closely behind.

As Omad, in full stride, approached the phalanx that were manhandling his friends, a jittery security guard pulled the trigger on his neurolizer, sending an indiscriminate blast into the crowd. A small child went down, and as she did, the Cereans rose up and attacked en masse. Justin barely had time to acknowledge his friend before the melee occurred. The guards were subdued quickly and the securibots destroyed, most before they could get off a single shot. The crowd took losses, but all in all it was quick, it was bloody, and it was recorded for all the system to see.

In the immediate aftermath of the skirmish Justin managed to make his way toward his exhausted, bloody, but now visibly relieved friend.

"How many times," asked Omad, wiping the dirt from his forehead, "am I gonna have to save your sorry ass? You know I'm not gettin' any younger."

Justin laughed and bear-hugged his liberator.

"As many times as I need, friend," he answered, "as many times as I need."

Mosh, Eleanor, and Neela—all of whom had also managed to make it through the skirmish with only minor cuts and bruises—joined up with Justin and Omad. After a few back slaps and hugs, Neela pulled Justin aside.

"Justin," she said, concern in her eyes, "we need to talk . . . now."

"What is it?" he asked, looking her over from head to toe. "Are you OK?"

"I'm fine, Justin," she answered, and then indicated the large crowd now gathering around them. "They're not."

Justin looked at her blankly.

"You need to talk to them, Justin. You need . . . to lead."

He looked around. Then made a wider sweep. Indeed, all eyes were on him. People were whispering and waiting.

He looked back at Neela and took her hands into his.

"You realize, my love, once this starts, there's no going back . . . for any of us."

Neela nodded. Justin saw, too, that Omad, Mosh, and Eleanor had also acceded. He took a deep breath and thought about what he needed to say, what he'd been waiting to say. He realized at that very moment that the first life of Justin Cord had only been in preparation for this—his one and true destiny. He would lead these people and, come hell or high water, do everything within his power to save them.

"Then let's do this thing," he said to the four people he now considered the closest thing to family. "Let's roll."

Omad, his crew, and the willing hands of a few dozen people quickly assembled a makeshift dais from the various pieces of junk still littering the battlefield.

Justin climbed to the top and once again surveyed the assembly. What had started off in the tens of thousands had, in the brief period of the melee and its aftermath, swarmed to well over a million. The entire Smith thoroughfare was filled, as were all the available balconies and platforms. Where possible, people floated aloft. The mediabots, too, were out in full force, and for once Justin was not annoyed by their presence; he was emboldened by it.

They were all eerily silent and waiting.

Justin realized that of all the crowds he'd ever spoken to before, of all the speeches he'd ever given, this would be the one that mattered most.

"I know you're worried," he began, "and maybe even confused. Well, you should be. They tried to take something from you." He could hear his voice skipping across the wide expanse of the park and onto the thoroughfare by way of a million-plus DijAssists. "You might not have known what it was, maybe you couldn't put your finger on it, but you knew they were trying to take something away . . . something important. In each and every one of you something was screaming for its life and rasping its last breath and you knew, *you knew*, it was too precious to let die. And so you fought."

"Many people," he continued, "will say that you fought to free *me* from a bunch of security goons. Nothing more. Nothing less." Justin shook his head derisively. "Maybe. But I'm not really that important."

The crowd murmured its disagreement.

"But if this were only about *me*," he continued, "you wouldn't have fought. If this were only about *me*, you wouldn't have risked your lives. And if this had only been about *me*," he said, making sure to do a complete 360-degree turn before delivering his next salvo, *"you would have lost."*

The murmurs suddenly diffused.

"This," he continued, "was about *you. You* fought to free *yourselves* from the tyranny of those far away. Those who would take from you your birthright, who would take from you your destiny as free and independent human beings. These same people tell you that they own a part of you. And because they own this part of you they can control your future and the future of your children and your children's children. They say they control the destiny of the human race and you have to accept your subjugation with a bow and silence." Justin paused again, not only to gather his breath but also to let the tension build. "Well, today you said 'no!'"

The cheers were deafening. Justin looked down from the dais at Neela, who had become lost in his words, too. He then looked back toward the demonstrators.

"Today you said your destiny is yours to make, your future is yours to take, and to hell with anyone who tries to take it from you!"

Wave after wave of cheering shook and echoed through the cavern in a sound never before heard in the history of Ceres.

"But be warned . . . they will not let this stand. I must tell you honestly that they will come for your freedom. They will come for your hopes and dreams. They will come for your future and for your very lives, because they cannot tolerate your . . . ," said Justin, lowering his voice from a roar to a whisper, *"freedom."*

Justin raised his arms up and wide. "Look . . . look at how they treated one free man. They certainly will not tolerate millions living with that very same freedom. They will come in all their fury to extinguish this spark of liberty made into flame. They will come with their ships and their nanites and, yes, their psyche booths to impose their slavery by force, now that they can no longer fool you into accepting it willingly. They will do that because they must. And mark my words . . ." Again Justin let the last phrase slip away through the thoroughfare. Only when he heard his voice stop ricocheting off the grand stone ceiling did he continue, "*they will FAIL!* They will fail because it's too late. You are *all* already free!"

And then Justin heard what he'd been waiting for. What he'd been trying to coax from Cereans rather than prompting them. What he'd wanted to have emerge from the depths of their hearts.

"One free man, *one free man, ONE FREE MAN!*"

He allowed it to reach a crescendo, saying nothing, doing nothing, and then, with a sudden hammering of his fist onto the rail of the makeshift podium, he screamed at the top of his lungs, "*Stop!*"

The chant was shattered, the spirit diffused. Exactly as he'd wanted.

"Don't you see," he now pleaded, "that that is no longer true? That I am no longer the 'one free man'? That I am no longer cursed by the truth of that terrible indictment? How horrible it was to see humanity so enslaved that there was only *one* free man. Well, let me tell you, freedom like that comes at too high a price. It was too lonely a prison, too heavy a sentence. I wept with the thought that if I was indeed the one free man, I might perhaps be the *last* free man.

"But you," Justin continued, once again doing a complete circle in the limited space of the dais, "you *all* saved me. Not just from GCI, who would have stripped my mind and turned me into an automaton. You saved my hope. And you saved my soul. By your individual acts of courage and defiance this very day, you've freed me from the curse of the 'one free man.' I will say it again for all to hear and rejoice. *I am no longer the one free man,* because, as of this day forward, *we are all free men.* All free men, *All Free Men, ALL FREE MEN!*"

The roar grew to a crescendo, and the enormous cavern once again magnified and expanded the cry. Only this time it was heard not just within the confines of thoroughfares deep in the heart of Ceres, it was heard throughout the entire system. Justin stood tall, shoulders straight, head held high. As he watched the crowd sway, and heard the thunderous chant over and over again, he felt a tension release within himself that he'd never realized was there. At long last, Justin Cord was finally free.

Epilogue

Shortly thereafter, Ceres declared its independence. The next system to declare was the Oort Cloud observatory. In its declaration the new leader, Kirk Olmstead, called on all other enslaved peoples to throw off their chains. In addition to consulting with the leader of the revolution, Justin Cord, Acting Director Olmstead called for an outer systems congress to meet in Ceres to draft policies on trade, government, and mutual defense.

In quick succession over 90 percent of all the settlements from the asteroid belt out declared their independence, and began sending delegates to Ceres. On Earth there was massive rioting, put down ruthlessly. The Moon and Mars stayed impressively loyal to the corporate order.

Justin Cord had not been at all surprised by the scope and speed of the revolution. He was now the leader of a vast space-faring nation that stretched from the outer reaches of the solar system back to the asteroid belt.

Justin was sitting in his office reviewing trade policies when his new assistant entered the room and stood at attention, barely able to suppress her grin.

"Yes, Catolina," he said, looking up from a large stack of papers. "What is it?"

"Sir . . . I mean, Justin, the centaur state of Chiron has just declared for the revolution."

"Excellent," answered Justin. "With Chiron aboard, in six months the last of the outer settlements will declare for us."

The weary leader then looked back down at his papers. It didn't take him long to notice Catolina still fidgeting in place.

"Was there something else?"

"Well, um . . . yes."

Justin indicated that she continue.

"Now that's it's all over," said Catolina, "I mean, that we're free and all . . . Well, what do we do now?"

With a smile strangely devoid of joy and mirth, and as cunning as that of a hungry wolf, Justin Cord gave her the answer.

"We stay that way."

DANI KOLLIN lives in Los Angeles,
California, and EYTAN KOLLIN lives in
Pasadena, California. They are brothers,
and this is their first novel.

Turn the page for an excerpt from

The Unincorporated War

Available in May 2010

A wistful chime reminded Justin that his cabinet meeting was about to begin. He turned around and there to greet him was his Chief of Staff, Cyrus Anjou, standing next to Omad. Cyrus was a Jovian who, mused the President, was actually quite jovial. The chief of staff's roots were almost as critical as his political ability. While Jupiter itself proved uninhabitable, its many moons—seventy in all, including the seven man made—where rich in mineral deposits, usable gasses, and water. Cyrus hailed from one such moon and Mosh had vouched for him from the days when Cyrus was director of GCI's Jovian mining operations and Mosh was his boss. Unlike most corporate climbers, Cyrus took his majority and stayed near his native Io rather than follow the ladder back to Earth where the real power lay. But that merely helped hide the absolute political ability the man had. The moons of Jupiter made up a large and powerful constituency and there was no better person to see to its needs than the current chief of staff. Justin never made it a policy to ask why Mosh vouched for anyone, he just accepted it gratefully and moved on to the next task. And there was always a next task.

"Mr. President," Cyrus said, bowing accordingly, "I'm glad this miserable excuse for a human being found you."

"Don't listen to the Jovian," Omad shot back. "It's that big red eye talking. They stare at it long enough and eventually go loopy." He then looked over to Cyrus. "Case in point."

"That big red eye, Mr. President, as you may well know, is a storm that's been raging on Jupiter for well over a thousand years and, I would argue, only slightly less volatile than my good friend Mr. Hassan."

"Eyesore," snapped Omad.

"Tall words for a pebble dweller."

The last insult was meant to demonstrate the Jovian disdain for belt dwellers whose planetoids were but a fraction the size of any one of Jupiter's larger moons. Omad wasn't deterred and Justin tuned out the banter, realizing that the worse the insults got, the more solidified the relationship became. He only stopped it once it got to the breeding habits of their respective grandmothers. The cease-fire lasted long enough for him to hear Neela enter the room from an adjoining hall. He turned around and greeted her with a grin.

"Is the First Free ready?" she asked.

Justin winced at his wife's use of the phrase, but knew he was powerless to stop it. Neela was the one exception to many of his rules. He only wished she would use that particular designation more judiciously.

"He is, of course, always ready to see you, most dear and delightful lady," answered the chief of staff, again bowing politely. Cyrus, noticed Justin, had a knack of making the most effusive language seem natural.

Neela smiled at the compliment. "The others are waiting in the dining room and after this meeting we're going to the fleet officers ball. We have the first dance."

"Gentlemen, that is my dear wife's way of saying that I can't be late."

"Indeed," confirmed Cyrus, "we should start."

Neela smiled in agreement and unconsciously smoothed a line in Justin's jacket, though no such line was obvious to anyone in attendance.

The four made their way to the adjoining room where there were greeted by Justin Cord's newly acting cabinet. Justin took his place at the head of the table with Cyrus sitting to his right. Neela, overly conscious of her special relationship to the president, preferred to sit opposite him. Omad sat near his old friend on the left and Mosh to the right of Omad. Eleanor's seat was left empty as she, Mosh informed the group, was currently volunteering with a paramedic unit of the Cerian fleet militia. Kirk Olmstead, the acting head of Special Ops, was also in attendance and, as usual, sat where he pleased, not caring if he ruffled anyone's feathers. Today he found himself between Neela and Joshua Sinclair, a Saturnian pilot who was visiting for the first time and, it was clear to all, was unsure as to why.

Olmstead had long ago made peace with his former nemesis, now president. Given the fact that Kirk had at one time tried to have Justin assassinated, his inclusion in the cabinet was controversial to say the least. But Justin had overruled his trusted compatriots under the old adage, "the enemy of my enemy is my friend." It also helped that Olmstead had been one of the first to declare his support for Justin's fledgling movement and had been instrumental in getting others in the outer alliance to sign on.

Padamir Singh of Ceres was also seated. He served as Justin's press secretary, but in truth was more of an adviser on all matters Cerian. Singh knew the colony inside and out, having been born and raised there, as well as enriched by a small fortune from many of his private ventures. Or, as Omad would recount to anyone willing to listen, Padamir was the most successful smuggler the asteroid belt had ever seen. Finally, pacing anxiously in the hall just outside of the meeting room was the congressman from Eris, Tyler Sadma. But he, reckoned Justin, would have to wait.

As drinks were served by a few attendant drones, Justin called the meeting to order.

"I'm afraid I can't take as much time in this meeting as I'd like. It seems the congressman from Eris is waiting outside."

"Yeah, I noticed that," said Mosh. "To what end?"

"Apparently his colony is on the verge of declaring immediate, universal, and unequivocal disincorporation." Justin held up his hand as everyone tried to speak at once. "Please, no matter how you feel, I have to deal with this issue very carefully. Don't throw any more fuel on the fire than you have to."

Per Justin's wish, all held their tongues.

"Now to the business at hand," he continued. "How did the first meeting of congress go?"

"The military bill was proposed and passed," answered Padamir. "All colonial forces will be fighting under the command of one unified fleet."

"Well, that went easy," said Justin.

"Too easy," said Omad.

"No reason it shouldn't have," answered Mosh. "Everyone wants to put on uniforms and salute each other. They figure the best way to win elections after the war is a nice command or two. But so you know, Mr. President, there will be a congressional committee to 'advise' you on choices for various ships."

Justin grimaced. "We expected that. Did we get the important thing?"

Mosh allowed the corner up his mouth to curl up a bit. Justin knew it to be a smile, though not everyone else did. "Slipped it in attached to the proviso authorizing the committee on naval appointments. All volunteers are signing up for *the duration*. Not for two years like most of the colonial militias had them in for."

"Amazing," said Neela.

"Not one complaint," said Mosh.

It seemed that every colony of the outer alliance was sending men and ships of every description to the capital settlement in order to help fight in what was being termed the "glorious" freedom war. Most seemed afraid that the war would be over before they got to the action. Justin used that knowledge to his advantage in order to get his proviso passed but secretly prayed that there would be little "action" for any of them to experience. He lived daily with the foreboding sense that his prayers would not be answered.

"Everyone thinks the war will be over the second Earth loses the first fight," added Padamir, "so why argue over a moot point? After all, it's common knowledge that the core planets are dependent on our raw materials. The corporations will force the corporate core to make peace. It's the beauty of the incorporated system," he said almost triumphantly, "trade is more powerful than war. Always has been."

"I pray you're right, Padamir," answered Justin, unconsciously tapping his fingers on a large black binder, "but if you're not, this little amendment will save us a lot of grief."

It was at this point that Joshua Sinclair held up his hand to speak.

"Yes, Mr. Sinclair?" asked Justin.

"Pardon me for interrupting, Mr. President, but what am I doing here?"

Justin smiled at the man's temerity. He would never have stood for it in his first life. Protocol wouldn't have allowed it. But that former life, and the close to three hundred years he'd spent in cryonic suspension getting to this one, was well over. On top of that, the belt was a different world entirely. Its greatest strength, Justin had realized, was people just like this pilot. It was also proving to be Justin's greatest headache.

"I believe we're ready to move on." Justin answered, looking to Cyrus for confirmation. Cyrus nodded in the affirmative.

Justin fixed his glaze on the impetuous pilot. "Fleet needs an admiral, Mr. Sinclair."

Joshua Sinclair almost gagged on his drink. "Hey, now wait just a minute," he said, slamming his glass to the table. "I agreed to command a ship. Damsah's left nut, sir, she's not even that big. Barely a frigate."

"Captain Sinclair, Joshua if I may," answered Justin, turning on the charm.

Sinclair nodded, realizing he may have overstepped. Realizing in fact that this Cord fellow may be new to these parts but he still wielded an awful lot of power.

"Your record speaks for itself," continued Justin. "You're a career mercenary with a very reputable company and twenty years commanding an assortment of ships."

"No disrespect, Mr. President, but you just described fifty other men in orbit around this rock."

"None taken, Joshua. And of course you're right. But there are other reasons as well. One, lets face it, it helps that you're from Saturn."

"Titan, sir," Joshua answered proudly.

"I was of course referring to the neighborhood," answered the President, "but I can certainly understand pride of birthplace."

Saturn, like Jupiter, was itself an uninhabitable gas planet—the second largest in the solar system in fact. And like Jupiter, over sixty moons surrounded it—Titan being the largest.

Sinclair smiled even though he'd just received a platitude.

"Your planetary system has sent far more recruits and ships than any other. Also, Karen Cho's on the committee and it's her job to appoint all these eager officers to their posts. Saturnian officers, Saturnian admiral. Makes sense, no?"

Captain Sinclair was starting to come around. "I know Karen," he said. "She'll keep her word if she gives it, but count your fingers when you shake her hand and if you sign a deal don't expect the pen back. . . . Why don't you let her appoint one of those eager lads to the job?"

Justin now opened the binder he'd been tapping on and perused the first page—more for show than clarification.

"I have the report here on the Spicer ring."

Sinclair shifted uneasily in his seat, reliving a bad memory. "All the more reason not to hire me, sir," he answered. "It states rather clearly my insubordination and untrustworthiness."

"Indeed it does, Joshua. However, what it doesn't state is your refusal to cause the death of innocents."

"War is a terrible thing, Mr. President. I disobeyed a direct order."

"First of all, it wasn't war at the time," answered Justin, "and second of all, if I ever give an order like that I'd expect you to disobey it as well." Justin then pointed to large image of the asteroid belt projected on the wall. "They all think it'll be a short, easy war. I look into your eyes, sir, and see that you think different. That's the type of officer I need leading the alliance fleet."

Sinclair grinned. "Of course it has nothing to do with the fact that I'm a hundred-percenter."

"Officially, not at all. I, as the President, have no position on how the various colonial governments deal with incorporation. That is a colonial matter having nothing to do with the Alliance."

"But unofficially it don't hurt," added Omad, speaking the words that his friend could not. The widening split between those who wanted the incorporated system thrown out altogether and those who only wanted it reconfigured had been growing daily. But Sinclair's point, noted Justin, was spot-on. Most Saturnalians as well as those living in the farthest reaches of the belt were inclined toward disincorporation. Having their new admiral so inclined would make things run that much smoother.

"I'm sorry, Mr. President," said Mosh somewhat gruffly, "but I will be heard."

Justin motioned for him to continue. He knew full well Mosh's position. In fact Mosh was on the cabinet not only because Justin trusted him, but also for the very same reason Sinclair was now being coerced. Mosh represented a large constituency who felt that incorporation was still the best system devised when it came to delivering the twin benefits of peace and prosperity. That Hektor and his ilk had debauched it was beside the point.

"Most of these 'no shares' or hundred-percenters or whatever you wanna call 'em," said Mosh, chill evident in his voice, "were miners with heavy majorities and close family ties making it possible to get their parent's shares. And from my understanding, parents unwilling to comply were 'convinced' otherwise."

Sinclair grimaced at that comment but, noted Justin with appreciation, held back from saying anything.

"And the five percent that would normally have gone to the government," continued Mosh, "reverted from the Terran confederation to the colonial governments—who in turn offered it up as a recruiting bonus. But even so, most of those so-called hundred-percenters have on average ten to fifteen percent unaccounted for, are therefore breaking the law of incorporation, and should be made to pay just compensation."

That was enough for Sinclair. "And who the hell," he bellowed, "is going to make them . . . *Shareholder*?"

"Gentleman," said Justin in a firm, yet quiet voice, "enough." Mosh and Sinclair snapped to, realizing that now was neither the place nor time to rehash their well-trodden positions.

"Right here," said Justin, closing the binder in front of him, "you can see the biggest threat to the Alliance. Truth is, if the Terran Federation left us alone we'd probably end up destroying ourselves. It's difficult enough having each colony insisting on special rights and privileges, but when you bring the emancipation question into the picture it gets downright intractable."

"It's an issue that won't go away, Mr. President," intoned Mosh.

"I'm not saying it's not open for discussion, Mosh," answered Justin, "only that here in this room we'll need to keep our heads."

"My own brother's a NoShare," added Padamir. "I've tried to talk reason to him; that we simply cannot get rid of a system that has worked well for centuries overnight and replace it with the hope that something better will come along. But he insists, as I suspect does Mr. Sinclair here, that it must be now."

"Mr. Singh," answered Sinclair, "no disrespect, but incorporation has been very good to you. You're hardly an objective observer. But that point aside, most of the outer colonies feel like your brother, though there is conflict among families even on Pluto and the other TNOs." TNOs, Justin had learned, referred to the Trans Neptunian Objects or asteroids in the solar system further out than Neptune. There were thousands of them, but the most notable were the dwarf planets of Pluto and its largest moon, Charon; Eris and its sister moon, Dysnomia; as well as the larger asteroids of Sedna, Orcus, Ixion, Quaoar, and Varuna—all with sizable and very vocal populations.

"True, Mr. Sinclair," answered Mosh, more evenly this time, "but as you're well aware, most of the belt is shareholder in outlook, but . . . not all."

"Which is why," interjected the President, "we cannot allow this issue to be taken up by this government. It will split and destroy us. We have to bury it for now. Without the Alliance we have nothing, are we agreed?"

One by one all present nodded their heads in agreement.

"Good," said Justin, "and congratulations, admiral. Your first order of business is to plan a raid on Mars with the Alliance fleet."